PRAISE FOR TERRY GOODKIND

'Each volume of The Sword of Truth proves more difficult to review than the last. There are only so many ways of heaping praise on a series that gets better and better… Goodkind's greatest triumph: the ability to introduce immediately identifiable characters. His heroes, like us, are not perfect. Instead, each is flawed in ways that strengthen, rather than weaken their impact. You'll find no two-dimensional oafs here. In fact, at times you'll think you're looking at your own reflection.'
SFX

'Everything one could ask for in an epic fantasy… Few writers have Goodkind's power of creation – phenomenal imaginative writing, exhaustive in its scope and riveting in its detail… Goodkind's worldbuilding will keep readers captivated.'
Publishers Weekly

'A rip-roaring epic.'
Daily Mail

'Wonderfully creative, seamless, and stirring epic fantasy.'
Kirkus

'His writing is nimble, clear, dimensional.'
Entertainment Weekly

'A tour de force of mesmerizing storytelling… The compelling prose weaves a magic spell over readers.'
Romantic Times Review

'Near-perfect pacing, well realized settings and superior descriptive narrative.'
VOYA Magazine

TERRY GOODKIND

THE CHILDREN OF D'HARA

An Ad Astra Book

Originally published in five parts:
The Scribbly Man (2019)
Hateful Things (2019)
Wasteland (2019)
Witch's Oath (2020)
Into Darkness (2020)

First published as one complete novel in 2021 by Head of Zeus Ltd
An Ad Astra Book

9 7 5 3 1 2 4 6 8

A catalogue record for this book is available from
the British Library.

ISBN (HB): 9781789541335
ISBN (XTPB): 9781789541342
ISBN (E): 9781789541328

Typeset by Divaddict Publishing Solutions Ltd

Printed and bound in Great Britain by
CPI Group (UK) Ltd, Croydon CR0 4YY

Head of Zeus Ltd
First Floor East
5–8 Hardwick Street
London ECIR 4RG

WWW.HEADOFZEUS.COM

'I want to introduce everyone to *The Children of D'Hara*, a new series that continues the story of the lives of Richard and Kahlan. This is a journey that began twenty-five years ago with the 1994 release of *Wizard's First Rule*, when Richard first met Kahlan that fateful day in the Hartland woods.

After The Sword of Truth ended, I knew there was more to Richard and Kahlan's story. Much more. A whole world more. For years, readers have asked me about Richard and Kahlan's lives after The Sword of Truth and, importantly, about their children.

While my masterwork The Sword of Truth concluded with *Warheart* – twenty languages and 26 million books sold – I was burning to tell readers more about Richard and Kahlan. For that reason, this new series starts immediately after The Sword of Truth ended. Without skipping a beat, readers will plunge back into Richard and Kahlan's lives.

So it is that I want to welcome you all back into The Sword of Truth's world with many of the characters besides Richard and Kahlan, such as the Mord-Sith, that we have come to love. Learn what the star shift has done to their world and what monsters now lurk in shadows. I promise an arresting, beautiful, and sometimes tragic adventure that will keep you glued to this irresistible story.'

—TERRY GOODKIND

BY TERRY GOODKIND

THE SWORD OF TRUTH

Wizard's First Rule
Stone of Tears
Blood of the Fold
Temple of the Winds
Soul of the Fire
Faith of the Fallen
The Pillars of Creation
Naked Empire
Debt of Bones
Chainfire
Phantom
Confessor
The Omen Machine
The First Confessor
The Third Kingdom
Severed Souls
Warheart

THE CHILDREN OF D'HARA

The Scribbly Man
Hateful Things
Wasteland
Witch's Oath
Into Darkness

THE NICCI CHRONICLES

Death's Mistress
Shroud of Eternity
Siege of Stone
Heart of Black Ice

THE ANGELA CONSTANTINE SERIES

Trouble's Child
The Girl in the Moon
Crazy Wanda

The Law of Nines
Nest
The Sky People

THE
CHILDREN
OF
D'HARA

1

"I have come to accept your surrender."

Richard's brow drew down as he leaned an elbow on the padded leather arm of the massive chair he was in. He was more perplexed than troubled.

The rotund man was wearing formal white robes ornately embroidered in gold designs that added an air of dignity to his pear shape. He stood patiently at the head of a line of supplicants stretching back into the distance of the enormous, vaulted room. Windows high up to the side let in streamers of hazy afternoon light that gave the vast room an almost spiritual quality. Fat black marble columns, variegated with red and gold veins, rose up in a tight row to each side of the long room. Gilded capitals atop the columns supported balconies where large crowds watched the proceedings along with the people on the main floor in the shadows behind the columns.

At the head of the room, behind Richard and Kahlan sitting in stately chairs at a heavy table on a raised platform, a ring of leaded-glass windows surrounded a two-story-high, carved white marble medallion depicting the long lineage of the House of Rahl. It was an impressive seat of power. Growing up in the woods of Hartland, Richard could never have imagined such a place, much less imagined himself sitting at the head of it.

Nearby, palace officials and their aides stood ready to assist with anything needed. Heavily armed men of the First File, between Richard and Kahlan and the rest of the roomful of people, did their best to remain inconspicuous, mostly staying out of the way toward the sides. Behind Richard and Kahlan, in front of the massive marble medallion, six Mord-Sith stood at ease.

Five of the Mord-Sith wore their white leather outfits. One, Vika, was wearing red. Richard had requested that they all wear white for the occasion so as to appear less menacing, it being a time of peace, after all. Vika had said that she was there to protect the Lord Rahl and if she looked menacing, all the better. Richard had long ago learned that life was easier if he let Mord-Sith have their way with petty issues. He knew that if it was vital, they would follow his orders. To the death if need be.

The people to each side on the main floor and up in the balconies, everyone from farmers to nobility, all fell silent as they waited to hear what the Lord Rahl would say in response to such an outlandish demand. The heavyset man in gold-embroidered white robes waited as well.

Beneath an elaborate white cloak pushed open in front by his substantial girth, silver chains around his neck just below the folds of false chins held a variety of small ornaments that reminded Richard of symbols of rank that army officers wore on their uniforms for formal occasions.

Richard remembered seeing similarly dressed people in an open tent down in the market at the base of the enormous plateau that supported the sprawling People's Palace. The people down in the market and tent city had been gathering for weeks to have a chance to witness the kind of event that had never taken place in their life-times—or to profit from it.

"My surrender," Richard repeated in a quiet voice into the hushed air. "My surrender of what?"

"Your world."

Some of the nearby soldiers and court attendants chuckled. When they did, many of the people watching joined in to giggle with them. Or, at least they did until they saw that Richard was not amused.

His gaze flicked to Kahlan, seated beside him behind the table where supplicants could place maps, contracts, and other documents for their review. Besides the white dress of the Mother Confessor, he saw Kahlan was wearing her Confessor face. Her long hair gleamed in the light coming from the ring of windows behind them. He couldn't imagine a good spirit looking any more striking.

Her beautiful features revealed nothing of what she might be thinking. Despite how unreadable and dispassionate she may have appeared to others, Richard could read the fire in that calm expression. Were she a wolf, her ruff would be standing up.

Richard leaned toward her, wanting to know why she seemed to be seething. She finally broke eye contact with the man and leaned toward Richard to speak in a confidential tone.

"This man is from Estoria. The medals and awards around his neck mark him as the consul general." She stole a brief look at the man. "I think I may have met him once or twice, long ago when he was less important."

"What's Estoria?"

"It's one of the minor lands in the Midlands that I oversaw as Mother Confessor. For the most part the people there earn their living as professional diplomats for hire. The consul general would be the equivalent of a king."

Richard frowned. "You mean they are diplomatic mercenaries?"

She nodded. "Strange as it sounds, there are those who need a diplomat to champion their cause. When they do have such a need, they will often hire an Estorian. Estorians sometimes argued the position of a patron before me on the council."

Richard was still frowning. "Who would have need of such services?"

"You'd be surprised. Anyone from a wealthy individual having a dispute with a ruler to a kingdom on the verge of war. Skilled diplomacy can in some cases resolve a dispute, or at least stall armed conflict indefinitely while talks drag on and on. Estoria is considered neutral ground, so they often host the different sides in complicated negotiations. Putting up such important guests and their entourage is part of how the people there earn a living. The consul general will often host elaborate banquets for each side of the negotiations. At separate times, of course.

"Estorians have a long history as professional diplomats. They live to negotiate. They are very good at it. It is often said that an Estorian would try to negotiate with the Keeper of the underworld himself to try to come to an agreement on a later departure from life. That's what they do—they negotiate."

"So what has you so upset?"

Kahlan gave him a look, as if she couldn't believe how dense he was being. "Don't you see? Estorians negotiate. They don't ever make demands. It's not in their blood."

Richard finally understood what had her hackles up. This man was certainly making a demand, and apparently such a thing was completely out of their nature.

He turned his attention back to the diplomat standing before the gate through the railing not far in front of them. A pair of guards in intimidating dark leather breastplates over chain mail stood at the railing to each side of the low gate to admit supplicants with documentation for review or anyone else Richard or Kahlan might gesture to come closer.

Inside the railing to either side were the phalanxes of palace officials in white or pale blue robes. They dealt with a diversity of matters within the People's Palace and even D'Hara at large. They seemed to relish minutiae. Once a person had come before Richard and Kahlan to state their case, make a technical request, or ask for guidance, they were often directed to one of the variety of officials who could handle the details of their concern.

A number of the people waiting in the long line of supplicants were representatives of distant lands who had come, usually dressed in ceremonial attire, not to ask for anything but simply to swear their loyalty to the newly formed D'Haran Empire. They all wanted to look their best at the banquets planned for later. Peace greased the wheels of trade. Being a willing and cooperative part of the empire made trade with all parts of the empire easier.

The man in the gold-embroidered robes showed no emotion as he waited for Richard's formal surrender.

"What are the proposed terms?" Richard asked out of curiosity, expecting some kind of diplomatic proposal that would turn out to be much less ominous-sounding and reveal what was really behind such an odd demand.

"There are no terms. The surrender must be unconditional."

Richard arched an eyebrow. That didn't sound like his idea of a diplomatic negotiation.

He sat up straighter. "What is your name?"

The man blinked, as if the question had been unexpected and totally irrelevant. For some reason he had difficulty looking directly at Richard. He averted his eyes whenever possible.

"My name has no bearing here and is unimportant in the matter before you," he said, confirming the bewildered expression on his face.

"Important or not, I would like to know your name."

Long bracelets dangled from the man's thick wrists as he spread his plump hands. His droopy eyes searched absently left and right, as if he didn't know what to do about the unexpected request. "I am only here with instructions to accept your surrender on behalf of my patron."

"Who is this patron?"

"The goddess."

Richard was taken aback. He had heard of goddesses only in mythology. He didn't think goddesses, in mythology anyway, hired professional diplomats.

"We are gathered here to address the issues of those who come before us. This 'goddess' is not here. You are." The patience left Richard's voice. "Give me your name."

The man hesitated, avoiding looking directly at Richard. He picked up a long lock of gray hair that had fallen forward over his dark eyes and placed it back down over the bald top of his head. He licked his finger and then smoothed the lock down to paste it in place.

"If it will help ensure that you comply with the demand of the goddess, my name is Nolodondri, but I am known by Nolo."

"Tell me, Nolo, why has this goddess not come in person to request the surrender of the D'Haran Empire?"

The man lifted the freshly licked finger to make a correction. "Not your empire, Lord Rahl, your world. And it is not a request. It is a command."

"Ah. My world. I stand corrected. And it is a command, not a request. Duly noted." Richard rolled his hand. "So you worship this goddess, do you?"

Nolo's brow twitched. "No, not exactly."

"What does that mean?"

"Would the sky expect the veneration of the ants on the ground beneath it?"

"Well then, why would this goddess send an ant to do her bidding instead of coming herself to make such a monumentally important demand?"

Nolo bowed his head slightly. "The goddess does not bother with petty tasks such as the surrender of worlds, so she directed me to come here to command compliance with her wishes."

Out of the corner of his eye, Richard could see Kahlan's aura darkening.

"You say that this was her 'command'—that I surrender my world?"

Nolo bowed his head deeper, as if Richard were dense. "Yes, of course. I thought that I had made that clear."

Cassia's white leather creaked as she leaned in from behind Richard's right shoulder to whisper to him. "Please, Lord Rahl," she said as she pulled her single blond braid forward over her shoulder as if holding her own leash, "I'm begging you. Let me kill him."

Berdine, also in white leather, leaned in beside Cassia. "Lord Rahl, you left me here, unable to protect you, for ages. I think I deserve to be the one to kill him."

"Maybe we can decide that later," Richard said to them with a small smile. "For now, let me handle this?"

Both rolled their eyes as they straightened, but they released their Agiels, letting the weapons hang from their wrists on fine gold chains, always at the ready.

2

Richard was doing this public audience only because Kahlan had asked him to. She had told him that allowing people to come before the First Wizard with petitions or concerns was an ancient practice. She had in the past overseen the wizards' council as Mother Confessor in a time when there had been no First Wizard. Because of that experience, she'd said, she knew the good it did.

Richard had protested at first, saying that a wizards' council was a thing of the past, and besides, this was now the D'Haran Empire, not merely the Midlands.

She said that made it all the more important. She had argued that the need was not a thing of the past and that as the Lord Rahl, the leader of the D'Haran Empire and the new First Wizard, he was far more important than a wizards' council had ever been. She believed that because he held absolute rule people needed to know that it was fair and just rule. For that to happen they needed to be able to witness that rule firsthand. This was one way, she had told him, of letting people know that as part of the D'Haran Empire their voice would be heard and they would be treated fairly.

Richard had always found it difficult, if not impossible, to go against Kahlan's advice, especially since it was almost always sound advice. As the Mother Confessor, Kahlan knew a great deal more about the protocol of rule than he ever would.

While Richard was no longer a simple woods guide, Kahlan, too, was much more than the woman he had met in the Hartland woods that day so long ago. She was the Mother Confessor—the last Confessor. She'd held sway over the Midlands council, and thus the

Midlands. Kings and queens trembled on bended knee before her. She knew about authority and rule.

They had fought a long and bitterly difficult war to finally bring peace to the world. In that struggle they had lost many dear friends and loved ones, as had nearly everyone else. She and Richard were each the last of their kind, and together they were the hope of their world.

In the end he had known that Kahlan was right about holding such an event.

For three days they had been giving an audience to people who had traveled from far and wide to come before the Lord Rahl and the Mother Confessor with their concerns, or to see others do so. While he found it tedious and most of the matters achingly trivial, he realized that the people who had gathered to see it done found it not only exciting, but riveting and reassuring.

For those gathered, it was, in a way, a celebration of the end of wars, a joyous gathering with those who had saved their world and brought them peace, a time when rulers from far and wide came to swear their loyalty to the empire.

Richard just wanted it to be over so he could be alone with Kahlan.

While most people who had come before them were sincere, even if some stuttered in terror to be standing before the Lord Rahl and the Mother Confessor, this man, Nolo, was unlike the others. As far as Richard was concerned, he didn't seem to represent any real danger. Richard thought that maybe he was simply senile or possibly deranged in his old age. Richard noted, though, that Kahlan thought differently.

There were a great many people waiting for their turn to speak with them. This man had already wasted enough of their time with his nonsense, but worse, he had clearly upset Kahlan. Before Richard could say anything else, the man spoke again.

"Lord Rahl"—the Estorian's voice turned harsh, losing the polish of polite diplomatic tolerance—"it would be in your own best interest if you surrendered your world without further delay. You can either do so voluntarily, thereupon to be executed in a humane fashion, or, should you refuse, you will be assassinated in a most brutal fashion."

Richard leaned forward, put both forearms on the table, and folded his fingers together. With such a direct threat, especially after such hard-won peace, but especially against Kahlan, this man had just crossed a line.

Richard's patience was at an end.

Many hundreds of people were crowded in on the main floor observing from each side of the petitioners who were waiting to be heard. Many more watched from the balconies. All of them leaned forward in anticipation of what the Lord Rahl might say or do. This was a memorable event in their lives—the very stuff of legend—and it now held the distinct air of mortal peril.

He thought that most people expected a prompt beheading.

Richard was just about to instead ask the guards to escort the crazy old fool out of the People's Palace and see to it that he and the rest of the people with him never returned, when Kahlan touched his arm. She was staring directly at the Estorian diplomat as she spoke in a low voice to Richard.

"Do not dismiss this threat, Richard."

Richard could see the aura around Kahlan snapping with faint, flickering flashes, not unlike lightning, dancing and crackling all across the haze of her aura. Since coming back from the underworld, he had found that he had access to his own inner power in ways he had never expected. One of those was that it gave him the ability to read Kahlan's aura, much the same as he had often been able to read the complex aura around a sorceress. But knowing Kahlan as well as he did, he didn't need to see her aura to know her mood.

He inclined his head toward her and spoke in a confidential tone while keeping his gaze on the chief diplomat from Estoria.

"I'm listening."

She finally turned to direct her fiery green-eyed gaze and that hot aura at him.

"Let me question him. Alone."

Richard hadn't expected that. "Don't you think we're getting a little ahead of ourselves, here?"

"No." She leaned closer and lowered her voice to a heated whisper. "You need to listen to me in this, Richard. Estorians are diplomats. It's their nature, their very makeup. I've dealt with them many times and I've spent time in their land among the people there. They don't believe in conflict of any type as a solution to anything. They believe that any dispute must be resolved through diplomatic negotiation. They simply don't believe in absolutes nor do they make unconditional demands. There is no black and white to them. They exist in a gray world of diplomacy.

"I've never once seen an Estorian behave this way. Never. Something is very wrong. You need to listen to me in this. This man is dangerous. Let me question him."

It was an instruction, not a request.

Richard briefly glanced over at Nolo before looking back at Kahlan. What she was proposing, for all practical purposes, was nothing short of an execution, if not of his living form at least of his mind. Richard knew she was dead serious. Kahlan never used her power lightly or without being absolutely convinced of the need. But still…

"Kahlan, do you—"

"I know kings and queens and rulers of every kind and nearly every land. I've never once heard of a goddess. Have you? This man has just as good as declared war on behalf of someone unknown to us and made an open, public threat to our lives if we don't unconditionally comply."

Richard knew she was right. He had been trying to convince himself that because the demand was so preposterous the old man had to be insane, senile, or demented, but Kahlan was right. They could not let this pass, or allow people to see them let such a threat pass.

He turned a raptor gaze back on Nolo. That look alone caused the expansive room to break out in buzzing and worried whispers. It caused Nolo to avert his gaze.

Richard lifted a hand, wordlessly commanding silence.

"I am the Lord Rahl," he said in a clear voice that carried back through the hall. "The D'Haran Empire is this world. They are one and the same. I rule the D'Haran Empire along with the Mother Confessor."

Nolo couldn't seem to help his amused smile. The fat folds of skin bunched under his chin as he bowed his partially bald head. "That is true for now," he said as he looked up, "but you are a mere man, a ruler with no successor. Your rule is a dead lineage." He gestured up at the marble medallion towering behind Richard and Kahlan. "You are the last of the Rahl line. She is the last Confessor. When you two die those bloodlines will die with you. Your kind and your rule are at an end."

Kahlan slapped her hand down on the table. The sound made everyone jump as it echoed back through the hall.

She shot to her feet. "Enough!"

The room fell dead silent.

People had always been fearful of Confessors in general, and the Mother Confessor in particular. Seeing the Mother Confessor angry had them giving ground as if driven back by a wave crashing to shore.

Kahlan swept an arm out, calling on the soldiers to the side.

"We will take this man to a room where we can have a private conversation."

Everyone in the vast room knew exactly what that meant. This was to be an execution and it was to be at the hands of the Mother Confessor herself, not some hooded axeman.

Richard rose up beside her, adding his silent backing to her words.

He took up Kahlan's hand and gave it a squeeze as if to ask if she was sure she wanted to do this.

She gave him a look of resolve he knew all too well. "After all we have fought for, Richard, all we have lost, you promised me that we were now entering a new golden age. I will not have anything take that golden age from all of us. This man has just threatened our lives. He has made himself an enemy of a peaceful future for everyone."

"He could simply be an old man who has lost his mind and is imagining things," Richard reminded her.

"He represents a threat to us, Richard—I can feel it in my bones. This is not a time to let down our guard. We need to know the nature of the threat. There is only one way to find out the truth with absolute certainty."

Cassia leaned in close to them. "I will go with her, Lord Rahl, and protect her while she questions this fool who would think to threaten you both."

Richard gave her a look. "Do you really think you want to be in the room when a Confessor unleashes her power?"

That gave the Mord-Sith pause. "She's going to... Oh... Well then"—she straightened—"I will guard the room from outside in case she should need me."

Kahlan, looking ready to go to war to stop a war before it could start, gestured to the guards.

"Bring him," she growled.

3

The thick carpet muted Kahlan's footsteps as she marched down the private corridor. Cassia hurried to keep up. Behind the Mord-Sith a heavily armed detachment guarded the man in gold-embroidered robes as if he were the most dangerous man in the world.

As far as Kahlan was concerned, he was.

A muscular soldier to each side gripped Nolo under his flabby arms, virtually carrying him along. His footsteps only occasionally kissed the floor. He didn't struggle or protest his indignation at such rough treatment. In fact, he said nothing.

Kahlan needed a place where she could be alone with the Estorian. As angry as she was, if she ended up having to use her Confessor power it could be a danger to anyone too close. The men escorting her had simply followed her without question into the maze of the palace interior. Having been driven by her temper, she suddenly realized, she hadn't given any thought to where she was going, and she found that she didn't know where she was. She stopped and turned back to the soldiers.

"I need a private room where I won't be disturbed. Do you know of one nearby?"

The guard immediately behind the two carrying Nolo lowered his pike to point with it past them to the right. "Take that hallway, Mother Confessor."

"Then where?"

He hesitated, briefly considering the directions, then changed his mind. "It would be easier if I just showed you."

Kahlan gestured for the man to take the lead. He hurried past them down the white-plastered hallway and then through several more turns that eventually led them to an expansive, round entryway elaborately detailed with moldings and raised panels all painted a creamy white. While pleasant enough, it had a sterile feel to it. In that broad entryway there was but a single room. It had a heavy oak door with iron strap hinges that, oddly enough, could be bolted from the outside.

The round entryway where they all gathered was easily large enough to hold several times their number. Black and white marble had been laid out to create a spiral design on the floor. At the center of the spiral sat a round mahogany table with five carved stone mountain lions for legs. A beautiful pale blue blown-glass vase, apparently meant for cut flowers, rested at the center of the table, but it was empty.

Kahlan had never been in this area of the palace before. But that wasn't saying much, since it could take hours to walk from one end of the palace to the other. The palace was really a small city atop the plateau and home to thousands of people. There were public areas and service areas as well as places and corridors that were for the exclusive use of the Lord Rahl, the master of the People's Palace and leader of D'Hara. The soldiers and the Mord-Sith used all areas in their duty to protect and serve the Lord Rahl. The service halls were guarded, but the private areas were heavily guarded, all by the elite members of the First File, the Lord Rahl's personal guard.

The soldier who had led them there tipped his lance to indicate the door. "This room is at the outer wall of the palace and is unoccupied, Mother Confessor."

"How do you know about it?"

He blinked at the question, as if surprised she doubted his knowledge of the palace. "All members of the First File must learn not only the layout of the People's Palace, but its security secrets. In times past the Lord Rahl would hold court in the great hall—the same one being used by you and Lord Rahl today. When a past Lord Rahl, Darken Rahl especially, didn't want a visitor to leave, this room was nearby and one he relied on."

"It's a prison cell, then?"

"Yes, although a comfortable one as prisons go. It's meant for higher-ranking people or dignitaries the Lord Rahl wanted held temporarily."

"Until they were executed?"

The soldier smiled. "Usually, Mother Confessor."

She marveled at how, despite all the changes, some things hadn't altered.

Kahlan didn't need to think it over. "It should do."

The soldier opened the door for her. When she extended an arm in invitation, the two soldiers holding the heavy Nolo lugged him in ahead of her. One of the other men lit a long splinter on one of the dozen reflector lamps in the expansive entryway, then lit the lamps on the walls and small bedside table within.

As the lamps were lit one by one they gradually revealed a rather small room that, without windows, ordinarily existed in total darkness. The walls were made up entirely of limestone blocks. Heavy beams held up the plank ceiling. There was minimal furniture, the largest piece being a simple, unpainted pine wardrobe. Several reflector lamps on the walls as well as the one on a bedside table now provided plenty of light, as well as an oily smell.

Kahlan looked more closely and saw that messages had been scratched into the soft limestone walls. The few she took the time to read were prayers for salvation.

"Leave him," she said to the men holding the Estorian. "Then I want you all to go back and protect Richard."

The two men holding him finally let Nolo's feet find traction on the floor. They were clearly reluctant to leave her alone with the man. Kahlan knew something was seriously wrong, but she was in no danger from a lone man. She was more concerned about the shapeless threat to Richard and the people in the great hall. Anything could happen.

Nolo had promised that she and Richard would be executed or assassinated. With all the private corridors heavily guarded to make sure that none of the thousands of guests slipped into them, no one could get to the private area where Kahlan was.

"I'm not so confident that would be what Lord Rahl would want, Mother Confessor," the bearded commander said. "I think he would want us to protect you."

"You're right about that, but I'm not in danger from a single man," she assured them. "You men know that, and no one else is going to get into this area. Richard has a great hall full of people all around him. For all we know, this man here could have brought assassins with him to carry out his promise. They could be anywhere among the gathered crowd. Richard is the one in danger at the moment. He must be protected. He is the Lord Rahl. He is everything to all of us."

That spread alarmed looks among the soldiers. "Do you really think that this man brought assassins with him who could be planning to strike in the great hall, Mother Confessor?"

"Can you assure me there aren't, and that my husband does not need more eyes watching over and protecting him?"

When none of them could offer any such assurance, she said, "Please see to my orders."

These men knew her. They'd fought beside her. They didn't need convincing.

After saluting with fists to their hearts, they left with new concern for possible trouble in the palace.

"You too," Kahlan told Cassia, shooing her with a flick of her hand. Kahlan paused to point a finger back at Nolo when he started to follow. "You stay right where you are."

The man didn't look angry, curious, or the least bit afraid. He stopped where he was and waited.

Cassia hesitated. "I promised Lord Rahl that I would watch over you."

"You can watch over me from the other side of that door," Kahlan told the Mord-Sith.

"But I—"

"I would advise that you stand on the other side of the entryway, or better yet stay back a ways down the hallway. I wouldn't want you to be hurt."

While Cassia certainly did want to watch over Kahlan, she had also volunteered to watch over Richard's beloved wife, a task of honor, but one that carried great responsibility. Even so, she knew the very real danger of a Confessor's power to a Mord-Sith. She couldn't protect Kahlan if she was unconscious.

"All right, Mother Confessor," Cassia said as she cast a last glance at the man standing not far away.

Kahlan followed her to the heavy door and then, once she was out, drove the heavy iron bolt into place to make sure the Mord-Sith stayed on the other side. She didn't want anyone interrupting her. Nolo waited calmly.

Kahlan had visited Estoria a few times, as had Confessors before her. Estorians were familiar with Confessors and their power. Like everyone else in the Midlands, they feared Confessors.

This man did not look afraid.

He should have.

"I believe you are the consul general?"

He bowed his head at being recognized. "We met once, years ago when I was in the diplomatic service. You were young, and not yet the beautiful woman you have become. You were with one of your sister Confessors at the time."

All of Kahlan's sister Confessors were long dead. She didn't want to ask which of the other Confessors it had been for fear of it dredging up painful memories of those who had died horrific deaths at the hands of Darken Rahl. Kahlan was the last of the Confessors… and ironically enough now the wife of Darken Rahl's son. Fortunately, the two men could hardly be more different.

"On whose behalf are you here to negotiate?"

His brow twitched. "I thought I had made myself clear. There is nothing to negotiate. You and your husband are to surrender your world unconditionally, at which time you will be humanely executed. Fail to follow those orders and you both will be brutally killed."

Kahlan heaved a weary sigh. "To whom are we to surrender 'our world'?"

"The goddess. I told you that."

"That tells me nothing at all. I don't know any goddess. Who is she?"

"She is the Golden Goddess," Nolo said.

That froze Kahlan in place. It was a long moment before she could find her voice.

"What does this Golden Goddess want with our world?"

"She is a collector of worlds."

Kahlan could only stare at the man.

"Where is she," she finally asked. "What land?"

Nolo looked a bit confused. "She is the Golden Goddess." His confusion turned to a glare. "She must be obeyed."

Kahlan pinched the bridge of her nose in annoyance. Nolo was going around in circles. Diplomats, and the consul general of Estoria in particular, were experts at obfuscation. Kahlan wasn't having any of it.

"I need a great deal more information than that. You need to explain this whole thing to me. All of it."

Nolo shrugged, as if perplexed. "I have told you everything you need to know, Mother Confessor. There is nothing more to tell or anything more you need to know. You have the command from the Golden Goddess and you must comply."

Kahlan showed him a humorless smile. "I'm afraid that there is a whole lot more I need to know, and one way or another you are going to tell me."

He looked mildly amused. "I'm afraid you fail to understand your position."

Kahlan's smile, as humorless as it had been, left. "What, exactly, do I fail to understand?"

"The Golden Goddess is going to have your world."

"Yes, you've already said that. But there is no force left powerful enough to challenge the peace that the D'Haran Empire has brought to the world. Wars that had burned for thousands of years have been ended. Lord Rahl ended them. There is no one left strong enough to challenge the empire or his rule."

"Yes, but what you fail to understand, Mother Confessor, is just how fragile that empire really is. You and Lord Rahl are the power that holds the empire's might together. Without you both, the empire— your world—crumbles. The Golden Goddess has merely to wait for you both to die, of old age if nothing else. So you see, should you both manage to somehow survive, the Golden Goddess will have this world in the end, one way or another.

"She would prefer not to wait for your eventual death, so she wants you both to surrender your world now. You can't win in this. It is time you recognize that and surrender."

"What the Golden Goddess fails to understand is that the House of Rahl has stood for thousands of years. It will continue to stand and to rule."

Nolo looked even more amused. "I think not. But I have an alternative for you, although not for Lord Rahl."

"Are you making a proposal of some kind?"

He showed her a devious smile. "Yes, a proposal. I would like to put forward a private negotiation just between you and me."

"What are you talking about?"

"Lord Rahl is not the only one at the dead end of his lineage. You are the last Confessor, the last of your line."

Kahlan folded her arms and peered down at him, but didn't answer. The line of Confessors was none of this man's business.

"You have been with Richard Rahl for what—years, now?"

"If you have a point, you had better get to it soon."

"The point, Mother Confessor, is that Richard Rahl has failed in his duty as a man."

She frowned. "What in the world are you talking about?"

"He has failed in all this time to give you a child to carry on not only the Rahl line, but the Confessor line as well. In all the times you have given your body to him, he has failed to put you with child. He is not a real man. He is weak, and his seed is obviously worthless. Your empire is on the verge of crumbling because of that and you don't even realize it."

Kahlan had been pregnant before, but had been severely beaten and as a result lost the baby. That was none of this man's business.

Nolo twirled a hand in the air, making his false chins jiggle. "In all this time he has failed to continue the Rahl line, and now his inability to father a child also threatens to be the end of the Confessor line as well. So you see, Mother Confessor, what you need—if you are to carry on the line of the Confessors—is a man who can give you a child."

He abruptly pumped his hips toward her in a lewd fashion, leaving no doubt as to what he meant. "I am here to negotiate for the service you need to continue your line. I am here to offer you my seed so you may conceive."

Kahlan's arms came unfolded in disbelief as her fists dropped to her sides. She thought that Richard must be right—this man was simply deranged.

"Even if I did need someone else to father a child," she said, her anger driving her to ask, "what in the world makes you think for a second that I would pick you?"

An arrogant smile further plumped his already plump cheeks. "I think you would be wise to select me for this task because I could negotiate with the goddess to allow you to live." He flicked a hand dismissively. "Lord Rahl, of course, would have to die."

"Is this what your goddess suggested?"

"No, of course not. This is simply my idea of sparing you the suffering that is to come if you don't agree to her terms. A way out, if you will, for yourself. I might be able to see to it that you could live to raise your Confessor child—the child I sire."

"You must be out of your mind," Kahlan said. "I would die first."

"That's hardly a wise negotiating position."

"There is nothing to negotiate." At the end of her patience, Kahlan gritted her teeth. "It is the threat from your goddess we are here to discuss, and nothing else. I have heard enough of your own nonsense and I will hear no more of it. Surely you must realize that, as a Confessor, I am going to insist on your cooperation in telling me everything you know about this Golden Goddess. This is not a negotiation, Consul General. You will not leave this room alive unless you tell me every bit of what you know."

He paced off a few steps, then turned back. "You are correct, Mother Confessor... in that one of us is not going to leave this room alive. You have made a foolish mistake in turning down my generous offer to negotiate on your behalf to spare your life. Since I am the only one who could have helped you and you are turning me down, you have sealed your fate.

"You are the one who will not leave this room alive."

Kahlan had a hard time believing that an Estorian would make such an open threat.

She believed it when he pulled a knife from a sheath at his waist under his cloak.

He charged toward her with the knife.

As he came crashing in on her, Kahlan thrust her hand out, her palm turned up.

It may have all seemed lightning fast to him, seemed that he had the advantage—but not to Kahlan. She had known that he had the knife and had let him keep it to see if he would dare to try to use it. Even with a knife and even had he been more agile and a great deal faster, he still would have had no chance against a Confessor. None.

But in the attempt, he had erased her last shred of doubt and sealed his own fate.

As the very tip of the razor-sharp blade touched the palm of her upturned hand, her Confessor power had already slammed time to a stop.

The tip of that blade felt less than a feather touching her palm.

Time was hers, now.

This man was hers, now.

While some of the other Confessors had needed to deliberately invoke their power, Kahlan never had. Her birthright was always there deep inside her, a coiled fury that had to be continually restrained rather than occasionally summoned. She had always had to tightly contain it lest it slip its bonds unintentionally. To use it, she had only to withdraw that restraint. It all happened in an infinitesimal glimmer of an instant.

This man had condemned himself when he pulled a knife intending to kill her. Worse than that, in her eyes, he had threatened Richard's life as well as the lives of all the people she and Richard protected.

She no longer saw the consul general, or even a man.

This was the embodiment of a shapeless enemy come to destroy their world—her world. This was the face of evil.

There would be no mercy.

If he recognized what was about to happen, he didn't show it. All she saw in his dark eyes was the twisted hate of his determined, lethal intent. She no longer felt anger, nor was there any sorrow for what she was about to do to this man. As angry as she had been at him moments before, as her power ignited all emotion vanished, replaced by an overwhelming void, a space between thought, between feeling, between instants.

Time was hers.

Frozen there before her, she saw every bead of sweat on his brow and the bald top of his head. She had enough time to have counted those droplets. If she had wanted to, she could have counted all the whiskers on his face.

She had an eternity of time as the full fury of her will came to life.

It was breathtaking, intoxicating, as if her entire being were being sucked into that avalanche of power as it crashed into the man thrusting his knife toward her.

Thunder without sound jolted the air… exquisite, violent, and for that pristine instant, sovereign.

4

"What do you think it could mean, Lord Rahl?" the gravedigger asked.

As he wrung his hands, his head hunched down into his shoulders with the anxiety of standing before the Lord Rahl as well as an array of officials and so many soldiers and spectators. Richard could see that the man's fingernails were permanently stained with the dirt he worked in every day, but more so from the dead bodies he routinely handled.

"How often has this happened?" Richard asked.

"Several times," the man said, suddenly becoming animated as he gestured with the hand holding his battered old hat. "The dead animals were found on all the graves twice last month alone. People are frightened."

"What kind of animals?" Richard asked.

The gravedigger spread his hands with a shrug. "All sorts of animals, Lord Rahl. Raccoons, a few foxes, cats, dogs, squirrels, chipmunks, pigeons, starlings, an owl, and other sorts of birds. Even some fish. All manner of animals. Some looked fresh dead, and some looked long dead, with everything else in between. Some still warm, some barely more than bones inside scraps of hide, some writhing with maggots. It has the entire town upset and they expect an answer from me as I have been entrusted to care for the graves of their loved ones, but I have no answer for them."

As the gravedigger was talking, Richard spotted a woman in among the petitioners pushing her way forward through the spellbound crowd as they waited to hear what the Lord Rahl would have to say about the alarming mystery of dead animals found on graves. People grumbled irritably but moved aside as the woman pushed them out of her way.

The statuesque woman looked to be no older than Richard. She had long, straight dark hair, parted in the middle, and the kind of achingly feminine features that could easily melt men's hearts, or just as easily turn intimidating enough to make them stutter. This was a woman who appeared to brook no one questioning her authority to do as she pleased, a woman who expected her orders to be followed without question.

While she was distinctively dressed, it wasn't the kind of attire worn by nobility. It had more the look of practical yet alluring traveling clothes. The black cloak draped over her shoulders was held together at the top with bone buttons connected by a short silver chain. The black dress beneath the black cloak revealed a figure that had all the men gaping at her. It looked like she was used to ignoring such looks.

As she finally made her way to the front of the petitioners, a soldier to each side stepped up in front of her, to stop her from coming any closer and interrupting as well as to remind her to wait her turn.

Without so much as a glance at the soldiers, the woman put a finger to their shoulders, first one and then the other. The soldiers' eyes rolled up as they crumpled to the ground at her feet. She stepped over them without missing a stride as she continued forward.

Richard lifted the finger of each hand resting on the table to signal the guards to each side not to interfere. This was a situation he needed to handle or it could get ugly.

The gravedigger still hadn't seen the graceful creature approaching from behind. "So what do you think, Lord Rahl? What do you think could be the cause of all those dead animals found on graves?"

The woman gently pushed the gravedigger aside. "Have you considered that maybe some boys are playing pranks?" she said to him.

The gravedigger suddenly saw her and shrank away.

Richard couldn't help smiling. That was what he had been about to say.

The woman had the strangest aura radiating around her. It had some elements he recognized and others he'd never seen before. Even had he not been able to see her aura, though, he could have told by her bearing alone that this was not a woman to be trifled with.

She opened the gate without invitation and stepped inside the railing.

"I have come a long way to see you, Lord Rahl. I did not realize that once I got here I would find that you are an idiot."

Those close enough to have heard her gasped.

Richard came to his feet as the woman boldly strode up the three steps onto the broad platform.

"What have you done to my men? If you've harmed them, you are going to find yourself in a great deal of trouble."

She glanced briefly over her shoulder to see the men still crumpled, unmoving, on the floor. She dismissed it with a flick of a hand. "They are merely asleep. No harm has come to them."

"How can I be sure of that?"

She made a face at the fuss and then snapped her fingers. The men suddenly woke, rubbing their eyes as if groggy. They realized where they were and quickly scrambled to their feet, looking embarrassed but no worse for wear.

"See?" she asked. "I don't lie."

Richard leveled a glare on her. "And who might you be?"

She waved the hand again, this time as if to say she was sorry to have forgotten to introduce herself.

"My name is Shale."

"And where have you traveled this great distance from?"

She flicked the hand back over her shoulder. "I come from the Northern Waste."

Richard had never heard of the Northern Waste. "Does it snow a lot in the Northern Waste?"

Curiosity creased her smooth brow. "Of course. That, among other reasons, is why it is called the Waste."

Richard gestured to her dark clothing. "Don't you kind of stand out in the snow?"

"Stand out...?" She looked down at herself and suddenly understood his meaning. She looked unexpectedly amused. The look flattered her features. "I see what you mean."

She lifted her arms and then turned her hands palm up while letting her hands gracefully glide down beside the length of her to her hips. As her hands descended, her hair remained the same dark color, but

her outfit transformed from black to white, making her look like some
sort of mythical snow queen.

"There. Better?"

The crowd gasped and buzzed at the sight. First a threat of
assassination, and now this display of magic. It was proving to be the
kind of exciting day they had come hoping for.

Richard now knew at least some of what he was dealing with and
what it was about her aura that had puzzled him.

He crooked two fingers, motioning for her to approach so that he
could talk to her privately without the gathered throng hearing them.
Only the five remaining Mord-Sith were close behind him, all in white
leather except Vika, who was in red.

Shale didn't seem the least bit intimidated by the Mord-Sith as
she came right up against the opposite side of the heavy table. Had
the table not been there he suspected she would have come close
enough to dance with him. Whatever else she was, this woman was
not shy.

"You have made a poor first impression, Shale," he told her.

She blinked in surprise at someone being so blunt with her. It was
obvious she was not at all used to anyone taking that tone with her.
Her gaze fell away as she blushed.

"I apologize, Lord Rahl," she said after a moment. "One of my bad
habits." She bowed her head. "If it pleases you, may I start over?"

"I tend to share that same bad habit," Richard said with a small
smile. "Why don't you tell me why you're here, and what's so urgent
that you would come up out of turn?"

She took a breath to settle herself before beginning. "As I said, I
come from the Northern Waste. It's a barren land far from here, a harsh
place to live, but there are those who live there, many like me because
they were born there and it's all they know. Others come because they
feel lost in the world and so they want to become lost in the Waste. It's
a harsh place to live, and a harsher place to die."

"And you are their leader? Their queen or something?"

She blushed again. "I don't have so important a title. I... watch over
them. They think of me as their shepherd, I guess you could say. I have

no title as such. I am simply known as Shale. For the people in the Northern Waste, that name is title enough."

He imagined it was. By the undulating, crackling look of her aura, he was sure it was.

"I think you are more than simply 'Shale'. You are a witch woman?"

She lifted her chin, looking a little startled. "Yes and no."

"What does that mean?"

"My mother was a witch woman, but my father was a wizard. That combination made me a bit of both. I am a sorceress—with the gift from my father's side—and a witch woman from my mother. I am told that such a combination makes me... unique."

That explained the aura. "Each of us is unique in our own way," Richard said.

Her brow bunched as she peered at him. "What an odd thing to say."

"Not so odd. Please go on."

"For some reason my parentage makes me adept at healing, among other things. The people of the Northern Waste depend on me for that ability, among those other things, when in dire circumstances."

"So why have you come here?"

"The Waste is a forgotten place, but it does have its advantages. When there were cruel rulers in the past, such as Darken Rahl, living in a forgotten place was not such a bad thing. With men like Darken Rahl in power, some would say it was a blessing. Men like Darken Rahl would have eliminated a woman like me."

"Or enslaved you."

"Could be. Men of power don't tend to like others with brains and ability. Especially women. I heard it said during the great war that you were different. And now word of the war ending has finally reached us. Word of a peace under the D'Haran Empire is welcome news.

"I have come to offer the loyalty of the Northern Waste to the Lord Rahl and the D'Haran Empire."

Richard bowed his head. "Thank you."

"But now that I am here," she said, her brow drawing down again as her voice took on a dark edge, "I find the new Lord Rahl is an idiot."

All the Mord-Sith flicked their Agiels up into their fists.

Shale noted it with indifference.

Vika, in her red leather, leaned in on Richard's left side to point her Agiel at the woman on the other side of the heavy table. "I indulged you the first time you said that. I will not allow the second time to pass."

Richard put his left arm out to stop Vika from launching over the table at Shale. "Let me handle this." He gave the angry Mord-Sith a patient look. "Please?"

Vika finally relented and moved back, but not as far as before, and she didn't drop her Agiel.

"I can let insults pass as they are merely words, but I would like to know the reason for it."

Shale put her fists on the table and leaned in toward him.

"What did that fat pig in white robes tell you?"

"Some crazy nonsense about wanting us to surrender our world."

"Didn't I also hear him say that you are the last of the Rahl line, and that your wife is the last Confessor, and that when you two die his goddess will then have our world?"

"Yes, that's right. What of it?"

Her expression hardened. "In other words, for this goddess to take over our world, your line must end, the Mother Confessor's line must end. You must die. Your wife must die. That man said as much, either by execution or assassination."

Richard nodded. "That's the gist of it."

"He said your wife needs to die," Shale repeated carefully as she cocked her head. "And you let her be alone with him?"

Richard stared at Shale a moment. He blinked.

"I'm an idiot."

"Nice to know we agree."

Just then, Cassia raced into the room, vaulted over the railing without missing a beat, and bounded up the steps to the raised area with the table. She gulped air, trying to catch her breath enough to talk.

"Lord Rahl! You have to come quick! Something happened! Something bad!"

5

Richard charged through the hallways and corridors behind a frantic Cassia toward the room where Kahlan had taken Nolo for questioning—a place where she could use her Confessor power without having to worry about hurting anyone else.

A lone man had never been a threat to Kahlan. Rather, her Confessor power made her an overwhelming threat to him. Richard couldn't imagine what could have gone wrong. Whatever had happened, he didn't want to waste time questioning Cassia—

He just wanted to get to Kahlan.

When Richard had raced out of the great hall, Shale had followed close on his heels. The rest of the Mord-Sith ran in a cluster behind them. Behind the Mord-Sith a large force of men of the First File flooded through the narrow halls and wide passageways like a raging torrent of dark water. All their weapons hanging from belts filled the halls with a metallic jangle.

As they abruptly spilled into a round entrance hall that was painted white, Cassia slid to a stop on the polished black and white marble floor.

"Here, Lord Rahl! This is where they are." Cassia frantically shook her hand toward a heavy oak door, then raced around a table with stone mountain lions for legs. "In here! I tried hard as I could but I couldn't get the door open."

Richard could hear eerie shrieks and howls coming from the other side of the door.

"Why is this door bolted on the outside?" he yelled at Cassia as he slammed the bolt back out of the way.

"It—it wasn't, Lord Rahl," she stammered in surprise. "I swear. We never bolted the door. As I stood guard, everything suddenly shook like lightning had hit the palace, but there was no sound of thunder. Then I heard screams and howling. One of those screams was from the Mother Confessor.

"I tried frantically to open the door to help her, but I couldn't. Maybe the door was bolted from the other side as well, I don't know, but this side was not bolted when I came to get you, I swear."

Richard tried to open the door as she was talking, but it wouldn't budge. After slamming into it with his shoulder twice, he knew it was too big and heavy, and with its massive metal strap hinges they were not going to simply break it down. Howls were still coming from the other side.

Driven by urgent need, Richard's right hand went to the hilt of his sword at his left hip. The rage from the sword was already rising to meet his. Those twin furies, his and the sword's, spiraled together into a storm of lethal power.

In a near trance of rage, their power joined, Richard drew the sword. The steel, with its dark metallic gleam from having been touched by the world of the dead, rang out as it cleared the scabbard and emerged into the air for the first time in what seemed ages. That singular, deadly sound echoed through the hallways and corridors.

Richard had thought that it would be a long time before he ever needed to draw this ancient weapon again. As had so often happened, that time had come sooner than he expected, but in a way it was profoundly gratifying to be joined with the sword's magic once more, to know that it was still there, to feel it rise to his call.

With a cry of fury, holding the weapon in both hands, Richard unleashed a mighty swing. The tip of the blade whistled as it arced through the air. The sword cut an explosive swath through both the massive oak door and the stone walls to either side as if they were no more than mere gossamer. In the relatively confined space, the sound of rock and oak shattering was deafening. Chips of stone, both large and small, as well as a shower of oak splinters, rained down on everyone. The table was covered in crumbles of stone debris. One of the broken iron strap hinges skittered off down the hallway.

As large stone blocks tumbled across the black and white marble floor, the top half of the door let out a groan and then dropped heavily to the ground with a loud thud. Richard kicked over the bottom half and dove sword-first through the billowing dust into darkness.

The room was dark as pitch, with only the meager light of the reflector lamps on the walls in the outer room spilling in through the blasted opening to light a small area of the floor directly inside. It wasn't much.

In that weak light, Richard saw the Estorian at the end of the room to the left, racing back and forth, crashing into one wall only to rebound and race toward the other, where he leaped up, landed his feet on the stone wall, then bounded back to crash a shoulder into the opposite wall. Back and forth he went at a frantic pace, screaming, howling, and shrieking the whole time. Richard could hardly believe that the rotund man could move with such speed and power.

In between the howls and smacking into walls, the battered Nolo paused briefly to throw his head back and bark like a dog. He seemed oblivious to anyone else being in the room. A mask of blood from crashing into the stone walls covered his face. A large scrap of scalp hung down, exposing bone. Blood ran in rivulets down around his ear. His once-white robes were now wet and red.

All of his wounds and broken bones didn't seem to bother him or slow him down in the least. He was apparently being driven by some frantic internal need. With his head split open and all the blood he had lost, it was a wonder he was still conscious, much less alive.

Richard frantically peered around the room, trying to see in the dusty darkness.

"Get some light in here!" he yelled back out through the ravaged doorway at the soldiers.

As he did, other big men ran in to capture the howling consul general. Four of them tackled him. Despite their combined weight and strength, they had trouble controlling him. In his frenzy he pushed all four men back, their feet sliding on the floor. They pounced again.

With a howl from Nolo, the whole lot of them tumbled to the floor. The man's arms flailed as he struggled to get free of all the powerful men grappling with him.

Shale rushed into the chaos and squatted, squeezing herself in between the soldiers struggling to hold the howling man down. She placed her hand, her fingers spread, over his face. He shook violently beneath it. He froze abruptly, blinked, and then his eyes rolled up in his head. He finally slumped into an unconscious heap.

Men with torches finally raced into the gloomy room, providing light, but the dust swirling around in the air still drastically cut the visibility. In the illumination provided by the sputtering flames of the torches, Richard was able to see that most of the furniture in the room had been smashed. Splinters from the broken furniture lay scattered all over the floor. A table on its side and a badly misshapen wardrobe were the only things mostly intact.

Richard could see light leaking in through cracks in the outer wall where some of the limestone blocks had been displaced. Those cracks allowed slivers of daylight to show through from outside. Kahlan's power unleashed in such a confined space had apparently buckled the blocks outward. She must have unleashed everything she had to have nearly blown out the stone walls.

Richard hunted frantically through the dusty darkness, upending the table that lay on its side, flipping over a tented rug, kicking a night table out of his way, searching. He finally spotted Kahlan in a far corner on the opposite side of the room to the right, behind the broken, over-turned wardrobe. In the murky light he couldn't tell if she was all right, or hurt, or even alive.

Richard grabbed a stubby leg of the wardrobe and heaved it back out of his way as he dove in close and knelt down in front of Kahlan. The wardrobe crashed to the ground and broke apart. The Mord-Sith rifled through the murky darkness, looking for any sign of threat.

Slumped back in the corner, Kahlan stared blankly out at nothing. Tears ran down her cheeks as she panted in pain. Men with torches came in close behind Richard to provide more light.

The left sleeve of Kahlan's dress had been completely torn off at the top of her shoulder. There were three long, deep claw marks starting at her shoulder and running down her arm to the bend in her elbow. The muscle had been laid open down to bone. Nolo wouldn't have been able to do that. It looked more like she had been mauled by a bear. As horrific as it looked, it at least didn't appear to have torn open an artery.

Richard, his heart hammering, fought his rising sense of panic as he saw, then, that there was a knife, its handle covered in blood like her white dress, buried to the hilt in the upper left side of her chest, near the top of her breast. There was also a deep, slashing knife wound across the right side of her rib cage from her armpit to her abdomen. The tatters of her dress, soaked with blood, were no longer remotely white. The gash had been deeply sliced open, the knife leaving nicks in each rib it crossed. There was so much blood he couldn't tell what other injuries she might have.

Kahlan was shaking and panting uncontrollably.

"It's all right, Kahlan. I'm here," he said as he gently pulled her toward him with his arm, sitting her up a little, holding her head to his shoulder while in one swift pull he yanked the knife out of her chest then quickly pressed his hand over her breast as he let his gift begin to flow into the wound to staunch the heavy flow of blood.

She let out a sob of pain.

"It's all right. I've got you."

"Did you see him?" she asked in a quavering voice as he laid her back. "Did you see him?"

"See who?" he asked as he was busy lifting parts of her torn dress aside to appraise her other wounds.

When she didn't answer, he looked up. She was staring off at nothing.

"See who?" he asked again.

She suddenly looked back at him, gripped his shirt at his throat in her good hand, and pulled herself close. Her green eyes were wild.

"The scribbly man... did you see him?"

Richard didn't have a clue what she was talking about, and right then and there it didn't really matter to him. No one had come out of the room, and he knew for a fact that there was no one else in there with them besides Nolo, soldiers, Mord-Sith, and Shale. She was probably delirious from loss of blood.

Shale knelt in beside Richard to help. Vika grabbed her arm to pull her back away.

Richard seized Vika's wrist. "Leave her be," he growled. "If not for Shale we wouldn't have gotten here in time to save Kahlan's life."

Vika nodded then, realizing he was right, and released her grip on Shale. "Sorry."

Shale quickly nodded, as if to say she understood how protective the Mord-Sith were.

Richard frowned, deep in concentration. "I'm stopping the bleeding from this stab wound… but I can feel something more than her wounds."

Shale pressed her hands to each side of Kahlan's head and closed her eyes, as if trying to discern what he was feeling.

"You need to stop what you're doing," she said with sudden urgency.

"What? She'll bleed to death!"

"No, you've already stopped the bleeding. Your gift is causing her pain."

"Healing causes pain as you lift their injury," he said. "I've healed her before when she'd been terribly wounded. I've done it before and I can do it again."

"Ordinarily you would be right. This is different." Shale seized his wrist and forcefully pulled his hand back. "Lord Rahl, you will make it worse if you do it that way."

"What do you mean, that way? I told you, I've healed her before. Healing is healing."

"Not this time," she said in a distracted tone. "You need to let me do this if we are to save her life. What you are doing will kill her." She looked up at him with frantic concern. "If you don't let me do this, she is going to die!"

Richard hesitated, then sat back up. "Maybe together we can—"

"No. You need to listen to me." Shale shot him a quick frown honed by years of authority. "I know you want more than anything to help, but trust me, in this case your gift will only make it worse.

"Why don't you go heal that lunatic? I'm sure you are going to want to question him about what happened in here. You can't question him if he dies. Right now he is our only link to what is happening and he is in bad shape. He didn't leave these claw marks. We need to know what did."

Richard felt sick seeing the bone in her arm where the meat was laid back. Even the white bone had long gouge marks down it. He ran his fingers through his hair as he sat back on his heels.

Shale obviously knew what she was doing, even if he wasn't at all happy about not being able to help.

Holding the sides of Kahlan's head, Shale used her thumbs to gently close her eyes. It was somehow less frightening seeing Kahlan with her eyes closed. When they were opened, he could see the terror.

Richard didn't know what she had seen, but it was clear how much it had frightened her. Kahlan was not easily shaken, but she was now.

Once her eyes were closed, her panting slowed to even breathing, though it was ragged with stitches of pain. Leaving Shale to work on Kahlan, Richard reluctantly turned to seeing about the unconscious Nolo. He wasn't really interested in saving Nolo's life, but Shale was right about their need to question him. Something other than Nolo had attacked Kahlan, and they needed to know what it was.

Questioning the man was what Kahlan had been trying to do with her Confessor ability. Richard had seen her use her power since the first day he'd met her. It was as profound a use of the gift as he had ever seen. There was nothing that could stand up against it… as long as what it was being used on was human. He couldn't imagine what had gone wrong this time.

The soldiers stepped back out of his way as Richard placed the flat of his hand over the bleeding head wound to make sure the skull wasn't cracked. He found that it was. He released a flow of healing power through his gift. He wasn't careful about being gentle with how he did it. He didn't care how much it hurt the man, only that he lived. He forced bone together to close the crack and stop the loss of blood and fluid.

Even so, lifting such a severe injury from anyone was not only difficult, but caused agony to the one doing the healing. The more severe the injury or sickness, the greater the pain.

He knew that Shale would be in far greater pain taking the agony of Kahlan's wounds into herself in order to heal her.

Richard was so concerned about Kahlan that he endured the stress of healing the man's cracked skull almost without noticing the suffering he took into himself. Once he had the underlying structure repaired, he replaced the flap of scalp, placed a hand over it, and sent a flow of his gift into the wound.

Richard found that the man had several broken ribs, a broken collarbone, and a broken wrist. The ribs were relatively easy to mend with his gift, but the wrist was unexpectedly complex to heal. It had to be done in layers, bone by bone, until everything was back in place and the wrist moved as it should.

By the time Richard had finished and finally stood, his face was covered with a sheen of sweat. Nolo would still be unconscious for a time, but at least he wasn't going to die.

"Take him to the dungeon," he told the soldiers. "Put him in restraints so he can't hurt himself. It was a lot of work healing him. I don't want him splitting his head open again. I'm going to want to question him and I want him to be able to give me answers."

The soldiers all clapped fists to hearts before bending to the task. Even with four men, one on each arm and each leg, it was difficult to lug the dead weight of the heavy man out of the room.

Richard turned his attention back to Kahlan just as Shale stood. She gripped Richard's arm as he came close.

"It's all right, Lord Rahl. I've put her into a deep, healing sleep. The worst of the danger is past. I think she will be fine, but I've only pulled wounds together to stabilize her until we can get her to her room, where I can finish the work."

Richard nodded. "What about those three gouges down her arm?"

"I closed them as best I could for now, but her injuries are going to take a great deal more work to set everything right. I will need to fix the underlying layers so that her arm will work properly. I will need to work further down into the stab wound in her chest. Fortunately, while it did severe damage, it didn't cut her heart and kill her. It can all be healed."

Richard stared down at Kahlan. "What do you think did that—left those gouges down her arm?"

Shale hesitated. "What I can tell you is that Nolo didn't make them." She looked back down at Kahlan. "We should get her out of here and to bed. She needs to be cleaned up and I need to continue my work."

Richard bent down and carefully scooped Kahlan up in his arms. He didn't want anyone else carrying her.

Holding her in his arms, Richard looked to the six Mord-Sith. "Cassia, Vale, Berdine, Rikka, Nyda—I want you all to stay in the room with Kahlan and watch over her. Vika, I'll let you continue to have my back."

"Yes, Lord Rahl," they said as one.

"And I want you all in your red leather."

Their expressions grim, they all nodded.

"Let's go."

6

Once Richard had gently laid Kahlan in their bed, Shale pushed in beside him to sit on the edge of the bed to lay her hands on Kahlan's chest to continue the healing. Richard backed away, feeling useless when he thought he should be doing something. He'd healed Kahlan before when she had been seriously hurt. It didn't make any sense to him that he couldn't do it this time. Shale had saved Kahlan's life by making him go see if she was safe, so he trusted her. He didn't now want to start being suspicious of her.

He and Kahlan were so close that in the past that bond only helped make healing all that much more powerful and effective. It seemed to him that it should be the same now. He didn't know why Shale thought otherwise.

Berdine lit lamps around the room and then closed the heavy drapes. Rikka and Vale brought in more wood and fed some of it into the massive fireplace across the room to take the chill out of the air. Summer was giving way to autumn. Nyda brought sheets and blankets and laid them on a table nearby in case they should be needed. Cassia filled a basin on a white marble-top table with fresh water. All the Mord-Sith looked grim as they went about making sure everything they were able to do was tended to. Everyone wanted to help Kahlan, and he suspected they felt as useless as he did.

The knife wound in Kahlan's chest was closed. It had damaged her lung, but he had started healing it immediately when he first found her. At least he had managed to stop the bleeding right away. Even so, she had lost a lot of blood. Shale finished working on the knife wound and then used her gift to push in air to inflate the lung once more so Kahlan could breathe easier.

The claw marks down her arm were already closed with Shale's gift, but because they were so deep the sorceress said they would require more structural work. For now she had merely closed them and stopped the bleeding. It was obvious to Richard how methodical the sorceress was in the way she went about her work. Those massive wounds would need the layers of muscles to be properly joined back together one at a time so that full function would be restored to Kahlan's arm. Shale had also pulled together the gaping flesh across her ribs and closed the wound.

Thankfully, Shale had put Kahlan into a deep sleep so that she wouldn't feel much of anything as the sorceress went about the work.

Richard now realized that peacetime had lowered his guard. For years he had been used to being continually on alert for any trouble. He had found peacetime a respite. Besides that, a single man had never been any danger to a Confessor of Kahlan's power before. The reality was that it all had caused him to let down his guard. Shale had been right. He was an idiot. He could not feel more foolish for having it pointed out to him by a stranger. Maybe it was her fresh perspective, but whatever the reason, Shale's alertness had saved Kahlan's life.

Even given all that, Shale was also a witch woman, and that concerned him. His familiar state of suspicion was back in full force. He and Kahlan had a long history of trouble caused by witch women.

"You can stay and watch if you like," Shale said to him as he stood beside the bed staring down at the only woman he had ever loved—the only woman he could ever love. "I don't mind at all, Lord Rahl, really, and I completely understand if that is your wish. You don't really know me, so I take no offense at any suspicion you might have." She almost seemed to be reading his mind. "She is in good hands. I swear. I will let no harm come to her." With a quick smile, she tipped her head at the Mord-Sith. "Neither will they."

She was gently reminding him that there was some kind of trouble that had attacked Kahlan and it was his job as Lord Rahl to get to the bottom of it, not stand around twiddling his thumbs, worried about Kahlan while he watched her work.

There were things that only the Lord Rahl could do, and he realized he should get to it before anything else happened.

Richard nodded. "I need to go question the other Estorians. I want to question Nolo, too, but I want Kahlan well and at my side when I do. She used her power on him. If it worked at all, he will answer no one's questions but hers."

Shale pushed up her sleeves before going back to work on Kahlan as Richard left to go looking for trouble.

7

At the outer gate to the narrow road that wound its way down around the plateau to the Azrith Plain, Vika was already waiting with two horses. He had absently expected it to be Cara. In the past, it would have always been Cara ready to accompany him. Seeing Vika jolted him out of his thought and worry about Kahlan.

Cara was gone. She had done as she had always sworn she would do. She had given her life to save his. A day didn't go by that he didn't miss her.

Now Vika had taken Cara's place, and with no less resolve. Still, Cara had been more than his protector and friend. He almost always knew what she had been about to say before she said it and what she was going to do before she did it. Kahlan and he had come to love her like family. She was family. Strange as it sometimes seemed, all the Mord-Sith were, even if some of them were still only coming to understand that.

"While you were taking the Mother Confessor to your room I took the liberty of telling the commander of the First File that you would want the other Estorians detained. I hope I wasn't being too presumptuous."

She gestured with a tilt of her head toward the men of the First File already on horseback, waiting off to the side beside a towering outer wall of the palace.

Vika had done that entirely on her own initiative, without orders, something Mord-Sith had been trained not to do. He couldn't help smiling. That was what Cara would have done.

"Yes that was presumptuous, Vika. Well done. You go right on being presumptuous."

As she swung her leg up over the saddle, he saw her smile to herself. It occurred to Richard that she was going to be just fine.

Once in the saddle, Richard rested his hands over the saddle's horn as he surveyed the sprawling tent city far below. Flags and colorful streamers flew from many a tent. Smoke rose from cook fires. Horses, wagons, and carts moved slowly through the confined spaces crowded with people. It was a festive occasion. Richard had already begun to think of it as a threatening one. He was beginning to wonder if they should cancel the public audience and disband the tent city.

Above them the palace rose up, its towering heights resplendent in a single shaft of late-day sun just peeking through a rare break in the thick layers of clouds. He could see people strolling across bridges between towers or on ramparts or looking out from taller sections. Other people on balconies outside many of the rooms met for conversation while they marveled at the views.

While most of them had never thought it would come, it was peacetime. Everyone seemed relaxed. Everyone seemed in a good mood. Richard, too, had been relaxed. Too relaxed.

As the clouds rolled together, they closed the gap and blocked off the sun. The day grew somber. The threatening sky matched his mood. The bottoms of dark, turbulent clouds lowered, silently drifting by, just beginning to brush the higher parts of the palace.

In the distance, the Azrith Plain vanished in a gloomy haze. On the plain below the plateau, in the muted light, the temporary tent city took on a drab appearance. Somewhere down there were the rest of the Estorians.

With two fingers Richard lifted his sword a few inches in its gold and silver scabbard to make sure it was clear before squeezing his legs against the sides of his horse to start it ahead at an easy trot. The cavalry fell in behind him and Vika.

Richard felt as if peacetime had abruptly come to an end. He was back in a familiar war-wizard state of mind. As they started out, the breeze lifted his gold cape, a part of a war wizard's outfit.

Along with the smell of approaching rain, the aromas of cooking reached all the way up to the top of the plateau. The smells made his stomach grumble. He realized he hadn't had a thing to eat all day.

The ride down the narrow road was the fastest way to get to the Azrith Plain. There were internal passageways through the interior of the massive plateau that could accommodate large forces of troops going down or coming back up, but they were not as fast as the road. As he and Vika galloped along, with a small army behind them, he could see the bridge already being lowered. They didn't slow.

With a tip of his head, Richard acknowledged the men lined up to the side with fists to their hearts as he and Vika raced by. These men prevented any attack from below ever making it up the road. With the bridge up, there was no way to get up the plateau from the outside. On the inside, the great doors could be closed if necessary to prevent access to the palace from within.

The tent city spread out down on the plain was a congested place filled with the racket of all the people crowded close together. Most people wanted their tents offering services and items for sale to be as close as possible to the opening that went up the inside of the plateau to the palace above. Not everyone wanted to make the long climb up. Most of the assembled crowd simply wanted to be present for the occasion or else to sell things to people who had gathered.

Ill-planned passageways among the tents served as roads. They had started out in the beginning as wide thoroughfares, but then people took advantage of that open space to set up their own smaller tents and stands to have a better spot along the roads to hawk their wares, sell food, and provide every service from farriers to palm readers to men who pulled teeth. With everyone staking out prime territory, it had eventually narrowed the roads. With all the people on foot, on horses, in wagons, and pulling carts, what passageways there were became clogged. It slowed Richard and his party considerably, as they had to take time to carefully pick their way through.

When people saw that it was the Lord Rahl, yet more rushed to push in close, reaching out to touch him, or touch his horse. Cheers rang out, as if the dark day had dampened their spirits, but now such an unexpected sight had renewed their optimism. Men waved their hats, women waved scarves, people held children up to see.

Richard did his best to smile and wave acknowledgment of the greetings. The people were all there because they were happy to have a world at peace all thanks to Lord Rahl and wanted to show their appreciation. He didn't want to extinguish their good spirits. While these people were in a sudden celebratory mood, Richard wasn't.

With a hand signal, he ordered the commander of the cavalry forward, and he asked to have the soldiers clear a path so they could make it through the growing throng of excited people before they were mobbed.

Some of the soldiers pushed off ahead, shouting warnings for people to move aside and make way, making it sound like it was for their own safety, and not merely an order for them to defer to an important man. That simple method worked better than harsh orders yelled at people, and didn't dampen their mood. It appeared that the commander had used some intelligent initiative of his own.

At intersections with side passageways, soldiers placed their horses to block off the roads to clear the way for Richard. As people moved back, it made progress considerably quicker. All eyes remained on Richard in his black and gold war-wizard outfit and gold cape flowing out behind, as well as the Mord-Sith in red leather. These people had obviously never expected the Lord Rahl himself to come down among them, down from the grand People's Palace to their grubby tent city. The presence of a Mord-Sith would add an air of danger to the story once these people eventually returned home.

On one hand, it was heartwarming to be down in the tent city. These were the kind of simple people he had grown up with. On the other hand, someone from down here had threatened him and Kahlan, and then tried to kill her.

When they finally reached the tent with its sides rolled up to the roof, there was already a large force of men of the First File there. They surrounded the tent, all with pikes lowered, all pointing at the small group of people clustered in the center of the tent. It would have been impossible for any of them to leave without being skewered on at least half a dozen steel-tipped pikes.

Richard swung down from the saddle and handed the reins to a soldier. He glanced up to see a sky darker-looking than it had been only a little earlier when he had left the top of the plateau. It wouldn't be long before the rains came and turned the temporary dirt streets through the tent city into a muddy quagmire.

The men guarding the Estorians formed an intimidating wall of dark leather and chain mail behind the pikes. The soldiers made way when they saw that it was the Lord Rahl and a Mord-Sith in red leather who needed to get through.

Although the people in white robes who were huddled together in the center of their tent didn't look like they were trembling in fear, they certainly didn't look at ease, either. He supposed that diplomats weren't used to dealing with direct threats of weapons pointed at them. Inside the broad tent, to the sides, were small tables and simple stools where they could discuss their services with potential customers. Quills and ink stood ready for signing agreements for their services. Everyone in the cluster of people wore white robes with varying amounts of silver embroidery; none of them were openly armed. A few women among them cowered in the center, surrounded by their men.

"What is it, Lord Rahl?" one of the men asked as he took a step away from his comrades. They all cast worried looks at the Mord-Sith in red leather. "Whatever the problem might be, it surely has to be a misunderstanding of some kind. There is no need for displays of weapons. We are all more than open to discussing the matter, whatever it is, and coming to a mutually agreeable resolution."

Richard's gaze swept over the group and then returned to settle on the man who had spoken.

"One of your group tried to murder the Mother Confessor," Richard said without preamble. "What would be your agreeable resolution to that?"

They all looked too shocked to answer or even profess their innocence. They certainly didn't look dangerous, but then again, neither had the pear-shaped Nolo.

"What can you tell me about a member of your group named Nolodondri?" Richard asked as he took an aggressive step closer, the palm of his left hand resting on the hilt of his sword.

They all took a step back as one. A wall of soldiers with leveled, steel-tipped pikes behind them just outside the open back of the tent left no real room for further retreat.

"Nolo? He is the consul general," the same man said. "Our leader."

"What is your name?"

The man swallowed. "Jason, Lord Rahl. I am an aide to the consul general."

"Why have you all come here, Jason?"

Jason gestured around at the small tables. "We only came to discuss our diplomatic services with interested parties. We are seeking work. As you can imagine, the end of wars that have raged throughout our lives has left us to look hard for people needing our services. Of course there is always need for diplomacy. This gathering seemed like a good opportunity to make ourselves better known in the empire at large."

"Why did the consul general come up to the palace?"

Jason glanced up at the plateau. He looked a little confused. "Nolo went up to the palace?"

Richard nodded without saying anything. He had learned as the Seeker that his silence and direct glare often did more to prompt answers than anything else.

"He left early this morning," Jason offered. "We didn't know he was going up to the palace, I swear. We assumed he was merely going around visiting those gathered down here to ask them to stop by to speak with us about our very reasonably priced services.

"Our plan has always been to be down here, among the great gathering, so that we might make valuable contacts. There was no plan for any of us to go up to the palace itself. That would provide no benefit for us, as we know that the palace would hardly need our humble services. It would be those who deal with you and the D'Haran Empire who might want our help and guidance in diplomatic matters. That kind of person or representative of an outlying district would be down here, not up there."

"Tell me about Nolo," Richard said. "Has he said anything out of the ordinary? Has he acted out of the ordinary?"

The people behind Jason shared looks. "As a matter of fact," Jason said, hesitantly, "he has been acting… a bit strange."

"Define 'strange,'" Richard said.

The man spread his hands as he tried to think of how to explain it. "Well, for one thing, the consul general has been going for walks. Mostly at night."

Richard frowned at the man. "Why is that out of the ordinary? Lots of people go for walks."

Jason suddenly blushed at having to explain it. "The consul general is a… well, a large man, I guess you could say. Because of his size he has bad knees. He has difficulty standing for any length of time, much less walking very far at all. But lately he has been going on walks—alone, by his choice, without any of his top advisors." Jason gestured to some of the men behind him in the more elaborately embroidered robes.

Richard's gaze swept across the huddled group again, pausing to take in the higher-ranking advisors. "Do any of you know why he went for these walks, where he went, or if he met anyone while out on these nightly jaunts?"

Everyone shook their heads.

"And no one questioned him about his knees and how they fared on these walks?" Everyone shook their heads again. "What else has he been doing that is out of the ordinary? Perhaps he said something about the walks, where he went, or someone he might have spoken with?"

Once again, everyone shook their heads.

Richard took a step closer, Vika, his ever-present shadow, moving with him. "What else, Jason, has the consul general done that you thought was strange? No matter how small it may have seemed, I want you to tell me about it."

Jason put a finger to his lower lip as he squinted in recollection. "Yes." He took the finger away from his lip and shook it as he remembered. "He did say something odd this morning before he left."

"Like what?"

"He said he had to go see the shiny man. But he didn't say it to us, exactly. He mumbled it to himself."

Richard frowned. "The shiny man. What does that mean, the shiny man?"

"I'm sorry, Lord Rahl, but I haven't the slightest idea. It was early this morning. He simply said that he had to go see the shiny man. We saw him say this to himself, then he left without saying a word to any of us. We didn't know what he meant and we certainly didn't suspect that he was going up to the palace. We were all bewildered by his behavior. We haven't seen him since."

8

Richard, his arms folded over his chest, leaned his shoulders back against one of the small granite columns that stood on each side of the corridor as he brooded. That corridor was the only way into the entry area outside the master bedroom. The single broad corridor led out to a network of passageways. Soldiers were stationed back a ways in that corridor as well as in every branching hall. The large entry area outside the master bedroom was elaborately decorated with raised panels of book-matched crotch mahogany polished to a high luster. Detailed layers of crown molding finished off the look.

Richard's gaze was locked on the double doors on the opposite side of the entryway. They were carved with ornate designs that mimicked the spell-form the palace itself was laid out to. Kahlan was on the other side of those closed doors. He was beside himself with worry about what was going on and why it was taking so long. If he could, he would have willed the doors open.

As he agonized about Kahlan, he also thought about his meeting with the Estorians. He didn't trust anything they had told him, even if he had to admit that on the surface it had all seemed to ring true. But these were diplomats who were versed in making any argument sound reasonable. For all Richard knew, they could be lying through their teeth and they could have all been part of an elaborate plot to assassinate him and Kahlan. Richard was no longer taking anything for granted. His suspicious, questioning nature was on full alert.

For the time being, the Estorians weren't going anywhere. Their tent had been rolled up by the soldiers and put in storage. Meanwhile, Richard saw to it that they all were placed in "guest" rooms and asked not to leave until the situation could be straightened out.

To ensure they didn't decide to leave, they were being heavily guarded with instructions that they remain confined. Richard didn't want them wandering off in case more questions came up, or if anything they said turned out not to be true. He especially didn't want them wandering around loose in the palace if it turned out they were part of an assassination plot.

Richard shifted his weight to his other leg as he waited. The soldiers stationed in the corridors had told him that Shale hadn't come out yet. Neither had any of the Mord-Sith in there watching over Kahlan.

Since it was deep in the middle of the night, Richard had sent Vika off, against her objections, to get some sleep. She complied, but grumbled as she stormed off like a pouty child sent to bed early.

The constant worry was wearing on him. He considered going in to see what was happening and why it was taking so long, but he didn't want to interrupt the sorceress if the healing was at a critical juncture. He knew from experience that in the very intense process of healing a seriously injured person, he wouldn't want someone coming up to tap him on the shoulder and ask how it was going.

Just then the door opened. It was Shale coming out.

Richard rushed across the elaborate, deep-blue-and-orange-carpeted entryway to meet her. She was once again in the black outfit she had been wearing when he had first seen her.

He knew that, with a witch woman, there was no telling what their clothing really looked like or for that matter what they even really looked like. They somehow had the ability to bend things into an illusion, or perhaps it was an ability to alter a viewer's vision to what they expected to see. Shota had been able to change her appearance at will. From his experience, a witch woman showed you only what she wanted you to see, or what you expected to see, not what was really there to see. Shale obviously had at least some of that same ability. He wondered how much she wanted him to see of her true self.

As she approached, before he could even ask, Shale lifted a hand. "Your wife is going to be fine, Lord Rahl. I am relieved to report that she is past the biggest danger. There is more I will need to do, but for now I want to let her get some sleep. For the rest of the healing she first needs a good night's sleep."

Richard craned sideways to look into the room before Berdine closed the double doors. She flashed him a smile that looked more brave than happy. He was able to look past her to see Kahlan lying in the bed, her hands folded over her stomach, her eyes closed. She looked to be resting peacefully. He was also relieved to see that she was in a clean nightdress, rather than her bloody white Confessor dress.

"What do you mean?" Richard asked, looking back at Shale. "What more do you need to do?"

The sorceress let out a weary sigh. "There was another puncture wound in her right side that we didn't see before because of all the blood. It was another wound from a claw—like the one that tore up her left arm. I think that whatever attacked her must have impaled her with a claw into her side to incapacitate her while it tore her arm apart with its other claw. It caused a kind of wasting damage to some internal organs."

Richard's alarm rose to a new level. "Wasting damage—you mean like from snake venom?"

"Something like that. Fortunately it moves through the victim more like molasses than venom so it's not as aggressive as a viper's poison would be. It's as lethal, just not as fast. I found that it had caused similar tissue damage in her arm."

"So then she's been poisoned?"

"Yes... but not exactly." Shale made a face, trying to think of how to explain it. She looked up when it came to her. "You know how when a cat claws you it may not look very bad, but then in a day or two your whole arm is red and swollen to twice its size?"

"I suppose so."

"It's something like that. More than an infection and less than poison. I'm able to heal it, but it's more complicated than simply healing an ordinary wound."

"But she is well, now?"

"She's resting comfortably for now. She still has damage and I will need to finish the healing. What is to come is a painful process of tearing apart tissues that have attached improperly after the attack and then setting them right. I healed those things that were urgent and I put her into a deep sleep so that she could rest more easily.

"Rest will help stabilize her so that her body can heal some of the other things on her own. Rest is a great medicine. Tomorrow, or maybe the next day, when she has a good dose of that medicine and is strong enough to handle it, I will be able to finish."

"But in the meantime, aren't those things not yet healed, or attached improperly, a danger to her?"

Shale smiled in a way that said she found his worry endearing but overwrought.

"Lord Rahl, trust me. I know what I'm doing. Everything is under control and proceeding as it needs to."

When he didn't seem all that relieved, Shale pressed the flat of her hand to his chest. He felt the warmth of magic meant to reassure him radiating from that hand through his body. While it was a nice gesture, he didn't appreciate it.

"I swear to you," Shale said, taking her hand back, "she is past the danger that threatened her life. When she has rested and regained enough strength I will finish it and you will have your beautiful lady back, good as before. All right?"

Richard nodded as he walked off a few paces, letting his fingertips drag over the smooth surface of the eight-sided marble tabletop sitting in the middle of the entryway. The colorful flowers in the three vases in the center lent a calming aroma to the entire room. It reminded him of the outdoors where he had grown up. He took a deep breath of that fragrance and let it out slowly, relieved to have his agony of worry eased somewhat.

"Thank you, Shale. You've saved her twice. First, when you alerted me to how careless I was being, and then with the healing."

As his grandfather had often warned him, peacetime was sometimes more dangerous than war. He had let his guard down. He could just imagine Zedd's scowl at him being so careless. He vowed not to let it happen again.

"I'm glad I was here to help," Shale said from behind him.

He looked back over his shoulder, giving her a more critical look. "Your clothes are black, again."

She knitted her fingers together in front of her as she twisted her mouth, looking up as she thought how to answer what was obviously a question.

"You don't know much about women's dress, do you?"

Richard shrugged at the strange question. "I know what I like looking at. But I have a feeling you mean something else."

She smiled. "Women don't like wearing the same dress as another woman to an important gathering—or any gathering, for that matter. It is well known that the Mother Confessor wears a white dress. While not the same dress, I still did not want to come before you both in the great hall appearing to disrespect her by also wearing her traditional white."

Richard was a bit surprised. "I guess you put more thought into it than I would have."

"That's because you're a man."

"And why did you come here in the first place?"

She was momentarily caught off guard. "You ask strange questions out of the blue, Lord Rahl."

"I am the Seeker." He tapped the hilt of his sword. "I carry the Sword of Truth. I ask those things which need asking. So why did you really come here?"

"I told you, I came to offer the loyalty of the Northern Waste to the D'Haran Empire."

"I'm not in a very good mood, Shale. That's an excuse. Tell me the real reason you're here."

9

Shale sagged a little as she wiped a weary hand back across her face. "I'd prefer not to have to get into it just now, not after what's happened today, and not after I spent so much time and energy in a difficult healing, but I can see that you aren't going to be satisfied until you know the truth. I will give you the gist of it, but ask that we discuss it in detail later, after I have had some rest."

Richard shrugged. "Fair enough."

"I admit there is more to why I'm here. You say you ask those things which need to be asked. There are things which I need to ask as well. I came for answers to those things."

"Such as?"

Her bewitching eyes looked up at him from under her brow. "Such as why are the stars not where they belong in the sky? Why are the stars all jumbled up so that I no longer recognize them?"

Richard let out a long sigh. "Oh, that."

Her look darkened. "Yes, that. I have a feeling that only you could be responsible."

Richard lifted a hand in a gesture reflecting his discomfort about the subject. "I had to initiate a star shift. It was an act of desperation."

"I see that you are going to make me chase you round and round and then strangle you until you answer." She gave him the kind of dangerously sober look that seemed unique to witch women. "What is a star shift, Lord Rahl," she said slowly and carefully, "and what was the desperation?"

"It had to do with an evil that had festered for thousands of years, and a war that had never really ended. An emperor from that time rose up from the grave, tearing the veil between life and death in the process. He intended to join the underworld and the world of life, foolishly believing he could rule over it all."

Her mouth opened in surprise. "Combining them would have only destroyed both!"

Richard's brow lifted. "Glad you grasp the problem. To stop him from finishing what he had already begun to do, I had to use the boxes of Orden for their true purpose—initiating a star shift."

"Boxes of Orden?"

"Ancient magic, constructed spell and all that," he said with a dismissive gesture that said that wasn't the important point.

"And that put this evil spirit back in his grave where he belonged?"

"It did," Richard said. "It healed the veil and ended the ancient war that had smoldered all that time only to finally reignite. I can't begin to know how many people died because of that evil man. People we all know and loved died. Too many good souls never had a chance to live their lives because of him. Many more would have died if I hadn't done something. Everyone would have died. I had to put a stop to it.

"I did it in the only way that could work. It changed our world, I admit that. But I don't regret what I did. It saved life itself."

"But how is it possible for the stars to be different?"

"The ancient magic I used was the only thing that had the power to close the breach and stop the worlds of life and death from imploding. It's a bit like a constructed spell. Once initiated, it runs routines according to its internal protocol. That power, once ignited, ultimately shifted the stars."

She looked even more upset. "But how could you have unleashed such a—"

"Had I not done as I did we would all be dead right now. Do you understand? Dead. Worse than that, the worlds of life and death would have come together and both would have ceased to exist. Everyone forever would have ceased to exist. We were all out of time. It was either the star shift or no world of life, simple as that. I chose life.

"Some of the changes caused by the star shift are known—such as the stars suddenly being unfamiliar to us. But it altered other things as well. We don't yet know the extent of the changes."

She peered up at him in dismay. "Are you sure? There was no other way?"

"None," he said with finality. "It wasn't a situation of my choosing. Like I say, it was an act of desperation."

Shale fell quiet for a time as she looked off, trying to comprehend such a monumental event.

"Besides being a sorceress," she finally said, her voice weaker, "I am also a witch woman. Some of my ability as a sorceress, such as healing, still works as always." She looked up expectantly at him. "But other things, such as my ability to see into the flow of time, seem to be lost to me. That ability is part of who I am, what I am, and now I can't call it forth.

"This is in part the reason I came to see you—to ask how soon can I expect my ability to see into the flow of time to be restored to normal?"

Richard let out a sigh as he considered how to tell her. "Part of the key to saving the world of life was that it was necessary to end prophecy. The star shift was a way to do that. I'm afraid that a witch woman's ability to see into the flow of time is a form of prophecy. I had to end all forms of prophecy."

"End prophecy?" She looked both dumbfounded and horrified. "How could you do such a thing? How could you possibly take it upon yourself to destroy such a fundamental part of the lives of so many people?"

"That's where you are wrong," he said, leaning closer, "and that was the key to our survival. Prophecy is alien to the world of life. It was long ago sent here from the timeless world of the dead. Having that corrosive force here in this world was part of how that ancient, dead emperor was destroying the veil separating life and death. I had to end prophecy by sending it back to the world of the dead where it belongs. The star shift was the only way of doing it. I'm afraid that your ability to see into the flow of time will never return."

Tears welled up in her eyes. "But that's who I am. It's part of me."

"An alien part," he said. "Would you keep an arm eaten away by gangrene because that dying arm was 'a part of you'? No. To preserve life you would cut it off before it could kill you. That's what I did.

Cutting off that arm would certainly hurt, but it would also keep you alive.

"Prophecy was never meant to be part of who witch women really are. It was a crutch that in part gave witch women such a fearsome reputation. Believe me, witch women can be plenty fearsome without needing to see into the flow of time. That alien ability was also sometimes the cause of great harm.

"In the past, the false prophecies of a witch woman nearly killed me, nearly killed Kahlan. Witch women have had otherworldly power for so long they came to believe it was part of them, but it's not. It was in reality death lurking within you. I've ended it."

He knew by her expression that he had not heard the last of it, so he thought he needed to end the argument before it could fester in her.

"It's done, Shale. There is no putting it back to the way it was, any more than it is possible for me to put the stars back where they were. The spell has run its course. It is over and done.

"Our lives have all changed—mine included. Life is about change. Change has both good and bad elements to it. You can either deal with the way things have changed and move forward, or you can let bitterness about what's lost in the past rob you of your future.

"I'm afraid that what happened here today with this business about a goddess is one of those bad changes brought about by the star shift. I don't like it and I don't yet know what it means, but we have to figure it out and deal with it."

She nodded distantly. "I guess so."

"When I was starting to heal Kahlan," Richard said, changing the subject to get her mind off it, "you told me that there was something else going on, and that if I kept going I would kill her. What was it you felt?"

"It was that poison I told you about. Those claws planted the infection or poison in her during the attack. One of my healing talents—I'm not sure I can adequately explain it—is that I can, in a way, see what is happening inside the person I'm healing. I could tell that your gift had a dangerous effect on that poison. I don't know if it was an intended effect or simply that the two could not coexist. They were oil and water, you might say. Had I not stopped you, the Mother Confessor would have gone on to suffer a lingering death, but only after it had killed you first."

Richard was taken aback. "Do you think it was deliberate? That it was meant for me?"

"When I first probed for her injuries, I could feel your gift seeping into her. I could also feel that malevolence being drawn to your gift. Your gift attracted it. Had you kept the contact with her, it would have used that link to seep into you and kill you as surely as a bite from a viper."

"Why didn't it react to your gift the same way?"

She shook her head. "I'm not entirely sure of the reason, but I could see that it was drawn to your gift. I was able to get around it, allowing me to come in behind it and choke it off. Our gift is different. You are a war wizard, I am, among other things, a healer. Maybe your aggressive ability with your gift drew it."

Richard paced off a short distance. "I guess I owe you a debt of gratitude. Not only have you saved Kahlan's life, it seems you may have saved mine as well."

"True enough. I guess it's fortunate I showed up when I did."

10

R ichard looked back over his shoulder at her. "What's the rest of the reason for you making such a long journey? I suspect there is more to it."

Shale confirmed that with a troubled sigh. "Some of my people have been killed in a very strange fashion."

"Killed by who?"

"Not who, what. We find remains—larger bones and the dirty end of a gut pile—much like a mountain lion might leave from a calf or lamb kill. And the head. It always leaves the head. We don't know what is doing the killing, but no horses or farm animals have been killed in this same manner. This is something that hunts people exclusively."

"Is the Northern Waste covered with snow yet?"

"It's early in the season, but the snows have already come to large parts of it. It has snowed in some of the places where victims were found."

"Snow would make for clear tracks. What do the tracks look like?"

"There were markings in the snow," she said, looking somewhat at a loss. "Markings, of a sort, I guess you could say, but not exactly tracks. The snow was disturbed by networks of conflicting lines. There were no tracks as such, no indication of what sort of beast it might be, just a crisscrossed matrix of lines."

"I presume you followed them?"

"They were only in the immediate vicinity of the kill. They came from nowhere and led nowhere. There are no footprints, no claw prints, no wing impressions of something landing. Just those slashes and streaks in the snow, and then, of course, blood and the bones that were stripped of flesh and left. Sometimes some of the clothes were left as well, but not always. We find the flesh stripped from the skull and the eyes sucked out, making it difficult to identify the victim. There simply were no tracks to follow and even these strange slashes never went very far. It's as if it simply appeared out of nowhere and then after the kill vanished into thin air."

Richard looked off, thinking out loud. "Right off the top of my head that doesn't make any sense. A gar could drop in on prey but they would have left plenty of distinctive prints. Same with a dragon. Anything I know of that's large enough to snatch up a person and spit out the bones would have had to have left tracks. Of course, I'm not familiar with all the beasts in D'Hara, and I know virtually nothing of the Northern Waste."

"Well, I can tell you that there has never been any beast in the Waste I know of that would leave these kinds of marks in the snow. There are things like wolves and such that will take a person, but this is very different."

"Any other strange things going on that might help give us the bigger picture?"

"There is something else that I'm pretty sure is related." Shale clasped her hands as she looked away for a moment. "Do you remember that gravedigger up in the great hall, earlier today?" she asked.

"The one who said they had found dead animals on graves?"

She nodded. "We have been finding dead animals on graves, just as he described."

Richard stared in shock. "You've got to be kidding."

"No. Not only that, but on a few of the graves we have also found people. Freshly killed people."

Richard stared at her. "Killed how?"

Shale looked up at him with a grim expression. "They were mauled just like your wife—clawed to death, eviscerated—only the thing that attacked them had time enough to finish the job. The difference is they weren't eaten like the other victims. Their remains were simply dropped on graves.

"I recognized the Mother Confessor's wounds immediately when I saw them. The dead people on the graves were infected with something that wasted away at the flesh and organs even after they were dead. That was why I knew to look for it in her. I felt sure she would be infected the same as the victims found on graves and I was right."

"Are you sure they were killed by the same kind of creature that eats their kill? What about tracks?"

Shale clasped her hands in front of her as she stared off in thought for a moment.

"There were those same odd tracks. It was the same kind of creature that killed them. I'm sure of it."

"Can you describe the tracks better? What did they look like?"

"Well…" Shale squinted as she tried to think how to be more specific. "Imagine if you took a very thin willow switch and smacked it against the ground over and over from every direction all around, hundreds of times—maybe thousands of times—as you moved along, always changing the direction of the strikes. We followed these strange marks, and over a short distance they gradually became less and less until there were no more, leaving only virgin snow."

Richard, his left palm resting on the sword, tapped a finger against the raised gold wire spelling out the word "TRUTH" on the hilt. "I can't even imagine what could have left marks like that in the snow. Except maybe someone with a thin willow branch hitting the ground over and over from every direction, trying to deceive you?"

She looked over out of the corner of her eye. "Then there would have been footprints all around as they whipped the switch against the ground. There were no footprints of any kind—none—just all those strange marks."

Richard was at a loss and could only shake his head.

"There's something else," she said in a troubled voice. "I have had murky visions of some kind of being. I'm sure it was the goddess spoken of by that man, Nolo. Shadows of her have visited me unbidden while I have been in meditation. That was another reason why, earlier today, I came forward when I did. I felt sure that the same visions I've had are the goddess he spoke of."

Richard found this to be disturbing news. "Were you able to learn anything of her in these visions?"

Shale opened her hands in a helpless gesture. "Nothing, I'm afraid. I only had this vague, shadowy image. It did not speak. I had no idea what it could mean until I heard Nolo speaking, and then I knew there had to be a connection, much like I knew when I heard the gravedigger talking about dead animals left on graves that the same thing was happening to us."

Richard's first thought was to wonder if the goddess was trying to control Shale the same way she was possibly controlling Nolo. That thought alarmed him.

"There's nothing you can describe from this impression? Nothing at all? Even the smallest thing might be helpful."

Shale shook her head. "Sorry, Lord Rahl. I'm afraid not. Except that it felt like perhaps she was probing. I might try meditating again and see if I can learn more."

"I'm not sure that would be such a good idea. That may have been what Nolo thought, too. I never really thought that anything good came from meditation. I suggest you not invite trouble into your head."

"You may be right. We can discuss it later. Right now I'm exhausted."

"Of course," Richard said. "You need to get some rest. It's going to be morning soon. There are rooms nearby. I'll take you to one. You can use it as long as you wish to stay."

"You need to get some rest as well, and I think it would be best if you take one of those rooms for yourself and sleep somewhere other than with your wife. Just for tonight. It would be best if she not be disturbed."

Richard didn't like the idea, but their bedroom was inaccessible except through the entryway he was in. Between the Mord-Sith in the room and the men of the First File all throughout the halls, nothing was going to get near Kahlan.

He let out a deep breath, resigned to sleeping alone. "At least she is going to be all right. That's what matters."

11

In the morning, not wanting to wake Kahlan if she was still asleep, Richard cautiously opened the bedroom door just enough to peek in. Vika, just behind him, leaned in over his right shoulder to have a look for herself. Cassia, just inside the double doors to one side, and Rikka, to the other, both turned to glare out at the intruder. When they saw it was him, their scowls relaxed.

Instead of seeing Kahlan asleep, Richard was surprised to see her just finishing getting dressed in a fresh new Confessor dress. The satiny smooth material, the square neck, and the way it hugged her shape were just as stunning as the first time he had seen her in the same kind of dress. He didn't think that there had ever been a better example of femininity and authority combined into one dress. He marveled at her every time he saw her in it. And more so when she was out of it.

Since she was awake and up, Richard opened the doors and strode into the room, happy to see her looking alert and well, but not at all pleased that she was getting dressed rather than resting.

"What do you think you're doing?"

She cast a brief glance his way. "Getting ready for the petitioners in the great hall."

Richard did his best to contain himself. "You aren't finished being healed yet. Shale says you need to rest so that she can finish what she needs to do. You can't go to the great hall."

She gave him a cold look. "I certainly can, and I am going to. You are going as well."

"Kahlan, finishing your healing is more important."

"That can wait. This is more important."

Richard was baffled. "What are you talking about? There is nothing more important than finishing the healing."

She took a long, aggressive stride toward him. "Everyone saw a lot of strange and frightening things yesterday. They don't know what any of it is about. Rumors will no doubt have already spread like wildfire. Those rumors and suspicions will undermine your rule and degrade our authority.

"Overnight, stories—embellished stories—will have spread throughout the camp down below. People will be worried and anxious and already believe that we are in great trouble.

"We need everyone to come back this morning and see that there was nothing to their fears and that it was only a minor interruption that we took care of. We must show everyone that the rumors are wrong and we have everything under control."

"Kahlan, I understand all that, I really do, but that's secondary. You can't—"

"The subject is not open to debate," she snapped as she turned to the tall mirror. She picked up a hairbrush from the dressing table.

For some reason, she looked to be in a bad mood and her displeasure seemed directed at him. He got the uneasy feeling that he was in trouble. He supposed she had every right to be angry that he had let her go alone to question Nolo without even suggesting that he go with her. They could have done it later, together. Richard should have been there close by. That was a mistake, and it was his mistake. It had nearly gotten her killed.

Kahlan abruptly turned back to him from the mirror where she was fussing one-handed with her hair. Her left arm hung mostly limp at her side. She shook the brush at him.

"After we have the audience with petitioners in the great hall and reassure everyone, we are going to go question Nolo. I trust that you have him locked up?"

"I do, but first Shale needs—"

"I don't recall offering you alternatives," she said in an icy tone.

This was not Kahlan. This was the Mother Confessor, who was not at all happy. Worse, it was all too clear that he was the center of her ire.

"Kahlan," he said softly as he slipped an arm around her waist, "I'm sorry I let you go alone with Nolo. It's my fault. I should have been a lot more cautious. I should have been there with you."

That seemed to only set her off. She pulled away from him and glanced around at the six Mord-Sith in the room.

"Please leave us." She gestured with the brush, shooing them all out. "Wait for us outside. We will be out shortly."

The six Mord-Sith shared looks and started filing out.

Berdine leaned close on her way by. "I think you are in trouble, Lord Rahl. She's been calling you 'my husband' ever since she woke up."

"Great," he muttered. "Get Shale and tell her Kahlan is up, then wait outside for us. Tell her to hurry."

Richard closed the doors behind them, trying to think of a way to talk Kahlan out of putting her well-being last. When he turned back to the room, Kahlan was brushing her hair with her one good hand as if she wanted to rip it out by the roots. She was now angry at her hair for not bending to her will.

Richard crossed their grand bedroom to be closer to her. "Kahlan, what's wrong?"

"What's wrong?" She turned to him in a fury. "What's wrong!"

"Tell me. Please? What is it?"

She tossed the brush on the dressing stand and rapidly closed the distance to him to start jabbing her finger against the center of his chest. "What's wrong is your promise, that's what's wrong!"

"Promise?" Richard was mystified. "What promise?"

She exploded. "What promise? What promise!" She jabbed her finger hard against his chest. "Your promise as a wizard!"

Richard was truly confused. He grabbed her wrist to stop her jabbing.

"Kahlan, I don't know what promise you're talking about."

"It obviously meant so little that you don't even remember!"

Richard heaved a sigh in frustration, trying to hold his own anger in check. "I guess not, so why don't you tell me."

She tried to jab a finger at him with her left hand, since he was holding her right wrist, but she couldn't hold the arm up on its own long enough. It fell limp to her side.

"You promised me a new golden age." Her beautiful green eyes welled up with tears. "That was what you said."

Before he could reply, she pointed toward the balcony beyond the heavy drapes. "You promised me that night, out there. You said that with the star shift everything had changed and that this is the beginning of a new golden age. I asked you if you were sure. You said that it was a promise that you were giving me as the First Wizard, and that wizards always keep their promises!"

"I remember," he said with an earnest nod.

"Do you, Richard? Do you even know what you were promising? I think you did. I think you were just saying something that sounded nice to make me feel good right then, when all along you knew the truth. The truth was something very different. You of all people are supposed to always be dead honest with me, but you were deceiving me. That's as good as a lie."

Richard frowned down at her. "I remember the promise of a new golden age, and I meant it. I don't know why you think I was deceiving you."

She gritted her teeth and then leaned in. "Nolo told me the name of the goddess that promises to take our world and slaughter us all. Do you know what she is called?"

"No."

"The Golden Goddess."

He was speechless at the news.

She started jabbing his chest with a finger again. "The Golden Goddess! You promised terror and death in a new age for our world under the Golden Goddess, that's what you were promising me!"

Richard snatched her wrist again. "She's called the Golden Goddess? Kahlan, I didn't know that. I swear, that's not what I meant."

"Wizards always keep their promises, often in the same way that a witch woman's prediction always turns out to be true… just not in the way you expected when you heard it, but true nonetheless. We are entering a new age of terror under the Golden Goddess. That's the golden age you promised me!"

Before Richard could answer, the doors burst open. It was an angry Shale. Her aura crackled with flickering flashes of fury as she marched across the room.

"What are you doing up! You need to be in bed and I—"

"We are going to the great hall to show our people that everything is stable and all is well," Kahlan said, cutting her off. "If my husband and I are not there it would only add fuel to rumors and create the impression that the Lord Rahl and the Mother Confessor couldn't handle things and we are being overwhelmed by trouble, which would mean they have no chance against such trouble. The rumors could get out of control and start a panic.

"We can't afford to leave people with the impression that things are out of control. I won't allow it. We will grant audiences to petitioners, as promised, in order to reassure people."

"Perhaps for a brief appearance," Shale offered as a compromise, "and then we come right back here to continue what I need to do to finish healing you."

Kahlan fixed the woman in a hot glare. "We will spend the day seeing petitioners. A full day, just as people expect. After that, I am going down to question Nolo. You may come if you wish."

Shale, looking concerned, reached out in an attempt to calm Kahlan down. "Mother Confessor, you need—"

"What I need is for all of you to stop arguing with me!" She started for the door. "If you want to come with me, then keep out of my way. Otherwise, stay here."

Richard shared a troubled look with Shale.

"This is not wise," the sorceress whispered to him.

"Neither is crossing the Mother Confessor," Richard told her.

With a grimace, Shale nodded. "We had better do as she wants and go with her. Whether she realizes it or not, she is going to need help. We need to be close by."

12

Throughout the day as they sat at the head of the great hall, beneath the massive medallion showing the lineage of the House of Rahl, Richard would occasionally lean close and whisper a suggestion that they call an end to the audience. Whenever he did, Kahlan would shoot him a cold look. She was determined to stay the entire day and show strength to not only the people gathered to speak with them and those who had come to observe, but also to the many palace officials. Those officials were important in conveying the proper mood to those they interacted with. To do that, they needed to be buoyed by what they saw.

It was not the first time Richard had seen Kahlan exhibit such determination to show strength to her people. She believed that showing leadership meant she had to rise above any personal pain.

In a way he was proud of her, and at the same time he was exasperated by her stubbornness.

After a long day in the great hall in which they answered one trivial concern after another, listened to the platitudes of kings and queens and heads of city-states, and accepted tokens of appreciation from the people of various parts of the D'Haran Empire, and after the boring normality of it all gradually doused the rumors that had flared up overnight, Kahlan finally stood.

In her confident, silky voice, she thanked everyone for coming. She told them what a great honor it had been for Lord Rahl and herself to host them at the People's Palace. She promised that they would try to make it to as many of the planned banquets as possible. She wished them a pleasant stay at the palace and a safe journey home when it came time for them to leave. She said that they would always be welcomed back to the people's house, the People's Palace.

As the applause, cheers, and clamor of conversation died out and people began to leave, Kahlan turned to Richard. She looked no happier than she had that morning.

"I need to question Nolo. Take me to where he is being held."

"How about you let Shale finish helping you first."

Kahlan turned to the captain of the guard. "Take me to where the prisoner is being held."

Clapping a fist to his heart, he bowed his head. "This way, Mother Confessor."

As the captain started out, Kahlan marched off right behind him, seemingly not caring if the rest of them came along or not. Richard and Shale had to hurry to catch up to her. The gaggle of Mord-Sith were right on their heels.

It was clear to Richard by the way she moved that Kahlan was in pain. Throughout the day she had used the arm that had been mauled less and less, and now it didn't look like she was able to lift it for more than brief moments. Occasionally she had pressed her right hand over her side. Despite that pain, she showed no sign that she might be reasonable and allow Shale to finish the healing.

It was obvious to Richard that there was something bigger driving her.

As they left the upper broad corridors of the palace proper, the passageways became more utilitarian, the stairways less grand. By the time they reached the lower portion of the palace, the narrow, low, simple stone passageways were dark and dank. It was quite the juxtaposition to the beauty and grandeur of the great hall where they had seen the petitioners earlier.

Down in the lower passageways, one did one's best not to touch the often dirty or slimy walls. As grim as the lower passageways were, Richard was thankful to be down there because that meant they were just that much closer to completing Kahlan's wishes so that Shale could finish healing her.

Torches carried by soldiers both leading the way and following behind lit the forbidding passageways with flickering light that made their faces seem to float along in the darkness. As they hurried down the long halls, the flames flapped and hissed. Besides the light, those torches filled the air with the sharp smell of pitch. At least that smell was better than the all too frequent stench of the dead rats.

Water seeping down through the stone ceiling left slippery, wet, green mold in places. The oozing water had over ages created yellowish growths down the walls in areas that almost looked like the type of formations that he'd seen growing in caves.

Unlike the rest of them, Kahlan didn't look at anything in the cavelike passageways. She kept her eyes ahead, her expression grim and determined as she marched along on her way to see the man who had promised to take her world into a new age of a golden goddess.

An age she believed Richard had promised her.

Richard didn't quite know what to make of that, but he was confident that when he'd promised her a new age, he hadn't meant it would be under the tyranny of some mysterious golden goddess. He was hoping that Nolo could provide answers and from those they could find a solution.

They all came to a stop at a solid iron door completely blocking off the dark corridor. The soldiers on station there were already working several keys in multiple locks in order to get it open for them. Unlike the soldiers from up top in the palace, these men stationed down below were grimy and dirty. Their faces were blackened with soot from torches.

Once the heavy door had been pulled back on squealing hinges, they saw that there were more armed soldiers on the other side. Those soldiers all stood with their backs against the walls to let the visitors pass. After stepping through the low doorway, they soon came to long runs of iron stairs that led down into a large chamber. Their footsteps and the clanking of weapons echoed all the way down the stairs.

The chamber at the bottom, constructed of granite blocks, was damp and had an off-putting smell. It was clear that things had died down here. Most likely, people. It tainted the place with the enduring stench of death.

A series of rust-stained iron doors with small viewing slits lined each side of the rectangular room. Fingers gripped a few of those slots from the other side. The captain of the guard shepherded the group to the lone door at the far end.

"We put him in here, Lord Rahl," the captain said.

Richard nodded. "Don't bring him out. We will go in to see him."

The captain gave a nod to the men guarding the cell. After a soldier unlocked the door, two others pulled it open and went inside to unlock a second door. Once that was open, they took in half a dozen torches each and placed them in iron brackets so the visitors would be able to see well enough.

As the soldiers placed the torches, Richard stepped in front of Kahlan to prevent her from going in first, as she had clearly intended.

Unlike the rest of the cells, this one was a relatively large room. By the row of manacles and chains pinned into the stone at regular intervals, the room was meant to hold a number of prisoners along the length of the wall, but now it held only one.

Nolo, heavily secured against the wall, was naked except for underpants stained with dried blood. Without his formal robes, all his body hair made him resemble a bear. That hair was also matted with dried blood.

Because they didn't want him crashing into walls and trying to kill himself, he had been tightly chained against the wall to prevent any further such attempts. An iron collar pinned in the granite allowed his head only inches of movement. A post held the collar away from the wall enough to prevent him from banging his head back against the stone. His arms were spread wide, iron bands pinning them against the wall at his shoulders and wrists in a way that prevented him from trying to hang himself to death in the collar. His legs and feet were secured with shackles and heavy chains. The smell of dried blood along with the sweaty man stunk up the room.

Nolo did not look at all well. His head hung as much as the tall metal collar would allow. His droopy, bloodshot eyes were open but stared unblinking down at the foot of the opposite wall, as if he were in a stupor. He showed no sign that he even knew that people had entered his cell.

"I want everyone out," Kahlan said as she stared at the man immobilized against the wall.

"Well, that's not happening," Richard said. "No way am I leaving."

"Me neither," Shale said. "I can clearly see that your injuries are causing you pain. I need to be close by, just in case you require help."

"I'm not leaving Lord Rahl in here without me," Vika said, defiantly.

The rest of the Mord-Sith chimed in that they weren't about to leave either of their charges alone and unprotected.

The muscles in Kahlan's jaw flexed as she clenched her teeth. She pointed at the door. "I would like the rest of you men to wait outside, please. Close the door. Kill anything that comes out that isn't us."

The captain's steely gaze shifted among those gathered. "Lord Rahl has his sword, these Mord-Sith their Agiels, and this sorceress her powers. What is it that you think could make it out that would still need killing?"

"Just wait outside, please," Kahlan huffed.

When the captain looked at him out of the corner of his eye, Richard gave him a nod to do as she asked. The soldiers clapped fists to hearts, if less than enthusiastically, and left them with the heavyset, nearly naked, hairy-chested man chained to the wall.

13

Richard moved in close to Kahlan as she stared at Nolo. He didn't know what was behind it, but he was done with her fit of temper and by his tone made it clear he wasn't going to put up with it down here with a man who had already proven to be dangerous. He gripped her upper arm as he leaned in close.

"You have a job to do—a job you were born to do. You can yell at me all you want later, but right now you need to do your job. Our people are depending on us."

Her heated expression relented a little. She seemed to get a grip on her emotions as she nodded.

"Tell me what happened," he said to her as he pulled her back away from Nolo toward the sorceress. "You still haven't told me what happened when you used your power on him."

She looked up into the resolve in his eyes, then glanced at Shale. Her expression finally softened, returning to the Kahlan he knew.

"When I begin to release my power, it's as if time stops. In that otherworldly moment everyone else seems to me like nothing more than a stone statue. There is nothing they can do to stop me, least of all the one I have unleashed my power on. Right then as that connection is made, I guess the easiest way to explain it is that it's like a discharge of lightning. Pure power. Pure, heady power. The release of it is ecstasy.

"Right then, in that singular instant as the power has been released from deep inside me, the person is already beyond redemption, their mind is already gone, but that is also when I am at my weakest. I had been furious at the trouble Nolo was bringing us after the terrible war had finally ended. That anger added strength to the power I released. It sent the tables and chairs crashing against the walls. I heard the stone of the walls crack as the discharge of power buckled them. The lights were blown out."

Her brow bunched together as she was remembering it. "But right then, in that frozen blink of time as the power was still exploding from me, as the flames in the lamps were still floating above the wicks, those flames were stopped dead in midair like everything else for that instant before they were about to be blown out. In an infinitesimal speck of time, all that would soon change and it would be pitch black. But right then there was still light.

"That's when it happened."

Goose bumps tingled on Richard's arms. "When what happened?"

She looked up into his eyes, haunted by what she had seen.

"That was when I saw the scribbly man."

The sorceress stepped closer and leaned in. "The what?"

"The scribbly man," Kahlan said. She put the fingers of her good hand to her forehead, obviously in distress at the memory. "That's the only way I can think to explain it."

"I don't understand," Richard said. "What do you mean by a 'scribbly' man?"

Kahlan heaved a sigh of frustration, letting the arm flop to her side. "You know the hard charcoal sticks that artists use to sketch with?"

Richard was frowning. "Sure."

"Well," she said, searching for words to explain it, "imagine if the artist were to scribble as fast as he could in the form of a figure, a man. No outlines, no shading or features, simply hundreds of scribbles, back and forth, up and down, round and round, fast as possible, filling in the arms, the body, the legs, and the head to make the dark shape of a man."

When they only stared at her, she used her hand to demonstrate, as if scribbling in midair. "Like this. Just scribbles over and over and over—fast as you can—so that after a moment on the paper all those scribbles combine into the rough, dark shape of a man. An impression of a man made entirely of scribbles. No outline, no details, just... scribbles."

Richard was beginning to get the image in his head. "You mean this figure you saw just before the light went out looked kind of fuzzy or something? Sort of dark and shadowy?"

Kahlan was shaking her head. "No, no. Not dark. Not fuzzy. Not shadowy. He was made up of scribbles in midair. Lines. Hundreds of lines. All kinds of loopy scribbles like you would make when holding that charcoal against the paper and scribbling to fill in a shape as fast as you could.

"As he came toward me, every tiny movement he made as his arms moved, as his legs moved to take a step, he was redrawn with new scribbles. He just kept being redrawn over and over, time after time, over and over every fraction of a second. Those scribbles he was made of came anew so fast it made him sort of blur as he moved."

Richard suddenly looked over at Shale. "What does that remind you of?"

The blood had drained from her face. "The marks I told you about left in the snow that looked like thousands of strikes from a switch."

"Or scribbles made in the snow."

Shale nodded.

Kahlan looked from one to the other. "What are you two talking about? I know it sounds crazy, but do you mean you believe me?"

"We believe you," Shale said. "I have seen people murdered—likely by this same creature, this scribbly man as you call him. Some were clawed to death."

"He had claws," Kahlan confirmed, nodding, the haunted fear returning to her eyes. "He stood upright, like a man, but he had claws. Three on each hand. They weren't black like the rest of him, like the scribbles. They were more defined, thick, solid."

"What color were they?" Richard asked.

Kahlan rubbed her injured arm hanging at her side as if suddenly chilled. "I don't know. A lighter color. Sort of a tan or yellowish color."

"Or sort of golden?" Richard asked.

Her gaze came up to meet his. "I guess so. I only just saw him, saw the claws... and then he was on me... tearing at me, ripping into me. It was terrifying."

"What do you think it could have been?" Shale asked her, breaking Kahlan's sudden transfixed daze at the memory. "Do you have any idea at all?"

Kahlan nodded. "I'm afraid I do." She stared off into the shadows for a time before going on.

"They are the monsters under the bed when you are little, the shape just caught out of the corner of your eye when you thought you were alone, the shadow of something in a dark corner that surprises you and then isn't there. They stop you dead with a knot of unexpected terror in the pit of your stomach. We have all seen glimpses of them. Never long enough to see them as I saw them, but it was them. I recognized it the instant I saw it.

"We've all seen fleeting flashes of them, the dark shadow just out of sight. They could briefly terrify us before but never hurt us because they came from so far distant. They were never able to fully materialize in our world so we saw only transient glimpses of them, the shape of them if the light was just right, if the shadows were deep enough... if you were afraid enough.

"I think that the star shift has brought us closer to their realm so that they now have the power to step into our world and hurt us."

14

Angry that Kahlan had been harmed by such a monster, Richard turned to Nolo.

"What was that thing that attacked her?"

Nolo stared blankly, his eyes unblinking, as if he had not heard Richard's question, or wasn't even aware there was anyone in the room with him.

"I've touched him with my power," Kahlan reminded him. "Whatever else happened as I did, I still unleashed my power into him. He won't answer anyone but me."

"... Or maybe the goddess," Shale suggested.

Kahlan's only answer was a worried look.

Richard gestured angrily at the portly man pinned to the wall. "We need answers. Ask him what it was."

Kahlan moved closer to stand in front of the prisoner.

"Nolo. Look at me."

He looked up at her as if just coming awake from a deep sleep. Long strands of gray hair meant to cover his large bald spot instead hung down in front of his face. As he saw her, his expression turned to utter devotion to the Confessor who had taken his mind.

Then, a cunning smile thinned his puffy lips.

Richard had seen plenty of people touched by Kahlan's power.

None of them had ever smiled.

"She sees you," Nolo said in a raspy whisper.

"She?" Kahlan asked.

"The Golden Goddess. She sees you standing there. She sees into your world." His voice was slow and sounded different than it had when he was in the great hall. If it even was his voice. "Your world will be hers. You should give it up now, and save yourself witnessing what is to come."

"Who is the Golden Goddess?" Kahlan asked in a calm voice.

"She is the collector of worlds."

Richard didn't like the sound of that.

"What does she want with our world?" Kahlan asked. "Why does she want it?"

"You can't win in the end," he said in that slow, raspy whisper, which ran a shiver up Richard's spine. "He is the last of the Rahl line. You are the last of the Confessors. Once you are both dead she will have your world."

"Can you get him to be more specific?" Richard asked. "These are just threats. We need something that will help us."

Kahlan nodded. "How will the Golden Goddess collect our world?"

"She will have your world. You can't win. In the end, no matter what you do, she will have your world. Running will do you no good. Surrender now and she will kill you first. She will pick your bones clean and then you will not have to see the horror that will come for your people."

Kahlan shook her head to herself.

It was obvious to Richard that this wasn't working. "He is not behaving as he should after he has been touched by a Confessor," he whispered to Shale, standing just to his right.

Without a word, Shale walked briskly up to the man and held his sweaty head tightly between her hands. Fingers spread, she pressed her thumbs against his temples. She lowered her head as she closed her eyes. Nolo's entire body began to shake, his chins rolled like waves in a storm, his fat belly jiggled, his teeth chattered.

After a few minutes, still holding the man's quivering head, Shale looked over at Richard. "She is using his vision. She is using him to look out through his eyes into our world."

"Well... what do we do about it?"

"This," Shale said.

Without any hesitation she dug her thumbs into the inside corners of his eyes. She gritted her teeth with the effort of scooping out his eyeballs with her thumbs. It was shocking to see such a gorgeous woman engaged in such a brutal act.

Nolo screamed his lungs out as she dug deep with her hooked thumbs. Shale at last ripped the eyeballs out. She pulled them away from the connecting tissues and then held one up in each bloody hand to show them. Nolo shrieked the whole time.

"There. That should fix the problem," the sorceress announced. She tossed his eyeballs off into a corner and then turned to a surprised Kahlan. "I've cut off her link. You will be able to talk to him now. The Golden Goddess is gone. Nolo's core is yours now to do with as you will."

Vika, next to Richard's left shoulder, leaned toward him. "I'm beginning to like her a lot more."

The other Mord-Sith nodded their eager agreement.

15

The man hanging in the restraints thrashed and screamed with the pain of having his eyes plucked out.

"Nolo, be still and listen," Kahlan commanded.

His agonized cries died out almost immediately in choking fits. He lifted his head, even though he could no longer see anything. Tears of blood ran from his ruined eye sockets.

"Mistress... please... command me."

There at last was the person Kahlan's power had taken. Shale had broken the Golden Goddess's link to the man. The veneer of her control was gone. Nolo hung nearly naked before the Confessor who had taken him with her power, fat, sweaty, smelly, and now unconditionally compliant.

"Tell me who this Golden Goddess is."

"She came to haunt me. She made me do things I didn't want to do," he confessed in a tearful voice. "I don't know how."

"I know that much," Kahlan said. "What else do you know about her? Tell me who she is."

"She is from another world. She is a collector of worlds. Her people are marauders. She finds worlds for them to raid."

"How does she get here?"

"I don't know, Mistress." He shrugged in misery because he couldn't adequately answer the question. "She has looked into our world before, but it was always far too distant for her kind to come here. Now, somehow, our world has come into her realm. It is now within her reach."

Shale motioned Kahlan to step over to her and Richard, out of earshot of Nolo. "This isn't making any sense. I can't believe he is really telling the truth."

"Someone touched by a Confessor's power has to tell the truth," Kahlan said. "They have no choice. Their mind, who they were, is gone. All that is left is unfiltered devotion to the Confessor who took them and to what she wants to know."

"That may be, but this can't be right. It doesn't make any sense. This Golden Goddess and her people can't travel to different worlds or"— she twirled her hand overhead—"roam among the stars. Such a thing is simply not possible."

"I'm afraid it is," Richard said, drawing her attention.

"What are you talking about?"

"Kahlan and I have both traveled to a different world."

"What world?" the frowning sorceress asked.

"The world of the dead," Richard said. "We went beyond the veil. We left the world of life, went to the world of the dead, and returned to our world."

"That's different," Shale declared in a fit of annoyance. "The world of life and the world of the dead are both here, in the same place at the same time. They are two sides of the same coin. Only the veil separates them. They function together. While it may have been an incredible feat, one I don't entirely understand, it's very different from what Nolo is talking about. He is saying that the Golden Goddess's people venture among the stars, visiting other worlds. That's simply not possible," she insisted.

Richard hooked his thumbs in his weapon belt. "I'm afraid it is. I know because I've done it."

Shale's disbelief was obvious. "You've traveled to other worlds."

"Well, not me."

"I thought not," she huffed.

"But I've sent other people to a different world."

Taken off guard, the sorceress made a face. "What are you talking about?"

"When we won the war with the Old World and defeated Emperor Jagang there were many people who didn't want to live here, in a world with magic. That had been what the war had been about—Jagang and his followers wanted to end magic. So, when we won the war, I sent those people who didn't want to live in a world with magic to, well, another world, a world without magic."

Shale planted her fists on her hips. "You sent people to another world."

"Yes."

"How?"

"I used a spectral fold."

She threw her hands up. "A spectral fold. Of course." She leaned in with an angry whisper. "What in the name of Creation is a spectral fold?"

"Well," Richard said as he pinched his lower lip, trying to think how to explain it as simply as possible, "it's a way of making different worlds that are far away come together so that you can step from one world into the other."

"Bring worlds together?" She stared with her jaw hanging. She finally gathered her senses. "Have you lost your mind? Such a thing simply isn't possible."

"It is," Kahlan confirmed. "Richard has already done it. I was there. I saw it done."

"How? And don't give me any of that spectral-fold nonsense. How could you bring another world, a distant world, together with our world so that you could step from one to another?"

"Here is the easiest way I can explain it. Imagine if you took a piece of paper and put a dot of ink on one side at the edge and then turned the paper over and put another dot on the other side of the paper, but on the edge farthest away from the first dot. You might say they are worlds apart and on opposite sides of the paper. Right? How could you bring those dots—those worlds—together?"

After a moment of thought, Shale folded her arms across her breasts. "You can't. You can't bring things together that are physically separated like that."

"Yes you can. You simply fold the paper around into a cylinder until the dots touch. Dots on different edges, and different sides of the paper, now touch each other." Richard smiled. "A spectral fold."

Shale looked off into the distance as she puzzled it out in her head. Finally, once she grasped the concept, she turned back to regard him for a moment with a stern scowl.

"You are a scary man, Richard Rahl."

"War wizards are supposed to be scary. Part of the job."

Shale seemed to compose herself as she came to grips with the notion of moving between worlds. "And so you think that is what the Golden Goddess and her people can do? A spectral fold? Bring our worlds together and simply step out of one and into the other?"

Richard shrugged. "I don't know. I'm only saying that I know it's possible to go between worlds because I've sent people from our world to another one. My half sister wanted to go to that world to start a new life. She left this world and went to that one to live without magic. So what I'm saying is that we can't discount what Nolo is telling us about them coming here from another world simply because we don't know how they're doing it."

Shale nodded, still thinking of how to reconcile what he had just told her with what she knew. She had a sudden thought.

"What if the scribbly man the Mother Confessor saw, and the tracks I told you about, are them in the process of stepping through. You know, like they are still in that interface between worlds. What if that was what Kahlan saw—one of them in the midst of coming into our world? What if what she saw was him still in transition between worlds?"

Kahlan looked between Shale and Richard. "That actually might make sense. It didn't seem like he was, I don't know, all there, I guess you could say. Maybe he was in the process of materializing here. Before our worlds were close enough, they used to try and we would only see a glimmer of them. Now they can come through, so that's what I saw here."

Richard considered it a moment. "That certainly might explain it. Why don't you see what else we can learn from Nolo?"

Kahlan left the two of them to go back to stand before the prisoner. "How will the Golden Goddess try to take our world?"

Nolo struggled to shrug against his helpless fear that he couldn't properly answer her. "I'm not sure, Mistress—I swear! I do know that she doesn't understand our world."

"What do you mean? Our language? Our ways? What doesn't she understand?"

"No, not those things. Of all the worlds she has found and raided, she has never before encountered a world like ours."

"You already said that." Kahlan made a face. "What doesn't she understand about our world?"

He cried out in terror that he had displeased her by not answering in the way she wished. "Forgive me, Mistress!"

"Pay attention. Answer the question. She has never encountered a world like ours. What has she never encountered before? What doesn't she understand?"

"Magic."

Kahlan was taken aback. "She doesn't understand magic?"

"She has never before encountered a world with magic. The gift—magic—confuses her. She has never seen magic before. She does not understand it."

Kahlan paused to look over at Richard. This was certainly unexpected. Then again, in a way, it wasn't. It was entirely possible that magic was unique to their world alone.

"The world Lord Rahl sent those people to was a world without magic," Shale whispered. "Her world must be like that. That would explain why she doesn't understand magic."

Kahlan nodded her agreement before she turned back to Nolo. "Does she fear it? Does she fear magic?"

"She doesn't know what it is. She is wary of it because it is an unknown to her. She fears you. You have power she cannot comprehend. That is why she tried to kill you, earlier. She will have you dead. But there is one thing she fears more than you and your power."

"What would that be?"

"She fears the shiny man most of all."

16

Kahlan frowned and leaned in as if she hadn't heard him correctly. "She fears what?"

"The shiny man." He tilted his head in Richard's direction. "Lord Rahl."

"She fears Lord Rahl most of all?"

Nolo nodded as he cried out, "Yes!"

"Why does she call him the shiny man?"

"His magic. His abilities. His power. His gift. His sword. Everything about him strengthens the magic of this world—especially his bond as the Lord Rahl with his people. That bond is open-ended, without limits. The shiny man lights this world with this strange thing: magic."

"How could his gift give the magic of this world strength?"

"The same way his bond powers the Agiel of the Mord-Sith in ways that we cannot see. But she sees it shining. She sees the shiny threads of it.

"Magic shrouds this world, veils it, obscuring her ability to see into it very well. For that reason she uses people here, peering out through their eyes, like she was seeing through my eyes in the great hall when I came before you to give you her demand that you surrender. She was watching you both through my eyes. Through that imperfect, murky vision of looking through another's eyes—through my eyes—she couldn't see what Lord Rahl really looks like. His gift makes him look shiny to her. That terrible shine hurts her vision. No one else looks like that to her, just him. That's why she calls him the shiny man."

Richard remembered the way Nolo had kept looking away from him in the great hall, avoiding eye contact. This would explain why.

"So she hates him," Kahlan said, "because of his gift."

"Oh yes," Nolo said, nodding furiously. "She hates him. She wants him dead. Your magic reinforces his gift. She hates you. She wants you dead. Once you both are dead then this confusing shroud of magic around this world will fade away and her hordes will have free run."

"But our magic protects us. Lord Rahl's magic can defeat them."

"Forgive me, Mistress, for not being clear," he whined. "They don't understand magic, so they are cautious… for now. But don't mistake caution for fear and especially not for weakness. They are anything but weak.

"Up to now she has only allowed a few of her kind through to our world, like the one who attacked you. Allowed them to come here to hunt, to feed, to probe, mostly far away from you both, far away from your magic, to test our species. As she learns more about our world, she will send more of her kind."

"But my magic protected me?"

"During that moment when one of hers struck out at you, it was because you were at your weakest, but even so your magic kept the one who came from being bold enough to slaughter you as swiftly as she had intended."

"What exactly is their purpose, though? Their objective?"

"Her kind considers us an inferior species. We are prey. They will hunt us like game. They will hunt us in ways we cannot even begin to imagine. Other worlds are merely sport to them. We are a new kind of species, a new kind of prey, one that is difficult to chase down and kill, one that has this strange thing, magic. All that makes us a new kind of sport for them, a more challenging sport. That excites them."

"There must be a way for us to show her that we are intelligent, thinking beings," Kahlan said. "You're a diplomat, tell us how we can reason with them to reach a peace between our worlds."

"Peace is repugnant to them. They regard themselves as a race of gods. They don't live in peace with any inferior species. They hunt them."

Richard thought it ironic that the consul general, a man whose life had been devoted to diplomacy and negotiation in pursuit of peace, was explaining why there could be no peace with these beings.

Kahlan still wasn't convinced. "There must be a way to persuade them that hunting the people here isn't right, that there are better ways to deal with each other even if we are different, even if they think we are inferior to them."

Nolo had been shaking his head as she spoke. "You are still thinking of them in human terms. They are not human. They are not anything like us. I don't know what they are but I do know they are not like us. They even reproduce differently."

"What do you mean, they reproduce differently?"

"For them reproduction does not involve bonding or love or any kind of pleasure. They simply replicate more of their kind through some sort of process as necessary to maintain their supremacy. They get no pleasure or satisfaction from it, and certainly no joy. There is no bonding with those they create.

"The pleasure for their species comes from the singular act of inflicting terror and then killing their prey. The best way to explain it is that terrorizing prey is for them much the same pleasure we get from the act of sex. Bringing terror is a complex act to them, filled with nuance and excitement. After a period of this enjoyment building up from inflicting terror, killing, you might say, is their form of orgasm.

"Sometimes they eat what they kill, sometimes they don't. Either way, the object is terror and then the climax of killing. That is the central pursuit of their lives, much like some depraved individuals here are driven to get sick pleasure out of torturing and killing animals. We are just animals to the goddess and her kind. They have no empathy for prey."

"So they prey on other worlds?" Kahlan asked.

"Yes. They search the worlds among the stars for hunting grounds. They have been to our world before, but it has always been too distant a place to come to and hunt successfully, or even visit except for the briefest of moments. Too short a time to kill. Now, our world has somehow come within reach. Now, they can prey on us."

"It is only magic, then, keeping them from flooding in and slaughtering us all?"

"Yes, Mistress. Only the magic of this world gives the goddess pause—but only for the time being. You may not realize it, but only the power of the shiny man and you, Mistress, hold that net of magic together around our world. You two are the nexus of magic in our world. Lord Rahl's bond, as shown through the devotion, gives strength and energy to the web of magic. Your gifts are what binds all kinds of magic together in countless ways and keeps it viable.

"Even so, as soon as they learn more, her kind will use this world as they have used others within their grasp—for the sport of killing."

"But surely she must know that we aren't going to let that happen. We will fight back."

Nolo nodded. "She is counting on that. Your defiance piques their interest. They know we have weapons and that we are often warlike. The shiny man is a war wizard, after all. The resistance that would be put up by our kind excites them, draws them. It will bring more numbers than usual. It will drive them to stalk every person in this world and hunt us to extinction.

"In the end, there can be no salvation for our world. If you do not surrender, she will become bolder and then hunt you both down and kill you. If for some reason you could elude her, even that is not a problem. If she so decided, she has but to wait. It is only a matter of time."

"What do you mean, wait?" Kahlan asked. "Wait for what?"

"Wait for you both to die. Each of you is the last of your kind. The last Confessor, the last Lord Rahl.

"When you die—whether she kills you, or something else does, or you die of natural causes like old age—then the obstacle of magic will crumble. Once it does, we will then be like any other world. They will drink our blood and eat our flesh and spit out the bones. When they have eventually finished us off, they will move on to another world."

"Maybe she will die before we do," Kahlan said. "Richard and I aren't that old yet. We have our lives before us. Maybe she is older than we are and she will go first. That means she can't really afford to wait."

"No, Mistress. She is already many times older than you, and she is only now entering the prime of her life, in many ways the same as you and Lord Rahl. The difference is she will outlive you both by centuries.

"Even when she eventually dies, others of her kind will take her place as she took the place of those before her. Having this world is not so much her objective as it is the driving force of her species. She will outlive you if necessary and then when magic dies they will have our world.

"Time is on their side."

Kahlan touched the square neckline of her Confessor's dress over the spot where Richard had pulled out the knife. "So, since this superior species failed to finish the kill, that's why you stepped in and stabbed me." It was not a question.

Nolo's face twisted with horror at the sudden mention of what he had done. "Yes, Mistress," he answered in a whimper.

Kahlan looked puzzled. "How were you able to stab me after I used my power on you?"

He sobbed and trembled at what he had done.

"Answer me," Kahlan said in a deadly calm voice that matched her Confessor face.

"Forgive me, Mistress, but that was not me, that was the goddess using me. The one she sent pulled back to their world before you were dead. She wanted to finish it. She wanted you dead. She didn't care how so she forced me ahead, forced my hand to drive the knife toward you. You blocked me. We fought, and even though you only had one good arm, you managed to get the knife away from me. You stabbed me—as you should have, Mistress. But with the goddess guiding me in the pitch blackness, as you came at me again I was able to twist the knife away from your grip. Once I had it, it was the goddess driving my hand to plunge the knife into you. It was the goddess, not me, Mistress. The superior species, not me. Thank the Creator it missed your heart and you weren't killed. Please, Mistress, I am telling you the truth."

"Where is she?"

Richard could tell that Kahlan was getting tired and frustrated.

"Where is this goddess?" she asked.

"In her world, Mistress."

"But where is that—where is her world?"

Nolo started to weep. "I don't know, Mistress," he said in a pitiful whine. "Forgive me, Mistress, I don't know how she moves from world to world. I don't understand those abilities any more than she understands magic. One way or another she will outlive you and then they will have our world."

"There is a flaw in her plan." Kahlan lifted her head a little. "Lord Rahl and I can have children."

"Children?" he said, leaning forward as much as the restraints allowed, as if staring with his bloody eye sockets.

"Yes, children," she said. "Those children will carry the power of the Rahl line and the Confessors. That's how it has always worked. That is how it was passed down to us. That is how magic will go on to survive in our world. Our magic will continue unbroken through them. It will always help to keep her kind away from our people. Magic will pass on and always protect our world."

Again he shook his head. "She sees that you have been together for enough time to have reproduced. She sees that you have failed to breed successfully and bring forth successors as others of our kind have. As mates, you both have proven to be barren. She sees that your lines of magic are dead ends, that your world is nearly ripe for the taking."

Seeing Kahlan standing there, in a dungeon, discussing such personal matters with this man who had tried to kill her made Richard feel profoundly sorry for her. The war had robbed them of the chance to have children. She never mentioned it, but he knew how devastated she had been to have lost the child the one time she had been pregnant. And then the world had nearly come apart. With their lives drawn into so much terror and death, they could hardly bring a child into the world.

He had been hoping that the new golden age would finally provide that opportunity for a family, but now, with this dire threat from the Golden Goddess... it looked like their chance for children had just slipped away.

"Just because we haven't had children yet," Kahlan said, "doesn't mean that we couldn't still have children to carry on our lines."

"She does not care."

Kahlan blinked. "Why wouldn't she care—that would ruin her whole plan to outlive our gift?"

"She does not care because the young of any species are commonly helpless, ours especially so. You may be hard to kill, but young ones are easy to kill. They do not yet have magic that can protect them. Infants are even easier to slaughter. Her kind lusts to kill the young of any species because they more easily succumb to helpless terror.

"If you were to have children that would only serve to excite their prey-drive even more. Your children would be irresistible to her. She would come for them, magic or no magic, and she would kill them the way we would step on a cockroach."

Tears welled up in Kahlan's eyes, fury twisted her features as her hands fisted at her sides. "I want your Golden Goddess dead! I want you dead!"

Richard straightened, not expecting her sudden proclamation.

At her words, blood began to run from the man's ears. His body shuddered violently, and then he slumped heavily in the restraints. Once touched by a Confessor's power, a person lived only to serve her. If she wished them dead, they complied without hesitation.

She had just wished him dead. It was as an execution.

This man had tried to kill her. He had driven his knife into her chest in the hope of stabbing her through the heart, even if with the Golden Goddess commanding him. For that, Richard wasn't at all displeased that he was dead. But he had the larger picture in mind.

He stepped close to put a hand on her shoulder. "Kahlan, why would you kill him? He may have been able to provide more information."

"The goddess will grant no mercy," she said as tears ran down her cheeks. "Neither will I."

That was the iron will that inspired them all and had helped win the war. Although he would have liked to have access to more information, Richard wouldn't change her for anything.

He could see that the ordeal, both physical and emotional, had drained what strength she had left. Her face grew ashen.

And then he saw a wet red stain at her side spreading through the white dress.

Shale rushed forward to help him just as Kahlan collapsed.

17

Even though she knew she was in a deep sleep, Kahlan could hear herself screaming.

The pain was unbearable. She wanted to die just to end the agony, but in the strange, confusing landscape of dreams, death eluded her.

She had been in this place before, in this strange, twisted world of abject agony that distorted everything into one single, focused fixation on wanting the pain to stop. She begged for the pain to stop, but the blanket of sleep only helped to keep her immobilized and helpless.

Her hands gripped fistfuls of the bedsheets. She twisted her fists as the pain twisted in her. She panted as fast as she could, trying to get the air she so desperately needed but failing. She thought she might suffocate in that state of powerless burning need.

Somewhere in the distance she heard a comforting voice reassuring her. It sounded like a good spirit. That thought jolted her with a new fear—a fear that she was already dead.

She realized, then, that in death such worldly pain would be a thing of the past. She knew firsthand that death held its own agonies, but physical pain was not one of them.

Kahlan began, then, to feel the suffering starting to wane. It was the greatest blessing possible to have the pain ease, even if only a little. Gradually, her screams died down to moans until after a while she could begin to catch her breath. Even through the haze of sleep, she was aware of at last being able to breathe again.

As the pain abated bit by bit, it allowed her to drift off into a deeper, more normal sleep, where everything faded away into a dream world of every worry, every bizarre, warped fear all blended together into the kind of stark fright unique to dreams.

Her deepest personal fears, fears that were new to her, would not leave her be, even in sleep. Not after what Nolo had told her.

After a seeming eternity spent in that suspended dream state, her eyes finally opened. She was covered in a sheen of sweat. She pulled the neck of the nightdress up, trying to cool herself. She knew she had been asleep for quite some time, but she had no idea how long it had been. The heavy drapes were drawn, so she didn't know if it was day or night, but at least she was in their bedroom, where she was safe.

Kahlan lifted her head a little and saw that Shale was sitting close by in a comfortable chair, her head slumped, her eyes closed, her breathing even. The woman was gallingly beautiful, with that kind of feminine voice that made Kahlan think she sounded like a frog in comparison. How was it fair that such an alluring woman could have a voice like that?

Kahlan wondered if Richard thought the sorceress was beautiful. She knew he had to.

She smiled to herself then, knowing that Richard thought she was the most beautiful woman in the world. Sometimes she thought she must have tricked him into thinking that. It was a wonderful feeling, though, having him be obsessed with her. It was a wonderful feeling being obsessed with him.

She wanted nothing more right then than to hold him, than to tell him. But how could she? She wished more than anything that she hadn't yelled at him.

When she tried to sit up and an unexpected pain made her gasp, Shale's eyes opened. The sorceress rushed to sit on the edge of the bed.

Kahlan felt a keen sense of comfort to have the woman close.

Shale put a compassionate hand on Kahlan's arm as she smiled down at her. "There you are." She smoothed Kahlan's hair back from her forehead. "There you are." She looked relieved and radiantly happy to see that Kahlan was alive.

Kahlan took up the sorceress's hand in both of hers and held it against her cheek. Her gratitude for Shale saving her life seemed unable to be expressed in any other way.

"Where's Richard?" Kahlan finally asked. "Where are the Mord-Sith?"

"I made Richard go get some sleep by threatening to use a spell to put him down if he didn't do it voluntarily. He grumbled but complied. The Mord-Sith wanted to stay, but I find it an uneasy feeling to do a healing that makes people scream in pain when their protectors are nearby with an Agiel in their fists. I made them go get some sleep, too."

That made Kahlan smile. She put a hand across her middle. "If you healed me, why do I still hurt?"

"Because your abdominal muscles have been cramping against the things I've had to do. They are just exhausted, that's all. Nothing to be concerned about. I've healed all your injuries and drawn out the poison left by the claws of that thing that attacked you."

"Thing?"

"You called it the scribbly man."

Kahlan nodded at the memory. "Right."

Kahlan squeezed Shale's hand. She felt a deep bond with the woman who had healed her. Healing often formed that kind of closeness. The deeper the healing, the deeper the sense of connection.

"Thank you," she said. It didn't begin to seem like enough.

"Glad I could help, and I'm thankful that you are well. It saved my life, too."

Kahlan's brow bunched. "What do you mean?"

"If I had let you die, that man of yours would have skinned me alive and fed my hide to the vultures."

Kahlan smiled. She squinted around in the muted light. "How long have I been asleep?"

"Two nights and one day between them. It's not yet sunrise."

Kahlan put a hand to her forehead. "Dear spirits…"

As she tried to sit up, Shale gently pushed her back down. "You needed the rest. Don't be eager to get up too quickly. First get used to being whole again. There is no rush."

Kahlan tested her left arm. It felt normal.

"Is Richard all right?" she asked, looking up with sudden worry. "Have there been any more attacks?"

"One," Shale said. "Lord Rahl put his sword through it and the door behind. His reaction was instantaneous, but it was gone as soon as it appeared. I don't know if it was harmed, but I can tell you that the door will never be the same. That man has some muscles on him."

Kahlan couldn't help smiling. "Yes he does."

She didn't know if she should feel proud of Richard for Shale noticing, or jealous that she did.

"But he's all right? It didn't hurt him?"

Shale smiled her assurance. "He's fine, if a bit frazzled about you. So far the Golden Goddess has not caused any further trouble."

"But she will," Kahlan said.

"Your man will fight her. That is what a war wizard does."

Kahlan smiled at the mental image of him. "He is our protector." He was everything to her.

Shale nodded. "Yes, he is quite the man." She let out a deep sigh. "I have to say, that kind of man could make my toes curl, if you know what I mean."

That unwelcome mental image taunted Kahlan's jealousy out of the corner. She didn't say anything.

A curious hint of a smile grew on Shale's perfect features. "Does he do that for you? Make your toes curl and your eyes roll back in your head as the muscles in your legs turn to stone?"

Taken off guard by such a personal question, Kahlan didn't answer. But Shale's smile widened when Kahlan blushed.

"He is my world," Kahlan said. "He is everything to me."

Shale lifted an eyebrow. "Then why haven't you told him?"

If Kahlan had blushed before, now she felt her face burning. "You know?"

"Of course I know. In healing you I am aware of things like that."

Kahlan let her head sink back against the pillow as she closed her eyes.

"Dear spirits, how can I tell him, now? He promised a new golden age. I was so happy. I was about to tell him... but then when I saw everything falling apart because of the Golden Goddess, I blamed him. I was so angry at him, as if it was all his fault. I accused him of lying to me. I was so excited, and then all of a sudden I was so angry at seeing our happiness evaporate before my eyes. I blamed him."

"It's understandable," Shale assured her. "He knows that you don't really blame him or think he was deceiving you. In your condition it's normal to be more emotional. Once you tell him he will understand and everything will be right between you again."

"I was pregnant once before," Kahlan said as she rolled her head away from the sorceress. "I lost the baby. We were both devastated. Now..."

"Now you will finally be a mother, Mother Confessor."

Kahlan looked back at her. "How can I bring a child into a world only to have it hunted and slaughtered by the Golden Goddess? How can I bring a child into a world full of trouble?"

"It's not like you have a choice."

Kahlan shook her head. "I don't know how I can tell him now."

"Well, he is going to find out eventually."

"I know, but..." Kahlan forced out a breath in frustration. "When Nolo said they would kill our child, I lost it. All I could think about was our child, our new life just starting to grow in me, and then..."

"Our child would be butchered by those heartless beings. How can I burden Richard with such a worry? With this unexpected trouble how can I tell him I'm pregnant with our child?"

Shale had the oddest look on her face, but she didn't say anything.

"Don't you see," Kahlan pressed. "Our world needs both of us now more than ever. We can ill afford a distraction like this. Everyone's life is at stake. This would cripple our ability to protect people."

"Magic helps protect our world. In order for magic to continue, for Lord Rahl's power, for your power, to continue and protect future generations, you must."

"I know, but someday. Not now, when our child would be hunted by vicious predators."

"You and Lord Rahl are not helpless. You must fight for your right to happiness and for our way of life. That is the way of the world. When is it ever a good time?"

"Yes, but don't you see? This is different with the Golden Goddess and her kind suddenly coming for us. I'm terrified to bring a child into the world right now. I'm terrified for that child."

Shale seemed to glow with a serene smile.

"Not just a child, Kahlan."

Kahlan frowned. "What do you mean?"

"Twins."

Kahlan blinked. "What?"

Shale put a hand over Kahlan's belly. "You are going to have twins. A boy and a girl."

18

"**A** boy and a girl?" Kahlan asked in astonishment.
    "Yes, that's right," Shale said with a single nod and a warm smile. "You are pregnant with twins."

Kahlan stared up with both excitement and a deep sense of dread. Having twins—a boy and a girl—would be like a gift from the good spirits. It was a way for Richard's gift and her Confessor power to live on into future generations. The House of Rahl would not die out. The lineage of Confessors would not end. It couldn't be more perfect.

Kahlan winced as she tried to sit up. She put an arm across her abdomen to comfort the unexpected pain of the attempt.

"Easy," Shale said, pressing a hand against Kahlan's shoulder to ease her back down. "Your injuries were life-threatening, and you've only just been healed, at least for the most part. Your body is still in the process of completing the final repair of those injuries. Your muscles have been tested to exhaustion. You need to rest to complete your recovery."

Kahlan put her hand over Shale's in gratitude for saving her life after she had been attacked. She had worked tirelessly to keep Kahlan from dying or losing the use of her arm.

Even though she was a sorceress, the woman looked entirely too young and beautiful to be so accomplished a healer. Her youthful beauty laid over a shadow of wisdom and authority—that odd combination of freshly bloomed femininity and seasoned shrewdness—gave Kahlan pause in the back of her mind that Shale was more than what was on the surface.

At the moment, though, Kahlan was tormented by bigger issues than the hints of things beyond the woman's beauty or her own mortality.

She gently pushed Shale's arm aside as she sat up and swung her feet down off the bed. She finally stood. Shale, sitting on the edge of the bed, rose up beside her, ready to steady her or catch her if her legs gave out. Kahlan willed herself to straighten up. She found that she felt better being on her feet.

The lavish bedroom was still and quiet, lit only by the soft glow of lamps and a low fire in the massive fireplace. Kahlan knew that most of the Mord-Sith would be out in the entryway guarding the bedroom. She knew that Vika, though, would be guarding Richard.

With the Mord-Sith standing guard outside and Shale in the room with her, the private sanctuary seemed safe enough. But the thing that had attacked and nearly killed Kahlan hadn't needed to come through the doors. After all, it had attacked her when she had been in a locked room. From that, it seemed that those mysterious predators could appear anywhere.

Weighed down by the worry of the new threat to their lives and their world, Kahlan slipped on a robe and then opened the double glass doors to the balcony. The Lord Rahl's quarters for countless generations—now her and Richard's bedroom—were high up in the People's Palace and heavily protected by the men of the First File, the Lord Rahl's personal guard. At the far edge of the balcony, the fluted white marble balusters and railings had wild black veins among gold flecks. The grand balcony jutted out far enough over the edge of the plateau for her to be able to stand at that railing and look down past the palace to the Azrith Plain far below.

Kahlan tightened her robe against the chill. Summer was drawing to a close. The cold was a harbinger of the harsh times ahead.

In the predawn darkness there was no view of the Azrith Plain. Many times, beneath the vast sky it was a beautiful sight, in a stark, barren sort of way. It was a view of the world without the robes of green hills, carpets of forests, or jeweled streams of sparkling water. Instead, it was rather pure in the honesty of its unadorned form.

In a way, it was a visual reminder of how cruel and unforgiving the world of life could be beneath the façade of beauty.

Now, though, there was nothing to see except when lightning flickered. The lamplight coming from the bedroom behind her illuminated falling sheets of rain.

It was a gloomy, foreboding view that matched her mood.

Kahlan wanted these two children—Richard's children—more than anything. She had known she was pregnant, but to learn that she was pregnant with twins nearly took her breath with the unexpected excitement of it. As much as she wanted these children, though, she didn't know if she could dare to hope that she would ever have them.

The sorceress came up from behind. "Winter has already come to the Northern Waste. It will be down here soon enough."

"Is that where you are from?" Kahlan asked, her mind sinking into cold, dark thoughts.

Shale nodded as she gently placed a hand on Kahlan's shoulder. "I know your concerns and fears," she said as if reading Kahlan's mind, "but these children, the continuation of Lord Rahl's gift and your power, are what will help keep our world safe into the future. This could not come at a better time."

Kahlan folded her arms. "It could not come at a worse time. Giving birth to them will only mean that they would be hunted and slaughtered by the Golden Goddess and her kind. Our world needs them, needs our lines of magic to continue in order to protect our people into the future, but for that reason the Golden Goddess cannot allow them to live." Kahlan stared out into the darkness. "She will come for them."

"Are you saying that you would seek out an herb woman who would murder those unborn children in your womb before the Golden Goddess can?"

Kahlan recoiled at the very notion of ending the lives of her two unborn children before they could be born. But that dark thought, not fully formed, had been lurking in the corner of her mind. The way Shale had framed it was starkly cruel, and it was, but still, Kahlan couldn't help wondering about the mercy of such an act.

A cold tear ran down her cheek. "I didn't say that."

"Mother Confessor, your pregnancy is a joyous thing. Having these two children will preserve Lord Rahl's gift into the future. It would mean that you don't have to be the last Confessor."

"There is no way to know if either of these two children would carry our gift. They could be skips. Magic does not always pass on to the children of the gifted. It frequently skips one generation, or even many generations."

Even as she said it, she knew that daughters of Confessors were always born Confessors. But not all the sons of the Lord Rahl were born wizards.

"And if they are gifted? If it is what is needed for magic to continue to be the link that protects our world?"

Kahlan wiped the tear from her cheek as she looked back over her shoulder. "What if they are not gifted? Then having these children would not preserve magic in our world. Though it would be my greatest joy to bear Richard's children and they would be loved no less, they may not be gifted. If they aren't, and especially if they are, they could only look forward to being born into a dying world preyed upon by the Golden Goddess and her kind with no hope for the future."

Shale showed a curious smile. "I don't believe the good spirits would play such a cruel trick at such a time of need."

"How can you be so confident?"

Shale's smile widened as she placed her hand against Kahlan's belly. "Because I can feel it in them."

Kahlan's eyes widened. "You can say for sure that they are gifted? Both of them?"

Shale nodded with conviction. "I can."

Kahlan looked away again, out into the darkness. While that was what their world needed in the long term, it only made the immediate situation far worse.

The Golden Goddess would be able to see their magic. She called Richard the shiny man because she could see his magic shining in him. These two unborn children of D'Hara would draw that evil to them.

For all she knew, the goddess could sense that magic growing in Kahlan's womb at that very moment and could very well already be coming to kill her. It occurred to her that the goddess had already sent her kind to kill Kahlan and these unborn children. Kahlan had barely escaped alive. The goddess would send others to finish the job.

They would not be so timid the next time.

"This is not the way I wanted it to be," Kahlan said in a whisper. "Any time but now. Even if by a miracle these children are born, their birth will be their death sentence."

19

"Mother Confessor, don't you say 'Rise, my child' to any who fall to the ground at your feet?"

Kahlan stared out at the sheets of rain gently billowing in the breeze. "I do."

"So, all people are in a way the children of the Mother Confessor, are they not?"

Kahlan absently nodded in answer.

"Your instinct, as the Mother Confessor, is to protect your people—your children—is it not? Isn't that in a way the whole point of that singular title?"

"It is," Kahlan said.

"And you just fought a long and terrible war to protect them all, did you not?"

Kahlan nodded again, not knowing what the sorceress was getting at. "It was a terrible war. A long and terrible war. But for life to prevail, I had no choice but to fight. My whole life I have been in one endless fight to protect people from evil."

"And now you must continue to fight to protect all your children, especially the ones growing in you, even though they are yet unborn."

Kahlan took a deep breath and let it out slowly as she turned back to face the sorceress.

"This is different. These children would never have a chance at life. They will be killed for who and what they are. The Golden Goddess has everything on her side. She will not give up. She has vowed that magic will end in this world, one way or another, and when it does, her hordes will hunt us to extinction."

Kahlan couldn't stand the thought of bringing these two new lives into the world only to subject them to the terror of being slaughtered by such relentless evil. She ached with fear and dread for them.

"They hardly have everything on their side," Shale scoffed.

Kahlan frowned. "What are you talking about? You heard what Nolo said."

"Richard is a war wizard. He will fight to stop the Golden Goddess and her race of predators. War wizards are born with that power, that gift, expressly to face threats, both those known and those unknown. His children carry that gift. The world needs them."

Kahlan slowly shook her head. "You don't understand. There is more to it. The Golden Goddess is not the only threat. There is another that in some ways is just as formidable."

Shale leaned in to rest her fingers on the baluster while searching Kahlan's eyes. "What are you talking about?"

Kahlan drew a hand back across her face, wiping away the tears. "I'm talking about Shota."

"Shota?" Shale's nose wrinkled. "Who is Shota?"

Kahlan pressed her lips tight for a moment before answering. "Shota is a witch woman."

One of Shale's eyebrows lifted. "A witch woman?"

Kahlan nodded. "When Richard and I first met her, she put snakes all over me."

Shale looked puzzled. "Snakes? Why?"

"To keep me from moving and getting close enough to use my power on her. Back then I needed to physically touch a person to take them with my power. I no longer have to be close. My power can now span such a distance, but back then it couldn't, so Shota wanted to keep me at a safe distance from her, and she knew how afraid I am of snakes. She said that if I moved, those vipers would bite me. She intended in the end for those venomous snakes to kill me."

"Had you threatened her?"

"No."

Shale looked even more perplexed. "Then why in the world would a witch woman want to kill you?"

Kahlan gestured, as if weakly trying to banish the awful memory.

"She said that if she were to let me live and Richard and I ever had a child, it would be a monster."

Shale looked even more puzzled. "What would give her that idea?"

Kahlan let out a deep sigh. "In the distant past there were dark times caused by male Confessors. The gift passed on from a Confessor mother would give these male Confessors extraordinary abilities and power. That Confessor power alone corrupted them, and they used it to gain power. They were brutes who cast the world into tyranny and terror.

"Because of that history, at birth any male born to a Confessor is killed. That awful duty fell to the father. It had always been that a Confessor took her mate with her power so that he would not hesitate to carry out those instructions. Fortunately, males born to Confessors became rarer over time, so such infanticide became rare. Richard is the first one to love a Confessor and not be taken by her power.

"Because he is not bonded to me in that way, but by love, Shota knew that Richard would never kill any child of mine. He admitted to her that he could never do such a thing."

"Does the power of a Confessor pass on to all female children?"

"Yes. Every daughter born of a Confessor is herself a Confessor. It's the way the power was infused into us when originally created by a wizard named Merritt. The first Confessor, the one he created, was Magda Searus."

"Are the male children also always born with the Confessor power?"

Kahlan bit her lower lip as she squinted into her memory. "I guess I can't say for sure. It was a long time ago. It could be that only some were born with the Confessor ability, but the ones who had it certainly caused enough suffering, so the male children of Confessors are never allowed to live."

"Then Shota's worry may be for nothing. Your son may not have that ability. He may have only Richard's gift. Since Confessors rarely have male children, it is likely the girl has your power, and the boy Richard's. Besides, even if he has that ability, you both would teach him to be a good person."

"Well, male Confessor or not, Shota said that if Richard and I have a child, it will have both my power and his, and as a result it would be a monster."

"So, she was going to use snakes to kill you? Seems like a lot of effort."

"She did it because snakes terrify me. She couldn't be reasoned with. She is convinced that everyone in the world will be terrorized by any child of ours. She wanted me to feel that kind of terror before I died.

"Richard made her stop. I hate snakes, but I can't say that I think much of witch women, either, although I have known other witch women who have helped me. One in particular, Red, helped save Richard, but I think that was largely out of concern for her own hide. Witch women are dangerous and nearly impossible to reason with."

Shale grinned as if at a joke only she knew.

"What?" Kahlan asked. "Something funny about that?"

"In a way," she said, cryptically. "Go on."

"Well, anyway, Shota vowed to kill any child of ours. She said the mixing of gifts would create a monster. You have just told me that my twins are gifted—with Richard's gift and with mine. Shota is right about that much of it."

"Witches aren't always right in quite the way you expect."

"Believe me, I know that well enough, but Shota has vowed to kill any children we have. Given the dark history, I guess I can't say that her fears of a male Confessor are unfounded. When I first realized that I was pregnant, there were nights I lay awake, haunted by the fear Shota's words had planted in my mind, that our child would be a monster."

Shale shrugged. "Look at it this way: since you are having twins, a boy and a girl, the boy will likely have Richard's gift, and the girl will be a Confessor. No mixing of gifts. No monster. See? Of all the things you have to fear, that shouldn't be one of them."

"Can you say for sure that the boy won't have both powers? Can you say that the girl won't? Can you promise me that?"

Shale hesitated. "I admit that I am not able to tell that much. I only know that they are both gifted."

"Well," Kahlan said, leaning close, "Shota will not wait to find out. She will simply come to see them dead. She only agreed to Richard's demand that she let me live on the condition that we don't have children. Richard never agreed to her demand.

"Because he never agreed to her demand, she warned him that she would kill me and the child if I ever became pregnant. Even if I do live long enough to give birth to them, she will come after these children and kill them both. She will be relentless.

"Shota is a witch woman. She knows things. She finds out things. I don't know how, but she does. For all I know, maybe she reads things in the stars."

"The stars are now in a different place in the sky," Shale reminded her.

"Yes, well, if I know Shota, she will somehow come to know that I'm pregnant with Richard's children. Shota made it abundantly clear that she believes mixing different gifts creates monsters." Kahlan leaned toward the sorceress to make her point. "You don't know what witch women are like."

Shale cocked her head as she narrowed her eyes. "What do you mean?"

"Well, for one thing, they are profoundly dangerous."

Shale's face didn't reveal what she might be thinking. "Is that so?"

"Yes."

Kahlan felt something brushing against her ankle. She looked down and froze.

There was a large white snake hissing, red tongue flicking the air, curling its fat body around her ankles, locking them together as it flexed and contracted.

Kahlan's gaze shot up to Shale. "You're a witch woman?"

Shale smiled in a way that Kahlan didn't like.

Now she understood that mysterious shadow of something behind the beauty.

20

"Indeed I am."

Kahlan's eyes widened. "That's not possible. You're a sorceress."

"My father had the gift. He was a wizard. My mother was a witch woman. My father's gift passed down to make me a sorceress, my mother's makes me a witch woman. I am both."

"I've never heard of such a thing," Kahlan said, her eyes still wide.

"Besides the fact that fewer and fewer gifted people were being born, making the gifted rarer all the time, the House of Rahl periodically purged D'Hara of the threat purportedly posed by the gifted still remaining. Richard's father, Darken Rahl, was one of the worst of the lot. He denounced the gifted as criminals and called for them to be eliminated for the good of all."

Kahlan, of course, knew all that. Darken Rahl viewed anyone gifted as a potential threat to his rule. It was, in fact, why she had crossed the boundary into Westland looking for help to stop him. That was how she met Richard.

"Darken Rahl found a way through the boundary and put the Midlands, my people, under the boot of his tyranny," Kahlan said. "He killed any gifted he could find. He hunted down and killed all the Confessors. Only I escaped. That made me the last of the Confessor line."

"That man terrorized the gifted of every kind," Shale said with a sad nod.

"So how did your parents escape his grasp?"

"They fled in fear for their lives and the life of their unborn child." Shale smiled in a sly manner. "The House of Rahl never went looking for such gifted people in the Northern Waste; it was too far away and too sparsely populated for him to bother with. Because Darken Rahl was preoccupied with his war to take over the world, populated areas were where his attention was focused, not such remote and useless places as the Northern Waste. My parents lived there in peaceful isolation, and there they had me.

"In me, their two abilities mixed together to make me both a sorceress and a witch woman. Two gifts mixed together." She leaned a little closer. "A monster, as you described it."

Kahlan forced herself not to look down at the snake compressing her ankles, preventing her from moving. "That's what Shota called such people, not me, and she was only talking about any child that Richard and I would have. She was talking about our gifts being mixed."

Shale's tone took on the quality of an interrogation. "So then, unlike most people, you don't think me a monster because I have two different gifts mixed together?" She arched an eyebrow. "Or think I'm trouble because I am a witch woman?"

"Of course not."

"Are you sure of that?"

"You saved my life," Kahlan said. "You didn't have to get involved. You didn't have to work as hard as you did to save me. You could have let me die and no one would be the wiser. You have proven you are no monster by your actions.

"My children wouldn't be, either, just because a wizard is their father and a Confessor their mother."

"Well, while you are right that witch women are quite dangerous, I am one witch woman who wants you to have those children. Just as my parents fled the tyranny of Richard's ancestors who tried to eliminate the gifted, I, too, want to live in a world where magic exists, a world where we all, despite the unique nature of our individual abilities, can have a future without a fear of being persecuted for who and what we are. A world at peace."

"That's what Richard and I want as well. You lived far removed from the war just ended, but that is what we both have fought so hard for, what we have both been committed to, in fact what the D'Haran Empire is all about."

"That's reassuring to hear." Shale didn't sound completely convinced. "But for that to happen you must have these children. They are the hope for magic to survive in our world, and in turn, for our way of life to survive. You must see to it that they grow and carry your power and Richard's gift into the future."

Kahlan felt relieved by at least that much of it, but the snake around her ankles had her not only unable to move, but afraid to try. She did her best not to think about that fat snake squeezing her ankles, even though she could feel the cold scales sliding across her bare skin.

"You are more than a sorceress and a witch woman. You are Shale. Without you I would have died, and the hope of passing our gifts on to future generations would have died with me. I would like very much for you to see my children not only when they are born, but when they grow into their power."

Shale's intense look finally eased, and she nodded. "Ah. Well then, I guess the snake needs to go."

"I think that would be for the best." Kahlan swallowed. "If I die of fright, I won't be able to have any children."

Shale let out a soft laugh. She gently rolled her hand to the side while bowing her head as if suggesting Kahlan look again. Kahlan glanced down. The fat white snake was gone. She let out a deep sigh of relief.

She didn't know if witch women could make real things appear, or if they only made you believe they were there. She knew that Shota could change her appearance as well as make things appear. There was no way to know what she actually looked like, or if you were looking at the real Shota. For that matter, now she didn't know if she was looking at the real Shale. That might explain the beauty overlaying the ageless wisdom. But Kahlan did know that Shota's snakes, at least, were real enough that their venom would have killed her.

With a finger, Shale lifted Kahlan's chin.

"It wasn't my intent to threaten you or frighten you. I simply wanted you to see that just because that witch woman, Shota, said that mixing magic creates monsters, that is not necessarily true."

"I think that sometimes it results in someone quite remarkable," Kahlan said.

"That is what I hoped you would understand. Your children will also be remarkable. I don't want you to let the fear that Shota planted in your mind become large enough to cause you to act on that fear."

"There is enough evil in the world without Shota inventing more from her twisted imagination." Kahlan fixed the sorceress with a determined look. "If Shota threatens my children, it will be the last thing she ever does."

"Good," Shale said with a satisfied smile.

21

Shale's smile left as a more serious look took its place. "But I didn't know that you had such little faith in Richard."

Kahlan frowned at the woman. "What are you talking about? I have total faith in him."

"Richard is the protector of the D'Haran Empire, is he not? His bond to his people and theirs to him is part of our world's protection. He has proven time and time again that he would fight to the death to protect our people."

"I know that," Kahlan said. "What's your point?"

"Well, what means more to him than anything else?"

Kahlan didn't need to think about it. "I do."

"And don't you think he would fight to protect you and your children? Don't you think he will use his gift and do everything in his power to protect them, even before they are born? Don't you think he would prevent this witch woman, Shota, from ever getting near you?"

"Yes, but—"

"Your children would be of one blood, yours and Lord Rahl's together. You must have faith in him to protect you. This is what he was born for. This is his highest calling. We are all in his hands. The Mord-Sith will always be there to protect you. I will be there if you wish it. You need to have faith in him to protect you so that you can worry about those two children."

Kahlan was baffled at what the woman could be getting at. "I do have faith in him. Complete faith."

Shale leaned in a little. "Then he needs to know that you are going to bear his children. You have been hiding it from him. He needs to be told that you are pregnant so that he can protect you."

Kahlan paced to the stone railing, to the very edge of where the rain was falling only an arm's length away. Lightning danced and darted among the roiling clouds, illuminating them from inside and the barren landscape far below in flickering flashes. Occasional distant, deep rumbles of thunder rolled across the plain.

"I will let you stand with me, help protect me, and if possible be there when I give birth," Kahlan said. "But there is one condition."

"What condition?"

"You must not tell Richard that I'm pregnant."

Shale let out a soft chuckle. "I'm afraid that he is going to find out. It's not the kind of thing you can hide."

Kahlan turned back. "For now I can. It won't begin to show for a while yet."

Shale looked confused. "Why would you want to hide this from him? I haven't known Lord Rahl long, but from what I've heard and seen, he would be overjoyed by this news. He would do whatever was needed to protect you and those unborn children."

"That is precisely why he must not know. At least for now. We can't afford to have Richard distracted from his job of protecting our world. He is a war wizard. He needs to find a way to eliminate this new threat from the Golden Goddess and her kind. All our lives—my children's lives—depend on him and what only he can do."

Shale, looking mystified, spread her hands. "But if he knows you are going to have his children, he will fight all the harder to protect them. That's what you want, isn't it—for your children to be protected?"

"That's the point," Kahlan said.

"What point?"

"You don't know Richard. He already feels guilty for letting me go alone to question Nolo. He thinks that what happened was because he wasn't there to protect me, even though he knows that, as a Confessor, a lone man has never been a threat to me before. He wrongly thinks he made a mistake in not protecting me. With me nearly being killed fresh in his memory, he will not want to again make what he feels was a mistake. If I know Richard, I bet that you had a time of it trying to get him to stay out of here so that you could heal me, am I right?"

Shale made a face as she sighed. "That's the truth." She looked a bit embarrassed. "As a matter of fact, when I first met him in the great hall, I told him that he was an idiot for letting you go alone to question Nolo."

"Well, if he knew that I was pregnant, that would only make him more determined to protect me. He would shift his focus away from where it needs to be right now. Protecting me would become his central focus. Don't you see? We can't afford that right now.

"Of course he can do both—protect us from this new threat and protect me, and he will—but if he knew I was pregnant, it would unavoidably split his attention. I have no idea how he will be able to solve this new threat from the Golden Goddess and her kind. That is for him to figure out. For our part, we dare not burden him with the additional worry of me being pregnant."

"But Mother Confessor, sooner or later it is going to become obvious."

"Yes, later," Kahlan said as she put a hand over those children. "But for now, it's not obvious. For now, we must let him do his job of figuring out how to protect our world. Right now, he needs to worry about everyone before it's too late and our children no longer have a world to grow up in."

"You realize, of course, that when he finds out he is going to be angry with you for keeping it from him."

"Better he is angry then, than we all die in the meantime because he is distracted."

Shale's smile returned. "And you will do *your* job of having these children in order to protect our world in the future."

"Yes, of course."

Shale thought it over for a moment before finally sighing. "All right. You have my word. I will not tell him. It will be up to you when you feel the time is right."

Kahlan held up a cautionary finger. "And you can't tell the Mord-Sith, either. I know how incredibly difficult it is to keep anything from Richard. If one of the Mord-Sith knew, he would soon after find out."

Shale rubbed her forehead with her fingertips as she turned and paced off a few strides before turning back. "All right. No one will know but you and me until you decide otherwise."

"Good. Thank you, Shale."

"But I hope you are prepared for how angry and upset he will be when he learns you have been hiding it from him."

Kahlan flashed a lopsided smile. "I'm not afraid of the big guy. I will smooth his ruffled feathers when the time comes."

22

Holding the scabbard and baldric together in one hand, Richard pulled open the bedroom door. When he did, Vika, who had been sitting on the floor leaning against the door, tumbled back inward. She jumped to her feet, quickly rubbing the sleep from her eyes. Holding her arms out to keep him behind her, her single blond braid whipped one way and then the other as she checked all around for any threat. It was obvious to Richard that she had been sitting on the floor, leaning against the door so that he couldn't sneak off without her.

Some of the other Mord-Sith must have warned her about him occasionally doing just that. There had been times when he had deliberately slipped away from Cara or the others, but not without good reason. Of course, to Mord-Sith, whose sworn duty it was to protect him with their lives, there was no such thing as a good reason to go anywhere without them. They didn't realize, or refused to accept, that when he did that it was most often to protect them from dangers they couldn't fathom or handle. The fact that he did worry about their safety was another reason they were so fiercely loyal to him.

"Any word from Shale or Kahlan?"

Vika shook her head. "No, Lord Rahl."

Shale had been healing Kahlan, and she didn't want Richard looking over her shoulder. At her insistence he had gone off to another bedroom to get some sleep. But with his worry over Kahlan, he had gotten precious little rest.

The soldiers, weapons to hand, were all looking off down the hall to Richard's left, ready to protect him from whatever they were concerned about. The men had been standing guard nearby outside the bedroom he had been using, and apparently something down that hallway had brought them in close to his room. Whatever had them on high alert had drawn their swords.

"What was that sound?" he asked as he slipped the leather baldric over his head to lie on his right shoulder. "I thought I heard something."

The commander of the detachment pointed with his sword down the hallway to the side. "We heard an odd sound as well, Lord Rahl, but I'm not exactly sure what it was. I'm pretty sure it wasn't a natural sound, like the creaking of the palace you sometimes hear."

Richard secured his sword at his left hip. The ornate gold and silver of the scabbard gleamed in the lamplight. He knew from the window back in the bedroom he had been sleeping in that it was not yet dawn.

Before he could ask the commander to describe the sound, Richard heard something new, loud and distinct. Even though it was some distance down the hall, it was clear that this time it was a bloodcurdling cry.

Richard immediately took off down the hall toward the source of the shriek. The entire group of big men of the First File abruptly fell in behind him.

Richard raced down the elegant blue and gold carpet of the broad corridor toward the sounds of yet more screams. Without slowing, he made a turn to the right down a narrower hall, following the frantic cries. It was hard to turn on the slippery stone, so he deliberately hit the paneled wall with his left shoulder and rebounded off of it to help him turn the corner down a narrower hall.

Vika shoved men to one side then the other as she pushed and squeezed her way through the cluster of big, heavily armed soldiers in order to get close to Richard. All of the men knew that Vika was Richard's personal guard, so they didn't try to stop her, even though the First File was also his personal guard. None were willing to challenge a Mord-Sith with an Agiel in her fist, especially not one dressed in her red leather.

The First File was the closest line of defense for the Lord Rahl. These men had worked all their lives to earn a place in the First File. They were all powerful men in chain mail and shaped leather armor. They were all experts in every weapon they carried. Each was deadly.

They were all the elite of the elite. Each would lay down his life before he allowed trouble to get a look at Richard.

Yet none wanted to disagree with a Mord-Sith who insisted she be closest to Lord Rahl. Like them, like all the Mord-Sith, Vika wanted nothing more than to protect Richard. For the Mord-Sith, their greatest wish was to die in their duty of protecting the Lord Rahl. It was a twisted wish, but then, the Mord-Sith were rather twisted women.

When Richard had released them all from their long history of enforced bondage to the Lord Rahl, they all chose on their own to stay right where they were. If anything, freeing them and giving them their lives back had only made them more devoted to protecting him, now by choice, not a lifetime of training, punishment, and compulsory duty.

The hall they were all racing down, while elegantly paneled with dyed maple, was dimly lit with reflector lamps spaced a good distance apart, leaving a lot of unsettling shadows. Following the sporadic, weak sound of pain and the occasional, otherworldly, echoing bellow, Richard passed dozens of rooms to each side before having to turn down another hall branching off to the left. The thick, dark mass of soldiers flowed through the halls behind him and Vika. The new hall he entered had only one lamp, back near the intersection, so they were all running into growing darkness.

Even before Richard drew his sword, the weapon's magic was calling to him, eager to join with his suddenly awakened anger at the unknown threat. The magic of the blade was impatient to join with the Seeker's fury and taste the blood of the enemy.

Knowing that he was getting closer to the source of the sounds, Richard at last drew his sword. The unique ring of steel as it was pulled free of the scabbard echoed through the confined space. What little light there was seemed to give the black steel a sinister glow.

Now, with that ancient weapon in his fist, there was nothing holding back the power of the sword's magic from flowing into him. Together, his fury and the sword's joined, ready to confront any threat, eager to meet the enemy.

Behind Richard, the soldiers' weapons clanged and jangled. The dim lamplight sent flashes of reflections off them into the darkness.

As they raced onward, darkness closed in around them. It grew hard to see. Even as they rushed ahead, the weak gasps had died out. The footfalls of all the men sounded like rolling thunder echoing through the narrow hallway.

Suddenly, Richard came upon the crumpled form of one of the men of the First File. A quick look told him that the man had been mauled. Great wounds were cut right through the leather breastplate and the man's rib cage, exposing his insides. His arms were shredded to the bone through the chain mail. He had no weapon in his bloody fists.

Richard looked up just in time to see a dark shape in the distance. He couldn't tell what it was, but it was moving away from them. When it paused to look back, Richard could just detect the lamplight from quite a distance behind him reflecting a dim gold color in the eyes of the predator.

Having already taken in the sight as he had approached the downed soldier, he bounded over the man without losing a stride and was off down the hall after the attacker.

The thing was swift and made no sound. In a fleeting moment, it had melted into the darkness. Richard charged down the dark hallway after it, determined not to let it get away.

Vika grabbed his shirt at his shoulder and pulled him to a stop. Her teeth were gritted in anger.

"What do you think you are doing?" she growled.

"I'm going after it!" Richard jerked his shirt free of her grip.

Before he could be off after the attacker again, she hooked an arm around his to keep him from getting away. "No, you are not going after it! It's all dark down there. We don't even know what that thing is. Did you see what it did to that man back there?"

"Yes, the same thing it had started to do to Kahlan. I have to—"

"No you don't! It wants you to follow. It's black as pitch down there. You wouldn't stand a chance."

Richard, as angry as he was about the man being killed, frowned at her. "What do you mean, it wants me to follow?"

Vika gestured angrily back with an arm. "Don't you see? It mauled that man within earshot of where you were sleeping. It wanted to draw you out and down here, into the dark. It wanted you to come after it."

"It could have just appeared in the bedroom and had me there."

"You heard what Nolo said. They want this world, but they are wary of your gift. They don't understand it. This one wanted to get you to do something stupid so that you would be vulnerable—just as the Mother Confessor was when one of them attacked her.

"They are using your empathy for your people to try to draw you to them. For all we know there could be an ambush down that hallway, waiting in the dark, with the intention of trying to overcome your magic. There could be dozens of them waiting down there to tear you apart."

The commander of the men standing close behind Richard smoothed down his thick beard as he caught his breath. "I think you should listen to her, Lord Rahl. She has a good point. It could have attacked any number of people asleep in the palace without being heard or discovered. Had it done that, we would only later find the remains. This attack on a lone sentry, near your quarters, only makes sense if you see it as a tactic to draw you out."

Vika bowed her head to the commander as if in respect for the man for agreeing with her.

Richard reluctantly forced himself to think through the fog of rage about their words. He had to ram the Sword of Truth back into its scabbard to quench the anger it was feeding into him. He took a settling breath.

Finally, he gave a nod to Vika. "You're right. Thanks for not letting me do something stupid."

"From what I hear from my sisters of the Agiel, that appears to be my full-time job."

Some of the soldiers chuckled.

"All right," Richard said. "Let's hurry and get back to that man to see if there is anything that can be done for him."

The commander gestured back with his sword. "The only thing you can do for him now, Lord Rahl, is to say some words as he is laid to rest. His pain and terror is at last ended. He is in the hands of the good spirits, now."

Richard felt terrible that the man had died guarding him.

"We need to search this hall and see if that thing is still down there," he told the commander. "If it is, we won't be rushing into an ambush. We will corner it. Have some of your men get torches."

Once close to a dozen men rushed back with torches, Richard moved quickly but cautiously on down the hall, looking for the killer. Men searched every room along the way. At each intersection two men were dispatched to scout side routes. The farther they went down the main corridor, the more the corridors branched off.

After a time-consuming, fruitless search, Richard finally brought them all to a stop. "There is no telling where that thing went. But from what Nolo told us, they can simply melt into thin air and go back to their own world. I suspect it's no longer in the palace."

"I'm afraid I have to agree," Vika said. "I think it's gone."

"But to be sure," Richard said, "I want the men to conduct a thorough search. Make sure they are in pairs at a minimum."

The commander nodded. "I will get more men and we will search this entire part of the palace."

Richard raked his fingers back through his hair. "I need to go check on Kahlan." He was still feeling the remnants of the sword's rage crackling through him. It was hard to douse such powerful anger once it had been ignited. "If the sorceress isn't finished healing the Mother Confessor, I will wring her neck."

"I'm sure she is doing her best, Lord Rahl," Vika offered in a quiet voice.

Richard nodded before addressing all the men watching him. "It looks like these predators are ambush hunters. They pick the moment to strike. That means we will always be at a disadvantage. It doesn't matter how big and strong you men are. If they catch you off guard, or alone, you will be like that unfortunate soldier back there—dead before you know what happened."

"Then it would seem prudent," the commander said, "that all men standing guard, no matter where, do not do so alone. There should be at least two men, maybe three, at each post. That way if the enemy jumps one of them, the others can attack it."

Richard sighed as he nodded. "That's the idea. Please see to it. In the meantime, I need to make sure the Mother Confessor is safe."

The commander clapped a fist to his heart. "This way, Lord Rahl."

"While I'm checking on her," Richard said as he started out, "I want all the officers of the First File gathered." He gestured to the left. "There's a devotion square not far away in that direction. There's too many men of the First File to pull them from their duties all over the palace and address them all at once, but by meeting with the officers they can pass my words on to their men. Have them gather there so that I can talk to them."

23

Kahlan, in the white dress of the Mother Confessor, was just emerging from their bedroom as Richard hurried into the entryway from the broad corridor. He could see that her arms were moving without pain. She was walking straight and tall, which told him that the healing had been successful.

When her green-eyed gaze locked on him, her expression brightened.

The Mord-Sith were all gathered in that round entry where they had been guarding the bedroom all night while Shale had finished the healing. Only Vika had gone with Richard to another room where he could get some rest.

A weary-looking Shale followed Kahlan out. Richard knew that such a healing would have been quite an ordeal for her as well as Kahlan. He could read in the sorceress's face and in her aura the toll it had taken on her.

Kahlan rushed into his arms and for a long moment he lost himself in that embrace, relieved beyond words to see her looking like herself again. As he was hugging her, he reached out with one hand to touch Shale's arm in appreciation for what she had done. She returned a proud smile.

"Did you sleep well?" Kahlan asked, holding his upper arms as she pushed back from the hug.

"Without you? Hardly at all."

Kahlan flashed him her special smile. "Now that Shale has finished healing me, tonight you will be back with me, and I will see to it that you do."

"There was an attack," he said, hating to break the spell of her smile.

Just that quick, the smile was gone. "What?"

"I'm pretty sure that it was the same kind of thing that attacked you—one of the predators sent by the Golden Goddess. The thing you called the scribbly man."

Kahlan's face lost some of its color. "Where? When?"

Richard pointed a thumb back over his shoulder. "A short time ago. It was one of the soldiers standing guard by himself down the hall not far from the room where I was sleeping."

"Was he severely hurt, Lord Rahl?" Shale asked from behind Kahlan. "Can I help?"

Richard shook his head. "I'm afraid it's too late to help him."

"Dear spirits, that's terrible." Kahlan frowned. "Why attack a lone man standing guard? That seems odd."

"I think because I was sleeping nearby."

Just then, a soldier of the First File rushed into the entryway breathing heavily. "Lord Rahl, Mother Confessor, are you both all right?"

"Yes," Richard said. "What is it?"

"One of the sentries standing guard down a hallway branching off from this corridor coming in here was just found dead."

"Did it look like he had been mauled by a bear?" Richard asked, his heart sinking.

"That's right," the man said, looking a little surprised. "There is no sign of whatever it was that attacked him."

"So, you didn't catch sight of it?"

"No, Lord Rahl."

"I heard a scream a couple of hours ago," Cassia said.

Richard turned to stare at the Mord-Sith. "And you didn't go to help the man?"

She frowned. "Of course not, Lord Rahl."

"Why not?"

"Because our duty is to protect the Mother Confessor. It could be that it was a diversion to draw us away from protecting her. We are not going to abandon our duty to keep her safe. The risk of doing so would be too great. It is the job of the First File to respond to such things."

Richard looked at the grim faces of Rikka, Nyda, Vale, and Berdine. None looked to think any differently.

"Lord Rahl," Berdine finally said, "we are here, in your place, to protect your wife. She is just as important to preserving the magic protecting this world as you are. I know you would not want us to be tricked into leaving her without our protection. We would not trust her to anyone else's care. We are the last line of defense. We would all die before harm could get a look at her, just as we would all die before harm could get a look at you."

"That's right," Cassia added. "I am sorry one of the men of the First File was killed, but that's all the more reason we should not leave our post guarding the Mother Confessor."

Vika looked to her sister Mord-Sith. "Lord Rahl sometimes gets crazy ideas to expose himself to danger. Fortunately, I was there to stop him from doing something foolish and dangerous only a little while ago, in a similar situation."

The rest of them nodded solemnly.

"Protecting him is often a burden," Berdine confirmed.

Richard was used to the Mord-Sith talking about him in such a way, right in front of him, as if he were a doddering old fool who could barely feed himself.

He turned back to Kahlan, spellbound by her green eyes, but needing to return to business.

"I asked the officers to meet us in a devotion area not far from here," he finally said. "With two men killed already this morning, I'm sure rumors will be circulating among the First File. We need to let them at least know the nature of the threat. We need to come up with a plan to fight it."

"They can appear out of thin air," Kahlan said, sounding skeptical that any planning could be possible.

"I know. That makes it difficult, but we've learned one thing. They are attacking targets around both of us to try to draw us out and into a surprise ambush."

Kahlan looked more than a little concerned. "It seems they can appear anywhere, so why wouldn't they simply attack us right there in our rooms, much like the way they did when I was alone with Nolo? Why not surprise us that way?"

Richard stared off for a moment, trying to reason it out in his own mind. He finally looked back at Kahlan.

"They are afraid of our magic. They tried a direct surprise attack on you when you touched Nolo with your power. They struck when you were at your weakest. Even though that thing ripped into you, I suspect that it vanished before finishing the job because at the same time your power was already returning. Nolo says they are fearful of our magic.

"Before, when Shale was beginning to heal you, I was going down a hallway that was dark because the lamps had gone out. One of them appeared suddenly. I don't know where it came from, or if it came out of nowhere. It was simply suddenly there."

"What did it look like?" Kahlan asked.

"It was too dark to get a good look at it. This dark shape suddenly came rushing at me out of nowhere. I had my sword out before it was on me and I was able to take a swing right through the middle of it."

Kahlan leaned in. "And then what? What happened? Did you kill it?"

Richard shook his head in regret. "Then it just wasn't there, as if it never had been. For an instant I thought I had only imagined the whole thing, imagined I had seen something in the dark—a shadow or a twist of the light. I wondered if I'd been scared by my own shadow. But I wasn't. Something was there. My magic—the sword's magic—must have scared it off. I suspect they are attacking people around both of us to test the limits of our powers."

"Or to try to test themselves against it," Shale said.

"That could be, too," Richard said in a worried tone as he paced off a few feet, thinking.

"We need to warn people of this new danger," Kahlan said.

"Can people defend themselves against these things," Vika asked, "these scribbly men, as you called them?"

Kahlan shook her head. "No, they can't. No one can, except maybe Richard and maybe me."

"Then what can be accomplished by telling everyone that our world is under attack from an unknown threat that will come out of nowhere to rip them apart and there's nothing they can do to save themselves? That would terrify people, which is exactly what Nolo said these predators seek: terror."

Richard rubbed his chin in thought. "I'm afraid Vika is right."

"Along with the First File, we are the steel against steel," Vika said. "You are the magic against magic, Lord Rahl. This is what you were born to do."

"These predators don't have magic," Richard reminded her.

"Well, they have something that enables them to get from their world to ours in order to hunt and kill us. You are the only one who can figure out how to fight beings that can do that."

"Right now, you can't worry about the people living in the palace," Berdine added. "You need to focus on stopping this threat, not managing panicked people."

"They have a point," Kahlan said.

"I'm afraid I have to agree." Richard let out a deep sigh. "The Golden Goddess and her kind are using our empathy for others against us to goad us into traps."

Kahlan shook her head in despair. "What can we do about that?"

Richard's gaze swept over the six women in red leather all standing at ease, watching him. "We have a secret weapon."

Kahlan frowned. "What secret weapon?"

"The Mord-Sith," Richard said with a wry smile. "They have no empathy."

The Mord-Sith all flashed self-satisfied grins.

24

Richard watched a school of gold-colored fish in a loose group gliding gracefully through the reflecting pool in the center of the devotion square, their long, flowing tails swaying rhythmically side to side as they slowly circled the large black pitted boulder sitting in the center of the pond. Vines, with delicate little blue flowers and roots fanning out in the water, grew up along the sides of the boulder, clinging to it, reaching for the light above. It was the way of life, it seemed, to always reach for the light.

The predators that hunted them, though, sought the darkness from where they struck.

Overhead, the roof above the pool was open to a gloomy gray sky. The heavy rain of the night before had stopped, but by the way the sky looked it could easily start again at any time.

Richard stepped up on the short blue-tiled wall that surrounded the square pool, and turned to the dozens of silent officers standing at attention in neat rows before him. Kahlan stood on the floor in front of him to the right. Three of the Mord-Sith stood at ease to her right, three more to Richard's left.

Shale stood off a little farther to the left, hands clasped before her, watching. Her hair, parted in the middle, wasn't nearly as long as Kahlan's, and it was dark, but like Kahlan's it gleamed in the flat light from above. Most of the men hadn't been able to avoid staring at her when they had come into the square. Shale had an arresting presence. She looked both alluring and intimidating at the same time, as if daring men to look at her and threatening them if they did.

Richard knew that was the witch woman in her. Witch women were dangerous. Shale radiated that danger even without intending to do so. For some witch women, like Shota, they intended every bit of that threat and more.

Most of the soldiers standing before them wore chain mail under shaped leather armor along with broad weapons belts holding at least a sword, a double-bladed axe, or a mace. Many had two weapons, some all three. A few of the men, specialists in close-quarters combat, additionally had metal bands with razor-sharp projections around their arms just above their elbows. Those projections could tear an opponent apart in seconds.

Richard clasped his hands behind his back as he began. "While we are all grateful that the long and terrible war has finally ended, we unfortunately find ourselves facing a new threat unlike anything we have faced before." His expression was grim as memories flashed through his mind. "And we have faced many terrible things before."

He could see the uncertainty on many of the faces. He knew that most of these men would have heard rumors. He wanted to end the rumors with what he knew.

"As I'm sure all of you have noticed, since the end of the war the stars in the night sky look completely different." Richard smiled a little as he gestured up at the opening through the roof. "At least, when you can see them.

"That is one sign that our world has changed in ways that we don't yet understand and can't predict, but what I do know is that somehow we have come within the reach of a new threat from a race of predators from another world. Their leader is called the Golden Goddess. They are not human. Their only motivation is to hunt, kill, and eat. To them, we are merely prey. Rabbits before wolves.

"There can be no reasoning with these predators, no treaty, no peace agreement, any more than the rabbits could insist on peace when the wolves are of a different mind. Although I can't yet explain it, they somehow come into our world and when they do, they come for only one reason. They come to kill. So far they quickly vanish back to their own world before we can kill or capture any of them."

"They have magic, then?" Commander Sedlak asked.

"No. In fact, they fear magic, or at least they're wary of it. That's why I want the tradition of devotions to continue. For now, that link to my magic is the only thing keeping them cautious. If they can kill the Mother Confessor and me, then they will no longer have reason to be cautious. They will flood into our world, where they will hunt humans to extinction."

"What do they look like?" another man asked. "Are they like wolves, or gar, or something like dragons?"

Richard shook his head in regret. "No one has seen what they look like. At least, no one who has lived to tell about it. I think they walk on two feet, although I can't yet say for sure. We know they have claws or talons that can rip a man to shreds. I'm sure you have heard about the men who have been killed. That is how they died."

Lieutenant Dolan lifted a hand, and when Richard nodded asked, "How do we fight them? Can they be harmed by our weapons?"

"Since they don't have magic, I would assume so," Richard said. "The problem is seeing them in time, and then reacting before they can strike or vanish back into their world. But they often eat what they kill. That means they are living creatures. If they are living, then they can die. Our job is to kill them—you men with steel, me, with magic. I intend to find a way that I can do just that. In the meantime, the First File is our first line of defense, here, at the palace.

"So far, because they are being cautious, they seem to favor using the cover of darkness and ambush. That means they are thinking creatures. We need to outthink them. I want all of you officers to convey what I am telling you to all of your men. We need all of the First File to understand what we know so far about the nature of what we face. Once I find out more, I will let you know.

"Because they strike so fast, I want no man patrolling or standing watch alone. There should always be at least two men on watches and when patrolling. Groups, when possible, would be even better.

"While I want you to spread the word among your men, I don't want any of you or your men to tell anyone else about this. That means those living in the palace and those visiting delegations who are in the process of departing. For now, this is privileged information for men of the First File alone."

Lieutenant Dolan frowned with concern. "You don't want us to warn people about a threat that could come out of nowhere to attack them?"

"And what good would that do?" Richard asked. "Right now, there is nothing people can do to keep themselves safe. That's our responsibility. Even locking themselves in their rooms won't help, because these predators can appear out of thin air right in those rooms. Telling people would only spread panic throughout the palace, and that would cause people to flee. These creatures are predators. Predators are driven to chase running prey. From what I know, there is nowhere safe, nowhere to run, nowhere to hide. Whether here at the palace, or in a far distant land, everyone is prey for this race of predators.

"As more attacks happen, there will soon enough be panic. But for now, our duty is to try to find a way to stop this menace, not scare the wits out of everyone without being able to offer a solution.

"For now, I believe the primary goal of these creatures is to kill the Mother Confessor and me so that our magic won't interfere with them marauding unchecked across our world. Not that they won't attack other people—there have been people killed in distant places—but I think those protecting us are likely to be their primary targets."

The bell atop the rock in the center of the pool rang, the first of three, calling everyone to devotion. As that sound reverberated through the palace, Kahlan signaled to Richard that she wanted to say something. He gave her a hand up onto the wall beside him.

All eyes were upon Kahlan, standing tall and proud in the satiny white dress of the Mother Confessor. "I regret more than any of you could ever know, having to call upon you men to fight again. Know that it is not by choice.

"Once again, we must fight for our lives and to protect the lives of our people."

As beautiful as Kahlan was, as intelligent, as kind, as wise, there was no one more ruthless in battle. These men all knew that. Many had fought under her command and followed her into bloody battle after bloody battle. For that reason, more than any other, she held a special place in the hearts of these soldiers. Silence hung over the gloomy devotion square as they waited for her to go on.

"The Golden Goddess, the leader of these predators, spoke to Lord Rahl and me. She is called the collector of worlds. She wants ours.

"To her kind, killing is a sport. They somehow go to other worlds to hunt and kill other species to extinction. That is the purpose that drives them. They get delight in clawing people apart. Our intelligence draws them as an added challenge for their hunts. They seek to inflict pain and terror.

"One of them ripped into me with its claws and nearly killed me. I barely survived. I can't begin to explain to you the pain and terror of being attacked by one of them."

She slowly shook her head as tears welled up in her eyes.

"These beings also lust to slaughter our children."

The room waited in dead silence as a tear ran down her cheek.

"They are hateful things."

Richard knew she didn't like to show weakness by crying in front of people. Now, she seemed to be having trouble controlling her emotions. She wiped the tear from her cheek, trying to compose herself before going on.

"We have no choice but to kill every last one of them, because if we don't, they will not stop until they have hunted us all to extinction.

"In the past have I asked some of you men to bring me the ears of the enemy. This time..." Kahlan gritted her teeth for a moment, the steel coming back to her voice. "This time, I want you to bring me the heads of these hateful things!"

With their fists raised in the air, a deafening war cry rose up from the men, reverberating through the devotion square.

25

O ther people from the palace, after the second bell calling them
to the devotion, began filtering into the square. At the third bell,
along with the Mord-Sith and officers at the front, everyone went to
their knees, bowed forward, and placed their foreheads to the ground.

In the hushed silence, as Richard stood watching, everyone in this
devotion square and at every other one in the palace began the words
they had repeated countless times throughout their lives.

"Master Rahl guide us," everyone said in one, sincere voice.
"Master Rahl teach us." Their voices echoed through the stone
corridors. "Master Rahl protect us." Those words were like a hot
knife through Richard's heart. He didn't know how in the world he
was going to protect them. All he knew was that he was the only one
who could.

The assembled crowd finished the devotion in that same joined,
haunting voice. "In your light we thrive. In your mercy we are sheltered.
In your wisdom we are humbled. We live only to serve. Our lives
are yours."

This, Richard knew, this bond of his people to him, and him to his
people, was what the Golden Goddess feared. It was empathy charged
with magic. It bound them together—the people as the steel against
steel and the Lord Rahl as the magic against magic. That unity made
them stronger. And yet, he didn't know if it was strong enough. What
he did know was that this bond was their only hope.

Away from the People's Palace the devotion was spoken once as
a reminder, a reinforcement of the bond. But since the palace itself
had been constructed in the form of a spell, the power of that spoken
devotion was amplified and reinforced. Because of that, at the palace,

the seat of power of the Lord Rahl, the devotion was recited three times, three times a day, a reflection of the magical power of nine.

Once the third devotion had ended, Richard signaled Lieutenant Dolan to remain behind as the men went off to inform the rest of the First File of the situation.

"I need to talk to one of the palace officials. Someone who knows about the people living here and about the guests staying here, if possible."

The lieutenant briefly twisted his mouth in thought. He looked from the devotion square off down the adjacent broad corridor.

"This wing of the People's Palace is where the Lord Rahl's quarters are located. It is also the section where the highest officials are located. Those offices are not far from here. I think the man you're looking for is Mr. Burkett. He oversees the administrators of each section of the palace.

"You may remember him from when you met petitioners in the great hall. He was there to help with details." The lieutenant tapped his chin with a finger. "Small chin. All top teeth."

Richard couldn't begin to remember all the people he had met, but he did remember most of the faces of the palace officials. He remembered that face if not the name. He had been an accommodating man, cheerfully helping with all the tedious arrangements and requests of the visiting dignitaries.

While the Lord Rahl issued sweeping orders, it was the palace officials who had to see them carried out. The People's Palace, after all, was more of a busy city atop the plateau than simply a palace. It was home to many thousands, not to mention the thousands more men of the First File.

"I remember him," Richard said with a nod. "Where is his office?"

"Why don't I take you there," Lieutenant Dolan said as he held his hand out in invitation.

Kahlan took Richard's arm as they followed behind the officer. Vika and Shale followed close behind them. The rest of the Mord-Sith, all in their red leather, were swept along in their wake. Richard was sad to see the Mord-Sith no longer in the white leather, as he had asked them to wear in the great hall to signify peacetime. With their red leather on, they now all looked deadly serious, and no longer the least bit peaceful.

The lieutenant led them up a broad staircase made of cream-colored marble. The treads were rounded over on the front edge from all the people who had climbed those stairs through the ages.

On the upper level, they crossed a bridge with short walls capped with speckled granite. Those short walls acted as solid railings to either side. The bridge provided a dizzying view of one of the massive main corridors in the palace. Glassed areas of the roof let the gloomy light filter down to brighten the vast space.

Far below, people going about their business moved along in every direction. Some walked at a leisurely pace, while others hurried. Many of these people lived and worked in the palace. Others had always dreamed of visiting the splendor of the People's Palace. Now that Richard was the Lord Rahl and the world was at peace, they felt it was finally safe to do so.

In places along the sides of the corridor below, there were shops, some with colorful awnings, that sold everything from herbs, to leather goods, to pottery, to trinkets so that visitors could remember their visit to the palace. There were also many different kinds of shops that sold food. There were butchers selling meat, farmers selling vegetables, and people who sold wild things they collected such as herbs and mushrooms. Many of the shops cooked day and night to supply meals. People could get cooked meat on a stick, deep-fried potatoes and fish in paper wrappers, and bowls of stew they ate at small tables right outside the shops. The aromas were intoxicating.

Once they were across the bridge and a short distance down the balcony that overlooked the grand corridor, Lieutenant Dolan finally came to a halt in front of an open doorway. He held his hand out, indicating that this was the place.

Richard rapped with his knuckles on the doorframe as he stepped into the room.

Mr. Burkett was hunched over a sizable desk that looked too small for all the stacks of scrolls, candles, a collection of official seals and sealing wax, and papers of every sort lying every which way. Maps of sections of the palace were pinned to one wall. Another wall held long lists of names.

The man jumped in surprise and then shot to his feet when he saw who it was. His blue-edged robes had three gold bands on the sleeves, marking him as an official of importance. In his haste to stand, he accidentally knocked several scrolls from a pile; they rolled off the side of the desk, then bounced across the floor. One of the open papers fluttered away as if it had flown off in a panic.

"Lord Rahl," the man said, grinning broadly as he tried to catch the paper that had taken flight, "what an honor to have you visit my humble office."

Richard caught the paper as it floated down like a leaf in autumn. He handed it to the man. "Mr. Burkett, I came because I need your help."

Vika squeezed into the room behind Kahlan and Shale. The rest of the Mord-Sith had to wait outside, because there wasn't enough room for them in the small office.

"Anything, Lord Rahl. Anything at all. How can I help?"

"Can you tell me, are there gifted living in the palace?" Richard held a hand out to Kahlan and then to Shale on either side of him. "Present company excluded."

"Yes, of course, Lord Rahl." Mr. Burkett had such a strong overbite that it gave his speech a distinctive, slightly slurred quality. "There are a number of gifted people living in the palace."

Mr. Burkett started rummaging through the papers on his desk, shoving piles aside as he mumbled to himself. He finally found what he was looking for and yanked it out from under stacks of other papers. He caught a wooden candlestand just before it toppled over. "Yes, here it is. We keep a list. Any gifted visitor is also required to state as much when they arrive so that we can also keep track of them because…"

"Because in the past the Lord Rahl was insistent on knowing who around him was gifted," Richard finished for him.

Mr. Burkett cleared his throat. "Yes, well, even though you are the new Lord Rahl and unlike in the past don't harbor animosity toward them, we still keep a list of who they are, as well as where these gifted people live..."

"In case their services are needed by the palace?"

The man's face brightened. "Yes, exactly."

Richard frowned. "How many are there?"

Mr. Burkett scratched his scalp as he reviewed the list for a moment. "Actually, Lord Rahl, there are not many. At least not as many as one would expect, considering the size of the palace and the number of people living here."

Richard knew that in the past the People's Palace could have been a dangerous place for any gifted to live, but its power also drew them.

Mr. Burkett mumbled to himself as he tallied his list. He finally tapped his paper. "There are not quite two dozen gifted living here, Lord Rahl, and one gifted visitor. A gifted woman and her ungifted daughter."

"Good. I need to speak with all of them right away. Could you see to it, please?"

"I have assistants"—the man gestured to the side—"in nearby offices. The palace is quite large, as you know. I can get them right now and we can divide up the task. That way it will help get it done without delay."

"Good. Have them gather at the library here on the top floor." Richard pointed out the doorway, past the Mord-Sith all leaning in watching and listening, to a spot across the other side of the main corridor. "The one over there, down at the end of that passageway by the white marble column. It's the library with the opaque glass on the doors and windows. There are rather ugly orange-striped chairs just outside, in the sitting area."

Mr. Burkett cocked his head. "You mean the library that is also a containment field?"

Richard was a bit surprised that the man knew what the place was, but then again, he supposed it was his job to know such things.

"Yes, that's the one. Considering the size of the palace I imagine some of the gifted will be quite a distance away, so tell them to meet me there following the afternoon devotion. That should give them time to get there. Tell them I said not to stop for the devotion, but instead get there by the time it's over. It's important that I talk with all of them as soon as possible."

The man bowed, revealing the shiny, bald top of his head with a rather unfortunate liver spot the shape of a daisy.

"Of course, Lord Rahl. It will be done." He hesitated, putting a finger to his lower lip. "Will you be sending soldiers with my men?"

"Soldiers?" Richard was a little puzzled. "No, why?"

"Well, it's just that in the past..." the man hesitated for a moment, then cleared his throat, "...when the Lord Rahl wanted the gifted rounded up, it often meant bad things, so the soldiers were necessary to make sure they heeded the call."

Richard nodded his understanding. Being brought to meet Darken Rahl in person was usually cause to be terrified. He knew that from personal experience.

Richard smiled. "Nothing sinister is going to happen to them."

"And if they still don't want to be collected to come meet with you?"

"Tell them that I need their help, that's all."

"And if they still won't come along?"

Richard sighed that the terror Darken Rahl had struck into the gifted still lingered. "Well, I guess if they don't come back here with your assistants, then you will need to have the First File escort them back."

26

As they all emptied out of the cramped office, Mr. Burkett turned toward the offices of his assistants. Richard watched the man hurrying away. He had a hitch to his step that looked like his knees were getting old and achy.

As Richard turned back, he saw a red-faced soldier running along the balcony toward them. He was a big man, with a barrel chest and powerful-looking arms. Richard could see his rank marked on a leather shoulder pad. He came to a stop a little farther away than he had intended when the Mord-Sith closed ranks in front of Richard and Kahlan.

"Lord Rahl, I need to speak with you."

"What's your name, Sergeant?"

He clapped a fist to the leather armor over his heart as he panted, catching his breath. "Sorry. I'm Sergeant Barclay, Lord Rahl. I was in the devotion square when you spoke to the officers. There is trouble and I had wanted to talk to you back there, but then Lieutenant Dolan led you away and you looked like it was important, so I decided to wait until you were finished with Mr. Burkett. I was just checking on my men while you were busy, and then I came back here right away to see if you had finished so I could have a word with you. Lord Rahl, this is important, or I would never think to approach you like this."

"I welcome men of the First File to always feel free come talk to me with important matters, so be at ease, Sergeant. What's the problem?"

He licked his lips nervously. "Well, I'm afraid that we found something. Something you need to see."

Richard frowned. "What did you find?"

"It's down there, Lord Rahl," the sergeant said as he turned and gestured vaguely down over the side of the balcony. He turned back. "I think it would be best if you came to see it for yourself, Lord Rahl."

Richard had important things he needed to do, but this man was clearly quite agitated about something. "All right, but I hope it won't take long."

Sergeant Barclay dipped a quick bow and started leading them all to the grand staircase. Once they were down on the main floor, he took them to a nearby set of plain-looking closed metal double doors. Two soldiers stood to either side, each holding a pike with the butt end planted on the ground. They all wore swords as well. They saluted as one with a fist to their hearts before two of them pulled open the doors for Richard and his group.

Beyond the doors was a service area closed to the general public. Simple hallways led off in each direction, from there to branch off to specific areas. Not far inside the main area was a flight of stairs with a utilitarian iron railing. They all followed as the man hurried down the stairs, two at a time in places. The sound of all their boots in the stairwell reverberated with a hollow echo.

Torches were placed at intervals in iron brackets to the side, creating wavering shadows. At each landing there was a door, presumably to passageways in each of the lower levels. There were two guards posted at each door, at each level, as they descended. The sergeant didn't pause to speak to them as he continued downstairs to ever lower hidden reaches of the palace interior.

Finally, at one of the small landings, the sergeant brought them to a stop. He motioned one of the men standing guard to open the door.

With a concerned look, the sergeant took in the anxious group watching him. "I just wanted you to see this first, so you can get your bearings and know where we are, and what we are near."

Beyond the door they emerged onto a landing in a section of the great inner staircase up to the palace. This inner shaft was how visitors to the palace got up into the palace proper—through the great door at the bottom and then up the interior stairs. The stairs up that interior shaft weren't continuous. The pathway with flights of stairs at intervals meandered along and around the contours and odd shapes of the near vertical walls. There were long flat walkways for stretches in areas. Some of those broad level areas had benches where people could stop and rest.

It was relatively dark in the area where they were standing, but Richard could see silhouettes of people not far off, going up on their way into the palace or going down on their way out. Since the audience in the great hall was over, a great many more people were leaving than arriving.

Much of the interior, being so vast and difficult to light, was dimly lit. There were torches and lamps along the climb to relieve some of the perpetual darkness of the interior underground, but there were also areas, such as the place they stood, where shadowed darkness prevailed. Many people carried simple, inexpensive candle lamps with them that they could buy from vendors along the way. Many did not, and simply skimmed a hand along the metal railing as they made their way across the dark areas.

It was such a long climb up from the Azrith Plain far below that there were shops along the way, carved out of the rock of the plateau in the more expansive level spots. Those shops sold many of the same things as the shops above. Many visitors became discouraged by the arduous climb and would stop at these shops for something to eat, to take a rest, or to buy a souvenir and then go back down.

"How far up is this along the interior passageway?" Richard asked the sergeant.

The sergeant led them back to the service stairwell and motioned the guards to close the door. "Above halfway up. Before, I had a man stationed at each one of these doors on the way down, guarding them so that people couldn't wander in here and have access to the restricted areas of the palace."

"One man at each post?" Richard asked, since there were now two men at each door.

The sergeant wet his lips. "Yes. The doors are always bolted from this side so that people can't wander in here, but we often had men guard the doors when a lot of people were visiting the palace, like now, just so that there wouldn't be funny business. You know how people get curious about locked doors."

Before Richard could question him, the man started out again.

"This way, please, Lord Rahl."

The sergeant continued on down the stairs, hurrying the entire way. After what seemed like an endless series of flights of stairs, they finally approached the bottom. Half a dozen men with torches waited there for them. Even the torches couldn't entirely banish the oppressive darkness. They hissed and sputtered, is if warding off the haunting silence. The smell of burning pitch helped mask the dank, musty odor.

Once Richard and his party had all joined the sergeant at the bottom, the sergeant signaled most of the men with torches to go on ahead. Then he tilted his head, indicating he wanted Richard and the rest of them to keep following as he led them all onward through a wider hall and then a dark passageway that reeked of stagnant water, mold, and dead rats. In places there were puddles of water they had to skirt or step over. Their footsteps echoed in whispers back from the darkness.

When the men with the torches stopped before a broad opening into pitch blackness beyond, Sergeant Barclay halted and turned back to all those following him.

"If it pleases you, Lord Rahl, I think the ladies should remain here while I take you on alone the rest of the way back in there to see it."

"See what?" Shale asked.

"Please, trust me on this." He paused to lick his lips nervously. "If you would, could you just wait here and let Lord Rahl come with me, alone?"

"Where Lord Rahl goes, I go," Vika said with finality.

The other Mord-Sith all looked to be of the same mind.

"You wouldn't have brought us down here if it wasn't something important," Shale said. "I'm going, too."

"Show us what you brought us down here for, would you, please?" Kahlan commanded.

The sergeant was about to object, but at the look of resolve in her eyes, he simply let the breath out and turned to Richard as if to implore him to intervene.

"Just do as she asks, would you, Sergeant?"

The sergeant took one more look around at all the determined faces, then nodded. With a sweep of his arm, he ushered a few of the men with torches ahead into the darkness.

"Watch our backs," he told the ones he left behind. They nodded and took up positions to each side of the entrance.

"What's in here?" Richard asked, wondering what the men needed to watch their backs from. In some of the broader areas Richard saw the shapes of stone blocks stacked in random places. "What is the purpose of this place?"

Sergeant Barclay looked back over one of his broad shoulders as he hurried onward. "It's an area where part of the foundation was constructed. The foundation is massive. I can't say for sure, but I believe this area was used to store construction materials—stone and such—during the construction of the palace. After it was finished the room was left empty, possibly so that the foundation could be inspected from time to time, or possibly it was simply not seen as worth the effort to fill it in."

As they hurried down the roughly hewn passageway, Richard could begin to pick up the unmistakable stench of death. Before long it was bad enough to make his eyes water. Shale and Kahlan tried to cover their mouths, but it wasn't much help.

"Wait," Shale finally said, bringing them all to a halt. "Wait just a moment."

She scooped up a handful of pebbles near the edge of the uneven floor. She spun her other hand around over the top of the hand with the pebbles. Finally, she held out her hand, palm up.

"Here. Each of you take one of these. I infused them with a powerful smell of mint oils. Hold it up to your nose to help keep from gagging." She looked to Kahlan. "In case any of us might have unsettled stomachs to begin with, I don't want any of us vomiting from the smell of death."

The three soldiers, Richard, and Kahlan each gladly took a pebble.

Kahlan held it to her nose and took a deep breath. "I've smelled the stench of death often enough. It's something you never get used to. This helps a little. Thanks."

The sergeant looked grateful for the menthol-scented rock. Richard certainly was. The Mord-Sith seemed indifferent.

Vale took one, smelled it, then handed it back to Shale. "Thanks, but I don't need it."

Shale arched an eyebrow as she glanced at Richard.

Richard didn't feel like taking the time to explain Mord-Sith to Shale. "Let's go," he said to the sergeant.

In a short distance, the smell of death became so overpowering that Richard was glad to have the salvation of the pebble that filled his nostrils with the strong aroma of menthol. It helped mask some of the sickening smell. Without it, it would have been difficult to continue. As it was, it was still hard to take.

The end of the crude passageway opened into a vast chamber. In the dim, flickering torchlight, Richard saw something ahead in the darkness.

"What is that?" He could hear buzzing, but he couldn't see exactly what it was.

Sergeant Barclay held a hand up urging them to wait as he went forward a short distance with a torch to show them what was there. Richard blinked in stunned astonishment when the torchlight lit the scene. Shale leaned forward, her eyes wide.

"Dear spirits help us," Kahlan whispered as her eyes welled up with tears.

27

What Richard was looking at was so incomprehensible that at first, he wasn't sure he could believe that it really was what he thought it was.

There in front of them, up against a dark, towering, rough-hewn stone wall near one of the monolithic footings of the foundation, was a massive pile of remains. It took a moment for it to sink in that the mass of the irregular heap were indeed remains, and that they were all human. Blood and bodily fluids had drained out in great, thick pools across the floor. Clouds of flies buzzed all over the chaotic pile while others drank at the edges of the thick liquid on the floor. In the shadows, what at first looked like the pile moving proved to be rats burrowing through the remains.

The stench was overpowering, even with the menthol stones Shale had made for them. The smell was sickening enough, but the sight of it added another dimension to his revulsion.

White bones or pieces of bones stuck out everywhere from the tangled jumble of spinal columns, smaller bones, clothes, guts, and connective tissue putrefying in the humid darkness. Most of the bones had had small bits of tissue still attached. Bloodstains gave most of the bones a dark patina. Many had been shattered to get at the marrow. Some were gouged with claw marks that Richard recognized from those he had seen on Kahlan's arm.

Here and there Richard spotted chest and shoulder plates from the leather armor of men of the First File. All of them he could see had been ripped apart by claws. That leather armor had afforded no protection from the power of the attackers. Tangled in among the remains were bloody sections of chain mail. Here and there weapons lay among the debris.

There were oozing masses of the dirty ends of viscera that had been tossed on the pile. They almost looked alive as maggots wriggled all through them. Larger bones of legs and arms, and even sections of rib cages, protruded from the continually moving soft mass. Many of the skulls, with rows of white lines gouged down into the bone from teeth that had raked the scalps and faces off of them, had rolled off the pile to litter the floor.

The pile of remains was slightly taller than Richard, and at least a dozen and a half feet across. A quick calculation in his head from the numbers of leg and arm bones, as well as the skulls, told him that these were the remains of possibly several hundred people.

It quickly became clear to Richard what this was.

"They brought their kills down here—or even live captives—to feed off them," he said to the sergeant. "They tossed the bones and things they didn't want to eat on the pile."

Sergeant Barclay nodded. "So it would appear, Lord Rahl."

Kahlan gasped back a sob as she pointed. "Those smaller bones are from children. It's not only adults. There are children among the remains."

A watchful Shale reached a hand out to steady Kahlan.

Richard finally turned his gaze from the horror to look at the sergeant. "How did you find this?"

The man let out a troubled sigh. "A number of my men were approached by people looking for missing loved ones. They helped search and took down the names. I knew something was odd when none of the missing people could be found. Not a one. We often encounter frantic people looking for a lost child or a relative. We almost always find the missing loved ones. But now, we weren't finding any of the missing people, not the missing husbands, not the missing wives, and not the missing children. It was like they all had simply vanished.

"That was strange enough, but then I realized that some of my men were missing as well.

"I started checking and soon discovered who the missing men were."

"Who were they?" Richard asked.

The burly soldier leaned closer. "The thing was, Lord Rahl, the missing men were the ones who were supposed to be guarding the landings on the way down here—the landings with the doors, like the one I showed you. The men had been posted to guard those doors to the inner areas of the plateau where the public comes and goes from the palace. There had only been one man at each post, and now those men were gone.

"So, I took a squad and we went searching. On our way down here, we found bloody handprints here and there, on the corner of hallways, at doorways, even along the walls. It was where the victims were dragged in here, still alive, trying to grab onto a corner or doorway, anything to try to help them get away. None did.

"We kept going, following the bloody smears and the blood that had dripped on the floor." He gestured to the remains. "Eventually we discovered this. I can only imagine how terrified these poor people were as they were dragged in here and eaten alive. Down here, no one would be able to hear their screams.

"I recognized a couple of the pieces of armor. They belonged to my men. Some have a mark that identify their owner. That's how I know who they were and that this was where they had vanished to."

Richard boiled with rage, and at the same time he was heartsick at the discovery. It was especially painful seeing that children were among the remains.

He also felt a rising sense of panic that everyone depended on him to stop this slaughter, and he didn't have the foggiest idea how he was going to do that.

"They were using this place as a base to hunt from." Richard gestured back up the way they had come. "After they killed your men, they used the doors out to the dark landings where people were coming and going from the palace. They were snatching unsuspecting people from the shadows on the landings outside those doorways."

"If ever there was a nightmare come to life, that is it," Kahlan said.

The sergeant nodded. "That was why I wanted to show you the dark landings beyond the doors when we were on our way down here. I wanted you to see where they were likely snatching most of the victims."

Richard took the torch from the sergeant, and alone stepped among the skulls—both of adults and children—scattered on the floor in order to get a closer look at the heap of remains. He had to walk through the sickening pools of blood and fluid. None of the others looked the least bit inclined to want to go with him, except, of course, Vika. She followed closely in his footsteps, her Agiel in her fist, as her analytical gaze swept over the scene.

Richard wanted to get a closer look to burn the full horror of it into his memory so that he would never fail to use every last bit of strength and resolve to stop these hateful things, as Kahlan had called them.

But more importantly, he wanted to see what he could learn about the predators who had done this. He squatted down next to a small skull. It was obviously from a child probably six or seven years old. The scalp and face had been mostly scraped off. Only a little patch of blood-soaked hair remained, above where an ear would have been. With a finger, he turned it around and around to get a better look at it in the torchlight.

The back of the skull was missing. Jagged marks revealed that it had been teeth that had opened the skull, most likely to get at the brains, as the skull was mostly empty.

He bent closer, holding the torch near to see better.

The deep gouges across the top of the skull and down toward the brow were made by a row of many, many sharp, pointed teeth all close together. By the way they were deeper in the center, and lighter and lighter as they moved farther to the side, it told him that the thing had a very large mouth. Only the front teeth had done this damage as they were raked across the bone. He looked around at some of the other skulls littering the floor. They had the same kind of deep gouges raking across the bone, indicating the same thing—a very large mouth with a lot of very sharp, pointed teeth, all close together, tightly lined up across the top and bottom jaws.

Vika shadowed him as he stood and returned to the others, where he handed the torch back to the sergeant.

"What did you learn?" Kahlan asked.

"Without realizing it, they have revealed a little bit about themselves. From the evidence left on the skulls, I can tell that rather than fangs like many predators have that would leave puncture holes, they have a lot of needle-sharp teeth, all about the same length, lined up closely together side by side. Some of the large bones were bitten clean in half, so their jaws are powerful. From the evidence on some of the skulls, it also looks like their mouths are big enough to gnaw on a skull, like we might bite at an apple. From the confusing mass of indistinct footprints, they don't wear boots. From the size of those prints I'd guess they must be half again my size."

"Dear spirits," Kahlan said as she slowly shook her head. "We are in a lot of trouble."

28

They left the site of the slaughter, grateful to be away from the gagging stench of death, and made the long, tiring climb mostly in silence. When they finally reached the uppermost landing of the service stairs, Richard gently grabbed the sergeant's arm and brought him to a halt.

"There is no way we will ever be able to identify all those people. You said you have a list of the names of missing people. I think it's safe to assume that the missing are those we saw down there."

The man nodded. "So, what do you want to do, Lord Rahl?"

Richard felt overwhelmed, frustrated, and angry. "We can't really bring the whole rotting mess back out of there for a proper burial. It would be to no real purpose, since we wouldn't have any way to put the remains of individuals together or identify any of them so that people could grieve and bury their loved one. There is no way we would know who we're burying or if the missing are for sure among them, even though it seems likely that they are. And we certainly can't bring their families down there to the site and tell them that their loved ones are likely among the remains in the pile. Seeing those remains would be more horrific to them than the torment of not knowing what happened to their loved ones. There is nothing we could do that would provide closure for people."

"So, what are you thinking?"

Richard wiped a hand across his mouth as he briefly considered. As much as he didn't like the idea of simply leaving the remains down in the lower reaches of the palace, he couldn't see that there was really any choice. There were catacombs under the palace where a great many people were interred. In a way, the victims were already buried underground.

"Their suffering is over. They are with the good spirits, now," Richard finally said to the sergeant. "I'd like you to get a group of men together. Have them collect stone and mortar from down in the lower levels. I saw supplies of that kind down there in some of the nearby rooms off the side passageways. Once you have the supplies you'll need, seal up the entrance to that chamber with the remains. Not just a simple wall. Those creatures could probably break through that and go back to using it again. You need to plug up the end of the passageway for a good enough distance that they aren't ever going to be able to break through it to get back in and use it as a nest. That will be the tomb for all those poor victims."

Sergeant Barclay nodded. "Then those creatures will know we are on to them, know we have discovered their lair."

"Good. I want them to know that they aren't as clever as they thought they were. And at least they won't be able to continue to hunt in the same way."

The sergeant tilted his head closer with a serious look. "Lord Rahl, there are many places like that in the lower areas of the palace. They may simply find similar places from which to hunt."

"Of course they will. We will have to be on the lookout for that now that we know what they were doing. We need to quickly deny them places they use wherever we find them. Maybe we can make them feel like the hunted for a change. We might even be able to kill or capture some of them. In the meantime, seal that chamber as a gravesite."

The man clapped his fist to his heart. "I will see to it right away, Lord Rahl."

As the sergeant hurried off through the service area to get a crew to take care of sealing up the tomb, Richard headed in the direction of the double doors that would lead out.

"We need to get up there to meet with the gifted," he told the others. "They likely will be waiting for us by now."

"What are you thinking?" Shale asked, sounding suspicious. "What do you want with the gifted?"

Richard paused before opening the doors out of the service area and turned back to the eight grim female faces watching him. Instead of answering her question, he asked her one. "Do you know how to join gifts from different gifted people to create more power?"

He knew that the Sisters of the Light could do it. He had seen it done.

Shale's smooth brow bunched together a bit. "I've never heard of such a thing. But to be fair, the only gifted people I knew were my parents."

Richard paused in thought for a moment. "That means you may not know how to do what a lot of sorceresses who have been trained are able to do."

Shale's lips pursed with displeasure. "Magic is magic."

"So it is," he said, offering her a small smile.

Kahlan took his arm and pressed her head against his shoulder as he started off toward the grand staircase. He put an arm around her waist and pulled her close as they went up the first flight to the broad landing where the stairs reversed direction to continue on up.

29

S hale hooked a hand around Richard's arm to stop him.

"Lord Rahl…" She sounded hesitant. "That sight down there, all those people… it was horrifying."

Richard frowned, not knowing if she had a point. "It was."

"Well, the thing is, you hope to be able to stop these predators. In the meantime, our world is steadily heading toward the day when people will be without the protection of your magic and without the Mother Confessor's magic. If anything should happen to either of you, then the future of our world would be doomed as the protective web of your gift holding all magic together disintegrates.

"The Golden Goddess may never send those of her race to have a big battle in which you can hope to defeat her. She may deny you that opportunity of a conventional war and instead continue to attack as she has been, terrorizing us with continual surprise attacks, maybe even wiping out small towns here and there so that everyone will be in the grip of fear. They will continue to feed on our people. As we wait for an attack that may never come, many more people will go missing, just as those people down in the darkness were missing.

"Your magic is the only thing protecting our world by keeping them cautious. The future survival of this world depends on that magic being preserved. Every day that passes increases the danger that you will be killed and our world would then lose that protection.

"As we learned through Nolo, the Golden Goddess can wait us out. If she chooses, she can wait for you to die of old age. You and the Mother Confessor grow older every day, and with your gifts destined to eventually die out, our world gets closer to dying out with you."

Richard was absently wondering what kind of gifted might be living at the palace and what abilities they might have that would be able to help them. He was only half listening to Shale ramble on with the obvious. He realized that even though she seemed to be talking a lot without saying much, she was getting at something.

"What of it? What's your point?" he asked, impatiently, needing to get to the library where the gifted would be gathering.

"Well, to keep any of that from happening, and to have your gifts live on to protect the future of our world, you and the Mother Confessor need to have children. It can't wait. You must have them now."

"Children! Now? Are you out of your mind?" Richard blew up in anger, flicking a hand in a gesture toward Kahlan. "I can't think of anything that could cause us more trouble right now and threaten to bring the sky down on us all, than Kahlan getting pregnant."

"But—"

"But nothing! You heard what the goddess said about the young and how she lusted to kill them. How can you even suggest that right now?"

"I can suggest it because every day you both get older. Just like everyone else, day by day the time when you can have children dwindles away. You must think of the future. You must have children. I think it's time."

"That's absurd. We're hardly old enough to suggest that we are running out of time to have children."

Seeing how angry he was, Shale wisely closed her mouth.

Richard raked his fingers back through his hair, trying to control his temper. "One day? Absolutely. But now? There is nothing that would do more to draw the dedicated ferocity of the Golden Goddess and her kind than us having children." He shook his head at the very idea, almost too angered by it to speak.

Shale's prudence ran out. "But Lord Rahl—"

"Tell her!" he suddenly yelled at Kahlan. "Tell her how that would compromise our situation and in all likelihood ensure the destruction of our world! The entire focus of the Golden Goddess would be to hunt down those children and slaughter them. That would unleash such wrath that it would ensure that Kahlan and I would be killed as well. It would be the end of magic in our world. All because of such a foolish impulse at a time like this. Tell her that we can't put such a notion ahead of us stopping this threat!"

Kahlan had gone pale, making him suddenly wish he hadn't yelled at her. He hadn't really been yelling at her, but rather the recklessness of such a suggestion.

"But, Richard—" she said in a small voice, almost a plea.

"Someday, Kahlan," he said, leaning down toward her, softening his voice. "Someday. But right now that is the one thing that could seal our fate and the fate of our world. It would be the single thing that would ensure our total annihilation. Such a thing would cause them to cease being cautious and unleash a full-scale, worldwide invasion. We would be overrun and slaughtered.

"Right now, their attention is on you and me as they probe our powers. Once we can learn more, discover ways to kill them and get control of the situation and hopefully stop them from coming to our world at will, then yes, that's what I want more than anything. But right now we have to use our heads, or we will all lose them like those people down below."

Kahlan nodded as she glanced at Shale. The sorceress had gone silent and red-faced. Richard didn't know what was wrong with the woman to even suggest such a thing right in the middle of such a crisis.

"Kahlan being pregnant would mean that the Golden Goddess could no longer afford to wait us out," he concluded. "Without a way to stop these predators, it would mean the end of us all."

Kahlan turned a look on Shale as she gritted her teeth. "What's the matter with you? Can't you see that Richard is trying his best to figure out how to stop this threat? We don't need to make his job any harder than it already is."

Shale looked a bit sheepish as she abandoned her argument. "I apologize." She gestured vaguely. "I was only trying to broach a subject that one day must be addressed. But I can see that now is not the time." Kahlan closed her eyes a moment as she took a deep breath. "One day it will be. Until then, let's not talk of it again—all right?

Richard has a job to do. He doesn't need us to pile more worries on top of those we already have."

Shale's lips pressed tight for a moment. Finally, she bowed her head. "Of course, you're right, Mother Confessor."

Richard gripped Shale's shoulder and gave it a jostle, along with a smile. "It's a wonderful idea, Shale, just the wrong time, that's all. No hard feelings?"

Shale shook her head, returning a bit of a smile.

Richard held his hand out to Kahlan. "Come on. We need to get up there to see what kind of gifted we have here in the palace. I'm hoping they are strong enough to be able to help us. I'm also hoping that at least one of them knows how to link others with the gift to make it more powerful."

Kahlan took his hand, but stood her ground, making Richard stop and turn to her.

"Richard, I'm feeling a bit sick after what we just saw down below. I think I will go lie down."

Richard was a bit puzzled, even though she did look awfully pale. Kahlan had seen horrific deaths before. It always made her more determined than ever. It was completely unlike her to want to go lie down.

"I don't think that's a good idea right now."

Kahlan frowned. "Why not?"

"Because it's easier for wolves to take down a deer if they can cut one from the herd. Better that we stay together. I don't want you to become one of the missing."

30

Without realizing it, Richard, in his distracted anger, had started taking the stairs two at a time, opening the distance back to most of the others. At a landing where he had to go around a newel post to the next flight of stairs heading up, when the others had lagged a little way behind, only Vika had kept up with him.

With all the shuffling footfalls on the stone steps echoing up and down the stairwell masking her voice, Vika leaned close to whisper to Richard as he slowed to let the others catch up.

"You're right, Lord Rahl, about not needing the additional worry of a pregnant wife and then children in the middle of a fight to try to save all of our lives. I could see that Shale also upset the Mother Confessor. I will tell the sorceress to mind her own business in the future and I will see to it that she does."

Richard, deep in his own thoughts, glanced back at the Mord-Sith. "That isn't necessary."

Vika didn't answer. She simply straightened her back and proceeded up the stairs with him as the others hurried to catch up. Richard knew that it didn't really matter if he told Vika not to say anything to the sorceress. She would do what she thought best to protect him so that he could do what he had to do as First Wizard. Steel against steel so that he could be the magic against magic. That consideration of the larger objective overrode whatever he might say.

Richard was certain that when she caught Shale alone, Vika would deliver a lecture at the end of an Agiel. He didn't want her to do that, but he knew he wasn't going to easily be able to stop that from happening. He also knew that if he tried it would end up causing more drama that he didn't need. He had bigger worries. Besides that, Vika was right. Shale should mind her own business.

He hoped that Shale was wise enough to keep a cool head and not argue with Vika. There were no Mord-Sith in the Northern Waste and Shale had no real idea of how truly dangerous it would be to tangle with one, Vika in particular. While Vika had assigned herself as his personal guard, any of the other Mord-Sith, for that matter, would be just as much trouble to cross. Now that Vika had seen how much Shale had angered him, she had, by extension, also angered Vika.

Such volatile behavior from Vika and her sister Mord-Sith was the price Richard had to pay for having given them their freedom. To the Mord-Sith, such freedom was worthless if they weren't able to exert it as they saw fit. In return for their independence, they protected Richard and Kahlan with their lives. He was beyond grateful for their protection, but at times it tested his patience.

At the head of the stairs, they emerged into a quiet section of the upper level. The top floor of this entire portion of the palace, where the Lord Rahl's quarters were also located, was reserved for the exclusive use of the Lord Rahl and any of his staff he designated as needing access. It was strictly off-limits to the general public. The First File patrolled the area at all times to make certain it was free of any unauthorized visitors.

Richard knew there were ancient books on magic in the library to be found up in this area. It was only one of a number of libraries reserved for the Lord Rahl. Some were in this section, some in other restricted areas. While some were considerably larger, this one was special in other ways.

He suspected that this particular library was the reason his ancestors hadn't wanted anyone else having unfettered access to this area of the palace. That, and they hadn't wanted just anyone nosing around. Considering the dangerous nature of the books in that library, Richard knew that he also had to keep access restricted.

While ungifted people wouldn't be able to understand those books or make use of them, if stolen they would bring a high price from the right people. Also, anyone gifted with even modest ability, should they try using those tomes, could accidentally invoke dangerous spells without realizing what they were doing.

Richard idly wondered if any of the spells in those ancient books could be useful to him in the present situation. He knew they contained powerful magic, but the problem was, he didn't know how to use much of it.

Having grown up in a place without magic he'd had no training in the use of his gift. But such training would have been of no real value. Because he had been gifted as a war wizard, his powers worked differently than in anyone else and training would have been of no help to him. Unlike other gifted people, his gift as a war wizard was linked inextricably to anger. Anger was a necessary tool in combat, and thus essential in a war wizard.

Still, since leaving the Hartland woods, he had learned a lot about magic, and he knew the danger of those books. He had read many of them, as well as many other books of magic in other libraries both at the People's Palace, and in other places. At times, such books had proved useful to him. They had explained much, and unlocked many secrets.

On the way to the library, they had picked up a fair number of men of the First File. With the new danger from the goddess and her kind, the officers wanted to make sure Richard and Kahlan were always well protected. Although it was at times awkward to be surrounded by soldiers, Richard, a loner by nature, knew it was necessary. While half a dozen Mord-Sith in red leather trailed right behind, one group of armed men checked the way ahead as another group marched along in the rear. Richard felt a bit like a prized pig being taken to a fair.

He understood that as the Lord Rahl he didn't have the right to needlessly put himself in harm's way, so he had grown somewhat used to being constantly protected. He was at least gratified to have Kahlan under that protection as well. As a Confessor, she had grown up with others rightly concerned about her safety, so it wasn't odd to her.

The corridor they were in had a thick carpet with a pattern of leaves in various shades of brown. The carpeting and sizable wall hangings gave the corridor a muted, calm feel. The carpet also quieted all the footsteps, which in turn only served to highlight the jangle of weapons and chain mail.

Along the way there were graceful wooden tables and comfortable chairs with studded metalwork on them. Most of the tables held vases, many with flowers. Some of the colorful blown-glass vases were quite elaborate and were there simply for their own beauty. Paintings along the walls showed forest scenes, lakes, and mountains. They reminded Richard of how much he missed being alone in the quiet of his woods. He missed those peaceful times when there was no one, and nothing, trying to kill everyone in the world.

It was a troubling concept to grasp, and it occurred to him that the calm beauty of the restricted areas was a way for the Lord Rahl to have his mind quieted in order for him to ponder unfathomable threats to the world.

It was amazing that in such a short time, they had gone from the lower levels with horrific sights, to such a beautiful and peaceful area. All in the same palace.

31

As they quickly made their way down the elegant corridor, Richard spotted the group of people assembled in the distance. Most were sitting on the ugly orange-striped chairs outside the library. There was a group of soldiers there as well, to watch over the guests in the restricted area.

As they got close enough for the group to see that it was Lord Rahl approaching, in his war-wizard outfit, gold cape and all, along with the Mother Confessor in her white dress, the guests all shot to their feet.

When Richard and his group were close enough, all the people, except the soldiers, went on to a knee, bowing forward, as was the old tradition when meeting the Mother Confessor. Richard saw a number of those people trembling. He didn't know if it was out of fear of him, or the Mother Confessor. He remembered after he had first met Kahlan, when they crossed the boundary into the Midlands, he saw people of every kind, including kings and queens, fall to their knees before Kahlan. Many of those, too, had trembled. Many people believed that a Confessor could steal their minds if she chose. In a way, that was true, but not in the way many people feared.

Kahlan came to a halt before the bowed, silent people.

"Rise, my children."

Everyone returned to their feet, but none of them looked any more at ease. None of them would look up into either Richard's or Kahlan's eyes.

"I want to thank you all for coming," Richard said in as friendly a tone as he could muster. Below the surface he was boiling with rage over the murders of so many people down in the dark recesses of the palace, but he knew he couldn't show that anger to these people. "It's an honor for me to finally get the chance to meet the gifted living here at the People's Palace."

One woman, with frizzy faded brown hair and in a plain, straight tan dress with no belt, held up a hand. When Richard nodded to her, she spoke in a meek voice.

"I am gifted, Lord Rahl." Her other hand settled on the shoulder of a girl with her back up against the woman. "But my daughter, Dori, is not. Also, we don't live here. We are merely visitors to the palace, come to watch the audiences you granted in the great hall the other day."

Richard supposed she wanted to make that clear just in case the Lord Rahl suddenly took on the disposition of Richard's father and decided to imprison the gifted who lived at the palace, or at least restrict their lives in some way.

Richard smiled at the woman. "I'm sure your daughter is no less of a handful, and no less of a joy, for being ungifted. The Mother Confessor and I are grateful that you came to visit the People's Palace."

That brought a smile to the woman. The smile looked to have surprised her at its unexpected arrival, causing her to blush.

The daughter, Dori, seemed to be even more shy than her mother. She wore a faded blue dress dotted with little white flowers and cinched at the waist by a thin woven cord belt tied at her hip. Her straight brown hair, parted in the middle, hung just short of her bony shoulders. She seemed too fearful to be able to bring herself to look up at the Lord Rahl towering above her. Richard studied her a moment as she turned her head, looking away to the side to avoid eye contact.

He finally clasped his hands behind his back as he strolled before the rest of the group, getting a good look at them all, and they at him. There were two older men with white hair and beards, one very old woman with short, wavy white hair, half a dozen young men and women still in their teens, and all the rest in a variety of years in between.

"You all are gifted in some way?" Richard asked.

Many of their eyes shifted to the half-dozen Mord-Sith standing off behind him before looking back and nodding, some slowly, some enthusiastically. Some even smiled with confident pride.

"Good. I'm truly honored to finally have the chance to meet all of you." He smiled again. "Perhaps some of you have known your gift as far back as you can remember. I was shocked, myself, when I first learned that I'm gifted."

That brought broader smiles to most of them and seemed to at least put others at ease to know he was human.

"Are there any among you who have been formally trained in the use of your gift?"

One of the older men, and three of the middle-aged women, lifted a hand.

"Can you tell me how?" Richard asked, pointing at the man.

He cleared his throat. "I was trained in prophecy, Lord Rahl. By an uncle who has long since passed away," he hastened to add.

"Are you gifted in any other way?"

The man winced a little, as if afraid to disappoint Richard. "No, Lord Rahl. Just with prophecy, I'm afraid."

"Are there any others among you who are gifted in prophecy?"

Everyone shook their heads. Richard turned back to the older man.

"And have you had any prophecy recently?"

He looked abashed. "I used to be visited by prophecy regularly, Lord Rahl, but I'm afraid that since the end of the war, I've no longer had any prophecies."

Richard didn't want to tell the man that he had ended prophecy, so instead he offered a smile. "All right, thank you for coming. If prophecy returns to you, please be sure to send word to me and perhaps I will call on you again, but that's all that I need for now." Richard held a hand out toward nearby stairs that led down to the public area. "Sorry to have asked you up here for nothing."

As the man thanked Richard and dipped a bow, Shale came up behind Richard to speak in a confidential tone.

"Lord Rahl, I think I can be of assistance."

"What do you mean?"

"I can very easily test each of these people for the scope of their ability and the specific talents of each. I believe it would make things go much faster, but more importantly we would get a true accounting of their actual ability, untainted by exaggerated boasting or imagined abilities."

"That makes sense. I've seen people before who thought they were gifted when they really weren't." He turned back to the waiting group. "Shale, here, is a talented sorceress. She is going to assist me by testing each of you to see if you have a specific ability I'm looking for."

Richard didn't really have a specific ability he was looking for, as he had already found exactly what he sought.

But he was interested in knowing if anyone gifted with considerable power was among the group. That kind of person would worry the Golden Goddess and might possibly be useful.

Shale started in the back and worked her way among the group. As she approached each person, she smiled and told them to simply relax. She then placed a hand to each side of their head, in much the same way a mother might hold the face of a beloved child. She tested Dori's mother, the woman who was visiting, last. Dori looked down and away, as if too shy to watch a sorceress at her craft.

Shale finally returned, taking Richard's arm on the way past and leading him back a number of paces, out of earshot of the group. Kahlan went with them, wanting to know what Shale had discovered.

"Well?" Richard finally asked when they came to a stop. "What did you learn?"

Shale looked disappointed. "There are a variety of talents among these people. One man started training in the craft of wizardry. His gift is weak and not adequate enough that it could be developed into much of anything. A few of the women have a talent for sorcery, but it is a bit hard to call it a 'talent.' It's more like a shallow hint. A number of them have minor healing ability. Some have a variety of other talents, but those talents are only latent, at best, and profoundly weak."

"Who is the strongest among them?" Kahlan asked. "Who has the most power?"

Shale briefly cast a glance back over her shoulder before turning a frown on her and Richard.

"In all honesty, I don't think that the whole lot of them have enough combined power to be able to light a candle."

"Really?" Richard was mildly disappointed, because he had been hoping, along with his true interest for calling them all together, to maybe find among them some who were gifted enough to possibly help defend them. "None of them have even a modest amount of gift?"

Shale shook her head regretfully. "I'm afraid not, Lord Rahl. I think the strongest healer among them might have the power to pull out a splinter, but that's about it. Many of them are quite proud of their gift, but not for sound reason."

Kahlan's attention was focused on Richard. "You don't look very discouraged."

Richard showed her a brief smile. "I'm not. I found what I was looking for."

Before she could ask what he had been looking for, he returned to the group. Shale and Kahlan followed, Shale looking puzzled, Kahlan with a look of growing concern.

Kahlan leaned in close from behind. "Richard, are you having one of your crazy ideas?"

"He gets crazy ideas?" Shale asked in a whisper.

"You don't know the half of it," Kahlan whispered back. "Trust me on this one."

Richard ignored them both and instead paused to take hold of Vika's arm and pull her close. He tipped his head down toward her and spoke with quiet meaning. "I want you to look after Dori's mother for me."

Vika understood the look and so didn't question the order. Her expression hardened. "Not a problem, Lord Rahl. I will take care of it."

Richard returned to stand before the group, hands again casually clasped behind his back. "I would like to thank you all for coming. We have everything we needed to know. We have learned that your abilities are all quite special. For now, you may go back to what you were doing. If we discover that we have need of your unique talents, we will contact you."

He held an arm out, indicating the stairway not far down the corridor, which was guarded by four soldiers with pikes.

Before the mother and daughter could leave with the rest of the group, Richard held a hand up to signal the woman to remain behind.

She frowned. "Yes, Lord Rahl?"

"Actually," Richard said, "I would like to speak to your daughter, Dori."

Dori's head was bowed, her gaze cast down at the floor; she was too afraid to look up at the big, scary Lord Rahl.

Richard went to one knee and leaned close. He put a finger under her chin to lift her face up toward him. She turned her eyes away, still afraid to meet his gaze.

"What is it you want?" she asked in a small voice.

"I would like to surrender," Richard said in a quiet, confidential tone that only she could hear.

The girl's eyes suddenly looked up at him from under her brow, and then she slowly smiled in a way that no innocent little girl ever could.

32

Vika stepped in front of the little girl's mother as she started to reach for her daughter. Vika lifted her Agiel and, with the weapon pointed toward the mother, began backing her away.

"What a very, very wise decision," the girl said in a low, husky voice. It was a voice that sounded as if it could crush bone.

Without looking back, Richard lifted a finger behind himself when he sensed Kahlan starting to come forward. At his warning, she stopped in her tracks.

"Please"—Richard rose and held out his hand in invitation—"let's go in here where we can talk in private."

Richard didn't wait for an answer or explain to the others. He strode to the room and opened the double glass doors without slowing, one hand on each handle as he swept into the room, his cape billowing out behind him. The girl glided in after him, glancing over to give Kahlan a murderous look on her way past. Once she was in the room, Richard turned and closed the doors. He twisted the lock so that no one else could enter. With the doors secure, he pulled the thick drapes over them. They had squares of special glass that people couldn't actually see through, but light could still come in. The drapes prevented that.

Dori, her back straight, slowly strolled around the center of the room, gazing at the walls of books, looking up and around, taking in everything as if viewing it from an alien world.

As large as the room was, it was actually one of the smaller libraries in the palace. All the walls except the one at the end with the glass were lined with shelves reaching up to a high, beamed ceiling. A brass rail with a ladder hooked to it ran past shelf after shelf packed tight with books of every size.

The tooled leather covers on some of the books looked timeworn. Even with their great age, it was easy to see the care with which they had been made to denote their importance. Richard knew, though, that the most dangerous volumes in the library looked simple and not at all important, and that the most important-looking books, crafted with great care and skill, were not actually all that special. It was a simple method the wizards of old used to throw off would-be thieves and those who had no business looking for dangerous spells. It was something, among a great many other things, that Zedd, his grandfather, had taught him.

Each side of the long room had three rows of freestanding bookcases. Some of the cases held enormous, oversize volumes. Some of the covers and spines of those had titles in gold foil. One of the cases had locked glass doors covering the entire face of it, further restricting access to the books it contained in a room that was already highly restricted.

The glass doors weren't simply locked. Richard knew that the books behind those glass doors were some of the most dangerous of the books in the library, books so dangerous that the wizards of the time when the library had been created did not want to trust the simple trick of making those books look unimportant. Those glass doors were sealed with spells that required considerable skill and Subtractive Magic to open.

Richard knew that many of the most dangerous books, those on the shelves and those behind locked glass doors, spoke of him. They called him by many different names. They spoke of him centuries before he had even been born. They expressed grave warnings, and profound hopes.

On the distant side of the room to Richard's left, beyond the rows of bookcases, there was a sitting area with three comfortable-looking chairs. Except that he couldn't imagine anyone using them, because they had the same ugly orange stripes as the chairs in the sitting area outside the library. Richard knew the true purpose of the ugly orange stripes.

In the center of the room, between the rows of bookcases to each side, stood a long, heavy oak table with massive turned wooden legs. A few wooden chairs sat at random angles around it, as if the people using them had just gotten up for a moment, but never came back. Richard had been one of those people.

A number of simple, unimportant-looking books lay open on the table. Richard was the one, quite a while back, who had left those books there. A few small stacks of books on the table were ones he had collected from the shelves and left there in case he needed to come back to search them for things that could help him. The whole library looked like a cozy, inviting place to read. But Richard knew that, like some others, this room was more than simply a library, and it was anything but cozy.

As Dori gazed about the room, he went to the end of the far wall on his right and pulled the heavy drapes across the tall windows made up of squares of thick, clouded glass. It was a very special type of glass that only the most knowledgeable wizards in an age long past knew how to make. It took not only Additive Magic to create such spiraled glass, but Subtractive as well, to say nothing of special knowledge and arcane skills.

"What are you doing?" Dori asked. She sounded annoyed and impatient.

"Just hoping to make you comfortable," Richard said over his shoulder as he made sure the drapes were light-tight.

When satisfied, he blew out the flame on one of the nearby reflector lamps. He smiled at her.

"I know how you prefer the dark."

"I have spent time with that woman, the mother of this body. She has magic," Dori added with growling distaste. "Magic is not the incomprehensible mystery I thought at first. I have observed the woman and it is not so strong a thing, this magic your kind has."

"No," Richard agreed with a sigh. "I suppose not."

He blew out the flame of another lamp on his way by. With the heavy drapes drawn over the windows and doors, only two lamps, one at either end of the room, were left to light the grand library. They were woefully inadequate for the task and left the middle of the room in deep shadows. Dori smiled her approval. Richard had to be careful not to run into the rows of bookcases.

"What are the terms for my surrender?" he asked as he returned to the center of the room.

"Terrrrms?" she rasped. "No terrrrms." The very word was obviously distasteful to her. "Surrender is unconditional. In return for saving me the trouble of having to hunt you down and kill you, I will grant you the indulgence of a quick death. It will be terrifyingly painful, of course, but quick. That is your reward for surrendering. That, and the knowledge that you will not have to witness what is to come for the rest of your world. You should be groveling at my feet in gratitude for sparing you that."

"What about the Mother Confessor?"

Dori frowned her displeasure. "She did not offer to surrender. Unlike you, she still resists the inevitable. She will again feel our claws, but this time, as she screams her lungs out, she will also feel our teeth as they rip her face from her skull. We will suck out her eyes and brains and gorge on her flesh. We will smear her blood on ourselves for the pleasure of the warm, wet, greasy feel of it."

Richard desperately wanted to draw his sword. Its magic was screaming for release. He denied that magic its urgent need. He controlled his own rage, as the Sisters of the Light had for so long sought to teach him. As he smiled at the little girl, it occurred to him that the Sisters would be proud of how far he had come.

What they wouldn't have understood, though, was how he was able to turn that fury inward. Richard blew out one of the two remaining lamps by the ugly orange chairs and then returned to the center of the room. In the murky light of the one remaining lamp off in the distance behind him, he could barely see Dori at the opposite end of the long table.

"Who are you, exactly?" Richard asked across the length of the heavy table. "It seems I should be allowed to know who you are, since I have agreed to surrender."

"I am the Golden Goddess."

Richard shrugged. "Well, I know that much. What I mean is"—he leaned in—"who are you? What are you?"

Dori effortlessly sprang up onto the top of the other end of the heavy oak table like something out of a nightmare. She slowly walked down the length of the table toward him, her heels clicking with each measured step, a predator locked on to its prey.

"I am the bringer of the tide of my kind," she said in a low, guttural growl. "A coming tide that will wash over your kind, wash over your world, and drown you all." She came to a halt above him at his end of the table. She glared down at him. "I am the Golden Goddess, the bringer of that tide."

In the dead silence, with shadows all around her, she slowly lifted both arms out at her sides and opened her fingers, palms up, summoning that tide forth.

First one began to appear, then another; then the whole room started coming alive with movement. It was just as Kahlan had described it, like scribbles in the air, dizzyingly fast lines upon swirling lines, faster and faster, arcing, looping, tracing through the air, indications of their shape and mass and size. Because it was impossible to make it all fit any notion of what was real, what was solid, what existed, and what didn't, it was a disorienting sight.

At least it was until those scribbly lines began to thicken, as if they were now being drawn in gooey, muddy water. Those thickening lines began to fuse together, revealing their true forms, until they finally materialized in the gloom all around him. The whole process took only seconds, but in those few seconds, the whole world seemed to change as it suddenly came alive with creatures more terrifying than anything he could have imagined.

"My children," Dori said in a low, menacing snarl as she held out her arms, this time in introduction. "They have come for you."

All around, more and more of those scribbles in midair were coalescing into dark, wet shapes, tall, massive, and muscular. They stood on two legs, hunched a little. He could just make out the claws at the ends of powerful arms. Steam or vapor of some kind rose from the black, glistening bodies. Globs of gelatinous material slid down off their lumpy, amphibian-like skin, dripping from the creatures to splash on the floor.

"Who are you?" Richard asked in a whisper as more and more of the creatures were continually materializing in the shadows all around, each one scribbles at first, then becoming its full form, until they packed the room with their tall, black, steaming, dripping shapes.

When their wide mouths opened and their thin lips drew back in a kind of snarl, Richard could see their long, sharp, pointed teeth. Those sharp white teeth stood out against the wet black bodies. Slime drew out in thin strands between the top and bottom teeth as they opened their mouths wider, hissing with threat.

"Who are you?" Richard asked Dori again, appalled at what he was seeing all around him. "I mean, who are your kind? What are you? What are you called?"

"We are the Gleeeee," she said, dragging the name out in a guttural growl that was bone-chilling.

Hundreds of them, it seemed, surrounded him, packed into every available space in the library, some even crouched atop the rows of bookcases, all leaning in toward him. The steam rising from their wet bodies collected like a cloud near the ceiling. Their lumpy black skin shimmered in the shadowy light. Their teeth clacked as they snapped their jaws at him.

"The Glee," Richard repeated.

"Yessss," she said as she grinned with evil intent.

"But how are you able to be in the body of this girl? How do the Glee travel from your world to ours?"

"I am able to put my mind into this body."

Richard frowned. "But how?"

"Because I am the one who presently serves as the Golden Goddess, my mind is able to go to those places where I send the Gleeeee. I am able to enter the mind of another. I am now in this pathetic, weak skin creature."

Richard gestured up at all the menacing creatures behind her. "And how are your kind able to come here, to our world?"

"We come." Dori cocked her head. "We collect other worlds. It is what we do."

Richard realized that, for whatever reason, he wasn't going to be able to get any better explanation out of her, possibly because she didn't know how they did it, only that they did. He guessed that maybe it was something like someone asking him how he breathed, how he walked, and how he was able to talk. Like her, he just knew that he did.

He gazed around at the hundreds of creatures packed into the library, their wet bodies sliding against one another as they vied for a better position, trying to get closer to their prey.

"Why did you need to bring so many just to kill me?"

"Because I wanted the Gleeeee to see that your magic is not to be feared so they can tell others. With caution about magic dispelled, we will become a tide that will wash over your world. I am the Golden Goddess. I am the bringer of that tide."

33

"What do you suppose he is doing in there?" Shale asked as she paused to gaze nervously at the double doors before turning her attention back to Kahlan.

The woman's pacing was starting to get on Kahlan's nerves. She knew that something was terribly wrong, and her heart already hammered in dread. Richard had wanted to see all the gifted in the palace, and when they proved to have very little useful power, Kahlan had thought he would be disappointed, but he wasn't.

It was obvious to her now that he'd had some kind of plan when he called all those gifted people up to the library area. Kahlan didn't know what that plan had been or what it was he had been looking for, but she did know that it had brought him what he had been seeking. Kahlan worried what his real reason could have been for wanting to see all the gifted. More worrisome, though, was what he could have really been looking for, and what he had found.

He was the Seeker, of course, and Kahlan had seen him do such inexplicable things before. Kahlan knew Richard, and she knew that he was focused on something. Something dangerous. Something so dangerous that he hadn't told her what he was really doing or what it was about.

Kahlan slowly shook her head as Shale stood over her, waiting for an answer. "If I know Richard, and I do, he has gotten some crazy idea into his head."

"Crazy idea?" Shale was clearly agitated by the answer and considered it unsatisfactory. "You said that before. What kind of crazy idea?"

"Lord Rahl gets crazy ideas sometimes," Berdine said, coming to Kahlan's rescue.

Shale paused in her pacing to stare incredulously at the Mord-Sith.

"How do you know that?"

"I know because I am Lord Rahl's favorite," Berdine explained with a grin.

Whereas the others were tall, muscular, and blond, Berdine had wavy brown hair, also pulled back into a single braid. She was shorter than the others, too, with a curvier, solid build. While she looked different from the other Mord-Sith, and had a rather flippant nature, she was no less devoted or deadly.

Shale blinked at the woman. "His favorite?"

"He doesn't have favorites," Kahlan absently reminded her as she stared again at the double doors. "He's told you many times, Berdine, that he loves you all equally."

Berdine beamed as she nodded. "I know. But he loves me more equally."

Kahlan could only shake her head. She didn't feel like indulging Berdine's nonsense. Kahlan knew that Berdine sometimes turned to the distraction of such seemingly inane banter when she was worried for Richard.

Kahlan was worried for him, too. She thought again about how she had heard Richard lock the latch on the double doors. Was he worried about someone interrupting them? Or did he want to lock Dori in for some crazy reason?

"What is she talking about?" Shale complained. Kahlan had learned over the years that sorceresses tended to complain a lot. It was part of their nature. An annoying part. "What does she mean about Richard getting crazy ideas?"

Kahlan, sitting on the front edge of one of the ugly orange chairs, hands in her lap, her back straight, finally looked up at Shale when she came insistently closer, expecting an answer.

Kahlan lifted a hand in a vague gesture. "Richard sometimes has crazy ideas. At least, they always seem crazy to us at the time, but they're not crazy to Richard. He is always running odd little bits of information and strange calculations through his head that none of us could possibly know about or understand and so the things he says or does can seem... crazy."

"That's the truth," Cassia chimed in. "I haven't known him as long as some of the others, but I certainly have seen him get crazy ideas."

A few of the other Mord-Sith nodded that they, too, were all too familiar with Richard's crazy ideas.

"It isn't just that Lord Rahl gets crazy ideas," Nyda explained. "The man *is* crazy. Stone-cold crazy. That's why he has crazy ideas. That's why he needs all of us to protect him."

Shale looked appalled. "You mean he does that a lot?" she asked as she leaned down toward Kahlan. "Get these crazy ideas?"

Kahlan glanced to the doors again before answering the sorceress. "I don't know. Sometimes he just does. A lot of times it's simply hard to imagine what he's thinking. He doesn't always have the time or patience to explain things. I don't know how to explain the ideas he gets in his head."

"That's because they're crazy," Berdine offered, helpfully.

Kahlan ignored her. "Sometimes when we all think we know exactly what we must do, then he suddenly does the opposite. Or he comes up with something out of the blue that no one expected or understands. Sometimes he does things as the Seeker that he knows he has to do, and we just don't know his reasoning, so it seems crazy to us, that's all."

"Like what?" Shale pressed.

Kahlan got up from the chair and went to the doors. She leaned close, putting an ear almost against the glass for a moment. She didn't hear anything. As she returned to Shale and Berdine she hooked a long strand of hair behind an ear.

Kahlan gave the sorceress a look. "Like deciding that to save the world he must end prophecy. Does that sound normal to you?"

Shale made a face. "No. I've never seen him do anything I would call crazy, but now that you mention it, that most definitely would have sounded crazy to me." She shook her head. "I have to say, it still does."

"Well," Kahlan said, gesturing at the locked doors, "now you have seen him do something else that seems a bit crazy."

Shale conceded with a sigh.

34

Kahlan glanced over at Vika, a ways down the corridor. The Mord-Sith had backed the girl's mother off quite a distance. The woman was wringing her hands in worry, peeking around Vika from time to time, trying to see what was happening with her daughter. Kahlan worried about that, too.

A few dozen men of the First File stood guard farther down in each direction of the corridor, well beyond the sitting area outside the library. The upper level of the palace was generally quite elegant. Most of it was calming and hushed. All the decorations and beautiful art contributed to that sense of tranquility. It seemed rather odd to her, considering the types of men who had been the Lord Rahl throughout history. In recent centuries, they had been a long string of tyrants, and the world was never calm and tranquil under their rule.

The one thing that didn't fit with all the tasteful areas of the upper corridor was the orange-striped chairs in the sitting area outside this particular library. They were terribly uncomfortable to lean back in and were so ugly that Kahlan didn't really like to sit on them.

"Why do you think they would have put chairs like this in such a beautiful corridor?" she said out loud to no one in particular.

Shale frowned at the question and then looked around at the chairs. "What's wrong with them?"

"What's wrong with them? They're grotesque."

Kahlan's feet hurt from standing, so, as much as she didn't like the chairs, she sat down again on the very front edge of one.

Berdine patted a hand in a familiar manner on the back of one of the chairs. "Richard's father, Darken Rahl, never liked coming up here because he didn't like these chairs, either."

Kahlan stared openly at the Mord-Sith. "Then why in the world didn't he order them changed? He routinely ordered the execution of countless innocent people. He delighted in throwing people from different lands into slavery and indentured servitude. He ruined lives across D'Hara and then the Midlands without a second thought. He ruled with an iron fist.

"So why, if he didn't like these chairs, wouldn't he order them removed, burned, and replaced with something else?"

Berdine raised her eyebrows, as if it were a silly question. "Because they have to be here." The way she said it made it sound obvious.

Kahlan pressed the middle finger and thumb of one hand to opposite temples in an effort to calm herself. She had a headache from thinking about the helpless terror of all those poor, innocent people who had been slaughtered down in the lower reaches of the palace. The tension of this new threat was getting to her. She knew that her pregnancy had something to do with it. She was in a constant state of worry for the two babies growing inside her.

She took a deep breath before asking, "Why do these chairs have to be here?"

"Because they have ugly magic."

"What?" Kahlan made a face at the woman. "Ugly magic? These chairs have ugly magic? What in the world kind of magic is ugly magic?"

"Well," she said, gesturing to the closed doors, "that room is dangerous. It's a repository, a containment field, for very dangerous spells. Darken Rahl rarely went in there himself. I'm pretty sure he was afraid of that room, although he never admitted as much."

"What does that have to do with these ugly chairs?"

Berdine shrugged. "There are inviting places everywhere." She gestured back down the corridor one way and then the other. "There are many comfortable, beautiful places outside other libraries to sit. You can sit and relax almost anywhere you like up on this level."

"Well then," Kahlan said with exaggerated patience, "who would want to sit here in these uncomfortable, ugly, orange-striped chairs?"

Berdine smiled. "Exactly."

Shale blinked. "You mean, these chairs are—"

"You mean, they're meant to discourage people from lingering here in front of that dangerous room," Kahlan said, suddenly understanding.

Berdine nodded with a smile that Kahlan finally caught on. "One time," she confided in both Kahlan and Shale, looking back and forth between them as if revealing a secret, "Darken Rahl said that a person would have to be crazy to use the room with the orange-striped chairs."

"Crazy…" Kahlan glanced to the double doors. "Crazy, like Richard."

Berdine confirmed it with a single nod of satisfaction. "You see? Ugly magic."

Kahlan stood to gesture toward the doors. "Does Richard know that this room is dangerous?"

Berdine snorted a laugh. "Are you kidding? Of course he knows. Back when Lord Rahl—your Lord Rahl, not Darken Rahl, not that Lord Rahl—asked me to help him do research on things he desperately needed to find out, he asked me to go to all the libraries throughout the palace to search the reference works referring to specific things he needed."

Kahlan frowned. "So?"

Berdine leaned in again, lowering her voice as if someone might overhear, even though there was no one other than Shale and Kahlan within earshot.

"So, when Lord Rahl asked me to search the reference books in all the libraries, he told me, 'Except the one with the orange-striped chairs. I don't want you going in that room—not for any reason. I will search that library myself.' That's how I know that he knew the place is dangerous. Of course, I knew it was dangerous before, because of Darken Rahl."

Just then an onslaught of piercing shrieks erupted. Along with everyone else, Kahlan looked toward the doors. It sounded like the shrieks of demons.

Then came a collective howl so horrifying that it made Kahlan flinch in fright. The horrible screech from beyond the doors echoed through the corridor. Everyone—the soldiers, the Mord-Sith, Shale, and Kahlan—all turned to gape at the library. The sound made the hair on Kahlan's arms and neck stand on end.

35

The hundreds of bloodcurdling shrieks joined into one collective howl that felt as if it tore the very fibers of Kahlan's nerves. Her heart pounded out of control in her chest. She knew that the slaughtered people down below had heard those same shrieks as they were being ripped apart. She knew because she had heard one of those horrifying shrieks when she had been attacked, one claw pierced into her side to hold her while the other claw ripped down through the muscles of her arm.

The wail of it made her freshly healed claw wounds throb in sudden pain. Kahlan covered her ears, trying to shut out the horrifying sound. Tears sprang to her eyes from the bone-tingling terror for her husband beyond those doors.

Then, the whole palace shook with a sudden jolt that nearly took them all from their feet.

The powerful shock that rocked the palace made Shale gasp. The Mord-Sith spread their feet and went into a crouch to keep their balance. Kahlan grabbed one of the high-backed orange-striped chairs for support. Some of the others fell over.

She saw the doors to the library shudder in their frame, but they held, and not even the glass broke from the violent jolt that had come from inside that room. It was, after all, a containment field, so she would have expected the doors to hold. That brutal jolt to the palace brought an abrupt end to the needful, murderous howls.

In one instant, Kahlan had to cover her ears, and in the next instant, everything went dead quiet. She lowered her hands from her ears.

"Earthquake?" Shale asked in the sudden silence.

Kahlan shook her head. "I don't think so. It was just one big jolt. I'm not sure, but I think earthquakes shake more. This was more like an explosion. And besides, it came from in there, not underfoot."

Shale looked confused. "But there was no sound of an explosion. How could there be no sound?"

"Outside a containment field you wouldn't necessarily hear the explosive release of profoundly violent magic, but you couldn't help but to feel it."

Shale gave one cynical shake of her head. "I've never heard of a containment field before. But I guess it's not the kind of thing to be found in the Northern Waste."

Kahlan hurried to the room and pounded a fist on the door. She didn't care if he was doing something and wanted to be left alone. That wish had suddenly been nullified as far as she was concerned.

"Richard!" When there was no answer, she pounded again. "Richard! Are you all right? What's going on?"

She stepped back when all of a sudden, the doors burst open. Thick black smoke billowed out and spread across the ceiling of the corridor. Men of the First File were already rushing to the scene from every direction. Glowing embers floated and whirled out with the sooty smoke.

Berdine and the other Mord-Sith ran toward the open doorway, followed closely by Shale. With all the black smoke, it was hard to see inside the room. Kahlan held an arm out to stop the others. She didn't think it would be wise to blindly charge into the room.

"Richard!" Kahlan called into the darkness, fearing the worst.

"I'm here," he said in a quiet voice as he seemed to materialize out of the swirling, inky smoke and burning embers. Kahlan expected the smoke to smell acrid. It didn't. Not at all. Oddly, rather than smelling like anything burning she had ever smelled before, it smelled like nothing so much as a stagnant swamp.

"Dear spirits, what happened? What was that explosion or whatever it was?" Kahlan asked as she gripped his upper arm. "It shook the whole palace."

Before he could say anything, Shale leaned around him to look into the room as the smoke was beginning to thin and clear. "Where's Dori?"

Rather than answer, Richard gave her a forbidding look, then turned and disappeared back into the swirling smoke, the gold of his cape swallowed by the murky haze. As the haze started to clear, the room began brightening. Apparently, Richard had opened the drapes over the windows.

Once there was enough light from those windows and coming in through the open double doors, Berdine, Nyda, Rikka, Vale, Cassia, and Vika pushed past Shale and then Kahlan to hurry into the room. Each of them had her Agiel in her fist. Ignoring the fetid smell from inside, Kahlan cautiously followed them in, with Shale right behind her.

The sight of the inside of the room was not at all what Kahlan had expected. She had expected nothing but a charred shell. Instead, it appeared mostly intact. The shelves she could see rising up all around into the smoke still hanging near the high ceiling looked relatively undamaged. The books were intact and all still on their shelves.

But it was clear that something in the room had been incinerated.

There were countless black splotches, as if countless clots of greasy soot had been hurled against the walls, the books, the shelves. There were splashes of that dark, grimy substance everywhere, on nearly everything. Hundreds of those masses had impacted against the walls of books all around, leaving them looking like hundreds of clusters of dirty, greasy ash had been blasted against them. All of those sprays of soot lumped up in the center of each splash, with a starlike pattern thrown out from that center. Wisps of smoke still floated up from each of those clots. The floor was covered with the still-smoking substance. It was so deep that Kahlan's shoes sank into it. As the smoke gradually thinned out, she could see the same kind of grimy splatters all over the ceiling.

Kahlan couldn't imagine what had made such an incredible mess.

"What in the world..." Shale whispered as she stared up at the dark disorder all around the room. She turned and frowned at Richard. "Where is Dori? The little girl you came in here with. Where is she?"

Richard fixed the sorceress in his raptor gaze a moment, and then went to the end of the table. There was a small pile of ash on the end of the table, but this particular pile wasn't black. It was gray.

Richard put a hand under the edge of the table and with his other hand wiped the ash off the table and into his upturned palm.

He took it to the sorceress. "Hold out your hands."

Shale regarded him suspiciously. "Why?"

The muscles in Richard's jaw flexed. "Hold out your hands."

Reluctantly, Shale finally did as he asked, lifting her hands, holding them together, palms up. Richard let the ash slowly pour into her hands.

"This is what is left of Dori," he said in a low, menacing tone. "Since you are such an advocate of bringing innocent children into a world in the middle of this terrible threat, where they will be helpless, where they will be hunted, where they will be subjected to horrors with no way to defend themselves, I want you to take the remains of this child to her mother, and tell her that her precious daughter was possessed by an evil force and died because of it."

Shale looked horrified. "Lord Rahl, I don't think I can—"

"Do it!" Richard yelled right into her face. "You think this world is safe for children and wanted Kahlan and me to have children despite the monsters that hunt us. This is the kind of thing that would await them. You take this child's remains to her mother, and you tell her that we are sorry but none of us could protect her daughter from evil—just like none of us could protect Kahlan and my children from this evil."

Kahlan wanted to tell him that it wasn't Shale's fault, but at the sight of Richard's anger over the death of a child, she was paralyzed. She was going to have to tell him sooner or later, but she wanted it to be a joyful announcement of her pregnancy. She didn't want to have such wonderful news come out when something had just happened that had Richard in a rage, or when someone else's child had just died.

Worse, apparently died at Richard's hands.

Shale, still standing with her hands out, holding the pile of ashes, swallowed. Seeing the look in his eyes, she finally nodded in resignation.

As Shale left to do his bidding, Kahlan threw her arms around Richard, hugging him close. She could feel him trembling. She didn't know if it was in rage, or from what had just happened in this room.

She wanted to tell him that everything was all right, now, but she knew it wasn't. Whatever had happened was only a small part of a much larger menace, and it had involved a child losing her life. At a loss for words, Kahlan simply hugged him.

"I'm sorry," Richard whispered in her ear. "I'm so sorry. I do want to have children one day. I just can't imagine bringing them into a world with what I have just seen."

36

Kahlan wanted to know what had happened—what he had just seen—but she didn't want to press him for answers right then. Richard would tell her in his own way, in his own time. For the moment, she simply put her head against his shoulder and her arms around his waist.

By the time Shale returned with Vika, Kahlan had come to realize that Richard's trembling was anger. He had come out of the library room shaking in rage and that rage was still charging his muscles with tension. Worse, he hadn't even drawn his sword and called forth its fury. It was purely his anger.

"I did as you asked, Lord Rahl." Shale's face had lost some of its color.

Richard nodded. "Thank you. I don't imagine Dori's mother took the news well."

"No, she did not," Shale admitted. "But she did tell me something I think you should know. When I told her what you said, that her daughter had been possessed by evil and died because of it, she didn't act surprised. She cried at the loss, of course, but then told me that Dori had been acting strange ever since arriving at the palace."

"Strange how?" he asked.

"Cold and distant. She said that was unlike Dori and she began to fear that her daughter had been possessed by something depraved. That was the word she used, 'depraved.'"

Richard stared off into distant thoughts for a moment. "I have seen too many mothers lose their children. With the great war finally over, I thought I had seen the last of it. But now I know otherwise. We have only seen the beginning of it."

"A mother feeling that something was off about her daughter is understandable," Shale said, apparently trying to distract him from grim thoughts. "A mother would know. But, how did you?"

Richard let out a sigh. "She wouldn't look at me."

Shale looked skeptical. "Children usually are too shy to look at strangers, especially an authority figure. Being shy is not exactly unusual, especially not when meeting a frightening person like the Lord Rahl."

"I realize that," Richard said, "but there was something about the way she avoided looking at me that wasn't quite natural." He thought about it a moment before going on.

"Remember when we questioned Nolo? He wouldn't look at me, either. The Golden Goddess used Nolo to demand that we surrender, and if we did she would in return offer us a quick death. Later Nolo told us that the Golden Goddess called me the shiny man because she found it painful to look at me because of my gift. I remembered the way he wouldn't look at me in the great hall the other day. That was the goddess not wanting to look at me."

"That's it?" Kahlan asked, throwing her hands up. "Just that she wouldn't look at you? Richard, that hardly seems enough to prove that the Golden Goddess was watching through Dori's eyes."

"Well," Richard admitted, "that, and what she did when I leaned down close and told her that I wanted to surrender."

"What?" Shale asked.

Richard nodded. "When told her that I wanted to surrender, she looked up at me and grinned."

Kahlan still wasn't entirely convinced that meant that Dori was acting on behalf of the Golden Goddess. "Children often smile at the strangest times. I've seen little kids smile at me as they were wetting their pants."

Richard looked over at her, shaking his head. "Not like this. This was as evil a smile as I've ever seen. Once I told her that I wanted to surrender and took her into the library, she dropped all pretense and there was no longer any question about it. The goddess was possessing Dori.

"I closed the drapes and blew out all but one lamp to make her more comfortable—to make the goddess more comfortable looking at me. The shy little girl was gone; there was only the contemptuous Golden Goddess."

"You mean she showed her true self because you told her you wanted to surrender?" Kahlan asked.

"That's right. She thought she had me where she wanted me—surrendering and ready to die. But the thing that was really making her confident was the mistake she made."

"What mistake?" Berdine blurted out, too curious to keep quiet at a lull in his story when he stared off into the memory.

Richard smiled at her eagerness. Berdine was an old friend, and the two of them had a special bond. Berdine was something of a scholar, and they had grown close when searching through books together for answers about things such as the omen machine.

Vika was Richard's personal bodyguard. She was muscular, strong-headed, and reacted instantly with profound violence to any threat to Richard. Berdine would also protect Richard with her life, but the two had known each other for a long time, and he really did love her, although not more than the others.

"The mistake the Golden Goddess made was in the choice of a host. I don't know how she can do it, and she wasn't able to tell me, but somehow, she invaded Dori's mind in much the same way as she had used Nolo. But this time she wormed her way in deeper and for longer."

"Why choose a little girl?" Kahlan asked. "Just to look less suspicious?"

Richard folded his arms. "No. She chose Dori because her mother was bringing her to the palace, where we are, but more importantly, because Dori's mother has the gift. The gift may not be strong in her, but the Golden Goddess didn't know that. The goddess is wary of magic, so she wanted to have time to observe the mother's magic and take the measure of it, thinking magic is magic—all magic is the same. So, she chose the daughter of a gifted person, a gifted person who was going to the palace where we live. She thought she had an additional stroke of luck when the mother was called up here to meet with me."

"Well, it actually was a stroke of luck," Shale said.

Richard shook his head. "Not exactly. I suspected that the goddess would want to get close to a gifted person, or even try to get in the mind of a gifted person. That's why I called all the gifted up here to meet with us.

"If she had invaded the mind of a gifted person, I wanted to give the goddess a chance to get close to me. I knew she very well might inadvertently make herself known by being afraid to look into my eyes. Dori was the one, though, who wouldn't look at me. When I leaned down and told her that I wanted to surrender, she took the bait—or at least, the goddess did. The reason I had invited all the gifted up to this place, besides suspecting the goddess might be among them, was that I hoped to get the goddess into a containment field if she was in one of them."

Shale slapped the palm of a hand to her forehead. "You mean you thought that you could kill the goddess?"

"I told you," Berdine said, "he gets crazy ideas."

"No, I didn't think I could kill her," he said in a mocking tone over his shoulder at Berdine. "And it wasn't a crazy idea. I was hoping to get more information out of her, maybe learn their weaknesses. Maybe find at least something we could use against them."

"So, you lied to her?" Shale asked, sounding as if that was somehow cheating.

Richard showed her a lopsided smile. "I sure did. I lied through my teeth. She bought it, too. The goddess is arrogant. She believes that she is so terrifying that I would be afraid, feel hopeless, and simply give up."

"All right. All well and good." Kahlan pointed impatiently. "But, exactly what happened in there?"

37

Richard pulled in a deep breath. "Well, the Golden Goddess decided, because of being around Dori's mother, that magic wasn't really so dangerous after all. Since she doesn't understand magic, she didn't grasp that the mother's gift wasn't very strong, and assumed that because the mother had magic, and that her magic wasn't very dangerous, then my magic and magic in general weren't really anything to be worried about.

"As I had hoped, she wanted her kind to come and see that there was nothing to fear from us, so she summoned a horde of them into the room. Hundreds. She wanted them to see how weak magic actually is by letting them kill me and then tell others, so that her kind would no longer need to be cautious."

Kahlan leaned in, expectantly. "What did they look like?"

He looked into her eyes. "It was just like you described it—at first, anyway. They first appear as what you called a scribbly man. But that is only the initial phase as they are coming to our world, not what they really look like. It's simply some kind of transitional phase as they begin to materialize here. It went fully dark before that one that attacked you completed its transition into our world, so you never actually saw what they look like."

In slack-jawed attention, Berdine impatiently rolled her hand. "So, what do they look like once they finish appearing?"

Richard appraised all the eyes watching him. Kahlan could see that he was reluctant to tell them. After having been attacked by one, she wasn't sure she wanted to hear the terrifying reality that all of those dead people below had faced.

"Bigger than me," Richard said, holding his hand up high

above his head to illustrate. "Muscular, long arms, each with those three claws, with almost black skin that... I don't know. They didn't have skin like us, and they didn't have scales. The best way I can describe it is that it reminded me of the skin of a newt, or salamander, or even a tadpole. They were wet and slimy-looking, with globs of gelatinous material that slid down off their lumpy, amphibian-like skin."

Berdine wrinkled her nose. "That's disgusting."

Richard nodded his agreement. "Some kind of steam or smoke rose up off of them as they became solid. I suspected that was somehow a consequence of traveling to our world."

Berdine hooked her first two fingers. "Do they have fangs? Like snakes?"

Richard shook his head. "No. They have long, sharp white teeth, all about the same, and a whole lot of them in a row across the top and the bottom jaw.

"I asked Dori what her kind was called. She said they were called the Glee. Except that when she said it, it came out like a long, croaking hiss. I can't pronounce it the way she did. But I can tell you, it ran goose bumps up my arms to hear her say it."

"So then when happened?" Kahlan asked when he fell silent, staring off into the memory of it.

He gave her a look with a smile, which she thought was a little odd.

"Then she told me that she was the Golden Goddess, the bringer of the tide that would wash over our world and drown us all. All of those creatures were packed into the room, gathered around, all leaning in toward me, all snapping their jaws full of those long, sharp teeth, all eager to tear into me once she gave them the word."

"And then what?" Berdine asked, impatiently rolling her hand yet again to urge him on when he paused.

"When she told me that she was the Golden Goddess, the bringer of the tide that would wash over us, I smiled at her, and asked if she knew who I was. Her eyes narrowed, and for the first time she looked uncertain."

Berdine leaned in. "What'd you tell her?"

"I said, 'I am the bringer of death.'"

Berdine laughed with excitement at that.

"And then what?" Kahlan asked.

"And then," Richard said in a quiet tone, "along with everything else alive in that room, I had to kill that child."

He paused for a moment before looking back at them and going on.

"I unleashed the full fury of that which I had been holding inside. In essence, I filled the containment field with an explosive discharge of Additive and Subtractive Magic linked together. Those two things don't mix. Without the containment field, it would probably have taken out this whole floor of the palace, possibly this whole wing."

"Did it catch them in time while they were still in our world? Did it kill them?" Kahlan asked, expectantly.

"Yes. That greasy black soot in there is all that's left of them. The goddess thought she had learned from Dori's mother that magic isn't anything to fear. I wanted to show her just how mistaken she was, so I unleashed my hate on those hateful creatures, the kind of hate that only a war wizard can unleash. I have only just begun to show them my wrath."

Berdine thrust a fist into the air. "Yes! That's my Lord Rahl."

The other Mord-Sith looked equally pleased, if less animated about it.

Kahlan leaned forward hopefully. "So, then you were able to kill the Golden Goddess as well."

Richard looked from the Mord-Sith back to Kahlan as he slowly shook his head. "I killed the little girl who was hosting her. But the goddess wasn't really there, in her. It's something like the way the dream walkers used people. Remember when you once tried to kill the dream walker by touching someone he was using, but he was gone as soon as you unleashed your power? This was much the same. She was only using the girl to look through her eyes and use her voice. The goddess wasn't physically there, in Dori. I only had an instant to act when she gave the Glee the command to take me or they would have all torn into me or escaped. I had no choice but to kill Dori along with all those hateful things."

He let out a long sigh. "But it accomplished two things. First, I learned that I don't believe that the goddess is able to enter the mind of a gifted person."

"Why do you think that?" Shale asked.

"Because she would have if she could have. As weak as Dori's mother's gift was, the goddess couldn't get into her mind. That is why she had to use Dori. That was as close as she could get."

"What's the second thing?" Kahlan asked.

"It takes them a second or two to materialize here, in our world. Then, when they get here, they have to grasp their surroundings, look for any threat, and take in their target. It's only an instant, but in that instant they are vulnerable.

"But to kill them after they were here and before they could escape back to their world, and more importantly to strike fear of us into the hearts of their kind through the eyes of the Golden Goddess, I had to kill Dori, too."

Kahlan put her arms around his neck, holding his head to her shoulder. "You had no choice, Richard. You had no choice."

"I know. I am *fuer grissa ost drauka*. I am the bringer of death."

38

"Are you sure they can't enter the mind of a person with magic?" Shale asked.

"I can't say I know that with absolute certainty," Richard told her, "but after talking to the goddess through Dori, I'm convinced that she isn't able to use the gifted—or she would already have done that. I believe she isn't able to enter our minds for the simple reason that her ability isn't compatible with our gift. Simply put, our gift won't allow her in."

Shale squinted with uncertainty. "Won't allow it?"

"While the goddess and the Glee can do what seems unfathomable to us—traveling to other worlds—I think that magic must block their ability to get past it and into our minds. That's why they were leery of the gift.

"They are predators. They hunt, which proves they have the ability to think and plan. And from the evidence of the dead we found down below, they work together. There are plenty of animals that are very dangerous, that stalk their prey and work together, but can't fathom magic. It stymies them."

"But you can't say with absolute certainty that they can't use the mind of the gifted," Shale pressed.

"Their primary goal is to eliminate me and Kahlan, right? So why not use you? If they could do it," Richard insisted, "then the goddess would have chosen to enter your mind, don't you suppose? You are close to me." He swept an arm around. "Or the mind of one of the Mord-Sith. They are even closer. If she was able to do that, then why choose a little girl? Because the minds of children are weaker, that's why," he said, answering his own question.

"But Nolo was an adult," Shale argued.

Richard smiled. "He was a diplomat, through and through. All of Nolo's people are bred to be diplomats, raised as diplomats."

Shale frowned. "So?"

"What adult mind is more simplistic and childlike than a diplomat's?"

Shale considered a moment. "I suppose you could be right."

"Killing me and Kahlan is her goal. When we're asleep, the Mord-Sith watch over us. If the goddess could use the mind of a gifted person, she would have already killed Kahlan and me by simply having a Mord-Sith do it while we were asleep. If she could have, she would have."

"I see your point," the sorceress conceded. She met his gaze. "Now that you mention it, as I said before, I had a murky vision of some kind of being when I was in meditation. It was just beyond awareness and I didn't know what it could be. That vague, shadowy image had to be the goddess trying to make a connection with me, but ultimately failing. You have to be right that they can't enter the mind of the gifted or she would have entered my mind right then and there."

"So, then we have learned something useful," Kahlan said.

Richard flashed her a smile. "Yes, we have. It means we can use the gifted to help us without worrying that the goddess could be watching what we do through their eyes. But now we also know that anyone ungifted here at the palace could be an unwitting spy. That means that the goddess could even enter the mind of any of the First File." He arched an eyebrow. "Not exactly safe having them watch over us while we sleep."

Kahlan looked around at the decidedly unsettled looks on the faces of the Mord-Sith. "That's an alarming bit of news."

"Do you know where there are more gifted who could be helpful?" Shale asked. "All those here at the People's Palace may have enough of the gift to keep the goddess out of their minds, but they don't have enough power to be of any use in defeating these things."

"The Wizard's Keep," Vika answered in Richard's place.

"That's right," he said, nodding at her. "If we can get there, then—"

Everyone turned when they heard twin screams echo up a stairwell not far down the corridor. They were the kind of screams that could mean only one thing.

Every one of the Mord-Sith immediately swung the Agiel hanging on a fine gold chain from her wrist up into her fist as Richard broke into a dead run. All the Mord-Sith were right behind. Richard and the Mord-Sith beat the soldiers to the stairs, but not Kahlan and Shale.

Kahlan was not pleased to be stuck behind so many hulking men as Richard charged down the stairs. As they reached the next level down, a service area, Kahlan saw past the men and the railing that the torches were out, as were the lamps. The only light was that coming down the stairwell.

In the shadows, she could see a dark shape flailing away at someone already on the ground.

Still four steps from the bottom, Richard leaped off the stairs toward the shadowy shape of the threat. His sword came out in midair, sending its unique ring of steel down the dark hallway. The blade, steel blackened from touching the world of the dead, flashed as it came up into the air.

Richard, screaming with lethal intent, swung the sword with all his might while still in mid-leap. The blade whistled as it arced through the air. A black arm lifted in defense, only to be severed.

As Richard was landing on his feet, the dark arm, with three massive claws at the end, spiraled through the air. At the same time, the rest of the creature turned back into scribbles as it vanished into thin air.

The Mord-Sith dove off the stairs after Richard, all of them striving to reach the threat. But it was gone before they could get to it. The Mord-Sith, along with the soldiers, charged off into the darkness, looking for any more of the Glee.

Two women were sprawled on their backs on the floor, clearly dead. The rib cage of one and the abdomen of the other had been ripped open almost to their spines by powerful strikes from those claws, leaving their insides spread across the floor.

Almost without pause, Richard stormed off down the hall right behind the soldiers, then sped past them, his sword in hand, hoping to catch more of the attackers.

Kahlan stood with Shale as the others raced away to make sure the dark hall was clear. Other soldiers collected torches and headed into the darkness. Shale leaned down to check, but it was obvious to Kahlan that no amount of healing would bring life back to the poor women. They were two of the palace staff, and had simply been going about their work when they had been cut down. Kahlan couldn't help thinking about their families. She wondered if they had children who would never see their mothers again.

As Shale looked up at Kahlan to say that nothing could be done, her eyes went wide. Kahlan realized that the sorceress was seeing something behind her. Without hesitation, Kahlan ducked and rolled to the side, just in time as claws swept past, flicking a lock of hair on the way by and barely missing catching her neck.

Shale thrust an arm out. From her hand a wavering glow to the air instantly left with a loud crack, like the crack of a whip. As Kahlan was rolling back to her feet, turning to face the enemy, the strike of Shale's power went right through the dark shape just as it was dissolving back into its own world. That magic hit a far wall and blew a hole through it, sending bits of plaster and stone flying everywhere. Kahlan could see the main corridor beyond through the hole.

She didn't know what sort of magic Shale had used. Kahlan had never seen anything quite like it. But then again, she had never seen a sorceress and a witch woman combined in one person.

Richard returned just as Shale rushed over to Kahlan to make sure she was all right.

"What happened?" he asked.

"One of them tried to get me," Kahlan said. "Shale saved me just in time. She tried to strike it down with her power"—Kahlan gestured to the hole in the wall—"but it was already vanishing and got away."

Kahlan and Richard were suddenly surrounded by Mord-Sith, but the threat had already passed. Soldiers closed in beyond the Mord-Sith, forming another ring of protection, swords all pointed outward.

"You're right," Shale told Richard. "They are thinking creatures. One of them attacked these two women to draw you away so that another could strike behind you at Kahlan."

Richard gritted his teeth in anger. "And I took the bait, leaving Kahlan unprotected." He thought better of what he said. "Except for you, of course. Thanks, Shale."

She offered a smile. "I just wish I had been faster. I almost had it. Next time I'll have to be quicker."

Richard sheathed his sword, helping to quench the anger in his eyes as he looked down at the arm on the ground. It had been severed cleanly just above the elbow, bone and all. Its skin was as he had described it—almost black, smooth and slimy. The blood was red. The bloody claw, with strings of tissue and clothes stuck in it from the two women it had killed, slowly closed and opened once in death before finally going still.

Kahlan was enraged that it had murdered the two women, and another one of them almost had its claws into her. "If I would have just been a second faster, I could have touched it with my power after it took that swing at me."

"Well," Shale said, "at least one of them went back without an arm. That's a good message to send back to them."

Richard didn't look pleased. "A message that will likely anger them. From what you said about there being killings in the Northern Waste, and other reports we've had, the Glee are randomly attacking people everywhere.

"But it's becoming clear that their main focus is to attack people around Kahlan and me in an effort to draw us into making a mistake. The goddess is becoming obsessed with killing you and me," he said to Kahlan. "They almost got you for a second time. We can't let that happen again. We have to deny them their plan while I try to figure out a way to end the threat."

"How?" Kahlan asked.

Richard ran his fingers back through his hair. "Everyone in our world is now in danger from the Glee, but the people here at the palace are in much greater danger because we're here. They are going to be targeted, just like these two women were, simply to try to draw us into making a mistake. As long as we're here at the palace, this place is going to be a killing field.

"Besides that, the goddess could be looking at us through the eyes of anyone in the palace." He passed a brief look over the soldiers with their backs to them, swords pointed out toward any threat. His meaning was obvious. The goddess could even be using one of the men of the First File. "It's too dangerous for the people here at the palace for us to be here, and it's too dangerous for us to be here. We need to leave.

"If we leave, the focus of the Glee will be to come after us. We need to draw them away from all these innocent people."

Kahlan's brow lifted with a sudden idea. She leaned in and spoke quietly so that the soldiers wouldn't hear in case the goddess was listening through one of them.

"We can leave in the sliph. In a way, the sliph enables us to do something like the Glee. It allows us to travel to a different place in our world in a very short time. Traveling in the sliph will get us far away from here and draw the attention of the goddess away from all these people. That kind of departure might even confuse the goddess."

Richard smiled at her. "Exactly. We need to leave at once."

"But go where?" Kahlan asked.

Richard's smile broadened. "To someplace with gifted who do have lots of power. We need to get to the Wizard's Keep. There are gifted there—real gifted. The Sisters of the Light are there, as are other gifted they are training."

"What are Sisters of the Light?" Shale asked, keeping an eye toward any soldier who might be listening.

"Sorceresses," he said before turning back to Kahlan. "We need to leave at once, before there are more attacks here and before the goddess can get one of us. If we leave in the sliph, that will confuse the goddess as to where we went and hopefully buy us some time."

39

Kahlan stuffed some of her things into a backpack on the bed as Richard did the same. They needed to get out of the People's Palace to confuse the Golden Goddess and lead the Glee away from all the innocent people there.

Kahlan was cautiously excited about being at the safety of the Wizard's Keep. Not only were there a lot of gifted people there, the Keep itself was filled with all kinds of protective shields. Any of the Glee that the goddess sent there would be in danger without realizing it. There were lethal shields in any number of places throughout the Keep that would incinerate anything that didn't belong there or have the proper magic to allow safe passage. The whole Keep would be a death trap for the Glee.

For the first time in days, Kahlan felt a glimmer of hope.

The Keep would also be a place of safety for her to have their children.

Once they were safely in the Keep and it would soon become obvious, Kahlan would finally be able to tell Richard that she was pregnant with twins. They would be safe there, with Sisters of the Light and others to protect her. The Keep had protective magic to protect from invasions. The whole purpose of the Keep was to protect the First Wizard and the gifted working there.

At the Keep, Richard would be able to figure out a way to stop the goddess. Kahlan didn't know why she hadn't thought of the Keep sooner.

The Wizard's Keep was also Richard's other ancestral home. The People's Palace had always been the seat of power for the House of Rahl, but the Wizard's Keep had always been the ancestral home to the First Wizard. It was his Keep. Part of its purpose was to protect him.

If it was safe enough to leave the Keep, Kahlan could possibly give birth to their children at the nearby Confessors' Palace, where she had been born. That was her ancestral home. There were people there who had known Kahlan since she had been born. If it was safe enough to leave the Keep, her dream would be to have her children at the Confessors' Palace. The daughters of a Confessor were always Confessors, so Kahlan would dearly love to have her daughter be born at the Confessors' Palace. The twins could then be raised in the safety of the Keep.

As a young girl, Kahlan had spent a great deal of time in the Keep, under the watchful eye of wizards. The Keep was a place of power for the First Wizard. It would protect his children. And, in turn, those children would continue their lines of magic to protect their world. That would bring life back to the Wizard's Keep the way it had been alive when she had been a girl.

Both she and Richard changed out of their official clothes and into their traveling clothes. Richard put some of his war-wizard outfit in his pack, but kept on the black shirt, the special weapons belt, and the broad, leather-padded silver wristbands with ancient symbols in the language of Creation. Kahlan didn't need to pack her Mother Confessor's dress, because the Confessors' Palace was there in Aydindril, near the Keep. She had other dresses of the Mother Confessor there, all the same silky fabric, all with the same square-cut neckline.

Her whole life she had grown up wearing the black dresses that all Confessors wore. Only the woman chosen by her sister Confessors wore the white dress of the Mother Confessor. Kahlan had been the youngest woman ever named Mother Confessor. It was a testament to the strength of her power.

When she and Richard emerged from their bedroom, all six Mord-Sith, all in red leather, were waiting out in the round entryway along with Shale. Each of the Mord-Sith had a small pack with her. Shale was dressed in her black traveling clothes with a black cloak draped over her shoulders and held together at the top with bone buttons connected by a short silver chain. She had her pack with her as well.

They were all obviously intending to go with Richard and Kahlan. That was fine with Kahlan, and she knew it would be with Richard, too. Of course, their wishes were irrelevant, because the Mord-Sith would have already decided that they were going.

Importantly, the goddess couldn't use them or Shale, so the Mord-Sith would be fearless guardians of her children. Kahlan was grateful that they were coming along to the Keep.

A large force of the First File, Lieutenant Dolan in command, waited off a ways in the wide corridor. With what had happened in the containment-field library, as well as the two women being murdered, to say nothing of the horrific discovery down in the lower reaches of the palace, the men all looked grim and tense. Kahlan couldn't help looking to see if any of them averted their eyes. None did.

"We need to get down to the sliph," Richard told Berdine confidentially, so that the soldiers wouldn't overhear. "I don't want anyone but us nine knowing where we are going."

She nodded. "I know a fast route. It will also keep us out of sight."

Richard nodded to her and then went down the hall a short distance to meet the man in command. "Lieutenant, I need to leave on an important mission."

The man tipped his head. "Of course, Lord Rahl. How many men do you want to take with you?"

"None. Right now I'm in too much of a hurry." At the look on the man's face, he added, "I will send for some of the First File when I can. In the meantime, you know the threat here at the palace. You know how dangerous these creatures are. As you saw, they bleed, so they can be killed if you can catch them in time before they can vanish."

The lieutenant looked uneasy. "While you were getting your things, there was another attack back not far away in one of the hallways branching from this corridor. Two of my men were killed."

The muscles in Richard's jaw flexed in anger.

"They need to eliminate Kahlan and me so that they can rampage unrestrained across our world, hunting our species to extinction. That's one reason we need to leave. By leaving I hope to confuse them. Since they are focused on us, the sooner we leave the palace, the less the danger to the people here. At least for now.

"Tell Mr. Burkett that the Lord Rahl has had to leave on an important mission. The man is used to taking care of the palace while the Lord Rahl is gone. He will know what to do. Help him in any way you can."

"I will see to it, Lord Rahl."

"With Kahlan and me gone, the First File will be the only protection for the people here at the palace. I don't want any of the First File to leave the palace for any reason. I'm counting on you and the First File to stand here in my place and protect everyone. I will be the magic against magic, doing what is necessary to end the threat."

Lieutenant Dolan, looking resolute, clapped a fist to the leather armor over his heart.

"The Mord-Sith will protect us from here on out. You and the men must see to protecting the people here."

The man reluctantly saluted again, tapping his fist to his heart.

Richard turned to Berdine. "Let's go."

40

Berdine immediately started down the corridor. The ranks of heavily armed men all moved to the sides of the broad passageway for her and her charges. Nyda went in front with Berdine. Kahlan, holding Richard's hand, was next, with Vika right behind her. Shale, Rikka, Vale, and Cassia took up the rear guard.

The entire way past all the soldiers to either side of the corridor, all standing with their backs to the wall to make room, Kahlan met the eyes of each man in turn. There was not one who averted their gaze. That much of it was a relief. She hoped they could escape the People's Palace without the Golden Goddess seeing them leaving through someone's eyes. As she had learned as a little girl being taught combat strategy by her father, King Wyborn, confusing the enemy was always a valuable tactic.

Berdine led them at a near run down side halls and narrow stairwells and through a labyrinth of dark and deserted passageways as they wound their way ever lower and across the restricted section of the palace. Everyone followed in silence. They all knew the dangers they were leaving behind and the ones they might encounter along the way. They watched for any threats as they moved as silently as possible.

Kahlan was excited to finally have a plan that she knew could work. The Sisters of the Light could be overbearing and full of themselves at times, but they were loyal to Richard and to life. They had fought valiantly in the war. She was confident they would face this new threat with determination and grit.

Kahlan wished so much, as she had so many times, that Richard's grandfather were still with them. Zedd had been an important part of her life ever since she met him. He had watched over her in ways that no other could. The wily old wizard had wormed his way into her heart from the first. But in a way, with Richard, she still had part of Zedd with her.

With a great sense of relief, they finally reached the sliph's room without being seen or being attacked. Kahlan had feared that the goddess would somehow try to stop them. But with only the Mord-Sith and Shale with them, there had been no eyes able to watch where they went, rendering the goddess blind. While the protection of the First File would be valuable, the risk of having the goddess see or hear what they were doing through one of them was now too great.

Without delay, Richard crossed the ancient room to the waist-high, round wall of the massive well. He leaned over the stone cap and put the silver wristbands together at his wrists. They began to glow brighter until Kahlan could see the shadows of his bones right through his flesh.

"Sliph!" he called down into the darkness. "I need you!" His voice echoed up from the well and around the domed room.

Shale looked especially tense, not knowing what to expect. Kahlan twisted her fingers together, worried that maybe the sliph might not come, or maybe she wasn't even there anymore. Shale, now knowing what Richard was doing, gave Kahlan a puzzled frown. Kahlan thought it would be best for her to wait and see it for herself.

As they waited in silence, pebbles and dirt on the stone floor started dancing as a vibration rose up from deep below. With building intensity, the whole room reverberated with a droning rumble. Dust fell from joints in the stone walls and domed ceiling.

With a roar of tremendous speed the silver sliph shot up from the depths of her well, stopping abruptly at the top rather than surging out. The silvery, liquid surface calmed, and then a lump of it rose up into the air. A beautiful silver face formed. A silver arm reached out and cupped Richard's face.

"Master, it is good to see you again," she said in her beguiling voice. "Come, we will travel. You will be pleased."

Richard held an arm back to the rest of them waiting by the wall. "We all need to travel. We need to go right away."

For the first time, it seemed, the sliph looked around and saw that there were eight women with him, or possibly she'd seen them before and simply didn't care about anyone but Richard. Now that she thought about it, Kahlan realized that was probably it. She fumed silently at the way the sliph smiled at Richard.

"All of you wish to travel?"

"Yes," Richard hurriedly said for everyone, as he motioned with an arm to urge them all closer. "We all need to travel. I would be very pleased if you would take us all. We're in a hurry."

Shale, looking quite alarmed, took a step back.

"Where do you wish to travel?" the sliph asked in that silky, silvery voice that for some reason grated on Kahlan's nerves.

"The Keep," Richard said. "I would be very pleased if you would take us all to the Wizard's Keep."

"I know the place," she cooed to him. "I can take you there. But you know you can't take that sword." She slipped her arm around behind him in a familiar way to touch the scabbard.

Richard pressed his lips tight for a moment. "I know. I'll have to leave it here until we can return."

He pulled the baldric off over his head. "Now that the blade has touched death," he told Kahlan, "I think I could take it, but with so much at stake, I fear to risk it." He leaned the scabbard up against the stone wall.

Kahlan didn't like the idea of him leaving the sword, but she remembered how in the past taking it with him nearly cost him his life. He was right, there was too much at stake.

"Come closer," the sliph said to everyone, her voice more businesslike, not nearly as soft and smooth as when she spoke to Richard.

All the Mord-Sith approached to stand before the stone wall of the well. The sliph's silver arm reached out, her fingers gently passing from one to another, brushing each forehead briefly.

"You all have what is required to travel."

Richard hooked Shale's arm under his and pulled her closer. Her eyes were wide with shock at seeing the sliph and hearing it speak. Such a creature, created by ancient wizards, was obviously something she had never encountered before, and she was more than a little wary of it. It had to be incomprehensible to her.

"Is this safe?" she whispered to Richard.

"It is for me," the sliph said with a smooth, silvery smile before sliding her silver fingers across Shale's smooth brow. Shale winced but stood her ground. The sliph pulled her hand back. "She cannot travel. She doesn't have the required magic."

"What is she talking about?" said Shale with sudden displeasure. "I'm a sorceress. I have the gift. Obviously, I have magic."

Richard shook his head. "You misunderstand. You need both Additive and Subtractive Magic to travel in the sliph."

Shale took a step back. "Subtractive Magic? Are you crazy?"

Richard waved a hand to dismiss her concern as he climbed up to stand on the stone wall. "I can give you enough of it to make it possible for you to travel. Don't worry. I've done it before."

As Richard was reassuring Shale, the sliph reached out to run a hand across Kahlan's brow.

"She may not travel," the silver face announced with a hint of distaste.

Richard had just helped Vika up beside him. He turned to frown at the sliph, then held an arm out toward Kahlan. "What are you talking about? Kahlan has traveled before many times. Of course she can travel."

"Not now."

Richard growled his impatience. "Why not?"

"Because she is pregnant. She and the two babies growing in her would die in me if she were to try to travel."

Richard turned with a look that locked Kahlan's breath in her lungs. Richard stood frozen with a look of shock on his face as he stared down at her. She suddenly felt hot all over. Her fingers and toes tingled. She thought she might pass out.

Kahlan forced herself to speak. "It's all right, Richard. You and Vika go. I will stay here. Shale and my sisters of the Agiel will protect me. I will have your sword. You must travel to the Keep to get help. You must. It's our only chance."

Richard hadn't moved a muscle as he stared at her. The room rang with a terrible silence. No one said a word.

The Mord-Sith were all staring at her, but Kahlan could only look into Richard's gray eyes.

She swallowed again, desperately trying to hold back tears as she took a step back away from the sliph's well. "I love you. Now go."

41

"You have to get to the Keep," Kahlan told Richard, fighting to get the words out past the lump in her throat. "Hurry. I'll be all right. Take the sliph and go."

Richard hadn't said a word. He seemed frozen in place, standing there on the top of the stone wall around the sliph.

"I'm sorry you can't travel in me, too, Mother Confessor," the sliph said in her silken voice while showing a smooth, silvery smile, "but you and your babies would die in me."

Kahlan thought the sliph sounded a bit too satisfied that Kahlan couldn't travel with Richard.

The Golden Goddess wanted to end Richard and Kahlan's line of magic. She would do anything to kill them both, but she would be especially ferocious about killing their children should they have any. Those children were more than Kahlan's longtime wish; they were a promise of a future with magic to protect their world.

Kahlan struggled to hold back tears of crushing disappointment that she couldn't travel in the sliph and get to the Wizard's Keep. The Keep was a place of safety. Besides the Sisters of the Light and other gifted people there, the Keep itself had powerful shields. The massive Wizard's Keep was designed to protect the First Wizard, and by extension his loved ones and children. They felt sure they would be safe there from the Golden Goddess and the Glee. Richard and Kahlan's children would be safe there to live and grow, to run through the halls, laughing, as Kahlan had done as a little girl, while Richard found a way to put an end to the threat from the goddess and her kind.

But because she was pregnant, Kahlan couldn't travel in the sliph. The Keep suddenly seemed very, very far away.

"I will take Lord Rahl," the sliph cooed. She circled a quicksilver arm around Richard's waist as he stood as if paralyzed on the stone wall of her well, staring down at Kahlan. "As you say, Mother Confessor, you can remain behind while I take him to the Keep."

Unable to stand the tension under Richard's penetrating gaze, Kahlan yelled, "Go!"

Despite her best efforts, tears were beginning to well up in her eyes. She knew she wouldn't be able to hold them back for much longer. She wanted him to leave before she lost control of her emotions.

Shale looked from Kahlan back to Richard. "I will protect her, Lord Rahl, while you go get help."

"We will protect her too," Cassia said as she nodded her agreement with Shale. She stepped closer to Kahlan. "With our lives."

Vika, standing on the wall next to Richard, said, "I will go with Lord Rahl and protect him."

Vika looked over at him, uncertain if she should jump into the roiling silver waters of the sliph ahead of him, or wait.

Kahlan's lower lip began to quiver. "Go and get help, Richard, would you, please? I'll have your sword. I know how to use it and it has served me well in your absence in the past. I'll have plenty of protection. I'll be fine until you can get back to me."

Richard finally pulled away from the silver arm the sliph had around him. When he did, it shrank back, seeming to melt down into the pool and become part of what looked like nothing so much as liquid silver sloshing in the well. The glossy silver face, which reflected the room around it, showed no emotion.

Free of the sliph's arm, Richard hopped down off the short stone wall and walked across the room, his raptor gaze seeing no one but her. Kahlan couldn't stop trembling. Dreading what he might say, she involuntarily backed away a step.

When Richard reached her, he softly enclosed her in his strong arms and then pulled her tight to him. She could no longer hold back the tears as she buried her face against him.

"I'm sorry, Richard," she blurted out. "I'm sorry I didn't tell you. I couldn't, not in the middle of—"

Richard pressed her head to his shoulder. "Hush now. No need to cry about something so wonderful."

"But—"

"I'm not leaving you for anything."

"But you must get to the Keep."

"We'll figure something out. I'm not leaving you, not at a time like this."

"I didn't want to tell you. You need to be able to protect us. I didn't want to burden you with this on top of everything else. I didn't want it to be a distraction."

Richard let out a soft laugh as he briefly hugged her tighter. "It's not a distraction, Kahlan. It's motivation." He pulled back, holding her by her arms as he looked in her eyes. "The sliph said babies. Not baby. Babies."

Kahlan nodded. "I'm pregnant with twins."

Richard's eyebrows lifted a little in surprise. His smile warmed her heart and, in that instant, dispelled all her terror and fear. She suddenly felt the full joy of it again.

"A boy and a girl," Shale said.

He turned a serious frown on her. "You knew?"

Kahlan put a finger against his jaw and turned his face back to her. "I made her swear that she wouldn't tell you. I guess I made the same mistake the goddess made up in the library."

His smile returned as he gazed into her eyes again. "What mistake is that?"

"I underestimated you."

His smile widened at that.

Kahlan grew sober. "But Richard, you still need to get to the Keep. You can't stay here if you hope to stop the goddess. That's what matters. There are gifted there who may be able to help. The Sisters of the Light are there. Maybe you could make a quick trip there in the sliph and bring back some of the Sisters."

"You are what matters," he said softly as he gently pulled Kahlan back into his arms.

She buried her face against him, now with tears of relief and joy.

"This is what we have been fighting for since we first met in the Hartland woods," he told her. "For life, for the right of life to continue. And then for our right to continue, for our own happiness."

Holding on tightly to him, Kahlan had never loved him more.

She should have known.

42

"What do you wish to do, Lord Rahl?" Vika asked. He finally drew back from Kahlan. "What my grandfather would have said to do, of course."

Vika pulled her single long blond braid forward over her shoulder and held it in her fist as she looked down at him. Finally, she hopped down off the short stone wall.

"I don't understand, Lord Rahl."

"Zedd, my grandfather, always said to think of the solution, not the problem. The problem is that Kahlan can't travel in the sliph. We're focused on that problem."

"I didn't know your grandfather." Vika looked at a loss. "I'm sorry, Lord Rahl, but I don't know what that means."

"It means that instead of thinking of the problem—that the sliph can't take us all—we instead need to think of the solution. I'm hoping we will be safe at the Keep—Kahlan especially—so we need to get there. If the problem is that she can't go in the sliph, the solution is that we have to get there another way."

Vika brightened. "I will get horses and supplies together."

Richard smiled at her. "Good thinking, Vika. That is the solution."

Shale stepped closer. "Lord Rahl, won't that be dangerous? Traveling all the way there? I'm from the Northern Waste, which has enough of its own dangers, but I've heard very ugly things about many of the places down here. I've heard that D'Hara is dangerous enough in its own right, but the Midlands is a savage and wild place and traveling across it can be quite perilous."

Kahlan knew the truth of that. When she used to travel the Midlands, she always had Giller, an experienced wizard, with her at all times for protection. Richard was a wizard, of course, and more powerful than Giller had ever been, but Giller did have the advantage of having been trained his whole life in the use of his craft and in the dangers of the Midlands.

Richard had been raised in Westland, far away from any knowledge of magic, and the gift didn't work the same way in him as it did in others. Unlike a typical gifted person, he couldn't necessarily call upon his ability at will—both because of his lack of a lifetime of training and because his gift was fundamentally different. Being the gift of a war wizard, his power came forth mostly as a function of rage.

"I can testify to the fact that the Midlands is indeed dangerous," Kahlan said. "But it's also a place of beauty and wonder."

Shale shot her a cynical look. "Beauty won't save us. The key word in what you said is 'dangerous.' We would have to cross a lot of dangerous territory."

"Well, it's obviously dangerous for us to stay in the People's Palace," Richard told the sorceress. "We will be under constant threat and unrelenting attack as long as we're here. Here, the goddess can keep an eye on us, so to speak, through everyone in the palace without the gift. That's pretty much everyone. She can watch us and pick a time to attack when we are at our weakest. We can never have a moment of safety, here.

"There are gifted at the Keep who may be able to help us, and perhaps more importantly, the Keep has numerous powerful shields of every kind that can protect Kahlan and the babies. There are some shields here at the People's Palace, but not nearly enough. It simply isn't safe for us here. We need to get to a place of safety so we can figure out how to combat this threat. That place is the Wizard's Keep in Aydindril. We can't go in the sliph, so we either walk or go on horseback. There is no other way. It's as simple as that."

Shale crossed her arms as she considered his words for a moment, visibly cooling as she did so. "You're right. We're not safe here. I can't offer any better suggestion."

Berdine scowled at him with fury in her blue eyes. "Well, I'm going, too. I'll not be left behind this time. I'm going."

Richard turned a smile to the concern that was so obvious in her expression. "Of course you're going. I wouldn't think of going without you, Berdine. We're all going."

"I'll organize a detachment of the First File to escort us," Cassia offered. "How many soldiers do you wish to take with us?"

With one arm around Kahlan's waist, Richard took in all the tense faces watching him. "None. We can't risk it."

Cassia leaned in as if she hadn't heard him correctly. "Can't risk it? Can't risk having protection? It's a long way across a lot of dangerous territory. A unit of cavalry and soldiers of the First File would act as a deterrent to those dangers. A show of force would prevent a fight from happening in the first place. The last thing we want is a fight. You or the Mother Confessor could be hurt or even killed in a fight. Why wouldn't you want to take adequate protection?"

"Because the goddess has the ability to use soldiers to spy on us, just the same as she can use anyone else. If she knows precisely where we are, she can send the Glee to attack us out in the open in the Midlands. Worse, just as she used Nolo to try to stab Kahlan to death when he was alone with her, the goddess could use one of those men to attack us when we least expect it. Whereas Nolo was rather inept with a knife, the soldiers of the First File are experts with their weapons. Those soldiers wouldn't be protecting our backs, they would be a threat when our backs are turned.

"The Golden Goddess only has to be successful once and Kahlan is dead. The goddess will then have accomplished her objective of destroying the chances of our magic living on. That would ensure the eventual extinction of everyone in this world."

"He's right," Kahlan said, the strength finally coming back to her now that Richard knew she was pregnant and was determined to protect her and the twins. More importantly, it was also clear from his reasoning that her pregnancy wasn't going to be the distraction she had feared. "It's not a matter of their loyalty. We know beyond any doubt that they are loyal. It's a matter of the ability of the goddess to bend them to her will and use them."

Richard turned back to the sliph. Her smooth silver face was still watching him, and the shiny surface of that face reflected the people watching both of them.

"Sliph, you may go back into your sleep. Thank you for coming."

"Even if the Mother Confessor can't travel, I can still take you to the Keep, Lord Rahl. Come, we will travel. You will be pleased."

"I would like that very much, but I can't leave Kahlan. I must stay to protect her. Since I can't have the pleasure of traveling in you, you may go back into your sleep until the day when I can travel in you."

Kahlan knew that Richard understood the unique nature of the sliph. He knew how to talk to her in a way that she not only understood but he could put it in a way that didn't lose her trust. Kahlan just didn't like the nature of the necessary flattery.

"Thank you, Master. I'm sorry you won't be traveling in me. You would have been pleased."

"Yes, I know I would have," he said. "I hope to one day soon have the pleasure of traveling in you. Until then, you may go back to be with your soul."

The silver face smiled. "Thank you, Master."

With that, the shiny silver face seemed to melt back down into the ever-moving liquid silver filling the well, and then the entire mass of her swiftly sank out of sight with accelerating speed.

Shale planted her fists on her hips. "Someday you are going to have to explain that to me."

"If you like," he said, "but I can tell you right now you will not be any more pleased to know the story."

When she let her arms fall back to her sides, Richard gestured around at all the women watching him. "From now on, the only ones we can trust are the nine of us. We all have magic that prevents the Golden Goddess from getting into our minds or seeing through our eyes."

"Do you really think that if we took soldiers who are loyal to you," Shale pressed, "that the goddess could actually use them?"

Richard shrugged. "Maybe not, but are you willing to risk it?"

"Are you willing to risk danger to the Mother Confessor by traveling dangerous lands?" the sorceress asked.

Richard frowned at her. "So then, you relied on soldiers for your protection in the dangerous Northern Waste?"

"No. I relied only on myself." Shale sighed when she realized what he had just done. "I see your point."

"You told me when we first met that when you were meditating you could feel some strange entity probing, trying to get into your mind, but it couldn't. Remember?"

"Yes."

"That had to be the goddess. Your gift protected you and she couldn't get in. None of the soldiers have the benefit of that protection. We in this room are the only ones we can trust to be free of the goddess's control."

Richard finally retrieved his sword from where he had left it leaning against the stone wall of the well. He slipped the baldric back over his head before attaching the scabbard at his left hip. He looked at each of them in turn. "Until we get to the Keep and the gifted there who may be able to help, it must be us nine against everyone else because everyone else is a potential threat."

Vika turned a sly smile to her sister Mord-Sith. "We are Mord-Sith. We have no desire to babysit soldiers, anyway." She turned back to Richard. "Unless you think it best to travel on foot, we are going to need to get horses. That's not a problem at the palace."

"Except that Lieutenant Dolan and the First File know we're leaving the palace," Richard said, "so they will likely assume we're leaving on horseback. That means we have to assume the goddess knows that as well and will be watching for it. But she won't know which direction we go unless the soldiers see us leaving. It would obviously be easier and quicker getting to the Keep if we had horses, but taking them would mean that soldiers would by necessity see us collecting them. Any number of the First File standing watch on the high ramparts would easily spot us leaving on horseback and know which way we went."

Kahlan's concern was evident in her expression. "That means the goddess could see all of that through any of their eyes."

Richard agreed with a nod. "Getting away on horses without being seen is a problem."

"Then stop thinking of the problem, and think instead of the solution," Shale said.

"What would the solution be, then?" Richard asked her.

Shale leaned toward him. "Think. Who do you have with you on this journey?"

The way the sorceress asked the question reminded him of so many gifted people who had taught him valuable lessons.

Richard shrugged, not sure what she meant. "We have the nine of us. Kahlan, me, six Mord-Sith—"

Shale flashed him a cunning smile. "And me."

43

The stables were partway across the sprawling city-palace. Once they had horses, then Shale would need to do her part, but before they reached the stables they needed to avoid being seen by people throughout the palace. Being spotted would expose them to the risk that the goddess could also see them and send Glee to attack.

To keep out of sight after leaving the room with the sliph's well, the nine of them had to make their way through a labyrinth of underground passageways and tunnels that few people other than the Mord-Sith knew about or used, then climb iron ladders in ventilation shafts and a series of ancient, rusty iron spiral service stairs. They managed to remain unseen the entire journey through the rarely used areas of the palace.

Nyda, in the lead, brought the party to a halt when she reached a small metal access door. She carefully pulled it open just enough to peek out. Once satisfied it was safe, she pulled open the door, letting short, wavy-haired Berdine go through first. The tall, blond Nyda went next. When Richard poked his head through, he saw that they were behind some of the storage buildings. Beyond was a staging area and then a number of buildings with stables. The buildings had roofs to protect them from the open sky above, which revealed fading daylight. The first of the strange, new stars in that sky were just beginning to appear.

Not far away, between the dark shape of the buildings to each side of them, was a large manure pile waiting for eventual use in the many gardens throughout the palace grounds. Besides the food transported in by vendors who brought it up the internal passage, the gardens and greenhouses in the palace were an abundant source of fresh food to feed all the people living in the palace. The manure fed those crops.

That large manure pile served to hide the nine of them, but because of the stink it wasn't a pleasant place to hide. Richard reminded himself that it wasn't nearly as bad as the horrific stench of the remains deep down in the foundation area.

"Something smells funny," Shale said.

Richard turned to her with an incredulous look. "Maybe it has something to do with this big pile of manure right in front of us?"

As Shale leaned out to peer into the distance, the sarcasm didn't seem to register with her. "No. It's something else," she murmured, half to herself.

"Like what?" he asked.

The sorceress's attention finally returned to him. She shook her head unhappily. "I'm not sure. It's not something I've exactly smelled before, but for some reason I feel like I should know what it is."

Richard realized she was serious, but it didn't make any sense and he didn't want to take the time to discuss the unknowable. Instead, he advanced in a crouch and then leaned out from behind a manure cart to survey the area. He wanted them to be able to get out of the palace and on their way to the Wizard's Keep without being seen. Anyone who saw them meant that it was possible the goddess could see them, too. If they could get away cleanly, then the journey to the protection of the Keep's shields and the gifted would be that much less hazardous.

In the distance Richard saw soldiers on horseback just returning from patrol, likely around the base of the plateau. Horses were also occasionally used in the palace's special passageways meant for mounted soldiers, enabling them to quickly get to distant areas or trouble spots. Sometimes they used ramps up through the inside of the plateau that were also used exclusively by troops. Less commonly they used the narrow road that wound around the outside of the plateau.

That was the road they were going to need to use to get down to the Azrith Plain. One of the problems with that was that there was a drawbridge with soldiers stationed at it. Richard was trusting that Shale had some witch woman's trick to make those soldiers think they were someone else, or even not see them at all. He didn't care what she did, only that it worked.

Vika pointed at stable workers taking the horses as the tired soldiers dismounted. "Over that way, where the man is lighting the lamps on the outside wall of the stables, is one of the buildings where the fresh horses are kept for men to take out on patrol."

Kahlan rested a hand on the hilt of the knife sheathed at her belt as she came up in a crouch close to Richard and Vika. As beautiful as Richard thought she looked in the singular dress of the Mother Confessor, she looked just as good to him in her traveling clothes with a knife sheathed at her side. Some of her long hair fell forward over her shoulder as she carefully leaned out to take a look.

"How many fresh horses do you think are in there?" she asked. "Do you think there are enough?"

Vika looked a little surprised by the question. "There are a lot of stables all throughout this one area. There are hundreds and hundreds of horses. I'm not sure of the exact number. With as many horses as I've seen here and other areas combined while living and working at the palace under Darken Rahl's rule there might even be thousands."

Richard was jarred by her saying "while living and working at the palace under Darken Rahl's rule." Before Richard defeated Darken Rahl, as under the tyrants of the House of Rahl before him, the work of a Mord-Sith living at the People's Palace was the work of torturing people for information or simply because the Lord Rahl wanted them tortured to death as punishment. The Mord-Sith were experts at keeping their captives on the cusp between life and death for prolonged periods of time to extend their agony.

The Mord-Sith didn't come by that work easily. They themselves were taken captive as young women and broken through years of the same kind of torture they learned to use on others. They became the chattel of evil men—property, weapons those men used for their own ends.

That training eventually drove those women to madness. Richard had once been the captive of an especially ruthless Mord-Sith, Denna, who had introduced him into that hopeless, surreal world of madness.

Vika's words had brought all those unwelcome memories unexpectedly flooding back to him. As he had done so often, Richard forced those memories from his mind.

"Vika is right," Berdine said as she snuck up closer behind them. "The palace must have at least a thousand horses in all. For all I know, it's possible the true number is twice that. And that's only counting the horses belonging to the First File."

"Then they shouldn't miss the dozen and a half we'll need," Shale said as she and the rest of the impatient Mord-Sith, ducking low, joined Richard.

Berdine gave her a reproachful look. "You think cavalrymen don't know every horse? Know how many there are, and which stables house them? They live with those horses. Many sleep in barracks at the rear of the stables so as to be at hand should they be needed on a moment's notice. They would miss one set of reins, to say nothing of a saddle. One missing horse would be noticed immediately."

"We aren't out to steal them," Richard said. "We merely need you to collect what we need. The stables provide horses and supplies to the Lord Rahl all the time. That's what you are doing this time as well. It's nothing unusual."

Vika nodded. "I got the horses for you the last time, remember?"

"When we went down to see Nolo's people," he said as he turned back to watch the stablehands leading the horses into the stables to unsaddle, water, and feed them.

Vika nodded. "That's right. I've been to the stables many times before. The soldiers and workers aren't going to dare to ask a Mord-Sith why she wants a dozen and a half horses and supplies. I've been here a number of times and they know it's always on orders from Lord Rahl. Not you, Lord Rahl—your father. That Lord Rahl. Anyway, they won't give a second thought to my request for horses and supplies."

"That hardly seems like the secrecy we need," Kahlan said. "The whole point is that we don't want the goddess to know that we're collecting horses, otherwise she will be watching to see where we are headed. If these men know, then it's possible if not probable she would know as well."

Shale gestured dismissively. "Leave that to me."

Richard looked over at her. "What can you do?"

"She's a witch woman," Kahlan reminded him in a low voice so that the stablehands wouldn't hear her.

Richard turned his frown toward her. "What does that have to do with it?"

Kahlan put a hand on the side of his shoulder. "Witch women are masters of illusion, remember? People see what a witch woman wants them to see. Red appeared beautiful and young to me, much like Shale, but she appeared to others as an elderly woman."

When Richard looked back over his shoulder at Shale, she showed him a sly smile. "Let me worry about the solution to this problem."

Richard realized that he knew what Kahlan meant. Witch women could make you see what they wanted you to see. More than once Shota had appeared to him as his mother. He knew what Shota looked like, or at least how she presented herself to him when she wasn't creating the illusion that she was his mother. But he couldn't be entirely sure if that was her real appearance or not. He suspected that the same thing was true of Shale.

"All right," he said to Vika. "Why don't you go and tell the stable master that you need a dozen and a half horses, with saddles for nine of them. And supplies. We will need traveling supplies—food, water, sleeping gear. He doesn't need to know who it's all for. Let him assume what he will. Have them hitched over there at that staging area. Once he gets what we need, we will let Shale do her part so we can collect the horses and leave. The sooner the better, so be quick about it."

Vika gave him the kind of smooth, confident smile that few people other than a Mord-Sith could do so well. "No problem. Wait here. I'll be back as soon as I arrange it."

44

Shale leaned in impatiently. "What could be taking her so long?"

Richard let out a frustrated sigh. "I can't imagine. They should have been able to have the horses saddled and the supplies ready long ago."

"Could the soldiers or stable workers be giving her any grief?" Kahlan asked.

Richard turned an incredulous look on her. "A Mord-Sith. Give a Mord-Sith grief."

Kahlan let out an exasperated sigh. "I guess that was kind of a silly question."

It had long since grown dark. For a time, the stars had been out, but as they waited clouds had rolled in. It was starting to smell like rain was on the way.

Richard leaned out a little, scanning the area, but he still couldn't see Vika anywhere. What was just as troubling, he couldn't see any sign that the stable workers were hurrying to carry out her instructions. He had long ago expected to see the freshly saddled horses brought out to the staging area while the supplies were collected and loaded.

Vika had walked over to the buildings, around the corner of one of them, and that was the last they saw of her.

"Maybe they're having trouble getting supplies together," Kahlan suggested. "Maybe they had to send someone down to the storehouses to get the kind of traveling food we need."

Richard nodded as he watched the entire area, looking for any sign of Vika. "I suppose that could be the case. It could be that the kind of supplies she asked for have to be collected from a distant storehouse.

But still, I can't imagine Vika not coming back and telling us what the delay was all about."

"Well, maybe she slipped and fell and hit her head or something," Shale whispered. "Maybe she's hurt and needs help."

Richard bit his lower lip as he considered. The same thought had occurred to him as well, but he hadn't heard anything. It seemed like if she had fallen, then in the quiet of the night they would have heard her calling out, or something. Besides that, there were a few stable workers occasionally coming and going from all the buildings. If she had fallen, it seemed like one of them would have seen her on the ground. A Mord-Sith in red leather would be hard to miss. Although, it had grown dark...

An impatient Berdine leaned close. "Lord Rahl, it couldn't possibly have taken this long. This doesn't make sense. She could have had a hundred horses saddled and out here by now."

"More than that," Kahlan added, "there hasn't been any sign that the stable staff are seeing to her orders. They all seem to be calmly going about their other work. No one is rushing to take care of the things she would have asked for. Surely men would have come running when a Mord-Sith demanded horses to be saddled. Besides that, we would have seen other people rushing off to get supplies. No one is rushing anywhere."

"You're all right." Richard scratched his eyebrow as he considered what to do. "Something is wrong, I can feel it. I need to find out what's going on."

He abruptly stood up. His feet were numb from squatting down for so long. He rotated each ankle in turn to get the blood started back into his feet as he looked around. All five of the Mord-Sith stood up with him. He turned to Kahlan and Shale, still crouched down behind the manure wagon.

"Berdine, you come with me. Shale, Rikka, Nyda, Cassia, Vale—in case there is some kind of trouble please stay close to Kahlan for now. For all we know, one of the Glee could have snatched her. It shouldn't take long to find out what's going on."

The four Mord-Sith squatted back down near Kahlan. If there was any kind of trouble, he knew that in a heartbeat they would all bring their Agiel up into a fist and at the ready to defend her.

Richard gestured. "Come on, Berdine. It all looks peaceful enough, so something is obviously wrong. Keep a sharp lookout for anything that doesn't look right to you. Be ready for one of those hateful things to pop out of nowhere."

Berdine nodded and then fell in beside him after he went around the manure cart and started across the open stable area. The aroma of haystacks near each building was a pleasant change from the smell of manure. They hadn't gone far when some of the men saw them. They all abruptly changed course from what they were doing and rushed over to Richard and Berdine.

"Lord Rahl!" one of them called back into the quiet night in case any of the other workers hadn't seen him. "It's Lord Rahl!"

So much for stealth, Richard thought. Men who had heard the call ran out of buildings. In short order there were fifteen or twenty men gathered around and more in the distance were coming.

"What can we do for you, Lord Rahl?" an older man with a flat cloth hat asked. "Do you wish some horses saddled and brought out?"

"Actually," he said, still looking around for any sign of her, "I sent a Mord-Sith to do just that quite a while ago. Her name is Vika. Why didn't you get the horses for her?"

The men all shared puzzled looks.

The older man pulled off his cap and smoothed back his thin crop of gray hair. "A Mord-Sith?" He frowned as he gestured at Berdine. "This would be the first of those ladies we've seen all night, Lord Rahl." He turned one way, then the other, looking around at his men. "Anyone see the Mord-Sith?"

The men all shook their heads, mumbling that they hadn't.

Richard gestured. "I thought I saw her go that way, by that building. Would some of you take a look, please, and make sure she didn't fall and hurt herself or something."

"Stranger things have happened," the older man confirmed.

Men ran off to do Richard's bidding. He saw some of then trot off to go between the buildings, checking where he said he had last seen her. It wasn't long before they all straggled by, looking disappointed and shaking their heads. They all reported that they had found nothing.

Richard put his hands on his hips as he looked around. It didn't make any sense. Vika couldn't have vanished into thin air. A frightening thought that had been in the back of his mind was beginning to seem like the most likely explanation. Could it be that one of the Glee had snatched her and taken her back to the goddess? That seemed far-fetched, especially since he didn't even know if that was possible. Finally, he had an idea.

"I need something to see with," he said to the gathered men. "Bring me a torch or lantern, please."

"We try not to have torches around the horses and all the hay," the gray-haired man said as he replaced his hat on his head. "We have plenty of lanterns, though."

When he gestured the order, one of the men rushed to retrieve a lantern. He pulled one off a hook on the corner of the closest building and rushed back to hand it to Richard.

"Thanks. You can all go back to what you were doing. I'll take it from here."

Lantern in hand, Richard marched off to have a look for himself. Berdine followed close on his heels.

Going around the building where he had last seen Vika, Richard started searching the soft ground looking for any sign. In the shadows between the buildings, and with the clouds, it was quite dark, but the lantern gave him enough light to see what he needed to see. There were a lot of footprints. Most of those prints were older, while a few were from the men who had just checked for Richard, looking for Vika.

Before long, the confusion of prints sorted themselves out in his mind and Richard found what he was looking for: prints from Vika's boots. He recognized the size and the shape. None of the prints from the men's boots looked similar. Had there been more light, he would have been able to recognize Vika's unique gait from the angle and depth of the impressions made by her boots, along with her height and weight.

He followed her footprints between the buildings to the end where she had turned behind the building to Richard's left. He also saw larger prints from a man, but it was hard to tell if Vika had been following him or he had been following her.

Then Richard saw something that made the hair on the back of his neck stand on end.

45

Richard squatted down, holding the lantern out close to the ground to better highlight the ridges and depressions. There, in the soft dirt, he could see where Vika had come to a stop, and a short distance beyond that, where she had gone to her knees.

His blood ran cold when he saw that the man's prints tracked around her while she had been there on her knees to turn and stand before her. In his mind, as he stared at the prints, Richard could picture a big man standing over Vika.

It made no sense, but the tracks were clear in the story they told.

"Someone has taken her," he whispered to himself.

Berdine leaned in with alarm. "Taken her? That's crazy. Who in the world could take a Mord-Sith?"

Richard gestured behind, then along the building, and finally to the prints on the ground before him. "Her footprints came from between the buildings, where I saw her go, then around behind the back of this building to right here."

Berdine smoothed a hand back over her hair as she straightened after peering at the ground. "If you say so, Lord Rahl. I can read books, but I can't read footprints."

"Well, I can. Look," he said urging Berdine to lean in again as he pointed. "See there, those impressions? That's where Vika walked up to here and right there is where she knelt down."

"Knelt down?" Her nose wrinkled skeptically. "Are you sure?"

"Of course I'm sure. See this?" He hovered his hand over the indentations made by Vika's knees. "See this depression? That's not a footprint. It's a knee print. It's deeper where her knees bend and gets shallower as it goes back toward her ankles. See those little round impressions? Those are from the toes of her boots as she was on her knees. She knelt down right here."

Berdine squinted in the lantern light. "I guess I can see what you're talking about. It does make sense now that you explain the depressions in the ground."

He touched the edge of the indentations. "See this? You can see where the wrinkles of her leather outfit as she knelt made these rows of little marks."

Berdine leaned in, looking more closely this time. "All right, I see what you're talking about now. But why would Vika kneel down in the dirt back here, in such a dark, out-of-the-way place?"

With his fingertips, Richard touched a couple of the other footprints. "These prints here are from a man who is big, but not as big as me. They come in here beside Vika's prints—not in front of or behind, but beside her prints—then..." He leaned over to point out the important part. "...then, see here? He walked around Vika right here, when she went to her knees. Right there. See that? See the prints turned around right there, the toes pointing toward her, right in front of her knee prints?

"That shows that he stood in front of Vika when she was on her knees."

Berdine blinked as the meaning of it all sank in.

"Look at these prints here. After he stood there in front of her, she got back up. See that sideways indentation? That's the side of the sole of her boot pushing the dirt sideways from her putting weight on her right foot as she got back to her feet in front of the man. That's her prints standing, then, right in front of where she had been kneeling, right in front of the man facing her."

Berdine was staring, her eyes wide. Her face had gone ashen.

Richard flicked a hand. "Then, the man's prints twist around and they both go off in that direction, down that way, with the man leading, Vika right behind him."

Berdine swallowed. Her blue eyes welled up with tears.

"He took her," she said in a meek voice choked with those tears. "Lord Rahl, he took her." She gasped back a sob. "It can't be, but that's the only explanation for why Vika would leave you without her protection, and why she would go to her knees like this."

Richard finally stood. He whistled for the others; then he looked down at Berdine. "Berdine, what are you talking about? Do you know something about this?"

She choked back another sob as the others rushed around the building and came to an abrupt halt, looking expectantly at the two of them. Richard signaled them to be quiet and wait.

"It can't be," Berdine said to no one in particular as she stared off in the direction he had taken her. "But it has to be."

She sounded forlorn and terrified. While Berdine was bubbly and cheerful, it was always filtered through a Mord-Sith's iron temperament. Richard had never seen her behave in such a normal human way. Human feelings were suppressed in Mord-Sith. But with Richard as the Lord Rahl, he always hoped that their humanity would return to them. He had seen a number of instances where it rose to the surface. This seemed to be one of those times, yet not a joyful one. It made him ache for all she had been through.

When he reached out and gently held her by her shoulders, he could feel her trembling. He shook her just enough to make her look up at him.

"Berdine, what are you saying? Do you know who took her?"

"Moravaska."

"Moravaska? Who is Moravaska?"

Her big eyes brimmed with tears. "Moravaska Michec."

Richard frowned at her. The tears began to run down her cheeks as she shook. He could only imagine what would make a Mord-Sith tremble in fear.

"Berdine, who is Moravaska Michec?"

Berdine wiped tears back off her cheek as she swallowed. Her eyes turned away from him in embarrassment for having shown such emotion.

"A bad man. A very, very bad man."

Kahlan gently circled a comforting arm around Berdine's shoulders as she looked back at Richard. "What's going on?"

When Richard saw the faces of the other Mord-Sith, there was no doubt that they all knew who Moravaska Michec was. But Berdine's reaction was the strongest.

He gestured to the tracks to explain it to Kahlan. "See here? These are Vika's tracks. She came around this building." He pointed. "She stopped and knelt down there. A man walked around in front of her while she was kneeling, and then the two of them walked away in that direction."

"Are you sure, Lord Rahl?" Shale asked, sounding more than a little skeptical. "You really believe you can tell all that just by looking at the ground?"

"Richard can track a cricket through a field of tall grass in a rainstorm at midnight," Kahlan said to the sorceress.

Shale arched a cynical eyebrow.

"Figure of speech," Kahlan said. "But Richard knows tracks. It's what he was raised doing, what he used to do as a woods guide. If Richard says that's what happened, then that's what happened."

Richard looked around at the Mord-Sith standing in a semicircle. "Who is Moravaska Michec?"

Nyda was the one who spoke up. "Michec was Vika's trainer. She was taken when she was twelve and given to Michec to be trained. He tortured her for three years. After that first phase of her training, he eventually tortured her mother to death in front of her, but after keeping her alive for a long, long time to numb Vika to another's pain. As her last stage of training to be Mord-Sith, when ordered, Vika had to torture her father, keeping him alive for a protracted period of time to demonstrate that she could keep a captive on the cusp of life and death for as long as she wanted. She was finally ordered by Michec to kill him. When she completed her training, and had been broken those three times, Michec took her as his mate."

Richard knew all too well about a Mord-Sith's training, but even so he stood in pain for a moment in the dragging silence. "Was Michec gifted?"

Nyda huffed. "Oh yes. That was part of how he was so easily able to control his trainees. Michec was feared here at the People's Palace.

Darken Rahl let him indulge his sick appetites, not merely with the Mord-Sith in training but on others as well. Darken Rahl ordinarily didn't trust having strongly gifted people around him, but Moravaska Michec was so loyal and devoted to the cause that Darken Rahl trusted him."

"Then that must have been how he captured her, here," Richard said. "With his gift and the power he had over her."

"She would have been kneeling in front of him," Nyda said in a flat tone that unlike Berdine's seemed devoid of all emotion, "so that he could have put a training collar back around her neck and attached a chain to it."

Richard knew all too well about the collar and chain.

In the terrible silence, Berdine, still turned away, said, "Vika wasn't the only one Moravaska Michec trained. Not the only one he took as his mate."

Now he understood Berdine's reaction.

"But Vika was with Hannis Arc," Richard said. "That's where I first came into contact with her. She was his most trusted protection, always at his side. When they had me captive for a time, I told her that her life could be her own. She eventually came to believe me. She's the one who killed Hannis Arc to join with us."

Nyda nodded. "Long before that, Vika belonged to Michec. He gave her to Hannis Arc on the condition that if and when he no longer had need of her services, she was to be returned to him. Hannis Arc liked the status of having a Mord-Sith at his side. But Vika always belonged to Moravaska Michec. She was his property."

Richard rested the palm of his left hand on the pommel of the sword in the scabbard at his left hip. "So then when she killed Hannis Arc, she was supposed to go back to Michec."

"Yes," Nyda said. "But she instead swore loyalty to you. Against all the training and despite being the property of Moravaska Michec."

Richard was incensed at such a concept. "She belongs to no one but herself."

"We have to go find her," Berdine said, the strength returning to her voice. "We have to."

"What we have to do," Shale said in a sympathetic but firm tone, "is get the horses and supplies we need and get away from the palace. It's dark. Sentries won't be able to see which way we ride off. I can help to make sure of it."

"That would mean the death of Vika," Richard said.

"A very long and torturous death," Nyda added.

Shale didn't shy away from Richard's glare. "Vika knows the possible price of her loyalty to you. She knows that her sacrifice might be necessary to protect you. It was what she chose. For your safety, for the Mother Confessor's safety, and for the future hope of everyone in this world carried in the gift of those babies, we need to get to the Keep. Delay would risk everything."

"We don't leave one of ours behind if there is any chance we can save them," Kahlan said with quiet authority.

"I understand, Mother Confessor, but—"

"We would come after you," Richard said in an equally quiet voice.

Staring up at him, Shale considered for a long moment. "I am a witch woman. No one would come after me."

"We would," he said without hesitation.

Her brow twitched as she seemed captured in his gaze, unable to look away. Finally, her voice returned.

"Let's go get Vika back."

46

The eight of them hurried through the halls and corridors of the palace urgently going after the ninth. Nyda and Rikka, both tall and blond, were in the lead, Richard, Kahlan, and Shale in the middle, with Vale, Berdine, and Cassia guarding them from the rear. They took the shortest route, which necessarily meant going through the public areas.

Even at night there were quite a number of people in the sprawling corridors. When they saw the five Mord-Sith in red leather, they kept their heads down and averted their eyes, wanting nothing to do with why they might be rushing through the halls. Richard couldn't help wondering if the Golden Goddess was also watching them. Right then, what mattered the most was not only getting Vika back, but stopping Michec from running free in the palace.

Without the Mord-Sith saying anything, Richard knew where they were headed. They were going to the Mord-Sith's traditional quarters. Vika would once have had quarters there. It seemed unlikely but possible that Moravaska Michec would have taken her back to her room and would be using the adjacent training room to punish her for ever thinking she could walk away from the master who owned her.

In places the cavernous corridors were open to the sky in order to fill the palace with light. Since it was long after dark, that left the lamps and the isolated, flickering light of torches the task of providing light in the corridors. Many of the shops located in the main corridors closed down at night, but a number of others stayed open for the customers who worked in the palace even in the dead of night. Each of the halls and passageways they used stretched nearly out of sight. Sometimes they took to the private passageways in order to take shortcuts.

Because the purpose of the shape of the palace was to function as a massive spell-form, there weren't convenient, direct routes from one place to another. At intervals, wide marble stairs provided a quick way up or down in order to get to other passageways that crossed over constricted areas so they could continue heading in the direction they needed to go.

In other places they passed statues of people in proud poses. The statues were made of carved and polished stone with different colors of veining, though they were predominantly white. In some areas the statues were twice life size. It had been a very long time since Richard had seen those particular statues. They reminded him in a way of the massive statue he had once carved.

Nyda led them past a sprawling square open to the sky above a small indoor forest. It was a large enough area that many of the trees were full grown, the branches reaching all the way up through the open roof. Mosses and ferns covered the ground. It was a convincing imitation of being outdoors in a beautiful grove. For a brief moment it reminded him of his forest home in Hartland.

"I've never seen such an indoor forest before," Shale said in amazement as they made their way along the path of clay tiles through the center of it. "I suppose there must be many different kinds of places here that would surprise me. I wouldn't have believed such a place existed inside the palace. Did you know this was in here?"

Richard nodded, not wanting to get into how he knew.

Nyda and Vale led them past an official palace dining room that never closed. It was for the exclusive use of the many people who worked at the palace, especially those who worked at night. Beyond the dining room, they hurried through the halls to another area open to the sky, with pillars supporting arches on all four sides.

Instead of a forest, under the open sky was a square made of short tiled walls filled with white sand raked in concentric lines around an irregular-shaped dark pitted rock in the center. On the top of the rock was a bell to call people to devotion—a devotion that now was key to keeping their world safe from the Golden Goddess and her predator race.

Devotions used to be hours long. Richard thought that was a waste of time and had shortened them to three repetitions, as was the custom when in the field away from the palace. He judged three repetitions to be more than enough to satisfy the magical connection between the people and the Lord Rahl.

When Nyda turned off the main corridor, she took them down a passageway that led them to a place Richard knew all too well.

"These are the Mord-Sith's quarters," Nyda said, in a quiet voice in case Michec should be in one of the nearby rooms.

"Do you know which one was Vika's room?" Richard asked.

Nyda gestured. "This one right here."

While everyone waited, the Mord-Sith with Agiel in hand and Kahlan standing beside Shale, Richard took a lantern from the wall and went in. With one hand on his sword, and the other holding the lantern, he checked the room. It was small, with a little training room beyond. He opened the wardrobe to be sure, but there was no one hiding in the room, and no place to hide.

"Empty," he said when he came back out. "We need to check all the rest of the rooms."

The Mord-Sith each looked in rooms, as did Richard. After checking several dark and empty rooms, he went into one with polished wood floors, a window with a pointed top and trimmed with simple drapes open to the darkness outside, and a bed with a blanket and pillow. Richard was abruptly staggered to remember sleeping at the foot of that bed, as well as being in it. Next to it was a nightstand with a lamp. On the other side of the small room were a simple table and chair. Next to a door into the training room were dark wood cabinets built into the wall. He opened the doors and found the cabinets empty.

He went into the training room to check. It seemed smaller than he remembered. A pulley in the ceiling had a rope that was attached at the wall. The floor had a drain for the blood. He stood frozen for a brief moment before turning away and leaving.

All five of the Mord-Sith silently watched him as he came out. They all knew it had been Denna's room. None of them said a word. They didn't have to. But he was glad they remained silent, because the last thing he would have wanted was for Kahlan to know whose room that had been.

"Nothing," he said. "It's empty. We need to hurry and check the others. If Michec is hurting her, the sooner we can get to her the better."

By the time they had finished checking all the rooms, they had found no sign that either Michec or Vika had been there.

"This is getting us nowhere," he finally said in frustration. "Do any of you have any idea where Michec could have taken her?"

All the Mord-Sith looked equally disappointed as they shook their heads.

"Do any of you have any idea where Michec's quarters used to be?"

Again, they all shook their heads.

Richard paced down the hall a short distance and then back, pinching his lower lip as he tried to think how they could find her in the enormous People's Palace. Everyone watched in silence as he paced.

His head suddenly came up.

"I know someone who should know where Michec would be."

47

Once on the upper level, they hurried along the balcony looking out over one of the main corridors. Rather than a railing, it had a short wall at the edge. They went past side halls and room after room until they finally reached the room Richard was looking for. He opened the door and then stood in the doorway, staring into the darkness within, his anger on a slow boil.

Coming back out, he looked farther down the balcony and saw light coming from one of the other rooms. Three soldiers of the First File on patrol coming along the balcony from the other way eyed the room on their way past it. Each big man had on dark leather armor over chain mail. Each carried a sword sheathed at a hip along with knives. One also had an axe held in a leather holder that covered the sharp blade edges. The wooden handle hung down, swinging freely as he walked. Each had a beard and strands of long dark hair that flowed down over broad shoulders. Their arms looked like they could have been carved from blocks of granite. They were the kind of soldiers that no one would want to cross, the kind of men of the First File who were widely feared.

Richard signaled and the three soldiers sped up a little, then came to a stop when they reached him and his group.

"I'd like you three men to come with me," Richard told them as he gestured back the way they had come.

They clapped meaty fists to their hearts and then fell in behind Kahlan and Shale, but ahead of the Mord-Sith. The five Mord-Sith were not happy about that, but let it go for the time being because Richard had already started out and they had to catch up as it was.

Shale leaned in close from behind so only Richard would hear her. "I thought the plan was not to let any soldiers see us?"

He knew what she meant. "When we leave, yes. But right now, we can't avoid it. There have already been hundreds of pairs of eyes on us all along the way coming up here. Don't forget, it's not only soldiers the goddess could use. She can use anyone who isn't gifted. For now, though, it can't be avoided. Worse, the goddess doesn't need to possess the person, she merely needs to take a look through any of those eyes to keep track of us. The people she used wouldn't even know she was doing it. Unless, that is, she exerted control over them to make them do her bidding, like she did with Dori— remember?"

Shale nodded with a grim expression on her beguiling features.

With everyone following behind, Richard hurried to the open doorway with light coming from inside. He paused with his hands on the sides of the doorframe.

A clean-shaven, middle-aged man was sitting behind a desk, bent over his work. A lamp sat on either end of the desk. The man blindly dipped a quill pen in an ink bottle as he focused on jotting notes on a collection of papers arrayed before him.

Richard stepped through the doorway and into the room. The Mord-Sith pushed past the soldiers, like going around giant oak trees, and came into the room behind Richard. The man working behind the desk finally noticed all the people and stood.

"Lord Rahl, you're out late. How may I help you?"

Richard thought the man might be rattled to have the Lord Rahl and a party that included soldiers and Mord-Sith show up at his door. Instead, he seemed calm and interested in what Richard needed. His blue-edged white robes of office with the gold bands on the sleeves were lying over a chair. The man apparently didn't care to wear them when he was working and instead was in his shirtsleeves.

"What is your name?"

The man bowed his head of thick, dark hair. "Edward Harris, at your service, Lord Rahl. I am second-in-command to Mr. Burkett."

"And where is Mr. Burkett? I need to speak with him at once."

"I believe Mr. Burkett has gone home for the day. But it sounds like it's urgent." Edward Harris gestured to the side. "His quarters aren't far away. I can take you there, if you wish."

Richard held an arm out behind him. "Lead the way."

Harris hurried around the desk, not bothering with his robes, and went out to the balcony area, where he turned to his left. At an intersection he led Richard and his party down a simple-looking side hall that turned away from the balcony. A short distance down the hall, he came to a door with Burkett's name on a small plaque to the side.

Harris lifted a hand toward the door. "These are his quarters, Lord Rahl. Do you wish me to wait?"

Richard nodded to the man and then knocked. "For now, yes."

When there was no answer, Richard knocked again, more insistently, and then a third time. Finally, he tried the door and found it locked.

Richard, what little patience he had now gone, threw his shoulder hard against the door. The door offered little resistance to his weight or mood. It stayed on its hinges as it banged back against the inside wall. Everyone stepped out of the way as splinters of the wooden doorjamb skittered across the floor of the hall. Knowing how upset Richard was, no one said a word.

Richard charged into the room without waiting for a greeting or an invitation. Burkett, in his stocking feet and still in his official robes, looked up with bloodshot eyes, but didn't get up from a chair at a table against the far wall. He had a bottle in one hand. The room was orderly and well-appointed with simple but comfortable-looking furniture. A dark doorway probably led to a bedroom. Richard didn't see a wife or anyone else in the apartment.

"I knocked," Richard said. "Why didn't you answer?"

"Because my workday is done," he said in a slur. "I don't like people bothering me after work." Burkett tried to set the bottle down on the table, but it took him three tries to find it. "What's the meaning of this, anyway? What is it you want?"

Richard seized the man by his tunic, lifted him out of the chair, and slammed him up against the wall. No one, including a surprised Edward Harris, said anything.

Richard clenched his jaw with barely contained anger. "I told you that I wanted to see all the gifted. You told me that you had all the gifted in the palace collected and sent to the library."

"That's what I did." Burkett licked his tongue out from under his overbite. "That was all the gifted living in the palace or staying here as guests, just as you asked."

Richard pulled the man away from the wall and slammed him into it again, banging his head hard enough to crack the plaster. His thin hair slipped off the top of his head where it had been covering his daisylike birthmark and fell down across his red face.

"You lied then and you're lying right now," Richard said through gritted teeth. "You didn't tell me about all the gifted."

Burkett tried, as best he could what with being held up in the air and hard against the wall by an angry Lord Rahl, to gesture his innocence.

"I didn't lie! I told you about all of them. I had all of them collected. All the gifted in the palace were sent to meet you up at the library, just as you asked. I saw to it. I have them all listed."

Richard lifted him away and threw him against the wall again. By now the shock was sobering him up a bit.

"You lied and you're lying now!"

Burkett's tongue licked out from under his overbite. "No, I'm telling you the truth. Those were the only gifted living or staying at the palace. Why would you doubt my word?"

"You keep track of everything going on in the palace for the Lord Rahl. That has always been your job. Your office keeps records of the visitors, the dignitaries, and the gifted living here. Especially the gifted. That was the most important duty you had for Darken Rahl, and you have a network of people everywhere who report everything to you, especially about the gifted, because Darken Rahl, like those before him, would not have tolerated you not reporting all of the gifted to him.

"You are the spider in the center of that web, and you know when anyone plucks one of those strands. I am the Lord Rahl now, and I asked for that same information you have always kept for the Lord Rahl. I asked you for all the gifted, and you deliberately didn't tell me about all of them."

"But I did, I swear! I swear I told you about every one of them. Every one!"

Richard cocked his head, gritting his teeth again as he put his face closer to the man. "You swear?" Richard asked. "Is that right? You swear?"

Burkett nodded furiously. "Yes. I swear."

"What about Moravaska Michec?"

The blood drained from Burkett's red face.

48

"Wait—what?" Edward Harris suddenly leaned in with alarm. "Do you mean to say that Moravaska Michec is in the People's Palace? Michec is here?"

"Yes. And your superior here knew it." Richard turned back to the suddenly silent man he was holding up against the wall. "Didn't you, Mr. Burkett? You knew. Didn't you!"

The man was clearly caught in the lie, his tongue nervously flicking in and out.

"I asked you a question! You knew Moravaska Michec was here at the palace when I asked for all the gifted to be sent up to the library, didn't you? Even though your duty is to report all the gifted to the Lord Rahl, you deliberately hid the fact that he is here, at the palace, isn't that right?"

"Well, I, I, I couldn't. You have to understand, I just couldn't."

Richard slammed him against the wall again, extending the crack in the plaster out on either side of his head.

"Why couldn't you tell me?"

"Michec was always loyal to Darken Rahl because they shared certain exotic… indulgences. As long as he left me and my staff alone, it was none of my business."

"What does that have to do with you not letting me know about him or sending him up to the library with the other gifted?"

"He thought you only defeated Darken Rahl because of luck. He was certain that your luck would run out in the war and that you would never be seen again. He would then step in and assume a place of power here at the palace. He said that he would use a spell to do something horrifying to me if I told you he was living here."

The muscles in Richard's jaw flexed at the thought of Vika being back in that man's hands. "I am the Lord Rahl. It is treasonous to deceive the Lord Rahl about someone scheming against him in his own house!"

Burkett winced as he nodded. "I know, I know, and I would have told you, but he threatened me if I ever did."

"How many times have you been to the devotions, Mr. Burkett?"

"The devotions? Why, three times a day, of course. Every day. I never miss a devotion."

"And you lied each of those times you swore loyalty to me, isn't that right, Mr. Burkett?"

"Not because I wanted to. Don't you see? It was because I had to. Michec said that if I told anyone, especially you, that he was living here and planning on taking away your power, he would kill me in the most painful way imaginable."

"I can understand people being afraid of magic, but as the Lord Rahl I am the magic against magic. You should have told me that he was here, and that he threatened you, to say nothing of his threats against my rule. I would have handled it and I would have protected you. That's my duty in the oath of the devotion. Now, because of your disloyalty, his schemes are threatening the lives of those loyal to me as well as the Mother Confessor, as well as everything we have fought for."

"Why didn't you tell me?" Mr. Harris asked of Mr. Burkett. "If you were afraid to tell Lord Rahl, I would have done it for you. Why didn't you simply tell me?"

Burkett stammered and flicked his tongue out, ignoring Harris, trying to downplay his breach of trust. "I, I didn't know he would hurt anyone, Lord Rahl. I swear. I didn't know Michec would hurt anyone."

Richard was not about to argue so obvious a lie. "What kind of gift does Michec have?" Richard demanded. "What kind of things can he do?"

Burkett looked past Richard to all the people watching him—the Mother Confessor, the soldiers, and the Mord-Sith. "Well, I, I, I'm not sure."

"I know all too well who Moravaska Michec is," Harris said when Burkett wouldn't admit what he knew. "I thought he fled long ago when you defeated Darken Rahl. I never expected to see that wicked man again. I had no idea he had returned."

Richard turned to him. "Do you know what kind of gift he has? Is he a wizard?"

Harris shook his head. "No, Lord Rahl, not a wizard. Moravaska Michec is a warlock. You know, a witch man."

"A witch!" Shale exclaimed as she stepped forward. With a finger, she poked Richard's shoulder. "That was what I smelled!"

Richard frowned back at her. "What?"

"At the stables, remember? I told you I smelled something that I thought I recognized. I did. I smelled a witch."

Richard turned back to Edward Harris. "Do you know where he would be?"

"Sorry, Lord Rahl, I don't." He lifted out his hands in frustration that he didn't have an answer. "You know how big the People's Palace is. There are probably a thousand places he could be living and we would never know about it."

Richard turned back to Burkett. "Where are his quarters? You knew he was here, so you would know where he is staying in the palace, or should I say where he is hiding. Now, where is he?"

Burkett licked his lips. "He said that if I told anyone he was here, he would do something terrible to me, something that would make me suffer before I died."

"You don't need to worry about a spell from Michec. He's not here. You need to worry about me. Once I find him, he won't be putting any spells on anyone anymore, because he will be dead." Richard shook the man again. "Now where is he!"

Burkett trembled as he panted. "He's, he's in a remote place where no one ever goes, down a level below where the tombs of your ancestors are located, in an area called M_{III}-B."

"M_{III}-B," Richard repeated, keeping his focus on Burkett although he sensed the Mord-Sith shifting uneasily and sharing a look.

Burkett nodded. "That's right, M_{III}-B. But a witch's lair down there will be a very dangerous place. You won't be able to get him out, not out of that place."

Richard dropped the man down in the chair. "Mr. Burkett, you are relieved of your position." He turned to the dark-haired man. "Mr. Harris, you are second in charge, under Mr. Burkett?"

"That's right."

"As of this moment, you are promoted to Mr. Burkett's former position."

"You can't do that!" Burkett cried out from the chair. "I know more about the palace workings than anyone! I have years of experience!"

"What good is any of it if you take orders from someone working against my rule, working against the peace of the D'Haran Empire? I came to you before and asked you for all the gifted, expecting you to be truthful. You schemed to deceive me. You lied to me."

"But I had to! I told you, Michec threatened me if I told anyone, especially you."

"It's done," Richard said, incensed by the excuses. "You are relieved of your position."

The man's fingers took refuge on the gold bands on the sleeves of his robes. "What position will you put me in, then?"

"None."

"You can't do this!"

"We fought a long and terrible war. Many, many people sacrificed their lives so that other people could live in peace and freedom. Even though I have fought and bled for them, everyone is free to dislike me if they so choose. But no one can be here if they are disloyal to the empire and plot against me or the Mother Confessor. No one."

Richard turned to the grim-faced soldiers. "See to it that Mr. Burkett is escorted from the palace as soon as he can pack his belongings. Watch over him as he does so. Come sunrise, I want him gone. He is banished from the People's Palace forever under penalty of death if he ever tries to sneak back in. Let your officers know my orders."

As one they all clapped fists to hearts.

"But, Lord Rahl, I made a mistake," the man pleaded. "That's all, just a mistake."

Richard turned back to Burkett. "We all make mistakes. I can understand and forgive mistakes. But this was not a mistake. You acted deliberately. This betrayal cannot be forgiven." The man started to speak, but Richard held up a finger, warning him not to say anything. "Count your blessings that I don't have you beheaded for treason."

Richard turned to the dark-haired palace official. "Mr. Harris, you are in charge now."

Edward Harris clapped a fist to his heart. "I will not betray your trust, Lord Rahl."

Richard briefly smiled his appreciation and then turned to the Mord-Sith. "Do you know this place called M$_{\text{III}}$-B?"

All five of them again shared glances.

Richard couldn't miss the troubled expressions. "Obviously, you do. What do you know about M$_{\text{III}}$-B?"

"Darken Rahl used to call it the Wasteland," Rikka said.

Richard had never heard of an indoor place with such a name. "The Wasteland? Why did he call it that?"

Rikka shared another look with some of the others. "He didn't understand the place and didn't care to. It's a vast, remote, isolated area. He didn't know why it was here in the palace. He rarely if ever went down there."

"He was afraid of it," Nyda added when Rikka didn't say it.

Richard's gaze shifted to her. "Why?"

For a moment, Nyda seemed to search for a way to explain it. "M$_{\text{III}}$-B is a strange, surreal place. It's a kind of self-contained labyrinth of confusing passageways and dead ends. It would be easy to become lost in there and never find your way out."

"It's so dangerous that it's not merely restricted," Rikka explained. "The whole area is closed off behind a series of locked doors. We can take you there, but if there is a witch man down in there, it is going to be beyond merely dangerous. Unlike Darken Rahl, Michec had a certain... fascination with the Wasteland. He used it often. As Berdine can attest, Michec is a very sadistic man. Some called him Michec the Butcher."

When Richard looked to her, Berdine reluctantly spoke. "The Wasteland is a place you wouldn't ever want Moravaska Michec to take you. When Darken Rahl ruled, the Wasteland was a kind of refuge for Michec. He used to take people in there where he wouldn't be disturbed. None of those people he took in there ever came back. If he took Vika in there..."

Richard gripped Berdine's arm and leaned close. "We're going to get Vika back. That's a promise."

Berdine swallowed her emotion. "I know you will try, Lord Rahl. But you don't understand Michec... or the Wasteland."

"Lord Rahl," Harris said, "MIII-B is more than a confusing and simply dangerous place. I can't imagine the purpose of it, or why it's down there, but I've heard that in the past somehow people have accidentally managed to get in there. Only a couple ever made it out. I don't really know about them, but the rest must have died in there. Anyone who knows it fears that place." He gestured at the Mord-Sith. "As they say, Darken Rahl may have been afraid of the place, but Michec used to go in there."

Richard wondered why there would be a labyrinth of any kind down in the lower reaches of the palace. In the Keep, yes, there were any number of such places, some of them so complex that it had been a thousand years since people had set foot in some of the confusion of rooms, but those areas had a defensive purpose as traps for intruders. He had never seen anything of the kind at the People's Palace, and even if it was somehow meant to be defensive, he couldn't imagine any strategic reason for it to be down in a lower area of the palace.

"With a witch man casting webs down there," Shale said, "that is only going to make it all the more dangerous, especially when we don't know the layout of this Wasteland place. He would be able to use that to his advantage to trap us and kill us."

Richard tapped his thumb on the scabbard at his hip. "A labyrinth of confusing halls and rooms is a real problem by design. We could get really lost in there. Since we don't know the layout of the maze, we won't know where we are once we're in there."

"I can help with that much, at least," Harris said, lifting a hand to break into the conversation. "We have maps of every area in the palace. There would be diagrams of M$_{III}$-B. That number is a charting designation."

Richard frowned. "You think you have a diagram showing a layout of that place, M$_{III}$-B? The Wasteland?"

Harris nodded with conviction. "I haven't seen that specific one myself, but there are plans of every part of the palace. They are necessary for a variety of reasons, from repair work to locating sources of leaks and every other sort of malfunction that needs to be addressed. I'm sure there would be one of M$_{III}$-B."

"Show us," Richard said.

Going for the door without a word, Edward Harris wove his way among the soldiers as they started for Mr. Burkett.

49

As they left Mr. Burkett's apartment, Kahlan felt shock and dismay over the discovery of how disloyal the man had been. In his position he had uncaringly put the lives of everyone in the palace at risk. His betrayal had led to Vika being taken, and she was now in the hands of the shadowy Moravaska Michec. With a gifted man possessing such powers holed up inside the palace, and in a perilous place, no less, it was now a situation beyond merely dangerous.

Kahlan knew that, in a way, Shale had been right that their purpose of getting to the Wizard's Keep overrode the life of one person who, after all, had sworn to protect them with her life. Vika was doing just that. She would want them to leave her and get to the safety of the Wizard's Keep.

The Mord-Sith always came after her and Richard without question or hesitation. Kahlan hated the thought of her in silent terror, thinking no help would be coming.

But at the same time, this was also about much more than saving Vika's life. Evil could not be left to fester and grow inside the House of Rahl. There was no telling what Michec would do once they left for the Keep.

As they reached the end of the hall where it came out to the balcony area, with Mr. Harris leading the way, Kahlan heard a commotion behind her. Along with everyone else, she turned to look back down the hall. Mr. Burkett suddenly bolted out of his room. Unbelievably, he ran toward them in his stocking feet, fist raised in the air, the three soldiers chasing after him. One of the men stretched out, snatching for

Mr. Burkett, but the wiry man twisted away. He was yelling drunken curses at Richard.

As the four of them raced out into the balcony, everyone turned to the threat. It wasn't much of a threat, though, so Richard didn't bother drawing his sword. He looked like he intended to simply hook the man with an arm and turn him over to the soldiers.

The Mord-Sith weren't so casual about the threat from an unarmed, skinny, older man. They all had their Agiel to hand and looked like they intended him great violence. As Mr. Burkett charged out of the hall, yelling that Richard had no right to remove him after his years of service, something out of the corner of her eye caught Kahlan's attention.

She heard their howls at the same time that she turned and saw them. Four or five Glee, in a tight group, had already materialized and were racing down the hall toward them with alarming speed, steam still trailing off their dark, wet bodies.

Just as they all turned to confront the threat, another group of the creatures they hadn't seen materialize crashed through the center of their group from the opposite side, catching them all by surprise. Everyone ducked as claws flashed by and wicked, pointed teeth snapped. With Glee converging on them all from both directions at the same time, several of the Mord-Sith were blind-sided and knocked to the floor by the tall, dark creatures going for Kahlan.

Richard's arm swept behind, circling Kahlan's waist. As he spun around, he took her from her feet and to the floor just as a claw swept by right over their heads.

A claw did catch one of the soldiers by surprise as he charged out of the hall after Mr. Burkett. It ripped through the leather armor and the flesh and bone under it.

Another one of the dark creatures swung at Mr. Burkett, ripping out his throat so deeply and with such force that the claw hooked his spine and threw the man flying. When he slammed into the short wall, his upper body flipped backward over the parapet. Mr. Burkett plummeted to the stone floor far below.

As the dark, slimy creatures attacked from both sides, the Mord-Sith, after having scrambled to their feet, rammed their Agiels into the center of the tall monsters. Kahlan knew they bled; when she heard the shrieks, she knew that they also felt pain. By the sound of their shrieks, they felt no less pain than any human would under an Agiel.

Richard grabbed the arm of one as it stormed through the midst of the group, clawing wildly at them. He twisted the arm around as the creature's weight carried it on past. Its arm wrenched around with enough force to partially rip it off. When it smacked the floor, the Glee began to dissolve into scribbles. In an instant it had vanished. Others the Mord-Sith caught also vanished before any more damage could be done.

A soldier swung his sword, taking the head off one Glee just before the wicked claws of another hooked his arm, tearing flesh from bone. Another claw ripped open his middle. The soldier fought in vain as he was being taken down and mauled to death.

Richard circled a powerful arm around the head of one of the creatures attacking the soldier. With a violent twist, he broke its neck. In such a sudden death, it failed to vanish back into its own world and instead fell sprawling on the floor.

Some of the creatures went into deep, froglike squats and then sprang up toward them with frightening speed. There seemed to be black shapes flying at them from everywhere. Kahlan ducked back just as jaws snapped, and the creature's pointed white teeth barely missed her face. She pulled her knife and hooked its leg, slicing to the bone. When it fell, Richard drove his sword through its spine.

Berdine jumped onto the back of one of them leaping for Kahlan and pressed her Agiel to the base of its skull. The slimy monster screeched, tipping its head back in agony at the same time as it turned to scribbles. Berdine, on its back with her legs around the middle, suddenly tumbled to the floor when it vanished from right under her. Another one of the monsters saw her at a disadvantage and jumped for her. Berdine managed to flip onto her back on the floor and strike up at the dark shape closing down over her. Caught on her Agiel, it, too, shrieked as it vanished.

Richard lopped off arms reaching for Kahlan. She could see the rage in his eyes, both his own and the power from the sword. As one of the tall creatures dove for Kahlan, he took a mighty swing at it, slicing it clean in two from one shoulder to the opposite hip. The two halves tumbled across the ground, one to each side of Kahlan. The insides spilled across the marble floor, spreading yet more blood and viscera underfoot.

Another one of the big Glee, running in with claws held high for a swing at Edward Harris, slipped on the blood. Instead of taking a lethal swipe at the man, it fell and crashed into him. The impact knocked him over the waist-high wall at the side of the balcony. Harris cried out as he tried to grab the edge, but he only was able to catch it with one hand as he fell.

Richard dove for the wall. At the last instant, as the man's fingers slipped off, he snatched Edward Harris's wrist, keeping him from a fall that would have killed him. As Richard held on to the man hanging down over the side of the wall, he stabbed at a Glee coming for him. Kahlan saw the sword erupt from its back. Richard pushed it off the blade with a foot. As the dying creature fell, another going for Richard tripped over it and met the same fate.

Kahlan reached for a nearby Glee to unleash her power on it. While she didn't need to touch a person, not knowing how it would work on these creatures, she wanted to make contact with it. Cassia slammed into it first, ramming her Agiel into its middle. The creature shrieked in agony, its head twisting violently, its long, dark, almond-shaped eyes going wide. Even as Cassia twisted her weapon to increase the pain, it was already dissolving back to its own world. Cassia screamed in rage that it got away before she could do more damage.

The slime from the creatures, which not only dripped off their smooth black skin but splashed across the floor when they fell and smacked down hard, was mixing with the blood to make for slippery footing. In their frenzied attempts to get at them, some of the Glee slipped and fell.

Richard swung his sword as two of the monsters feinted one way and then the other, trying to find a way past his blade to get at him, knowing he was pinned to the short wall as he held on to the wrist of the man over the edge.

Shale slipped and fell just as she cast an arm out, sending out another wavering crack of power. It blew the shoulder and arm off one of the creatures trying to get at Richard, throwing black flesh and bloody bone up high into the air. The dark shape stumbled around in shock as it dissolved into scribbles and vanished.

The remaining soldier slashed through several more of the tall, dark Glee trying to get at Richard. The Mord-Sith had formed a defensive ring around Kahlan. The way Richard was holding on to Edward Harris had him pinned to the short wall so that he couldn't fight effectively, but he couldn't let go or Harris would die. The Glee all knew it.

"Help him!" Kahlan screamed.

The Mord-Sith reacted to her order and attacked the creatures from behind as they tried to rip into Richard. Here and there the victims screeched in pain briefly before they vanished. Their numbers were being whittled down, making it easier to fight back against them, but if they connected with either claws or teeth, they could do lethal damage.

Everyone, it seemed, was frantically fighting for their lives. Then, almost as soon as the battle had started, it ended with the last two creatures escaping by vanishing into thin air.

The bodies of several mangled or decapitated Glee lay sprawled on the floor. Everyone panted in exhaustion after the brief but frenzied fight.

Richard sheathed his sword as he turned to the man over the edge of the wall to get another hand on him.

A soldier stood in front of Kahlan with his feet spread, ready to protect her with his life. When he saw that the attackers were gone, the soldier ran to the short wall and leaned over, grabbing the man's arm to help Richard hold on to him. Together he and Richard hauled Edward Harris up and back over the wall. His shirt soaked with sweat, he flopped down, leaning against the wall to catch his breath.

Across the broad corridor, on the balcony that mirrored the one they were on, some people were running for their lives while others stood pressed against the short wall, where they had been anxiously watching the fight. People were running for safety down in the expansive corridor below, too, while many more were gathering around the crumpled body of Mr. Burkett and a severed black arm from one of the creatures.

Kahlan rushed to Richard. Like everyone else, he was breathing heavily.

She put a hand on his chest, thankful that he was all right. "I think that must have taken a few years off my life."

He gave her a knowing smile. "Me too. For a moment there, I thought they had us." He gestured to the two downed soldiers. "Unfortunately, not all of us survived the attack."

Shale shook gore and slime from the hem of her dark dress as she came closer. "I've been righteously frightened often enough in the Northern Waste, but life here at the beautiful, glorious People's Palace is a lot scarier. Those of us still alive still came very close to death today."

Richard seemed to understand her meaning. "As soon as we can leave we'll be a lot safer. Right now the goddess can look through the eyes of any of the thousands of people here and know where we are at any given moment so she can send attacks when we are vulnerable.

"But we can't simply leave a threat here that is just as deadly. If we left now, Michec could stab us in the back, so to speak. If he cast a lethal spell that killed Kahlan, hope for the future would end right there. Just because the Glee are a threat doesn't mean this one isn't just as dangerous and we can ignore it."

Shale nodded with a sigh.

Kahlan saw soldiers of the First File running in from both directions, weapons drawn.

Just as Richard turned back to Kahlan, the air of the hall not far off shimmered with a mass of swirling lines that could mean only one thing.

Kahlan's eyes went wide. There had to be well over a hundred of them, the steam rising off their glistening black bodies as they suddenly materialized, it seemed, at a dead run.

50

In a heartbeat, from not far off down the corridor, a massive mob of the huge, dark creatures with steaming, soft, dark, slippery skin raced toward Richard and his party. They had materialized all bunched together in a writhing, howling mass. At first, all the waving arms reminded him of nothing so much as a dark mass of wriggling worms. As they ran, gelatinous globs slid off their naked bodies to drip and drop all over the floor.

Mouths wide, they roared with ravenous intent, their howls echoing through the vast, multilevel corridor.

Their large, glossy, almond-shaped eyes seemed nearly as black and wet as their soft, moist flesh. When a thin, semitransparent third eyelid blinked in from the inside corner of each eye, the membrane gave their eyes a slightly milky appearance.

In an instant, Richard's emotions went from exhausted relief to full fright. He had thought it was over, but now there were suddenly many times the number of Glee as in the attack that had just ended. He took a quick look over his shoulder. None were coming from behind. At least not yet. The soldiers back in that direction were still a long way off. They would never reach Richard and those with him in time.

All of those claws were terrifying enough, but even more frightening were the nasty, oily faces of the creatures. The thin wet skin wrinkled as their wide mouths gaped open, lips pulling back from long, needle-sharp teeth that glistened with stringy slime. The mouths full of white teeth stood out all the more against the dark mass of the creatures.

The few dozen soldiers racing to Richard and Kahlan's defense from that same direction were suddenly beset by the tall dark shapes slashing away at them with hooked claws. They ran through the midst of the soldiers, overwhelming them with sheer numbers and brute force. The soldiers tried to fight back—even taking down a few of the Glee, which were then trampled underfoot—but they were being hopelessly engulfed and overrun.

Before the Mord-Sith could launch toward them, before Richard had time to think about it, he reacted out of instinct born of white-hot rage.

He thrust both hands toward the threat.

Clarity came to him in a frozen instant in time.

His birthright, that core of his gift deep within that he hadn't been aware of growing up, but that he had come to know intimately when in the underworld, erupted forth as if it were wild fury brought to life.

In that fraction of a second, everyone seemed to be moving in a dreamlike state so slow that he could see the shock on every face as this sudden new threat materialized out of thin air. The fear and stark terror of what was coming for them was clearly evident on each of those faces. The Mord-Sith, though, lived to defend Richard and Kahlan with their lives, so their fear was layered over with grim resolve, a kind of acknowledgment that they were already dead, so they might as well take down as many of the enemy as they could before there was no power left in their muscles or blood in their veins.

Richard had time to look at each of their beautiful faces, each an image of intelligent beauty, reflecting what could have come of these women had they not been taken at a young age and twisted into killing machines. But now that was what they were, and that visage overlaid whatever else might lie beneath.

In that silent, otherworldly state, everyone seemed to Richard to be moving so slowly so as to almost be statues. He could see the fiercely determined expressions on all of the soldiers as the Glee around them ripped at them with claws and teeth. The whole scene, that instant in time, seemed frozen in midair.

At the same time, Richard could see all the ravenous, wrinkled faces of the Glee—big eyes, small nostril holes, enormous mouths and teeth—all of them struggling in the thick mass, tumbling over one another to be the first to get at Richard and Kahlan. It wasn't a drive for glory, as a soldier in battle might have, but rather a voracious, communal hunger to kill, like beasts needing to feed.

Richard knew without a doubt by seeing their big, almond-shaped eyes that their gazes, frozen in that moment in time, were mostly fixed on Kahlan. They had also been sent for Richard, but more importantly, for her first. Their claws were all reaching out, trying to be the first to hook her, to be the first to rip her open, to sink those needle-sharp teeth into her flesh.

They had been sent to eliminate not merely Kahlan, but the children she carried, the hope she carried.

He could see in her face that Kahlan knew it as well.

From within the crackling cocoon of power, Richard could see it all, watch it all, as everyone moved only the width of a hair with each lazy tick of time.

A kind of sparkling, spiraling, hissing haze swirled up around him, colors flashing up and down within it. Eddies of light rippled through it. Tiny flashes, sparks of energy, ignited all throughout that haze, uncountable numbers glowing with glittering fluidity. Each of those embers sparked out, only to be reborn and set off yet another cascade of glimmering flashes. It was dazzling. The center of the vortex was warm and protective; it was the energy of his own gift expanding outward.

It reminded him of the first time he stood on Zedd's wizard's rock, the way the light threatened to ignite the air around him and the air itself rotated with a dull roar as it swirled like smoke. It engendered that same sense of wonder, that same recognition of unimaginable power being gathered together, of a world he had never known existed coming into being.

He could just see in his peripheral vision that Kahlan, knowing they were coming for her, had straightened her back, the Mother Confessor ready to release her own power. But Richard knew beyond any doubt that in this case, with as many of the dark creatures as there were charging through the soldiers to get at her, she didn't stand a chance.

None of them did.

Only one thing could stop what was but a heartbeat away from becoming reality. He knew that in two heartbeats, they would all be dead.

Unless he stopped them.

Power, ignited by the spark of his rage and fueled by the singular gift he carried, filled every fiber of his being, swelling through him, around him, a summoned haze of lethal force. It felt hot, sharp, and violent, as if it were erupting from his very soul and tearing its way through him, eager to get to his hands, eager to do his bidding.

In that quiet, clear instant of inner cognition, of wild rage and hate materialized, he also had time to reflect on everything he had been taught, everything he had read, and everything he had seen about the use of the gift. It was all there in his mind, the memories ready to serve his need. In that instant, it felt as if Zedd were there with him, because this was something Zedd had intimately known and understood.

Now, Richard felt it. It was him. It was wrath itself.

Through it all, even as memories of Zedd warmed him, the thing that stood out in his mind, the thing that mattered, was that he was a war wizard, born of a long line of those rare men.

He had always fought that reality. He had always tried to both master it and avoid it, never comfortable with who he was. But in that crystal-clear instant sparked by raw danger, it all came together.

This was his purpose, his calling, his need.

To his other side, Shale was also lifting a hand to use her power. He knew, in the silence of that soft yet unborn instant inside the swirling haze of rage sparkling all around him, that not only was it not enough, but it wasn't going to be fast enough. What she was able to do couldn't begin to match the speed and enormity of the threat. At most, she would only have time to take out one or two of what looked like well over a hundred attackers before the attackers overwhelmed and killed them all.

As much as he admired her courage, this was not for her to do. This was not for the soldiers to do. This was not for the Mord-Sith to do. This was not for the Mother Confessor to do. This was vastly more than any and all of them could begin to do.

This was for Richard to do.

In his mind he realized that the totality of it, while at first seeming overwhelming, simply required a computation of position, distance, degree of angles, numbers of each threat, and their rate of speed as they closed the short distance to their victims.

While the entirety of it was a complex algorithm of various factors, it was, at the same time, a known equation. He knew the foundational formulas from the language of Creation, from notes in a book he had found by First Wizard Baraccus, *Secrets of a War Wizard's Power*, written expressly for Richard three thousand years before he had been born. There was also the underlying work done by Baraccus on azimuth observations, and what Richard had learned from the many other books he had read—even *The Adventures of Bonnie Day*, written by Nathan Rahl—as well as a variety of formulas in the Cerulean scrolls, and several useful ratios from a book his grandfather had once found in the Keep, *Continuum Ratios and Viability Predictions*. There were computations of gradient angles affected by speed that Richard had already made the same instant he saw the perspective and distances while computing reflective effects of what he intended. He had to factor in the power that he would bring to bear and how it would affect every one of the calculations.

He saw all of those calculations and computations in his mind's eye in a flicker of time. They were done almost as soon as he saw what would be necessary.

Those calculations came together with instinct honed from every experience in his life, from every battle he had fought, every person and creature he had killed. He wondered why he had never realized it in quite that same way before.

Even as he wondered, he knew that his time spent in the eternity of the underworld—when he had straightened out tangled connections in his gift—had given him inestimable insight he could have gained nowhere else but in the world of the dead.

All of that power crackling around him, was him. It was a creation of his gift. He had brought it into being. It was his to direct. It was his to wield. It was an extension of his fury.

In that instant, at the peak of the swirling haze of colors and flashing points of light surging up from his soul, Richard unleashed his rage.

The air between him and the creatures distorted as it was violently compressed to an infinitely small point. Throughout the palace, through every open window and door, every place open to the sky, air rushed in to fill the void he had created up on the balcony by that sudden compression. It abruptly sucked the air from the lungs of everyone around him, instantly forming ice crystals around their noses and mouths. Their eyes bulged from the sudden pressure difference.

Richard leaned his body forward, arms out, projecting and directing his gift through his hands to push that point he had created toward the enemy. It shifted in among them as they were helplessly suspended in that moment frozen in time. Near the focal point of that pressure gradient some of their chests ripped open from the internal pressure of the air violently escaping as it tried to equalize the pressure in the vacuum around that compression point. Some of their eyes burst.

As Richard pushed that compression point through their midst to position it where it needed to be in the center of the mass, the tissue nearest the steepest portion of the pressure gradient vaporized. From his point of view, what Richard saw was a hole being tunneled right through the creatures, and unfortunately the soldiers, through flesh and bone and steel as he pushed it to where it was going to need to be. Flesh around the vaporizing tissue shredded as it was sucked in toward the point.

But that was only in the first infinitesimal fraction of time before he released the heat and energy he had pulled from the air he had compressed into that point.

Richard, that power's origin, its genesis, its creator, its commander, gave it what it needed: command.

He pushed his hands out with the effort of pressing that point of concussion not only tighter but also into the midst of the Glee.

When he at last released that compressed energy at that central, infinitesimally small point, it expanded with such a violent detonation that it shook the palace and knocked everyone except Richard from their feet.

The heat of the explosive expansion ignited the air itself. Countless shards of elemental fire, like splinters of white-hot burning glass, tumbled, spun, and flew everywhere inside the expanding discharge of energy. Those glowing splinters of heat flared through everything within the shell of the expanding central point. Flesh, bone, blood, even the steel of the soldiers' weapons, all fragmented into burning particles that blazed from white hot, to red, to ash, all in one explosive instant.

Richard, though, could see it all drawn out in its full dynamic display.

The air that had been sucked into the palace now had to leave, driven before a violent shockwave. The pressure that had built up broke windows in its brutal rush outward. Air that had been sucked from lungs suddenly rushed back in with a thump and an involuntary gasp.

In that instant of release—the center of it located in the center of the mass of Glee—the concussive energy violently reoccupied the void around the central point with such force that everything ignited in something akin to wizard's fire, but not concentrated and not actually fire in the same magic-generated sense. This was something else entirely. This was elemental heat and force, a forge of a war wizard's power unleashed.

To Richard it all was a predetermined, programmed formula unfolding in deliberate stages that he had calculated the instant before releasing the energy he had gathered. To anyone else seeing it happen, it was a sudden detonation that filled the corridor with a blinding flash and thunderous blast, and in that pristine instant of release, they would have felt the hammer of force against their chest as they saw the Glee explode into ash.

Richard felt it all as an extension of his rage unleashed, exquisite, pure, and profoundly violent. It was glorious.

In the ringing silence that followed, the greasy cloud of ash that had been the Glee floated through the air, gradually drifting down.

There were sooty piles of it similar to the ones left in the library's containment field, even if created in a different manner. There were splatters and smears of it against the walls, the pillars, and on the short wall at the side of the balcony. It covered the floor in a thick mass like the aftermath of a black blizzard.

Amid that devastation were also the gray, ashen remains of the soldiers of the First File who had been coming to protect them. They had been there, caught up in the center of that maelstrom of energy Richard had released.

He had ached with sorrow, even as he had released his power, knowing it would also kill those brave men.

51

In the hush as time returned to normal, those with Richard slowly tried to gather their senses. The ones still conscious held their heads, groaning in pain from the pressure he had created both in the compression of the air and in its explosive expansion.

Richard alone stood unaffected, gazing first for a time at the ashen remains of the Glee and the soldiers, then around at everyone else.

Rikka and Cassia looked to be unconscious. Nyda, Vale, and Berdine were just sitting up, holding their heads and taking deep breaths. Shale put a knee to the floor as she steadied herself before trying to stand.

Richard bent to help Kahlan get up. Like everyone else, she looked stunned. As consciousness gradually returned, she blinked, trying to collect her wits. He lifted her to her feet. Still trying to get her balance, she leaned against him for support.

"Richard," she managed as she winced, panting to catch her breath, her hands grabbing hold of his arms, "what... what just happened? I thought we were all dead. How can we be alive? What did you do?"

"Not the kind of thing I would want to do outside a containment field, but I had no choice."

"Where are we?" Rikka asked, sounding groggy and only half awake.

"It's all right," Richard said as he grabbed her hand when she lifted it and then helped pull her to her knees.

Shale, still on her knees, gestured. "You destroyed them all." She squinted at the mass of black ash not far away. "You destroyed them all?"

She seemed confused. People down on the main floor who had also been knocked from their feet were groaning as they began to get back up. Being farther away, they didn't feel it with the same severity, but they were still affected by what had happened. Such an event expanded for quite some distance beyond the lethal radius.

When Richard looked up, he saw that across the vast corridor, on the balcony that mirrored theirs, a lone Glee stood motionless, claws at its sides, watching.

Richard stared across at it. The lone Glee stared back. For a long moment, they just stared at each other. It didn't try to come closer, or for that matter, do anything. It appeared that it was simply observing.

And then, as the tall black creature and Richard stood gazing at each other, it dissolved back into its own world.

Richard couldn't begin to imagine what that had been about.

Kahlan looked around and saw everyone finally getting to their feet. With their hands, they felt their chests, checking themselves over, expecting to find injuries, but there were no injuries to find. Back down the corridor behind them, the soldiers that had been rushing to their assistance were likewise all trying to regain their senses. Some had to steady themselves on a hand and a knee as they pulled themselves together. Some of the men helped others up.

Kahlan looked around, surprised to see that everyone was alive. The Mord-Sith appeared unhurt. Edward Harris leaned back against the short wall a moment, catching his breath. The remaining soldier of the three shook his head, as if clearing the cobwebs.

Kahlan's thoughts seemed to tumble in fragments as she tried to piece together what had just happened. She had seen the mass of Glee materialize, and she had known they were all going to die.

It almost felt as if time itself skipped a beat, then something violent happened. It felt to her like it had been a dream. For a moment she couldn't breathe, as if the wind had been knocked out of her, then she remembered suddenly gasping in a breath and feeling life return to her only to lose consciousness.

In a way, there were elements of what had just happened that reminded her of when she released her power. But this time, she knew that it was quite different, and that somehow, in some way, Richard had just used his gift to save them all.

One instant they had been about to die, then the next instant, it seemed, she was waking up on the floor. Down the corridor she could see that the Glee were no more. There was only the greasy ash remains similar to what she had seen in the containment field in the library. She knew without a doubt that these Glee had not had the chance to return to their own world.

She finally hugged Richard, laying her head against his shoulder. "You saved us, Richard. You saved us all. I don't know exactly what just happened, or how you did it, but you saved us."

Richard, staring off at the ashen remains of the soldiers who had died with the Glee, nodded.

"Sometimes," he said in a soft, intimate voice, "I wish I didn't have such ability and everyone else wasn't depending on me to protect them. Sometimes I wish I didn't know the things I know or couldn't do the terrible things I can do.

"Sometimes," he said, staring off at nothing, "I wish I was just like everyone else."

"But you're not, Richard. You're not. Remember what I've always told you? You can be no more than who you are, and no less." She put a hand to the side of his handsome face. "Remember?"

He smiled a little as he nodded.

"I know what you mean, though. Growing up I often wished I hadn't been born a Confessor, that I was just like everyone else, that I was simply a normal girl. I've had to do terrible things with my ability. I've had to unleash my power against people I wish I hadn't needed to kill. So I understand what you're feeling. But with me, I've had a lifetime to come to terms with it. You will, too."

Richard touched the side of her face, gazing into her eyes. "I know."

He sighed as he seemed to remember himself again and all the others. "Berdine? Are you all right?"

Berdine, bending to retrieve her Agiel, grinned at him. "I knew you would save us, Lord Rahl. I wasn't worried at all."

"Well, I was worried enough for all of you," Shale said. "If you had any sense, you would have been scared witless."

"If it's any consolation," Cassia said with a smile, "I was just a little bit worried."

Shale harrumphed. She came closer and peered up at Richard, as if seeing him in a new light. "Lord Rahl, someday when we have the time, I would like very much for you to explain to me precisely what you just did."

Richard, one arm still around Kahlan, holding her close, shrugged. "It was just some simple calculations."

"Uh-huh." She cast a critical look over at the greasy, black, ashen remains. "Simple calculations. Yes, of course. I can see that." She planted a fist on her hip. "Then how is it that you can turn a raging mob of monsters to ash, and yet you can't seem to light a lamp with your gift?"

Richard shrugged. "The lamp isn't trying to kill us all."

He turned to the soldier still with them. "When those men down there gather their senses and get over here, they can help you take care of this." He gestured around at the carnage still left all over the floor from the previous attack. The remains continued to leak blood and fluids in ever-growing pools. "I need to see to some urgent business."

With a steely look, the man clapped a fist to his heart.

Richard gestured off at the destruction he had created. "I'm truly sorry about those men. They didn't deserve to die. They especially didn't deserve to die by my hand."

The soldier glanced briefly at the ashen remains. "You had no choice, Lord Rahl. You just preserved any hope we have for all of us to survive, for all of us to have a future. These monsters want to hunt and kill us all. Grieve for those fallen men of the First File but know that they were doing what they believed in and what they chose to do."

Richard gripped the man's shoulder. "Thank you. You got some of them, too. You did good, too." He gestured to the remains of the two who had fought off the Glee when Mr. Burkett had been fleeing. "You and your two brothers-in-arms."

The soldier nodded his appreciation.

"Mr. Harris," Richard said, as he took Harris's arm and helped pull him the rest of the way upright, "take us to the place with the maps of the palace you told us about."

"At once, Lord Rahl." He hesitated. "And thank you, Lord Rahl, for before." He pointed over the side. "For catching me."

"'Master Rahl protect us,'" Richard quoted from the devotion. "Just doing my job. Now let's go."

52

Edward Harris wasted no time as he led Richard and everyone with him to one of the grand marble staircases to begin their descent from the upper level to the secure lower vault where the palace design plans were located. Because it was so open, this was one of the few staircases that didn't echo with all their footsteps. Instead, the whispers of conversation drifted up to them.

When they reached the main floor, Richard saw large numbers of people gathered in small groups all around the expansive corridor, engaged in worried talk about what had just happened. Richard could see soldiers and workers in the distance dealing with the remains of Mr. Burkett as well as a broad area covered with greasy ash—the remains of the Glee Richard had killed.

The hushed conversations, fearful talk, and tearful stories tapered off and died out when the Lord Rahl, the Mother Confessor, and the alluring Shale marched through their midst with five Mord-Sith in red leather escorting them. The eyes of hundreds of people watched them making their way along the corridor. Some were probably surprised to see the Mother Confessor in traveling clothes and wearing a long knife at her belt. Business at the shops had come to an end after many of the customers as well as the people working in the shops had fled in fear for their lives.

Richard wondered if the Golden Goddess was watching through any of those eyes, and if another attack would suddenly appear out of nowhere, possibly with many times the numbers sent for the last attack. He hoped the goddess had been watching through someone's eyes and had been discouraged from the notion that simply sending large numbers would bring her success. Richard feared it would, but maybe if she saw the ashes of hundreds of her kind up on the balcony it would discourage her.

Everyone with him watched nervously for another attack. Down in the corridor the Glee could kill hundreds. For the time being, though, they seemed to be focused on killing Richard and Kahlan, not the people in the palace.

Richard knew that by now a great number of people—both those seeing the battles play out up on the balcony, and others watching from the upper galleries—would have finally seen the frightening Glee. There was no more keeping it secret. Talk of such sightings, the deadly battle, and power unleashed by the Lord Rahl against the howling monsters would be spreading to every corner of the palace. By morning, everyone would have heard about it. Everyone would be talking about little else.

He knew that fear would have many people either holed up in their quarters or fleeing the palace. There was no safe place anywhere in their world, of course, but the people didn't know that. As far as Richard was concerned, his job was to worry about finding a way to stop the threat, not to give them comfort and assurances.

As they quickly moved down the corridor, he wondered about the lone Glee he had seen off on the opposing balcony, just standing there, watching him. Richard feared to imagine what that was about. Something about the look they shared still haunted him.

At the least, that silent observer had seen Richard turn more than a hundred of its kind to ash. If it had been there as a spy for the goddess, then it had some bad news to report back to her. He didn't know if such a report would strike fear into her heart, or merely make her angry and even more determined. What he did know was that appeasement wasn't an option.

Turning off the main corridor, Harris, in the lead, finally took Richard and company out of the public areas and out of the sight of so many people. He wondered if she would think of watching them through Harris's eye. Once they were in the restricted areas, he took them down a series of hallways and corridors.

Kahlan, almost having to run, put her arm through Richard's as she leaned close. "We will get her back, Richard."

Richard nodded. "As long as I'm alive, we will."

"Don't put it that way," she admonished. "Not after what just happened back there."

Richard forced himself to show her a smile as he briefly hugged her close with one arm.

Four soldiers standing guard over an even more highly restricted area saw him coming accompanied by Mord-Sith. They saluted with fists to hearts. Richard was aware that it would only take one ungifted person, like one of those four soldiers, for the goddess to see where they were going.

Richard didn't have any idea how the goddess selected a person to use as an observer. He hoped that maybe it took her a bit of time to find a new person.

"Just because we're in the restricted corridors," he told the rest of those with him, "doesn't mean we're safe. The Glee can show up in here just as easily as they did up on the balcony. Stay alert."

The Mord-Sith, all spinning their Agiels at the end of the fine gold chains around their wrists, nodded.

Inside the next set of doors was a simple stone service stairwell that echoed all the way down four flights of stairs. At the bottom there was a small room with a locked door. Harris, who fortunately had keys for such doors, hurriedly unlocked it. Beyond, a broad hallway stretched off into darkness.

"People don't have any reason to regularly come down here, so it isn't kept lighted," Harris explained. He gestured to shelves. "We'll need to take some of those lamps."

He collected one of the dozens from the shelf, then lit it with a splinter he caught to flame from another lamp mounted to the wall outside that door. Each of the Mord-Sith collected a lamp and let him light theirs from the same splinter.

Harris pointed off into the darkness. "Down that way is where all of the palace plans are kept."

Nyda stepped out in front of the group. "Wait here. Let me and Vale go check, first."

Richard was in a hurry, but considering how many surprise attacks they had experienced, he decided to let them do their job. He tilted his head for them to go on ahead, then watched as the bubble of light moved with them down the long, dark stone passageway until they reached double doors the end.

Nyda's voice echoed when she turned and called back to them, "Clear."

Richard knew that there was no such thing as clear. The Glee could show up anywhere, but at least he knew they weren't waiting for them down in the darkness. At least, not yet.

"Let's go," he said as he started out.

The rest of the group followed down the passageway of gray stone to the gray-painted, broad metal door. There was an odd kind of lock built into the door that required moving a series of five levers sticking out of the metal covering up or down to one of several dozen specific, marked positions. Once the man had the levers properly positioned, he pulled up on a heavy lever to draw the bolt back. The hinges squealed in protest as it swung open. The air that escaped smelled musty.

"What do you do if you forget the lock sequence?" Richard asked. "Or if you go missing and they need to open the door?"

Harris shrugged with a smile. "There are a half-dozen palace officials who know the lock sequence, but if none of them could be found and if it was important enough, then I guess the soldiers would simply break it down. It's not like a vault door, such as the one to get into the inner shaft of the plateau, and it's not protecting a treasure of gold. It's a strong metal door, but with enough effort I would guess it could be broken down. The lock is basically meant to keep out people who might be snooping around where they don't belong. An enemy who wanted to attack the palace, for example, could make good use of all the plans and diagrams in here. That's why it's locked."

"I guess that makes sense," Richard said as all of the Mord-Sith rushed in before the door was even fully opened.

"Did Mr. Burkett know the sequences for the lock levers?"

"Of course. Him and then six of his assistants, including me."

Richard didn't say anything, but Mr. Burkett had already proven he was willing to betray the interests of the palace. Richard had wanted him out of the palace and banished forever. But considering that he knew the lock combination, not only to this place but, Richard had to assume, to many others, it was probably a good thing that he was dead.

Once inside, Shale swept out her arm to light all the lamps placed liberally around the surprisingly vast room. It was a lot bigger than Richard had envisioned. Arches all around the outside walls were held up by unadorned stone pillars. Three more substantial pillars down the center of the room held up the row of arches that in turn held up the vaulted ceilings.

Between each pillar against all the walls, crosshatched boards created what had to be thousands of uniform, diamond-shaped cubbyholes for all the rolled-up diagrams. A series of at least a dozen large tables sat in the center of the room, each big enough to spread out one or more of the diagrams. Richard couldn't even begin to guess at the number of rolled-up plans.

Harris went to the right, to the nearest series of cubbyholes holding rolled plans. He pointed up at the label in the top of the arch.

"See? Everything is numbered and labeled so you can find the plan you need if you know the section name in the palace. If you don't, there is a map of each floor over there where each section is labeled. This section between pillars and the ones next to it are all 'W.' We need sections with 'M' at the top."

The five Mord-Sith spread out, going around the room, looking at the letter at the top of each arch.

"Here they are," Cassia called out from the far-right corner. "Section M."

"See here?" Harris asked when they reached the section she had found. "They're organized in vertical rows. Here are rows A and then rows B and so on. Depending on the number of areas with rolled plans, those rows might continue on the other side of the pillar."

He trailed his finger down one row and then down two more before he leaned in to check the numbers on the bottom of the cubbyholes. He had to go to the end of the section they were in; then he pulled out a long, rolled plan. At the nearest table he spread it out, putting weights each table had on the sides to keep the plans from rolling back up.

He pointed. "See, it's written here, down at the bottom. 'M$_{\text{III}}$-B.'"

Richard, standing at the edge of the table, looking down at the diagram, leaned in a little. Everyone to either side leaned in, looking with him. Richard was the only one who actually knew what he was looking at.

He stared at what he was seeing, hardly able to believe it.

"What's wrong?" Kahlan asked. "Your face just turned white."

"Lord Rahl, what is it?" Shale asked in the dragging silence.

Richard's gaze traced all of the passageways, the rooms, the circular halls, the dead ends, the entrapments, the false helix, the lateral routes, the complex of twinned and tripled passageways, checking, hoping he was wrong.

He wasn't.

"We're in trouble," he said, not really having intended to say it out loud.

53

"Why are we in trouble?" Kahlan asked, alarmed by the way he was acting. He seemed not to hear her. "Richard, why are we in trouble?"

She finally had to put a finger on the side of his jaw and turn his face toward her to get him to pay attention.

"What?"

"You said we're in trouble. Why are we in trouble?"

Richard straightened and took a step away from the table as he raked his fingers back through his hair.

"Richard," Kahlan said again, this time with exaggerated patience, drawing his name out to make him look at her, "what do you see? What is it?"

He stared at her for a long moment. "It's a complication."

"Well, I can see by the weird and confusing design of the place that it looks incredibly complicated. But what do you see?"

He was shaking his head even as she was talking.

"No. You don't understand. It's a complication." He swept a hand out over the plan. "This kind of design is called a complication."

Shale looked exasperated. "You mean it's an exceedingly complicated maze? We all can see that. Is that what you mean to say?"

"No," Richard said, irritably, as if no one was really paying attention to what he was saying. "No. I mean it's a complication."

"Richard," Kahlan said, pinching the bridge of her nose with a finger and thumb as she let out a composing breath, "I know you think that should explain it, but we don't understand what that means to you. You need to tell us what you mean by that. What are you trying to say?"

Kahlan knew that Richard's unorthodox way of thinking often

galloped so far out ahead of what they saw, taking into account things only he knew about or understood, that he often seemed to make no sense. It was one of the reasons the Mord-Sith, along with others, sometimes said he acted crazy. It seemed that way to people because they didn't understand what was in his head.

"It's a complication. That's what this kind of design is called. That is the name for it: a complication." Richard lifted an arm, indicating everything above. "This whole place is laid out atop a spell-form drawn on the ground."

"The People's Palace," Kahlan said, nodding, "yes, we know that. We know the palace is a spell-form."

Shale leaned in, holding a hand against her arm. "A what? A spell-form? Now what are you talking about? You're beginning to sound as crazy as him."

Richard squinted at her in a way that told Kahlan he was having a hard time believing Shale would ask something so basic. "You know... a spell-form."

Shale folded her arms and straightened without saying anything, clearly not understanding and expecting him to explain.

Richard took a settling breath to back himself up. "Well, you know what a Grace is, right?"

"A Grace?" Shale squinted with uncertainty at what he was getting at. "Well yes, my mother and father taught me to draw a Grace when I was little. I know what a Grace is. What does that have to do with anything?"

Richard leaned toward her a bit. "A Grace is an example of a spell-form. The lines that make up the Grace, the design of it, is called a spell-form." He moved his finger around in the air before him as if drawing a Grace. "When you drew the Grace you were drawing one example of a spell-form."

It was Shale's turn to frown. "I don't know what you're talking about. A Grace is a Grace is a Grace."

Richard threw up his hands in exasperation. "A Grace is a spell-form! Like any spell-form it can be drawn in different ways for different purposes."

"Different purposes? Now what are you talking about?"

"Think of the spell-form this way. Imagine a plan drawn for a building. That's called a building design, right? But the resulting building can be different, depending on how you draw the design. Do you see what I mean? It can have more rooms or more floors drawn on the design and the resulting reality in brick and mortar will be a reflection of how the design was drawn."

She stared openly at him a moment. "So, a spell-form, such as the Grace, can be drawn in different ways?"

"Of course. Didn't your parents warn you never to draw it in blood? Or out of order?"

"Well, obviously."

"That's because a Grace is a spell-form, and like all spell-forms, since they involve magic, if not drawn correctly they can cause great trouble. There are certain spell-forms that are lethal if drawn incorrectly or in the wrong order. Some, like the Grace, if deliberately drawn by a strongly gifted person in certain ways other than the formal procedure like you were taught, can be used to invoke any number of things."

"Any number of things?" Shale was still frowning as she watched him. "Like what?"

"Well, drawn by the right person, in a specific order and manner, a Grace can conjure up the world of the dead. The Grace is only one of many examples of spell-forms, some of them very minor and relatively unimportant and some quite consequential."

Shale shook her head to herself. "I'm afraid that where I grew up the gifted were few and far between. I never learned anything about spell-forms, other than what my parents taught me about how to draw the Grace."

Richard cooled a bit, turning sympathetic. "I understand. I grew up in a place without magic. I've since had to learn about it. One of the things I had to learn is the language of Creation. The language of Creation actually uses some elements of spell-forms because it's representational language."

"Representational language?"

"Sure. If you see a simple drawing of a bird, it conveys a whole array of meaning—a concept—without needing words, right? That's how the language of Creation works. It conveys meaning and concepts through symbols, designs, and emblems rather than words."

She looked intrigued. "Someday you will have to tell me more about the language of Creation, but for now, what is the important point about this particular spell-form?"

Richard pointed a finger toward the ceiling, rotating his hand around to indicate everything above them. "The People's Palace is laid out in the shape of a giant spell-form, the purpose of which is to give the Lord Rahl more power when he is here, in his home, also called the House of Rahl. That makes the People's Palace a place of power for the Lord Rahl."

"More power? More power like what?"

"Like when I turned all those Glee to ash. I was in part aided by the power of the spell-form of the palace itself. It helped me by adding energy to what I did—because I am the Lord Rahl. That's the purpose of the way the palace was originally designed. Like a castle has thick walls and defensive parapets and ramparts, the People's Palace was built on a giant spell-form drawn on the ground. That spell-form gives it its shape and is its means of defense for the House of Rahl by augmenting their magic."

Shale blinked as she thought about it. "No wonder the halls are so confusing."

"Not if you know the specific spell and the language of Creation. If you do, the layout of the palace makes perfect sense. It's elegant in its simplicity... as a spell-form."

"Sure, perfect sense," she mocked. She gestured at the plan on the table. "So then, what's this business about a complication?"

Richard turned back to the diagram as he let out an unhappy sigh. "A complication, which is a spell-form, is an ancillary element of the principal spell-form to which it is attached. In this case, it's a subordinate, supporting spell-form, meant to add power to the rest of the spell-form that is the palace. You might say it's like extra descriptive words in a sentence."

"So it is a spell-form that exists on its own and it can also be a supporting element of another spell-form?"

"Yes and no," Richard told her. "This is a specific type of spell-form called a complication. It's not meant to ever exactly exist on its own. Its purpose is to add capability to the spell-form to which it is attached."

"Then it has a purpose for being here, for being built into the palace," Kahlan said.

"Yes."

"So then why does it have you so worried and upset?"

Richard took a deep breath. "The simplest way to explain the problem is that in the language of Creation, the primary elemental component of this particular spell-form means 'chaos.' That means that this spell-form adds an element of chaos to the power of the palace spell."

54

"Chaos," Kahlan repeated. "In what way?"

Richard lifted a hand as if to say that it was unknowable. "It adds its power to the main spell to which it is attached in chaotic ways, meaning there is no way to predict what it will do. That makes the primary spell-form of the palace more dangerous to enemies of the House of Rahl."

Kahlan wasn't at all sure how such a spell would work. "Why would a chaotic element make the main spell-form more dangerous?"

"Because if a wizard—a Rahl here at the palace—uses his magic against a gifted enemy, the palace spell-form amplifies the power of the web he casts."

"All right," Kahlan said. "That makes sense."

Richard held up a finger. "But a dangerously gifted enemy will know how to counter magic. See the problem?"

Kahlan, trying to follow, frowned in concentration. "No."

"The spell-form of the palace is a known, specific spell-form and for someone powerfully gifted and experienced, it is therefore predictable in how it amplifies a Rahl's power. Predictability means it can be anticipated and if it can be anticipated it can be countered. If a Rahl's magic is countered, then it is rendered ineffective against the enemy, right?

"To solve that predictability problem, what the creators of the People's Palace did was to add in this chaotic complication."

"You mean it's like gravy on a meat pie?" Shale asked.

Richard smiled at her sarcasm. "Sort of. Lumpy gravy, and you don't know what's in the lumps."

He held out a hand toward the plan on the table. "In this case, this complication's function is to make the web cast by the Lord Rahl and amplified by the primary palace spell chaotically unpredictable. That makes it nearly impossible for a gifted enemy to defend against. See? It's hard if not impossible to put up a defense if you don't know what's coming."

"That's incredibly devious," Kahlan said as she thought about it.

"Indeed it is," Richard said with a nod.

"Then having it here within the palace must not be so dangerous," Shale said as she paced off a short distance, considering, and then returned. "After all, it's been here for millennia, hasn't it? And it was meant to help a Rahl. So why do you all of a sudden think it's such a problem?"

Richard wiped a hand back across his face. "Well, because it's not simply a complication drawn in sand or blood meant to attach to another spell-form drawn in sand or blood to cast a web. This one is huge, and it exists in stone and mortar, not in the dirt drawn with a stick. That means we're going to need to actually go inside the complication." He leaned closer to her. "Inside it."

"We're inside the palace spell-form right now," Shale said with a shrug.

"Hens and hawks. Both birds, not the same animal."

Kahlan was beginning to grasp his concern. "So that's why Moravaska Michec would hide in there? Because it's like he's hiding in a giant thorn hedge?"

Richard nodded. He turned to Edward Harris. "Could you please get me the plans for this region of the palace—the surrounding areas? And the levels above and below?"

After consulting the palace map, the man went around the room, pulling rolls of the appropriate plans out of their cubbyholes, holding them under an arm as he collected all the ones needed. Once he had them all, he spread them out on the adjacent tables, putting weights on the sides to hold them open. Following along behind him, Richard reviewed each one, looking increasingly upset with everything he saw.

"What?" Kahlan finally asked as he silently studied one, then another, then went back to the first, then to the last. "What do you see?"

His brow lowered as he leaned in over the plans laid out on all the tables. "This thing is even more extensive than I thought at first. This complication spell isn't technically two-dimensional, so it's not a single floor, but actually a number of floors that are involved, all of it self-contained in its own compartmentalized, separate location. Look here," he said, pointing, "this is the whole restricted wing of the palace where the complication is located, and all of this is the complication. It's enormous. I mean, really enormous. Not simply in terms of length and width, but on multiple levels.

"It's one gigantic, three-dimensional labyrinth. I can easily see why people who went in there became lost and were never seen again. If you became disoriented, and didn't understand the nature of the layout, it would be easy to get lost and never find your way out. That's why I needed the plans. I need to understand them so that we'll know where we are once in there.

"This kind of spell-form, being chaotic, is naturally unpredictable, so the builders deliberately kept it totally isolated. When the palace spell uses it, it becomes involved and has purpose."

He gave both Shale and Kahlan a deadly serious look. "But when it's idle and left to its own devices, since it's a chaotic element, it's unpredictable."

"Unpredictable," Kahlan repeated, folding her arms as she looked from his raptor gaze down at the plans, seeing the maze of halls and rooms and staircases in a new light. "We get the concept. It adds chaos to the palace spell."

Richard was shaking his head. "No, I mean it's unpredictable in and of itself."

Kahlan frowned her skepticism. "Are you saying this place made up of confusing halls and rooms can do things on its own, independent of the palace spell?"

Richard nodded. "Exactly. In the right circumstances, this kind of spell-form would be semi-sentient."

Shale's jaw dropped. "What! Are you actually suggesting that it's alive?"

Richard waved a hand, dismissing the notion. "No, no, it's not alive. I oversimplified what I meant. Its specific purpose is to decide on its own, because it's a chaos spell-form, how to add power to the primary spell-form. See what I mean? Because it has the power to decide what to do and when, that process makes it seem to mimic life. When I used my power, and the palace's spell added power, this complication likely added some unpredictable, violent element, making what I did to the Glee functionally more lethal. That makes it virtually impossible to defend against."

Richard leaned in, giving them both a serious look again. "But when idle and left to its own devices, a spell-form of this nature doesn't simply sit there. It's always active, a pot always on the boil, so it can do dangerously unpredictable things, such as entice people in."

Shale made a face. "Why? Why would it entice people in?"

Richard stared at her for a long moment. "As a self-generated activity—as entertainment, you might say. Not exactly, but that's the best way I can explain how its function appears to us. Absent direction from the primary spell-form, it boils up and acts on its own, kind of like a curious child when left alone. It starts doing things as a way to fulfill its primary purpose. It's a hammer, and pretty soon, if not used, it starts to think everything is a nail. When we go in there, we are the nail."

"Dear spirits." Kahlan put a hand to her forehead. "Why in the world would they build something that dangerous into the palace?"

"Because it has a valid purpose," Richard said. "If left entirely isolated, it's not an issue, and that is what was intended. See here? The complication is not only off-limits, but completely isolated. The builders put it on dedicated levels off to the side, diagonally, under the tombs. To further isolate it, they built in locked doors preventing people from even getting to the stairs down to the complication. It can't hurt you if you don't go near it."

"How can it hurt us?" Kahlan asked. "What can it do to us if we go in there?"

Richard shook his head. "I don't know. All I can tell you is that whatever it does will be unpredictable."

"Then we should leave," Shale announced. "You've just done a thorough job of explaining why this complication spell is incredibly dangerous.

"This isn't your primary objective," she reminded him with a shake of her finger. "Your duty is to get yourself and the Mother Confessor to the safety of the Wizard's Keep. The future of magic and the lives of everyone in our world depend on it. The safety of children yet unborn depends on it. Your gift, the Mother Confessor's gift, your unborn children, are more important than getting Vika out of there."

"I hate to say it," Rikka said, "but the sorceress has a point. Like all of us, Vika knows the risks of protecting you. As terrified as she rightfully is of Michec, she would want to die at his hands rather than have you put your life and the life of the Mother Confessor at risk to come in there after her."

"I agree," Vale said. "Your safety and the Mother Confessor's safety are what matters. We should avoid this danger and get to the Keep."

Nyda nodded her agreement. Cassia did so next. Berdine turned her face away and nodded.

"You don't understand," Richard said. "Yes, I want to get Vika out of that man's clutches, but this is about something more important. If Moravaska Michec is what you all say he is, then once we leave, he will undoubtedly strike at our backs when we least expect it. He could sabotage our cause just as effectively as the Glee in ways we can't even imagine. He doesn't want me to rule as the Lord Rahl. If we leave and he takes over the palace…"

"Richard is right," Kahlan said. "You don't leave a powerful enemy hiding in your home to come at you when you're asleep."

"Why would Michec be hiding in this complication thing?" Shale asked. "Wouldn't it be dangerous to him as well?"

"Not if he understands it," Richard said.

"He did," Nyda confirmed. "He often took captives in there."

"He's hiding in there, waiting for the right time to kill you," Berdine said. "Taking Vika proves it."

"Well, that place down there isn't called the Wasteland for nothing," Harris said. "We always did our best to keep people away from the section. Somehow people still got in."

Richard nodded. "The spell-form self-generates things to act on as a way to carry out its destructive, defensive function. I guess you could say it practices killing by enticing unsuspecting people in there and killing them. Moravaska Michec isn't unsuspecting, so the spell-form is in a way his protection."

Harris shook his head. "I just don't see how, with it being behind all kinds of locked doors and guard posts, people still manage to wander in there."

"The complication has the ability to undo locks," Richard said. When they all stared at him, he added, "Because locks are part of the palace, and so is the complication, it's very possible it can unlock the doors."

"If people die in there," Shale asked Harris, "then how do you really know that people find their way out there? I thought that people never returned from that place."

"Well, over the years a few people have wandered out," he said. "They all died, however, shortly after escaping. But before dying they reported seeing corpses in there, or human bones. I'm not sure what they died of because the First File was responsible for such things, but I know that since it's their responsibility to keep everyone away, the soldiers were quite alarmed to discover people coming out."

Shale finally let out a deep sigh. "I can see that I'm not going to be able to talk you out of going in there, and probably for good reason. But if it's that dangerous, then I think the Mother Confessor shouldn't go in. I will protect her while you go in and deal with Michec."

Richard shook his head. "I appreciate the thought, but that's not a good idea. For all we know, he could be expecting that and while I'm in there trying to find him, he could actually be lurking out here in order to strike at Kahlan. Besides, as you said, he's a witch man. You're a witch woman."

Shale arched an eyebrow. "You seem to know everything, so now you need me?"

"I hardly know everything, Shale. I do know I need your ability. We're stronger together. In our own way, we each help fill in the blanks. I agree that it's dangerous for all of us to go in there, but the situation we have on our hands now is that it's more dangerous for us to split up and more dangerous yet to simply leave this witch man lurking in the maze down there. Taking Vika was his first act of war against us. He very well might have done it to get us to run."

Shale folded her arms as she looked away in thought. "I hate to admit it, but I think you may be right."

"So how are we going to deal with him?" Kahlan asked. "He is a witch man. We know all too well how dangerous witch women, like Shota, can be. For all we know, he could be much more powerful. Plus he has us at a disadvantage because he has been living and hiding in there for a very long time. He knows the layout and how to use the complication to his advantage. He's had time to plot his revenge. How are we going to be able to deal with someone like that?"

Richard gazed into her eyes. "If I have to, I will strangle him to death with my bare hands."

55

"That's the passageway, there, Lord Rahl," Nyda said in a low voice. "Beyond lies the Wasteland."

"Just so you understand," Rikka told him, "Vika is most likely dead by now. Michec would not want to let you have any hope of saving her. He would want to use her death to make you feel powerless against him. His specialty is making his victims feel helpless."

Richard shook his head as he stared off into the darkness. "A man like Michec has bigger designs than killing Vika. His desire is to eliminate me. To do that, he will need her alive as bait."

Rikka let out a deep breath. "I have to admit, that's a possibility. He must feel you are vulnerable."

"You mean because of the goddess?" Kahlan asked.

Rikka nodded. "He has a way of knowing things. He would have chosen this time to strike while you already have an incredibly difficult situation on your hands. He came and took Vika before we could leave in order to keep you here."

Richard checked a side hall as they went past. "All the more reason we can't leave and allow him to have free run of the palace. There is no telling what sort of treason he could be up to."

While Richard and those with him were on their way to find Michec, he had sent Edward Harris back. Harris swore that he would oversee the staff until Richard's return.

He also swore to investigate any influence by Moravaska Michec among the palace staff. Richard told him that if he found any connections, to have the First File deal with it harshly.

It had been a long way down to where the tombs were located, and then another long journey to the isolated section MIII-B. The eight soldiers at the guard station at the first of the locked doors reported no activity.

They admitted that in the past people had been discovered beating on the locked doors from the other side. The doors were opened to release those people, but strict orders said that under no circumstances were they to go in beyond the fourth locked door, even to look for others.

When the soldiers opened the first massive door and Richard stepped inside, glass spheres in brackets began to glow. The soldiers, carrying lamps, were surprised. Richard wasn't.

The soldiers weren't the only ones surprised. Shale gaped at the glowing glass spheres. "What in the world...?"

"Light spheres. They were created by ancient wizards," Richard told her. "They can still be found in a number of isolated places, not only here at the palace."

Standing beyond the first door, inside the lighted area illuminated by the spheres, Richard turned to the soldier.

"Do the other men also have keys?"

The soldier looked a little puzzled. "Yes, Lord Rahl."

He really didn't want any of the men getting any closer than necessary to the spell-form of the complication that waited beyond the fourth locked door.

"Then give me your keys. I'll return them when we come back out."

The man looked apprehensive. "Lord Rahl, we have men here who can escort you for protection."

Rikka gestured around at her sister Mord-Sith. "What do you think we're here for? Just to look pretty?"

"That's not..." The big soldier took one look at her glare and cleared his throat. "I can see that you have adequate protection with you." He glanced back at Richard, eager to look away from the displeased Mord-Sith. "We will be at our post should you need us, Lord Rahl."

"Have you or the others seen anything out of the ordinary recently?" Richard asked the soldier.

"Out of the ordinary? No, Lord Rahl. It's been as quiet as a tomb down here. Always is."

Richard nodded, thanking the man, and then closed and locked the first door. It felt ominous being beyond that first barrier on their way into what he knew to be a dangerously unpredictable spell-form.

"What really bothers me," Richard said as he pulled the key from the lock, "is how Michec was able to come and go from this place. It appears he may have been hiding down here for a long while, waiting for the right time to strike. But no matter how long he's been here, he would need to come out from time to time for supplies. And, he obviously went up to the stables to capture Vika and take her back in there with him."

In the silence, Richard turned back to look at the rest of them. "So, how was Michec coming and going?"

"Maybe there's another way in and out," Kahlan suggested as they reached the second vaultlike door. "You know, a secret entrance of some kind. Maybe a service entrance."

"That wouldn't be necessary," Shale said.

Richard had to turn keys in two sets of locks in the second door, and then lift a long lever to draw back heavy bolts.

He turned back to Shale. "What do you mean? Why wouldn't it be necessary?"

He pulled open the second door. Beyond was another small, empty room made up of rough stone blocks. Light spheres in four brackets began to glow as they all stepped into the room.

"This Michec character wouldn't need a secret way in and out. He's a witch man." Shale shrugged, as if that should explain everything. She glided a hand over the top of one of the glowing glass spheres. "These light spheres, as you called them, start glowing a faint green, getting brighter as we get close, to then glow with a warm yellow-white light when we're even closer and like now, when I put my hand on it."

"They react to the presence of the gift," Richard said as he unlocked the two locks on the third door. "Between you, Kahlan, and me, they have what's needed to make them glow. Now, what do you mean about Michec not needing a secret way in and out?"

Shale's brow twitched. "I told you. He's a witch man."

"So?"

"Witch women are masters of illusion. As a witch man, I can't even imagine how powerful he might be. That kind could easily create an illusion that he wasn't there. That's how I intend to get us away from the palace without the soldiers, and thus the goddess, knowing we are leaving or which direction we were going. Don't you remember that I said I would take care of it?"

Everyone stared at her. Richard pulled open the door, revealing the same sort of plain room and the substantial fourth door on the opposite wall. That last one had four locks—two on each side. Instead of a lever, it had a wheel in the center.

"You can do such a thing?" Kahlan asked.

"I'm a witch woman. Of course I can. If I can make snakes appear and disappear from around your ankles, don't you suppose I can make people not see us leaving?"

"Snakes?" Richard turned to Kahlan. "What's she talking about?"

Kahlan waved off the question. "So then Michec could cast a web so that the soldiers wouldn't see him coming and going?"

Shale frowned her incredulity. "You two really don't know much about witch women, do you?"

"What about the locks?" As soon as all of them had stepped into the little room Richard pulled the third door closed and then locked it.

"I'm not sure." Shale's face twisted in thought a moment. "Could be any of several methods to defeat them."

"Like what?" Richard pressed.

"Well, one simple way would be to cast a web to make the guards curious enough to come to check on things and unlock all the doors, giving him the chance to slip in before they are satisfied there was nothing there, and lock the doors."

Richard didn't like to think how easy it would be for someone gifted in such a way to create trouble. "But to get back out, would he be able do that from beyond four locked doors? Could he somehow make the guards come back to unlock all the doors so he could get out? And wouldn't they get suspicious when they were unlocking the doors so often over nothing?"

Shale looked back at the third door Richard had just locked as she considered. "I'm not sure, but there's an even simpler explanation."

"Like what?" Kahlan asked.

"He could have used a concealment spell so the guards wouldn't see him and then simply taken a set of spare keys, like the ones you borrowed."

Richard grunted unhappily. "You're right. That certainly would be easier. Then, all he would have to do is cast a concealment web to go unnoticed as he came and went?"

Shale nodded. "That's the idea."

Richard unlocked the locks on each side of the final door and then started spinning the wheel in the center. As he did, it drew the heavy bolts back from the iron doorframe set into massive stone blocks to each side.

"It certainly looks like the builders went to a lot of trouble to make sure no one got in here," Kahlan said.

Richard pulled on the door. "Unfortunately, they didn't take witch men into account." The door was so heavy that he had to tug on it several times to start it moving. Once it did start, it slowly glided open on silent hinges.

With the door standing wide open, they all stood and stared in amazement at what lay beyond.

56

There before them, beyond a wide space that stretched off for quite a distance until it vanished into darkness on each side, stood a tall wall made up of huge blocks of age-darkened stone. As with the sides, the light failed to reach far enough up for them to see the full height, but from remembering the plans, Richard thought it rose possibly three stories high. The width of it was far greater.

It almost appeared as if they were standing before a massive castle, as imposing as any Richard had ever seen, as if it had already been there for eons when the House of Rahl came along, and then it had been left in place and the palace built around it. He knew, of course, that wasn't the case, but that was the impression it left him with.

In the center of the wall was a great doorway surrounded by a series of stepped stone arches jutting out from the face of the wall. Each of those stone arches, some carved to look like rope, some with repeated designs, was layered on top of a broader one behind. The mass of those intricate, layered arches was so thick they stood out several feet from the wall. The stacked arches surrounding the wooden wall with the door had to be a couple of stories tall.

A wall of age-darkened oak with large hammered-iron studs laid out in a grid pattern was set back far enough in the deep opening of the enormous arches that it almost made it look like a vestibule. Iron straps crisscrossed over the face of the heavy oak door in the center of that wall. Iron studs pinned where each of the straps crossed connected them solidly together. The strap-hinges looked large enough to easily hold up the weight of the door. There were no locks in the door; there was simply a big iron ring in the center, held out in the hooked beak of a cast bronze eagle head, presumably used to pull open the door.

"Why do you suppose there would be such an elaborate and imposing entryway beyond the four locked doors?" Kahlan asked. "After all, who is going to see it?"

Richard shook his head as he studied the wall and the entryway, looking for anything suspicious. "I can't imagine." His brow twitched. "Unless it's to pay homage to the spell."

"You have to be kidding," Shale said.

Richard merely flashed her a brief smile.

They all shared looks before Richard finally ascended three monolithic slabs making up the stone steps to get up to the door. He hesitated, wiping his palms on his pants before using both hands to grip the big iron ring held in the eagle's beak. The door glided open, almost willingly, to reveal just the beginning of a dark corridor beyond.

"Are you sure about this, Lord Rahl?" Rikka asked.

Rather than answer, Richard walked through the doorway and into the dark corridor. As glass spheres to each side began to glow, he could see that it was a vast passageway that stretched off into darkness in a gentle curve to the right. He was pretty sure he knew which curved element it was from the spell-form of the complication. Grimy-looking stone walls rose up high to each side. Ornate crown moldings at the edge of the ceiling appeared to be carved from stone as well.

The corners of the ceiling and even joints in the stone of the walls had layers of dirty cobwebs that waved slightly as the air moved when they walked in.

The floor was covered with a variety of darker marble tiles in a spiraled gridwork pattern. Big squares holding stone mosaics were set into frames of large marble tiles. The designs of the floor swept off into the distance, elaborate, yet dimmed over time by dust and dirt. The gloomy stone making up the walls appeared to be just as grimy from many centuries of accumulated dust. The walls and the floor were so dark they seemed to suck up the light. All the grout lines in the marble floor were packed with millennia of dirt that helped to darken the whole floor.

Michec might have been a warlock who could cast concealment spells, but as far as Richard knew, he couldn't fly, so he had left footprints in the dusty floor just like any mortal. A pathway through the dirt and dust told Richard that the man had probably been hiding down in section M111-B for some time, since his coming and going had nearly cleared the grimy dirt away down the center of the broad passageway.

Richard spotted smaller footprints near the side, as if a lost woman had kept a hand on the wall for guidance as she walked haltingly on her way farther in to answer a calling from the complication spell. The light spheres wouldn't work unless you were gifted, so unless she carried a lamp, she would have been blind in the total darkness, driven on by a compulsion she didn't understand.

From the well-worn path through the dust, Richard couldn't help but wonder how many times Michec had gone up into the palace proper and what he done on those occasions. He did know that one of those times he had captured Vika.

As Richard moved farther into the corridor, everyone followed silently. Richard held a hand back, touching Kahlan to make sure she stayed close. Nearby glass spheres in iron brackets all the way down the corridor began to glow when they got close enough, making it seem almost as if they were alive, the light welcoming and escorting them in, but the somber stone passageway was so murky that the glass spheres didn't do much to illuminate anything beyond their immediate area.

Before long, as the corridor curved off into the distance, they encountered rooms randomly placed to each side. At each room, since they had no light spheres, Richard took one of the plentiful spheres from a bracket in the hall and carried it with him. The rooms were various sizes, dark, and all were empty. They were elaborately trimmed with complex molding, some with patterned stone paneling, but there was no furniture.

"Why in the world are there rooms in here?" Shale asked, sounding annoyed by the uncanny uselessness of the rooms.

"They're actually representations of nodules in the complication," Richard told her. "If you were to draw this spell-form in the dirt with a stick, these would be little tick marks you would make along the main, sweeping line of the spell. Their number and spacing has meaning to the complication. But since the spell-form is so big, it appears that rooms serve that purpose."

"The rooms aren't close enough to share walls," Kahlan noticed. "So what's in the space between the rooms?"

Richard peered around in another of the empty rooms. "Good question. I have no idea, but since the empty space between the lines and nodes of the design doesn't serve a function, I suspect those spaces are simply filled in with rubble or possibly stone blocks."

When they finally came to a closed door on the left, Kahlan stopped and pointed in alarm. "Look. There are fingers sticking out from under that door."

Richard turned the latch and pushed the door partway open against the weight of a desiccated corpse of a woman lying on the other side. The body looked like it might have been there for many decades, possibly centuries. Coils of long hair were still attached to the almost black, leathery skin of the skull. The full dress was so layered in dust that it was hard to tell what color it had been. The arms sticking out from the sleeves were bones covered in thin, leathery skin that was just as dark as that on the skull.

The delicate, dried-out fingers of one hand were extended under the door in a feeble, dying effort to somehow open the door. The woman, probably dying of thirst, had given up in that spot as the life went out of her.

"Why would she be doing that?" Kahlan asked. "Reaching under the door like that?"

Richard leaned in far enough to look at the other side of the heavy door to confirm what he suspected. "This branch of the spell-form, behind the door, flows in only one direction: in this way."

Kahlan gave him a questioning frown. "So?"

"So, because it's a one-way element, you can go into the room because that's the direction of the flow. The door doesn't have a handle on the other side, so once you go in and the door shuts, you can't open it to come back out."

"Why wouldn't she break the door down?" Shale asked.

Richard arched an eyebrow. "It's a one-way element of the spell-form. Besides having no handle on the other side, this is an awfully heavy door for a small woman to break down. But even if she had been strong enough, it would also likely be blocked by the spell's magic to prevent anything flowing out."

"Such a trap door is dangerous!" Shale objected. "Why in the world would the builders have put that in here?"

"They were building a complication, not a palace attraction for visitors," Richard said. "No one is supposed to come in here. People aren't safe anywhere in here." He leaned in a little, giving her a look. "Not anywhere. That's why there are four locked doors protecting the place. That alone should tell you something important."

Shale's mouth twisted a little in concession. "I guess you have a point."

"Just keep that in mind," Richard told them. "Everywhere in the complication is dangerous in ways that we often won't even realize. So don't wander off to look at anything. Stay close and keep a sharp lookout."

57

After the heavy door pulled closed on its own, like the lid on a coffin, Richard, Kahlan, Shale, and the five Mord-Sith continued on in silence until they finally reached the end of the long, curved corridor. There was a passageway going off to the right and another to the left. The way straight ahead was blocked by a tall, flat metal door.

"How do we know where we need to go from here?" Kahlan asked.

"Since I don't know where Michec would be, or where he has Vika, I don't, actually," Richard told her, "but since we haven't come across any sign of either one, yet, we have no choice but to go farther in and keep looking.

"The hall to the left is essentially a dead end unless you correctly make a complicated series of choices necessary to get through the maze to an open element in the spell-form. If you make a wrong choice, you could wander around in there for a very long time before finding your way out, if ever. From knowing the complication and having studied the plan Harris showed us, I can tell you that this hallway here, to the right, if you make the correct turns, goes through a series of intersections until it eventually connects to the way ahead on the other side of the node behind this door and then deeper into the complication."

"So both the hall to the right and this door eventually meet back up?" Kahlan asked.

Richard nodded.

"What's behind the door?" Shale asked.

"If we're where I think we are in the complication, it's a node that should eventually link to a convergence of branches. In the spell-form as you would draw it, it's made as a circle with a line through it. That hall to the right is a way to get around this constricting node, but it's a lot longer way around. The quickest way into the heart of the spell-form is straight ahead through the doorway and across the node. Although it's longer, I think the safer way would be the hallways to the right."

"So if this isn't a room, then why is there a doorway here?" Kahlan asked.

"I don't know for sure, but I imagine it's a way to physically complete the circle of the node to match the way the spell-form is drawn."

Kahlan eyed the dark passageway to the right. "Well, I get a bad feeling about this hallway, here, to the right."

Shale looked from Kahlan to Richard. "Pregnant women have good instincts. I suggest you pay attention to them."

"I always trust Kahlan's instincts."

Richard opened the tall, heavy, flat metal door in front of them. As he did so, light spheres to either side beyond began to glow. They all stepped in and stood in a tight cluster on a small landing inside the doorway and stared out at the colossal octagonal room that came into view as the light spheres brightened.

The vast space stretched high up into darkness. There were no windows Richard could see. As soon as he realized that he was reflexively looking for windows even though windows would be pointless down here, he became newly aware of how deep underground they were, below even the tombs of his ancestors. That awareness brought back his old dread of being trapped in confined spaces underground.

A broad stone walkway built in the form of an arched bridge spanned across to another door on the opposite side of the octagonal room. The walkway was six or eight feet wide. Richard leaned out and looked down at the drop-off under the bridge. He couldn't see the bottom in the darkness below.

There was no walkway around the perimeter of the room to the other side. If they wanted to proceed, they would have to cross the bridge over the ominous pit.

Kahlan pressed a hand over her nose. "The smell of death is awful in here."

Richard took a light sphere from a bracket on the wall, held his breath, and leaned out, looking over the edge again. Even with the light sphere it was still too dark to see anything.

"The stench is too powerful to merely be some dead rats or small animals. It has to be the rotting corpses of people."

"How do you lose your balance on a walkway that wide and fall off?" Shale asked. "There is no railing, but still…"

Richard gave her a worried look. "Well, if they were moving through here in darkness, they could have simply stepped off the edge without realizing it."

Because of the smell of rotting flesh, and their need to get on with finding Michec, Richard didn't want to spend any more time in the octagonal room than it would take to get across.

Even though the bridge was plenty wide enough, everyone stood pressed up against the door at their backs. The gagging stench of death was so oppressive it made them all hesitant to proceed.

"Maybe we should go around after all," Kahlan said.

The landing they were on had a twin across on the other side of the bridge. There was a closed door at the other end of the bridge that looked the same as the one at their backs. On the walls all the way around the octagonal room were stacked stone moldings, as if at the base of the wall, as well as crown moldings, but there was no floor or ceiling. They were merely decorative. The unpleasant thought occurred to him that tombs were also decorated.

Carved medallions stood out on each facet of the octagon-shaped room. Richard leaned over the edge to peer down the walls. He could see that there were similar carved medallions far below, and also up high on the walls, both almost in darkness, both denoting other levels of the complication. The stone of the room, like the rest of the place they had seen so far, was covered in dark, dirty, gritty, mottled splotches, almost like lichen that grew on rocks. In some places it was draped with filthy cobwebs.

"I think we should trust your first instinct," Richard said. "After all, the other way around could have even worse things than this."

"Well, this is just ridiculous," Shale huffed, obviously nervous about the stone bridge. "Do you mean to tell me that this is part of a spell-form? Like you would draw in the dirt with a stick?"

"Actually, yes," Richard said. "Like I explained before. It's a kind of decorative element in the complication."

Shale's hands fisted at her sides. "Why in the world would the builders decorate this spell-form?"

It was clear that she didn't like the place one bit. Richard couldn't say that he blamed her. But it wasn't like they had a choice.

"Well, the People's Palace is similarly built in the shape of a spell-form laid out on the ground. It has a lot of beautiful, grand decorations—columns, arches, statues—that aren't needed for that spell-form. Things like that aren't really a part of the spell-form, so I can only assume the builders wanted to make it beautiful or interesting."

Shale scowled. "You call this beautiful?"

"No," Richard admitted. "I'd say this place looks—"

"Dangerous," Kahlan said as she stared out across the bridge.

Richard squeezed her hand. "The whole complication is dangerous, so that would make sense."

"Do you have any idea where Michec would be?" Shale asked.

When Richard gave a questioning look to the Mord-Sith, they all shook their heads.

"I don't either," Richard told her. "From the plans, this place is enormous. I can tell you that this is only the very tip of one edge of the spell-form, and it comprises several levels. Michec wasn't in any of those rooms behind us, so obviously he has to be deeper in." Richard pointed down. "By the footprints in the dust, he comes and goes this way, across the bridge. That would make sense, since the most straightforward way deeper into the heart of the spell-form is straight ahead across the bridge."

Nyda stepped out past Richard. "We'd better go across first and check, then."

Richard was about to object, but all five of the Mord-Sith pushed between him, Kahlan, and Shale and started across the bridge before he had a chance to argue.

Vale was the last one in line. She looked back over her shoulder. "Just wait there a minute until we check out what's beyond the door."

As she turned back to catch up with the others, the stone in the middle of the bridge abruptly shattered and began to fall away. Loud cracking noises came from the rest of the stone. Vale had to leap off one of the big blocks as it tipped and began to tumble into the darkness. Nyda and Cassia grabbed her arms and pulled her onto the far landing with them just as the rest of the stone bridge gave way underfoot and all dropped into the pit.

Clouds of dust rose up as the stone fell with a roar. Large blocks of stone, parts of blocks, chunks, lumps, and flakes all cascaded down into the black abyss.

The Mord-Sith all pressed their backs against the door as even the edge of the landing they were on began to crumble. To keep from falling, they opened the door and stepped back into the dark doorway.

Shale, Kahlan, and Richard backed up against their own door in disbelief as they watched the dust billowing up. They could hear the large blocks hitting the bottom somewhere far below in the darkness.

The five Mord-Sith stood in surprise across the room, in the dark doorway, staring back through the clouds of dust at Richard, Kahlan, and Shale. He was at least relieved that they all made it safely to the other side.

Shale was beside herself. "I thought this was a spell-form! How could that happen? It's obviously not drawn in the dirt collapsing into a big hole in the middle of it, is it?"

"No, it isn't."

"Then what just happened?" the sorceress demanded.

"Chaos." Richard drew his lower lip through his teeth. "The complication just did something chaotic."

Shale stared back at him. "Or it was a trap laid by Michec."

"Either way," Kahlan said, "we can't leave them over there and us over here. We need to all stay close together."

"You're right," Richard said. "All of you... wait there," he called across to the five Mord-Sith. "We'll go around and come meet you over there."

58

Kahlan followed closely behind Richard as he moved quickly down the side hallway. Shale brought up the rear, watching over her shoulder so that they wouldn't be surprised from behind. None of them said anything about it, but they were all worried about what could have caused the stone bridge to collapse. After all, it had been there since the palace had been built, and it certainly hadn't looked like it was weak.

They were even more worried, though, about the Mord-Sith being separated from them. After all, Michec had separated Vika from them. The bridge giving way felt too much by design.

Despite being in a hurry, Richard stopped briefly at each room they encountered. Each time he took a glass light sphere from a nearby bracket and used it so he could quickly check inside the dark rooms. Most were empty. Several were not.

The first one they found that wasn't empty had a mummified corpse of a man. Even though his clothes were covered with a thick layer of gray dust, they could still see that the dead man was wearing a fancy outfit. Under his embroidered coat there was a shirt with ruffles at the neck and cuffs, that Kahlan recognized as likely a sign of nobility. Expensive-looking rings were still on three of his fingers.

"Do you think," she wondered aloud, "that some of your wicked ancestors might have put people they didn't like behind the locked doors of this complication to let them wander around, looking for a way out, only to eventually die a slow and terrifying death in the darkness?"

Richard, on a knee taking a quick look at the dead noble, looked back over his shoulder. "I never thought of that, but you certainly could be right. What better way to rid yourself of a pesky detractor vying for power than to put them down here where they would never be found? I think that Darken Rahl, though, favored more public demonstrations of his displeasure."

Kahlan nodded. "He liked to make examples of people, so these bodies are likely from long before his time. The ones we've seen so far look to have been down here for hundreds of years."

In several places on their way down the hall, they came across yet more desiccated remains with leathery skin, and a few that were mostly bare bones. All the bodies, though, were still dressed in clothes. They found both men and women where they had finally collapsed and died. It was surprising to Kahlan to see how many people had managed to get into the remote place. Or were locked in. Despite the numbers they had found, she supposed that given the timespan it was rare for anyone to find their way in.

When they reached an odd-shaped room, Richard stopped to look in with the aid of the light sphere. Kahlan saw skeletal remains in a far, acutely pointed corner. Before Richard saw the remains, Kahlan was sure she saw the bones move.

"Look," she said, pointing.

Richard took the light sphere closer. He bent over at the waist to look, then straightened.

"Just bones. Did you see something?"

"I saw them move," she said.

"Did you see what Kahlan saw?"

Shale shook her head. "I didn't see them until she said to look."

"Might have been a trick of the light. The light the spheres give off can be strange at times."

Richard turned back and with the toe of a boot pushed at the bones. They collapsed inward with a hollow clacking sound. The skull toppled off the spine and rolled a short distance. Richard used his boot to push it back toward the rest of the remains. After it stopped, facedown, it slowly rolled back over, as if to look up at him.

"Whatever did that, we don't have time to worry about it," he said as he left the room. "We need to get to the Mord-Sith."

Kahlan knew she had been right about the bones moving, and the way the skull had rolled back over was creepy, but she was more worried about getting to the Mord-Sith before Michec did. He had already captured Vika, so he obviously had the gifted ability to deal with Mord-Sith.

As they took a turn at an intersection and rushed onward down yet another gloomy, filthy stone corridor, Richard abruptly stopped. Kahlan noticed a room to the right. The door was closed, but Richard hadn't stopped to look in the room.

He instead stood frozen, staring ahead at something.

"What is it?" Shale asked from behind his left shoulder.

"I thought I heard something..."

All of a sudden, Kahlan heard a roar from somewhere off down the corridor. Blinding light ignited in the distance and rushed out from around a corner.

Richard drew his sword. The sound of the steel being freed from the scabbard was drowned out by the wail of the fearsome fireball as it grew in size and speed.

Richard dropped to his left knee. Holding the sword's hilt in his right fist, he grabbed the tip of the blade with his left hand.

"Get behind me!" he screamed at them. "Get behind me!"

As he was saying it a second time, the corridor out ahead filled with a bigger explosion of expanding, whirling fire. The yellow-orange flames boiled up as the blaze spilled over the top of itself in its reckless, onward rush. The fire completely filled the corridor as it raced toward them.

Kahlan could feel the heat given off by the inferno. Black smoke swirled in great swaths with the flames breaking through as the fire erupted and rolled toward them down the hallway.

Richard held the sword up like a shield. "Get behind!"

Kahlan crouched down behind him. She had seen Richard use the sword very effectively as a shield against conjured fire.

Shale obviously had not.

As Richard again yelled for them to get behind him, Shale charged at Kahlan, ramming a shoulder into her middle, colliding with such force that it lifted Kahlan from her feet and drove them both into the closed door to the side. Their combined weight smashed the door off his hinges. It fell out ahead of them as together they both flew through the doorway.

Rather than hitting the floor, Kahlan felt herself falling through space.

She realized as she saw the yellow-orange light through the doorway far above her that there was no floor in the room.

Kahlan had just started to scream when she hit the water.

59

Hitting the water was an icy shock that helped drive out what little air Kahlan still had in her lungs from Shale crashing into her.

Shale still had her shoulder in Kahlan's middle with an arm around her waist as they plummeted down underwater. Shale had thought she was saving Kahlan from the blast of conjured fire. Instead she had driven them both into the unknown.

As they hit the water, Kahlan heard Shale's head hit something hard. It made a terrible clonk of skull bone on something just as hard.

As Shale went unconscious, she lost her grip on Kahlan. Kahlan tumbled under the water, unable to get a breath, and lost track of up and down. She panicked with complete disorientation, not knowing which way was up toward the air. She thrashed at the water but, being underwater, her arms couldn't move very fast.

She felt something slimy slide past her arm.

She was desperate to pull in a breath, but she knew that if she tried to breathe, her lungs would only fill with water and she would drown. Her throat had clamped closed with the terror of being underwater. She didn't know which way to swim to get to the surface.

Thrashing wildly, blind, desperate for air, Kahlan thought suddenly of her two babies. Were they to die in this forsaken place? Was she to be yet another corpse left for good in this awful place? Were her two babies to die before they had a chance at life?

As her mind started going black, her arms and legs lost their power and slowly stopped their frantic thrashing. As her body went still, she finally bobbed to the surface. When the air hit her face, she gasped it in. She was horrified by what else she gasped in. Coughing, she had to spit out a mouthful of bugs. The surface was covered with floating mats of beetles. They crawled up onto her face as she struggled to keep her head above water.

As she swiped the fat bugs off her face, she saw that light came from the doorway, but it was up above her. It was too high up for her to reach for the threshold. She could feel the legs of the beetles getting tangled in her hair as it floated out on top of the water. They clung to her floating hair as if it were a raft.

Kahlan gasped and gulped air as she struggled to tread water enough to keep her head above the surface. Big, glossy, hard-backed bugs swam into her mouth. She spat them out and tilted her head back to get a breath. The surface of the water was covered with the beetles. More scrambled up on her face as soon as she swiped them off.

Overhead, she saw fire roaring past the doorway, sending flickering red, orange, and yellow light down into the dark place where she struggled to keep her head above the choppy surface of the water. She couldn't seem to stop the beetles from crawling over her eyes. They tried to burrow into her nose.

As she got more air and was able to think more clearly, she jerked around, left, then right, looking for Shale. The raft of black bugs floated over her face on waves she stirred up. She didn't see the sorceress anywhere. She knew that as soon as the fire above stopped, it would be pitch black.

Fearing to lose a second of the light, Kahlan upended herself and dove under the water to try to find Shale. The water was murky, so she couldn't see far, but at least it got most of the bugs off her. With her eyes open under the water, even though the visibility was poor, she could see that the water was full of all kinds of debris. She had to push things aside as she searched.

Kahlan had to surface, gasping in air for a moment, more beetles trying to cling to her face when she came up; then she upended and returned to searching underwater. She swam down and down, thinking the sorceress might have sunk to the bottom, but she didn't have enough air to reach the bottom and she didn't have any idea how deep the water really was. She desperately raced up to the surface again and gasped in some more air, swiping the clinging bugs from her face before getting a big breath and then going back down.

As she pushed the underwater debris aside, she saw that some of it was the handle and hinges of the door they had broken through, slowly sinking with wood still attached.

Then, when she grasped something to get it out of her way, she suddenly realized that she had her fingers in the eye sockets of a partly decomposed skull. She pushed it away as forcefully as she could.

As she did, something long and dark slid through the water close by.

Just as she was starting to head for the surface again, she spotted Shale's hand. Kahlan grabbed the arm floating motionless in the water and with all her strength swam upward toward the light.

She broke the surface just as she was running painfully out of air. She pulled in lungful after lungful of air as she worked to paddle with her feet and one arm, trying to keep Shale's face above the water. Wooden chunks of the broken door, covered with the beetles, floated nearby. The big black bugs crawled up onto Shale as if she were an island. Kahlan spat out more of the fat beetles.

"Breathe! Breathe! Shale! Breathe!"

Kahlan thought that the sorceress might have gasped in some air and spat out some water, but as the light faded, it was hard to tell.

And then, the fire above was completely extinguished, leaving them alone in the dark, dirty water with the big beetles crawling all over their faces. The sound of Kahlan's splashing echoed around her. It stank so bad that she was reluctant to breathe in the air, but she desperately needed it.

"Richard," Kahlan cried out. "Richard! Help!"

He suddenly appeared in the doorway up above. He was on his hands and knees, peering down into the darkness.

"Here," he called down. "Catch this."

He tossed a light sphere down toward her. Kahlan held Shale's head above water with one hand and struggled to keep her own head above the surface, having to swipe the bugs away from her mouth and eyes as best she could. The sphere wasn't what she needed. She let it splash down close by and sink.

"Shale's unconscious!" Kahlan called up. "We're in water! I can't hold her up much longer!"

As the light sphere Richard had tossed down sank, it lit the water under her with eerie green light. When it did, Kahlan saw a long dark shape glide silently past.

"Richard!" Kahlan yelled, on the ragged edge of panic. "Help! There's something in the water!"

Once he realized the situation, Richard pulled the baldric off over his head. Gripping the empty scabbard in one hand, he leaned out and held the rest of it down toward her.

"Grab hold!" Richard called down.

Kahlan turned over and backstroked with one arm to try to pull Shale closer to the dangling loop of leather that was the baldric.

Splashing the water as she reached for it, she missed it over and over as it swung back and forth just out of reach. She suspected that up in the hallway lit by the light spheres, he probably couldn't see down where she was and didn't realize that he wasn't holding it still enough.

When she finally reached the vertical wall below the door, she managed to hook an arm through the baldric. The fat black beetles scuttled up her arm and onto the baldric. For a moment, she simply held on and panted from the effort of keeping Shale's head above the churning surface of the water. Large, floating mats of the hard-backed bugs collected around her. Kahlan had never felt so dirty in water before.

"Can you put the loop of the baldric around her?" Richard called down. His voice echoed around the empty space above the water. "See if you can put her arms and head through and I'll pull her up."

With great effort, Kahlan managed to slip the broad leather baldric over Shale's head and then, one at a time, under both arms so that she finally hung limp in the sling. As soon as she had the loop of the baldric around her, Richard pulled up on the scabbard, taking up the weight of the unconscious woman. Slowly, hand over hand, he pulled the scabbard up, lifting Shale's dead weight. Water and big bugs sluiced down off her. Finally, Richard was able to get a hand on the baldric. Once he did, he was able to grab it with both hands and lift.

He managed to pull the unconscious sorceress up to the doorway's threshold and drag her in.

As soon as Richard was able to pull the loop of the baldric off her, he lay back down and, holding the scabbard, lowered the loop of the baldric down to Kahlan.

Kahlan frantically reached for it. Bugs tried to crawl up her nose. She had to swipe them away.

As she reached for the baldric again, the slimy thing under the water coiled around her legs and abruptly pulled her under. She only had time to gasp in half a breath. It filled her mouth with wriggling bugs.

60

As she was pulled under, Kahlan sacrificed some of her air to blow out the mouthful of clawing, clinging bugs. She could see ghostly, glowing green light below from the sphere that Richard had thrown down.

The thing compressing around her legs suddenly spun her around, over and over, making her dizzy and nauseous. Then it began whipping her around under the water like a rag doll. She was helpless to fight against the power of it.

Kahlan thought of her two babies. At the thought, terror for them, more than for herself, overwhelmed her. This wasn't only attacking her; it was trying to kill them as well. She tried to swim toward the surface, but each time she did, the thing that had her by her legs tightened forcefully and yanked her back under. It was hard to keep her eyes open to see because the water burned. Things under the water, some hard, some squishy-soft, bumped against her as she was flung helplessly about.

She saw torn parts of bodies suspended in the water as she was dragged past. She saw an arm still attached to a shoulder with a couple of rib bones and dangling flesh. A hand, the tissues where it had been ripped off at the wrist waving gently in the water, floated past her face when the thing that had her paused for a moment. She also saw other, unidentifiable meat with patches of skin or hair drift by under the water. She just wanted air.

Desperate to get away, Kahlan pulled the knife at her belt. With all her strength, she bent herself over to reach the thing that had her legs. Every time she stabbed it, it tugged her, jerking her straight as it dragged her through the water. As the thing thrashed, spinning and pulling her around in dizzying loops, she briefly broke the surface of the water.

Gasping in air, she saw Richard dive off from the doorway above. She heard him hit the water just as she was violently yanked back underwater so hard she feared it might rip her legs off. She wondered if that was what had happened to the disembodied limbs she'd seen floating in the turbid water.

With the way the thing sharply whipped her around, Kahlan again began having trouble telling up from down, and even more trouble holding her breath. She was exhausted, making it more difficult all the time.

Each time it slowed, giving her some slack, she frantically swam for the surface. She managed to break above the water for just long enough to gulp in another breath before the coil around her legs tightened painfully and submerged her yet again. It almost seemed as if it wanted her to get a breath to keep her alive so it could continue to play with her, like a cat playing with wounded prey, encouraging it to try to get away so it could pounce again.

As she was pulled back down with frightening speed, she suddenly felt Richard's hands grab on to her. He dragged himself downward along the length of her, clutching at her clothes hand over hand to pull himself down far enough to reach the muscly body coiled around her legs. She saw that he had a knife between his teeth. The powerful thing that had hold of her effortlessly dragged them both through the water, Kahlan feet-first, Richard, holding her leg with one hand, face-first, as they were both twisted around and around.

As the snakelike tentacle flexed, tightening painfully, she saw Richard start to hack away at it with his knife. He stabbed the fat gray tentacle over and over. With each stab she could feel the thing flinch and twist, its powerful muscles constricting more each time.

Since it still wouldn't release her, Richard sawed at it with his blade, trying to cut it off her. The blade opened great, gaping wounds, but the creature pulled away before he could finish cutting it off her. Gouts of dark blood poured out, filling the water with inky clouds. Richard clung to her leg and kept stabbing away, over and over and over, desperately trying to get it off her.

Then he was gone, shooting toward the surface for air. In what seemed like only an instant, he was back with renewed determination, hacking away more furiously than ever as Kahlan could feel herself going limp, her vision dimming from lack of air.

At last, with the slimy tentacle slashed and cut nearly in two and bleeding profusely, the pressure on her legs flexed once more and then finally relaxed. Richard kept cutting and stabbing until it finally fell away, freeing her legs. Once it did, with him helping her, Kahlan swam for the surface. She broke above it, her lungs burning, finally able to gasp in air, bugs clinging to her face and hair. She didn't care anymore. She just wanted to be able to breathe.

Richard surfaced beside her, gasping for air along with her. "Let's get out of here."

Kahlan wondered how, but she didn't have the energy to ask.

With an arm around her, under hers, Richard helped her swim over to the side. He hooked the baldric with a hand. "Can you climb up."

Kahlan was gulping air, too exhausted to answer or even swipe the crawling bugs from her face, nearly too spent to tread water enough to stay afloat. She shook her head.

"All right," he said. "I'm going to climb up. As soon as I start up, put your arms through the baldric, like you did with Shale. Once I'm up, I'll pull you up after me. Do you think you can at least do that much?"

Kahlan nodded, unable even to say "Yes," unable even to use her fingers to rake the hard-backed bugs from her face.

She managed to grab the dangling leather strap with a hand as she watched him climb up the baldric and leather belt until he reached the doorway and then drag himself the rest of the way out. He immediately turned around, his head and arms hanging over the edge, water and big black beetles pouring off his hair, to grab the leather belt.

"Put your arms through the loop. Kahlan—you have to put your arms through so I can lift you. You won't be able to hold on, otherwise. You need to loop it under your arms."

Kahlan tried. Her arms wouldn't respond to her wishes. She was so spent from fighting for her life as she was being dragged under the water and whipped around when she tried to stab the thing that her arms felt as heavy as lead. She tried, but she couldn't lift them.

"Kahlan! Put your arms through!"

She felt numb. It was starting to seem unimportant. She didn't even have the strength to claw at the bugs trying to crawl their way into her nose. She tried to blow them out, but that didn't work. She just wanted to drift into eternal sleep and not have to fight any longer.

"Kahlan, do it for our children!"

She looked up at his face in the dim light. "What... ?"

"Put your arms through. You have to do it to save the twins!"

The twins... That thought sent a searing jolt of panic through her. She couldn't let them die before they had even been born just because she was exhausted. That was no excuse.

With a final effort, she struggled awkwardly to flop her arms through the loop of the baldric, finally lunging up enough to hook it around her under her arms. That was all she could do. The big black beetles scurried up her arms and up the baldric.

As she hung limp in the leather strap, she could abruptly feel herself being lifted. Water and bugs sluiced off her body. The toes of her boots dragged slowly up the stone wall as she was pulled up clear of the water. She could hear Richard grunting with the frenzied effort of pulling her up as fast as he could. In her mind, she was helping him, but her body wasn't actually doing anything useful to help.

The loop of the leather baldric lifted her until she saw over the threshold of the doorway. Richard gave another mighty pull, lifting her another few feet, then managed to get first one arm around her, then another. Once he had her in his arms, he straightened to lift her up and out. He fell back with her through the doorway, hugging her tightly to him, him on his back, Kahlan sprawled atop him.

What looked like hundreds of fat black beetles fled off them both and scurried across the floor, going for cracks in the stone walls at the sides of the hallway.

Kahlan could feel his heavy breathing and her own as she clung to him, thankful to be alive. He had saved her. He had saved the twins. The terror leaving her body left her trembling.

After she had recovered for a moment, she pushed away and frowned in confusion. "Who held the scabbard for you to climb back up? Did Shale wake up and hold it?"

Richard sat up with her. "No." He gestured. "I saw that something had to have ahold of you because you kept being pulled under with such force. I put the blade through the metal loop where it attaches to the scabbard, then I stuck the sword in the stone floor for an anchor point. After that, I tossed the rest of the baldric over the edge and jumped in. I was hoping it would be long enough. Fortunately, it was." Then he said, "By the way, here is your knife back. You managed to stick it in that thing."

61

Kahlan crawled over to Shale. The soaking-wet sorceress was lying on her back in a puddle of water. Her face was ashen. Kahlan felt the side of her neck and was alarmed to find that while the sorceress still had a pulse, her breath gurgled with water.

"She thought she was saving me from the fire," Kahlan told Richard. "That's why she pushed me through the door."

Kahlan slapped the woman, hoping to revive her. She shook her shoulders, but Shale still didn't respond. A few bugs hiding under her collar and hair ran out. At the sides of the hall, there were masses of the glossy black bugs trying to get into the spaces between the stone blocks and the floor. Kahlan pulled out one tangled in her own hair and tossed it against the wall. She flicked one off as it crawled across Shale's face.

"She risked her life thinking she was saving me and the babies from that fire. We have to help her. It doesn't sound like she's breathing right. It sounds like maybe she has water in her lungs. What can we do to help her?"

Richard leaned over, putting his ear close to her mouth for a moment, listening to her breathing. "You're right, she's in trouble."

He quickly placed a hand in the center of her chest and another on her forehead. He closed his eyes as his head lowered in concentration. For a time, as Kahlan watched, nothing seemed to be happening. Each of Shale's breaths gurgled with water.

Kahlan then saw a warm glow around each of Richard's hands. It lit his veins, pulsing with each of his heartbeats. The glow warmed in color as it began to flow through into the sorceress, pulsing with the power of Richard's gift. For a long time, Richard didn't move and neither did Shale.

Richard had healed her before, so Kahlan knew how good he was at using his gift to heal. When he had done it to her, it had brought her back from the cusp of death. She hoped it could for Shale as well.

Then, after a time, Shale abruptly gasped in a deep breath. She rolled to her side, hoarsely coughing out water. Richard put both hands on her back, letting his power continue to flow into her, helping her clear her lungs of the water until she was finally able to take in breath after breath more normally. Between breaths, she spat out more water.

Richard finally sat back on his heels as they waited, giving the sorceress the time she needed to recover and gather her wits. After a short time, she was finally able to get air free of water in and out of her lungs.

"What happened?" Shale managed to ask in a grating voice as she panted. She lifted both arms, looking at the sleeves of her dress as they dripped water. "Why am I all wet?"

Richard stood and retrieved a glowing sphere from a nearby bracket on the wall. It grew even brighter in his hands. With one hand, he held the light sphere out through the doorway to show her.

Shale staggered to her feet, finally standing with Kahlan's help. Once she had her balance, she went to the doorway to see what he wanted to show her. She put a hand on the doorframe for support as she leaned in a little and looked down into the gloom.

"Water? Why is there no floor? What is water doing down in there?" She shot Richard an angry look. "Why would there be water in there? That's just crazy!"

"I don't know," he said. "What I do know is that the complication spell-form doesn't call for it. It could simply be a deep pit that over time filled with water."

Kahlan wondered if it could be something else.

"Well, that's just—"

"I told you to get behind me," Richard said, cutting off the sorceress's heated rant before it could get a good start. He lowered his head, giving her a serious look from under his brow. "You should have listened to me. I knew what I was doing. My sword acts as a shield against conjured fire. You would have been safe behind me, but instead, thinking you were protecting her, you dove with Kahlan through this doorway. I appreciate that you thought you were saving her from the fire, but as you can see, there is no floor and you both ended up nearly drowning. Had it simply been a deep pit, you both could have fallen to your deaths. In a way, it's fortunate that the pit is filled with water."

"Very foul water," Kahlan added. "We both were fortunate that Richard was able to help us get back out. He pulled you up while you were unconscious. He saved your life."

Shale looked between the two of them, appearing mortified. "I could sense myself at the veil. How did you manage to bring me back from the brink of death? What did you do?"

Richard arched an eyebrow. "You aren't the only one who can use your gift to heal."

Shale had calmed down considerably. "Thank you. None of that could have been easy."

"It had to be Michec who conjured that fire. We must be getting close, so he tried to kill us. Fortunately, you and Kahlan survived your little swim."

Shale put her hand to her head and winced. "Why does my head hurt?"

"You hit your head on something down there when we fell in," Kahlan told her. "I think you cracked your skull on a decapitated head that was bobbing in the water."

Shale made a face that revealed her disgust. "There are human remains down there?"

"Yes." Kahlan shuddered as she flicked a waxy white chunk of flesh off her leg. She could see that it looked like human skin on one side of it. "But what I don't understand is how some kind of creature could be living down there."

"Creature?" Shale asked, her alarm rising again. "What creature?"

"I don't know. I thought it might be a snake nearly as thick as my leg that had me, but with the way it whipped me around under the water, I think it had to have been something big and powerful that grabbed me with a tentacle. Richard attacked it with his knife and managed to get it off me. But how could something that big live down there? Other than the random person who fell in, and a lot of bugs, what would it eat?"

Shale considered briefly. "I suspect it might not have been a real creature."

Kahlan's jaw dropped. "Not real? Are you kidding me? It was real enough to whip me around underwater and nearly drown me."

"I think you must be right that a monster of that size couldn't live down there." The sorceress gazed off down the hall. "A witch man could have conjured such a thing. Michec probably knew we fell in and conjured it. That's the most likely explanation. It had to be him trying to kill you."

"Considering how real it behaved, how powerful it was, and how it reacted and bled when Richard cut it, if it wasn't real then how are we to be able to tell what's real from what's not?" Kahlan asked.

Shale regarded her with a grim expression. "With any kind of witch that powerful, you often can't."

"Then how can we possibly fight back?"

"When you are fighting the illusion, you are, in a way, fighting the witch. When you cut the thing attacking you, slashing it as Lord Rahl apparently did, you are, in a way, harming the witch, because the illusion is partially an extension of them. Odd as it may seem, it's not entirely an illusion, not an independent creature. It's conjured but also real and as such, in certain aspects, connected to them."

"We don't have time to discuss it right now," Richard interrupted. "We're all alive. We need to go after Michec. I have a feeling that Nyda, Cassia, Vale, Berdine, and Rikka don't have any defense against the man, otherwise he wouldn't have been able to capture Vika. Come on. Conjured fire and creatures, real or not, I need to catch him before he can get far."

"What are we going to do when we catch him?" Shale asked.

"Kill him," Richard said without pause as he started out.

62

Richard lifted his arm out to the side to keep Kahlan and Shale back. He could tell by the route they had taken that they were near the heart of the spell-form. They all felt the increased sense of danger.

He wanted to carefully peek around the corner to see what lay ahead, and he didn't want either Shale or Kahlan showing themselves. Not that they were going to be able to sneak up on the witch man. He obviously knew they were coming after him. Besides whatever gifted ability he might have, their mere presence made the light spheres begin to glow. Even with their faint green glow off down the halls, it was hard to see, because the stone walls of the passages in the complication were so dark it seemed to suck up the light.

While the lights beginning to illuminate made it possible to see, it would also alert anyone to their presence, which made stealth impossible.

Even before looking, Richard felt something. He couldn't quite determine what it was he felt, but it gave him a feeling of dread in the pit of his stomach. He decided that the feeling had to be from the continual state of heightened tension. His grandfather would have told him to fear what he knew, not what he was afraid of. But Zedd hadn't ever given him any advice on complication spells or witch men.

Richard slowly moved his head out just enough so that he could see down the dark passageway with one eye.

In the faint green glow, he saw something down low far off down the dark stone hallway. He couldn't quite figure out what it was.

As he squinted, he suddenly realized what it was he was looking at.

Richard let out a curse under his breath. He held up a finger without looking back to prevent Kahlan asking what would have made him use that kind of language.

As slowly and quietly as possible, Richard drew his sword. The gleaming black blade hissed with lethal fury as it came out of the scabbard, its power joining with his own rising anger, eager to be unleashed on the enemy. It was a contest as to what lusted to kill Michec more, Richard's rage or the sword's.

Kahlan leaned in close behind him. "What is it?" she whispered.

He looked back over his shoulder. "I think I see the Mord-Sith."

"You think?" Shale asked.

"What about Michec?" Kahlan whispered. "Do you see him?"

Richard peered into the distance, then looked back over his shoulder. "No. There is a broad opening of some kind. It's a lot wider than a doorway or an intersection with a hall. There is light coming from inside—light from light spheres. That means there has to be someone inside. I'll give you one guess as to who that would be."

"No need to guess," Shale said. "Not only can I smell him, I can sense him with my gift. I can sense how powerful he is. Let me tell you, it's an uncomfortable feeling."

"I know," Richard said. "I feel it too. Stay behind, and out of the way of my sword. If I can get close enough, I intend to separate Michec's head from the rest of him."

"Do you think it's a good idea to simply go in there?" Kahlan asked.

"Not really, but I doubt he is going to come out and surrender. I don't know how else we will have any chance of eliminating him other than going in there after him. Since he conjured fire, that means he can defend against it, so I can't burn him out."

With Kahlan and Shale following close on his heels, Richard came out from around the corner and moved carefully but swiftly down the hallway. He looked back from time to time, as did the other two, checking for any threat from the rear. He didn't see the witch man anywhere, but he couldn't yet see into the room. It was likely he was hiding inside.

As they reached the broad opening of the vast room, lit from within, they found what Richard feared he had seen.

The five Mord-Sith were lined up on their knees just in front of the broad entrance, each with both hands held out, their Agiel resting in their upturned palms.

Keeping an eye on the room beyond, Richard touched Berdine's shoulder, the first of the five kneeling side by side in a row. She didn't react. He urgently whispered her name as he waved his hand in front of her eyes. She didn't so much as blink. He shook her shoulder; she didn't react.

"Any idea what he's done to them?" he asked Shale.

Shale knelt in front of Berdine and placed her hands to either side of her head. Berdine stared ahead without seeing, without blinking, without moving. After bowing her head a moment, Shale finally stood and let out a troubled sigh.

"Nothing. I sense nothing. They might as well be statues."

"How is that even possible?" Richard frowned at her. "What does it mean?"

Shale regretfully shook her head. "He has somehow blanked them out. That's the only way I can explain it. Berdine doesn't give off any sign of life. I can see that they are alive, but I can feel no sign of life in her. Despite their eyes being open, they are not conscious."

Kahlan gently shook Berdine's shoulder. There was no reaction from the Mord-Sith.

"The only way you are going to get them back is if you can get Michec to release them," Shale told them. "They are captives of his power."

"What if I simply kill him?"

Shale shrugged. "That would work."

Richard couldn't imagine what the witch man could have done to make the five Mord-Sith kneel and offer their Agiel.

He really didn't want Kahlan coming with him, but there was little choice—he judged it more dangerous to leave her behind. Michec would probably love to catch her alone and capture her. That would give him even more power over Richard.

"Can you do anything to block what he can do?" he asked Shale.

Her hopeless look told him all there was to know.

"If I can get close enough, I can use my Confessor's power on him," Kahlan said. "That would render him harmless."

"With his ability, he'd likely incapacitate you the way he did the Mord-Sith," Shale told her. "I don't know if it would even work on him, but you would never get the chance to try."

"Just stay clear of my sword," Richard said as he made his way past the five unmoving, kneeling Mord-Sith. "Shale, if you can do anything to slow him or hinder his ability, please do."

63

As he moved between the five Mord-Sith and through the opening, the glass spheres inside brightened enough to reveal what was in the room. As he took in what he was seeing, it felt like Richard's heart came up in his throat.

The room was a central complex in the complication spell. Because of that, it was huge. But that was not what was so terrifying about the room.

In a gridwork pattern about eight or ten feet apart, throughout a large portion of the room, in row after row, bodies hung on chains by manacles on their wrists. In the ghostly green glow from spheres around the room, it almost looked like a forest in an eerie fog; the bodies resembled tree trunks. The silence was haunting.

Besides the gagging stench, it was clear from their condition that the people hanging from chains hooked to the beamed ceiling were long dead. Some of the bodies were charred a bubbled black from head to foot. Most, though, had been skinned alive, their flesh in a bloody pile beneath their feet. The heads, from the neck up, still had their skin, presumably to preserve the expressions of stark terror and pain frozen on their faces. Their hands, held by manacles around their wrists, also had skin, making it look like they were wearing pale gloves. Everything else had been carefully skinned, even the toes. With the red muscles and white tendons exposed, the figures all looked grotesquely naked.

Her face contorted in disgust, Kahlan held a hand over her mouth and nose, the same as Shale. The stench of death was overpowering.

Richard's rage relegated the smell to a distant distraction.

All those bodies hanging motionless above bloody piles of their skin, a mist drifting among them in the near darkness, with the faint green light from all the light spheres filtering among the carcasses and casting multiple fingers of shadow across the floor, was just about the creepiest thing Richard had ever seen. This had obviously been done by a deranged person who very much enjoyed the grisly work.

As Richard moved into the kill room, through the forest of motionless, hanging bodies, he spotted a faint movement in the distance. He wove his way quietly among the hanging corpses, sword held in both hands, ready to kill Michec.

As Richard came around one of the stiff corpses, he suddenly came face-to-face with Vika. His breath caught and he froze in his tracks.

She was naked, hanging in manacles hooked by a chain to a bolt in one of the beams of the ceiling. Her red leather had been thrown aside. Unlike all the others hanging in the room, she was still alive, if barely, and still had her skin. Her brow tightly bunched, her eyes tracked him as he moved in among the corpses.

Tears streamed down her cheeks, blood down her chin.

She had obviously been beaten to within an inch of her life, but far worse, there was a knife slit that had opened a wound in her belly. A long length of intestine had been pulled out of that incision. It hung down in front, along one bloody leg, some of it at the end coiled on the floor in a puddle of blood beneath her feet.

The end of Vika's Agiel was sticking out of the open wound in her belly, the fine gold chain hanging down from the end.

Had Richard not been so enraged at what had been done to her, he might have thrown up.

"Please," she whispered, hardly loud enough to be heard. "Please, Lord Rahl… kill me. Please…"

He stepped close. "Stay with me, Vika. I'm going to take care of you."

Her whole body shook slightly, partly from the beating and the open wound in her belly, but mostly from the pain her Agiel was giving her. It had been pushed into the wound, into her exposed insides, to add unrelenting agony to everything else he had done to her.

Through her pain, she managed to whisper, "Lord Rahl… run…"

Richard started to reach for the Agiel, to pull it out and at least stop that much of her pain, but he stepped back when he heard a soft chuckling. With a hand, he urgently shepherded both Kahlan and Shale around behind him, backing them up to give himself room to use his sword.

He couldn't tell where the chuckling was coming from. It seemed to echo out from everywhere. As he looked all around for the threat, dark smoke, clinging low to the floor, glided in under the hanging corpses. It snaked slightly as it moved among the bloody piles of skin. It seemed almost alive, the way it moved.

As it came close, it gathered into a thick, greenish-gray cloud. That increasing mass of murky smoke rose up, so heavy it obscured everything beyond it.

Richard took a mighty swing with the sword through the smoke. Wisps of it curled away when the blade passed through and disturbed the air, but there was nothing solid in it.

He heard the soft chuckling again. He gripped his sword tighter as he stepped back from the tall, hazy mass of smoke.

The smoke seemed caught up in a sudden wind, and with a swirl, as if something had passed close by, it spun as it faded away into the air.

When it was gone, there was Moravaska Michec standing before them.

He was a big, barrel-chested man past his middle years. His face was coarse, as if made up of chunky blocks of clay that had hardened together before being refined into proper features. His heavy brow nearly obscured dark eyes peering out from narrowed eyes. A dark, pockmarked complexion scarred his cheeks and bulbous nose.

He wore what had once been white robes, similar to the white robes Richard remembered Darken Rahl always wearing. But Michec's white robes were stained with what looked like years of blood and gore, as if they had never been washed. Richard could understand why Nyda said that he was called the Butcher. It looked much like he was wearing a butcher's apron.

Richard could easily understand the other reason, hanging all around the room, why he was called Michec the Butcher.

There was a cloth stole, such as a priest would wear, around the back of his neck and draped down over the front of his shoulders. It was embroidered with layers of designs in golds and purples. Richard guessed that it had denoted his high rank back when Darken Rahl ruled. But like his robes, it was soiled with blood and dark stains.

The man's full head of short hair was salt-and-pepper, and stuck up from his scalp in greasy spikes. The thick mass of his beard, confined for the most part to the rim of his broad jaw and chin, had been braided into dozens of long, fat strands hanging to mid-chest. They looked like nothing so much as snakes hanging from the rim of his face.

His fat fingers, ending with jagged, broken nails, were stained with messy black muck under the nails and in the crevices and wrinkles, obviously from many years of his sadistic fixations.

His sly smile conveyed abject cruelty.

"So tell me," he said as he gestured all around. "Really, was this your plan? To simply walk in here and kill me? That was your plan? You think yourself that powerful? Powerful enough to rule, to protect those loyal to you?" He clucked his tongue with amusement. "My, my. Such arrogance."

Richard didn't answer. His mind was spinning with a thousand thoughts. For some reason, though, it felt like he couldn't connect those fragments of thoughts, couldn't make his mind work.

The man's cunning smile widened. "You are all probably wondering why your meager abilities aren't working. Well, I must confess: I spelled this room. And you simply walked right in here, distracted by my collection of pretty people. So you see, like the Mord-Sith, you three aren't as powerful as you imagine yourselves to be, because in here, even what powers you do have are blocked." He lifted his heavy brow. "Just like all your pretty little Mord-Sith. Not even your bond protected them."

Richard tried to summon the gift he knew was there, somewhere, deep inside, but it simply didn't respond. By the look on Shale's face, she was having the same problem.

Michec gestured to Vika. "She's mine, you know. Darken Rahl himself assigned her to me for training. After that, she was given to me. I only loaned her to Hannis Arc. He was supposed to return her. When he died—because of you—she was obligated to come back to me. An inviolable duty she chose to ignore." A dark look came over his features. "I am seeing to it that she fully regrets her disobedience." He reached out and with the tip of his first finger pushed the Agiel a little deeper into the gaping belly wound.

Vika's eyes rolling back in her head; her chin quivered as a shudder of agony went through her.

"I will similarly deal with her equally disloyal sister Mord-Sith." He glanced toward the opening into the room where they were kneeling before looking back at Richard. He smiled with menace. "Once I deal with you and your lovely wife."

He lifted a hand as he walked off a few paces, then turned back. "Once I do, I will be richly rewarded. You see, the Golden Goddess has become... annoyed, shall we say, by your stubborn resistance." He stepped closer. "I assured her I could handle the situation. We came to... an arrangement."

Richard was horrified to learn that Michec was working with the Goddess. Even though he was filled with rage, he couldn't make his gift respond to that fury. Try as he might to call it forth, it felt like there was nothing there. Whatever kind of spell the witch man had used, besides blocking his gift, it also made Richard's thinking foggy.

Michec swept a hand around in a grand fashion, as if proudly showing off his years of dedicated labor.

"As you can see, my work continues. It was interrupted by you, Richard Cypher, the pretend Lord Rahl. For that, you will suffer, I can assure you.

"But the goddess, you see"—he smiled with meaning at Richard as he pointed a finger toward Kahlan—"wants more than anything to hold the bloody remains of the two children growing in her belly. I assured her she will have her wish."

Richard came unhinged.

With a cry of rage, he abandoned his attempt to use his gift and instead went for the man, sword-first.

64

It felt to Richard like they must have been walking for days. The Azrith Plain seemed endless. Richard's mouth was so dry from thirst that he could hardly swallow anymore. His tongue stuck to the roof of his mouth. The air felt hot, but there was no sun. He judged that it must be sometime after twilight by the odd, purplish light laced with streaks of green. He was glad to finally be gone from the People's Palace and on the way, but he was so thirsty he could hardly think of anything else.

"Is there any water left?" he asked Kahlan.

"No."

He seemed to remember, then, that he had told her to have the last few swallows. But why didn't they bring more?

For what seemed hours, they trudged on across the parched ground. Despite how long they walked, it never seemed to get any darker. The sky was black above them, with the color of a purple bruise farther down where it met the horizon.

"Why didn't we bring horses?" he asked. "This would be easier if we had horses."

"You said we didn't need them," Kahlan said in a flat tone from behind him somewhere.

Richard squinted, trying to remember why he didn't think they should bring horses. That seemed strange. It was going to be a long journey. Horses would have made it easier, and they could have carried more water.

They had already been traveling for what seemed days and days. As they marched ever onward, the night seemed endless. The Azrith Plain, so barren and empty, seemed endless. He wished they had brought horses. And more water.

"Do you want to stop?" he asked.

Kahlan didn't answer. She was probably so thirsty she didn't want to talk. He felt too thirsty to bother asking again, so he slogged on.

It was hard to walk, because his legs hurt. His back hurt, too, but more than anything, his shoulders ached something fierce.

After endless walking, he at last began to see trees out ahead. He did his best to pick up his pace. He started to run for them, because trees meant water. Despite how hard he tried, his legs moved like they were mired in molasses.

When he finally reached the trees, he found a brook, as he had known he would. The water looked clean and cool. He fell to his knees and started scooping up water, drinking and drinking and drinking from his hands.

But the water, no matter how much he drank, didn't do anything to quench his thirst.

Kahlan and Shale stood watching him, as if he had lost his mind.

"Aren't you thirsty?" he asked as he looked back over his shoulder at them. "Don't you want to get a drink?"

Kahlan shrugged and knelt then. She cupped her hands, bringing water to her lips. She drank and then scooped more water, to drink that as well. It ran between her fingers. He watched as she drank, wishing that he could satisfy his thirst the way she seemed to be able to do.

He tried it again. Nothing. No taste, no wetness. Nothing. He put his face under the water, guzzling. It simply wouldn't quench his terrible thirst. It angered him, because it looked so good and felt so good in his hands, so good against his lips. But he might as well have been drinking sand for all the good it did him.

He rushed to his feet when he saw Kahlan walking on ahead. He had to protect her and the twins. Even if he couldn't get a drink to satisfy his thirst, he had to protect her.

That was all that mattered: protect Kahlan.

Richard saw that his wrists were bleeding. He stood and stared at them. He couldn't make sense of it.

When he looked up, he saw his skinny grandfather standing on a rock in among the trees.

"Zedd?" Richard blinked. "Zedd, is that you?"

"Indeed it is, my boy."

His familiar, wrinkled face, his skin and bones under his simple robes, looked so good that it made Richard ache.

"Zedd... what are you doing here?"

He peered at Richard in that way that Richard knew well. "To help you, of course, my boy. I have come to help you."

Richard suddenly broke into tears of joy at seeing his grandfather. He had thought he was dead, but here he was, alive.

"Listen to me," Zedd said.

Richard nodded, still choked with tears. "I'm listening."

"You have to get out of here, Richard."

Richard looked around. In the dim, greenish-purple light, he couldn't see much.

"Get out of here?" Richard frowned at the warm and familiar face of his beloved grandfather. He loved the old man so much. "What do you mean, I have to get out of here? We're on our way to the Wizard's Keep. We have to get to the Keep where it's safe while I figure out a way to stop the Glee."

"You're not going to get there this way. You have to get away from here, first."

Richard glanced around and then took a step toward his grandfather, so close he knew he could reach out and touch his wild, wavy white hair if he wanted to.

"Get out of here? Why? Where are we?"

Zedd smiled in a sad way. "Don't you know, my boy?"

"No," Richard said, his mouth so dry he could hardly talk. "What is this place?"

Zedd looked at Richard in silence for a long, loving moment.

"Richard, you are in the Wasteland."

The word "Wasteland" jolted Richard so hard that he gasped and opened his eyes. He saw blood running down his arms from the manacles clamped tightly around his wrists. His shoulders were in terrible pain. With a sense of dread and alarm, he realized he was hanging from the ceiling among the corpses.

He had been hung from the ceiling gridwork of iron pins, facing Vika. Barely conscious, she trembled in agony as she watched him through slitted eyelids. He could read the look on her face. It said he shouldn't have come after her.

Richard twisted and looked over to see Shale on his left, hanging unconscious in manacles.

He looked to his right, then, and was horrified to see Kahlan also hanging in manacles chained to the ceiling. Unlike Richard and Shale, she was naked. Her face had lurid bruises on it. Her left eye was a painful-looking shade of purple and almost swollen shut. Blood from her mouth dripped in strings from her chin. She was trembling as tears ran down her cheeks. She didn't look over at him.

At the sight of Kahlan hanging helpless in the forest of dead bodies, Richard went wild, thrashing around, trying to break free. He drew his knees up, bent himself in half, gripped the chain and lifted his legs up over his head to push his feet toward the ceiling to try to pull out the anchor bolt. The ceiling was too far to reach. His legs flopped back down and he swung helplessly. The attempt extended the wounds in his wrists. Fresh blood ran down in little rivulets. He had no idea how long they had been unconscious and hanging from the ceiling.

Michec stepped into his field of view. "My, my. The Lord Rahl himself, the man who defeated the great Darken Rahl. You hardly seem so big and important now, do you?"

Richard gritted his teeth in rage at himself, at how stupid he had been to underestimate Michec and let them be captured. He desperately wanted to kill the witch man. He struggled to pull his bloody hands through the manacles so that he could get them around the man's throat. Despite how slippery the blood was, the iron bands were far too tight for that to work.

"I was more than angry that you ruined the empire that Darken Rahl was building. It was going to be grand. You only defeated him through trickery, not through strength. You are weak and undeserving to take such a great man's place." Michec smiled with hate. "But now, the Golden Goddess and her kind will build a better empire, a world that will serve as their hunting ground. I will run it for them."

When the man lifted a hand back, Richard was horrified to see the tall, dark shapes of at least a dozen Glee step out of the shadows of the hanging, skinless corpses.

Michec twined one of the beard braids around a filthy finger as he stepped away from Richard to stand in front of Kahlan. He grabbed her face, gritting his teeth, squeezing so hard she cried out.

"For your husband to truly understand how worthless and undeserving he is as a leader, I am going to let him watch me skin you alive." He pulled out a knife and as he looked into her eyes, he licked the blade. "Please do scream for him, would you? As soon as I finish, these Glee will claw those two babies from your womb as you hang helpless and watch them do it."

Three of the glistening Glee came forward on their long, muscular legs, clacking their claws, eager to get at her. Kahlan's eyes went wide in terror as one of them pressed its sharp claw against her belly and hissed in her face.

Michec used the back of his hand to urge the dark creatures back. "Not yet, my friends. You must wait until I finish."

The Glee reluctantly stepped back.

"After I have skinned her, then you may rip out her babies. You have my oath, the oath of a witch man."

That seemed to satisfy them and they retreated farther back into the shadows to wait until he was done.

Michec leaned in close to Kahlan, smiling at her, inches from her face, as he cut through the skin along the side of her throat.

"Shall we begin, Mother Confessor?"

Gazing into her green eyes, Michec worked two fat fingers in through the pocket he had cut and under her flesh to get a good grip on her skin. Panting in terror, Kahlan let out a shriek that felt like it ripped Richard's soul.

65

Kahlan's scream not only felt as if it ripped Richard's soul, it overwhelmed him with shock and terror. He couldn't understand or remember how he had come to be hanging in a room full of skinned corpses also hanging by their wrists from the ceiling, but he realized it had to be a spell of some sort cast by the witch man, Moravaska Michec. More than that, what had happened or how it had happened didn't really matter. All that mattered was what was, now.

A quick glance to his left showed Shale, manacles around her wrists, likewise hanging on a chain attached to the ceiling and facing in the same direction he was. She appeared to be unconscious and so could be of no help.

The same distance to his right and facing in the same direction, toward all the hanging corpses, Kahlan struggled in panic at what was happening, at what was about to happen. The smell of all the dead bodies hanging in a grid pattern throughout the room was not only sickening, it was overpowering.

Despite how much Kahlan thrashed around, making her wrists bleed all the more as the manacles cut into her flesh, Michec had a firm grip on her flesh, with his fat thumb on the outside and two fingers in under the slit he had cut in the skin at the side of her throat so that he could begin skinning her alive.

Richard clearly remembered Michec saying he had spelled the room to block their gift. That had to be the reason she hadn't used her power on him. The thought of Moravaska Michec skinning Kahlan alive was more than Richard could take. He tried to reach his own gift, but when he did, it felt as if nothing was there. He simply felt empty.

As long as Michec's spell blocked their gift, his gift could be of no help.

Directly across from Richard, Vika, as naked as Kahlan, hung helpless in manacles facing him. Despite the agony she was in from the gash Michec had made in her abdomen to pull out a length of her intestines, and the Agiel he had pushed into the open wound to increase the torture, she was clearly distraught watching Kahlan in the clutches of that evil man. A man who had once owned Vika.

"Master," Vika called out in a weak voice, but a voice that Michec heard.

Annoyed, he turned a frown back over his shoulder at her, expecting to know why she would interrupt him.

"Master," Vika managed again in a shaky voice.

"What!" he shouted in anger at being interrupted before he could begin skinning Kahlan alive.

"I'm trying to warn you. You've made a terrible mistake."

The witch man's expression darkened, but curiosity caused him to take a step back from Kahlan. He wiped his bloody fingers on his filthy robes as he turned toward Vika. His blocky features were tight with displeasure at being called away from what he was so eager to do to Kahlan.

Richard sagged in the manacles with relief that Vika had managed to stop him, if only for a moment, from what he had been about to do. Kahlan sagged as she watched, fearing his return.

Michec moved closer so that he could hear Vika's weak voice. "Warn me about what?"

"Master, it is my duty to tell you that you have made a dangerous mistake."

"What mistake?" When she failed to answer immediately, he pushed her Agiel in a little deeper, making her gasp as her head tipped back in agony. "What mistake!"

Richard could see the muscles in her legs tense. She clenched her teeth and held her breath for a moment, doing her best to endure the increase in agony caused by her Agiel.

Panting to get her breath, Vika finally brought her head back down. "The same mistake made by Darken Rahl. The same mistake made by Hannis Arc. The same mistake made by Emperor Sulachan. The same mistake made by so many others."

Moravaska Michec, angry to be told he was making a mistake of any kind, stepped close and grabbed her Agiel. He twisted it back and forth, sweeping it around inside the wound in her belly, making her cry out involuntarily as her eyes rolled up in her head with the pain, unable to endure it, yet unable to do anything to stop it. Her legs trembled; her feet shook. Richard ached at seeing how helpless she was.

Michec released the Agiel and gripped one of the ropy braids of his beard between a dirty finger and thumb. One brow arched over a dark, angry eye. "What mistake would that be?"

Her muscles stood out iron hard from the torment of the Agiel jutting from the open wound. She finally managed to gasp in enough air to speak. She stared at him with wet, sky-blue eyes. "The mistake... of underestimating Lord Rahl."

Michec gestured irritably toward Richard. "Him? He is not worthy to be called Lord Rahl."

"Call him what you will. Call him a mere woodsman if you will. But it is my duty to warn you, Master, that you have made a fatal mistake."

"First, I underestimated him, and now I've made a fatal mistake?"

Her jaw trembling in pain, tears running down her cheeks, Vika nodded.

Michec's brow drew down over his cruel eyes. His arm lifted in a grand gesture. "And what fatal mistake do you imagine I've made?"

Vika had to pause to swallow back her agony. "You did not kill him when you had the chance. Richard Rahl does not make the mistake of trying to teach his enemies lessons. He does not keep them alive to lecture them and gloat. He simply kills them."

Even though Vika was advising Michec to kill him, Richard had faith that she was doing it for good reason. He realized it was a distraction to make Michec stop before it was too late and he started skinning Kahlan alive, even though it meant he would turn his formidable wrath on her. Richard feared for Vika but was beyond grateful for her intervention.

When he saw movement out of the corner of his eye, a quick glance revealed that Shale was at last awake. In that quick glance they shared, they both knew the despair of their situation.

Michec stared at the Mord-Sith briefly, as if considering her words, or possibly what more painful torture he could inflict, then huffed a brief chuckle. The snakelike braids of his beard swung around with him as he turned and stared at Richard a moment. The greasy spikes of salt-and-pepper hair stood out against the pale greenish light from the glass spheres around the room. Michec flicked a hand dismissively toward Richard as he looked back at Vika.

"I appreciate your loyalty in trying to warn me of danger, but you underestimate me. The famous and powerful Lord Rahl is quite helpless against me. No one escapes a witch's oath."

"He is gifted. I have seen him kill with his gift."

Michec's derisive smile distorted his coarse features. "Gifted? I've blocked his gift"—he thumped a fist against his own puffed-up chest—"the same as I blocked your ability to use your Agiel against me, and I blocked the ability of the other Mord-Sith, and I blocked this witch woman's gift, and I blocked the Mother Confessor's power. No one but me can use their power in this room. So, you see? You are quite wrong. He is hardly a danger to me, now. His questionable 'powers' won't help him. He is under the decree of a witch's oath."

"I am telling you, Master, you have made a fatal mistake. You arrogantly think to give him a show of your superiority, and in that arrogance, you have let your chance to kill him slip away. You will not get another chance."

Michec turned a look of raw hatred toward Richard. He slowly closed the distance from Vika, his glare fixed on Richard the whole time. He paused briefly to glance once over at Kahlan with lust for what was being delayed. She glared back with loathing and defiance. He smiled, pleased by that look. He finally came to a stop before Richard to look up at his helpless prize.

"Dangerous, are you?" He planted his fists on his hips as he glared up at Richard with contempt. "Then maybe I should take the advice of my loyal Mord-Sith, and—"

As hard as he could, Richard kicked the witch man in the face. His boot connected with bone. Richard didn't know if it was skull or jawbone, but Michec's dead weight toppled back. He landed hard on his back and lay motionless, sprawled on the floor, his arms out to the side. He looked to be out cold.

Her brow bunching with the effort, Vika flashed Richard a shaky smile through her pain. "I bought you time. Now get out of here."

"Richard..." Kahlan said.

He looked where she was looking and saw the dark shapes of the Glee cautiously stepping out of the shadows of the hanging, skinless corpses. Like those corpses, Richard also hung helpless from manacles around his wrists. Those creatures would not wait for Michec to come around and finally finish his work with Kahlan so they could have her.

He knew they would take the opportunity to have what they had come for—the babies in Kahlan's womb.

66

Richard looked from the dark, glistening shapes of the cautious Glee back in among the shadows and hanging corpses to the unconscious form sprawled on the floor in front of him. Had he been able to brace against something solid when he kicked Michec in the head he might have been able to kill him. Hanging helpless, he had done the best he could. At the least, the big man was out cold for the moment.

Richard knew he had only a small window of time before either Michec came around or the Glee decided that this was their opportunity to take what they wanted.

Richard pressed his knees together and lifted his legs out in front of him, then let them fall back. He did it several more times to get his whole body to start swinging back and forth, each time pumping his legs to get each arcing movement higher and higher. The chain grated in protest as the top link pivoted from the fat eyebolt in the ceiling. Once he was swinging back and forth as much as he could, he threw his legs around to his right and kept contorting his body, changing that pendulum motion to rotation. As he swung his legs, he twisted his whole body around, swinging faster and faster, building momentum.

Once all the slack was gone out of the chain as he continued to turn it with his body, the links couldn't resist the strain and they started folding over on top of one another. The more he spun, the more it twisted the chain and the harder it was to keep the rotation going. As he spun the chain, it continually increased the pressure of the manacles on his wrists. They cut painfully into the flesh. He gripped the chain above the manacles to try to take some of the pressure off his wrists as he spun. Richard ignored the pain and kept swinging his legs around and around to force the chain to turn, hoping something would have to give way. As he did, the links continued to bunch and knot up.

Suddenly, the pressure was too much, and the eyebolt in the ceiling beam let out a snapping sound as the rusty threads finally broke their bond to the wood. With the threads broken free, the twisting force caused the bolt to begin to turn, unscrewing it from the wooden beam. The age and corrosion of the threads caused them to want to bind up and made it difficult to keep up the turning force. Despite the difficulty, Richard knew he couldn't stop, or he might never get it going again. He kept swinging his legs around and around to keep the eyebolt unscrewing. He didn't dare rest for fear it would bind up and stick.

Although Michec still lay unconscious on the floor, Richard knew the man could come around at any moment. But right then there was a bigger concern. With each rotation he could see the Glee advancing across the room to get to Kahlan. He knew that with one powerful swipe of their claws they could rip her open. By Kahlan's rapid breathing, he knew she was well aware of that imminent threat.

All of a sudden, the turning eyebolt broke free of the beam. Richard crashed to the floor. He quickly scrambled to his feet as several of the dark shapes were going for Kahlan.

He grabbed the heavy chain in both hands and started swinging it around over his head. The first two Glee saw that he was now free and a threat, so they turned away from Kahlan toward him, eager to attack. Richard whipped the chain around and cracked it against the side of the head of one of them. The big eyebolt at the end of the chain split its skull and sent the creature sprawling.

Before the second could get to him, he swung the chain again. Because the second Glee raced in closer, he couldn't hit it in the head with the eyebolt at the end of the chain. Instead, the chain caught the side of its neck. The heavy eyebolt and the rest of the chain continued their flight, and the chain wrapped twice around the creature's neck. Richard immediately yanked the chain before the Glee could grab it or get its balance. The force of that pull twisted its head around, breaking its neck. Like the first one, the second fell dead before being able to vanish.

Suddenly there were more Glee coming for both him and Kahlan. He shortened his grip on the chain and stood far enough in front of her that he wouldn't accidentally hit her as he continued swinging it around. The speed of the heavy chain was deadly. He took down the Glee as fast as they could come.

"Shale!" Kahlan yelled. "Do something to help him!"

"My gift doesn't work any more than yours does," the sorceress called back. "Don't you remember? Michec blocked our power in this room."

Richard knew there would be no help coming. It was all up to him to stop the threat or Kahlan would die. They all would die.

As masses of the Glee converged and all came for him, he threw himself into the battle. He kept the chain spinning overhead fast as he could, whipping it against the creatures as soon as they were close enough. The eyebolt at the end of the chain whistled as it swept through the air. Almost as fast as he downed one and another got close enough, he cracked the heavy eyebolt against its skull. Most slowed and stayed back out of range. Others came for him, thinking they could duck under and evade the chain. He saw sharp white teeth snapping at his face. He caught the chain and doubled it over so he could swing it at them like a bat. That doubled the weight of each impact.

As he was fighting off a number of Glee at the same time, one of them somehow suddenly got in close. Before it could claw him or bite his face, Richard threw a loop of the chain over its head and around its neck. He put his knee between the thing's shoulder blades and hauled back on the chain, letting out a yell with the effort until he felt and heard the windpipe crush in. Once it did, he kicked another of the tall, dark creatures back and immediately hit it in the head with the doubled-over chain.

Richard lost himself in a world of seemingly endless, bloody battle. The rhythm of what he was doing soon became what he knew so well. It became the dance with death.

He killed the creatures as fast as they could come at him. Those that were severely injured and were able vanished back into their world. The air in Richard's world was filled with howls and shrieks of the enraged creatures and of the wounded and dying. The floor was slick with blood and slime of the dead.

Panting from the effort, Richard paused, looked around for more of the enemy, more targets. He suddenly realized that there were no more Glee still standing. A number of them lay dead, many sprawled over the top of others. The last of the howls and shrieks still seemed to echo in his head.

He raced back to the witch man to strangle him with the chain before he could wake up.

Michec was gone.

67

Richard quickly looked around, hoping to be able to find and catch Michec before he could get away, but he was nowhere to be seen. He gritted his teeth in rage that the witch man was no longer there on the floor. He had to kill the man before he could do anything else to them—before he could kill them first.

"Did you see where he went?" he asked Kahlan and Shale.

Both shook their heads.

Before doing anything else, Richard rushed to Vika and yanked the Agiel from the gaping wound in her belly. She gasped. Holding the Agiel sent a jolt of pain up through his elbow, making him flinch. The blow of pain felt as if he had been hit in the back of the skull with an iron bar. It made his ears ring. He could not imagine the agony of having that weapon jammed inside an open wound.

He tossed the Agiel on the floor, then touched her bloody, trembling leg as he looked up into her wet eyes. "Hold on, Vika."

"Kill me," she pleaded. "Please, Lord Rahl. There is no hope for me now. Please, end it."

"Just hold on," he said. "I'm going to help you. Trust me."

Angry that he couldn't kill Michec right then and there, he dragged the heavy chain attached to his manacles over to his sword and baldric, which lay under where he had been hanging. He had to grab the arm of one of the dark, slimy creatures lying over the bottom half of the scabbard and flip it over and off the weapon. He started to pull the sword out of the scabbard with his hands, but because they were chained closely together, he had to hold the scabbard between his boots to be able to draw the blade the rest of the way out.

A familiar sensation stormed through him. He felt a fool.

With the hilt held in both hands, it was with great relief that he felt the anger of the sword's magic join his to blossom into full rage. He immediately turned and swung the sword over the sorceress's head. Sparks flew as the blade shattered the iron chain and sent links flying. Shale dropped to the floor.

"Hold your hands out," he told her.

When she did, and she saw what he was about to do and that she didn't have enough time to stop him, she gasped in fear as she turned her face away. The blade whistled through the air as it came down in an arc and hit the manacles with a glancing blow to the side of her wrists. It was enough to shatter the metal bands. Shards of hot steel skittered across the room bouncing along the rough stone floor.

Shale, somewhat surprised to still have her hands, was relieved to finally have the horrible devices off. She rubbed her bleeding wrists.

"Hold Kahlan for me," he told the sorceress before she had the chance to thank him.

Shale hugged her arms around Kahlan's legs to lift her weight a little. As soon as she did, Richard took a mighty swing at the chain holding Kahlan up by her wrists. The iron links blew apart when hit with the singular blade, as if made of nothing more than clay. Hot, broken bits of chain sailed off through the air.

Together Shale and Richard lowered Kahlan down to stand on the floor. She held her hands out as she turned her bruised and bleeding face away so Richard could break the manacles from around her wrists. In relief, once they were off, she threw her arms around his neck. Richard returned the hug as best he could with both of his wrists still in manacles, and while doing so let healing magic flow into her just long enough to ease her pain a little. The rest would have to wait.

When he released her to turn and look for any threat, she sank down to the floor in a squat, elbows in tight at her sides, holding her head in her hands, comforting the painful wounds Michec had inflicted but also thankful for at least the little healing Richard had done. He put a hand on her shoulder, relieved that she was safe, at least for the moment. Without looking up, Kahlan reached up to grip his hand a moment.

He understood the wordless meaning in that touch.

Then, with Shale's help holding the Mord-Sith's weight, Richard used his sword to break the chain holding her. As soon as he did, he immediately moved to help Shale carefully lower the Mord-Sith to the floor. Shale and Kahlan both held Vika's arms as he shattered the manacles around her wrists.

As the metal shards were still bouncing across the stone floor, a sound made him turn toward the back of the vast room.

There, in the distance beyond the hanging, skinless corpses, he saw the air come alive with masses of scribbles as hundreds of Glee began to materialize, pouring out of nowhere into a mad dash toward them. They went around and among the hanging dead like a raging river flooding around rocks on their way to Richard, Kahlan, Shale and Vika.

Without pause, still in the haze of rage from the sword, he turned to face the threat. Shale seized Kahlan in a protective hug, turning her own back to the danger.

Still lost in the dance with death from fighting the last onslaught of Glee, Richard acted without forethought.

He went to his right knee. Holding the sword in both hands, he thrust it out toward the mass of dark shapes coming for them, teeth clacking, claws reaching, as they screeched with murderous intent.

From somewhere deep within, his war-wizard birthright, his instinct, his raging need took over. That inheritance of power shot through his grip on the hilt, adding destructive force to the sword's rage. Light ignited from the tip of the sword. The room shook with a crack, as if the sword had been hit by lightning.

The horizontal wedge of light that flared from the tip of the sword came out razor thin and as sharp as his blade. The blindingly bright flash of flawless white illumination was so flat and thin as to be insubstantial, like a glowing pane of glass, yet at the same time it was pure menace.

Everything that razor-thin flare of light touched was instantly severed.

Corpses were sliced cleanly in half through bone and flesh as that flat blade of light effortlessly flared through them. The stiff bottom halves of the bodies thumped down to the floor.

That same wedge of light cut through the Glee like a hot knife through silk. There was no escaping the instantaneous, blindingly bright knife of light.

Dark, severed legs collapsed. The top halves of slimy torsos, arms still flailing, tumbled across the floor, spilling their insides as they crashed down. Some of the Glee clawed at the floor, trying to reach him. Since they were without legs and losing blood at a catastrophic rate, those efforts quickly died out as life left them. It all happened so fast that none of them managed to dive to the floor to evade the cutting light or vanish back into their home world.

The Golden Goddess would never hear from the attack force.

The instant that sheet of light ignited, everything before it was sliced in two. Almost as soon as it had ignited, the flat wedge of light extinguished. It had only lasted an instant, but that was all it had taken.

Even though the light was gone, the room still reverberated with the crack of thunder it had created. Slowly, even that sound died out, to leave the room in ringing silence. What looked like hundreds of Glee lay in a tangled, bleeding mass, a few arms still weakly clawing at the air. In another moment, even that residual muscle movement ceased, and the room went still as Richard, motionless on one knee, the manacles still around his wrists with the chain attached, head bowed, held the sword out toward the vanquished threat.

When he finally stood and turned back, he saw Shale standing stock-still in wide-eyed shock. Kahlan, who only a moment before had been bracing with the sorceress for the swift death about to descend upon them, let out a sigh as she sagged in relief.

68

"Richard," Shale finally whispered into the haunting silence, "how in the world did you just do that? For that matter, what in the world did you just do?"

Richard had no real answer. Truth be told, he was at a loss to understand what he had just done, much less explain it to her. He had simply acted out of instinct—a war wizard's instinct.

"I ended the threat," he said in simple explanation, without trying to embellish with guesses about what he couldn't explain.

"No... well, yes, but what I mean, is how could you possibly do that? That was clearly magic. Michec blocked us from using our magic in this room. For that matter, how did your sword work? Your sword shouldn't work in here either. You shouldn't be able to use your gift in here."

Richard arched an eyebrow at her. "And you believe that?"

"Of course." Her brow tightened. "I could feel that I couldn't use my gift. It was blocked. How were you able to use yours?"

"He's not a wizard, but he used Wizard's First Rule."

Her face twisted with bewilderment. "Wizard's what?"

Richard wet his lips. "I don't think that a witch man even as powerful as Michec could do something like block us from our gift. But you were afraid it was true, so you believed it. By believing it, in a way you made it true. You blocked your gift because in your own mind you believed a block was there. You expected to be blocked from your ability. I don't think Michec really has the ability to do such a thing. At least not to us. To the Mord-Sith, yes, because he was a trainer to Mord-Sith, but not us. Sometimes a trick is the best magic."

"But how did you know?"

Richard showed her a crooked smile. "A lesson my grandfather taught me. I just wish I hadn't been so slow to remember the lesson and realize what was really happening. If I had realized that lesson sooner, I would have been able to kill Michec while still hanging from the chain.

"Without thinking, while I thought my gift was blocked, I expected the magic of the sword to work when I grabbed the hilt. When it did, I suddenly realized there couldn't be a block or I wouldn't be able to feel its power bonding with me. It was just a trick. I had been believing it because I was afraid it was true."

Shale shook her head. "I wish I had realized it. I could have done something."

"We all believed it because Michec is a scary character. That's how such a trick works. It has to be convincing. Michec is convincing, but he has limitations."

Richard turned to Kahlan and held her bloody face gently in his hands. He kissed her forehead, relieved beyond words that she was safe, at least for the moment. He hated to see all that blood on her face. He briefly released a flow of Subtractive Magic as he held her head between his hands, making the blood on her face vanish and easing a little more of her pain.

"Do you think you can hold on for a bit?" he whispered to her. "I need to help Vika."

Kahlan nodded. "Michec did no serious damage to me. Don't worry about me. You have to help Vika if you can."

As Richard turned, an astonished Shale hooked his arm. With her other hand she waggled a finger at Kahlan. "How did you make the blood on her face vanish?"

"Subtractive Magic. I told you. There is no block on our gift." He held both hands out, still in the manacles. "Now, show me I'm right by using your gift to get these off me."

Giving him a dark look, she opened her mouth to question him, but then put her hands around the manacles. She closed her eyes as she concentrated on the task. Richard heard a snap as the lock on the metal bands broke. He twisted his hands, and to his great relief the manacles with the chain still attached fell open and dropped to the floor.

"Thanks. See? Your gift was there all the time." He gestured toward the opening to the room off in the distance. "Now, keep a sharp lookout for Michec. He's out there somewhere and he is not going to so easily give up. I have to help Vika before he shows up again."

The sorceress tightened her grip on his arm. Her eyes reflected the pain of sympathy, and regret. She hesitated briefly, then leaned in close and spoke softly so that Vika wouldn't hear.

"Lord Rahl, her wounds are too grievous to heal. Healing is part of my ability, something I've done my whole life. I know what is possible and what is not possible. There is nothing that can be done for her. You must believe me that I know what I'm talking about. She cannot be healed of a gut wound that serious, to say nothing of what else he did to that poor girl.

"But beyond that, even if it were within the scope of the possible, a complex healing takes many hours. An extremely complex healing can take days. Michec is still down here, somewhere. He is not going to give up on a witch's oath. He will come back after us all. Do you think he won't kill Kahlan as well after he is finished with her?"

Richard frowned at her. "Are you saying we should run? That I should flee because of a witch's oath?" He gestured around at the room full of skinned corpses, some of them now sliced in half by the magic he used to stop the Glee. "That I should abandon the People's Palace to Michec knowing full well what a monster he is and what he will do?"

"No…" She shook her head in exasperation. "No. It's not that. It's just that with such grave danger to you and the Mother Confessor—and to your children—we don't have the luxury of that much time for a futile attempt to heal Vika. Nor can you afford the distraction of a protracted attempt that is doomed to fail in the end. The most you can do for Vika now is to grant her the mercy of a quick death. She has earned that much."

Richard bit back his anger at her words and instead said, "Let me handle this."

Seeing the look in his eyes, Shale finally relented with a nod. He gently pulled away from her grasp on his arm. Kahlan, then, touched him with an expression of anguish over the grim situation. Richard looked at both of them briefly, at the pain he saw in their eyes. The resolve they saw in his eyes kept them both from saying anything.

And then, something back in the darkness caught his eye. Past Kahlan and Shale, in the distance, in the dim greenish light, he saw a single Glee just standing there, watching. He remembered seeing a single Glee before, after a previous battle when he killed a large group of them.

He stared at the dark shape. It stared back.

And then it did the oddest thing. Without moving, it turned its hands over and spread the three claws of each hand and just stood there like that for a moment. He saw, then, that the Glee's hands were webbed between each claw.

It wasn't at all an aggressive posture. If he didn't know better, he would say it was acknowledgment of Richard and what he had just done. As soon as the Glee knew they had made eye contact, and it had shown him its webbed hands, the air turned to scribbles as it vanished back into its own world.

Richard wondered if it could possibly be the same one he had seen before, the same lone Glee. Or if it was a scout of some sort come to see what had happened and report back to the Golden Goddess.

He also wondered why the Glee would have webbed claws, if they were predators.

Whatever its purpose, Richard didn't have time to consider it any longer. He had much more important things to tend to.

His gaze refocused on the two women in front of him. "I have to help Vika."

69

The naked Mord-Sith lay in a pool of her own blood on the rough, cold stone floor below where she had been hanging. Bits of broken chain were scattered across the floor. Her single braid was soaked red from that blood. Her red leather outfit lay on the far side of her.

Vika's pale face was a landscape of bruises, open wounds, and strings of blood from a beating. Richard could see that both her cheekbones had been broken from blows. One of the bone fragments stuck out through the skin. He could hardly contain his rage at what the witch man had done to her. He could also hardly believe that she was still alive. He knew, though, that if he didn't do something soon, she wouldn't be alive for long.

He reminded himself that the time would come, but now was not the moment to focus on his anger at Moravaska Michec. Now, it was about Vika, and what he hoped to be able to do.

She was trembling ever so slightly. Her eyes were closed as she struggled against the crushing weight of pain. A glistening, bloody mass of her intestines lay up against her side, still attached by a knotted length of gut coming out of the gaping wound in her abdomen. He had a hard time believing that she wasn't crying in agony.

During their training, Mord-Sith were kept on the cusp of death for days on end. Richard knew that such twisted training made them more than merely tough. They all knew death well. They all danced with death in their own, private way. It was that training, he thought, and only that training, that made her able to endure it, and probably was keeping her alive.

Vika's eyes opened as Richard knelt down close beside her.

"You did good, Lord Rahl. I knew you would think of something if I could just buy you a little time." The inside of her lips had been gashed open on her teeth when Michec had struck her with his fists. He could see how much it hurt her to speak, despite doing her best not to let it show. "I hope you don't think I was really urging him to kill you."

"No," he quietly reassured her as he put a hand gently on her shoulder, "no, I knew what you were doing."

She let out a breath in relief.

Richard smiled down at her through the pain of empathy at seeing her in such a condition. He gently brushed a strand of blond hair back from her eyes as she gazed up at him.

"You are the one who did good, Vika. It was all your doing. I couldn't have done it without you. You saved Kahlan and me—and our children."

"It was my great honor," she said. "I'm afraid that it is my time, now. I know the cusp of the world of the dead well enough. I have returned from that place more times than anyone has a right to. I am looking out at you now from the brink of that dark place. The world of the dead calls to me. My time has come to go beyond the veil. Thank you for rescuing me from Hannis Arc and for allowing me to serve you."

Richard shook his head. "It's not your time, Vika. Don't even think that. You must live. I need you."

She rolled her head from side to side. "It is too late for me now. I know that. Please don't try to soothe me with the false kindness of a lie. I know better."

"I am the Seeker of Truth. It is no lie. I wouldn't do that to you. If I thought it was too late for you, I would tell you so."

She smiled the littlest bit. "Not even you can heal me or hold back the world of the dead. But I would be eternally grateful if you would spare me any more suffering in this life and send me swiftly on to the next."

"Vika—"

"Please, Lord Rahl. End it. I am ashamed to admit that I am not strong enough to endure this any longer and I don't have the strength to end it myself. I hate for you to see me so weak. Please. Grant me the mercy of a quick death."

Richard swallowed back his anguish. It was hard for him to see her beg for death.

"I asked you to trust me. You must do that now. I am the Lord Rahl. We are bonded in an oath—you to me and me to you. Your life while in this world is in my hands and just as it is your duty to serve and protect me, my duty is to protect you. More than that, I need you. You have given me your oath of loyalty. Remember that oath now and put your trust in me. You must hold on for me."

Before she could object, Richard laid a hand gently on her brow. He closed his eyes and bowed his head, letting his power flow into her. Vika gasped as she felt the hot rush of it. He didn't try to heal her, or even relieve her pain. He knew that would be futile right then. For the moment, he could only give her strength to help her endure her injuries and hold on until he could do more to try to save her.

When he opened his eyes and lifted his head, he was looking into her intense blue eyes. He smiled at the look in those eyes.

"There is the Mord-Sith I know." He touched a finger to her lips before she could speak. "My strength is your strength. Now, hold on for me."

A tear ran from the corner of her eye as she nodded.

Richard rushed to his feet. He might have given her some added strength, but he knew he didn't have much time. Strength alone would not keep her alive.

A short distance away, Shale, keeping a watchful eye on him, was just finishing helping Kahlan get her clothes back on. Kahlan's eye was still bluish black and swollen shut. Her wrists oozed blood, as did Shale's wrists, as did his own.

"Watch for Michec," he told them both. "He is still down here, somewhere. We are going to need some time without being interrupted."

Shale eyed him suspiciously. "Time for what?"

Kahlan was just finishing buttoning her shirt. When Richard didn't answer, she offered her own answer. "Time for a crazy idea, I suspect."

Shale looked to Richard and then back at Kahlan. "What crazy idea?"

"I can't begin to imagine."

"Kahlan, I need you to do something." With an arm around her shoulders, Richard pulled her closer. He didn't have time for questions. "I know you are hurting and you need to be healed. So do Shale's wrists. We will take care of that, I promise. But right now, stay here with Vika. I don't want her to be alone. Hold her hand. Just be with her until I get back."

"Where are you going?"

"To get the others."

Shale gestured off toward where the rest of the Mord-Sith knelt at the opening to the kill room. "Michec blocked them. Do you believe it is the same kind of trick of magic that he did with us?"

Richard sighed as he looked off among the hanging corpses toward the opening to the room. In the distance, between some of the skinned bodies, he could just see the red leather outfits of a few of the kneeling Mord-Sith.

"No. He was a trainer of Mord-Sith. I don't know exactly how such things worked, but as a trainer he would possess very real power over them. I'm sure Michec really was able to block them off from everything."

"Then what are you going to do?" the sorceress asked.

"I'm going to pull them out from beyond that block. Now wait here with Kahlan, please, and stay on guard. Michec is out there, somewhere, and sooner or later he is going to come after us. I'm worried he might slip back in here and surprise us."

"When you see him are you going to scythe him down with light from your sword like you did to the Glee?" the sorceress asked expectantly. "That would certainly be effective."

Richard's mouth twisted with frustration. "I would if I could, but I don't actually know how I did it. I simply reacted. In that instant of desperation I can only assume my war-wizard heritage took over, assessed the nature of the threat, what tools I had at hand, and what powers could be brought to bear, then it did what that instinctual part of my ability concluded would be the most effective response. I don't know that for certain, but it seems the most logical guess. I do know it wasn't a conscious act."

Shale briefly considered his words. She finally gave him a serious look. "Then what are you going to do if you encounter the witch man? He has powerful magic."

Richard gazed back with an equally serious look. "I guess I'll have to take care of him the old-fashioned way."

"The old-fashioned way? What's that?"

Richard arched an eyebrow. "I'll just have to go all emotional on him."

Shale's mouth twisted with displeasure as she looked over at Kahlan. "You were right. A crazy idea."

70

Just before he reached the broad opening back out to the corridor, Richard paused, sword in hand, to carefully lean out and look in both directions. He could feel the word "TRUTH" formed by the gold and silver wire-wound hilt pressing into his palms. Blood ran down from the painful, throbbing wounds on his wrists, onto the hilt of the sword, and then down the blade to drip from the tip. His blood always made the sword's magic lust to meet the enemy. He had often used his blood to give the sword even more motivation.

Looking out, he didn't see any sign of the witch man. He worried how Michec might be able to hide himself in plain sight. After all, the first time Richard had seen him he had seemed to materialize out of smoke. Fortunately, Richard didn't see any smoke, either. But he had no way of knowing what other powers Michec might be able to use to hide himself.

Richard had kicked the man in the head pretty hard, but he didn't know exactly where his boot had connected or how much damage it had done. All he knew was that he had used all his strength to do it. With the way it had knocked the man out cold, it had to have done some damage, but Richard didn't know if it was enough.

Michec was most likely hiding somewhere nursing his injuries. Richard knew nothing about witch men and wondered if it was possible for him to heal himself. Unless the kick had done serious damage, it wouldn't keep him down.

Someone that filled with hate and a lust for power wasn't about to let his prey slip away, so Richard knew it wouldn't be long before the witch man came out of nowhere to attack them. When he did, Richard knew, the man would be out for blood. But until then, he had at least a small window of opportunity to try to save Vika.

The other five Mord-Sith were still kneeling in a line in the broad opening, hands held out, their Agiel, still attached by the fine gold chains around their wrists, resting across their upturned palms. They all stared blankly ahead. Richard knew that despite their lifeless appearance, they would all feel the pain of those Agiel.

Richard didn't believe it had been a trick that put the Mord-Sith into such a state of oblivion. This was a result of Michec's abilities both as a witch man and as a trainer of Mord-Sith. Richard didn't know what those abilities entailed or how he had come by them, but he knew they were very real. It was just one more cause for concern. While young women were chosen for their innocence and compassion, he suspected that trainers of future Mord-Sith were chosen for their obsession with cruelty.

All he knew for sure was that he had to get the five Mord-Sith back from that lost place before he tried to heal Vika, and he needed to hurry; Vika couldn't last much longer.

He put his hand on the red leather on Berdine's shoulder. She didn't respond. She had belonged to Michec once, so his control over her would be the strongest. Through his hand on her shoulder Richard could feel the painful hum of power coursing through her from her Agiel. That power was fueled by their bond to the Lord Rahl, not Michec, and therein lay the source of his hope.

He could also sense, through that connection, that she was in pain. That pain was likely worsened by the block. It saddened him, too, to feel her hopelessness.

Richard squatted down, keeping his hand in contact with her shoulder. He knew how to heal with his gift. He had, a number of times, connected to people who were injured or sick and let his ability flow into them. He began to open that same mental gateway deep within himself.

"I am here with you, Berdine," he said into her ear. "As Mord-Sith, your loyalty and bond are to me as the Lord Rahl for as long as you wish to serve me. No other may claim dominion or authority over you. No one. Not now, not ever. Moravaska Michec is an enemy of the D'Haran Empire and I am the leader of that empire. I now dissolve any block he placed in you and place instead the protection of my gift to block him from ever again using his power over you."

Richard removed the rest of his own internal restraints to let the full healing force of his power rush into her so she would not only hear him, but feel him, feel his gift, feel his bond to her and hers to him, and be able to feel the raw pain of the block the witch man had left in her mind melt away into nothingness.

He stood, then, and held the point of the sword over her upturned hands to let some of his blood drip from the tip of the blade onto her palms.

"With my bond and blood oath I reclaim you from that witch."

Berdine gasped. Her head jerked up. Her eyes came open. She blinked a moment and then shook her head as if gathering her senses, trying to understand where she was. Finally, she stared at the blood on her palms and then looked up at Richard.

"Lord Rahl…"

When Richard smiled, she suddenly shot to her feet and threw her arms around him in relief.

"You saved me! You came for me and you saved me! I knew you would."

Richard patted her back and then pushed away. "We don't have much time. I need to get the others back as well."

He went to each Mord-Sith in turn and repeated the procedure until all five of them were jolted out from behind that block Michec had put in their minds. None of the others hugged him the way Berdine had, but they were all clearly thankful that he had come for them and succeeded in breaking the witch man's hold over them.

"Where is Michec?" Rikka asked as she stood and looked both ways down the corridor.

"I don't know," Richard said. "We are going to need to hunt him down, but first I have to help Vika."

"You found her, then?" Nyda asked, expectantly.

Richard nodded. "I'm afraid that the news is not good, though. He hurt her bad."

Richard hurriedly led them back through the forest of nearly skinless corpses. The Mord-Sith all looked about dispassionately, taking in the exposed red muscles, white ligaments, and faces frozen in horror and agony. They were all familiar with Michec's work. When they spotted Vika, though, they were clearly angry.

"Michec did this to her?" Cassia asked in a whisper as she leaned in close.

Richard nodded. "We need to help her."

Nyda turned an incredulous look back over her shoulder at him. "Help her?" A look of sudden understanding came over her. She lowered her voice. "Oh, I see now what you mean. Lord Rahl... would you rather one of us do it, then? She is a sister of the Agiel, after all."

Richard cocked his head. "Do what?"

Nyda looked clearly uncomfortable. "You know. End it. A quick twist of my Agiel and her suffering will be forever over."

Richard held out his hands, forestalling any such idea. "No, no. You don't understand. We have to heal her."

71

The five Mord-Sith shared a look but didn't say anything. They all knew that these kinds of injuries were well beyond healing. Richard hoped to prove that belief wrong.

Kahlan was kneeling beside Vika, with Shale on the other side. Each was holding a hand of the gravely wounded Mord-Sith.

"We need to get on with the healing," Richard told them. He looked around to make sure all of them were paying attention. "We have to hurry. Here is what we are going to do."

Shale looked up at him. "We?"

Richard nodded as he gestured for all of the Mord-Sith to gather round closer to Vika so he would only have to explain it once.

"Michec is down here somewhere," he said, looking to each of their faces in turn. "He could show up at any moment, so we can only do this if we're quick."

Shale clearly looked confused. "Healing grievous wounds, if it was still within the realm of possibility and if it could be done at all, would take a day at least, likely many days for all I know."

"You're right," Richard said. "We don't have that kind of time. Neither does Vika. So trying the conventional way of healing that you know so well is simply not an option. Not only that, but like you, I seriously doubt that it would even work. Whatever we do must be done quickly."

Kahlan looked puzzled as to what he could be talking about. Shale was looking at him as if he had lost his mind.

"Quickly," the sorceress repeated. "You intend to heal her quickly. Of course." She looked up at the ceiling as if speaking to an audience in a gallery. "That makes sense."

Ignoring Shale's remark, Richard wiped a hand across his mouth as he turned around, staring off in the other direction for a moment, trying to think how he could explain it to them without causing them to panic. He turned back.

"I think I have a way that we can heal her if we all do it together. All nine of us together."

"Lord Rahl," Berdine said as she gestured at her sisters of the Agiel to each side of her, "we don't know anything about healing. I think most of us have been healed at one time or another, but we can't heal anyone. We can't use magic—other than that which the Lord Rahl gives us through our bond in order to use the power of our Agiel and all that involves."

Richard knew quite well how much Mord-Sith hated anything to do with magic. "Yes you can," he insisted. "But in a unique way. I'm afraid that it will be dangerous, though. Dangerous to all of us. Still, I think it has a chance to be successful."

"You 'think'?" Shale held up a hand to stop him right there. "First of all, I can't imagine what you are talking about, but more importantly, you and the Mother Confessor have a responsibility to the two children of D'Hara she is carrying. Our job is to protect her from danger, not put her in it."

"This is to protect her," Richard insisted. "You need to listen to me. You all need to listen to me. You need to see the bigger picture, not just this one moment, this one risk. It's important that Vika live because she is vital to our survival. There are nine of us. If we lose Vika, then there are only eight."

Kahlan squinted. "Does this have something to do with the Law of Nines?"

Richard gave her a firm nod. "Yes."

"The law of what?" Shale asked. "I think you said something about that before."

"I did." Richard pointed a finger up at the palace above them. "In one of the highly restricted libraries up in the People's Palace, there is a book that deals with the power of numbers as it relates to the use of the gift. It says that there are various cardinal numbers, some of them very powerful in how they affect magic.

"Nine in many ways is the most important number. In the right circumstances it can alter and increase the power of magic. In some cases it can even invoke some powers of magic. In rare cases there are even powers of magic that can be brought about in no other way.

"The number three is associated as an element of the number nine, and so also important. It's part of how we use magic. For example, the devotion is repeated three times. There's a reason for that. Those three repetitions reinforce the magic in the bond itself because they invoke the Law of Nines."

Berdine looked puzzled. "But three isn't nine."

"But there are three devotions spoken, three times a day. Three threes are nine. See what I mean? Three is a constituent component of nine. It adds power to an already powerful number."

"So you think that because there are nine of us, our power is greater than any one of us alone?" Kahlan asked.

"Among other things," Richard said, relieved that she, at least, grasped what he was talking about.

"What other things?" she asked.

Richard gestured overhead. "We are in the People's Palace, drawn in the shape of a spell-form to give the Lord Rahl more power. On top of that, we are also inside a complication, designed to make the Lord Rahl's power, aided by that spell-form, more effective. The Law of Nines makes a third element. All three of these things—the Law of Nines, the palace spell, and the complication—give me the best chance to save Vika.

"I have to take this opportunity while I have all those elements on my side."

Kahlan leveled a look at him. "We also have things that work against us. Besides Vika's wounds being grave, Michec is down here somewhere. He could show up and attack us at any moment. And then there are the Glee."

Richard nodded. "I didn't say it would be easy, or that there aren't risks." He leaned closer to her. "But if we lose Vika, we lose a powerful element of protection for you and the babies in getting us to the protection of the Wizard's Keep. To preserve that power of nine, we need Vika with us. We can't begin to imagine right now how and when we might desperately need that added bit of help afforded by the Law of Nines. As small as that bit of magic may be, it could be enough to make the difference when it matters most.

"Because of the Law of Nines, the nine of us together have a kind of cumulative ability that none of us alone would have. Neither Shale nor I by ourselves have the ability to do a healing of injuries as life-threatening as the ones Vika has."

Shale was giving him a look, part skepticism and part analytical interest. "So, because of this Law of Nines, you think all of us together can somehow heal her?"

"In a way, yes."

"In a way." Shale folded her arms. "How?"

"We need to all join hands. Shale, you will be holding Vika's right hand as you were a moment ago. Then all the Mord-Sith will line up around Vika, all holding hands. Kahlan will be at the end of them, then me. I will be holding Vika's left hand with my right, in that way linking us all together. When we are joined in that ring, I believe the Law of Nines will give me what I need to help me heal her."

Shale still had her arms folded as she glowered at him from under her brow. "And how long do you think this will take?" By her tone, she was clearly growing even more suspicious of exactly what it was he intended to do.

"From our side it will be almost instantaneous. That's the advantage of what I plan to do."

Kahlan leaned in, her suspicion now exceeding Shale's. "From our side? What exactly are you saying?"

Richard didn't want to fool any of them, but at the same time he had to tell them at least part of what he intended. "Once we are linked, I will use all our combined gifts to stay connected to Vika in the underworld."

Jaws dropped.

Kahlan reached out and gripped his arm. "What?"

"It's the only way."

Shale's arms had come unfolded as she leaned in along with Kahlan. "The only way to do what? Die with her?"

"Well, I should hope not," Richard said, offering a smile to her surprise. That clearly wasn't what any of them expected to hear. "You have to trust me on this. It's the only way to have the time we need to do this."

Only Kahlan understood. "Of course… but Richard—"

"Of course what?" Shale interrupted.

Kahlan cast a worried look at the sorceress. "The underworld is eternal. There is no such thing as time in an eternal world, because with no beginning and no end there is no way to measure it or determine how much time has passed. What might be an instant here could be days, or even centuries in the underworld."

Richard could see that Shale was about to unleash a hundred questions and a thousand objections. He didn't want to hear any of it.

"I intend to save Vika, the same as I would save any of you. I view this as necessary to help us get Kahlan and these children of D'Hara to the safety of the Keep. It needs to be done. We are wasting time."

In the underworld he would have an eternity of time, among other things.

"I want everyone to kneel down around Vika in a circle," he told them. "Shale, you take her right hand. The rest of you join hands like I explained. Kahlan, you take my hand."

"Lord Rahl," Vika said in a weak voice as they all knelt around her, "I don't want to endanger any of you. Please don't—"

"It endangers us more if we lose you. As the Lord Rahl I judge that this is what we must do. Now, put your trust in me." Richard gestured to the others. "Everyone, join hands."

72

Richard picked up Vika's Agiel, which he had pulled from her gut wound earlier and had thrown on the floor.

"Vika, I want you to hold this in your teeth. I gave you some of my strength, before. Do you think you can do that? I need you back at that place."

Knowing that he meant that place on the cusp between worlds, she nodded. In a way, the pain of an Agiel was an insane kind of familiar comfort to a Mord-Sith. Richard had already tensed the muscles of his abdomen to help him endure the pain of holding the Agiel. Unlike the Mord-Sith, he found no comfort in such pain. When he held it out in front of her she pulled her lips back and clamped her teeth down on it. Her pupils dilated as the wall of pain hit her and her jaws clenched tighter.

He didn't need to tell her to bite down.

Once he saw that she had, he carefully picked up the small pile of her intestines coiled on the floor beside her. He did his best to carefully wipe off any specks of dirt or crumbled rock. Once he had inspected them to see that they didn't have any foreign matter stuck to them, he stretched out and pushed the tips of his fingers into the wound in order to spread open the sides to give him room to guide the warm mass back inside her abdomen.

Her eyes wide, Vika stared at the ceiling as she trembled. Each breath was a ragged pull; then she would tighten her muscles and bear down again until she needed another breath.

"All right, that's the worst of it," he told her.

She nodded without looking over at him. It didn't look like it had helped with the pain. Her face had gone a bloodless white, telling him that, if anything, the pain was worse.

He put a bloody hand on her shoulder. "Hold on, Vika. It won't be long. You are already on the cusp. The pain of the Agiel will help you take that final step through the veil. I will be holding your hand. I will be here, but also with you, and watching over you when you cross over."

The last part wasn't exactly true, but he needed to say it for those listening, especially Kahlan. This was no time for questions he dare not answer honestly.

"When you get to that place beyond, to that world, it will be tempting to let yourself go into that forever world," he told her. "Believe me, I know. You will find comfort there in being free of the pain, free of misery, fear, and worry—free of everything. You will want to let yourself drift away into that eternal world where struggles of life are a thing of the past and you can be at peace. If it's all too much for you, you have my permission to accept that world."

He didn't want her to make that choice, but he wanted to give her a choice to be better able to endure what she was about to face. He knew that by having the option of a way out, it sometimes helped endure a hard choice.

"But I need you, Vika. Kahlan needs you. Our children need you. D'Hara needs you. So I hope you will have the strength to let me heal you while your spirit is there and then return to us."

She finally looked over into his eyes and nodded. He could see her doing her best to fight the pain of both her injuries and the Agiel she held clamped in her teeth.

"This is insanity," Shale said in a low voice.

Kahlan looked like she might agree, but she didn't say so. Richard knew that despite her well-founded fear, Kahlan was doing her best to put her trust in his judgment that what he was doing was necessary to help get their unborn children to safety. He fervently hoped that her trust was warranted.

Richard looked up at the sorceress on the other side of Vika. "You may be right. I do know that without you to make up nine of us, this will likely fail. But just as I'm not forcing Vika to do this, I'm not forcing you to be a part of it, either. If you can't commit to helping me, to helping us all, and especially to helping Vika, then that must be your choice. Either way, I intend to attempt it, with or without you, but without you, without the Law of Nines as an aid, my chances of being successful go down. So it's up to you." He leaned a little closer to her across Vika's body. "Choose."

Shale's gaze took in all the Mord-Sith on their knees around the supine Vika. She met Kahlan's gaze for a long moment, but Kahlan, despite the bruises and the eye swollen nearly shut, was wearing her Confessor's face. Finally Shale looked down at Vika, the Agiel between her teeth as she did her best to draw each breath. At last, she looked back up at Richard.

"I didn't come all the way from the Northern Waste to deny you my help now. You are the Lord Rahl. Do as you must. I will support you."

Richard smiled his appreciation. "All right, I want everyone to concentrate on Vika. Imagine giving her your strength and imagine her being whole again. Shale, please add what ability you have at healing to mine."

"Do you really think that will help?" Cassia asked. "Us concentrating on Vika, I mean? We can't do magic."

"You're not doing magic. You are magic, through the power of the Law of Nines and through your bond to me. You are part of that whole. It's that whole that matters.

"You and your sisters have all been on the cusp of death. You remember being partway into that world, don't you?"

Cassia looked grim. "More times than I care to remember."

"When you are on the cusp, you are actually partially in the underworld, or you couldn't really know that you were on the cusp, now could you? Vika knows. She is there now at that threshold, at the brink of death itself. She told me that she was already in some ways looking out at me from the world of the dead. It is that experience of being on the cusp that you bring to the circle. It is that experience of coming back into the light of this world that we need. Vika is crossing over as we speak.

"Now please, all of you, just do as I ask. I have to save her while I still can. We are all holding hands to give Vika a link back to this world. You know both. This is a time when we show how much life means to us all. You all are her sisters and her way back."

Vika squeezed his hand at his words. As she trembled from the pain of the Agiel clamped between her teeth, a tear rolled from the corner of her eye. Holding her hand, he could feel the pain pulling him under with her. He had to will himself to ignore it to do what needed to be done.

Richard squeezed Kahlan's hand. Her wrist was still oozing blood. He needed to heal that as well, to say nothing of the obviously painful, swollen bruises on her face.

Once they all had gone quiet, with their eyes closed and heads bowed, Richard turned his mind to what he needed to do, to what he couldn't tell them he was going to do. He took a deep breath against the enormity of the task ahead of him.

If he was to have the time necessary to do what needed to be done, the only place with enough time was a place without time.

He remembered all too well dying and going beyond the veil. He remembered all too well being in the world of the dead. As he concentrated, he embraced the devastating pain of the Agiel radiating up his arm to the base of his skull as motivation to help him go to that numb place of refuge from the pain of life. Thankfully, the others, because Vika's Agiel had never been used against them, could not feel the pain he felt from it.

With the overpowering need of being free of pain pushing him ever onward, he used the power of his gift to do one of the most frightening things imaginable.

He willed his heart to stop.

He ignored the crushing pain that started radiating from the center of his chest by concentrating instead on the pain of the Agiel that didn't let up even though his heart had gone still.

He felt Kahlan's hand tighten on his as she sucked back a sob of fear for him, not really realizing what he had just done.

The world faded away. Kahlan's grip seemed to dissolve as his muscles went slack. Richard saw darkness beyond darkness.

He heard the faint sound of voices—the countless voices of the dead from beyond the veil. As he sank into that dark void, swirling masses of souls swept through a darkness blacker than black and began to surround him. In that void, ghostly arms and writhing fingers reached for him. Hints of light wheeled around him. He held on to Vika, knowing that she was seeing the same thing.

Richard did his best to ignore the voices and the reaching hands. He did his best not to recognize the spectral faces. He couldn't afford the distraction of familiar voices, familiar faces, familiar emotions and longing.

Despite his best efforts, those he had killed, evil people who fought in the world of life for the cause of death, smiled out at him from the darkness as they swept in closer, eager for the chance to rip and tear at his soul. Claws sank painfully into his spirit. As they tried to drag him down among them, Richard held onto an awareness of the light from above, of the light of Kahlan's soul and those with her beyond the veil. As he did, evil lost its grip on him and sank away. He pulled Vika up with him, away from the terrible evil that lusted for them both.

As they rose up through endless darkness, the multitude of souls appeared to be nothing more than the soft flickers of stars massing and moving together like folds of gossamer in a faint breeze, rippling, twisting, rolling as one insubstantial mass. Even as they revolved around him, a curtain of eternal inhabitants of darkness, they knew he did not belong.

But they wanted him to.

They whispered to him, promising him the end of pain, the end of sorrow, the end of a life of constant struggle. They whispered to Vika as well.

He had but to let himself accept what was all around him.

He knew that they were also appealing to Vika to join them in their eternal rest. He knew how much those whispers and tender touches would lure her toward their world for all eternity. He knew how she ached to accept their call.

Richard circled a comforting arm around her shoulders as she gazed about in wonder, the pain of the world of life far distant. In this dark world, she was free of the mortal pain of her injuries, even if her physical form was not yet free of those injuries. Richard held her close, silently reassuring her that he was with her, not letting her feel alone.

When she listened to him, the darkness shifted, the souls twisting away as if in eddies from a current sweeping past, carrying them with it. Richard held Vika close as the two of them drifted through layers of darkness teeming with spirits. Those streams of darkness carried them through rolling undercurrents formed out of nothing. All the time the soft glowing mass of souls followed along, distant, hesitant, yet drawn to them, these alien beings in their world. It was bewitchingly beautiful and terrifying all at the same time.

Richard had to remind himself continually of Kahlan's hand in his, still back there beyond the veil in the world of life, and his love for her. She and the other souls there with her were his anchor—and Vika's anchor—to the world back beyond the veil.

He had to remind himself of their two children back in the world of life. The twins needed him if they were to be born and their Graces were to be completed. And they all needed Vika. He wanted more than anything to be back with Kahlan, and with her unborn babies.

To do that, he needed to get on with the job at hand.

As Vika turned to him, not knowing what to do, not knowing what choice to make, he reached into himself to the depths of his gift, into the network of connections linking his magic to his soul, linking it to the world of life, searching for the exact gossamer threads he needed.

At the same time, he reached into Vika with his gift. Were they still in the world of life, she would have let out a gasp at the power of it.

73

Kahlan, her eyes closed, her head bowed, tried to focus her thoughts on Vika, hoping it would somehow help Richard heal her and at the same time keep her grounded in the world of life. Berdine, to Kahlan's left, held her hand in a tight grip that revealed her fears. Kahlan knew that, like her, they were all terrified by what Richard was doing. It involved magic that none of them understood and they all feared. Kahlan was only obliquely familiar with it, and her understanding of it was in large part theory. Sometimes, she had to put her trust in Richard even when she greatly feared what he was doing.

As the room grew deadly quiet, she couldn't seem to calm her anxiety.

In that silence, Kahlan heard a sound that didn't belong.

Oddly enough, it sounded like something wet.

With sudden realization of what it was, she opened her eyes, despite Richard's instructions, and glanced back over her shoulder. In the dim, greenish light beyond the forest of hanging corpses, she saw dark shapes running as yet more scribbles were forming in the air.

"Richard!" When he didn't respond, she screamed his name again.

Richard slumped, partly bent over on his side, one hand reaching back to hold hers, the other holding Vika's hand. Kahlan saw, then, that Vika had stopped breathing. She urgently pulled away from Berdine to put both hands on the side of Richard's chest, shoving him, trying to wake him from his state of deep concentration.

With a jolt of horror she realized that Richard wasn't breathing, either. She was momentarily confused, unable to understand why he would not be breathing.

If she lost him because she went along with his crazy idea, she would never forgive herself. The twins would never forgive her.

Despite her worry for him, there was no time to figure it out. She had to do something about the dire threat coming into their world from across the room. As she sprang to her feet, she stole a quick glance back to check that the sword was there at Richard's left hip. Once she saw it, she dropped down and grabbed the hilt. The blade rang, hot with rage, as she yanked it free of the scabbard. She knew that rage all too well.

"Shale!" Over on the other side of the still Vika, the woman's head was bowed, her eyes closed. "Shale!"

The sorceress's head jerked up. "What—"

More of the dark, wet shapes materialized out of nowhere to rush forward, their bodies steaming as they came around the hanging corpses. Clear, gelatinous blobs slid off them and splashed across the floor. She realized that was the wet sound she had heard at first.

"Do something!" Kahlan screamed at the sorceress in order to be heard over the sudden sound of murderous shrieks and howls from the Glee, excited at finding her vulnerable with no witch man to stop them.

One of the monsters, apparently the one she had heard materialize first, was out well ahead of the others. She leaped back as wicked claws swiped at her, first one and then the other in rapid succession. Kahlan had been trained in the use of a sword growing up. She reacted instinctively. She swung the sword around and brought it down with all her might, lopping off the second arm that had taken a swipe at her, severing it between wrist and elbow.

The creature recoiled in surprise and pain, drawing back the stump. In that seemingly frozen instant, she immediately used the opening to drive the blade through its chest before it could use its other claw on her. The tall, dark shape dropped to its knees. The sword, still through its body and jutting out its back, was pulled down and almost out of her hands as the creature sank to the floor, already dead. Kahlan grunted with the effort of putting her boot against it and pulling the blade back out as the dark shape toppled over.

Dozens more Glee came charging out from among all the hanging bodies. Bloody sword in hand, Kahlan turned to the sorceress, now alert and on her feet.

"Do something! Richard's not breathing! He can't help! I can't stop them all! You have to do something!"

Shale was already lifting her hands. With her eyes closed, her fingers twisted this way and that as she held her hands up before herself. When she opened her eyes, they had turned a strange yellowish color. Her long dark hair fell forward over her shoulders as her head and brow lowered, as if having no need to rush.

The dark material of the top she wore bunched above the leather forearm shields. Beads and small chains with strange amulets hung below a black leather bodice. A loose wrap skirt of dusky dappled colors was open at her left hip, revealing dark traveling trousers tucked into boots. The trousers had a variety of pockets and equipment straps.

Kahlan always thought of Shale as the sorceress who had healed her and saved the lives of her unborn children. She felt a bond to the woman because of that. But in that instant, her hands lifted up before her dark glower, her fingers swaying snakelike, Shale looked every inch a lethal witch woman. It was a frightening glimpse of pure menace.

As Kahlan swung back around toward the advancing threat, sword at the ready, the floor suddenly came alive with snakes that seemed to materialize up out of the stone. The sight was as alarming as it was impossible.

She gasped as the writhing creatures slithered around her feet as they rushed toward the Glee. They brushed against her ankles as they went over her boots. Some of them glided in waves right over Richard's legs. There were so many the floor seemed to have suddenly come alive with movement.

Most were frighteningly big. While they weren't all the same color or type, most of the biggest were white. A few had brown patterns of scales. Some of the smaller black vipers had yellow bands with white and red rings. Others were a rust color, and a few of the smallest were no bigger around than her finger and as black as death. They were all shockingly fast.

Kahlan didn't know what kind of snakes were white, but these all had the broad heads and snouts of vipers. Red, forked tongues licked at the air as their bodies moved in writhing waves as they raced ahead. She saw that rather than round pupils, all of these snakes had slitted pupils.

Kahlan stood motionless, sword in hand, fearful that if she moved, the snakes still slithering around her ankles would turn and strike at her. As much as she hated and feared snakes, these didn't seem the least bit interested in her. From all around, the hundreds of vipers were all headed toward the Glee.

Shale hadn't moved. She stood with her hands lifted, her fingers slowly twisting with the effort of doing something that appeared extremely difficult. The witch woman's eyes had turned a darker yellow, and Kahlan could have sworn that they, too, had vertical slits for pupils, but before she could get a good look in the dim light, she had to turn back to the howling threat charging in toward them.

As a tall dark shape in the lead dove toward her, Kahlan brought the sword around in a mighty arc, lopping off its head. She had to turn and pull her hips sideways to avoid being knocked down as the headless monster toppled past her. The head bounced along atop the mass of snakes. In reaction to it landing on them, the snakes, with lightning quickness, turned and struck at the head with their fangs, so that as it tumbled along the floor, it became balled up in snakes.

Shale stood with her hands lifted, motionless other than her writhing fingers. Kahlan stole a quick glance and saw that all the Mord-Sith looked to be unconscious. Vika looked to be dead, as if she could no longer will herself to fight for life.

But far worse, that quick glance told her that Richard had clearly stopped breathing. At first, she had thought maybe he was holding his breath in concentration, but he would surely have responded to her calls, if not the threat from the Glee, if he could.

The mass of tall, slimy creatures slowed their advance, seeming unsettled by all the snakes racing toward them across the floor. First a few and then all the Glee came to an uneasy halt. They didn't look like they necessarily feared snakes, but the numbers and their behavior clearly had them concerned.

As they came to a halt, the racing snakes in the lead were finally close enough to strike. They lifted up and drew their heads back, the rest of their bodies whipping around forward for support, and then, jaws opened wide, they struck with lightning speed. As yet more came in, they threw themselves at the Glee. Fangs sank into the soft, dark flesh. The vipers struck at ankles, at legs, and the larger ones that could strike higher went for arms and the lean, muscular bodies.

When the vipers sank their fangs into the Glee, they didn't let go to strike again. Instead, they held on, their heads flexing as they pumped venom into their victims. The Glee, at first confused, then alarmed, were now in full fright, as each of them had dozens of vipers on them with more striking all the time. In mere moments, they were all covered with wriggling snakes. Arms weighed down by snakes that had sunk fangs into them became too heavy to lift. As they staggered back, the snakes wouldn't let go. The stricken Glee dragged the weight of snakes with them as yet more leaped up to join in the mass attack.

Other long, massively thick snakes, with mottled patterns of brown, black, and tan, coiled themselves around legs, progressively rolling the coils up the legs of the victim, finally wrapping their fat bodies around the chest and neck. Once they had made it up the dark, slimy body, they began rhythmically constricting. With each breath the victim took, the snakes tightened their bodies. Kahlan could see the panic in the big glossy eyes of a Glee, the third eyelid blinking in as it struggled to breathe. Each time the Glee breathed out, the snake tightened, preventing the Glee from getting a full breath. In this way, the powerful snakes worked to progressively suffocate the victim.

Some of the Glee, with snakes already attached to them as yet more vipers leaped at them to strike, began to vanish, retreating back into their own world. The snakes that missed an intended target that was suddenly no longer there dropped to the floor and without pause turned their attack to others still there. As many of the Glee vanished back into their own world, they took the snakes, with fangs firmly sunken into them, back with them.

Others had become so fearful of the attacking vipers that they didn't seem to have the presence of mind to flee. They fell back under the weight of snakes attached to them. Once on the floor, they were even easier prey. The Glee shrieked in pain and terror, swiping at vipers going for their faces. None of the invading Glee escaped the attack. Everywhere, snakes continued to attack, sinking their fangs into any victim they could get to.

As the last of the Glee still able were vanishing, Kahlan turned and fell on Richard. She pounded her fists against his chest.

"Richard! Richard! Come back! You have to come back!"

He didn't respond. He seemed lifeless. Kahlan had thought he meant that he was going to go to the cusp of the world of the dead with Vika. Clearly, he hadn't. He must have made some kind of miscalculation and crossed over into the world of the dead.

Or else he had done it deliberately.

And now he was trapped there.

"Shale, help him!"

Kahlan saw Shale, instead of responding to Kahlan's urgent call, sinking to the floor. The witch woman looked to be blacking out from exhaustion. The effort of conjuring all those snakes to attack the Glee seemed to have taken everything she had.

"Well, well, snakes, is it?" a gruff voice behind Kahlan said. "Witch women do seem to have a fondness for their snakes."

Kahlan spun to the terrible voice she knew all too well.

Michec extended an arm down toward the writhing mass of snakes. One of the larger white vipers coiled itself around his arm, slithering up and around to settle itself over his shoulders. He stroked its head affectionately. The snake flicked its tongue and seemed to be content with its new master.

Michec casually swished a hand, and the hundreds of snakes massing around his feet began dissolving. He lowered the one draped over his shoulders to the floor, where it glided away until it, too, vanished.

74

Kahlan gripped the hilt of the sword tighter in both hands even though she remembered full well that it had somehow done Richard no good. If he hadn't been able to use the sword effectively against the witch man, she didn't know how she would be able to do any better. Still, it did make her feel better to have a weapon in her hands. She could feel the word "TRUTH" on the hilt made out of the gold wire wound through silver wire pressing against her palm. It was a reminder of all she and Richard had gone through since they met in the Hartland woods, all because of Darken Rahl, and now, all this time later, she faced one of his henchmen. It felt almost as if Darken Rahl himself was reaching out from the grave to continue to haunt them.

And like Darken Rahl, the witch man had some kind of powers that had counteracted the power in the sword and enabled him to capture Richard. She remembered Zedd telling him that the sword wouldn't work against Darken Rahl. She could only imagine that the same protection against the Sword of Truth might extend to Michec.

Still, it was all she had, unless she could unleash her Confessor's power on him. Not only was he keeping his distance, but it also seemed risky to attempt such a thing on someone with abilities she had never encountered before. She knew that there were rare people on whom her power had no effect, or an unpredictable effect. It could be that Michec was like that. If she had to, though, she fully intended to attempt it.

She started circling to Michec's left to draw his attention away from Richard, Shale, and the Mord-Sith, who were all on the floor and unresponsive. It seemed that when Shale used her ability to the extent she had against the Glee, it sapped her strength until she could recover. That was something Kahlan understood all too well. When she used her power, it took her time to recover. She didn't know what the problem was with Richard, and that worried her greatly.

For all practical purposes, she was the only protection for the others, and she was alone with this madman. By the look on his face, he clearly relished the idea of catching her by herself. As she slowly moved to the side, she watched for any opening in case she had to try to use her power on him.

She worried, too, that Michec might have had something to do with the condition of the others. The memory of being helpless with him about to skin her alive was all too fresh in her mind. Right then she felt very alone and vulnerable.

"Again with the sword?" Michec, seeming amused, arched an eyebrow over one eye. "You think yourself better with it than your husband? Well, should we see?"

He stomped a foot in her direction, bluffing that he was going to charge at her. Kahlan didn't flinch back. Instead she thrust the sword out at him, hoping to catch him off guard. She didn't know if the magic of the sword would work against him, but the razor-sharp blade was in itself formidable. He easily stepped back out of range of both her and the sword. Her caution kept her from following through and pressing the attack.

He grinned with menace. "Ah, a fighter. Good for you. I enjoy skinning fighters." He gestured at all the corpses behind him. "Makes it so much more satisfying when they finally find themselves helpless. I like to look into their eyes when I begin and they know that there will be no stopping and no rescue."

Kahlan didn't need to imagine such terror; she had been there. She wanted nothing more than to kill this monster.

She kept the point of the blade up and at the ready. She could feel its power singing through every nerve fiber in her body. The sword wanted the man's blood, but not as much as Kahlan did. She resolved that when he eventually came at her, she would try to run him through or use her power. What really concerned her was that he knew she was a Confessor but that didn't seem to bother him in the least. If both the sword and her power failed to stop him, well then, at least she would not go down without a fight.

She noticed, then, as she forced herself to look into his cruel eyes, that his face didn't look the same as she remembered. The shape was different. His features had always looked thick and blocky, but the area around his left jaw and ear appeared even thicker. She could see traces of blood left in the folds of his ear. It looked like he had wiped off blood that had been all over the side of his face.

She also saw that the filthy white robes he was wearing were stained with fresher blood up at the neck, as if it had run down onto his robes. That blood was not from a victim. It was his.

The injury had to have been from when Richard kicked the witch man in the head. She wondered just how much damage Richard had done. A kick that hard to his head, if in the right spot and if Richard had been able to make solid contact, would likely have broken the mandible. That would certainly explain why his speech sounded a little slurred, and also why he had been gone for a while. He had probably been hiding somewhere while he did what he could to repair the damage enough with his magic to keep going. As much as he tried not to show it, she could see by the way he kept his shoulder protectively forward that it was hurting him. She realized that might give her an opportunity.

But then, on the other hand, a wounded animal was more dangerous, and Michec certainly was an animal.

Together, with Michec glaring at her and Kahlan with the sword up at the ready and glaring back, they continued slowly revolving as if locked together. Michec seemed entertained by the dance as he waited for her to make the first move, or to make a mistake so he could overwhelm her.

Of course, it was also possible that he simply enjoyed the game.

As they slowly moved in unison, his dark eyes peering out from narrowed eyelids were about as intimidating as any she had ever seen. But she also thought she saw caution there. She hoped that Richard had managed to hurt the man more than she knew.

She also felt the weight of responsibility. It wasn't just her life she was protecting; it was the twins' and everyone else's. If she tried something and it turned out to be the wrong move, they would all be dead.

For the moment, as she and Michec both stared each other down, each waiting for the right moment to strike, she decided that if she saw the right opening, she would have to act.

His gaze, then, flicked down to something that caught his attention. His intimidating glare took on a hint of confusion.

Kahlan glanced down, looking for what it was that had him so distracted. She didn't see anything out of the ordinary.

"See something you don't like?" she asked. "Thinking twice about how this blade can cut you?"

He cocked his head as he appraised her with one eye. "I see you have managed to have your wounds healed while I was… away for a time." He arched an eyebrow. "I will soon remedy your return to good health and have you screaming your lungs out down here where no one other than your husband can hear you and no one will ever help you."

Her wounds? She didn't know what he was talking about.

She glanced down again, and then she saw it.

In the heat of the confrontation, she hadn't realized that her wrists were no longer cut up and bleeding from the manacles. They were completely healed and looked as if they had never been severely gashed. She reached up just long enough to feel that the left side of her face wasn't bruised and swollen, nor was it throbbing in pain. The cut along the side of her neck was gone as well.

He gestured behind at all the skinless corpses without taking his eyes off her. "As you can see, I have quite a talent. The time has come for me to demonstrate."

75

Just then Kahlan caught movement out of the corner of her eye. It was Vika, naked, with her Agiel between her teeth and a knife in her fist, charging in at a dead run. She was a picture of muscled fury.

At the last instant she rammed the knife into Michec's side, catching him off guard. Kahlan had thought that she would use the Agiel between her teeth, but she must have been more interested in cutting him open the way he had cut her.

He let out a terrible cry of pain and surprise as he fell away from her attack to escape her blade.

Michec twisted and spun to get some distance as she tried to cut him again, but missed. He clamped a hand over the wound. Kahlan could see the wet red stain under his hand growing on his filthy white robes.

He saw, then, the same thing Kahlan saw. As hard as it was to believe, Vika was completely healed. She didn't have a stitch of clothes on and they could clearly see that she looked in perfect health. The flesh of her abdomen was flawless and looked never to have had so much as a scratch. Kahlan couldn't imagine how her intestines could have been put back as well as they had and how such a gaping wound had completely closed.

In her hunger to cut Michec, Vika must have just had time to grab her knife from the sheath attached to her leather outfit. She screamed in fury as she scrambled to dive at him again and drive her blade into him again, but her bare feet slipped on the slime and blood all over the floor from the Glee. She leaped back up to her feet almost immediately.

The witch man moved faster than Kahlan would have thought his bulk would allow, spinning around twice so that Vika, on slippery footing in her bare feet, missed him when she took a swing and tried to slash him again. Though he escaped her stabbing him a second time, the first cut had obviously done damage. Because of his girth, Kahlan suspected that the blade had cut only fat and muscle. She didn't think it had gone deep enough to damage internal organs. Vika had apparently been going for his kidney. Had she hit it, that would have stopped him or at least slowed him down enough for her to be able to finish him. As it was, he was still on his feet and while hurt, it was not enough to stop him.

Seeing an opportunity with Michec wounded, Kahlan cried out in fury of her own to startle him as she charged in at him sword-first. Even if the magic didn't work against him, the sharp blade would. Ordinarily, Kahlan would have been unsure that it would be so simple that she could kill him with Richard's sword, but the way Vika had driven her knife into him had clearly hurt the man. From behind Vika came flashes of red leather as the rest of the Mord-Sith raced to Vika and Kahlan's aid.

Hurt from Vika's first strike with her blade, Michec held one hand back to comfort the wound as he desperately swept his other hand up as if lifting a curtain before himself.

As his hand came up, the glass light spheres abruptly dimmed.

And then, the quickly waning light revealed nightmarish creatures densely packed together coming at them out of nowhere, all of them reaching with fury and lust.

They were terrors from a child's nightmares, larger than a person, most with veined, membrane wings like bats. Those wings stretched and flapped. At the first joint of the leading edge of their wings they had a large, hooked claw that raked the air as they swept their partially folded wings forward, trying to snag Kahlan or one of the Mord-Sith.

The pale, wrinkled, ulcerated flesh of the monsters was hairless. In places that flesh looked rotted away, exposing gooey green slime and fibrous tissue beneath, like the damp, rotting, decomposing tissue of a corpse. They glided in just above the floor, their wings flapping to enfold their prey. As they got closer, they opened huge mouths full of fangs.

Their jaws opened wide as they roared, so wide that it distorted and stretched the skin of their faces. That flesh tore in places, exposing the decomposing sinew beneath. Under the tears in the stretched flesh she could see their jaw and cheek bones. Flesh hung in ragged flaps as it ripped apart when their mouths stretched even wider to snap at Kahlan and the others frantically backing away.

Kahlan and all the Mord-Sith continued to scramble back, trying to avoid being caught by the grotesque creatures as they hurtled in out of the rapidly gathering darkness. Their deafening howls echoed through the room. In the fading light, Kahlan saw that the creatures were not all the same. Not all were winged like bats.

Some of the things had no wings, but instead had long, skeletal arms. They grasped at the air with bony fingers as they rushed in, reaching for Kahlan and the others. Some were missing part of their skull, exposing the festering brain and internal structures. Some of the forms had only scraps of skin attached to bones. That kind, their joints separating from the effort, ripped themselves apart as they struggled to leap through the air to be the first at Kahlan and the Mord-Sith.

Others, with long gangly limbs, crabbed sideways across the floor, ducking in under the winged creatures. Others staggered with stiff limbs and a halting gait. Most of their mouths opened impossibly wide, as if they intended to devour Kahlan and the others whole in one bite.

It was a collection of creatures beyond imagining. None of them could possibly be anything that existed in the world of life.

And yet, Kahlan realized that she had seen these things before.

A whole army of the monsters charged in at her, wings made of stretched skin flapping, raptorlike claws extended, lips pulling back in snarls over fangs. As Mord-Sith leaped toward her to help, Kahlan swung the sword, ripping through the monsters. The sword seemed to tear them apart rather than cut them. Their bodies disintegrated as if made of crumbly dirt and dust. Flesh and bone fell to pieces as she swung the blade as fast as she could.

It was growing so dark so rapidly that she already couldn't see the women fighting near her. But she could see the glowing red eyes of ever more of the things coming for her. She swung the sword as fast and hard as she could, knowing that if she stopped, they would be all over her. No matter how many she destroyed, their numbers pressing in at her seemed to multiply.

Only brief, terrifying moments after the battle had started, the room was plunged into total darkness. The blackness was filled with the terrible angry howls and ravenous screeches of the things coming at her and the others. Kahlan used their cries to find them, swinging the sword around when she heard them trying to get behind her. She had no hope but to keep fighting.

The darkness was so complete that the red glow of their eyes went dark, too, so that she could no longer even tell where the swirling mass of creatures were. In desperation Kahlan kept swinging the sword, hoping none of the Mord-Sith were close enough to get hit by the blade. She could feel the resistance each time it crashed through the monstrous things. She felt bony bits and reeking, wet scraps smacking into her as they disintegrated.

And then, when she knew that all hope was lost, the air suddenly seemed to explode. Flames filled the room, twisting, spiraling, rolling as if inside the inferno of a blast furnace. It was so bright Kahlan had to close her eyes and cover her face with a forearm against the blinding light and intense heat as she turned away. She feared she would be consumed in the conflagration.

Instead, the billowing flames were gone almost as soon as they had erupted, so fast that they didn't burn her as she had thought they surely would; they didn't so much as singe her hair.

As the flames vanished and the room was once again plunged into blackness, the air was filled with a swirl of burning embers that slowed and finally drifted down, sparking out as they touched the stone floor. In the faint light of those glowing embers, Kahlan saw the Mord-Sith nearby, like her with their weapons held up defensively.

After a moment of total darkness and dead silence once all the burning embers were gone, the light spheres around the edge of the room slowly began to brighten again. In the faint greenish glow, she could see that all the corpses were still hanging throughout the room. She had thought they might have been ripped to shreds by the ravenous creatures or burned to cinders in the flames, but they looked untouched. Apparently, the beasts had only come for the living and the flash of fire was too brief to consume the bodies.

But the fire had incinerated the creatures, burning them to ash. It left behind the stench of sulfur.

"What were those things?" Vale asked in a panting whisper.

Kahlan knew what they were but was afraid to say it out loud.

"Where did he go?" Rikka asked in a heated voice as she and the others raced around, searching among the forest of bodies for the witch man.

Cassia dropped to the floor to look under all the hanging corpses to see if Michec was hiding behind one of them, perhaps in the distance. She finally jumped back up.

"I don't see him anywhere."

Shale raced up, coming in protectively close to Kahlan.

"What in the world were those things?" Nyda asked as she worked to catch her breath. "I've had nightmares that haven't been as scary as that."

Shale cast a sidelong look at Kahlan. "I can only conjure snakes. Apparently, the witch man has the power to conjure demons."

"Demons! Like from the underworld?" Nyda shook her head. "That can't be true."

"I've seen such things before," Kahlan said.

Nyda looked incredulous. "Where?"

"In the world of the dead," Kahlan finally told them in a troubled voice.

"You can't be serious," Shale said.

They all looked at Kahlan expectantly, awaiting more of an explanation.

"They're called soul eaters."

"Soul eaters!" Berdine exclaimed. "How could Michec bring demons from the underworld into the world of life?" She swept an arm out. "And what happened to them at the end? It was like they were suddenly exploded and burned to cinders."

"I have no idea," Kahlan said. "But from the smell of sulfur it seems clear to me that Michec somehow opened the veil enough to pull those things into this world to do his bidding."

"It doesn't matter, now. They're gone." Vika grabbed Kahlan's arm. "We have to help Lord Rahl. He healed all of us. We have to help him."

When a last, quick check around the room confirmed that Michec was nowhere to be seen and they knew that he wasn't about to set upon them again, Kahlan rushed over to Richard, dropping to her knees to see if he had started breathing yet. She was alarmed when she found that not only wasn't he breathing, he had no pulse.

"Richard!" She pounded his chest with her fist. "Richard!"

Shale leaned in close. She put a hand on his forehead, closed her eyes, and was silent for a moment.

The sorceress at last drew her hand back as if the touch had burned her fingers. She looked up at Kahlan, her eyes reflecting her horror. "He's... gone."

The Mord-Sith stared at her in stunned silence.

"He's not gone," Kahlan insisted. "He just needs our help to find his way back."

Shale's eyebrows lifted in disbelief. "From the dead? How do we help him do that?"

"He's not dead." Kahlan swallowed back her rising sense of panic as a vision of her children never knowing their father flashed through her mind. "He's just lost."

Shale gave the Mord-Sith watching her a troubled look before she looked back at Kahlan. "And how do you propose that we get him... unlost?"

76

Kahlan pressed her fingertips to her forehead as she frantically ran through memories and what she knew of the underworld, trying to come up with a way to get Richard back from that dark place. She stubbornly refused to believe the finality of it. She couldn't let herself believe the finality of it. But while she believed it might be possible to get him back, she also knew that the window to do so—even if it still existed—was rapidly closing.

At last, her head came up. She looked to all the faces watching her.

"The Law of Nines. Richard said that the Law of Nines is a trigger for magic."

Shale threw her hands up. "How is that supposed to help us? He is with the good spirits, now. He is beyond what we can do with magic."

"But for a precious bit of time, he still has a link here, in this world." Kahlan gestured. "Everyone gather around. Shale, you go on the other side of him and take his hand. I'll take this one." She urgently motioned the Mord-Sith to all come in closer. "The rest of you, kneel down around him and hold hands between Shale and me. We need to link us all together with Richard between me and Shale."

While they clearly didn't understand what it was that Kahlan thought they could do, they all gathered around Richard anyway, taking up each other's hands even though they all looked confused as to why they were doing it, hoping that somehow she knew some secret solution and could do what none of them could imagine.

"We all need to bow our heads and close our eyes," Kahlan told them.

Vale leaned in expectantly. "And then what?"

"And then... think about Richard. Think about how much we all want him back. How much we all need him back."

The Mord-Sith shared skeptical looks.

Kahlan thought of something else. She released his hand and picked up the Sword of Truth. She placed the hilt in his hand, then put her hand over the other side and intertwined her fingers with Richard's, locking their hands together around the hilt of the sword. The word "TRUTH" on her side pressed into her palm. She knew that the same word on the other side was pressing into Richard's palm. That physical sensation was intimately familiar to both of them. More than that, the Sword of Truth was an ancient weapon with unfathomable magic. She hoped that magic would also help guide Richard back to them.

Tears ran down Vika's cheeks as she watched Kahlan position the sword. "If we don't get him back, I will never forgive myself. He did this for me. He came after me. I told him not to, but he did it anyway. He shouldn't have. I wish Michec had killed me, then Lord Rahl would not have done what he did and he would be here, alive, and with you all. He would be where he belongs."

"No, he wouldn't," Kahlan said, knowing how distraught the Mord-Sith would have to be to show such emotion. "None of us would be here. We would all be dead."

Vika wiped a tear back from her cheek. "What are you talking about?"

"When Richard found out that Michec had taken you and that he was here at the People's Palace, he wanted to get you back, but more than that, he knew as the Lord Rahl that we couldn't leave the witch man here when we leave for the Keep. You, of all people, know what Michec is capable of. He was devoted to Darken Rahl and hated that Richard was now the Lord Rahl. His ambition has no bounds. There is no telling what he might have done, but we do know that he would have worked to defeat all we have fought for. He has the power to undo all the good we have worked to bring about.

"We had to go after that monster. Yes, Richard wanted to rescue you, but he would have gone after Michec even if you were already dead. He had to. We came down here, into Michec's lair, and he was somehow able to capture us. That's not your fault. Richard was going after Michec one way or another, with you or without you."

"Yes but if I had already been dead—"

"Then you couldn't have saved us." Kahlan was shaking her head. "Don't you see? All the rest of us would have been captured whether or not you were alive. But since you were still alive, you were able to interrupt Michec when he was about to start skinning me alive. That gave Richard time to stop him. You saved our lives, Vika."

"Kahlan's right," Shale said. "I think it was that Law of Nines thing he told us about. It caused a change in the outcome. The nine of us together had an effect on what would otherwise have happened."

Kahlan leaned in a little toward the distraught Mord-Sith. "That's why Richard came after you: because we need you. Your life is important to all of us. We all need each other. There is power in the nine of us together. I thought he was only going to the cusp of the underworld to help you somehow, but for whatever reason, he crossed over."

"He came after me," Vika said, fighting to hold back her tears. "That's why he crossed over. He did it to heal me."

Kahlan gave her a hurried nod. "He saved you for a reason. Now, we need to save him."

"How?" Shale pressed, frantic for some kind of reason to believe it could really work. "He crossed over through the veil. We all know what that means. Dead is dead. How in the world do you propose to bring him back from the dead?"

"Dead is not always as dead as you might think." Kahlan gritted her teeth against the fear of giving in to the finality of such thinking. "Richard is not dead. Not yet. Not with finality. He has done this before. He's just lost. There is no sense of direction or scale in the underworld. It's eternal in every direction. He will be trying to come back to us now that he is finished with what he needed to do there, but he needs the light of our souls to find his way back."

"But how can we reveal our souls to him when he's on the other side of the veil?" Shale asked.

"Like I said before, Richard told us that the Law of Nines is a trigger for magic of great power."

Shale looked far from satisfied. "But how—"

"Enough! We're wasting what precious little time we have! Bow your heads," Kahlan ordered, her patience at an end, "and give him a way back before he is gone too long and can't ever return."

A worried Berdine glanced over at Richard. "Are you sure he hasn't already been gone too long?"

"Do it!" Kahlan yelled, her frantic fear powering her voice. "Do it now. Think of Richard and how much he means to each one of you and how much we all need him back. We need to show him the light of our lives on this side to guide him back through the veil. He is the completing link for the Law of Nines, the last one that makes nine of us. He is the Lord Rahl. Our bond to him as the Lord Rahl is our connection to him. Now use it.

"Rikka, Nyda, Cassia, Vale, Berdine, Vika, you have all been to the cusp before. Do that now if you can so that you can bring us all closer to that world."

When Kahlan was sure that all of the rest of them were following her orders, she finally bowed her own head.

She refused to allow herself to fear it wouldn't work. Richard would see the light of their souls on their side of the veil and it would help guide him back. She knew it would.

Just before she let herself slip into the memory of what it was like in that other place, she had a last twinge of fear that Michec might show up and, seeing them all vulnerable, slaughter every last one of them right then and there where they were kneeling.

Among the corpses, the room was dead quiet as she brought up a memory of the world of the dead, and her love for Richard, the father of her two children. Three, she corrected herself. One was gone now, but the twins were still growing in her.

She remembered, then, the first time she knelt before him and swore on her life to protect him. She had been the first ever to swear loyalty to him.

Her breathing along with everyone else's slowed almost to a stop.

77

Kahlan seemed lost in a quiet, lonely place on the fringes of panic when she heard Richard gasp in a breath.

She looked up into the life in his gray eyes, startled at him returning so abruptly. He smiled at her, too busy getting his breath to speak right then. Her fears, which she had been keeping under tight rein, were unexpectedly dispelled. Joy rushed in to displace despair.

Kahlan needed something more than words, though. She fell on him where he sat, holding him tight, feeling the life in him as his big arm came around to embrace her and pull her tight against him. It was salvation, redeeming her as she had been about to give up all hope.

"Lord Rahl!" Berdine squealed. "You're back! You're really back!"

He nodded, still panting.

Shale looked astonished. "How are you here? How is this possible?" The way she said it made it sound as if his return was almost unjust, a violation of everything she believed.

Richard swallowed, still catching his breath. He looked around at the forest of dead bodies, the empty vessels for souls now gone, perhaps, Kahlan thought, seeing them in a new and sympathetic light.

"I was lost. It's beyond dark, there." His haunted tone reflected everything behind those words. "I didn't know where the veil was, or how to find my way back. Then I saw the cluster of light of your souls, the glimmer of your lives gathered together around me to show me the way back. That was what I needed."

Berdine shook a finger at Kahlan. "That's just what she said would bring you back!"

Richard chuckled. "I'm glad you listened to her. You all brought me back. Thank you."

"The Law of Nines was the key," Kahlan said.

Richard nodded, still drawing deep breaths. "It was the trigger for magic that made it work."

Shale leaned in, looking bewildered to see him alive after being so clearly dead. She held up her wrists before him.

"We're healed." It sounded like an indictment. "Not just Vika. Kahlan and my wrists, and her face—we are all healed."

Richard nodded. "I know. I healed Vika, then I healed the rest of us as well." He ran a finger down Kahlan's once bruised and swollen cheek and then held up his own wrists to show them that they, too, were no longer cut and bleeding.

Shale seemed to be bursting with questions. She started one, only to stop and start a different one. Finally she was able to settle on one and get it out.

"Lord Rahl, how could you have healed Vika? Her wounds were well beyond healing, but even if they hadn't been quite so horrific and had been within the realm of the possible for healing, it would have taken many days to do such a complex healing. How is it possible that you healed her of such grievous wounds in the blink of an eye?"

Richard gazed into her eyes, looking for a long time as if gazing into her soul. "It was far more than the blink of an eye. The underworld is eternal. It never ends, so there is no such thing as time there. I could have taken months to heal her for all I know—there is no way to tell. In fact, it felt in many ways that I was there for that long. But here, despite how long I was there, only moments had passed. That was how my body survived until my soul could return. I was still connected to it through the Grace. There, those moments are an eternity that gave me the time to do what I needed to do. In a way, I was working in both worlds at the same time."

The answer appeared to be worse than no answer to the sorceress. "Working in both worlds?" Shale pressed a hand to her forehead, looking exasperated as she tried to imagine the unimaginable. She pressed her palms against the side of her head, elbows up, looking like she feared she was descending into madness. "How is that even remotely possible?"

Richard shook his head as he sighed. "The only way I can begin to explain it is that there, in the underworld, I'm able to see and touch the threads of my gift in ways that I never could here, in this world. You might say that the lines of the Grace are revealed to me when I'm there.

"Those tendrils are more pure, more amazing, than any of us realize of ourselves. Things I could never do here, things I couldn't even imagine doing, I can do there by touching the right strands in that line from Creation. It is beyond wondrous."

He gestured toward Kahlan's belly. "Those two lives growing in Kahlan are in the process of connecting all the countless filaments and fibers that will make up the lines of the Grace within each of them. We draw a representation of the Grace, but it is so much more than those simple diagrams. Each line is complex beyond our ability to comprehend.

"When I was beyond that outer circle of the Grace that represents the beginning of the underworld, I was able to see and touch those fibers, those strands and filaments, that connect us all to Creation. It's more than merely life, Shale. It is all of Creation, the totality of it all. It is life and the absence of life, all connected within the Grace which we each have within ourselves."

Shale bowed her head as she closed her eyes, fingers against her forehead. It looked like it was beyond overwhelming for her to fit it all into her understanding of the nature of the world of life. Kahlan reached over and put a hand over the sorceress's other hand in her lap, giving her confusion and disbelief a bit of silent empathy.

"Believe me, I, too, have trouble comprehending it all."

Even though Kahlan had been in that place, and understood some of what Richard said, he had been born a wizard, and he had a much deeper understanding of all those things. It was hard for her to remember the time when she had first met him, and he knew nothing about magic, and she had to teach him some of what she knew about it. He had come a long way. His understanding of it all had at some point surpassed hers. In some ways, it was hard to even grasp the reach of his awareness.

Vika was already up, hurriedly pulling on her red leather outfit. "Somehow, Lord Rahl, 'thank you' hardly touches it. You told me to be strong and hold on for you and you would take care of me. You were as good as your word. You always are.

"I find what you did impossible to understand and hard to believe. It also makes me appreciate not only life, but the bond, more than ever before and in ways I never did before."

She gestured to her sisters of the Agiel after pulling a red leather sleeve up her arm. "We have all been to the cusp before, but this was different. This was seeing the threads of life, as you put it. I've seen the Grace drawn before, but when we were there, you showed it to me within myself." She searched for words. "You touched my soul. I now understand your bond to each of us as never before. You are the magic against magic. I am honored to be back in the world of life so that I can be the steel against steel for you and the Mother Confessor."

Berdine stood and helped tighten and buckle some of the straps on Vika's outfit. "For today," she said to Vika, "it's all right with me for you to be Lord Rahl's favorite."

Richard shook his head with a smile. "I don't have favorites. I love you all the same."

"I understand that, now," Vika said with a nod.

"Don't pay any attention to him," Berdine told Vika, ignoring Richard. "He says that all the time. It's not true. For today, you deserve to be his favorite for hanging on to life so you could be here to help us all."

"Richard," Kahlan said, eager to get back to the important matter at hand, "Michec is still down here somewhere. We need to find him."

Richard agreed with a nod as he stood and slid his sword back into its scabbard. "Let's go."

78

They all moved cautiously through the eerie green light and the still, hazy trails of smoke left from the fire that consumed Michec's underworld minions. Those long, hanging tendrils of smoke swirled around them as they made their way among the forest of corpses and the stench of the dead, eager to be away from the place.

"While you were still in the underworld," Kahlan told Richard from close behind him, "Michec conjured demons that nearly killed us all."

Richard paused at the opening out into the hallway and looked back at her. "I know. I saw the prophecy that he was going to do that. He has the power to somehow open the veil just enough to pull some of those things into the world of life to do his bidding."

"Wait." Shale stepped closer, her hackles up again. "What do you mean, you 'saw the prophecy that he was going to do that'? You said there is no more prophecy. I have been able to see into the flow of time my whole life. Now I can't. While I'm not at all happy about it, you said it is because you had to end prophecy to save the world of life."

Richard leaned out and peered both ways down the hall as far as the visibility from light spheres in brackets on the walls would allow.

"Well, while for all practical purposes that's true," Richard said when he pulled his head back from the edge of the opening, "it's not technically accurate that I ended prophecy. Prophecy is an underworld property and as such it was harmful being here in the world of life, so I sent it back to the underworld where it belongs. In so doing, it ended prophecy in this world, the world of life. But prophecy still exists in the underworld. It can't be destroyed. It's a functional part of the underworld. Think of it as an elemental part of eternity playing out every possible outcome as events branch into the future."

The more he talked, the more Shale's agitation seemed to bubble up. "Yes, I know, the flow of time and all of its many tributaries that I used to be able to tap into. But if you banished it, how were you able to see it and how could you possibly use it?"

"I'm the one who sent it back to the underworld. I was just in the underworld. See what I mean?"

Shale was still frowning. "No."

Richard took a patient breath. "Because I was there, in the underworld, where it exists, I had access to prophecy. So, among other things, I took advantage of it while I was there. Since I'm the one who sent it home, it has a certain... familiarity with me."

"Oh, so now it's alive?"

"It's complicated."

Shale cocked her head. "But you used it?" The way she said it made it sound as if she thought that quite unfair, considering that she no longer could. "You used prophecy?"

"Yes, that's right. Prophecy is frequently misunderstood." He turned back to lean toward her a little with an intimidating look. "Even among witch women. I'm a war wizard. Part of my gift is prophecy. That means I can understand prophecy in ways that no other, including witch women, could ever begin to comprehend.

"So, while there, I took the opportunity to access it. When I did, I found a prophecy flowing out of present events that revealed that Michec was going to open the veil enough to pull some of those underworld beings into the world of life.

"I could see that it was a forked prophecy—a this-or-that type. I knew I had to act to block the wrong fork or you would all die. So, when he pulled them through, I was ready."

Kahlan grabbed a handful of his shirtsleeve. "You were ready? What does that mean?"

"It means that when he fulfilled the first part of the prophecy and pulled those creatures through into this world, at the appropriate moment, I was able to shift it to the alternate fork by blasting them back to where they came from."

"That was the fire?" Berdine asked as she leaned forward in rapt attention. "You blasted those things apart from the underworld? You burned them to ashes?"

Richard nodded. "Sorry I couldn't have been quicker. It was rather... difficult to do from where I was at the time."

"But how?" Berdine asked, caught up in the story. "I mean, if you were there, how could you do that here?"

"The Grace," he said. "Everything is connected through the Grace. Those creatures were the souls of evil people. But they had once been created through the spark of life that is the Grace. I used that interconnection of everything in order to destroy their existence in this world where they don't belong. In much the same way I used my ability from there to heal Vika, here."

"If you could do that," Shale asked, folding her arms as if she had caught him in a mistake, "then why couldn't you simply come back through the breach in the veil that Michec created."

"I could have." Richard sighed. "But then I wouldn't have been able to destroy those things and you all could easily have been killed. I had to make a choice—return to fight them and maybe end up having us all be killed, or destroy those things in the world of life before they killed you all. Had I chosen to come back to fight them, the prophecy was not favorable. So, I did what I was sure would work.

"In the end, I was able to do both things, destroy those things and return, because Kahlan thought of a means to show me the way home again. She gave me a path back. It was a much better path than the one Michec had created. His was ugly. Hers was profoundly beautiful."

After checking the hallway again, Richard motioned to the rest of them. "Come on. We have to catch up with Michec. Everyone keep your eyes open. There is no telling where he could be hiding or what he might try to do."

"The goddess sent a horde of Glee," Kahlan said into the silence of the dimly lit hallway. "Shale got rid of them by conjuring snakes." She realized it sounded like she was tattling on the sorceress. Maybe she was.

Richard looked back with a frown. "Really? How?" he asked the witch woman.

"Ah," Shale said with a sly smile, "so now you want to know how I did something that you don't understand and can't do?"

"That's right. I would very much like to know how you could do such a thing. It sounds extremely useful. So, how did you make snakes appear?" Richard asked as he gestured ahead, indicating they were going to need to take the hallway that forked to the right.

Shale shrugged, looking rather smug about it. "I thought them into existence."

Richard paused at the next dark intersection of stone passageways, bringing them all to a halt again so he could look in both directions. "You thought them into existence?" He turned back to her. "How does that work?"

"I am daughter to a witch woman. As a witch woman myself, I can bring thoughts into physical reality by breaching the separation between thought and reality."

Richard was the one who now looked astonished. "You mean to say that you can think things into existence? It's not just an illusion of something, like snakes? They are real?"

"In a way. Those things we bring into reality, because they are a physical manifestation of our thoughts, are in a way part of us. Because of that, they are also in that way connected to us."

Richard was still staring at her. "But I still don't get how you can make thoughts real."

Shale shrugged again, but this time looking earnest. "Remember when you said that a plan for building the People's Palace and the complication was a way to make the spell-form real? The results of that plan, or spell-form, depend on how you draw it, with how many rooms, how many floors, and so on. In other words, the plan is thought, the building follows the thought into reality."

"That's incredible," Richard said, looking genuinely fascinated.

"Not so incredible. At least not to me. You seem to have breached the veil between the world of the living and the world of the dead—now that is incredible. A witch's ability is to breach the veil, you might say, but only between thought and reality. If we can think it, in certain cases, we can make it real."

Kahlan remembered all too well those snakes Shale brought into reality. It gave her shivers just thinking about the slithering mass of vipers. She had another thought.

"So then, those vipers the witch woman Shota put on me before could really have killed me?"

Shale gave Kahlan a hard look. "Absolutely."

Kahlan took a deep breath at the thought. "If it's something you can do, then why did you collapse at the end. Were you simply exhausted from the effort?"

"Partly," Shale said as they all started down the dark hallway once more.

She looked uneasy about the question, but when Kahlan kept staring at her, she went on. "When we think something into being, as I said, it is in a way part of us. It is a creation of thought, our thought, and in that way still connected to us. You could even say it remains an integral part of us."

"So?" Kahlan asked as she watched Richard pick a light sphere up out of a bracket and hold it out ahead as he poked his head into a room to the right.

Shale gave Kahlan a troubled look. "I didn't recall those thoughts. They were taken away."

Richard looked back over his shoulder. "What?"

Shale licked her lips. "The snakes attacked the Glee. They were killing them. That was what I intended, why I thought them into existence because I knew they could be deadly. Since the Glee can somehow vanish back into their own world, I knew the danger of doing such a thing. But I only had an instant to do something. It was the only way I could think to stop them before we were all killed."

Richard's brow lifted as he smiled. "In other words, it was an act of desperation?"

Shale nodded unhappily as they started out again. "I guess you could put it that way."

"So what's the danger part?" Kahlan pressed.

"Well, the problem was, once they were attacked, many of the Glee began to vanish back to their home world, the fangs of many of the snakes, now creatures that existed, holding fast onto them. When they vanished, they took those snakes with them."

Richard stopped and turned back. "Why is that a problem?"

"Once I think them into existence, they act according to their nature. They do what the real creature would do. In this case they viciously attacked what I consciously thought of as their prey. In a way, they are real creatures, yet they aren't. Because they were conjured from my thoughts, they acted according to my will. Ordinarily I would simply withdraw the thought that brought them into existence, and they would cease to exist.

"But because there were so many Glee, I had to react out of desperation. I conjured hundreds of them, all at once, and because the snakes were attacking, doing what they do by their nature, they were on the Glee when many of those monsters went back to their own world. I couldn't withdraw the snakes because there were still Glee coming for us. The Glee that vanished took many of the snakes with them."

Richard shared a look with Kahlan. She knew that he had realized something significant, but she didn't know what. It was a look she was all too familiar with. She knew that if she asked, he wouldn't yet be ready to tell her what he had now realized.

Shale swallowed. "When they were taken away like that, rather than me withdrawing the thought"—she rubbed her arms—"it feels like something is being ripped out from inside me. It was a rather... brutal sensation. That sensation overwhelmed me, and I lost consciousness for a time."

Kahlan glanced over at Richard. "That's when Michec showed up."

"He wanted to humiliate me for only being able to conjure snakes," Shale said. "So he made the snakes vanish and brought those demons up from the underworld to show me his power and superiority."

Richard looked like he had just had another thought. "Can you bring anything bigger and more frightening than snakes into existence?"

"It isn't big and scary that matters," Shale admonished. "What matters is what works."

Richard let out a sigh as he started them all moving ahead again. "That's true enough."

"The snakes worked," Shale said. "They did as I intended. They kept the Glee from slaughtering us—from slaughtering your two children."

Richard nodded his appreciation as he moved into the darkness ahead.

Kahlan put a hand on the back of Shale's shoulder in appreciation for what she had done, even at great cost to herself.

79

Richard cautiously followed a long, curved passageway, watching for anything out of the ordinary as things ahead gradually materialized out of the darkness. In some places the passageway ascended a half-dozen steps beyond stone columns holding up barreled ceilings that denoted more important sections of the spell-form. In some of those places ornate decorations meant to indicate dominant and subordinate flows of magic within the spell-form had been carved into the stone walls.

Along the way Richard checked each room they came to, leaning back and pushing closed doors open with a foot. While he did find long-dead, mummified corpses in a few, there was no sign of the witch man in any of them. He didn't expect to find Michec in any of those rooms, but he still had to check them just in case.

"Do you know where we're going?" Cassia asked in a whisper that seemed appropriate in such sinister, ornate passageways.

Richard simply nodded as he kept going.

At regular intervals massive stone archways separated sections of what was an important element of the spell-form from less significant supporting elements. In places those elements and thus the archways and sections of passageways could be quite complex, reflecting the intricacy of the complication itself.

It still felt disorienting to him to be back in the world of life. Solid ground was hard to get accustomed to again. He had begun to fear that he would be forever imprisoned in the underworld. He cherished the memory, though, of seeing the light of Kahlan's soul when he had been in that dark world. It was a wondrous thing that was like seeing the light of her love for him visualized.

But now that he was back, even that memory seemed very dreamlike and distant. It was just as well those memories faded away since such a place was best forgotten.

As they passed under another soaring archway with columns of gray stone carved into ornamental spiral forms, it opened into a broad room with eight sides. A column in each corner supported a rib holding up the complex vaulted ceiling. On each of the other seven walls before them there was a stone archway just like the one they had entered under.

"Lord Rahl," Vika said in a quiet voice that betrayed her concern, "Moravaska Michec captured all of us. You know what happened then. If we're going after him, well, I mean, what good will it do? Aren't you worried that he will simply capture us again? He likes to play with his captives, but this time I don't think he will make that same mistake again before he kills you and the Mother Confessor."

"I hate to admit it," Kahlan said as she leaned in closer, "but Vika is right. He already had us all once and it seemed effortless. If we catch up with him, he might just as easily have us all in his clutches again."

Richard looked to all the worried faces. "Do any of you know the mistake we made?"

The Mord-Sith all shook their heads. Kahlan bit her lower lip. She didn't have an answer either.

"Sure," Shale said. "The mistake we made was coming down here after him in the first place when we should have been on our way to the Keep."

Richard smiled. "No. The Mord-Sith know what we did wrong, don't you?" he asked them.

They all looked puzzled.

"What happens," he asked them, "when someone tries to use magic against you?"

They all huffed as if it were a silly question.

"If they were foolish enough to do that, then we would capture them by the very magic they tried to use against us," Nyda said.

"Michec is no Mord-Sith," Cassia objected.

"No, he's not," Richard said. He looked from one to the next. "What is he, then?"

Rikka shrugged. "A witch man."

Richard shook his head. He gestured to Nyda. "What is he?"

Nyda shrugged. "Like Rikka says, he's a witch man."

Richard shook his head again. "No. Berdine, what is he?"

She made a face. "He's a bastard witch man."

Richard smiled then looked at Vale. "What is he?"

She lifted her hands out in frustration. "He is called the butcher?"

Richard finally looked at Vika.

"Think, Vika," Richard said. "What is he?"

She frowned in thought as she shared a long look with him. Finally her eyes lit with understanding. "Michec is a trainer of Mord-Sith. When I encountered him up at the stables, I immediately tried to use my Agiel on him. That was my mistake. It was over in that instant. He had me. That was how he did it."

"That's what happened to me!" Berdine said. The others nodded that they, too, had tried to use their Agiel against him.

Richard snapped his fingers. "Exactly. In order to train Mord-Sith, Darken Rahl must have instilled in him the same power instilled into a young woman when she is initiated into the sisterhood of the Mord-Sith. They are given power, through the bond, to use a person's magic against them to capture them.

"I once made the mistake of trying to use the magic of my sword against a Mord-Sith. I made that same mistake again when I tried to use my sword against Michec. He captured me the same way Denna did the first time I tried it."

Shale looked a bit sheepish. "I tried to use magic to stop him as well."

Kahlan was frowning. "I don't remember what happened, but I guess I must have tried to use my ability against him. Used against a Mord-Sith, that would be a very bad death. So why didn't my power work against him?"

Richard looked at her with a sad smile. "He isn't a Mord-Sith. He is a witch man and Darken Rahl gave him the ability to capture those with magic. I'm afraid that I made the same mistake as the rest of you."

Kahlan let out a heavy sigh. "That's how he had us all."

Richard's gaze passed over them all. "So don't make that same mistake again."

"I cut him with my knife," Vika said. "Since that's not magic, he couldn't capture me again. Now he's wounded. So we can hurt him, just not with our Agiels or with your magic."

"Exactly," Richard said. "Using your knife was the right thing to do. But now he's a wounded animal. Now that we understand what his trick was, remember not to try to use your Agiel on him. If you get the chance, use your knives. But that shouldn't be necessary. I will take care of him."

"Not with your sword," Kahlan admonished in alarm.

"No, not my sword. But I will take care of him."

"Lord Rahl," Vika said with a serious look, "promise me that you will let me cut him."

He looked into the iron in her eyes. "You got it."

He had a sudden thought and looked at Shale. "Can you use your ability as a witch woman, not to make something come into existence, but to make something go out of existence?"

Shale looked confused. "What do you mean?"

Richard gestured at the stone column they were standing beside. "Well, for example, could you make this column, or this wall, cease to exist? Make them disappear?"

Shale made a face like he must be crazy. "Of course not."

Richard let out a disappointed sigh. "That's a shame. All right." He gestured into the eight-sided room. "He went down one of the other seven corridors leading out of here. Which hallway did he take?"

Shale's dark expression returned. "How am I supposed to know?"

"You said you could smell a witch. Smell the air at each archway entrance and see if you can smell which one he took."

The dark look left Shale's face. She blinked. "Oh. That's a good idea, actually."

Richard smiled. "And here you thought I was crazy."

Shale smirked. "Not entirely. Just somewhat."

They all followed as Shale started around the large room, pausing in the entryways to sniff the air. She stopped at the fifth archway she came to and spent some time smelling the air. Finally she lifted an arm, pointing.

"He went this way."

80

Following the corridor from the octagonal room, they came to a complex of passageways. Leaning in a little to look into each of them, Richard saw no light spheres. He knew all too well that there were few places as dark as it was underground. Except, of course, the underworld. But that was an entirely different kind of darkness.

In their situation, light wasn't just safety, it was life, so when Shale pointed and before venturing into the blackness of the opening to the far left, Richard lifted one of the glowing glass spheres from a bracket and took it with him. Each of the Mord-Sith followed his example. Together the group of spheres cast a warm yellowish light a good ways into the distance.

Shale tilted her head toward the first narrow hall to the left. "This way. I can smell the witch man."

Berdine looked bewildered. "I don't smell anything other than dust and dankness. What does he smell like?"

Shale gave her a look like it should be obvious. "He smells like a witch."

"Ah. That makes sense." Berdine turned her face back toward Richard and rolled her eyes.

Now, instead of their Agiel, each of the Mord-Sith had a knife in her fist. While Mord-Sith were formidable enough with an Agiel, years of training made them more than a little dangerous with a blade. They knew how to cut a person both to cause pain, to cripple, and to bring a swift death, and they weren't timid about doing either.

Richard didn't want to dissuade them from keeping knives in hand, but he knew that it wasn't time yet. The witch man was still quite a distance away and moving quickly. Soon enough he would go to ground.

Kahlan didn't have her knife out, but from time to time she rested her palm on its hilt, making sure it was still there. Shale did the same. Richard had never seen the sorceress draw her knife, but he suspected she was just as talented with it as she was at so many other things. For that matter, he sometimes thought she could wound with a look.

Richard didn't bother with his knife. He wasn't going to use it.

At each room they encountered, one of the Mord-Sith, holding a light sphere in her free hand, slipped in to check for the elusive Moravaska Michec. They had no luck. Richard knew they wouldn't but he let them check anyway because it was easier and faster than an argument or having to explain.

"The smell of him is getting stronger," Shale told them. "We're getting closer to him."

Rikka and Cassia took that news seriously and went out ahead to check in the darkness.

"All I smell is dust and dampness," Berdine said to no one in particular.

Richard didn't bother to tell the Mord-Sith to stay behind. They would likely have ignored the order, and besides, he knew that while Shale said they were closer, they weren't yet close enough.

Michec had spent years down in the complication. He had trapped people in it, he had kept them prisoner in it, he had turned victims loose in it so he could hunt them. As a result, he knew the place like the back of his hand. Fortunately, because Richard had spent time studying the drawings Edward Harris had shown them, he had a map of the complication in his head and was able to know exactly where they were. He could envision all of the intersections and passageways ahead of them.

Besides knowing the corridors, Richard understood how the wounded witch man thought, the choices he would likely make, and why. As they came to branching passageways, he knew other things as well, and made sure they went the right way. Shale confirmed his conviction at each of the intersections he took without asking her.

In some places they came to large rooms they had to pass through. Those were secondary nodes in the spell-form. Some had smaller rooms off to the sides. He knew Michec wasn't in any of them, and for the sake of safety from other dangers, he wouldn't let the Mord-Sith check them. It took a look from him for the Mord-Sith to follow his order and stay out of those rooms.

The witch man was leading them through the most dangerous parts of the complication, hoping they would venture into an ancillary node, the way Kahlan and Shale had dived into a room without a floor that had turned out to be filled with water. Richard didn't want the Mord-Sith running into trouble by entering places he knew were dangerous, but not necessarily why. When the Mord-Sith again wanted to check, Richard had to reassure them that Michec had gone on ahead, and not to look in those places because they had dangerous magic. Mord-Sith didn't want anything to do with magic and so didn't argue.

Because he knew the place so well from the plans, Richard knew that Michec was trying to draw them into a trap. Because the man was wounded from Vika cutting him, he would want to get to a place that would give him an advantage. He would want a place that could help him surprise them and trap them with magic. Richard worried about what kind of magic Michec had at his disposal.

For those reasons and more, Richard knew that the witch man was deliberately heading for a complex dead end. He didn't really need Shale's nose to tell him which route Michec was taking, but he let her point out the correct choices at each intersection or cross corridor they encountered. Each time she confirmed what he suspected, it further narrowed down the possible outcomes toward the one he had believed from the first.

With Kahlan being pregnant with the twins, Richard didn't at all like the idea of taking chances. She had lost their first child. If she lost the twins because they went after the witch man, Richard would never forgive himself. Even so, he knew that the bigger risk was in leaving Michec for some other day. In a way, that was the mistake the witch man had made by leaving Richard alive.

While Richard already knew a great deal about what lay ahead, there was no telling precisely what Michec might be able to do, or what harm he might be able to cause. At the same time, they didn't really have a choice. It was either try to surprise and fight Michec now, on Richard's terms, or fight him later at a time of Michec's choosing and after he had recovered. He might be a dangerous wounded animal, but he was also a weakened animal, so their best chance was to go after him before he could recover.

When they came to a place with four closely placed openings into dark passageways at one side of a spacious room, and one passageway on the opposite side, Shale immediately started for the far-right opening of the four.

Richard reached out and grabbed her arm. "Not that way."

She shot a puzzled look back over her shoulder. "But I can smell that he went this way."

"Don't stand in the opening, yet." Richard guided her to the passageway to the left of the one she had been about to take. "We are going to need to go this way."

"Why wouldn't you want to follow him? We've been following him all this way. If you really want to catch him, he went that way. Why stop now?"

"Because that's a special kind of dead end. It's a twinned spiral. It's a deadly part of the constructed spell-form. He intends to use it against us, and trap us in there."

81

S hale looked even more bewildered. "What do you mean, he intends to trap us in there? How do you know this?"

Rather than answer the sorceress, Richard turned to Vika. "I need you to do something for me."

Vika pulled her braid forward over her shoulder and held it in one fist as she nodded eagerly. "Yes, Lord Rahl?"

"You need to do exactly as I say."

She added a confused look to Shale's. "All right. What do you need me to do?"

Richard gestured, pointing a thumb back over his shoulder at the opening beside the one Michec had taken. "I'm going after Michec down this way."

"But Shale said he took the other passageway."

"I know what Shale said." He pointed, then, across the broad room to another corridor by itself. "I need you to go down that way."

After she looked back over her shoulder to where he had pointed, her expression turned dark. "You promised me I could cut him."

Richard nodded. "And I meant it. Until then, if we are to have a chance, you need to listen to me, and do exactly as I say."

Vika pulled both leather sleeves down tighter as she considered for a moment. "All right, I'm listening."

No Mord-Sith would ever have dared to hesitate at any order Darken Rahl, or any of his predecessors, gave them. To do so would have meant a swift death. Richard, on the other hand, was pleased that Vika had hesitated. It was just another indication that she was beginning to think for herself.

"Go down that passageway, there, until it forks," he said, waggling his hand across the room. "When you get there, take the left fork. A short time later you will come to a steel door. Behind it is another major node. Remember the one we crossed before? The one with the stone bridge?"

Vika nodded. "The bridge that collapsed."

"That's right. Go through that door, cross the bridge and through the steel door on the other side—"

"Is this bridge going to fall in, too?"

"No. At least, I don't think so. Now listen. You need to go through the second steel door on the other side, then take the hallway to the left at the first intersection you come to. Go past two wooden doors on the right side of the hall, then take the next hallway to the right immediately after the second door, go to the fourth wall bracket with a light sphere—"

"What if there aren't any light spheres? Some of these passageways don't have them."

Richard shook his head as he waved his hand for her to be quiet and listen. "There will be light spheres. At the fourth light sphere, take it out of its bracket and throw it on down the hallway as far as you can."

She blinked, not sure she had heard him correctly. "If I do that, it will be pitch black."

"That's right. After you throw the sphere, then turn back and stand there in the darkness."

Vika leaned toward him, confused by the strange order. "Stand in the darkness. Just stand there?"

"Yes. Facing the way you came from, take one pace from the center of that hallway toward your left. Keep your knife in your right hand. Then wait."

The Mord-Sith leaned in a little more toward him. "Wait. All right. Wait for what?"

"You'll know when it happens."

"But you promised me that I would—"

"Vika! You need to follow my instructions exactly!"

She straightened at his sudden tone. "Yes, Lord Rahl."

"Do you remember it all?"

"I think so."

"There can be no thinking so. You must remember it exactly and follow every bit of it as I laid it out. Repeat it back to me. And hurry, we don't have much time."

"Much time for what?" Shale interrupted.

Kahlan hushed her. Shale pressed her lips tight with a look of dissatisfaction as she crossed her arms and remained silent.

Vika looked from Shale back to Richard. She gestured behind. "Take this passageway to the fork. Take the left fork to the steel door. Go through the steel door, cross the bridge, and then go through the steel door on the other side. Take the left hallway at the second—"

"First," he corrected, holding up a finger. "Take the left hallway at the first intersection you come to."

Vika was nodding, trying to commit it to memory. "The left hallway at the *first* intersection. Then go past two wooden doors on the right side of the hall. Take the next right immediately after the second door, go to the fourth light sphere, take it out of the bracket and throw it as far as I can down the hallway, then turn back and stand there in the darkness."

"That's right. Then what?" he asked her.

"Facing the way I came, I'm to take one step to my left, then wait. Oh yes, and hold my knife at the ready in my right hand."

"Good." Richard grabbed her by her shoulders. "Now repeat it back to me again. You have to get it right, Vika. If you take a wrong turn down here we'll likely never find you. If you take a wrong turn you will die all alone like all the dried-up corpses we've found down here. I suppose that would be better than dying old and toothless in bed, but dead is still dead."

Vika smiled that he knew what Mord-Sith always said was their worst fear. Then she nodded as she looked up at him and repeated the instructions. She hesitated in a few places. Once she finished, Richard made her repeat it again, then another time until he was sure she had every turn correct.

Shale's suspicion was clearly evident in her expression. "How do you know all this? How do you know all these places, these corridors, and where these turns are?"

"I studied the plans of this place, remember?"

"Yes, but that doesn't explain how—"

"We don't have time to discuss this," he said, cutting her off and letting her know by his tone that he wanted her to stop asking him questions.

"What about your promise that I could cut him?" Vika asked. "Why can't I go with you so that I can—"

"Do you think I would lie to you?"

That made her blink. "No, Lord Rahl."

"Good, because I wouldn't. Now get going. We don't have much time. Hurry, but don't run or you might make a mistake."

After a brief look at her sisters of the Agiel, she turned and rushed off on her mission, her red leather quickly vanishing in the dim distance down the passageway.

Richard turned back to the suspicious sorceress. "I need you to think something into existence."

Startled by the unexpected request, Shale cocked her head. "What do you want me to think up?"

"Something that will distract Michec. Something that will throw him off. Maybe even scare him."

"I told you. He isn't afraid of snakes."

"I didn't say snakes. I said something to distract him and hopefully scare him."

"I don't know that I can conjure something big and scary enough to worry a witch man."

"You told me that it isn't big and scary that matters. What matters is what works. That's what we need: something that works. I need you to think up something that will get Michec's attention. Alarm him. Something that will distract him—distract and hopefully frighten him. If you can make him scream and frantic to get away that would be perfect."

Shale looked on the verge of panic. She lifted her arms and let them flop down at her sides.

"And how in the world do you suggest I do that!"

"Use your head, Shale. It will come to you when you need it. I know it will. I trust you. Now, I need you to go about three dozen paces down the next passageway over, the one he went down, but no closer—I don't want him to know you're in there—then set loose whatever it is you can conjure and send it on down the rest of the way to attack him. After you do that, come back here to this passageway and come after us as fast as you can. I may need you to help with something else. I'm not sure yet."

Shale stood staring at him with her jaw hanging. "You're not sure, yet," she repeated in astonishment.

"We're wasting what little time we have," he told her. "We can't let this opportunity slip away. We may never get another. Get over there, count your heartbeats until you get to a hundred, then do what I asked. Conjure something formidable and send it on down the hall, then hurry over here to us." Richard turned to the others before Shale could object or argue. "The rest of you, come with me."

Richard left Shale to do as instructed as he led Kahlan and the five remaining Mord-Sith to rush into the twin to the spiraled passageway Michec had taken in order to trap them.

82

Richard brought Kahlan and the five Mord-Sith to a halt. Before any of them could speak, he crossed his lips with a finger.

"If you must speak, do it quietly."

Kahlan glanced over at the wall. "Michec is on the other side?"

"Yes."

"Then what are we doing here?" Kahlan asked. "Shouldn't we be over there if we hope to catch him? How do you hope to get him from here?"

Richard smiled. "Wait. You'll see. And remember, don't try to use your power on him. Get your knife out. I doubt you will get the chance to stab him just yet, but you need to be ready in case."

He turned to the stone wall separating the passageway they were in from its twin where the witch man lurked, waiting to capture them. He looked to the right, to the stone pillar not far away, and then to the one to the left, to judge his relative place between them.

"What are you looking for?" Kahlan asked as she watched.

"I don't have time to explain it. Just watch."

Once he was sure he was in the correct spot, as the six women watched, Richard put his fingertips lightly against the wall and slid them over the stone, looking for the right place. When he found the joint between the stone blocks he was looking for, a joint deeper than the others, he followed it to a similarly deep vertical joint and then went to one knee as he followed that one down. In the silence as the others watched him, he traced all the joints at that area of the wall, making sure they were the ones he needed, and being certain of their layout.

Once he was sure he had found the right place and he was sure of the arrangement of the individual blocks, he turned to the women watching him. "As soon as Shale does what I told her, we're going to go through here and try to catch Michec off guard."

Berdine's nose wrinkled in disbelief. "How are we going to get through a solid stone wall?"

Instead of wasting time answering, Richard took hold of Nyda's arm and pulled her closer to the wall. He squatted down, drawing her down with him. He looked into her blue eyes to make sure she was paying attention. When he was sure she was, he traced a stone block about knee height, showing it to her. It was square, each side about as long as his forearm.

"When I tell you, I want you to side-kick this stone block."

She looked at him with a wary expression. "And what am I to do once I break my ankle?"

Richard shook his head. "Don't worry. I'm going to fracture key places in the wall first to weaken everything. It's beveled to balance where it is, so when the rest of the wall comes apart and you kick it, it will be enough to tip it and cause it to give way. It won't take a great deal of force, so you don't have to worry about hurting yourself.

"This block is a critical structural element, but I can't take care of all the right places by myself. I'm going to need you to take care of this one. Once I fracture the wall, freeing it from the stone above, and then you kick it, that block will tip and will fall through and the rest of the wall will come falling down."

He looked at her and then the others to make sure they were all paying attention. They were all more than merely paying attention. They were mystified.

"All of you, be sure to stay clear and get back—especially you, Nyda—once the stone blocks start collapsing. I know the wall is going to come down, but I don't know where all the stone blocks will fall. Many of them are heavy and could severely injure or even kill you if they fall on you. We can't risk that, so be sure to stay clear."

As they were all trying to comprehend what he told them, Richard drew his sword. He tried to draw it slowly enough that it wouldn't make a sound Michec could hear. Still, the unique, high-pitched ringing sound the blade made coming out was almost painful as the magic answered his call. Richard winced as the sound reverberated through the hall, hoping it wasn't so loud that it could be heard on the other side of the stone wall.

Once the sound died out Richard put his ear close and listened for anything from Michec. When he heard nothing but silence, he placed the point of the blade at a key joint low on the wall, and then he waited, listening for the right time.

Kahlan leaned in, unable to stand the tension any longer. "Richard," she whispered, "what are we waiting for?"

He lifted a finger for her to wait as he heard Shale's footsteps in the distance as she came running.

As soon as he heard Michec scream over on the other side of the wall, he said, "That."

Gritting his teeth with the effort, Richard put all his weight against both hands on the hilt and shoved the sword through the low joint between two of the stones. The stone grated against the blade as it slid in. Once it was through, with all his might he pulled the sword upward. Stone popped and shattered, sending small bits flying. After he had cut as far as needed, he pulled the blade back out of the joint.

He could hear Michec, on the other side of the wall, curse and yell. Between angry curses, he let out short screams. As the witch man was struggling with whatever Shale had thought into existence and set upon him, Richard used the hilt of the sword to tap the stone blocks. As soon as he heard a hollow sound that confirmed the loss of integrity, he sheathed the sword.

He looked at Nyda. "Wait until I hit the wall and then kick that stone."

Nyda gave him a single nod. Richard took a step back and, hoping he was right, threw himself at the wall, grunting with mighty effort. As soon as his shoulder hit the stone with his full weight behind it, he could feel the blocks under his shoulder give. Joints popped and shattered as blocks began to tip. As stone started coming apart, he looked back at Nyda.

"Now!"

Nyda threw a swift kick at the stone block he had shown her.

With a cracking sound the stone gave way as if it had no strength at all. Nyda leaped back out of the way. As the wall caved in, Richard almost fell in with it. He regained his balance and jumped back just in time as blocks of stone and broken chunks of rock came crashing down with a rumbling sound. A great cloud of dust billowed up. All of them coughed out dust.

As soon as enough of the stones had collapsed, Richard dove through, toppling a few blocks out of his way to make the opening larger. Some of the stone blocks crashed down to the sides while several others tumbled in ahead of him. He could sense the Mord-Sith charging through right after him. Even as he was going through, more stones, having lost their support, toppled over. Some of the big blocks of stone hit the floor and shattered, sending fragments sliding underfoot.

Richard charged through the rolling clouds of dust. As he emerged on the other side, he spotted Michec. The man looked shocked by the wall collapsing right next to him, and even more so by Richard and the Mord-Sith suddenly storming in at him.

But the shock of seeing them was only secondary to the witch man's plight. What had him in a real panic was the cloud of angry wasps swarming around his face. He was frantically swinging his arms, swatting at them, and trying to swipe dozens of them off his face as they were stinging him. His face was already a mass of angry red welts. His eyes were nearly swollen shut.

Shale and Kahlan came through the dust cloud, both with knives at the ready. With the wasps swarming around his head, Michec took in all the people coming for him with knives.

He immediately turned and raced away, swatting at the wasps as he ran. Richard heard him laugh even as the wasps were stinging his face. Richard knew why the man was laughing. It was the reason he had been waiting in this particular trap of a dead end that delighted him.

Instead of going after Michec, Richard grabbed Kahlan's arm and tossed her behind him, in the direction Michec had run.

"Something very bad is about to happen," he said as he turned to her. "Go. All of you. Go."

"What's about to happen?" Shale demanded.

"Go! I need you all out of the way!"

All of a sudden, a sound Richard had heard too many times before filled the passageway behind him.

Glee shrieked with rage as they came racing out from far off down around the spiraled end of the trap. Hundreds of them filled the corridor. Their screams echoed off the stone walls. Steam rising from their wet bodies rolled along the ceiling.

He knew that the Glee, with their long, muscular legs, could outrun them and would love nothing more than to run down their prey. Running would be the death of them.

83

The slimy, dark creatures were packed into the corridor so tightly they were jostling each other and having trouble scrambling forward as fast as they wanted. Many of them were clambering to go over the top of others so they could be the first to get at Richard, Kahlan, and the rest of them. Richard knew that as much as they wanted them all, they were especially keen to get their claws into Kahlan.

He had no intention of running, but he needed the rest of those with him to get out of harm's way. Looking over his shoulder, he saw them all hesitate.

Needle-sharp teeth snapped. Long arms flailed. Claws reached and raked the air as they shrieked their bloodlust to get at them.

Richard waved his arms at the others, urging them to get back. Not only did he want to make sure the Glee didn't get to Kahlan, he needed all of them back out of the way.

"Go! Run!"

As Shale and Kahlan hesitantly turned to run in the same direction Michec had gone, the Mord-Sith swept in to surround Kahlan. He saw that, at last, they were all running.

Richard turned back to face the enemy racing toward him from around the spiraled end of the corridor where they had been hiding. There were so many of them they were in each other's way and having trouble going as fast as they wanted. Richard hoped that delay would give him the time he needed.

The shrill, angry sound of the steel coming out made Kahlan and the rest of them all stop and turn back to see what he meant to do. They all knew that there had to be hundreds of Glee coming, far too many for him to fight.

Richard looked back over his shoulder. "Keep going!"

They all backed away, none of them willing to leave Richard to fight the threat alone. They didn't realize that he had known that Michec had the Glee hiding back in the spiral, and he didn't have time to explain his intentions to them.

He was worried that they were going to interfere. "Don't stop! Keep going!"

Shale flung her hands out, sending a shimmering wave of light slamming into the mass of the enemy. The arms of several were blown off by Shale's power. That blast of magic ripped straight through maybe a dozen dark bodies before it dissipated. Although it cut down some of the Glee, it was insignificant in relation to their numbers. The mass of the monsters simply ran right over the top of the fallen dead.

"Stop!" Richard yelled back at Shale. "You're going to hit me. I need room! Leave this to me and get back!"

When she nodded her understanding and he was sure that she wasn't going to do it again and accidentally kill him, he turned back, hoping he hadn't lost what little time he had. He needed to act before the shrieking creatures got to him.

Richard turned to the side and took a mighty swing with the sword. The tip of the blade whistled through the dank air. With all his power behind it, he sent the blade crashing through one of the fat columns on the side of the corridor opposite the hole he had created. The massive capital, with its support column abruptly gone, dropped straight down to the floor and shattered, sending shards of stone flying.

Even as some of the stone of the column was still toppling, he rushed to take out the next fat column. As soon as a powerful strike from his sword had shattered the second stone support on that side of the corridor, he rushed to the wall beside the jagged hole he had made. With several more swings, he took down the supporting columns on one side of that opening and then on the other side.

Because the wall had been compromised, it caused yet more stone to drop down. Both capitals fell and rolled back down the corridor toward the Glee. The whole area filled with thick, choking stone dust.

He could see that it covered some of the wet, leading Glee in the dense pack coming for him, turning them from black to gray.

After that brief look, Richard turned and started running, arms spread wide, ushering the others, who had only gone a short distance, out ahead, urging them to hurry.

"Why would you do that?" Kahlan asked, confused as to why he would waste the time to take out a pair of columns on each side of the corridor.

"Something I learned in the underworld."

She cast a look back over her shoulder at him as she ran. "What?"

"Keep going. Provided I was quick enough, you'll see."

And then he heard the painfully piercing, distinctive sound of massive blocks of granite cracking. It made a ripping, crackling sound something like rolling thunder but higher-pitched as the fractures raced through the stone, making a popping sound as they went.

Richard couldn't help slowing down to turn and look. He had to be sure. If it didn't work, they were going to be in a lot of trouble. Everyone else stopped with him to look behind.

Back down the corridor, with the key support elements of the fat columns suddenly shattered, the huge ceiling blocks of stone, as wide as the corridor, had nothing to hold them up. All at once they began to fall free. The sound was horrific, and despite their desire to get away, Richard and the others all stood transfixed by the astounding sight.

The closest block came crashing down first, crushing the leading Glee. Blood and gore shot out from under the block as it hit the stone floor. A few arms, their reaching claws still twitching, stuck out from under the immense block of granite that only an instant before had been the ceiling of the corridor.

As soon as that first massive ceiling block had started falling free, the second, with its support now gone, immediately broke loose and started coming down, then the third, then the fourth, and then each of the rest of the ceiling blocks all the way back through the spiraled dead end came crashing down in swift succession.

That dead end became a killing field as the massive blocks of stone, each as wide as the corridor and nearly as thick, plummeted down with a thunderous sound in a series of deafening booms that reverberated through the passageways. The whole place shook with jolt after jolt as the massive granite blocks came to ground, each crushing the Glee packed into the hall on back into the spiral.

It all happened so suddenly and so swiftly that Richard doubted any of the Glee had enough time to vanish back to their own world. He was pretty sure that every single one of them had been crushed to death instantly as the ceiling of the entire corridor crashed down on top of them. He almost felt sorry for them. Almost.

Kahlan stood in stunned silence beside him, looking at the massive block of stone that now completely filled the corridor, blocking off what had once been beyond. The corridor now had a new dead end, one much closer. Clouds of dust that had been forced out from under the blocks as they fell now filled the passageway, some of it still swirling through the dimly lit air.

The Mord-Sith stared in awe at what had just happened.

Shale turned to him. "How did—"

"Come on," Richard said, cutting her off. She looked like a thousand questions were bottled up inside her. "We can discuss it later. Right now we need to catch Michec. Stay behind me."

With that, Richard pushed his way through the knot of Mord-Sith and raced out ahead of all of them.

84

Richard needed to be the one to get to the witch man first. He realized, though, that even while Michec was already injured and now being tormented by wasps, he was still profoundly dangerous. The biggest worry was that Richard had no idea what the man was capable of in spite of his condition. He was aware that they could easily get caught up in a trap, so they had to be on the lookout for things that they weren't expecting.

Richard only knew that he needed to kill him before he could use any of his dark talents. He especially needed to kill the man before he could harm Kahlan. And, with the Glee showing up everywhere more frequently all the time, they needed to be done with the witch man so they could get to the Keep.

Richard sprinted down halls and corridors, watching for anything unexpected as he took turns instinctively from the mental map in his head and also from his knowledge of where the witch man was headed. Eager to get at Michec, Richard didn't wait for the others, and had soon pulled out a substantial lead over the rest of them. Checking back over his shoulder from time to time, he made sure not to get too far ahead of them lest they lose sight of him and not know which way he went.

If any of them fell behind and made a wrong turn down in the confusing maze of the complication, it could easily be fatal. He just wanted to stay far enough ahead that Kahlan and the others wouldn't fall into the witch man's grasp before Richard could get his hands on the man.

Richard was well aware that Michec was running in a blind panic, taking the swarm of wasps with him, running haphazardly, taking turns at random but still intent on where he was going. He simply wanted to get to a place of safety. That was fine with Richard, because despite the witch man's random course he knew where Michec would end up. Every once in a while, he could hear Michec in the distance, crying out and cursing as the wasps stung a particularly tender spot on his face.

Richard slowed a little to let the others get a bit closer. His blood was up and he wanted to get to the witch man, but he didn't want to let his anger cause him to run out too far ahead and have the others lose sight of him. He looked back over his shoulder at Shale as he ran.

"Those are your wasps, right?"

Shale nodded.

Richard gestured to let them know his intended direction before he cut down a narrow hallway to the right. "Why isn't he simply making them vanish? Kahlan said he made the snake you conjured vanish."

Shale ran up closer to him so she could speak without having to yell. "Because I intended the snakes for the Glee. I didn't know that I needed to shield them against a witch man's magic. I shielded the wasps, though. And, I made sure they were plenty angry. Only I can withdraw them."

Richard slid to a halt and looked up a set of broad stairs to the left. It was a shortcut that would gain distance on Michec, but it would take them away from his route for a time. He knew that was risky, because Michec, in his distracted state from the wasps, might deviate in his route and end up going someplace Richard wasn't expecting. But he needed to get to Michec before he could escape. The shortcut was the best way to help close the gap.

Decision made, he started up the stairs two at a time.

"When we get close to him," he called back over his shoulder to Shale, "I need you to withdraw the wasps so they don't sting us as well."

Shale nodded as she ran up the stairs after him. "Don't worry about the wasps. I'll make sure they're gone as soon as we catch him."

At the top of the short flight of stairs, a corridor branched off to each side. Richard paused to make sure Kahlan wasn't lagging behind. She wasn't. The Mord-Sith were surrounding her. Reassured, he went straight on down the dark center corridor between the other two. After a short distance the corridor came to stairs that descended back to the original level, where he again took a right.

As he raced down a corridor with dusty marble columns supporting a barreled, plastered ceiling, he slowed and turned as he trotted backward so he could see all the others.

"What magic is Michec liable to use against me when I catch him? Any guesses?"

Shale turned her palms up. "I've been asking myself that same question. I don't have an answer. I don't really know anything about witch men, except that they are witches. That's bad enough, but from what I've seen so far, I suspect he can do things I can't even begin to imagine."

"Do you think you will be able to do anything to counter whatever magic he might do?"

Shale shook her head as she hurried along. "He can't make my wasps vanish. There are limitations for a witch using their power against another witch, which limits what I can do. He is likely to shield anything he does so I can't stop it. You're a wizard, why don't you do something?"

Richard sighed unhappily. "All right. I will just have to deal with whatever he does, if I can't kill him first. But I need you to be ready to at least create light. Conjure a flame in your palm or something—I don't care, but I will need light to see. It's going to be pitch black when I catch him."

Shale blinked in surprise. "How do you know that?"

"Prophecy," Kahlan told her. "Richard was in the underworld, remember? There is prophecy in the underworld. Do you think a war wizard would fail to avail himself of any opportunity to gain an advantage against an enemy?"

Richard grinned at her in answer. He thought she was not only the most intelligent person he knew, but sometimes it seemed she could read his thoughts.

Shale looked alarmed. "You mean to say you have been acting on prophecy?"

"How do you think I knew that spiral corridor was packed with Glee waiting to ambush us? Would you rather I knew nothing about it and walked into Michec's trap?"

"Well, no," she admitted.

As he went past the second wooden door on the right and slowed down, he hushed her before she could ask any more questions.

"From now on," he told them all in a low voice, "try to move as quietly as you can. Michec won't be far ahead, now. He is down this passageway here, to the right. Rikka, Vale, Cassia, Nyda, Berdine, be ready to use your knives on him to protect Kahlan. Shale, be ready to provide light."

They all nodded as they started out after him down the hallway to the right. As they went farther in, the first light sphere began to brighten, showing them the way. As it was dimming behind them on their way past, the second began to glow. Richard slowed to a stop.

He held up a hand for everyone to be still as he listened into the dark distance. When he heard the echo of heavy breathing, he started running as fast and quietly as he could. He motioned for the others to stay back a ways. He didn't want Michec to snatch Kahlan or anyone else and use them as a hostage. Kahlan had a knife and knew how to use it, but he didn't want it to come to that. The witch man was unpredictable, had magic, and, after all, had called all those Glee back in the spiraled corridor to lay a trap for them.

As the second light sphere dimmed in the distance behind, they hurried past the third, and then beyond, on into darkness.

85

Richard had to judge the distance to the bracket where the fourth light sphere would be by counting his paces between the previous brackets. He began to smell the witch man even though he couldn't see him. He didn't know what a witch was supposed to smell like, but a big man sweating from running and from fear and panic was a smell Richard had no trouble recognizing.

He moved forward a little on his tiptoes. Before he had gone far, as he listened for the wasps and the heavy breathing, trying to judge the exact distance, a big hand came out of nowhere and backhanded him, knocking him back several steps. The surprise, more than anything, knocked him off balance.

Richard immediately regained his footing and dove in the direction of where he now knew Michec was standing. As he crashed into the man, he managed to get an arm around his neck. Michec twisted and struggled to break away. Richard reached up and gripped the wrist of the arm he had around Michec's neck and then used it to help increase the pressure. He knew it would be only moments until the blood supply was cut off to cause unconsciousness.

"Shale! Light!"

All of a sudden, the walls to each side ignited in flame.

In the bright light of the leaping flames, Richard saw Vika standing right in front of them, knife in her right hand.

"Now!" he yelled at her.

As Richard struggled to hang on to the brawny man trying to wrestle his way out of the choke hold, Vika slammed her blade into the witch man's belly. She grabbed the hilt with both hands and grunted with the effort of pulling it sideways, ripping him open.

Vika pulled the blade back and then thrust her left hand into the gaping wound. She pulled her bloody hand back out holding a fistful of entrails. She twisted her body to yank out a long, glistening length of intestine. Michec gasped with the shock of what had just happened.

The corridor suddenly lit with a blindingly bright flash of white-hot light that ignited around the witch man. Richard and Vika both were thrown back, slammed into the flaming wall. They landed on their backs and slid a short distance across the floor back up the corridor. It felt to Richard like they had been struck by lightning.

Richard and Vika both were momentarily stunned by the shock of the blast. Every nerve in his body rang with pain. Richard rolled to his side, his arms going numb. He was blinded by the intensity of the flash.

Michec, lit by the wavering flames of the walls, glared down at them both. He started to draw his hands up. Richard suspected he was going to fry them with another lightning-like strike. He knew that if he did, it could kill both him and Vika.

Despite the pain, Richard forced himself to jump to his feet, and without an instant's delay he crashed into Michec, grabbing him with both hands around his throat. The full force of the impact threw Michec's arms back, stopping him from what he had been just about to do to them. Richard knew that he couldn't allow the man to gather his wits and his power or it would all be over.

With all his might he rammed the big man into the wall. He gritted his teeth with a growl as he used all of his strength to lean in and force Michec's head back into the flames. Richard could smell the witch man's spiky hair burning. Michec reacted to the pain of the fire by thrashing wildly, trying to get away, but Richard held him tight as he used all his strength to choke the life out of him. His muscles bulged with the effort.

Something as thick as his leg whipped around Richard's middle and forcefully yanked him back. Despite his best effort, he couldn't hold on. Richard saw the red leather of some of the other Mord-Sith charging in for Michec, but another blindingly bright flash of light threw them back to land at Kahlan's and Shale's feet.

As Richard was dragged back, with the thick thing squeezing the air out of him, he thought that it had to be a tentacle of some sort, like the one he and Kahlan had fought in the water. He couldn't see its source. He put his hands on it to try to push it away and found that it wasn't soft, like living tissue, but rough and hard, like a rapidly expanding tree root.

As he twisted his body, trying to get away from its grasp, he saw yet more of the tendrils sprouting up out of the floor, breaking the stone apart as they rose up, growing fatter as they rose up. Before he was able to do anything about the one tightening painfully around his middle, another, lengthening and curling as it grew up out of the floor, coiled around his legs. Yet another rose up to grab his arms.

The rootlike tendrils grew in thickness and strength as they threw yet more coils around his arms and legs. He looked over and saw that the same kind of tendrils were climbing up Vika, thickening rapidly as they encased her, squeezing the air from her lungs.

Michec panted, trying to recover his strength. Wisps of smoke rose from his singed hair and the back of his robes. A long length of bloody intestine hung down to the floor. Blood from the gash soaked his filthy robes and began to puddle around his feet.

He grabbed hold of the intestine in his fist, and with a flash of knife-like light from his other hand severed it and cast the length aside as if it was no longer needed. He lifted a hand out to each wall, and the flames started to dim as the fire rapidly began to extinguish.

Michec turned to Vika. "Seems you made the same mistake you warned me of. Trying to teach a lesson of revenge rather than simply killing me. I am no longer going to bother with lessons for any of you. I'm just going to kill you all."

Suddenly, the corridor shimmered as a wave of light shot through the air. Richard could no longer move his head, but he could turn his eyes just enough to see Shale, Kahlan, and the rest of the Mord-Sith running in to help. The wavering light hit Michec, staggering him, but it failed to do any visible damage. He took a few steps back as he regained his balance and his senses.

Richard could feel the roots around his chest constricting. Every time he breathed out, they tightened, taking up the extra space, so that he couldn't get his full breath back. Each time he exhaled, it ratcheted him another notch toward suffocation. He tried panting with shallow breaths, but even those were being squeezed out of him.

Michec cast a grim look over the people trying to kill him and then lifted an arm. When he did, it brought up a wall of fire of his own. The searing flames blocked the advance of the women. Pleased that it drove them back, Michec turned and hurried off down the corridor, disappearing into the darkness.

The roots that had Richard and were growing thicker by the moment had finally cut off his air. His vision narrowed to a pinpoint of light in the center of blackness. He could hear Vika also struggling unsuccessfully to breathe.

A flash shower of rain came out of nowhere and dumped buckets' worth of water in the corridor, extinguishing the fire that Michec had used to block the others from coming after him.

Kahlan, Shale, and all the Mord-Sith raced to Richard.

"Hold on," Kahlan said as she frantically started sawing away with her knife at the roots and vines that had encased him.

Out of the corner of his eye he could see the red leather of a few of the others rushing over to try to help Vika.

"I can't use magic on this," Shale said as she desperately cut at the roots with her knife. "I can feel that Michec shielded them and his magic can overcome whatever I try to do. We have to do it with our knives. Hold on."

Kahlan gritted her teeth as she furiously cut through a thick root. Fortunately, it was relatively soft, rather than woody, and she was finally able to sever it, releasing the pressure and allowing him to at last draw a breath. His vision started to return from the blackness. He gasped air, angry at himself that he had let this happen.

It took some time before Richard and Vika were finally cut free enough that they were able to untangle themselves from the network of fibrous tendrils.

Once back on his feet, Richard lifted the sword a few inches and let it drop back, making sure the scabbard hadn't been bent or crushed and that he would still be able to draw it.

"Michec is pretty badly wounded," Richard managed to say between deep breaths. He winked at Vika. "Vika managed to hurt him more than I did."

Vika smiled her appreciation that he had kept his promise to let her cut him good.

"Vika has lived up to the honor as your favorite for today," Berdine said.

Richard wanted to respond but didn't feel up to it right then.

"We need to go after Michec," he said instead. "I want to kill him in case he doesn't bleed to death. Is everyone all right?"

A quick glance revealed nods all around.

"All right, then, let's go."

86

L ook," Rikka said, pointing. "Blood. And I can see more out ahead."
"There's quite a lot of it, too," Cassia said as she leaned down, taking a better look. "That will certainly make it easier to follow him. At some point it should start slowing him down, too."

Richard thought about it briefly and then turned back to Shale. "You can conjure things. So can you conjure blood?"

Shale frowned a little as she considered the question. "I've never thought about it before, but now that you ask, I imagine so. If nothing else, I could conjure a pretty good imitation of it."

"Go ahead and try." Richard gestured down at the long drizzle of blood on the stone floor. "See if you can make a blood trail that looks like that one."

Shale lifted her hands, her fingers wavering as she closed her eyes a moment in concentration. A wet swath of blood appeared on the floor, looking very much like the splash beside it that Rikka had found.

"Like that?" she asked as her eyes came open and she dropped her arms.

"Yes, that's good."

"Obviously," Shale said, "you are suggesting that the trail of blood may be a trick?"

Richard put a hand on his hip as he tried to put himself in Michec's place and think what he would be likely to do. "We have to assume that it's a possibility. He's wounded. He doesn't want to have to fight us right now. He would want to divert us until he can deal with his injuries. The best way to do that would be to lead us into a trap. There are certainly plenty of those down here."

"You mean like the spiraled dead end."

Richard nodded to the sorceress.

"How did you know that you could bring the ceiling down like that?" Shale asked, finally getting back to the question she had been burning to ask.

"When I studied the plans, I saw it there. The plans were drawn so that such a trap would be constructed when the place was originally built. The way it was constructed, that ceiling was designed to fall to either trap or crush people. You just had to know how to initiate the trap. When I studied those plans, I could see how the trap could be triggered. It wasn't too hard. You just had to know the weak spot."

Shale arched an incriminating eyebrow. "And did you also see the Glee hiding back in there on those same plans?"

"Of course not," Richard said, waving a hand dismissively. "I saw that in a prophecy while I was in the underworld."

"Ah. Again a prophecy." She gestured for him to continue. "And what else did you see?"

"I saw a prophecy that revealed where Michec would go. That's why I had Vika go there and wait—so that she could stab him just as the prophecy said she would."

"Then why wasn't he killed right there and then?" Kahlan asked. "If it was in the prophecy, why didn't it end right there as the prophecy said?"

Richard let out an unhappy sigh. "Because it was a forked prophecy. I saw that he would go to that spot, Vika would stab him, then we would either kill him or, if events took a less likely turn down the other fork, he would escape. Unfortunately, we are in a complication. A complication has an effect and it can twist events in prophecy.

"It fell the wrong way for us and events in that prophecy ended up taking the other fork. That fork was less clear and soon ends without resolution. Forks in prophecy often aren't always resolved in the particular prophecy where the first fork occurs. If it takes one of those secondary forks, then you need to find another prophecy that picks up where that particular fork left off. That's often the problem with prophecy."

"So then, on the fork in which he escaped, where does he go next?" She looked off down the passageway, as if she might chance to see him. "When and where will we be able to catch him? Could you at least tell that much?"

Richard wiped a hand over his mouth. "That particular prophecy ended either with his death, or his escape down the other fork, but that prophecy didn't go down that secondary fork. I would have to look for the next prophecy in the chronology to hope to be able to reestablish the event line and tell where he went after he took the fork in which he escaped. I didn't do that because once prophecy starts forking, the possibilities multiply exponentially."

Kahlan gave him a dark look. "If you're thinking of returning to the world of the dead so you can look for that prophecy, you can just forget it. These two children need their father."

Richard flashed her a reassuring smile. "No, I promise you on my word as a wizard, I have no desire or intention of returning to the underworld to look for that prophecy."

Kahlan leaned in and gave him a quick kiss on the cheek. "That's my boy."

"So what do we do now?" Shale asked. "Follow this blood trail, or assume it's a trick?"

Richard put a hand back on his hip, staring down the corridor, thinking. He at last turned to her.

"Send your wasps after him again. Let's see where they go."

Shale looked off into the darkness. "I can do that, but we won't be able to follow them for long. They fly fast."

"Let's see if we can follow them long enough to see if they follow the blood or take a different route."

"How are you going to have the wasps follow him if you don't know where he is or which way he went?" Berdine asked.

Shale's mouth widened with a sly smile. "Wasps have an excellent sense of smell. I will give them his scent and they will find him."

"All right, good," Richard said. "Send them."

Shale again lifted her hands and waggled her fingers.

She opened her eyes. "Done."

Richard looked off down the hall and saw where the buzzing swarm appeared and headed off down the corridor.

"Come on," he said as he started running. "We need to keep sight of them as long as possible."

87

Just as I thought," Richard said as he came to a stop when he saw the swarm of wasps flow around a corner to swoop down and disappear in a low, round passageway made of brick. He gestured ahead, then to the round opening at the side. "The blood trail goes that way, but the wasps went down here. The blood was a trick."

Vika leaned down, looking into the circular passageway where the wasps had gone. "There aren't any light spheres in this tube. We'll need to get some and take them with us."

Taking her cue, the rest of the Mord-Sith raced up the hall, and each lifted a glass sphere from a bracket and brought it back.

"What is this place, anyway?" Kahlan asked as she leaned down a little so she wouldn't hit her head as she peered into the dark, brick pipe. "It doesn't look like anything else we've seen down here."

"The complication is a low place beneath the People's Palace." Richard gestured off into the pipe she was peering into. "This is the lowest place in the complication. Water seeks the lowest level. This is an emergency drainage shaft in case there is ever torrential rain and the water manages to overwhelm the drainage system up above and flood all the way down here. This pipe drains the complication if needed."

"That makes sense for water," Kahlan said, "but why would Michec go this way?"

"He's injured. I think he went in here to hide."

"How can he hide in this shaft? It's round. There's no place for him to conceal himself."

Richard glanced over at her. "He's counting on us believing that. I've seen the plans. I know better."

Before entering the round passage, Richard looked over at Shale. "Don't forget, we can't directly use magic on the witch man, even when he is wounded. He has already proven that. But when you sent wasps after him, he wasn't able to capture you."

"I think that's because I wasn't using magic against him, as I did the first time. I created angry wasps with a desire to attack. I wasn't personally attacking him directly."

"That seems like a questionable exception," Kahlan said. "Are you sure he can't turn your magic back on you like the first time?"

Shale pressed her lips tight a bit as she considered briefly. "No, no I don't think so. The first time was a direct attack. The use of the wasps and the fire I made on the walls to each side of the passageway so Richard could see were tangential. Because they were indirect, that broke the link back to me. It doesn't give him a direct route to return to the source, namely me, with his own power."

"I hate magic," Berdine muttered. "It makes no sense."

Richard flashed her a brief smile and nod of agreement before he turned to the others. "We all survived back there because there were nine of us, and together we are stronger. We can't directly use magic, but there is strength in all of us together. Remember that if we can find him."

Like everyone else, Richard had to bend at the waist to be able to fit into the drainage pipe. Berdine, being the shortest, only had to tip her head forward a little in order to fit. Because the drainage shaft was round, and they were crouched over, they had to use their hands on the brick at the side from time to time to keep their balance. As they went farther in, the round shaft started going downhill in a gentle slope in order to drain the water.

In places water from above seeped through a series of round weep-holes in small blocks of stone set into the brick and accumulated at the bottom. The farther they went, the deeper the flowing water became, but it never reached more than ankle deep and since it was moving rather than stagnant it didn't stink. When they came to side drains that emptied into the main drain they were in, Richard stopped.

"Which way?" Vika asked.

Richard thought through the plans in his mind. He looked back at all the faces watching him in the eerie light of the glass spheres.

"We need to get to the low point. This way, straight ahead."

"Couldn't you be wrong about where he would have gone?" Shale asked. "For some reason I can't pick up his smell anymore. Couldn't he have gone off down one of these pipes to the sides?"

"Of course," Richard said without looking back as he started out again. He noticed dead wasps floating in the water.

"Then he may be planning ahead and instead of going where you think he is, he could be lurking in one of those side drains and be waiting for us in the darkness."

Richard looked back over his shoulder but didn't say anything as he kept going. He knew she was right, but he had a gut feeling born of growing up tracking wounded animals. He thought that he knew where Michec would have gone to ground.

After moving through the drainage pipe for a time, he turned back again and crossed a finger over his lips.

"We're close," he whispered. "Try to move as quietly as possible."

He cautiously led them ahead until they reached a square opening in the floor of the drain tunnel. Water that was draining along the pipe from both directions cascaded over the edge and down into the darkness. He was glad to hear the sound it made, because it would help cover any sound they might make.

Richard leaned toward the others, holding out his arms to gather them all in close so they could hear him. "This is the place. I think he's down in there."

Kahlan glanced over at the square opening. "What is this opening?"

"Any water that makes it down here drains into this rock drain."

"But what is it?" Kahlan asked.

"It's a massive pit filled with crushed rock. At the sides, near the top, it has a number of small pipes leading to the edge of the plateau in case there is ever too much water for the rock drain to hold. Unless it's a huge flood, the rock pit will hold all the water and let it slowly dissipate without damaging the foundation."

Shale craned her neck to look over at the dark opening. "What makes you think Michec would have gone down there?"

"Because he's an animal. Animals go to ground when they're injured. They instinctively seek out a hole to hide in. It makes them feel safer."

Shale looked skeptical. "Michec may be a beast, but he is also a person who is able to think. More than that, he's a cunning person. People act differently than animals. You are just guessing that he's down there hiding in a hole. He may be long gone."

Richard bent over and scooped up some dead wasps. He held them up before her as he lifted an eyebrow.

Shale stared unhappily at the dead wasps, and then looked around, noticing that there were many more all over the floor. "Making conjured snakes vanish is one thing. They weren't shielded. Killing conjured things that are shielded is altogether different. I can't even begin to guess at his abilities and how dangerous he is."

"How far down to the bottom?" Kahlan asked.

"There would be no reason for the top of the rock to be down deep in the pit. I believe the rock should come up pretty high. I doubt we could all stand up straight down in there."

"Why not just let him bleed out?" Kahlan asked. "Why risk going in after him?"

"Because Shale said he just did something he shouldn't be able to do." Richard gave Kahlan a sympathetic look. "I'd like nothing more than to simply let him die in misery down there. But for all we know about his abilities he might be able to heal himself enough to survive. He didn't seem concerned about cutting off the length of intestine hanging out of the gash Vika cut in him. We would never know if he managed to survive and would never expect him to come after us another time—until he unexpectedly showed up and killed us."

"If we're going down in there, I think it would be better if the Mother Confessor waited up here," Cassia said. "It would be safer than her going down in there with us."

"And what if I'm wrong?" Richard asked. "What if while we're down in an empty dry pit looking for him, he's really up here somewhere and he sneaks up from behind and murders her?"

The worry showed in Cassia's expression. "There is that."

"The nine of us need to stay together," Richard told them. "There is no telling what Michec might do. Besides that, it may take all of us to kill him. Look at what he did with those vines. It took all of us to escape them."

Kahlan turned to Shale. "Would his injuries limit his ability to use magic?"

Shale sighed. "I would like to think so, but since I don't even know how powerful he is when he's healthy, there is no way to be sure how much his injuries would limit his powers. Worse, even if his gift is limited, for all I know it still may be more than enough to kill us all. I think it best if we assume his present abilities are still quite lethal."

"We need to go down there and eliminate him. That's all there is to it," Richard said. "There is supposed to be an iron ladder going down there. Kahlan, after we jump down, you take the ladder."

She started to protest. "But—"

"You're pregnant. If it's a bigger drop than I think, I don't want you to take a bad fall and lose the twins. No unnecessary risks."

"You're right," she said in resignation. "The ladder it is."

Richard gestured around at them all. "The rest of you gather around the opening and then all jump down with me, all at once. Except you, Cassia. Stay behind and follow Kahlan down to guard her back. Once we're down there, we can't waste time finding him. We need to be quick. The more surprise we have on our side, the better. We don't want to give him time to do something that could stop us."

He looked around until he got nods from everyone. "Enough talk. Let's go."

88

Richard landed hard on both feet, Shale right beside him. Fortunately, it wasn't any farther down than he had thought. All the Mord-Sith, each with a light sphere, landed to the sides. Richard saw Kahlan hurrying down the iron ladder with Cassia right behind her.

Concerned at not seeing the witch man, Richard immediately started looking into the darkness in the distance, trying to spot him. There were simple, square stone posts at regular intervals throughout the expansive pit. The posts held up arches that in turn held up the low ceiling. The loose, ragged rock filling the pit tried to twist his ankles with every step, making it difficult to walk on.

Richard worried that the witch man might have heard them and could be hiding behind one of the massive stone supports, ready to surprise them with a lethal attack.

Without needing orders, the Mord-Sith all immediately started spreading out in an ever-widening circle, going farther into the darkness with their light spheres, searching for the witch man. They checked behind each stone post as they moved swiftly into the distance. Richard didn't want one of them to encounter Michec alone, so he stood ready to react if any of them spotted him.

Vika suddenly cried out and pointed. "There!"

Richard and the others turned and raced across the uneven rock and past several stone posts to catch up with her. As she held up the light sphere, it revealed Michec slumped in shadows of a dark corner like a spider waiting for prey. His robes were soaked in blood from the waist down, but he looked as merciless and menacing as ever. He sat up straighter but didn't try to stand under the low ceiling.

Vika, with a cry of rage, ran in and heaved her light sphere at him as hard as she could. Michec thrust out a hand. The glass sphere shattered explosively in a thousand sparkling shards.

He snarled a curse and flicked a hand toward the Mord-Sith. Vika screamed as a blast exploded the crushed rock she was on. The discharge of his power threw her flying back through the air. Rock flew in every direction.

Most of them had to stoop or duck under beams so as not to hit their heads as they ran toward the corner. As they got closer, Michec lifted his arms out to the sides, his fingers pointing up, and bursts of fire erupted from the floor in front of them. The heat drove some of them back as they shielded their faces with an arm, not just from the flames but also from the flying rocks.

Richard didn't slow. As he ran toward the corner, he dodged around every shower of fire the witch man ignited in his way. The others darted around the roaring columns of flame, trying to keep up with him. Kahlan, not far away, kept pace with him as she, too, wove her way through the sudden explosions of fire. The roaring flames lit the square posts in orange-yellow light. There seemed to be fire flaring up all around. Richard ducked first one way and then another, snaking between posts and fire as he raced for the corner.

Michec suddenly cast his hands out with great force. The rock of the floor blasted up at Kahlan, throwing her through the air to land on her back. Richard's heart felt as if it jumped into his throat at seeing her skid along the jagged stony surface. He saw several of the Mord-Sith thrown back with her in the same explosion of rock.

Richard kept the stone posts and fire between himself and the witch man as best he could to conceal himself as he rapidly closed the distance. When Michec suddenly turned and caught sight of him leaping through a fount of fire, he swung his hands around toward Richard. But it was too late. He was already there.

Richard dove in atop the man, seizing him by the throat.

Gritting his teeth in fury, Richard squeezed with all his might. As he did, the witch man swept both arms up. As Michec lifted his clawed hands, dark, rootlike branches sprouted from the stone walls on each side of the corner. Bony black tendrils grew like skeletal arms from the walls with frightening speed. The fingers of woody vine lengthened to grab Richard's wrists, pulling with powerful, conjured strength.

Mord-Sith dove in on each side. Nyda grabbed one of Michec's arms. Vale fell on top of the arm beside Nyda, helping her push it downward. Berdine fell across his legs to help hold him down. Rikka and Cassia, covered in stone dust, suddenly appeared and dropped onto his other arm, pinning it down so he couldn't lift it higher, but it was already too late. The rootlike tendrils wouldn't let go of Richard's wrists, and in fact grew thicker and pulled with more power. He fought against them, trying to put pressure on Michec's throat.

Vika reached in beside Richard with a knife to cut the witch man's throat above Richard's struggling grip. Before she could get the blade on his throat, a sudden, deafening blast threw her through the air again, this time even farther. She landed quite a distance back. Richard heard her grunt as the air was driven from her lungs when she slammed into a stone post.

Shale, not far behind Richard, lifted her hands, her fingers slowly waggling. When she did, as her eyes slowly rolled up in her head, more of the woody vines sprouted from the stone walls above the ones Michec had conjured, coiling around the ones holding Richard's wrists. Fingerlike branches grew out of the ends of the arms she created and grasped the thick, dark roots that continued to curl around Richard's arms.

Shale, her eyes half closed, worked her fingers. As she did, the rootlike arms she had summoned struggled to pull back on the dark tendrils that had a firm grip on Richard's wrists and forearms, preventing him from crushing Michec's windpipe. Despite Shale's efforts, the vines the witch man had conjured wouldn't let go. Richard's hands shook from the strain of trying to strangle the man against the power trying to pull them back. Yet more vines sprouted from the walls to either side. They were dark in color, like the first ones, so Richard knew that they, too, were the work of the witch man.

In his mind's eye, he remembered the sight of Kahlan hanging by the shackles, her beautiful face bruised and swollen from a beating

Michec had given her. He remembered the witch man telling him how after he was finished skinning her, he would let the Glee rip the two babies from her womb while she was still alive.

Those horrific memories fueled his fury as his hands shook with the monumental effort to overcome the woody vines trying to drag his wrists back. Richard screamed with rage as he struggled to choke the life out of the witch man. The tendrils holding him started to crack and come apart. Even as he tried with all his might, and even as he was able to start to break the hold on him, he knew it wasn't going to be enough.

All of those around Richard struggled along with him. He could see the sweat and effort on the faces of each one of the Mord-Sith trying to hold Michec's arms to prevent him from lifting them to call forth even more horrors. When Nyda managed to pull her knife, it suddenly flew from her hand and clattered against a post.

With a cry of effort born of rage, and determined to end it, Richard managed to press in harder on Michec's throat. He could feel his thumbs starting to compress the man's straining muscles.

"Wait!" the witch man cried out. "Lord Rahl—wait. Listen."

Richard didn't answer. He didn't care what Michec had to say. His actions and life had already revealed the truth about the nature of the man. Richard simply wanted him dead.

"I can see now that I was wrong. You really are rightly the Lord Rahl. I can see that now."

Richard struggled all the harder.

"Lord Rahl! I was only following orders!"

Richard didn't dare to waste any strength to ask the man whose orders he was following. To each side, the Mord-Sith grunted with the effort of holding the man's powerful arms. He was so strong that he lifted all four a few inches off the floor.

"I will swear loyalty to you!" the witch man cried out. "I will swear loyalty to your empire! Let me go so I may serve you!"

Richard wanted to tell him that he could serve him best by dying, but he didn't dare spare any effort to speak. Try as he might, with the conjured hands holding his wrists back, he couldn't close his grip enough on the man's throat to crush his windpipe and kill him.

"Let me live and I will serve you just as I served your father. I will protect and serve your wishes! Just let me go and my life will be yours to command. I can be useful to you! Please, Lord Rahl, allow me to serve you!"

In answer, teeth clenched tightly, Richard tried all the harder to crush Michec's windpipe. He could see the Mord-Sith to each side losing their grip as the witch man managed to start to lift his arms and turn his hands up.

89

Richard's muscles burned with exhaustion as he fought against the vines trying to pull his arms away. He knew he wasn't going to be able to hold on much longer. The Mord-Sith to each side were having even worse problems. The danger to all of them increased with the strain of pulling every breath.

Richard should have been able to strangle the man by now. It was obvious that the witch man's powers were somehow energizing him with desperate strength beyond that of a normal man so that he was able to overcome all of their efforts. It was clear that they were all now locked in a struggle to the death.

"Forgive me!" Michec cried out. "I was only following orders!"

Richard glared into Michec's dark eyes as he struggled with all his might to strangle him. His hands shook with the effort. His muscles burned.

Richard didn't want to give the man the satisfaction of asking whose orders, but the witch man told him anyway.

"I was only following the queen's orders!"

Richard didn't know what queen the man could be talking about, but he didn't believe him. Michec would say anything to escape. Richard wondered if maybe he was talking about the Golden Goddess, but she was described as a goddess, not a queen.

Kahlan appeared to the right of Richard, covered with dust from the rock the witch man had blasted up at her, trying to kill her. Blood streamed down her face from several wounds.

A strange look of bemused calm came over the witch man's swollen, red face. "If you think this witch's oath begins and ends with me, you are a fool."

That time, Richard couldn't resist asking, "What are you talking about?"

"Ask your witch," he said with a sneer.

Kahlan suddenly dropped in beside Richard, using her full weight to drive her blade between two of Michec's ribs and into his heart. She let out of cry of rage as she pivoted the handle of her knife from side to side, slicing through his heart.

Michec's eyes went wide.

Kahlan, gritting her teeth, keeping her knife pressed hilt-deep in his chest, put her face in close to his, looking into his startled eyes.

"Think to harm my babies, do you?" she growled. "I deliver you now into the hands of the Keeper of the underworld. He will take you into darkness you can't begin to imagine. You will never see the light of Creation again. All those innocent souls you tortured to death will now torment you for all eternity."

Michec's mouth worked, trying to beg for mercy, to explain, but no words came forth. The panic and terror in his eyes was clear. He had never had a shred of mercy for the panic and terror of his victims, and now Richard, Kahlan and the others with them had none for him.

Vika, covered in stone dust and with a gash across her forehead that had her face covered in a mask of blood, knelt to Richard's left. Without pause, she rammed her knife into the side of Michec's neck. Blood oozed rather than spurted out from the artery she severed. His heart could no longer pump blood.

The surprise in Michec's eyes slowly faded as the life went out of them until his stare was blank and empty. The bony hands holding Richard's wrists released their grip on him as they crumbled into dust and vapor.

Shale, her eyes still closed, dropped to her knees, clearly drained from the effort of trying to pull back on the vines that had so powerfully held Richard's wrists. Exhausted, she put a hand down on the rock for support.

Finally, Richard sat back on his heels, letting his cramping hands drop to his lap. He looked around to see everyone panting along with him from the effort. Despite being battered, and some of them bleeding, none of them seemed seriously hurt.

He finally circled an arm around Kahlan's neck and pulled her close. He brushed hair back from her face and kissed her forehead, then hugged her tight, grateful that she was alive and not seriously hurt. She took her bloody hand from her knife in Michec's chest and with both arms hugged him back, silently thankful to be alive and have the ordeal over.

At last, after a brief time to hold Kahlan tight, get his breath back, and be thankful that she was safe, Richard finally struggled to his feet. He helped Kahlan stand. All of the Mord-Sith untangled themselves from their grips on the dead man's arms and legs.

"You did it, Lord Rahl," Berdine said as she gazed hatefully down at the dead witch man. "You killed the butcher."

Richard shook his head. "No, we all did. It took all nine of us. The Law of Nines had more power than even a witch man."

The Mord-Sith looked pleased that he included them. Shale, with a hand on her knee to help her stand, managed to show a weary smile along with them.

They all backed away a short distance to stare at the dead man, all of them still having some difficulty believing the monster was finally dead. It had been a monumental struggle, but the witch man would no longer bring terror and pain to anyone.

Spotting something he didn't like, Richard gestured to the bloody body slumped in the corner as he looked over at Shale.

"Burn him to ash, would you please?"

Shale looked a little surprised by the request. "Why? He's dead. What do you think he can do, now?"

"I don't know, and I don't want to find out. You're good at conjuring fire. Do that now. End it. Burn him to ash."

Shale turned an uneasy look from Richard, to Michec, and back. She suddenly seemed both distressed and apologetic.

She shook her head. "Lord Rahl, I am a witch woman. I can't burn another witch. Never. That act has terrible significance."

Richard felt his anger heating. It made no sense to him.

"Even a man as evil as this?"

She couldn't seem to look him in the eye, so she stared off at the dead Michec. "I know that he was a monster, but he is also a witch. I wanted him dead just as much as the rest of you, and I helped with that to the best of my ability, but I can't burn a witch, not even a dead one. I just can't."

Richard was surprised, but it was obviously something profoundly personal to her. He wondered why, but rather than asking her he deemed it best not to force the issue.

He laid the palm of his left hand over the hilt of his sword. When he did, he was surprised to feel the magic from the sword stirring, trying to join with him. He surmised it could be that the sword's magic sensed his lingering rage at this evil man and all the horrific acts he had committed.

And then, as Richard looked over at the dead man staring back at him with dead eyes, he saw it again, a glint of something, some spark of light in those dead eyes that shouldn't have been there.

In that instant, he envisioned the horrors starting all over again. He saw everything they had just won suddenly slipping away from them. He saw that threat to Kahlan and their children reawakening, as if Michec were somehow trying to strike out at them one last time from the world of the dead before he would sink away into its eternal darkness.

From somewhere deep within him, without Richard consciously summoning it, the primal rage of his birthright awakened. With his left hand still on the hilt of the sword, drawing on all the ancient power of the weapon, he cast his other hand out, opening his fist, instantly igniting wizard's fire. The rotating bluish-white ball of flame shook the room with a reverberating boom as it exploded into existence. Seemingly at the same instant it came into being, it shot across the room, wailing with a piercing shriek as it lit the stone posts and all the stunned faces on its way to the source of Richard's ire. The sound of it was deafening as it hurtled the short distance to that target and burst apart on impact, splashing sticky fire over the body of the witch man.

Wizard's fire burned with a fierce intensity and purpose unlike any other fire. The roaring flames burned white hot at their center.

Shale wrinkled her nose at the stench of burning flesh. The Mord-Sith didn't.

In mere moments, the soft tissue was consumed in the ferocious blaze. Once the soft tissue had burned away, the wizard's fire continued to sink inward until it covered the bones, engulfing them in the savage flames until they, too, began to break apart and finally turn to ash and collapse into a brightly glowing heap. Only then did the fire, its work done, finally extinguish.

Everyone stood in stunned silence at what they had just witnessed. The heat from the wizard's fire had even partly melted the stone wall behind where Michec had been slumped.

"I didn't know you could do that," Kahlan said in a soft voice as she stared at the aftermath.

Richard felt a bit stunned himself. "Neither did I."

Shale looked shaken by what she had just seen. "I've heard whispered stories of such a thing. I never imagined I would live to see it with my own eyes."

Richard stared at the pile of ash that was all that remained of a henchman for Darken Rahl, a witch man who had been determined to kill them all, glad it was finally over.

The sorceress turned to him with a grave expression. "How did you do it?"

Richard slowly shook his head as he stared at the still-glowing pile of ash and asked her a question instead. "Did you see that glint of light in his eyes?"

Shale was taken aback. "No."

"I have no idea how I did it," he finally told her. "When I saw a spark of light in his dead eyes, I simply acted."

He knew that such an ability would be more than useful against the Glee, but it had all happened in an instant. He had absolutely no idea how he had brought it about.

After a moment of silence, Kahlan circled an arm around his waist. "Can we please get out of this wretched place?"

Richard smiled down at her as he looked into her beautiful green eyes. "Sure."

"We can now safely be on our way to the Wizard's Keep," Shale said, still looking a bit shaken.

"We've been down here an awfully long time," Cassia said. "We need to get some food."

Berdine grinned. "I could eat."

90

On their way out of the vast maze that was the complication, they passed between two columns at the end of the corridor and entered a sizable area with dozens of glass spheres in iron brackets lighting a formal stone floor made of black and white marble squares. The walls had decorative tiles. To each side there were a pair of white marble columns supporting tall arches with ornate carving. Richard knew that although it was a node, this one was a benign junction in the spell-form.

As the group crossed the large area and then passed between the two columns on the opposite side where the corridor continued on, something made Richard lag behind and then look back up over his left shoulder to where he could see through the tall arch to a part of the upper level where it crossed the lower one they were on.

A single Glee stood there in that gallery, looking down, watching. Somehow, Richard had known it would be there.

As the others continued on, carrying with them the soft murmur of conversation, Richard slowed to a stop and stared up at the dark figure. He realized that it hadn't been watching all of them. It had only appeared to watch Richard. Its third eyelid blinked as they stared at each other.

Richard couldn't help simply standing there, looking up at the still figure, the way it stood still looking down at him. He wondered if it could be the same individual he had seen on several previous occasions.

Almost as if in answer to the question in Richard's mind, the Glee bowed its head. Richard was stunned to see it do so. It made no hostile move. It didn't give him any other indication of its intentions, only that single bow, almost as if out of… respect.

And then it simply turned to scribbles and vanished back to its own world.

Left standing there staring up at an empty upper level, Richard had absolutely no idea what the sighting could possibly mean, but he felt a deep conviction that it had, in fact, been the same individual he had seen before. Of course, he had no way to know for sure. But if it really was the same one, he had now seen this particular Glee three times. The previous time it had spread its claws to show him that they were webbed. This time, it didn't. It bowed its head instead. On none of those occasions had it shown any sign that it intended to attack.

If anything, Richard felt that on each occasion it had simply been observing him. Each time Richard had spotted the lone Glee, it had been after he had killed large numbers of its kind. And yet it did not try to attack him. This time, though, it showed up after they had killed the witch man. The thought occurred to him that not only was it a witch man, but a witch man who had made some kind of pact with the Golden Goddess.

He wondered if it could be an observer for the Golden Goddess, reporting back on any observed weakness. So far, all it had to report was a lot of dead Glee and now a dead witch.

Another thought occurred to him that ran a chill up his spine. It made him momentarily stop dead.

"Richard?"

He blinked and looked down at the corridor to see Kahlan standing there, turned halfway back, waiting for him.

He immediately trotted to catch up with her. As exhausted as she was, she managed to flash him her special smile. As exhausted as he was, he couldn't help returning a smile, even if he didn't think he could in any way match the radiance of hers. It warmed his heart to see that smile, her beautiful face, the love in her eyes.

He took her hand and hurried to catch up with the others at a shorter archway complex held up by polished but dusty marble pillars to either side. Just beyond were four openings in a wall of rough stone.

"Which way, Lord Rahl?" Vika asked. The gash on her forehead had stopped bleeding, but her face was still a mask of blood. It matched her red leather.

Richard gestured. "The one in the middle."

She looked toward the wall and then frowned back at him. "There are four openings. There is no middle one."

Richard nodded toward the openings. "Take the second from the right. Once into the darkness where you can't see it yet, it forks. The others don't. That makes five passageways. Take the left fork and that will be the middle one. It's a concealed shortcut."

Vika shook her head. "Only the Lord Rahl could see what no one else can."

"It's not magic. I saw the plans beforehand."

"So did I," Vika said. "All I remember of them is that it was a confusing mess."

"It isn't nearly so confusing for me but only because I understand spell-forms and the language of Creation."

"I hate magic," Berdine muttered.

The rest of the Mord-Sith nodded their fervent agreement.

Richard couldn't help smiling his joy that they had all survived.

"We'll be up and out of here shortly," he told them. "Then we can all get cleaned up. Vika, you can finally wash the blood off your face."

She shrugged her indifference. "I don't mind blood."

"Well, we are going to be up in the palace soon, where there will be other people. Seeing blood on a Mord-Sith in red leather scares people."

"As well it should," Vika said without a hint of humor.

These women were still mad, but he was encouraged that at times they showed glimmers of their humanity. At other times, though, they were simply stone-cold mad.

"What about getting to the Wizard's Keep?" Shale pressed. "The witch man is dead, so we can now safely leave the palace without having to worry about him sabotaging our cause in your absence. We need to be on our way at once. It's not safe for us here. The sooner we leave, the better. We can clean up later."

Richard sighed. "It would probably be best to get something to eat." He glanced at Berdine. She flashed him a smile. "It would also be good to get a proper night's rest."

He hooked a thumb behind his belt as he considered. "But with the extreme danger of the Glee attacking us unexpectedly while we're still here, that would not be the safest thing to do." He tipped his head toward Shale. "You have a good point. If they discover that we're still here, they will continue their attacks. There is no telling how overpowering the next attack might be. We might not be able to stop them the next time. If they win just once, all is lost.

"The safest thing to do, the thing that would best protect Kahlan, the twins, and the future of our way of life, would be to do as we first intended when all this started and leave immediately in darkness."

"You mean the plan when Michec captured me?" Vika asked.

Richard nodded. "The threat from Moravaska Michec has been eliminated, but the threat from the Glee most definitely hasn't. We need to get back to our original plan of getting away from here and to the safety of the Keep."

"I think I should be able to gather horses and supplies this time without any nasty surprises," Vika said with a clear tone of relief.

"And I will make sure that we leave unseen so that the Glee won't know where we went," the sorceress said. "That should give us some breathing room."

"It should be well after dark by the time we can get the horses and supplies," Kahlan said. "While not the best for traveling, leaving in the dark would certainly help us evade any spying eyes."

"Let's get to it, then," Richard said, as he started ahead.

As they finally went through the last of the locked doors, the guards were there to greet them.

"Lord Rahl!" exclaimed the first one to see them. Along with the rest of the men, he stood up straight and tall as he saluted with a fist to his heart.

"I hope everything went well for you?" the man asked.

"We accomplished what we needed to do," Richard said without elaboration, locking the door behind them.

Berdine grinned at the guard. "We killed a witch."

He blinked in shock. "A witch? But how could a witch possibly get in there?"

Richard handed the man the keys Michec had been using. "As it happens, he was also a pickpocket."

91

By the time they made the long walk through the public areas of the palace where they had to worry about being seen by the goddess through the eyes of all the people in the halls, then along the routes hidden from the public where they didn't have to worry about the goddess seeing them, and then they were finally back up at the stables, it was deep in the night. After the ordeal down in the complication, they were all exhausted, but escaping without the Glee knowing that they were gone—or where they had gone—was more important than sleep. They were all eager to make good their escape sight unseen and be on their way.

None of them talked as they waited in hiding up at the stables. They were preoccupied with their own thoughts and no one was much in the mood to talk. They knew they had an ordeal ahead of them and dangers they couldn't yet imagine.

Vika rushed back behind the manure wagon and leaned down. "Everything is ready, Lord Rahl. Horses with supplies are gathered in the staging area. I told them that it was for a distant but routine patrol. I didn't want them to know it was for you."

Richard smiled. "Good thinking, Vika."

"Besides the travel food that will keep, the kitchens had just finished a late-night meal for staff, so I was able to get us some freshly cooked food for when we're able to stop."

Berdine grinned. "I guess you are a favorite to all of us today."

Richard ignored Berdine and looked back over his shoulder at Shale. "All right. Do what you need to do to hide us from the men in the stables so we can leave unseen."

Shale gave him a look that was part witch woman and part sorceress.

"What do you think I've been doing? I wanted to make sure we weren't discovered waiting back here. We can go anytime. They won't so much as notice us. Even if the Golden Goddess searches their minds, there will be nothing of us there for her to find or see. We just have to be sure not to linger, lest the spell wear off."

Kahlan leaned in. "Is there anything special we need to do? Anything we need to wait for?"

"No," Shale said as she stood. "We can mount up and be on our way. But the spell won't last long."

The witch woman walked out into the open and past a man headed to one of the stables. The rest of them cautiously followed her toward the waiting horses, feeling more than obvious. Richard looked around as they made their way across the grounds, but none of the stable workers appeared to notice them. They walked right past a man carrying rakes and shovels toward the first building. The man was whistling softly to himself and didn't even look up.

When they reached the horses, they all checked the gear, and made sure the saddle girth straps were tight. They tested the security of the saddlebags and the sacks tied to each of the horses. The horses seemed calm. They were used to late-night patrols.

Richard hooked an unstrung bow and a quiver stuffed with arrows on the back of the saddle of one of the larger horses. When he was finished checking that everything was secure, he moved forward, keeping his hand on the side of the horse so it would know where he was. He spoke softly to it and finally stroked its neck. The horse tossed its head in response, as if to say, "Let's go." It was hard to tell in the weak light of lanterns hanging on the fronts of buildings, but the animal looked black.

Kahlan stroked the nose of the mare right behind, then scratched its forehead. It whinnied softly and nuzzled its head against her in appreciation of her gentle touch.

All of the others made similar quick introductions and, once done, mounted up. They all urged their horses ahead at a quick walk through an arched opening in a nearby inner wall. As they rode, Shale, swaying gently in the saddle in tune with her horse's movements, held her hands out to the sides, palms up. She had already told Richard not to worry, that she wouldn't fall off, that the horse would watch out for her safety. She assured them that it was what she needed to do to be sure that no one saw them.

After they went through the massive gates in the outer wall, they finally emerged at the road leading down the side of the plateau. The walls of the palace soared overhead. Richard slowed his horse to get closer to the witch woman. Her eyes were closed as she rode with her hands held out to the sides.

"We're starting down, now," he told her as he placed his horse strategically between her and the edge of the cliff.

"I know," she answered, sounding unconcerned.

It made him a bit nervous to see her ride with her eyes closed and not holding on to anything, although her body moved fluidly with the rhythm of the horse's gait. As they made the first switchback turn in the road that wound its way along the nearly sheer walls of the plateau, he looked over the edge, down into the darkness of the Azrith Plain far below.

"It's a long drop. Maybe you should keep your eyes open?"

"The horse knows where it's going," Shale murmured.

"But still… don't you want to watch to make sure your horse doesn't, I don't know, ride off the edge in the dark?"

"No. I'm afraid of heights. Better that I don't look."

Richard sighed. "Have it your way. Not much to see in the dark, anyway. But we're going to be at the drawbridge soon. We don't want those men to recognize us."

"Send one of the Mord-Sith ahead to tell the soldiers to lower the bridge for a patrol," Shale instructed. "When we go past them, they will see only soldiers on their way out to patrol. They will not recognize us or remember what we look like."

Richard called Rikka forward and told her to do what Shale said, then he hurried his horse to catch up with Kahlan. Rikka rode out ahead of them to have the soldiers lower the drawbridge. He could see it in the distance, lit by a series of lanterns.

As they rode across it, their horses' hooves clopped over the heavy wooden planks. A few of the men casually tapped a fist to their hearts. It was a greeting to fellow soldiers on their way out on patrol and not at all the more formal way they would have saluted superiors, especially the Lord Rahl. Richard was glad to see by that casual salute that none of the men recognized them.

It wasn't long before they left the lamplight on the bridge far behind. The light from the palace high above them at least showed enough of the road to keep them from stepping off into a dark void.

By the time they reached the bottom of the plateau and the road leveled out onto the flat ground, Richard had finally started to relax a bit. As they rode out onto the Azrith Plain, Shale at last lowered her arms and opened her eyes.

Richard looked back over his shoulder to see the sprawling People's Palace atop the enormous plateau. It seemed to blot out half the sky. Walls, towers, and ramparts rose up impossibly high. Torches, lanterns, and fires lit the palace. That firelight reflected off the low clouds enough to keep the darkness from being total.

While there wasn't light enough to make out much of the features of the flat terrain and sparse vegetation, there was enough for him to see the shadowed shapes of everyone with him atop their horses. He was glad for that little bit of light, because he wanted to make sure that they stayed close together and that none of them accidentally became separated. They needed to stay together.

While the heavy cloud cover did reflect a little light, the farther they went the darker it became out on the vast plain. The only thing he could see well was the glowing palace in the distance behind them. He didn't like riding horses in the dark, because if they happened to step in a hole, they could break a leg, but with the little bit of reflected light off the clouds, he thought it was an acceptable risk and one they had to take, at least until it got too dark to continue.

They kept on riding in silence for a time after the palace was no longer visible behind them. He knew that they all felt a sense of vulnerability out in the flat, open country, but Richard wanted to make absolutely sure that they would be far enough out of sight of anyone up in the palace looking out over the plain, so he kept them moving ahead.

When he was just able to make out some kind of feature ahead of them, some distortion in the ground, he dismounted and had everyone do the same, then walked his horse forward rather than let it ride blindly into possible trouble. As he walked carefully ahead, he could just make out that the ground dropped away into some kind of shallow gully, but he couldn't see it as well as he'd like.

"Shale, can you light a small flame so we can see what this is?"

She handed the reins of her horse into the care of one of the Mord-Sith, and then she came forward. When she lit a small flame above her upturned palm, it was just enough to see the lay of the land. Slightly to the right, the ground slumped away, leading down to the bottom of what looked like a wash worn through dry ground by flash floods.

With Shale providing that small flame for light, they all filed down into the gully.

"This area is low enough that if there is anyone in the surrounding area, they won't be able to see us," he told them.

"Should we look for material for a fire?" Cassia asked.

"No," Richard said. "A fire would reflect off the clouds and reveal our location. Anyone near would also be able to smell the smoke. We can light some travel candles to see by so we can have something to eat. If memory serves me, I think Berdine is hungry."

Everyone laughed.

"Well, I admit," she said, "the aroma of that fried chicken has been driving me crazy."

After they broke out small candles in tin carrying housings, Shale lit them all, and they used the meager light to scout the area. A small stream through the gully bordered with scraggly vegetation and a few clumps of grass provided a place to picket the horses and finally gave them the opportunity to clean up and tend to wounds. The horses had eaten back at the stables only hours before, so Richard decided to save their valuable oats for when needed. After the horses were unsaddled, they munched on what clumps of grass they were able to find.

Once they found a suitable place to sit, they all gathered close together around a few of the travel candles, then eagerly unpacked the food. It was still warm and smelled wonderful.

Richard was well past tired, and he knew the others were as well, but he was hungry.

"We need to set up watches," he told them. There were still dangers to be worried about. "Two people on each watch. That should let us all get a halfway decent sleep."

"There are nine of us," Kahlan said. "How do you want to manage that uneven division?"

"You're pregnant. You don't need to stand watch. You need the sleep for the twins."

Kahlan opened her mouth, about to protest, but her better judgment apparently got the better of her. She pushed her long hair back over her shoulder. "All right. As tired as I am, I'm not going to argue. Neither are the twins."

Richard smiled to himself at the thought of them. "Vika, you and I can take first watch. Then however the rest of you want to divide up is fine."

They all grunted their agreement as they ate chicken.

"Can you pass me some of that hard cheese?" Kahlan asked.

Richard looked up from his piece of fried chicken. He finished chewing a mouthful and then swallowed.

"I like cheese," he said, "but you hate cheese."

"I know," she said, seemingly unable to explain it, "but for some reason I'm really hungry for cheese."

"Cravings," Shale said with a smile.

Richard looked over at the sorceress. "What?"

Shale gestured with the bones of a chicken wing toward Kahlan. "She's pregnant. She is having cravings."

Richard blinked at the sorceress. "But she hates cheese."

Shale's smile widened. "Well, apparently, at least one of her babies likes it."

92

As dawn broke in the east, they all ate a quick breakfast to finish off the chicken. The low clouds let rays of light through a band of sky at the horizon. The bottoms of the clouds turned pink at first, then gradually a deep purple.

Kahlan was eager to have another piece of cheese. She knew she hated cheese, but for some reason it tasted wonderful. She couldn't explain it. She supposed that Shale was right that at least one of her babies had a taste for it. As she ate it, she rubbed her belly.

"This is for you," she told them.

After they had packed up their bedrolls and gear, they saddled their horses while Vale and Cassia were off on a short scouting patrol to make sure there were no surprises lurking about. One of them went off in each direction to check the gully, since that was the only place where they couldn't see for miles, unlike the rest of the desolate Azrith Plain. It was a quick reconnaissance and they both returned to report seeing nothing and finding no footprints. While many people came to the People's Palace from all over much of D'Hara, in the direction they were headed across the Azrith Plain the land was deserted and there was no civilization before reaching the Midlands.

As Kahlan struggled to lift her saddle up over her mare's back, Richard rushed over to help. Kahlan was strong. It seemed odd to her that she was having trouble lifting her saddle. She decided that with all they had been through down in the complication, the encounter with Michec, and having only a short sleep, she was simply tired.

Richard stepped in beside her, taking the saddle out of her hands. "Here, let me help lift that."

He hoisted the saddle up onto her mare, and she got to put a hand on his back as he pulled the strap underneath and tightened it. She was glad for the chance to touch him, to feel a connection to him. After all that they had nearly lost, it was reassuring to touch him and see him smile. Though it was going to be a long journey, it would be a joyous one to not only be away from the constant threat of attack but to be with Richard.

She grinned as she looked up into his gray eyes. "We're going to have babies."

He bent and kissed her. "I will always protect them, and you. We'll teach them to be good people. I promised you a golden age and I still intend to keep that promise."

Darkness unexpectedly crept into her thoughts. "What about the Golden Goddess? Maybe you are mistaken and that is the golden age that is coming. She is in another world. How can we possibly defeat her? How can we stop her from coming for our children?"

Richard sighed, his smile fading with the change of subject. He didn't have an answer, so he didn't try to lie to her.

"I promised you I will protect them, and I will."

"I know. You will think of something," she said, forcing cheerfulness into her voice, trying to sound optimistic and bring back his smile. "I know you will."

His smile made a brief reappearance.

She gazed out toward the still-dark horizon to the west after she saw that the others looked like they were about ready to leave. "Which direction?"

Richard took a quick look off into the distance to the dark horizon. "Aydindril is northwest from here as the crow flies. That would be the obvious choice, but with a formidable mountain range lying across the straightest route from here to Aydindril, mountains where the boundary once stood when we were growing up, that's a problem. The boundary may be gone, but these mountains still present a formidable barrier."

Kahlan shuddered at the mention of the boundary. When it had come down, it had unleashed Darken Rahl and the might of D'Hara on the Midlands. It had been the end of a long peace, the end of all the other Confessors, and the beginning of a horrific war. But the boundary coming down had also brought her to be with Richard. The world was so different now, but those mountains reminded her of the way things used to be.

"It's possible we could find a way across those mountains," Richard said, "but if we found a pass, it would be a dangerous crossing. Any high pass across that range would likely mean we would need to abandon the horses at some point. And that's if we can find a such a pass.

"It's also possible we could wander around in those mountains and never find a way across. Much of that range rises thousands of feet in nearly sheer rock walls. While it would theoretically be the shortest distance to Aydindril, I think trying to go that way would mean we would have to go on foot, spend a lot of time only to come to impassable cliffs, and even if we eventually found a way over it would end up taking longer. Not only that, but like I said, if we can find a pass up in those mountains, it's likely to be dangerous."

Kahlan stared off to the west. She knew those mountains, and she knew he was right. "It's the heat of summer down here, but high up in those mountains weather could be a big problem."

He nodded as he checked a saddle strap under the stirrups and then tipped his head more toward the left. "Southwest will get us to the Kern River. There will be a road along the river. It would provide an easier way over into the Midlands. It's longer, but easier traveling and a lot less of a risk."

Kahlan sighed as she looked toward the northwest, toward her home, toward the Confessors' Palace, where she had been born, and where the Wizard's Keep waited. She hadn't realized how much she missed home. Now that they were going to Aydindril, she felt a sense of excitement to get there. The idea of having her children born where she had been born sounded wonderful to her.

"If we go too far south to cross the Kern we will end up in the Wilds." She lifted an eyebrow at him. "You know what that's like."

Richard grimaced as he nodded. "Well, maybe if we spot any possible gaps in the mountain range, we can find a way across long before we have to go that far south."

Kahlan nodded. "And if we can find a way across the mountains before we have to go too far south, we will end up in populated parts of the Midlands, where we can get any supplies we need. That will make our travel easier. Even if we do have to abandon the horses to get across, we can get horses in those lands."

"There is that," he said. "But don't forget, we need to stay out of sight of people as much as possible."

"You're right." Kahlan sighed. "It sounds like for now we need to head southwest through the desolate parts of D'Hara to get beyond at least the largest of the mountains. To the south they aren't as formidable as they are up here to the north."

"We will stay as close to the mountains as practical but still in areas that allow us to make good time. That way, I may be able to find a way over the mountains and into the Midlands sooner rather than later. Once we cross over, we can head north to Aydindril." He smiled at her. "If there is a pass, I'll find it. I am a woods guide, after all."

Kahlan returned the smile. "I guess we have a plan for now."

As eager as she was to get to the Keep, she knew they had to be smart about it. There was a lot of wild and dangerous country between them and where they needed to go.

"Everyone ready?" Richard called out.

Shale climbed up in her saddle after confirming that she was ready. The Mord-Sith mounted up, also letting him know that they were ready. When Kahlan saw Nyda yawn, it made her yawn, too.

In short order they were on their way. They rode up out of the gully and then headed southwest across the featureless plain for the rest of the day. As the sun started to sink off to their right, Kahlan was just able to make out a ragged, pale blue line of mountains in the distance, outlined by the sun as it sank behind them. She guessed those mountains would still be a number of days' ride if they went directly northwest, toward Aydindril, but with the way they were heading to the southwest to skirt the highest of those mountains, it would likely be many days before they were close to the long spine of the mountain range where Richard could start looking for a way over it. The sooner he could find a way, the shorter their journey would be and the sooner they would reach the safety of the Keep.

The frustrating thing was that they were going farther away from Aydindril all the time because the imposing mountain range prevented a more direct route. She told herself it couldn't be helped.

As tired as she was, it made Kahlan feel good to at least be headed home, even if indirectly, and, hopefully, the worry of the Glee would be left behind them.

It excited her to be heading home with her two unborn children of D'Hara. She hoped to raise them for a good part of their childhood where she'd grown up, where she had first discovered the excitement of the natural world around her.

As they rode, she couldn't keep her mind from drifting back to thoughts of Michec, when she had been hanging from the manacles as he was about to skin her, and the threat that the Glee were going to rip her babies from her womb.

Unexpectedly, the memory of the glint she had seen in the dead witch man's eyes just before Richard burned him to ash began to haunt her as she rode.

Witches had a way of never letting you feel entirely free of their reach.

93

Kahlan laid the reins down on her horse's neck and then rested her wrists on the saddle horn. She sat quietly, waiting, as Richard stared off at something. They had been riding since first light, and she was getting saddle-sore. As she waited, she put her hands on her sides and stretched in both directions as best she could.

Whatever it was he was staring at had Richard looking troubled, so much so that his behavior was beginning to spook her. She didn't like it when he turned quiet like this. It usually meant trouble.

A light mist tingled against her face, feeling like icy little sparkles. The weather had been gloomy for the past three weeks. Or was it four? The monotony of it was getting to be mind-numbing. Somehow, she felt as if she was losing count of the days as they made their way endlessly through a quiet wood of tall pine and fir on their way southwest.

Soft streamers of hazy light angled down in long shafts among the towering tree trunks, illuminating the veils of mist floating in the occasional breath of gentle breeze. Here and there small stretches of granite ledges broke up through the forest floor. A light fog moved silently among some of the fern beds between the rock outcroppings. The towering canopies of the trees left it somber and deathly quiet down on the forest floor. Because of the perpetual shade, little brush grew, leaving the ground open among the trees.

Down where they were, with the thick canopy so far above them, not even the wind reached them. While it was quiet now, she had on some days heard the distant sound of the wind gusting far above them. Sometimes, in the drizzle, the only sound was water that collected on the pine needles letting go and dripping down to splatter on the large leaves of moose maples. She was tired of huddling under rain gear.

It never kept them completely dry, making for miserable travel. She ached for the warmth of sunlight.

Everyone else waited behind Richard and Kahlan as he silently studied something. She was getting impatient.

"You know, for some reason, I feel like I've seen that rock before," Kahlan said to break the silence. She swiped accumulated mist off her brow. As she flicked the water off her finger, she gestured ahead. "That one there, the one that looks like a big nose on the side. It looks familiar."

Richard finally turned a troubled look back toward her. "That's because you have seen it before. This is the third time we've come this way."

Kahlan blinked in disbelief. Richard grew up as a woods guide. The forest had been his home for much of his life. He didn't lose his bearings in the woods.

"How is that possible?"

He turned away toward the rock again. "I don't know."

"What's the problem?" Shale asked from behind them.

Richard stood in the stirrups and looked back at the others. "Do any of you recognize this place?"

Baffled, Berdine glanced around. "Recognize it? How could we? Trees all look the same. How could we possibly recognize one place from another?"

Nyda looked about. "The woods all look the same to me, too."

The rest of the Mord-Sith all nodded their agreement. Mord-Sith weren't exactly familiar with forests, so Kahlan wasn't surprised they thought that trees all looked the same.

"So what's going on?" Shale asked, clearly getting impatient.

Rather than answer her question, he asked her one instead. "What direction are we heading?"

Perplexed, Shale lifted an arm to point out ahead. "Southwest. We've been heading southwest for weeks."

"I don't know a whole lot about the woods," Cassia said, "but I'm pretty good with direction. Shale is right. We've been heading southwest the whole time. Straight as an arrow," she added.

Shale regarded him with a curious look, sensing that something was amiss. "Do you for some reason think differently?"

"No," Richard said, "I agree, we've been heading southwest for a long time."

"So what's the problem?" the sorceress asked.

"The problem is, despite going in the same direction the whole time, straight as an arrow, as Cassia put it, this is at least the third time we've been in this exact same spot. Without a road or path, we are moving randomly among the trees, so even traveling in a big circle we wouldn't necessarily come across the exact same ground. Yet this time we did. If fact, this is the third time we have been in this same place in the woods."

The Mord-Sith, now alert, all looked around. Shale rode her horse forward, closer to Richard and Kahlan.

"What are you talking about? That's impossible."

Richard gestured ahead. "Do you recognize that rock?"

Shale wet her lips as she hesitated. "As a matter of fact, I might. I seem to remember it because it looks like a nose growing out of the left side."

"You mean we've been traveling around in a big circle?" Vika asked as she rode her horse up on the other side of Richard.

He nodded. "I believe so."

"We can't afford to waste time riding around in circles." Shale was beginning to sound more than a little aggravated, as if she thought he was doing it deliberately. "I thought you were a woodsman, or something."

"Or something." Richard sighed as he laid both wrists over the horn of his saddle. "All I can tell you is that as far as I know, we have been riding southwest for weeks, but this is at least the third time we've come across this rock. That can only mean that we are traveling in circles."

Shale glanced around suspiciously. "Well, have you seen hoof prints from all our horses to confirm your suspicion? If we've been here before, there should be some signs to confirm it."

Richard shook his head unhappily. "No, I haven't. But I know we've been in this spot before. I can't explain it, but I'm telling you, we are somehow going in circles."

"Maybe it just looks like another rock we saw before," Berdine suggested. "The rocks all have different shapes, but a lot of them are kind of similar-looking—like the trees. Maybe this one only looks similar to ones that you've seen before."

He gestured around at the woods. "Look at the type of forest we're in. It never changes."

Berdine wrinkled up her expression at what he could be talking about. "Of course not. Woods are woods. They all look the same."

"No they don't," Richard said with quiet disagreement. "At least, they shouldn't. As you travel you move into different areas. Vegetation changes. Trees grow different sizes with different soil conditions. Rocks and the terrain change from time to time. Sometimes windfalls will create openings for a meadow, or a tree nursery to spring to life. But the woods we've been in have not changed since about the time we entered them."

"Now that you mention it," Kahlan said, "the woods have been looking pretty much just like this for weeks, now. That is odd. We should be getting somewhere, but it doesn't seem like we are."

Richard nodded. "That's because we are somehow riding in a big circle."

"Well, except for the first day, it has been cloudy and drizzly for the entire time," Vika said. "It has been too overcast to see for sure where the sun is in the sky, and down here, under the cover of trees, it is even harder to tell."

"You're right, but the sun isn't the only way to tell direction," Richard said. "More than that, though, something feels wrong."

Shale squinted at him. "Like what? What are you suggesting?"

Richard sighed as he shook his head. "Maybe it's been too long since I've been in the woods. Maybe my skills have gotten rusty and something is confusing my sense of direction."

Kahlan thought that highly improbable, but she didn't want to say it out loud.

94

After another week of long days of traveling, or maybe it was longer, Kahlan couldn't remember for sure, they again arrived at the same rock that looked like it had a nose on the side of it. This time, though, they were positive it was the same rock, because the last time they had been there Richard had scraped a big X on the side of the nose. When they saw that X again, everyone's heart sank. No one doubted any longer that they were indeed traveling in a big circle, and no one had an explanation, least of all Richard.

The only good thing was that they had seen no other people, although that might have been a welcome relief, and importantly, they had seen no sign of the Glee.

"All right," Richard said, "I don't know how this can be possible. It makes no sense, but it makes less sense to keep doing what clearly isn't working. We have to do something different."

Kahlan could see how frustrated he was. "Like what?"

"There are a number of ways to make sure you are maintaining your direction of travel. The best way is to use landmarks to keep you on course. A prominent ridge or mountain are a good way to keep your bearings. Even high ground can give you sight of some landmark to use, even a distinctive tree. But in these woods, we can't see anything like that. We're going to have to do something else."

Berdine made a face. "What else is there to do then? With the clouds we can't be sure of the direction of the sun. We can't see any kind of landmark except these trees, and they all look the same."

Richard didn't argue the last point. "We are going to have to use plot lines to make sure we are going in a straight line. These woods are fairly open, the ground is relatively flat, and without much vegetation down low we can see for quite a long distance."

"How does that help us?" Vika asked.

"There are nine of us. That is an advantage we can use. We need to spread out in a straight line. When the last person in line can see at least the next two are lined up in a perfectly straight line ahead, then the next person goes out ahead. Guided by hand signals, they will go left or right so that the ones behind can ensure that they are positioned in a straight line and that the people in front of them are always in a direct line of sight. Everyone has to be lined up with at least three people visible ahead to make sure our line is straight.

"Once all of us are strung out in what we know to be a straight line, then the last person in line can go forward and take the lead, with the first few of us in line making sure they are positioned properly on that straight plot line. In that way we keep leapfrogging a line that we know to be straight, and we can keep it straight going forward.

"I don't know what the problem is, but for some reason these woods are confusing us—confusing me—and we aren't traveling in a straight direction. I don't know the cause, but this should solve the problem. It will be slower traveling, at least for a while, but once we get beyond this problem area, we should be able to spot landmarks. When we do, then things will return to normal."

Shale gazed around at the woods as if scrutinizing them for the source of trouble. "Do you think it could be magic of some sort causing this strange aberration?"

"I don't know what the problem is," Richard said. "But by doing this we should be able to get beyond this troublesome area to where we need to be traveling, no matter the cause. That's the solution."

Once they had a plan, they wasted no time in implementing it. Richard was right, it did slow down their progress, but going around in circles was not really progress. Kahlan was glad that everyone seemed pleased by this new tactic. It also relieved the monotony of the long days of travel only to keep discovering that they weren't getting anywhere.

After they kept leapfrogging along their line for a number of days, Kahlan noticed that the terrain began to change. There were more rock outcroppings and they were larger, indicating that they were making it out of the strange woods. They eventually came to a small lake they had never seen before. After being in under the gloomy canopy for so long, they were all relieved to look out over the water and up at the open sky.

They dismounted by the shore to have a quick meal and a brief rest. Kahlan sat close to Richard. They were all relieved to simply be able look out at a new landscape as they ate some travel biscuits and dried meat.

Farther on, they came to some deadfall that again opened up the forest to the sky. The heavy clouds persisted, but at least the rain and mist had stopped.

The next morning, Richard took a deer with a clean shot with his bow. It took some time to skin and clean the deer, but they were all eager to give up a morning of travel in order to have some needed fresh meat. Travel biscuits and dried meat were getting old.

After riding for the rest of the afternoon and as darkness began to gather, they finally stopped to make camp for the night. Kahlan was more than relieved to finally be able to get down out of the saddle. She walked around a bit to get the circulation moving better in her legs. Her pregnancy was beginning to make riding a horse uncomfortable.

As with every night so far, even though they were at last in a seemingly new place, there was no especially good defensive place to camp, so they had to again settle on a flat place among the trees. After picketing the horses and giving them some oats, they all trampled down the ferns and scraped the ground clear of forest debris to make spots for their bedrolls. There had been ample small streams for water whenever they made camp in the strange woods. Fortunately, now that they were out of those woods, all the recent rains meant that the streams were both plentiful and full.

"Why is it, do you suppose," Shale asked as she trampled some of the small plants, "that we came to that same rock again, with your mark on it, but we have never come across one of our campsites again? Doesn't that strike you as odd?"

Kahlan could tell that Richard's patience was wearing thin, and he had a time keeping his composure at the question.

"Your guess is as good as mine," he finally told her. "I need to collect wood."

The Mord-Sith noticed his quiet annoyance and busied themselves with clearing the ground for a place for the fire and collecting stones to make a fire ring. Kahlan knew they were all hungry, but no one said so. The mood was tense and none of them wanted to test Richard. For that matter, neither did Kahlan. She knew that something was bothering him.

Richard stacked wood for a fire over strips of birch bark and small sticks wiped on pine sap for kindling. He looked up at Shale and gestured. She knew what he meant and, with a flick of her hand, ignited a healthy flame in among the kindling. After the fire was burning hot he added new wood and after a time raked some of the glowing coals to the side and used them to cook some of the meat.

They used their knives to make long, sharp poles from young saplings in order to skewer and cook pieces of meat. Richard sliced off generous portions of the venison backstrap. It was the tenderest cut and everyone was eager to eat, but they merely said thanks when Richard handed each of them a piece and stuck them on their skewers. He set a number of chunks aside for anyone who wanted more. A few of the Mord-Sith hardly charred the outside of their pieces before sinking their teeth into the meat. They all moaned with pleasure and rolled their eyes at the taste.

The meal did as much for everyone's spirits as it did for their stomachs.

95

Thank you, Lord Rahl," Vika said, "for providing us this meal."
"Yes, thank you," Berdine added. "It's delicious!"

Between chewing, the rest of them chimed in with their thanks. Even Shale voiced her gratitude. Richard didn't say anything, but he did smile at them all, even if Kahlan thought it looked forced. Now that it seemed they were finally moving into new territory, no longer in the strange wood, and back on course, as well as having a good meal, everyone was feeling better.

"Although we've spent a great deal of time with you," Richard said to Shale without looking up, "we actually don't know much about you. Are your parents still alive?"

Kahlan instantly went on alert. His recent mood suddenly made sense to her. Although it was an innocent enough question, and no one else would have thought it was anything unusual, she recognized the subtle difference in Richard's tone of voice. That single question told her that Richard had asked that question not to make casual conversation, but as the Seeker.

It also told her that he knew the answer before asking the question. She didn't know what he was up to, but she knew she would find out soon enough.

Shale's gaze shifted uneasily among the rest of the group gathered close in around the warmth of the fire. The nights were getting colder and the wet chill seemed to go right to Kahlan's bones. The only real relief she got from shivering was when she could cuddle up against Richard during the nights.

"No," Shale finally answered. "My father passed a few years back." Her gaze drifted down to the flames. "My mother when I was younger."

Kahlan glanced around at all the faces watching the witch woman. "Mine too," she said into the uncomfortable silence. "My mother died when I was young. I know how terrible that is."

"Your mother was a witch woman, right?" Richard asked in a quiet voice, still without looking up. Again, Kahlan was aware that he already knew the answer, but for some reason he asked it anyway.

Shale nodded and devoted herself to pulling meat off with her teeth and then chewing. She clearly looked uneasy.

They all ate in silence for a short time.

"Tell me how your mother died," Richard said at last.

Kahlan glanced up. There it was.

She had been right about her instinct. This time, though, it was not a question, it was a command.

With their heads down, the Mord-Sith shifted their eyes among themselves. No one said a word. The death of a mother was not a pleasant subject for any of them, and not something they talked about. But they all recognized this as something different.

"What does it matter?" Shale finally said. "She's dead. That's all that really matters."

Richard didn't look up as he used a finger and thumb to pull a strip of meat from the chunk on the skewer.

"She was burned as a witch, wasn't she?"

Shale swallowed. "Lord Rahl..."

"Tell me what happened."

"Why do you wish to bring up such terrible memories?"

"Tell me what happened," he said in the same flat tone, still not looking up. The command in his words was clear, and Shale knew it.

Kahlan looked around at the Mord-Sith. They were all trying to look invisible. Except Berdine. She was watching attentively.

Kahlan reached over and put a hand on Shale's knee. "You are among friends. Sometimes it helps to talk about such things among those who care about you."

After a time, Shale finally let out a deep breath.

"All right." She leaned her skewer with a large chunk of meat ready to be eaten against a rock. "It was a harsh time in the Northern Waste.

The crops had done poorly, so there weren't going to be enough reserves for the coming winter.

"The migration of the caribou had moved too far away that year for some reason, and the hunts were unsuccessful. The rains had swollen the rivers, and so catching salmon, the way we usually did, didn't go nearly as well as usual. Ducks and geese were nowhere to be found. Elk, bighorns, black bear, antelope, deer were all scarce. Even the rabbit population had been nearly wiped out by people desperate for food.

"It is said that such times come along every once in a while. The animals seem to know it will be an especially harsh winter, so they change their usual habits." She shrugged. "It is the way of nature. The animals for some reason pick a different route, a route they think will be better, or start sooner, and as a result the people in the place where I lived couldn't find enough meat or fish to salt or smoke for the winter.

"My father went to try to see what he could do to help. You know, go to other places to try to barter for meat, offer his services in return for supplies we badly needed. My mother was a healer, so she stayed to take care of people.

"My father had a hard time finding any kind of help anywhere close, as they were having similar troubles, so he had to travel farther. He was gone for a long time. So long that people thought he had left for good. People started to whisper that he had run away from my mother."

Shale stared off for a time before going on. "Rumors fed on themselves. Gossip led to yet more gossip, all the time getting wilder with ludicrous ideas."

"That's a dangerous stew," Richard said. "So then they started to say that it was all because of a witch woman in their midst?"

Shale smiled sadly. "Yes. They said that she drove all the animals far away. Other gossip said that her incantations and spells had deliberately driven the fowl and fish away." She looked up briefly. "My mother didn't do 'incantations,' but that made no difference to them. They said she did and so people believed it."

"Why would they think she would do that?" Berdine asked. "You know, chase the animals away. If she was a healer and helped them, why would they think she would do such a thing?"

Shale shrugged self-consciously as she rubbed her arms. "My mother had always cared for their needs. She was a kindhearted woman. Too kind. They began to see her kindness as somehow sinister. They said she was devious, hiding her cruelty behind a smile and her offers to help, when really, she intended them harm.

"As winter closed in, the rumors grew worse. They said that she had caused some of the new babies to be born dead, or their mothers to die in childbirth. They said that those things could only have been my mother's fault."

Kahlan slowly shook her head as she held the skewer over the fire, roasting another piece of meat. "Those aren't rare occurrences. Birth is a difficult process. Newborn babies don't always live, and mothers sometimes die in childbirth."

"True enough, but people refused to see it that way. Once they got it in their heads that it was a witch causing their troubles, there was no changing their minds. It was easy to blame her when there was no way to know the real cause. Soon, everything bad that happened had to be the witch's fault. There could be no other explanation, and none were sought or tolerated.

"My mother only had kindness in her heart and was horrified by the things they accused her of. She wept in despair. Her whole life, she had worked to show people that as a witch woman, she could be of help to them, that she could be a good part of their lives, that witch women needn't be feared. She always taught me that as witch women it was our duty to serve the needs of others, that we must devote ourselves to their betterment.

"She didn't believe it was necessary or much use to argue with people. Quarreling wasn't in her nature, and besides, she was aware that it would do no good. She had done good and expected her actions to be enough proof of her true nature. When she didn't wish to argue with people to deny the accusations, they somehow saw that as proof that she was guilty. When she finally did deny some of the more horrific accusations, they somehow saw that as proof of wackiness. Nothing my mother said would dissuade them of their beliefs."

She fell silent and stared into the flames, into the memories.

"So they burned her alive," Richard said.

Those words jolted Kahlan. This was where the Seeker had been headed. She just didn't yet know why.

Shale nodded as she continued to stare into the flames. After a moment she cleared her throat.

"There came an unexpected warm spell that lasted weeks. During that unusual weather people started coming down with a sickness they had never seen before. Some of the weaker people, old people, and infants died in delirium from the fevers. They wouldn't allow my mother to attend to the sick, saying that she was actually the cause of it. With every death, anger grew.

"In the middle of a dark night, they showed up and dragged my mother and me out of our home." Shale glanced up. "I was a witch woman, too, after all. I was being trained in the evil ways of a witch by my mother, they said. Everyone was yelling and screaming to kill the witches. I was terrified.

"My mother pleaded with them—calling most by name, as she had healed many of them at one time or another, saved many of their lives before, birthed their children—that she would admit to anything they wanted if they would simply leave me be.

"They were having none of it. They said both of us were witches and we both needed to burn.

"They threw me in a wood box, where firewood was stored, and nailed it shut to make sure I didn't get away until after they were finished with my mother and could come back for me. The sides had open slats for air circulation, so I could see out. Inside that dark box, crammed in atop the firewood, I watched what they did. I can still remember the smell of that firewood box.

"The men tied my mother to a long wooden rail and made her wait there on the cold, wet ground, helpless, as they built a huge, roaring fire in the center of town. The whole time she called them out by name, begging them to spare her daughter. That was all she cared about. While the men built the fire, women surrounded her, calling her names as they spit on her.

"And then three or four men lifted each end of the wooden rail and walked it over to the roaring fire. As everyone cheered, they heaved that rail with my mother tied helpless to it atop the blaze.

"In my dreams, I still hear her screams."

Shale stopped then, working to maintain her composure.

"Then, after my mother's screams finally stopped, they came for me…"

Shale stopped there, and it seemed she might not go on as she stared into the flames, seeing dark memories. Her face was stone.

"Then," she finally said, "I taught them why they should fear witches."

"How many of them did you kill?" Richard asked.

Shale shrugged. "I didn't keep a count. Once I broke out of that box, with my mother dead, I knew my life had changed forever. Her lessons of kindness had earned the hatred of people and gotten her murdered.

"I first took down the ones who had been guarding me to make sure I didn't escape. Once I started on the rest, some managed to run and get away. But I knew who they all were. After I finished with those I caught near the fire, I hunted down every last person who had taken part in murdering my mother. I saw to it that not one of them had an easy death."

Richard tossed another stick of wood in the fire. "And so that is why you can't burn a witch, not even one as evil as Michec."

Shale nodded slowly as she stared into memories. "That is why."

"What happened when your father finally returned?" Kahlan asked.

Shale huffed. "What do you think happened? He was devastated. He didn't approve of what I had done, but he understood it. He was a hollow man after that. The life had gone out of him. His wife was dead and his daughter, the witch, had killed half the people in our town."

"What about everyone else after that?" Richard asked. "Not everyone took part in your mother's murder. And there were other people in the Northern Waste, other settled places. I presume you had to move, but you continued to live in the Waste."

Shale looked up at him, fire in her dark eyes. "After that, in the new places we moved to, I continued to help those in need. I healed people as my mother had taught me. I birthed babies. I attended the sick and did what I could when something could be done and comforted those for whom nothing could be done. I proved to people that I had a good side, a kind side.

"But from that day on, everyone in the Northern Waste knew the name Shale. What they hadn't realized when they burned my mother was that I was more than merely a witch woman, like my mother. I am also a sorceress, and that made me oh so much more dangerous.

"Needless to say, there were no more witch burnings. Those living in the Waste fear to even have that thought. Those in the Waste know that I am a witch in every sense, and more.

"They know that I don't live by their grace; they live by mine."

Bitterness soured Shale's expression. "You just don't understand what it is like to see your mother burned to death."

The witch woman stood, then, and walked off into the darkness.

96

Kahlan found Shale a short distance away, standing alone among a stand of birch trees, staring off into the darkness. She put a comforting hand on the witch woman's shoulder and gave it a gentle jostle.

"I'm sorry for all those terrible things that happened," Kahlan told her.

With her fingertips, Shale wiped a tear from under each eye. "Thank you. It's just that he doesn't understand what it's like to see your mother, a good woman who never harmed anyone, burned to death."

Kahlan leaned in and whispered. "Oh, but he does."

Shale shook her head as she looked over at Kahlan. "How could he?"

Kahlan squeezed with the hand on Shale's shoulder. "When Richard was a boy their house burned down. His mother burned to death inside. Richard couldn't save her."

Shale clearly looked shocked. "I had no idea."

"As with you, it's not a story one is eager to tell."

"Then why did he want me to tell it?"

Kahlan pursed her lips, trying to think how to explain it when she herself wasn't yet entirely sure.

"This is about something more," she finally said. "When I first met Richard, Darken Rahl had invaded the Midlands. I came looking for the help of a Seeker. Richard's grandfather was a wizard, but Richard never knew it. His grandfather also happened to be the great wizard who had long been the caretaker of the Sword of Truth, an ancient weapon of great power.

"I urged Richard's grandfather to name a new Seeker. Because of the great need, he finally agreed. To my shock, he gave the sword to

Richard and named him Seeker. Not because it was his choice, but, as he told me, because by Richard's actions and his life, he had revealed himself in a hundred little ways to be the one who had been born the true Seeker of Truth.

"That is how he came to have that ancient weapon and the title Seeker. The Sword of Truth is more than merely a weapon. It carries with it not only great power, but great responsibility that transcends the man alone. Only a true Seeker could understand that, and not use it merely to seek power for himself. That is how he came to be bonded to that singular blade.

"Richard always seeks to understand things, to seek answers. It's his nature, the way he was born, not something created in him by that weapon. The questions he asked you were not to hurt you, but because he needs answers to pieces of a larger puzzle.

"I don't know what that puzzle is—I often don't at first when he gets like this—but I do know we are all in grave danger and he sees something in the large picture about that danger that the rest of us don't see. He is seeking answers; he is not seeking to hurt you. You are part of that larger picture, and as such, part of the solution. He needs to know every facet of how you fit into it all.

"Richard knows very well that there are forces beyond life and death. Despite Michec being dead, Richard has concerns about the very real possibility of a threat of some kind, somehow surviving Michec's death. That is why he asked you to burn the witch man's body. He considered it essential.

"When you refused, that threw him off. It made no sense to him why you wouldn't do something that, in his mind, was so obviously necessary to ensure our safety. He is fighting—we are all fighting—against evil, and in that fight, there can be no quarter given, no mercy granted. He had to know why you refused so he can reassure himself that your reasons were sound.

"You just did that, and in so doing you showed us that you also fight evil, don't give quarter, and don't grant mercy to those who are undeserving."

It surprised Kahlan when Shale turned and gave her a hug. "Thank you, Mother Confessor, for explaining it to me in a way that I could understand, not the way he would have done it."

Kahlan smiled as they parted. "All of us—all nine of us—have lost our mothers when we were yet too young. The Mord-Sith all live with the horror of what was done to their mothers. Richard lives with the horror of his mother burning to death. My mother was lost to the horror of a terrible disease, but the loss hurts no less. We all lost our mothers and we all understand your pain. Never doubt that."

Shale nodded. "You are the Mother Confessor to us all, now."

Kahlan smiled. "Come on back and finish eating. You need your strength. We have a long and dangerous journey ahead of us. And, knowing Richard, he has more questions. Richard always has more questions. Sometimes it can be exasperating, but it is never done out of malice."

As they walked together back through the birch stand and into the flickering firelight, everyone watched the two of them return, but were apparently reluctant to ask what had happened.

Shale rubbed her hands together, hesitating before saying anything. "I didn't finish my story," she finally told Richard in a much calmer tone as she offered him a smile. "Would you like me to tell you the rest?"

He returned the smile. "I'd like that."

Shale took a deep breath as she sat again and folded her legs. "Well, not everyone where we lived had been a part of that mob. Many hid in their houses, afraid to speak up against those filled with bloodlust, afraid to be accused along with my mother, afraid to be treated the same by people possessed by such fanaticism."

Richard shifted his legs to get more comfortable. "Human beings have an infinite capacity for ignorance and intolerance. As a result, they can be profoundly dangerous. Others rightly fear them."

"Indeed that's what happened," Shale said as she held her hands out before the fire to get them warm. "I treated the people of the Waste with help and kindness, just as my mother taught me, but only when they merited it. I didn't hold against the innocent the sins of the guilty.

I treat each person for who they are. I treat evil people for what they are. It's as simple as that, and why I'm feared in the Northern Waste. Those who simply don't wish the help of a witch woman, I leave to themselves."

Richard smiled. "I, too, have met good people who didn't want anything to do with magic. That doesn't make them bad."

Shale couldn't help nodding at their shared experience with those who rejected or feared magic.

"News reached even the Northern Waste of the terrible things that had happened to the south of us. Fortunately, for the people there, we were far from the horrors of the war.

"From what I heard, though, I learned that you were one of those who fought against mindless brutality and hate, that as the Lord Rahl you fought that everyone might be able to live their own lives free of mindless persecution. While that was part of why I wanted to come here, there just seemed to be something more driving me to come."

"More?" he asked, looking up. "More, like what?"

Shale shrugged. "I don't know. Just an internal uneasiness, a nagging sense that I needed to come south. I'd like to think it's because after all that I learned about you and the Mother Confessor, I wanted to be a part of what you had created, to feel that my life and my abilities were worth something valuable to you, whereas they weren't by many others. Also I felt I had to warn you and the Mother Confessor of the strange killings that, as we all learned later, turned out to be the Glee."

"We are glad you came, and we are in your debt for that and for so much more," Richard said in a soft, kind voice that somehow melted away the hard feelings of the questions.

"I know now, after the Mother Confessor spoke with me, that you are the Seeker. I didn't really know much about that before, or what it meant. I understand, now, that as the Seeker you are asking all these questions for a reason, not out of malice, even if I don't yet understand the reason. So, please go on and ask what you need to ask. I know now that you must have some deeper purpose."

Richard smiled as he handed her another piece of meat. "Berdine ate the piece you left."

"I thought she was done!" Berdine protested. "I didn't want it to go to waste, what with it already being cooked and all."

Shale let out a bit of a laugh as she took the meat and skewered it. "That's all right, Berdine. Easy enough to cook another. So what do you want to know about, Lord Rahl?"

"I want to know about the things Michec said just before he died."

As she held the chunk of meat on her skewer over the crackling flames, uncertainty colored her features. "He said something? I'm sorry, but I didn't hear him say anything. I was concentrating with all my strength, trying to hold back those vines he had around his wrists. He intended to also try to strangle you with them. Only by me holding them back was I able to stop him from conjuring more in order to do just that."

"Oh. Well, it's understandable that you were preoccupied."

"So, what did he say?"

"He said he was only following orders—the 'queen's' orders."

Shale frowned darkly at him from across the fire. "What queen?"

Richard shrugged. "I don't know. So then you have no idea, either?"

She pushed her dark hair back over her shoulder. "Not a clue."

"He also said, 'If you think this witch's oath begins and ends with me, you are a fool.'"

"Ah. I can see why that would be bothering you and why you wanted to know more about me." Creases tightened between her eyebrows. "But I thought it was his witch's oath that he was going to kill us."

"Apparently not. He said it didn't begin with him, and it wouldn't end with him. I think he was telling the truth."

"That is disturbing." She considered a moment. "What do you think it could mean?"

"I don't know." Richard looked up with that raptor gaze of his. "He said to ask you."

Shale looked startled. "Me! How should I know?"

Richard shrugged as he pulled off a strip of meat. "That's what he said. What do you know about witch's oaths?"

Shale rested her elbows on her knees as she thought it over. "I didn't know any witch women other than my mother. She never spoke of a witch's oath, as such. What do you think he meant?"

Richard shrugged. "From the way he put it, as if it was something quite solemn and serious, it sounded to me like he was saying that once a witch gives an oath, it is somehow the duty of every witch to see to it that such an oath is carried out."

Again, Shale looked surprised. "I can see why you were disturbed by the things he said. But I'm afraid I just don't know anything about such oaths." Her eyes narrowed with a memory. "Now that you mention it, though, my mother sometimes said that she had given an oath to help people, and that as a witch woman it was my duty to follow that oath. Out of respect for her, I often felt compelled to help people. Do you think that was what she meant? That it was a witch's duty to follow such an oath?"

"I'm afraid I don't know a whole lot about witch women," he said. "I was hoping you could fill in some of the blanks."

"Sorry. It's as puzzling to me as it is to you."

"Did you see the glint in his eye, after he was dead?"

She paused her chewing. "Glint? No, I saw no such thing."

"I did," Kahlan said, suddenly feeling alarmed.

Richard looked over at her. "You saw it too?" When she nodded, his brow drew down. "Then it wasn't my imagination."

"Maybe I was just too far away to see it," Shale suggested.

Richard fed another stick of wood into the fire. "Whatever it was, he is nothing but ashes, now."

Kahlan couldn't help wondering if such a witch's oath somehow lived on.

97

D on't you think it's too early for me to be showing?" Kahlan asked the sorceress.

Shale glanced over from atop her horse. "There is no rule about such things. Different women start showing at different stages of a pregnancy. Some show much earlier than others."

"There was that strange wood," Cassia said from behind, "so it may actually not be as early as you think."

Kahlan cast a worried look back over her shoulder. "What do you mean?"

Cassia arced an eyebrow as she leaned forward in her saddle. "Tell me how long you think we were there, going in circles?"

Kahlan thought about it a moment. "I'm not sure."

"Exactly," Cassia said. "Last night when we made camp, I took stock of all of our supplies. I thought we should have plenty still left, but we've used up almost all of them while we were still in that strange, misty wood."

Kahlan stared back over her shoulder. "That seems unlikely."

"Check them yourself if you don't believe me. With as much as we took, they should have lasted us all the way to Aydindril, even going the long way. But they're almost all gone and we haven't yet even crossed the mountains."

When Kahlan thought about it, she realized that Richard had been having to find them a lot of food to supplement the travel supplies. She had thought that maybe it was because she had been eating as much as any three of them put together. But with the unborn babies, she seemed to need to eat a lot.

The deer meat was long gone. They had fortunately been able to catch a lot of fish, as well as rabbit, pheasant, a few turkeys, and even a big snake. Kahlan hadn't eaten any of that, though. Because of the food they had managed to catch along the way, they hadn't needed to rely solely on their traveling supplies, so Kahlan hadn't paid much attention to them.

Not only had they been catching a lot of the food they needed, but they had needed to spend considerable time to get that food. Fishing took time. Tracking animals took time. Hunting and cleaning their catches took time. Richard had taught all the Mord-Sith how to make snares for them to set at night, and while often successful, that took time as well.

"It can only mean that we were going in circles in those woods a lot longer than we thought," Cassia said.

Kahlan looked over at Shale. "What do you think?"

Shale sighed unhappily. "To tell you the truth, I've been wondering the same thing Cassia is wondering."

Kahlan didn't know what had gotten into the two of them. "You mean because of how big I am?"

"Yes, but it's more than that." Shale gave her a sidelong look. "I don't know how to put my finger on it, but there was something strange about those woods."

"Well, of course there was," Kahlan said. "We kept going around in circles."

"There's more to it than that alone." Before she went on, Shale leaned forward a little and patted her horse's neck when it began dancing around impatiently. "Now that we're out of there and at last into different country, hilly country with views of the mountains to the west and such, I realize that it wasn't just foggy in that forest. Thinking back on it, I realize now that my mind felt foggy as well.

"I don't know how to explain it, but my connection with my gift felt… different, somehow. I didn't even realize it until much later. I recognize now that I wasn't feeling myself back there or thinking clearly. I don't know exactly how to explain what I was feeling, but I guess I would say I felt disconnected from my gift. That may be why

I didn't realize that there was a problem with those strange woods. Something was shrouding that sense."

Vale caught a red maple leaf as it drifted down and held it as she gestured around at the nearly bare tree branches and the decaying leaves on the ground. "And doesn't it seem too early to all of you for the leaves to have all fallen?"

Kahlan realized that the leaf Vale had caught was one of the last few colorful leaves that had hung on to the bitter end of the season. Most had long since fallen. The bare branches and the chilly bite to the air made her keenly aware of what had been making her vaguely uneasy. Somehow they had jumped right over autumn into early winter. The change to autumn came a little early up in the mountains, but they weren't yet up in the high country, and it wasn't changing to early autumn, it was already early winter.

"We had to have lost more time back in those woods than we thought," Shale said. "Somehow autumn vanished behind us and winter is already bearing down."

"It was a strange place," Rikka confirmed from behind. "I feel like I didn't really wake up until Lord Rahl got us out of there."

"Speaking of Lord Rahl," Nyda said, using the opportunity to walk her horse up closer, "what do you think could be taking him so long?"

Kahlan couldn't imagine. She had been trying not to worry about that very thing.

"He and Vika have been gone way too long," Berdine said. "I think we should go after him."

Kahlan hooked some of her long hair behind an ear as she looked back. "He told us to wait here while he scouted ahead."

Berdine leaned forward in her saddle to gesture. "That's the other thing. Why would he do that? It doesn't make any sense. He is always saying that the nine of us have to stay together because of his magic law thing."

"The Law of Nines," Kahlan murmured. "But now that I think about it, it did seem like maybe he was looking a bit restless and distracted, like something was wrong." She turned back in her saddle to look at all the Mord-Sith in their red leather. "Did any of you pick up on that?"

After sharing blank looks, they all shook their heads.

"We don't know his small mannerisms nearly as well as you do," Nyda said. "You would be the first to recognize it if he was acting differently."

Kahlan idly rubbed her palm on the saddle's horn as she started to remember the odd little signals that told her something was bothering him. She hadn't put them together at the time. She should have.

"Now that I think about it, why wouldn't he tell us all we could go ahead and dismount, if he was planning to be gone this long?" That was one more thing that confirmed to her that she had good reason to worry.

"Do you want to go look for him?" the sorceress asked.

Kahlan thought it over briefly, finally forcing out an unhappy breath. "No. The woods in this area are pretty dense. There are low spots with bogs making it a maze to get through. We don't know the route Richard took. He knows where we are and how to find us as long as we stay here. We shouldn't take the chance on going a different way and getting separated."

Too troubled to sit still any longer, she swung her leg over the back of her horse to get down. "But I'm tired of sitting in the saddle."

The rest of them agreed with her sentiment and were happy to dismount. After staring off into the distant woods for a while longer, Kahlan tied the reins of her horse to a branch so she could pace. A few of the others sat on a nearby outcropping of granite ledge covered with colorful splotches of lichen, and a couple of the others on a log. Kahlan saw a squirrel, up on a branch, chirping down at them to get out of its territory.

As she paced, she had a sudden thought. "When we were in that wood, do any of you remember seeing any animals?"

Shale thought it over briefly. "No, as a matter of fact, I can't say that I do. But now, when I try to remember that strange wood, for some reason, the memory of the place seems dim and distant, like a dream you forget later on."

Cassia snapped her fingers. "That's it, exactly. That's how I feel thinking back on it. Like it was a dream. Now that I think about it, I can't even say that we were really there."

The others agreed about that part of it. None of them, though, could remember ever seeing any wildlife.

Kahlan looked up at the bare bark of the maple trees. To the right, a breeze rattled the exposed branches of the birches. As she stared around at the thinning trees, she ran her hand over the swell of her belly.

She unexpectedly began to worry about how long they had actually been there in those woods, traveling around in big circles. It made her apprehensive to realize that she could be a lot farther along in her pregnancy than she thought. If that was true, how was she to judge when the babies would be due?

"There were no birds," she said at last, picturing the place in her mind. "I remember thinking at the time that it was strange that I didn't see any birds." She looked over at the others. "Anyone remember seeing birds there?"

No one did.

They sat around, or paced, for what had to be several more hours, growing more edgy the whole time. Picking at the reindeer moss on the rough trunk of an oak tree, Kahlan glanced up and saw the sun sinking low in the sky. Like time itself, the day was slipping away on them. She worried that Richard wasn't back.

As she was flicking a piece of moss off the tree, Kahlan heard something. She rushed forward a few steps, peering into the distance. Everyone looked expectantly toward the noise off in the shadows. They were all relieved when they saw Richard and Vika on their horses riding back into view among young pines.

As soon as they reached Kahlan and the small group, rather than apologizing for how long it had taken them, Richard and Vika hurriedly jumped down off their horses.

"We have a problem," Richard said without any greeting.

Kahlan looked from Richard's face to Vika. Both of them were sweaty and looked pale.

"What is it?" Kahlan stepped closer and gripped his forearm. "What happened?"

As they all came closer to gather around Kahlan, Richard ran his fingers back through his hair as he tried to think of a way to explain it.

"We ran into the boundary."

Kahlan squinted as she leaned in toward him. "The boundary? What boundary?"

He gestured irritably back over his shoulder. "The boundary. You know, the boundary." Then he gestured off at the mountains to the west. "Remember the boundary that used to run down those mountains between D'Hara and the Midlands? Like the boundary that was between the Midlands and Westland—the one you came through with Shar. That boundary."

"Who is Shar?" the sorceress asked.

Kahlan flicked her hand and shushed the woman.

She was having difficulty in her own mind making sense of what he was saying. He was pretty upset. She thought he had to mean something else and she just wasn't understanding him.

"What did it look like?"

Richard threw up his hand. "You know what the boundary looks like, Kahlan! As you get close it becomes a big green wall. The closer you get, you start melting into it, the green grows stronger and then turns dark. The voices on the other side start to call to you. You start seeing their faces—faces of people you know, people calling you by name."

Kahlan looked over at Vika's ashen face. "You saw the same thing?"

The Mord-Sith swallowed. "When we got close enough, the surroundings disappeared as everything turned dark. My mother called to me from the other side of that dark wall. I saw her." Her eyes welled with tears. "She reached out for me." Vika swallowed back the tears again. "I tried to go to her. Lord Rahl pulled me back just in time, or I would have been lost."

Shale looked exasperated. "What in the world are you people talking about? What in the name of Creation is a boundary?"

"It's nothing from Creation." Richard took a breath, trying to regain his patience so he could explain it. "Think of it as a kind of fracture in the world of life. It lies like a curtain across the land. That curtain is death itself in this world. If you were to walk far enough into it, it's like walking off the edge of a cliff and falling into the underworld."

The sorceress stammered as if such a thing were unreasonable. "But what if someone comes along and walks into it without knowing what it is?"

Richard leaned toward her. "Then they die, right then and there."

Shale's gaze shifted about uneasily, as if she was searching for some kind of answer that made sense to her. "Well, how long is this curtain of death? Can't we simply ride around the end of it?"

Kahlan could see the muscles in Richard's jaw flex as he gritted his teeth.

"That's why it took Vika and me so long to get back," he finally said. "We rode a long way in each direction trying to see if it ends somewhere. It doesn't. If you go to the right, it goes straight west. To the left it starts hooking back up this way as it goes to the northeast."

"Could we all go farther than you were able to go and find an end, do you think?" Kahlan asked.

Richard gave her a look she understood all too well. "Could we have done that with the boundaries before? The ones between our lands? Could we have gotten around it that way? Their nature is to be a boundary, to restrict passage, so while I can't say for sure, but knowing what the boundary from before was like, it isn't likely that it has an end we could simply travel around. It completely blocks us from our plan of going south to get around the worst of the mountains."

Kahlan searched around for a solution. "Can't you find us a way through, like you did before?"

Richard had obviously already considered that and had an answer ready. "That boundary was failing. This one isn't. It's much more powerful than the last one I saw. We aren't going to be able to get through it."

"Then what are we going to do?" Kahlan asked, feeling a rising sense of panic at the thought of having her children exposed, out in the middle of nowhere.

The Glee were likely to be somewhere behind, looking for them. They needed to get to the safety of the Keep before they found her and the twins. Every moment they were out in the open increased the danger.

Richard averted his eyes and reluctantly gestured to the west. "We have no choice but to go west, directly over that imposing mountain range. We have no choice."

"Well," she finally said, trying to find a reason for optimism, "if we can find a way over the mountains, that would be a shorter route to get to Aydindril."

The sorceress wasn't about to be placated. "Show me this boundary thing."

98

Richard reined in his horse and pulled it sideways to block the others. "It's too dangerous to ride our horses any farther," he told them. "We need to get off here and go the rest of the way in on foot."

Once they had handed the reins of their horses to the Mord-Sith, he told them that he wanted them all to wait where they were and take care of the horses. They weren't happy about leaving Richard and Kahlan without their protection, but because it involved dangerous magic, they were happy to keep their distance. Only Vika insisted on coming with them. Richard agreed with a nod.

Richard led Shale, Kahlan, and Vika on foot forward through an eerie stand of dead spruce. The silver-gray skeletons stood in dried, cracked, black ground that had once been thick mud. The grove of spruce was devoid of all but a few stubby, bare branches draped with long trailers of dull green moss that hung motionless in the dead-still air. The place smelled as dead as it looked. Kahlan walked behind with Vika, gazing warily around at the dead trees.

The ground descended gradually into a wet area growing thick with bog weed that now had died off until next spring. The long reeds around the open water had previously been blown over by heavy gusts of wind and were likewise brown and dead. It was difficult to slog their way through the tangled mat. Small, unseen things darted away in the murky water.

Bugs buzzed around their heads. Kahlan had to use her fingernails to pull out biting flies crawling on her neck under her hair. From time to time Richard and Vika tried to swish the cloud of insects away. It did little good. They all swatted at the flies that bit them. Shale held her dark cloak tightly closed against the insects. That morning there had already been a frost, so she knew that while the bugs were a nuisance, they would all soon be gone with the first hard freeze.

Kahlan didn't hear any other sounds, but she kept looking around for anything unexpected. She was sure the place had to be full of snakes so she was careful of where she stepped.

As they came up through thick grasses onto higher ground, Richard lifted a hand to bring them all to a halt.

"This is the place."

"This is what you're worried about?" Shale looked off in both directions. "I don't see anything."

"Stay where you are and watch," he said.

He walked forward cautiously. As he did, Kahlan could see a green glow, at first hardly perceptible, form around him. It grew brighter in the area immediately around him until after a few more steps it brightened to a sheet of glowing green light that looked like it was pressing in around him. The ominous, wavy, distorted green wall grew larger with every step he took. The green light was stronger close to him and faded away to the sides and above.

Kahlan was able to see the forest and sky beyond the lighter portion of the wavering green light. As Richard finally turned and walked back to them, the green glow faded until he was far enough away, where it vanished completely.

Kahlan folded her arms, feeling a little sick at seeing such a thing again. She never thought she would. She did her best to force the terrible memories it brought back from her mind.

"What does it feel like when you get close like that?" Shale asked in a low voice, finally concerned. "I don't see why you say it's an opening to the underworld. I admit, it's strange-enough-looking, but it doesn't look like a wall of death, as you described it to us. It's just that unusual green light."

"You would know why if you got close to it," Vika told her.

Shale stared at the Mord-Sith a moment, then turned back to Richard. "I need to get closer. I need to be as close as possible if I'm to try to sense the nature of its magic."

Richard nodded his agreement. "Now that I've shown you that much of its characteristics, I'll take you in so you can see it and feel it for yourself." He gestured to Vika. "Why don't you wait here."

The Mord-Sith nodded. "Seeing it once is enough for me."

Shale didn't look the least bit reluctant to see what didn't look all that frightening from where they were. When Richard started out, Kahlan, knowing what was coming, walked beside Shale.

"Easy, now," Richard said as he finally locked arms with the sorceress.

"What are you doing?" she asked.

"Just keep hold of my arm. I'll stop you when we've gone far enough."

"What do you mean, when we've gone far enough?"

Despite her reluctance, Kahlan locked her arm with Shale's other arm. "It's best if you let us hold on to you. You'll see."

As they walked closer and a faint green glow began, it was different-looking than when they had watched from the outside as Richard walked close by himself. It almost felt like it was humming. Shale looked up and then to the sides.

As they went farther in, Kahlan started hearing that awful, high-pitched buzzing sound, like a thousand bumblebees. With each step, the sound became not only louder but deeper in tone. Kahlan knew, though, what the sound actually was. That knowledge ran a shiver up her spine.

As they continued in, the green light deepened in color. The woods all around became darker, too, as if it were twilight.

Abruptly, an entire sheet of green materialized, the greenish glow everywhere around them. Kahlan looked back. She could no longer see the others. The woods and everything beyond had been swallowed in darkness. The cloud of insects dispersed rather than go any farther in.

"Easy," Richard warned them as he stepped carefully.

After a few more steps, the green vanished as the whole world darkened to black. It felt like a moonless, starless night, where she couldn't see her hand in front of her face. The buzzing vibrating deep in Kahlan's chest was so strong that it was starting to make her feel sick to her stomach.

She put a hand over her babies, suddenly worried, wondering if it was a mistake to take them close to such an evil place.

The darkness abruptly became a distinct, darkly transparent wall, like looking out on a night through glass that had grease smeared all over it. Kahlan could see the shapes moving beyond.

"This is as far as we dare go," Richard said.

Kahlan realized that she was putting pressure on Shale's arm to draw her back. She eased up on the pressure to let her go farther forward. The sorceress needed to know what they were really facing. They had to let her get a little closer.

Shale's jaw fell open as inky black shapes swept by, close, in the gloom on the other side of that dark wall. Kahlan knew they were specters in the deep, the dead in their lair. The swirl of inky shapes was at first bewitching, but Kahlan knew better.

She felt overwhelmed by the darkness and then began to feel that old sense of longing for what lay beyond. She heard voices murmur her name, calling to her. Kahlan knew they would be calling to Richard by name. By the way that Shale's eyes opened wider, she knew they were calling to her by name as well. Those thousands of distant voices of the souls beyond were the buzzing they had heard at first. Now, each of those sounds resolved into uncountable individual voices, the appeals of the dead.

When Shale cried out and tried to lift her arms toward the dark wall, Richard and Kahlan had to forcefully pull her arms back. She let out a long, mournful wail. As they pulled the sorceress back, she struggled to reach out toward the dead, to get to them, trying to tear herself out of Richard's and Kahlan's arms. As they dragged her back, she dug in her heels, not wanting to be pulled away from what she saw.

When they were far enough back, Shale sagged in their arms, weeping. Knowing the agony of what she had seen, Kahlan felt a pang of sadness for her. She wished they hadn't had to show it to her, but she needed to see it to truly understand. Richard and Kahlan had to continue struggling, pulling the sorceress back away from the wall of death.

When they were far enough back, to where Vika waited, Shale finally grasped the magnitude of what she had seen and reacted in horror to what she had tried to do. As she fell to tears, Kahlan took the sorceress in her arms.

"Think of something else," Kahlan told her. "Shale, listen to me. You have to think of something else. Try to remember every town you passed through on your way to come to the People's Palace. Think. Try to remember them in order."

After a few moments Shale pushed back and swallowed. "I'm all right."

Hooking her arm through Shale's to be safe, Kahlan ushered her back away until they reached the others.

She finally stood on her own, wiping tears from her cheeks. "I've never in my life felt magic that powerful."

"It's not something pleasant, that's for sure," Richard said. "I have absolutely no idea why it's here. All I can tell you is that it shouldn't be. As far as I know, there is no one powerful enough to call up that boundary. I'm sorry for what you saw in there, but I felt that you needed to see it, feel it, for yourself."

Shale stared in wonder at him. She looked too stunned to speak. Kahlan knew, though, that it wasn't the world of the dead that had her looking so shocked. It was something else.

The sorceress abruptly reached out and put fingers to Richard's temples. "Hold still."

Richard turned a worried glance toward Kahlan, as if to ask what to do.

"Do as she asks," Kahlan said. "Hold still."

From not far away, the Mord-Sith, looking in ill humor, all watched. They didn't particularly like anyone but Kahlan touching Lord Rahl. It aroused their protective instincts. Kahlan held a hand out low in their direction, letting them know it was all right and to stand down.

All at once, Shale drew both hands back with a gasp, as if the touch had burned her fingers. She took a step back away from Richard, clearly in fear.

Kahlan was alarmed by her reaction. "What is it?"

Shale's terrified eyes looked from Kahlan back to Richard.

"Shale," Kahlan asked again, "what is it that you sense?"

Shale blinked at her. "It's him."

Both Richard and Kahlan shared a bewildered look.

"What are you talking about?" Kahlan asked. "What's him?"

Shale gathered her long, dark hair together and held it in both fists. She drew her lower lip through her teeth.

Her face had gone ashen. "It's his."

Growing impatient, Kahlan made a face. "His what?"

She hesitated. "The boundary. It's Lord Rahl's magic."

Richard closed the distance to the sorceress and grabbed her by an arm. "What are you talking about?"

"You created this, this…" She waggled a hand toward where they had just been. "…this boundary. This fracture in the world of life. This opening into the world of death. It's your magic that created it. I can feel it. I can feel your gift in its composition. You did this."

99

Richard gritted his teeth as he tightened his grip on her arm. "What are you talking about? What do you mean I'm doing it?"

Shale swallowed at the fire in his eyes. "As a sorceress I can sense a person's individual gift, much the way you can recognize a person by their voice, or their eyes. Your gift, like everyone's gift, has a unique feel to it, except yours is more recognizable and distinctive to me than most. The gift that empowers that wall of death, that boundary as you call it, is your gift."

Richard stared at her for the longest time. "That's impossible. I don't have any idea how to create such a thing," he finally said.

Shale pulled her arm back. "I didn't say you did. But the feel of your gift is unmistakable to me. It is your gift that brought up that boundary wall."

Richard growled in frustration. "It can't be. I would have no idea how to do such a thing."

"It's in your blood," Kahlan told him.

They all turned to her. "Your grandfather created the original boundaries," she explained. "He's the only one who could have. The awareness of the organic process involved with using his gift to create the boundaries must have somehow, in some way, been passed on to you along with his gift. You are a powerful and gifted war wizard, in many ways one of the most talented ever to live. Although you have never created a boundary before, the ability to do so is surely inborn in you."

Richard pinched the bridge of his nose, trying to get a grip on the anger clearly boiling right at the surface. His head finally came up and he tried hard to maintain his composure.

"All right, let's say that I have the inherent ability. Fine. But I didn't do it. I would know if I used my gift to create something this profound."

"I think that has to be true," Shale agreed. "But that means that someone else used your gift to pull up that curtain of death across our path."

He stared at her for a long moment. "If I didn't do it, then who could have?"

Shale looked at a loss to explain it. "I'm sorry, Lord Rahl, but until now, if I hadn't felt it myself—with my own gift—I would never have imagined such a thing was even possible. But then again, having been raised in the Northern Waste, my knowledge of the gift and all its capabilities is limited to what I learned from my father and mother. All I can say is that it has to be that someone powerful is usurping your gift.

"I can only imagine that it would take great power to do such a thing. You said there is no longer anyone powerful enough to do such a thing. But you told me before that gifted people can join their abilities together in order to do what none of them could do alone. Remember?"

His fists on his hips, he nodded. He stared at the sorceress for a time, his sense of reason finally rising up through his anger. He cooled considerably.

"That has to be the explanation. It has to be gifted people joining their power to be able to do this. That means that we're likely not dealing with a single gifted person, but a group of them."

"One gifted person, or a group, it has been done." Kahlan spread her arms in frustration. "Either way, at this point the more relevant question is *why* would they do such a thing?"

"If they wanted to kill us, it's highly unlikely that those powerful enough to do such a thing would think we would be foolish enough to simply walk into the boundary and be killed." The calm demeanor of the Seeker was back. "The strange wood wasn't life-threatening, it simply slowed us down. The boundary they put up must also be meant to stop us, not kill us. After all, stopping people from passing was the purpose of the boundaries."

"But why?" Kahlan asked.

He paced off a ways, then turned and came back with a look that worried her. "I think they don't want us getting away with the twins. I think their purpose is to keep us from going to the Keep where the twins would be safe."

Kahlan looked off toward the new boundary. "That's a frightening thought."

Richard let out a sigh of resignation. He held up a hand as he thought out loud.

"We can't get through that boundary to get any farther to the southwest in order to go around the mountains, so at this point our only two choices are to either go back to the People's Palace or try to get to Aydindril by going straight northwest over the mountains. Back toward the palace, we will be attacked relentlessly by the Glee. They are determined to slaughter us. If we try to get to Aydindril by trying to get over those mountains, I can only assume we will encounter those who are doing all of this."

Kahlan felt a rising sense of panic. "They want the babies."

"We will all protect the twins," Shale said.

With one hand on a hip, Richard rubbed his forehead with the fingertips of his other hand as he paced off a ways before finally returning to look at Shale.

"If it's my gift doing this, then is there a way for you to... to, I don't know, cut my gift off from it so that the boundary will lose its viability and come down?"

Shale looked off toward the boundary, as if she could still see it and hear the call of the dead.

"I suspect that now that it's up, it no longer needs your magic to persist. Once it's up, it's up. After all, once your grandfather used his gift to create the ones before, they were there and they didn't then need his gift to continue to exist, did they?"

"No," he admitted. He let out a sigh. "What matters is that someone doesn't want us to go south to take the twins out of reach." He gestured toward the mountains. "We have nowhere else to go except that way."

"Then it's surely a trap," Vika said as she stepped forward, unable to remain silent any longer. "We shouldn't indulge them and walk into their trap. Especially since they have already proven that they have enough power that they can use your gift."

Richard gave her a curious look. "Since when have the Mord-Sith not wanted to run headlong into trouble?"

"If it was me, and the others, we would do so in a heartbeat and without a second's thought." Vika gestured at Kahlan. "But the Mother Confessor carries the children of D'Hara and our hope for the future. It is for her that I am reluctant to take the risk."

"Well," he said, wiping a weary hand over his face, seeming a little surprised at how much sense she was making, "whoever used my gift has to be off that way. We don't know what other unexpected things they might do if we don't find them and stop them. Better on our terms than theirs."

Kahlan felt trapped by the unknown. "But they obviously want us to try just that so they can get our children."

Richard looked sympathetic but determined. "All the more reason we must find them and put a stop to it. The only way to protect the twins is to stop whoever is doing this, or just like the Glee, they will come after us in another way when we least expect it."

Despite the terror of the implications, Kahlan knew he was right. She tried to sound positive. "I guess if we can stop this threat and, in the process, find a way over the mountains, we will end up much closer to Aydindril and we will reach the Keep all that much sooner."

Richard smiled. "That's what I'm hoping." He gestured to the mountains. "The threat is that way. There are nine of us, so we have the Law of Nines on our side. The sooner we find and eliminate the threat, the better. With winter closing in those mountains will become even more treacherous. We need to get over them before the worst of it sets in. We can still make some distance before we need to make camp for the night so I think we should press on."

He looked around at all the faces watching them. "Just be aware that going through those mountains will be difficult and dangerous even if we can beat the weather, and even without the threat that's out there."

Everyone gave him a grim nod.

With the decision made, everyone mounted up.

As soon as they started out, Kahlan rode up close to Richard so the others wouldn't hear her. "I can tell by that 'Seeker look' in your eyes that you might know who could be waiting for us in that trap up there in those forbidding mountains."

He rode in silence for a time before he gave her an unreadable look. "I have a nasty suspicion, but I'm not ready to say it out loud, yet."

"Richard Cypher," she admonished in the name she knew him by when she first came to know him and fall in love with him, a name that touched on deep history and meaning for them both, "don't give me that. Tell me what you're thinking."

He gave her a look for using that name and then rode on for a time before answering. "I think we're making it too complex. I think it all boils down to one simple question."

Kahlan stared over at him as she swayed in her saddle. "What question?"

"When he was dying, Michec said that the witch's oath didn't begin and end with him. So who, then?"

Kahlan felt an icy jolt of realization wash through her veins.

"Shota."

100

As they followed the natural lay of the land to begin the ascent up into the mountains to try to find a pass, the forest thinned as it struggled to grow among the granite ledges and masses of rock that rose up all around. The exposed rock was covered in colorful medallions of lichen. Fluffy moss and small plants with deep green, heart-shaped leaves grew in low clefts in the ledges.

In the more rocky places, scraggly trees struggled to hold on to the rock with roots like claws. The roots grew in fat, twisting clusters over and around walls of stone and down over granite that looked like disorderly stacks of giant blocks. Ferns found a home in the crooks of those roots, and in the ferns, dirt collected to allow spotted mushrooms and other small plants to grow. Thin trailers of vines hung down from small ledges in the stone. Where water seeped down sheets of sloped granite, green slime grew, and in the laps of rock that collected the water small, colorful frogs waited for bugs.

Squirrels in the upper branches followed the progress of the invaders, chattering warnings as they leaped from branch to branch. Mockingbirds flitted about, or called out as they flicked their long tails. Richard saw ravens perched on branches high up in the larger spruce trees, watching them pass below. When they took to wing, the massive trees left plenty of space for them under the canopy to swoop through the forest. They sent out loud calls as they soared among the trees.

Richard heard a strange moan from Kahlan. He slowed and turned in his saddle.

"What's wrong?"

Kahlan doubled over. "I think I'm going to be sick."

He leaped off his horse when he saw her start to slump to the side and begin to slide off her saddle. He rushed in under her just in time to catch her fall enough to ease her limp form to the ground. The others all jumped off their horses when they saw her go down.

Kahlan crossed her arms over her middle as she let out a groan of agony. As Richard brushed her hair back from her face so he could see her eyes, he saw that she was covered in sweat. Her pupils were dilated. She looked up at him with panic in those green eyes.

"What's wrong?"

She clutched his sleeve, pulling herself up toward him, and opened her mouth, but she couldn't bring forth words before the pain overwhelmed her and her arm went slack. Her eyes rolled up in her head as she sagged back to the ground.

He put a hand to the side of her face and called her name again. He didn't think she had even heard him that time.

Shale rushed in and urgently dropped to the ground on the other side of Kahlan. The sorceress took one look at Kahlan's ashen face and immediately started unbuttoning her shirt stretched tight over her round belly.

"Loosen her trousers," she told Richard. After a quick look, she said, "Get them off. She's bleeding."

Richard felt numb. He did as the sorceress asked and then sat back on his heels. He didn't know what to do. He had never felt so afraid and helpless.

Shale placed the flats of her hands on the sides of Kahlan's belly, then on the top and near the bottom. She lifted Kahlan's eyelids, looking into her eyes. She put an ear to Kahlan's chest and listened to her heart and her breathing.

She looked up at last, her expression grim.

"She's miscarrying."

Richard blinked, the words seeming to come at him from some faraway place.

"What?"

"She's losing the babies."

"She can't," he said.

Shale looked up at him with as bleak an expression as he'd ever seen. "If we don't act quickly, we are going to lose her as well."

Richard sat frozen in terror, his skin feeling icy cold with goose bumps. He couldn't lose her. She couldn't lose her children.

Shale placed one hand on Kahlan's belly and the other on her forehead. She muttered a curse under her breath.

Richard looked up at the Mord-Sith all standing around them, as if to implore their help. They looked as alarmed and lost as he felt.

Kahlan groaned again as she folded both arms across her middle and sat halfway up with the cramping pain that made her cry out. She muttered something incoherently.

Shale put an arm under Kahlan's head and helped her ease back down. Vale rushed to her horse and quickly returned. She reached in to hand the sorceress a folded blanket. Shale put it under Kahlan's head. Someone gave Richard another blanket, which he laid over Kahlan's bare legs. Sweat was pouring off her face despite the chilly air.

"But she will be all right," Richard insisted.

Ignoring his words, Shale finally sat back up on her heels. "I need you to do something."

"Anything. Name it."

"I need you to get me some mother's breath."

Richard's mind felt blank. "Mother's breath?"

Shale glanced up, giving him a look as if to say she didn't have time for questions. "Yes, it's a plant with leaves that—"

"I know what it is," Vika said. "I grew up in mountainous country. That's where mother's breath grows—in the high country."

Richard looked around frantically. "Would there be any around here?"

Vika took a worried look over her shoulder at the mountains towering above them. She pointed.

"It grows much higher up, near the tree line. There is already snow in a lot of places up there. Mother's breath dies out when the snows come."

Richard shot to his feet, snatching up the reins to his horse. "We need to get up there and find some."

Shale looked up at them both. "I need the whole plant, roots and all."

Vika cast a troubled look up the mountain. "It's liable to be covered in snow by now. Snow kills off mother's breath until it comes back in the spring."

Shale shook her head vehemently. "It can't be dead and dry. If it's not still living and supple it turns to a poison that would kill her."

"It's an extremely rare plant." Vika hesitated. "I've only seen it a few times in my whole life. It doesn't grow in many places. What if we can't find any?"

Shale gave them both a look. "She's losing the babies. I don't know if I can save her. Go find the mother's breath. It's her only chance, now."

"What about the twins?" Richard asked.

Shale pointedly wouldn't look up at him. "Go. Hurry."

Richard and Vika shared a look; then each stuffed a foot in a stirrup and leaped up into their saddles.

"The rest of you," Richard said, gesturing to the Mord-Sith, "watch over them until we're back."

He looked down at Kahlan. Her eyes were half closed. She trembled in pain. She truly did look like she was dying. Richard swallowed and gestured to Vika.

"Let's go."

101

When hands gently lifted Kahlan from the ground, she came awake. Not fully awake, but awake enough to be aware of the red leather of a number of Mord-Sith surrounding her. She was aware, too, of the pain. That terrible, deep pain that told her that her pregnancy was in serious trouble.

Overriding the pain was a sense of helpless panic that there was nothing she could do about it.

In her dim, dazed vision, she saw Shale leaning close. Kahlan grabbed her sleeve.

"The babies... are they all right?"

Those carrying her by holding the edges of the blanket she was lying on paused as Kahlan desperately held on to Shale's sleeve. Even in her semiconscious state, she caught the sidelong glance the sorceress gave some of the Mord-Sith.

"Hurry and get her inside," Shale said to the others.

Kahlan looked around as they started out again. Her vision grew dim at times, but she could see that they were carrying her into some kind of crude shelter. When she rolled her head to the side, she saw a lean-to wall at the back. It looked to have been hastily constructed of sapling poles covered in pine and spruce boughs. The Mord-Sith gently laid her down on a bed of grasses and fern fronds. The whole shelter was roughly made from materials at hand, but at least it helped protect her from the cold wind.

Cassia knelt down beside her and laid another blanket over the top of the one already there to keep her warm. It was cold out, but Kahlan felt hot. She was already so hot she was sweating. She had to blink sweat from her eyes.

Shale turned a little and cast a hand outward, sending flame into wood that had already been carefully stacked for a fire behind her. As soon as it blazed up, Kahlan felt the added warmth of the crackling flames.

The next moment, she was overcome with a flash of cold shivers. The sheen of sweat suddenly felt like ice on her face. At least the lean-to helped reflect the heat back now that she was suddenly cold.

Moments later, though, the heat again felt oppressive. Sweat once more poured off her face and stung her eyes. As soon as she didn't think she could endure how hot she was, she turned back to shivering with sudden chills. The breeze that made it into the shelter felt icy.

When the sorceress passed close enough, Kahlan once again grabbed her sleeve. "Shale, talk to me. I'm burning up one moment, and the next I'm freezing. What's going on?"

"You have a bit of fever."

"But are my babies all right?"

Shale patted her shoulder and flashed a brief smile. "You need to rest. That is the best thing you can do for them right now. Please, Mother Confessor, you need to lie still."

Instead of following instructions, Kahlan tried to sit up. The sorceress rushed to push her back down onto a pillow made of a folded blanket.

"You must not try to do that, Mother Confessor. Just lie still. Try to go back to sleep."

"I'm not going to go to sleep until you tell me what's going on. Are my babies all right?"

Shale pulled her lower lip through her teeth as she considered whether or not to answer the question. She shared looks with some of the others standing over Kahlan.

"Shale?"

"You are having some difficulty. Nothing that can't be set right."

Set right. From Shale's tone of voice, Kahlan didn't know if the sorceress believed that it could be "set right." Kahlan looked around. Given the Mord-Sith's grim expressions, she didn't think they did.

"Where is Richard? Why isn't he here? He should be here with me. What happened? What's going on?"

Shale sighed as she realized from the confused panic in Kahlan's voice that she wasn't going to settle for anything less than the truth.

"You are having some difficulty with the pregnancy."

Kahlan was already aware of that much of it. "Difficulty? What does that mean? What difficulty?"

"The babies are in danger of miscarrying."

Kahlan blinked. "But I can't lose them."

Shale pulled the blanket up a little, tucking it under Kahlan's chin. "Lord Rahl and Vika went to find a plant I need to heal you—to save your babies. Once he returns with that herb, I will make you a medicine that should set you right."

Kahlan clearly caught the word "should." It wasn't a word that inspired confidence.

"What plant?"

"It's called mother's breath."

Kahlan had grown up in the Confessors' Palace and the Wizard's Keep. She didn't know much about the woods and plants, except what Richard had taught her. When she had been young, wizards, too, taught her a little about herbs. She couldn't remember ever hearing of mother's breath.

"Will he be back soon, then?"

Shale smiled. It was clearly forced.

"Just as soon as he finds me some mother's breath so I can make you all better. You need to lie still until then. You will make it worse for the babies if you try to move too much. Lying still is the best thing you can do right now to help them."

Suddenly fearing that she might be hurting them by trying to sit up, Kahlan relaxed back onto the makeshift bed. She did feel better at hearing that Richard was going for a medicinal plant. Richard knew a lot about healing herbs. She appreciated the Mord-Sith and the sorceress being there, but what she really wanted was Richard at her side, telling her that everything would be all right.

Kahlan stared up at the roof of pine and spruce boughs, searching for courage to ask a terrible question.

"Am I going to lose my babies?"

Shale leaned in, her face tight with concern. "No, no, Mother Confessor. I don't want you to have such a thought. I'm with you, and Lord Rahl will be back with what you need. Now that we have you inside a shelter and out of the cold wind, the best thing you can do for the twins is to rest until he returns. It's important for the babies that you don't try to move right now."

Kahlan felt a tear running down the side of her face. "Please, I can't lose them. I've already lost my first child." She fought to keep control of her voice. "I can't lose the twins. Tell me what's going on. Don't lie to me to try to make me feel better. Being kept in the dark is not helping me. I want to know the truth of what's happening."

Shale regarded her with a long, solemn look. "All right, I suppose you have a right to know." She took a deep breath before she began. "For some reason the babies are trying to be born before their time. It's too early. I don't know the reason this is happening. I have seen this occur before in women I've helped back in the Northern Waste.

"The truth is, if they are born now, they will die within minutes, if they are even born alive. With the way this kind of thing goes, that would be unlikely."

Kahlan stared up at the woman. She heard the words, but she was having trouble understanding them. This couldn't be happening. Everything had been going well with her pregnancy. These were the children of D'Hara. They had to be born and grow up to protect their world.

Kahlan realized she was panting in fear as well as pain. "But you've handled this kind of thing before, haven't you?" she asked Shale. "You said that you attended many births, even difficult pregnancies. You've seen this before?"

The sorceress nodded. "That's right. From the time I was young, I went with my mother and she taught me to use my gift to help where it was necessary. I would guess that I've attended hundreds of births."

"But what about trouble like I'm having? Have you helped with that as well?"

Shale pursed her lips, considering for a moment.

"I told you I wouldn't lie to you, and I won't. I've seen situations like this maybe six or eight times."

Kahlan looked up expectantly. "And were you able to help? Were you able to save the babies?"

Holding Kahlan's gaze, she slowly shook her head.

"I'm afraid that in every case like this that I've seen, despite what I did, not one of the babies survived."

Kahlan swallowed back her fear. "What about the mothers?"

Shale, with a grave look, shook her head again. "None of those mothers survived, either."

Kahlan's muscles went slack. Her weight sank back. The world seemed to be spinning.

That was the end, then. The end of everything.

Shale put a hand gently on Kahlan's shoulder. "But we have things on our side that I didn't have any of those other times."

Kahlan looked up. "What things?"

"In every one of those cases someone had to come to get me, so I wasn't there from when it started. With you, I was right there at the beginning, so I was able to use a bit of my gift to try to stabilize the situation right from the first—before it was already too late, the way it was with those other women."

"Can you heal me, then? Heal the twins? Can you do something for us?"

"Before I came here from the Northern Waste, I would have said no, it is beyond what is possible. But since I have arrived, I have seen things that I would not have thought possible. I have seen Lord Rahl heal wounds that could not be healed. I have seen you bring him back from the dead. I have seen Lord Rahl do things that I used to know with certainty could not be done.

"If you and Lord Rahl have taught me anything, it is that we are all more than we may think we are, that we should never give in to despair and defeat, that we should never give up.

"I intend to save you and the twins, even if I have never been able to do such a thing before. That is the long and short of it. I will keep all three of you alive until Lord Rahl returns with the herb that can reverse what is happening so that you can carry the twins until it is time for them to be born."

Kahlan felt more tears run down the side of her face. "Thank you," she whispered.

Shale leaned in and placed one hand on Kahlan's forehead, and the other on her swollen belly.

"Now, I am going to put you into a deep sleep in order to slow down what is happening. I will do everything I can to help the twins stay in the safety of your womb until your husband returns with the mother's breath. When he does, it will heal you.

"Until then, you need to sleep. The next time you wake, if I am half the sorceress I think I am, half the woman you have taught me to be, you will be well on the road to being set right."

Kahlan wanted to say something, but before she could, magic swiftly brought darkness that took her.

102

Richard lifted his shoulder, trying to shelter his ear from a frigid gust of wind. His fingers and ears ached from the cold. As the sun sank behind the mountains, not only was the light fading fast, but the temperature high up in the mountains seemed to be dropping even faster.

The cold, though, was the least of Richard's concerns. He urgently needed to get even higher up in the mountains to the tree line to find the mother's breath plant if he was to save both Kahlan and their unborn babies.

Vika had told him that mother's breath had odd, lopsided leaves. She held up her fist with the back of her hand facing him. "The shape of the leaves looks like this. If you ever saw it once, you would never forget it, but it's rare. I've only seen it a couple of times in my life, and then only up in the mountains near the tree line."

Richard dared not let himself worry about how rare it was. He just needed to get up to where it grew so he could search for it. He told himself that he was going to find it, and that was that.

The tree line, though, was still quite some distance away and much higher up the mountains. It was slow going trying to find an uncharted way up among the rocks and often dense trees of the steep and rugged terrain. It was difficult enough in the day, but he knew that in such mountainous country where there were no trails, it would be virtually impossible for the horses to climb once it was dark.

He also knew from Shale's urgency that time was critical to Kahlan's survival, so darkness or no darkness, one way or another, he intended to press on. Since the horses couldn't continue on in darkness, as soon as he found a place to leave them, he intended to keep going without them.

An all-too-familiar memory came to mind. Zedd had always said that nothing was ever easy.

Richard forced the thought from his mind as he turned his attention toward an opening between a stand of young spruce trees. Beyond was a jumble of rock with just enough space for the horses to pass through. It was the only way he could find that looked to have any chance to lead them higher.

Richard was using all his knowledge and experience as a woods guide to find a way to steadily make it to higher ground. Occasionally, game trails helped. Even so, without a real trail, they had a number of times come to the base of impassable cliffs that forced them to find another way around so they could keep going up. Other times, what had looked like a good route ahead ended at a drop-off that forced them to backtrack and find another way in order to keep going.

Richard tried to scan the mountainside higher up while his horse carefully picked its way over the loose rock between tall rock formations rising up to either side. Water seeped down the faces of some of the speckled rock, leaving green and brown streaks. Plants growing in the cracks hung down in places, making it look like green walls. Tangles of roots here and there made the footing tricky. He wanted the horse to hurry, but he knew that it was climbing as fast as it could. It was almost as if it could sense his urgency.

As they made steady progress ever higher, they entered low clouds. The soft gray blankets rolled over the jutting towers of rock as if trying to find a way down. As they climbed upward into the clouds it made the granite the horses had to walk over slick and the footing dangerous. In places the horses had difficulty on the steep ground only made worse in the wet. Their hooves slipped repeatedly before they could find adequate grip.

He knew that in such steep country going back down would be considerably more difficult for the horses than going up. It would likely be too dangerous in many places to ride down. For much of the way down he knew they would have to do the descent on foot, letting the horses pick their way without having to also deal with a rider who would make it more difficult for them to balance.

But first they had to find the plant Shale had sent them for. That was all that mattered.

Vika followed behind without comment. She was his sworn protector, after all, and in addition to wanting to find the mother's breath, as Mord-Sith, Richard's safety was her first responsibility. She knew how desperate he was to keep going despite how dark and dangerous it was getting, so she didn't object. With the way the trees found places to grow in among the rocks they were picking their way over, even without the fog the canopies were too dense for them to see higher up and how much farther they would need to go.

Not long before, through an opening in the trees and despite the thickening fog, in a rare moment of clear sky he had been able to catch a brief glimpse of the mountains towering above them. Through that opening in the trees he had seen that the tree line was still a great distance away.

As it grew darker, he was having trouble picking out a passable route. On top of the darkness, the fog was making it difficult to see very far. Besides cutting visibility, the fog was creating an icy mist that was both miserable and slippery.

As they came up into a broad area that was somewhat level, their progress blocked by a fragmented granite wall, Richard frantically looked for a way up. Worried they were again going to have to backtrack, he suddenly spotted something in among the trees atop that vertical granite barrier.

"I think I see a trail."

Vika rode up beside him and frowned. She looked to each side, seeing that there was clearly no way around.

"A trail? Are you sure?"

Richard pointed up at the top of the granite. "Look over there to that split in the granite wall. I think it might be a way up."

"We can't take the horses up that. It's way too steep."

"Yes, but it looks like there are boulders and rock jammed into that crevice that would allow us to climb up it on foot. Look at the top of the wall over to the left by that mass of tree roots coming down over the edge. What do you see?"

Vika rested her wrists on the horn of her saddle as she stood in the stirrups and leaned forward, squinting up at the top of the wall.

"That's strange. It's foggy and hard to see, but it looks like it might be several stones stacked atop one another."

"Exactly." Richard dismounted. "It's a cairn."

She frowned over at him. "What's a cairn?"

"It's a way to mark a trail in difficult areas where it would be easy or even dangerous to get lost and go the wrong way. If I'm right, and it's not something natural, it would mean we have come across a long-forgotten trail."

Vika held her long, single blond braid in her fist over the front of her shoulder as she frowned up at the top of the wall. "Why would there be a trail up here?"

"It could very well be an old trail leading over a pass. It has to be from before the boundary that ran up the spine of these mountains. If I'm right, it may be a way not only to get up higher to the tree line, but to get over these mountains. It could be a trail that leads over a pass and into the Midlands."

"The horses can't get up there, that's for sure."

"You're right about that," Richard said as he dismounted.

Once on the ground, he started to unbuckle the saddle girth strap. "We are going to have to leave them and go the rest of the way on foot. If it really is a trail, this would be an incredible stroke of luck. Once we find the mother's breath and heal Kahlan, then we might even be able to get over the mountains on this trail. That would save us a lot of time getting to Aydindril."

Vika scanned the area before she climbed down out of her saddle. "It's pretty flat here, but what if the horses wander off?"

"It's a risk we will have to take. Let's get the saddles and tack off them," he said.

"Should we take anything with us?" she asked.

Richard nodded. "We'd better at least take our packs."

"We should also take some dried meat and whatever supplies we can carry," she suggested.

"I have some oats tied to the back of my saddle. I will leave some of it out for the horses. That should keep them around." Richard gestured to the left. "There is a little water running down off the rocks over there. It's collecting enough for them to get a drink. After we get the saddles off we need to break out the travel candles. The light is fading fast, but if that really is a trail up there, the candles will help enough that we should be able to keep going."

Vika glanced up toward the mountain they could no longer see. "Candles in the tin traveling cases won't provide much light."

"With the fog, even if it was still light out, we wouldn't be able to see very far anyway. With the candles you can wait at that cairn up there while I scout ahead to see if I can find the next one. When I do, you can come catch up and then wait at that one until I find the next. In that way, if it really is a trail marked with cairns, we can keep going even in the dark."

Richard dragged the saddle off his horse and set it on a rock. As Vika did the same, he spread some oats on a flat area of rock. The horses were eager to eat. After giving them a pat on the neck, he swung his pack and his bow up on a shoulder. Vika untied supplies from her saddle. She hoisted her pack up onto her shoulder.

Once Richard lit a strip of birch bark with a steel and flint and it flared up into flame, he then used that to light the candles. They immediately started out into the foggy darkness, climbing up the narrow split in the granite wall.

103

Not long after daybreak they had made it up near the tree line and left the trail to search for mother's breath among where the snow had started to stick in patches. As eager as he was to find the plant, he had to be careful when he moved across the rocky ground they were searching. If he fell off the mountain, he wouldn't be able to help Kahlan, and in the place where they were searching, there was certainly a danger of falling. With the fog now down below them, there was no telling how far it was down some of the drop-offs.

The trail they had found was marked well enough with cairns and took a route that made for much easier climbing, at last saving them a lot of time. Richard was sure the trail had to have been laid out long before the boundary between the Midlands and D'Hara had gone up because, like the mountain range, the boundary divided the lands, so there would have been no purpose for a trail over a pass that would have been cut off once the boundary was there. It was fortunate that the cairns were still standing after all that time, and even more fortunate that he and Vika had happened across it.

It had worked surprisingly well for Vika to wait at each cairn they found while Richard went ahead to find the next one. Then she would climb to him by the light of his candle and wait at that cairn while he went on ahead to find the next. It was slow going to do it that way, but still a lot faster than wandering aimlessly up the mountains and having to backtrack from dead ends or being forced to climb in difficult and dangerous areas, especially when there was no way to tell if after a lot of hard climbing it would end up providing a way to continue. Sometimes it didn't.

They had climbed on the trail, following the cairns, throughout the entire night. Richard was too driven to find the plant that could save Kahlan to stop and sleep. Vika was Mord-Sith. Mord-Sith were trained to do without sleep.

Once it had gotten light enough to see, they had been able to make much faster progress following the trail. But their method of continuing to cover ground throughout the night had helped make critically important progress. Now that they were finally up to where the trees were thinning out and they had daylight, they left the trail to search at the base of where the snow had begun to stick, hoping to find mother's breath not yet killed by the ever-descending snow line.

"Lord Rahl!" Vika called out.

Richard had been using his hands to help keep his balance on the steep ground as he searched under brush and the lower sides of rock ledges that were still free of snow. Shale had told him that she needed living plants with their roots; she couldn't use them if they had been killed by the snow.

He stood and looked off to his right. "What is it?"

"I found it!"

It felt as if his heart came up in his throat. He scrambled over a rounded projection of rock and through several patches of snow, then held on to low-growing, thick juniper brush to help keep from sliding down loose scree.

Richard found Vika sprawled on her belly in front of an opening in the rock. The rising sun was at their backs, so it lit the entrance to the small cave.

Vika pointed. "Look! It's mother's breath. It's protected in here from the snow, so it's still alive."

There were three plants to her left, where she was pointing, and a couple more to the right side, just inside the cave's maw. They had fist-shaped leaves just as she had told him. She had been right; after seeing those odd, lopsided leaves, he knew they were a plant that he would never forget. Just inside the opening of the cave, where Vika was on her belly, wouldn't quite be high enough to stand in, but it was enough to protect the plants.

Richard looked deeper and suddenly saw what Vika hadn't noticed in her desperate search for the rare plant, and her excitement at having found it.

In the snow to either side of the cave, and in the soft ground of the entrance, were the prints of a large cat. Farther back in the cave, where rays of the rising sun reached, he spotted a variety of bones.

Farther still, back in the darkness, Richard saw a pair of eyes reflecting the light.

When he thought he heard the low rumble of a throaty growl, he drew his sword.

Vika looked back over her shoulder when she heard the distinctive sound of his blade being drawn. "What's the matter?"

Richard gestured with his sword. "There's a mountain lion back in there."

Vika froze. "What do we do?"

Richard carefully put one knee down beside her and leaned in, holding the blade protectively out over the top of her. He put his left hand on the back of her shoulder to keep her down as he spoke quietly, so as not to alarm the animal hiding back in the darkness.

"Dig up the three plants right there by your left hand. Shale said she needed the whole plant, so dig out the roots. We need to get all of the roots you can dig out. Three plants should be more than enough. Leave the other two on the other side to help them regrow. While you dig these three out, I'll watch and make sure that mountain lion stays back."

"All right," she said as she quickly pulled her knife from the sheath at her side, drove it into the ground, and used it to help her start digging.

With her fingers and the blade she dug down through the relatively soft, rocky dirt, frantically flicking it back like a badger digging a den. As she worked, the animal back in the cave crept forward into the light enough for Richard to see its face and yellow eyes. It was indeed a formidably large mountain lion, and by its low, rattling growl, an unhappy one at that.

The creature drew back its upper lip, revealing big teeth, as it opened its mouth a little to let out a louder guttural growl. As it took another step forward with a big, broad paw, Richard poked the blade toward its face just enough to make his defensive intentions clear.

It took two steps closer, head hunched down, ears laid back, eyes locked on him. Powerful muscles in its shoulders flexed as it growled while taking another step closer.

"Don't make me kill you," Richard said to the beast. "I don't want to kill you, but I will if I have to. Just wait a moment until we're done here and then we will be on our way."

For the time being, the blade was keeping it back. The mountain lion stopped, almost as if it understood his words. More likely, it understood the blade in its way.

Vika dug with her fingers as fast as she could, throwing the dirt back, trying to dig down and expose the roots without damaging them. All the while Richard and the mountain lion stared each other down.

Vika clawed at the ground and was finally able to bring the first plant out of the deep hole she had dug. It had a long, thick taproot. She got almost all of it out, shook the dirt off the roots, set it aside, then went back to excavating the other two. Richard could see that it wasn't easy digging while on her belly, but she worked as fast as she could, letting out little grunts of effort. Her fingers were bloody, but that didn't slow her down.

Richard carefully reached down with his left hand, as he kept the mountain lion at bay with the sword in his right, and set the mother's breath already out of the ground safely up on a small ledge that formed the roof of the cave. When Vika, panting with the effort, brought out the second, he took it from her and set it up with the first. Having loosened the ground as much as she needed to with her knife, she returned it to the sheath and went back to clawing out the dirt around the roots of the third mother's breath plant and flicking it behind.

"Got it!"

With the third plant in her left hand, Vika squirmed back. When she was back far enough, she got to her hands and knees under the protection of Richard's sword and collected the other two as he continued to guard her.

After she had the three mother's breath plants clutched in her hand, the two of them slowly retreated from the mouth of the cave. The mountain lion matched their movement, slowly slinking out with them while maintaining a safe distance, until it emerged from the darkness and into the light.

Richard gripped Vika's arm with one hand and pulled her behind him while he held the sword out with the other. Together they moved off to the side away from the angry animal.

Once they had left it enough room to escape, the mountain lion emerged from the cave, gave them a long, uncomfortable look, and then gracefully bounded off to their right, over the snow and among the sparse trees.

"It's heading toward the trail," Vika said as she pulled out a blanket to wrap up the plants. "That's an odd coincidence."

Richard watched where the mountain lion was slipping away. "We're long and well past the realm of coincidence."

104

Quiet darkness was settling into the woods when Richard spotted Nyda on watch long before she spotted him and Vika. When she finally did see him, she ran out and whistled a birdcall he had taught the Mord-Sith to alert the others that they had returned.

Rikka then emerged from the thick underbrush behind him. He hadn't spotted her. He was glad to see that they were using the tactic of positioning one person on watch so as to be spotted and distract anyone approaching. If it turned out to be a threat, the one still hidden could then take out that threat from behind. Even though he was glad to see them using their heads, he had more important things on his mind.

Richard and Vika were both exhausted from the long ride up the steep terrain, climbing the trail in the dark the entire night before, the hunt along the steep and difficult ground for the mother's breath, the tense encounter with the mountain lion, and then the difficult journey back down the mountains to where they had left Kahlan, Shale, and the rest of the Mord-Sith.

As they galloped into camp, Richard leaped off his horse. Berdine ran in and took the reins of both horses as Vika jumped down and handed Richard the blanket with their precious cargo. Shale was adding a stick of wood in the fire when she saw them ride in.

She stood and then rushed to meet them, brushing crumbs of bark from her hands. "Do you have it?"

Richard flipped open the blanket to show her. "How is Kahlan?"

Shale gently lifted out all three plants, using it as an excuse to divert her gaze. She looked amazed that they had actually found some mother's breath.

"Three! This is wonderful, and you managed to recover them with their taproots intact. I had dared not hope you would find even one. This is exactly what we need."

"I asked how Kahlan was."

Shale looked up from under her brow. "The Mother Confessor is asleep."

Richard gently grabbed Shale's upper arm. "I asked how she is."

The sorceress considered the intensity in his eyes briefly before answering. "She was losing the babies and her life along with theirs. The only thing I could think to do until you returned with the mother's breath was to use my gift to immerse her in a form of very deep sleep. I had to put her in that place between life and death. You called it the cusp. My hope is that inducing such a profound sleep will slow down all the functions in her body enough to keep her from miscarrying. It was the only way I could think of to save her and the twins. So far, she still has the babies and she is still breathing."

"But she will be all right." It came out more like a command than a question. He didn't like to hear that the sorceress had pushed Kahlan to the cusp between life and death. He didn't like it one bit. But he didn't want to second-guess her decisions. He knew the extent of the emergency, and that Shale would do everything she could to save Kahlan. "Now that we have the mother's breath, will she be all right?"

The sorceress hesitated. "I hope so. At least for now she and the twins are alive and together. With the mother's breath we have a chance. Now, I must hurry and prepare the medicine she needs."

"What can I do to help?" Richard asked as he followed close behind her as she hurried back to the fire.

Shale paused and considered a moment, looking toward the lean-to beyond a crackling fire before gazing at the three plants resting in her hand.

"I need to prepare the remedy, but that is going to take several hours. Since you were able to bring three plants, and considering the seriousness of the situation"—she handed Richard the one with the longest taproot—"maybe there is something you can do to help. Take this one, go to her, break off the bottom tip of the root, and then let the milky fluid drip into her mouth. She needs to swallow it. Do it only when you have it over her mouth so you don't waste any. It is a very rare and precious substance."

"If I'm going to let some of the milk drip into her mouth, why do you need to prepare a remedy?"

Shale didn't shy away from his gaze. "Lord Rahl, please do as I ask, and hurry."

Richard was concerned that she was deviating from the plan of preparing the plants first. He knew a great deal about plants and herbs, but he didn't know anything about mother's breath or how it needed to be prepared. He did know that there were plants that when prepared properly could heal. But he also knew that when raw and not properly prepared they could kill.

"Will it harm her to give her the raw milk of the plant? Are you sure you shouldn't prepare it first?"

Shale touched her fingers to the hollow of her neck as she considered it a moment. It was apparently a question that worried her, too.

"To tell you the truth, I can't be sure. I've never heard that mother's breath is poisonous, but also, I've never heard of giving a miscarrying woman the milk of the plant raw, rather than in a prepared remedy. I do know that the healing power of the plant lies in the milk." She held up a hand and rubbed her first two fingers together with her thumb. "It's a sticky substance, much stickier than the milky sap in any other plant. I believe that sticky quality is what may be the key to how the plant helps stop a miscarriage.

"I was told by an herb woman I knew that she believed the sticky milk of the mother's breath plant strengthens the bond the mother's body has with the unborn babies, keeping them in her womb. But to be honest, I've never heard of the milk being given raw. My thought is that women are always given the prepared potion but that may be because living plants are never at hand, whereas the preparation can be made up ahead of time and kept in stock, sealed in jars, ready for when needed in an emergency."

"Then to be safe, why not just wait until you can prepare the plants the way you were taught?"

Shale gave him a meaningful look. "Because it took you a long time to find the plant. Too long. I realize that's not your fault, and it is remarkable that you were even able to find it at all, but as far as the life of the Mother Confessor is concerned, it took too long. That's the reality.

"The only reason she hasn't miscarried and she is still alive is because I was there right when it started and so I was able to put her into that deep state of sleep before it had advanced too far. Traditionally the remedy is prepared by an herb woman for those times when it is urgently needed. That is often later when a healer has been summoned, so much time would have already passed by the time any help reached the mother. My intention was to prepare the plant in that way. But it took you a long time to return. Too long."

"But if you were to prepare it—"

"To be honest, Lord Rahl, even though she is in a deep sleep, I don't think your wife can last long enough for me to prepare the plants. My hope is that the raw milk will stop the miscarriage and keep the three of them alive and together until the preparation is ready. For all I know, the raw milk might even work better and then the prepared potion wouldn't even be needed.

"But what I can't say is that it won't do harm. In my judgment we have to chance it."

"It's a big chance," he said.

"It is," Shale agreed with a nod. "I leave the choice to you, then. You are her husband and would know best what her wishes would be. You decide for her. What would she want you to do?"

Richard didn't have to think about it. "She would say that it's the only chance for her and the babies, so we have no choice but to try it."

Shale offered him a brief smile. "Hurry, then, and give it to her."

Richard gripped the plant in his hand as he nodded. "How long will it take you to prepare the other two?"

She looked over at the fire. "To boil it down and prepare the remedy will take a few hours. I think you have made the right decision in the meantime. You must give her some of the raw milk now."

Richard looked down at the plant she had handed him. "Could it hurt her? Could it hurt her if it's raw, or hurt the babies?"

"I already told you that I just don't know." The sorceress glanced over the fire to the still Mother Confessor. "But I think that the problem may actually be if it works too well."

Richard frowned. "What do you mean?"

Shale looked back at him. "I mean that it may bind the babies into her so well that it may prove difficult for her to give birth."

"Well then, maybe—"

"Lord Rahl, there is no time. It is already long past when she should have been given the potion that I have yet to cook. By all rights, she shouldn't even still be alive. I doubt she will be for much longer. If you have made your decision, then you must do it now or she will be lost."

Richard let out a troubled sigh as he gently gripped the plant in his fist. He knew that there was really no choice. He just wished it were not a choice he had to make.

Shale put a hand on his forearm as if to steel him. "Hurry now. Go to her."

105

Richard's fear for Kahlan had him feeling like he was watching himself from somewhere high above the campsite as he rushed around the fire to the lean-to. If he had made the wrong decision, he could very well be about to poison the only woman he had ever loved, the only woman he ever could love.

He found Kahlan laid out just under the shelter of the lean-to on a bed of grass. She was covered with blankets. He marveled at how exquisite she looked in her deep sleep. It was the perfect innocence and beauty of a child. He hoped the sleep was a peaceful one. He knew, though, that if Shale really had succeeded in putting Kahlan in that nowhere place between the world of the living and the world of the dead, it was anything but peaceful there.

The Keeper of the underworld would be whispering promises to her, urging her to take that last step and enter his eternal realm of rest. Richard knew all too well that it was a seductive call and difficult to resist. But he knew, too, that she would be trying with all her will to resist so that her babies would have the chance to live. If she was able to resist that longing to be free of pain and suffering, it would be for them.

Cassia was there as well, on the opposite side of Kahlan from the fire, sitting on the ground beside her, holding her hand in both of hers. As Richard knelt down beside her, Cassia offered a hopeful smile as she moved back out of the way.

"How is she?" he asked back over his shoulder.

Cassia's voice was heavy with anguish. "She hasn't moved since Shale put her in a deep sleep. I was relieved, though, when she did because the Mother Confessor was struggling terribly in pain. I ached myself at seeing her in such agony. At least she is breathing more easily, now."

Richard nodded and turned back to Kahlan. He pushed her chin down until her mouth fell open. With his thumbnail, he clipped off the bottom of the taproot. One drop of the milky white sap dripped on her cheek before he could get the tip of the root over her mouth. As he held the plant over her with one hand, letting the milky fluid slowly drip into her mouth, he swept the drop up with a finger and wiped it onto the inside of her lower lip.

Even though she was still not conscious, Kahlan's tongue worked at the contact with the milky fluid. When the dripping slowed to a stop, Richard pushed up on her jaw to close her mouth. He knew she needed to get it into her stomach, so he was relieved to see her swallow.

After she had swallowed a few times, he opened her mouth again, then snapped off the taproot halfway up. When he did, more fluid again began running out, dripping into her mouth. Once the flow finally stopped, he closed her mouth again until she swallowed, then opened it and snapped the root off where it turned to the green stem. An even more plentiful, thicker flow started to drain from the rest of the plant. He understood, then, why Shale had told him that it had to be a living plant. A dead and dried-up plant would have no milky sap.

When the flow stopped, he worked his fingers to gradually wad up the plant in his fist. He squeezed to force out as much fluid as possible. When he was sure the dripping was finished, he handed the crumpled plant to Cassia.

"Take this to Shale. There may still be some milk in the plant that she can add to the medicine she's making."

Cassia nodded and then raced off to take the crumpled plant to the sorceress. Sitting on the cold ground beside Kahlan, Richard watched as Shale tore the plant into small pieces and added it to the steaming pot she already had cooking on the fire. She reached into a pocket of her trousers and pulled out a pouch. From the pouch she added a few pinches of some kind of powdered preparation to the pot.

As she stirred the boiling potion, Richard lay down close beside Kahlan to help keep her warm. He gently ran a hand over her round belly, hoping she would know that he was there with her. As much as he wanted to stay awake, he was exhausted and soon nodded off into a troubled sleep.

He hadn't been asleep long when he heard Shale speaking to some of the Mord-Sith. He sat up and rubbed his eyes. The brief nap had done nothing to banish his exhaustion. To his side, Vika sat on the ground, watching over him and Kahlan. He knew that she had to be just as tired as he was.

"Why don't you lie down and get some sleep?"

"I will," she answered. "But not until after the Mother Confessor gets the medicine Shale is preparing."

He looked over at Shale, squatted down beside the fire, leaning over the pot she had set on the ground, continually stirring the preparation. She lifted the stick out, letting the concoction drip off to test its consistency. She dipped her little finger into it to test if it had cooled enough. Apparently, it had. She gave an order to one of the Mord-Sith. Vale quickly stood and rushed to one of the saddlebags. She dug around until she came up with a piece of cloth.

Shale urged both Nyda and Vale to hold all four corners of the cloth. When they had, she slowly poured the pot of liquid in the cloth to filter the preparation and let it drip into a tin cup she had placed on the ground. Once the liquid had mostly dripped through, she took the cloth and twisted it around and around. She grimaced with the effort of squeezing out all the remaining liquid.

When she was finished, she threw the cloth and its contents onto the fire. Blue and green flames and glowing sparks shot up from the cloth as it burned, lighting the trees all around in flickering, colored light.

After dispensing with the filter cloth, she picked up the cup and hurried to Kahlan. She knelt down on the other side and set down the cup before putting a hand to Kahlan's forehead, checking on her fever.

"That's good. Her fever is down," Shale told Richard. She gestured. "Sit her up for me."

He carefully and gently scooped an arm under Kahlan's shoulders and lifted her. Kahlan's head slumped to the side. Shale straightened her head and then put her fingers on Kahlan's temples with her thumbs over her eyes. She softly spoke some kind of chant. Richard couldn't hear the words well enough to understand them. He doubted that even if he could hear them well enough he would have known what the words were. He assumed it was some sorceress's—or even witch's—spell. Sorceresses, and likely witch women, often relied on spells.

Whatever it was, it caused Kahlan to gasp in a deep breath along with Shale. Richard noticed that Shale synchronized her breathing with Kahlan's for a moment. Finally, the sorceress took her hands away and Kahlan opened her eyes.

Richard jumped a little in surprise. "Kahlan!" He was excited to see her awake. "How are you feeling?"

The sorceress swished a hand. "She can't hear you. She is still in that deep place. I don't want her to choke or drown when I give her the preparation."

Indeed, Kahlan seemed completely unresponsive. Though her eyes were open, it didn't seem like she saw anything. Still, Richard felt hope at seeing her beautiful green eyes. There was life in them, and that was cause for hope.

As he held Kahlan up, Shale brought the tin cup with the milky potion to her lips. As she tipped it in, Kahlan began to drink it. It took a while for her to slowly drink it all. When she had, Shale took the cup away and motioned for Richard to lay her back down. As he did, Kahlan's eyes closed once more.

Shale stood and let out a weary sigh. "Now we must let the mother's breath do its work—both what you gave her and what I prepared. When it has done all it can, and if it is enough, she will wake on her own from the deep sleep and be fully back in the world of life. Until then, let her rest. Tonight determines if she will survive this ordeal or not. Until then, we all need to sleep to be able to face what tomorrow holds."

Richard couldn't take issue with that. He nodded as Shale went to her nearby bedroll. She looked exhausted. Richard was as well, but he was worried that the medicine might not work. He was terrified that he might lose Kahlan this night. But at least she seemed to be resting peacefully. What terrified him more was that she might instead rest peacefully for eternity with the good spirits.

He leaned close. "Life is a struggle," he whispered to her. "Fight for me, for us, for our children."

When he was finished and sat back up, Cassia touched his shoulder. "Berdine and I will watch over her tonight. You and Vika need to get some sleep."

Richard didn't want to sleep. More than his better judgment, it was his exhaustion that made him lie down beside Kahlan. He kissed her cheek and then gripped her hand in his.

106

Richard was having a wonderful dream that Kahlan was kissing him. As it always did, the feel of her soft lips on his seemed to open up the feminine half of the universe to him. It was a profound completion of his reason for being. It made him whole.

As he was kissing her, something made him open his eyes. He abruptly realized that it wasn't a dream.

It was not yet dawn, but through the trees he could see the eastern sky just beginning to brighten a bit. Her hair had fallen down to flow around his face. Flickering firelight gave her face a warm glow as she pulled back and looked down at him with that radiant smile he knew so well.

"You were sleeping so peacefully, I didn't want to wake you." The smile widened with mischievousness. "But I couldn't resist kissing you."

Richard let out a deep breath of relief as he embraced her, holding her tight to him. His fears melted away in that moment.

He finally gripped her shoulders and lifted her back away from him. "How do you feel?"

Her mouth twisted playfully. "Pretty good now that I've had a kiss."

"No, I mean everything else." He looked at her skeptically. "Are you all right?"

She shrugged. "I feel surprisingly well, actually. I think I was having a terrible nightmare and it felt like I was asleep forever in some faraway place. I didn't like being in that place. While I was sleeping, I thought I heard you say that life is a struggle, and I should fight for you, for us, and for our children. So I did and woke up."

Seeing that Kahlan was awake and up, Shale threw off her blanket and rushed around the fire. "Mother Confessor! You're awake. How are you feeling. Don't try to stand. Any pain? Are you hurting anywhere?"

Kahlan struggled to sit up as Shale tried to push her back down. "I feel like I've had a very long and restful sleep, actually. I feel fine." As the Mord-Sith rushed up around them, Kahlan frowned. "Why is everyone acting so strange?"

"You don't remember?" Richard asked.

Kahlan made a face as she half smiled. "No. Remember what?"

"You... were having difficulty with your pregnancy," Shale said.

Kahlan's face suddenly went ashen. "What?"

The sorceress waved her hands to dispel the fear from Kahlan's suddenly pale expression. "No, no, everything is fine, now. Lord Rahl found a plant I needed to make you some medicine and it fixed you right up. It was not a big thing, really. You were exhausted and just needed a bit of medicine and rest, so I helped you go to sleep. Don't worry, everything is fine, now."

Kahlan looked skeptically at all the faces watching her as she ran a hand over her round belly. "Are you sure?" She looked under the blanket. "Where are my trousers?"

When everyone was silent for a moment, Rikka finally spoke up. "I washed them for you, Mother Confessor. I dried them by the fire. They are ready whenever you want them."

"I made some breakfast," Berdine said with a big grin. "I thought you would be hungry when you woke up. We have fresh fish and rabbit. Which do you prefer? I have to say, I like the rabbit best."

"Well, actually, I am pretty hungry. The fish sounds good." She tipped her head to look out of the lean-to. "It looks like the weather is no better."

Richard glanced out. "At least it's not snowing down here. Fortunately it's not raining any longer, either. At least for now. The weather in these mountains can change in an instant, but I don't think it's going to be getting much better for a while."

"Well," Kahlan said, "we need to get moving south to try to find a way to get around these mountains if I'm to have these babies at the Wizard's Keep."

"There can be no going south," Shale said with a frown. "Not with that boundary wall of death thing."

"The boundary..." Kahlan's brow twitched a little as she put a hand to her forehead. "That's right. I seem to have forgotten that we had run into the boundary..."

"Lord Rahl found a trail leading to a pass over the mountains," Vika said, hoping to dispel Kahlan's sudden concern.

Kahlan's mouth fell open. "A trail over a pass? That would mean the boundary wouldn't matter and we can cross the mountains here. That would get us directly to Aydindril." She looked up hopefully. "If there is a pass, we could get over the mountains right away. That would significantly shorten our journey."

"The sooner the better," Shale said. "You aren't getting any less pregnant. I would feel a lot better if we weren't out in the wilderness when the time comes to give birth."

Kahlan still seemed somewhat confused. "So then I'm all right? The twins are all right? Was I having some kind of trouble?"

Some of the Mord-Sith exchanged glances. Everyone noticed that Kahlan seemed not to remember what had happened. Richard could see no reason to tell her how close she had come to losing the babies, to say nothing of her life. It would needlessly frighten her to know how grave the situation had been. From the looks on all the other faces, it seemed that none of the rest of them thought it would be a good idea to tell her, either.

Berdine suddenly smiled brightly. "Lord Rahl found a plant that made you all well again."

Kahlan looked over at him and put a hand on his chest. "Was it any trouble?"

"None at all," Vika said from behind Richard.

Richard wasn't as happy about the pass as the rest of them. It seemed everything had been conspiring to force them to cross the mountains in this place. Someone was behind the strange woods they lost so much time in. Someone had usurped his ability and used it to put up those boundaries. Kahlan had begun to miscarry and he had to find a very rare plant to save her and the babies. There just happened to be some of those very rare mother's breath plants up the mountain trail they just happened to come across.

Whatever hidden hand was behind all of the recent events seemed determined to get them up into these mountains. And there just so happened to be an old trail for them to use.

"As soon as we have something to eat then we should probably get going," he said. "There is no telling how long this break in the weather will last. It would be good to make some distance while we have the chance."

She flashed him a smile. "I would like that. The sooner we are to Aydindril the better. I feel well rested. I'm up for some traveling."

"I'm afraid it's going to be a difficult journey," Richard cautioned her. "It's a demanding climb from here to get to the trail, and the trail itself is not an easy one. I'm afraid that once we get to it, there is no way to take the horses up that trail and over that pass."

"Well," she said, thoughtfully, "I expect the horses will enjoy their freedom. I'm sure they will be glad not to have to carry us and all our gear any longer."

Richard smiled. Kahlan always tried to find the bright side of things. He was sure she was worried about what lay ahead for them, but she didn't want to show her concern. As the Mother Confessor, she always tried to keep everyone positive. Richard wasn't feeling nearly so positive. As pregnant as she was, it was going to be a difficult journey on foot.

Worse, he knew that they were being guided by a hidden hand.

107

Fat snowflakes drifted through the still, cold air, dissolving away the instant they touched Richard's face and the backs of his hands. Dark, brooding clouds overhead seemed to hang still in the pass, casting the day in gloomy light. Richard could just make out the smell of woodsmoke. They all lay in a line on their stomachs in the fresh snow, heads just high enough to peek over the edge of the ridge in order to squint into the distance.

Richard was not liking what he was seeing.

"Why would such a strange place be way up here?" Rikka asked.

Nyda pulled the small willow stick she had been idly chewing from her mouth. "Maybe it's a stroke of luck."

"It's not a stroke of luck," Kahlan said, clearly as unhappy as Richard was at what they all saw in the distance.

"Why not?" Nyda asked. "Shelter, warmth, food, rest. That sounds like a stroke of luck to me. What could be wrong with that?"

"It's a trap," Richard said in a distracted voice as he peered into the distance. "That's what's wrong with it."

Nyda put her chew-stick back in her mouth as she let herself slide back down the snow-covered slope a little ways, retreating from the edge of the ridge so she could sit up without taking the chance of revealing herself to anyone beyond. She planted a boot against the base of a birch tree to halt her slide. "You really think so?"

"Everything that has happened has contrived to put us up here, on this trail, with nowhere else to go," Vika said with obvious displeasure as she looked over the edge of the ridge, watching into the distance with the rest of them. "Do you really think that coming upon this place is just chance?"

Nyda sighed. "I suppose not."

"This is the trap that has been pulling us in ever since we left the People's Palace," Richard said.

With a cunning look, Nyda spun her Agiel up into her fist. "Maybe I should go take a look."

"Not a good idea," Vika said.

Nyda dropped her Agiel, letting it hang from the gold chain around her wrist. She pulled the stick out of her mouth again. "Why not? A Mord-Sith might be the right thing to set the mood up there and change our luck."

Vika looked back over her shoulder. "The Law of Nines, remember? We need the nine of us to stay together."

"Vika is right," Richard murmured as he watched for any sign of people. He was sure that the Golden Goddess was still searching for them, so he didn't want anyone who might be out beyond to see them. There was no telling how many eyes the goddess could be looking through as she frantically hunted for him and Kahlan.

The town in the distance, off through the heavy timber, had been built hard up against the pass, spanning the broad distance from one towering bluff to the other, some of the buildings piled up on top of one another in what looked like an unplanned, haphazard fashion, making them appear hunched together against the elements. It was hard to tell at such a distance, but it looked like there was a stone wall built all the way across the pass, entirely blocking the way through. He supposed it was possible it was simply built that way to take advantage of the lay of the land. But in his gut, he knew there was more to it.

The massive fortress town grew right up behind the stone wall, the wall itself so high it rose up above some of the treetops. The tree line and barren ground above overlooked the town from each side of the wide pass.

As far as Richard could tell, the only way over the pass was through that walled fortress. He had trouble imagining the reason for a fortress in such an isolated place. Of course, it was possible that it wasn't really a fortress at all, and it only appeared that way from a distance. Again, his gut told him that wasn't the case.

Up inside the wall built across the pass and beyond the jumble of structures, he could just make out a much taller, more impressive-looking structure of some sort. It looked like maybe it was made from a pale-colored or white stone.

It had to be a difficult life in such a remote place. As such, it seemed an odd place for a grand structure of any sort to be towering in its midst.

Richard didn't think there could be more than a few thousand people at most living in the town. The smell of woodsmoke told him that the place was not abandoned. If it was not abandoned, then the goddess might be able to use the people living there to finally spot and attack them.

Unfortunately, the only way across the pass was to go through that fortress town.

Kahlan put her hand on his forearm. "I don't like it. Like you say, it's a trap. Everything that has happened to us since leaving the People's Palace has been leading us right to here."

Richard nodded. "I'm afraid you're right."

She rolled a bit to the side, looking like it was uncomfortable to be lying on her swelled belly. "So what are we going to do about it?"

In the middle distance, on the path leading through the snow-crusted trees and among the rocks rising up from the thick white blanket of snow covering the ground, and across another snow-covered rise, he could just make out the tracks of a big mountain lion. He didn't have to wonder if it was the same one he and Vika had encountered when searching for the mother's breath.

"Well," he finally said, "Zedd told me once that one should not willingly walk into a trap."

Shale scowled over at him. "Is that another one of your Wizard's Rules?"

Richard looked over and showed her a crooked smile. "If it isn't, it should be."

"Is that all of what Zedd had to say about it?" Kahlan asked.

"Actually," Richard said, "the rest of it is 'unless you have no other choice.'"

"Well, it looks to me like this would qualify as 'no other choice,'" she said.

They all turned to look up at the gray clouds when rumbles of thunder echoed through the mountains. The low, ragged clouds that were silently gliding in obscured the higher peaks, and by the looks of them, they promised some bad weather.

"I grew up in mountains like this," Vika said. "Thunder and snow high up in the mountains are a worrisome pair."

"So what are we going to do?" Kahlan asked, ignoring Vika's comment and obviously growing impatient. "I'm not in favor of walking into a trap. Someone wants my babies. I don't intend to simply walk in there and hand them over or have them taken from me. But I'm cold and I want to get beyond these mountains and down into Aydindril, where it will be warmer. We can't lie here forever watching that place."

Richard let out a long breath. The rising breeze carried away the cloud of that breath as he appraised her green eyes. "I agree." He showed her a smile. "I have a plan."

Kahlan arched an eyebrow. "A good plan?"

He wasn't in the mood to debate the merits of it. He was more concerned about avoiding whatever kind of trap waited for them in the walled stronghold blocking the pass. He was also concerned about the way the wind was coming up and the weather was closing in. The night before had been miserable huddled in the protection of a quickly built pine-bough shelter, with no fire, as they ate some of their dwindling supply of dried meat and hard travel biscuits.

"First," he said, "I need to know if you're up for a difficult attempt to get over these mountains in order to avoid walking into the trap that's waiting for us."

Kahlan frowned at him. "What are you proposing?"

Richard put an arm over her shoulders and pulled her close so she could sight down the length of his other arm to where he was pointing.

"Look at that notch to the left side of the pass, just before the slope of the second mountain over starts to rise up again. See what I'm talking about?"

Kahlan squinted into the distance. "I can't tell for sure. You always could see better than me. And you know more about such country than I would."

"Well, there's an indentation in the side of where that mountain rises up." He gestured to indicate the slope on the left side of the pass. "That notch is higher than the pass with that walled town built across the trail, but it might be a way over the mountains without having to go through the town. See? Up there not far above the tree line."

"I see it," Shale said as she pushed in close on the other side of him, finally seeing where he was talking about.

"I see it too," Vika offered.

"What of it?" Kahlan asked. "What are you thinking?"

"Like I said, it might be a way over the mountains. A way to skirt that walled fortress built across the pass."

"You mean a way to skirt that trap?" the sorceress asked.

Richard nodded. "Yes. I think it could give us a way to avoid walking into a trap and instead go right around it. If it is a way across, we could avoid anyone seeing us, and we just might be able to make our own luck and get over the mountains and into Aydindril and then to the Wizard's Keep."

"Then what are we waiting for?" Kahlan asked, blowing some warm breath into her cupped hands again.

"I'm waiting for you to tell me that you're up for it. It's going to be a difficult climb. It's not a trail, so we will have to make our own way. It will be hard climbing."

"I'm pregnant," Kahlan said, "I'm not helpless, and I'm not eager to spend any longer up here than necessary. Let's get going while we still have light."

108

The light was fading fast by the time they got closer to the notch Richard had spotted from back in the forest. Some of the way was steep and dangerous. They had struggled to make it through the snow up above the tree line.

In several places Richard had to climb up, lie on his stomach, and then reach down to help Kahlan, because her pregnancy made it more difficult for her to pull herself up, and also Berdine, because her arms weren't long enough to reach the edge. Once, when there was no practical way around, Richard had to quickly fell a pair of trees so they could cross a deep chasm. As they got higher, frigid winds funneled through the canyons to sting their faces with ice crystals.

In spots the thick blanket of snow hid deep ravines and rifts in the uneven, rocky ground. After Kahlan sank up to her armpits in one of those rifts, and he and Vika had to pull her up and out, Richard cut a long staff and took the lead, testing for ground under the way ahead to make sure it was solid. He cut a similar staff for Vika. She walked beside him, and together they tested the ground ahead. He had the rest of them follow in his and Vika's footsteps so that they wouldn't drop into a hole where they could easily be hurt, or worse.

As they got closer to the towering mountain, it was easier to see the notch in its lower slopes. The sun was setting beyond, to the west, where they needed to go, and even though it was cloudy, the brighter light of the western sky silhouetted the shape of the mountain to reveal the cut in the rock.

"Numbers mean things, right?" Berdine asked as they trudged through the snow. "I mean, like the Law of Nines. You said before that numbers have meaning."

Richard looked back over his shoulder. "Yes, sometimes. Why?"

Berdine squinted, shielding her eyes with a hand as she peered up at the gray sky. "Well, there are thirteen ravens circling us. Does that mean something? Thirteen?"

"They've been following us since we left the trail," Richard said.

"Really? I didn't notice them before," Berdine said, her voice trailing off as she turned, looking up. "But now that they are overhead, I noticed them going around in a circle as they follow us. So, does it mean something that there are thirteen?"

Richard poked his staff into the ground ahead, testing. "Hard to tell. A lot of numbers have meaning. Some are more important than others. It often has to do with circumstances surrounding the numbers or even the context that makes the number significant. I can tell you, though, that ravens are crazy smart, and they are as curious as cats."

"Oh," Berdine said, not really knowing if that answered her question or not. "I just thought that maybe thirteen meant something."

Richard glanced back over his shoulder at the witch woman. Her face was unreadable. He decided not to get into it and instead started out again.

Like the rest of them, he was bone-tired. Walking in deep snow was a lot of work. Kahlan was following behind Vika, trying to walk in her footsteps, but even though the person ahead was breaking a trail, it still took a grueling effort to pull each leg out of one hole and put it in the next. He could see that Kahlan was near to dropping from exhaustion. He wanted to stop and rest, but with the day drawing to an end he knew she would want to keep going while they still could, and she would want even less for them to stop because of her.

There was still enough light for them to see their way by the time they made it to the notch. As they worked deeper into the cut through the mountain he had seen earlier, sheer rock rose up to each side. It looked like slabs of the granite making up the mountain had broken off and fallen away, leaving the opening for them to make it through. The fractured rock created small shelves that allowed snow to build up, making white ledges that stood out against the gray rock.

In the sky between the soaring granite walls, he could see the thirteen ravens circling high overhead. Sometimes ravens followed hikers, hoping to snatch small animals such as voles that were flushed out by the noise and vibration of people walking.

He didn't think these ravens were looking for voles.

Richard was relieved to see ahead that there was easily going to be enough room for them to make it through the opening, although the snow had built up in the sheltered gap between sheer walls, making it deeper and progress even more difficult. But at least it was a way to finally get across the mountains and around the trap. With the light fading fast they were all eager to get through the opening before they had to stop for the night, so, despite their exhaustion, they pressed on through the deep snow.

No one wanted to waste their breath to talk. No one wanted to give up until they were at last through. Each of them struggled to simply put one foot in front of the other.

To make matters worse, the wind had picked up and snow was beginning to fall harder all the time. It collected on their eyelashes and it had to be blinked away to see.

Every few difficult strides through the deep, packed snow, they had to pause to get their breath in the thin air of the higher altitude. They were all keen to get far enough to finally see beyond and confirm that they had indeed managed to find a way across the mountain range by skirting the trap of that strange fortress town across the pass.

Richard expected that once beyond the walls to each side of the notch and finally on the way down, they would all need to at least stop and rest, if not stop for the night, but he would prefer to press on long enough to make it down to the tree line and get back into the shelter of the forest before they stopped. He could see the tops of trees beyond, so he knew that the ground descended just ahead and the next day they would finally be able to start down out of the cold and snow of the towering mountains, down to where winter hadn't yet fully taken hold.

As Richard poked his staff in the snow ahead and took another step, the air all around unexpectedly began to glow green. There was no mistaking that color for anything else.

Vika, her head down as she wearily plodded forward, was out a little ahead of him. She took another step and a hard, green wall lit in the air all around her.

Richard reached out, grabbed her arm, and yanked her back before she even realized what she had almost walked into. She looked up, stunned to see that she had nearly entered the world of the dead without even realizing it. She had been so focused on making headway that she was only watching the pole she was using to check the ground where she wanted to put her foot next.

They all stood stunned, staring at the greenish glow to the air before them. There was no need to talk; they all knew what it meant. They all felt the same sense of bitter disappointment.

Kahlan dropped to her knees in tears. Richard pulled the blanket she had around her shoulders up tighter around her ears to keep her warm. He hugged her, then, holding her head to his shoulder. He hated to see her in a state of such despair and on the edge of giving up. Shale touched her shoulder, as did several of the Mord-Sith. They all felt that same sense of wordless despair, but Kahlan seemed to be the one who most exemplified what they were all feeling.

"It's clear that we can't go any farther," Richard said as he looked up at the rest of them all huddled around. "We need to go back."

"I'm so tired…" Kahlan wept.

"The sun is down and it's getting dark fast," Richard said. He looked up at the others. "We need shelter for the night. We need to get her warmer. I'm sure we can't make it back down to the tree line. These rock walls offer some protection, but not enough."

"We need to go back just far enough to be clear of this boundary of death and then make a snow cave," Shale said. "We do that often in the Northern Waste. It's a quick way to have shelter and it can save your life on a cold night."

Still holding Kahlan's head to his shoulder, Richard nodded. "That would make the most sense."

Shale pointed. "That spot just back there, where the snow is drifted up against the jog in the face of the rock wall, would be good. The snow will be deeper there and compacted from the wind that drove it in there."

"Let's hurry and get it done before it gets too dark," Richard said. "We'll all feel better when we can get out of the wind and have something to eat."

Directed by Shale, the Mord-Sith began digging into the tightly packed snow. Once they had a good start on a cavern, Shale had them stand back. With them safely out of the way, the sorceress cast her hands out, sending a roaring stream of orange and yellow flame into the cavity. It curled around, melting the snow in deeper. She held her hands out, to keep the fire going, until it had melted a big enough space down inside for them. The snow walls to the side that had been melting quickly froze into a glaze of ice.

Richard glanced up at the black clouds through the snow that was beginning to fall in earnest, swirling around in gusts through the split in the mountain. "The storm is upon us. We need to get out of the weather."

Shale nodded. "Take the Mother Confessor into the back, against the rock wall. It will be warmest against the rock from the heat of the fire. It should be hot enough to let us all get warm. The ice walls will keep the heat in for a while, and I can use my gift to warm the rock when we need it."

"That sounds wonderful," Kahlan said through chattering teeth.

109

At first light they dug their way out of their cozy snow cave. After they all emerged, they began making their way back down the mountain to the shelter of the forest. Their breath drifted slowly in the bright, clear air. The fresh snow from the night before had completely covered their tracks with a new layer, making it even more difficult to walk than it had been the day before. The momentum of going downhill, though, was a bit of a help. Still, it took a lot of effort to make it back down to the forest and below the ridgeline where they had first spotted the town built across the mountain pass.

"What are we going to do?" Kahlan finally asked when they stopped to rest on a rock outcropping that was blown clear of snow but was ice cold.

It was a question they all had on their mind, but no one else had wanted to ask.

Richard scanned the thick woods. "We need to make a good shelter, clear some snow away, and build a fire. We all need food and rest to get our strength back."

"No," Kahlan said. "What I meant is what are we going to do about the boundary stopping us? I don't see any other way but to go to that town to get through the pass."

Richard shook his head. "I'm not ready to do that. We know there are people there. If the goddess can use them, we could suddenly find ourselves fighting an army of Glee. We need to avoid that at all costs. We need to recover and think this through before we do anything."

"So, what are we going to do, then?" Kahlan pressed. "We obviously can't go back."

Richard gave her a look. "We are going to make camp."

He didn't want to tell them what he had in mind. So instead, he went about cutting some young trees and stripping them of limbs to make poles. He used one of the bigger poles to span between the crotches of a couple of trees and used a vine to secure them. As he cut down more saplings the Mord-Sith placed them against both sides of the one bigger pole spanning between trees to make a roof of sorts, leaving a space on one end for an opening to get inside. Richard made sure the space inside was big enough for all of them.

He finally gestured. "Shale, could you clear the snow away in front of the door for a fire?"

The sorceress used fists of air driven by her gift to blast the snow from the ground for their shelter. It cleared the snow down to the forest floor. Scraping away wet leaves and branches uncovered solid rock that was broad enough to be a good place for a fire.

Some of the Mord-Sith went about collecting pine, spruce, and balsam boughs to place against the poles to form a roof to protect them from the wind if it came up again and hold in the heat. It took several hours to complete the roof.

While they were doing that, a couple of the others collected dried deadwood for a fire. They stacked up the wood and as it began growing dark Shale sent fire into the stack. In short order they had a good blaze going. The fire crackled as it burned the pine, sending sparks swirling up into the air.

While Richard set fishing lines in a nearby stream, and Kahlan squatted before the fire warming her hands, Berdine, Vale, and Rikka spread out all the bedrolls inside the shelter. There wasn't a lot of room inside, but the tight quarters would help keep them all warm. Nyda and Cassia brought more dried wood from the surrounding woods and stacked it to the sides so there would be a supply throughout the night. The crackling fire lit the trees all around, sending sharp shadows into the darkness.

After they had collected enough wood, they all gathered around the fire for a meager meal from the supplies they still had left. They were all hungry and there was only sporadic conversation as each of them tore off pieces of dried meat and salted fish. It wasn't very enjoyable, but at least it helped quench their gnawing hunger. They scooped up snow in tin cups and set them close to the fire to melt the snow for drinking water.

After they had all eaten, the Mord-Sith decided on watches. Richard let them talk him into sleeping the whole night. He knew he was going to need the rest. Once their meager dinner was finished, they all crawled into the shelter, except Vika and Nyda, who had first watch.

Richard hugged Kahlan close to him. He ached all over from the strenuous hike up to the notch and back, and he knew she felt just as sore. It was a lot of effort that had in the end been for nothing. They were all disheartened that their way had been unexpectedly blocked by the boundary. At least it felt good to have Kahlan tight up beside him. He enjoyed the quiet pleasure of holding her as long as he could, but in mere moments, sleep took him.

At the first hint of light, Richard woke when he heard Rikka putting more wood on the fire. He sat up and stretched as quietly as he could. Kahlan was still asleep. But when he started to climb out from under the blanket that had been around both of them, she woke up.

He told her to go back to sleep. He was relieved that she lay back down while he made his way out of the low shelter. He searched around until he found some tender saplings, then set to work. He used his knife to split them and then bend them around to make a hoop. With a supply of leather thongs from his pack, he wove a net across the loop of wood.

About the time he finished, everyone woke up and came out. They dug travel biscuits from their packs and had a quick bite to eat as they all rubbed sleep from their eyes.

"All right," Kahlan finally said, "we're rested. So what are we going to do now?"

Richard, his forearms resting on his knees, chewed the hard biscuit for a moment before answering.

"Well, you all are going to camp here and get some rest."

Shale, Vika, and Kahlan all looked up suspiciously.

"And what do you intend to do while we all 'rest'?" Kahlan asked.

"I'm going to go into the mountains on the other side of the town. I'm going to see if I can find another way around."

"You mean you are going to go see if the boundary is over on that side, too," Kahlan said, obviously realizing what he was up to.

"We need to know for sure if there is a way through or not."

"Then we should all go," Kahlan said.

Everyone else shifted their gazes between the two of them, not wanting to get in the middle of what was Kahlan's obvious displeasure at the plan and Richard's clear determination.

"No," he said, "we should not all go. I can travel faster by myself. There is no reason to expose you to the dangers and the difficult hike if it turns out to be for nothing, like it did on the other side. If I find a way through, I'll come back and by then you all will be rested and ready to travel."

"You're not going alone," Vika finally said. "I'm going with you."

"Not this time."

"Why?" Kahlan said. "Why can't you at least take Vika?"

"Because with me gone, I want everyone else to be here to protect you, that's why."

Vika clearly looked upset. "Lord Rahl, I—"

"I want you to stay here and protect the Mother Confessor. We don't know what dangers might be about. She carries our children, our hope for the future of our world. I want her protected." He stood, lifting his pack, slinging it up on one shoulder. He picked up his bow from where it was leaning against the shelter. "The subject is not open to debate. Check the fishing lines. Hopefully you can all have some fresh fish. I'll be back as soon as I can."

"You said that we have to all stay together," Berdine said, "for that Law of Nines thing."

"I'm doing what I think best," he said. "It doesn't take nine of us to trudge through deep snow to scout the terrain. Scouting ahead is what I'm good at."

Berdine pointed off through the trees to where the ravens had roosted. "Can you at least shoot a few with your bow so that their number will be less, like ours will?"

"It can't be done," Richard said.

"Why not?"

"Because the ravens would not allow it."

Berdine wrinkled up her nose. "Not allow it? What are you talking about?"

Richard gestured to the birds perched on branches in the pines. "Watch."

He turned his back on them as he quickly strung the bow. He gripped it in one hand as he pulled an arrow from the quiver over his shoulder. He quickly nocked the arrow in the string, and then turned around toward the ravens. Before he could even raise the bow to aim, all the ravens started squawking as they took to wing and, in an instant, had vanished back into the trees.

Richard cocked an eyebrow at Berdine as he replaced the arrow in the quiver and hooked the bow over his shoulder.

"Like I said before, ravens are crazy smart. But those are not merely ravens. I want Kahlan protected while I'm gone." His gaze swept over everyone watching him. "Is that clear?"

Once Shale and all the Mord-Sith nodded, he sat on the edge of the rocks and bent to tie the snowshoes he had made to his boots.

"That's pretty creepy," Berdine said as she looked again to see that the ravens had vanished. "It's like they're watching us."

"They are, so they will be back," he said. "Now, all of you watch over Kahlan for me until I get back. Please," he added.

Without waiting for them to raise objections, Richard started out, pleased to discover how well the snowshoes worked. It would make it a lot easier to cover ground quickly.

110

As he expected, one of the thirteen ravens left the others to follow him as he quickly made his way through the woods. It flew through the forest, weaving in and out among the branches as if they weren't even there to get out ahead of him, and then with a quick flutter of its black wings settled on a branch to wait for him to pass underneath. As he did, it would turn its head to look down at him with one black, glossy eye.

The bird's black eyes reminded him of the eyes of the Glee. It was wearisome the way there was always someone or something watching them so that they were never completely alone, to know instead that they were always being observed for any sign of weakness and for the right time to attack.

He knew that if he wanted to, he could kill the raven—what he had done before with the bow was just to show the others that these were not merely wild ravens so that they would be on alert—but he also knew that killing it would accomplish nothing, so he didn't want to reveal his ability before it became necessary.

Besides, the animal itself was innocent. It was merely being used, much the same way the goddess looked through the eyes of unsuspecting people. He actually rather liked ravens, although they were often quite noisy.

Richard was happy to find that the snowshoes made for much easier progress over the snow. They weren't perfect, but they worked. Rather than his legs sinking in with each step, he could simply walk on the surface almost as well as he could on the bare ground.

He didn't know why he hadn't thought of it the day before as they had struggled to make their way up the mountain to the notch he'd spotted. He guessed that he was letting himself become too focused with worry of what was going on and with what he had been hoping would be their way out. He supposed that he simply wasn't thinking straight.

He reprimanded himself that such lapses could be fatal. They were in a lot of trouble, more trouble than any of the others realized, and he needed to think clearly. That was the only thing that was going to save them.

He wasn't concerned about leaving the rest of them back at camp. He knew they weren't in danger there. The danger was in that fortress town built across the pass. That was where the spider waited at the center of this web.

They had discovered that to the left of the fortress town in the pass the boundary blocked their way. He needed to see if there was a way around the pass on the other side so that they could make it to the Wizard's Keep without having to go into that fortress. He had to know if they had a choice or if the boundary continued on to the right of the town.

As the day wore on, he continued to push, making more progress than he ever could have if he had let Kahlan and the others come with him. Kahlan never complained about the physical challenges, but with her being pregnant it was difficult for her to push as hard as she would like to or as hard as he could alone. Before she had become pregnant with the twins, he would never have had any doubt that she could keep up with him. At times, if anything, he had trouble keeping up with her. But he knew that now she couldn't.

When he finally made it above the tree line, he stopped and turned back to see the raven sitting on a bare limb, watching him. He turned and started ahead, panting with the effort and the thin air at this altitude.

After a time, he paused and with a hand shielded his eyes from the bright sunlight as he scanned the mountainside. While the place he spotted was far from ideal, and he knew it likely wouldn't be a way they could cross the mountains, he headed for the spot anyway, because it would serve his purpose to confirm what he suspected. In such a life-and-death situation, he dared not leave any stone—or escape route—unturned.

It was sometime in the mid-afternoon when he had to remove his snowshoes to start climbing bare rock that had been blown mostly clean of snow by the howling winds. At least those winds were now calm. It was hard climbing, but he was able to keep going without stopping to rest. Some of the places were so high that he had to jump and grab an edge with his fingers and then pull himself up. After such places, he had to lie on his back and catch his breath in the thin air.

His legs ached, and the altitude was not only causing him to become easily winded, it was starting to make him feel sick. The answer, he knew, was to reach the place that would tell him one way or the other what he needed to know, and then he could start back down.

As he pulled himself up and over the top of another ledge, he saw that the way ahead was relatively flat and would be a lot easier walking. As he started across, he could see trackless forests of trees crusted with snow blanketing the slopes beyond, on the way down. It would be impossible to climb down the cliffs on the other side of the place he had reached, but that wasn't important for now, so he kept going.

Partway across the broad ledge, he abruptly had to stop when the air all around him lit with green light. Another careful step and the wall of green appeared all around him.

It was the boundary he expected to find but had hoped he wouldn't. He found no joy in confirmation that he had been right.

Richard backed away from the boundary until it became invisible again and he could see beyond, then sat down on a knee-high section of ledge. He put his face in his hands, disheartened at the discovery. He had known the boundary would in all likelihood be there. Finding it removed all hope that they could avoid what he knew waited for them in that fortress built across the pass.

When he looked up, he spotted the mountain lion sitting on its haunches some distance away, its color making it blend in well with the rock. When their gazes met, the animal rose up and stretched, arching its back with its paws stretched out in front. Long, sharp claws came out from its paws as it stretched, scraping across the rock. The big cat stared at him the whole time.

Richard lifted his sword a few inches to make sure it was clear as he stared back at the sleek creature. He let the weapon drop back in its scabbard, sending a clear message of his own.

"Tell your mistress that I'm coming for her," he called out to the mountain lion.

The creature stared at him for a moment longer, then turned and trotted off.

Richard knew who it was going back to.

He now knew for certain that they had no choice.

111

When Kahlan, sitting in front of the fire to stay warm, heard one of the Mord-Sith let out a birdcall, she stood. Shale rose to her feet beside her.

"Do you think it's Richard?" the sorceress asked.

"Yes, it's him. Nyda would have made a different call if it wasn't, if it was a stranger or some kind of trouble. He's finally back."

Cassia glanced back over her shoulder to the woods in the direction of the birdcall, then put another stick of wood on the fire before standing. A spit over the fire had rabbits roasting. The cooking meat smelled good, but Kahlan, wringing her hands expectantly, was too worried about what word Richard would bring to them to be hungry.

When she spotted him coming out of the trees with Nyda, she ran to him and threw her arms around his neck. Her loneliness and worry of the day melted away at the sight of him. Something about being pregnant made her want to be close to him all the more.

She kissed his neck. "I'm so glad you're back. I was so worried."

Even though she was relieved that he was safe, the grim look on his face had her stomach once again feeling like it was tightening in knots. She gestured back to the fire.

"Cassia and Vale set snares and caught some rabbits. There were also some fish on the lines you set out before. You're just in time so that we can have a good meal together. We all need it. Come and have something to eat. You must be starving."

She could tell that he was deeply troubled, so she didn't want to press as to why just then. She knew that he would soon enough tell them all what he had learned. By that troubled look, though, she knew it would not be good news.

He put his arm around her waist as they walked together to the fire and then sat cross-legged on the bare ground. The fire had been going since the day before, so it had warmed the rock they were all sitting on, making it a cozy refuge from the cold.

Cassia tore off a big piece of meat from one of the already-cooked rabbits sitting beside the fire to keep it warm. She grinned as he took the meat from her.

"We used snares—like you showed us," she told him.

Richard returned a smile. "I'm proud of you. You did good."

"So are you going to tell us where you went and why?" Shale asked, obviously not willing to wait for him to decide to tell them in his own way and time.

"I had to confirm that the boundary was also on the other side of the town blocking that pass. It was. It runs off in both directions."

That bit of news was disheartening, but not exactly unexpected.

"It wasn't worth all of us going just to find that out. Going alone I made good time and was able to confirm it quickly," he explained. "That means that we now know that the boundary makes a big loop all the way around us, and likely around the People's Palace as well. It's a noose drawing tighter around us."

Berdine leaned forward. "Drawing us into what?"

Richard took a bite of rabbit as he looked into her eyes and then gestured back over his shoulder with the piece of meat he was holding.

"Drawing us into that fortress built across the pass. I suspect that if we stayed out here, the boundary would close in around us until we had no choice but to go in there or die.

"Someone in there didn't want us getting away—getting to the Wizard's Keep, getting to where they couldn't get their hands on us."

Kahlan didn't say anything. None of it surprised her. It angered her, but it didn't surprise her.

"But why?" Berdine pressed as she tore off another piece of meat and handed it to him.

"Isn't it obvious?" Kahlan said in a quiet voice as her gaze sank to the crackling flames. "To get the children of D'Hara that I'm carrying."

When she glanced up, Richard was looking into her eyes. From the look in his gray eyes it was obvious he agreed with her.

"If that boundary is covering all that territory," Shale said, "then what happens when people come upon it. There are people traveling between places. There are merchants and traders that travel between cities. Some people have business that requires them to travel. People are going to encounter it. What happens when they come to the boundary?"

"If they are unlucky or foolish enough to walk into it, they die," Richard said with finality. "As you get close the boundary starts giving off that green glow as a warning, but not everyone knows what it means. If they are too curious and keep going in to try to find out what it could mean, then once they take one step too many it will be too late for them to turn back."

"Doesn't whoever is doing this care about the lives taken by the boundary they created?" Cassia asked.

"No," Richard said. "They want what they want and that's all there is to it. They obviously don't care if it costs the lives of innocent people."

Shale threw up her hands. "Who? Who is doing all of this? It has to be more than one person. No one person would be powerful enough to use your gift to put up that boundary of death. You said before that gifted people could join their gifts to do things that none of them alone could do. It has to be a number of people doing it. But who?"

"Someone seriously committed" was all Richard would say.

Kahlan knew that he knew who waited for them in the fortress town.

Shale lifted her hands and let them drop into her lap in frustration. "It's not just the boundary. It's also that strange wood we were lost in for so long. I suspect they not only created that but also started the Mother Confessor miscarrying to keep us from getting far. I just don't know who could be doing all of this."

Richard gave her a look. "You will find out soon enough." He turned to the Mord-Sith gathered around. "Pack up everything. We're leaving."

"Now?" Kahlan asked. "It will be dark pretty soon."

"I'm done wasting time and I'm done letting other people control us. The skies are clear. The moon will be up soon. The moonlight reflecting off the snow will easily provide enough light to see our way. We're going in there now when they won't be expecting us and putting a stop to this."

112

The snow crunched underfoot in the cold, still air as they made their way up the path marked by cairns. Kahlan could smell woodsmoke mingled with the aroma of balsam and spruce. Richard and Vika led the way, poking their staffs into the snow ahead to make sure it didn't hide any deep holes. Kahlan and Shale followed behind them, with the rest of the Mord-Sith guarding the rear. If the fortress up in the pass had sentries, they hadn't seen any, yet.

The moonlight on such a clear night was proving to be more than enough to help them see their way. It was a little harder to make out the lay of the land in the dark pools of moon shadows as they passed under dense canopies of trees, but with the light reflecting off snow they were still usually able to make out the trail well enough.

In a particularly dense, dark section of the woods, Richard had Shale light a torch he made so they could see. Since they were going to the town in the pass, they would be seen soon enough, so it no longer really mattered if they were spotted by the light of that torch. When they once again emerged into bright moonlight, Shale turned the torch down and doused it in the snow.

It turned out that the fortress town they had spotted from that ridge the day before was a lot farther away than they had initially thought. As a result, as they finally drew closer after a long and strenuous hike and were better able to see the details of it, it became obvious that it was not only much larger than they had initially thought, but more complex.

At parts of the wall to either side, the wall itself continued up to become the walls of multistory buildings, their square windows looking out over the approach to the pass. Those windows looked to be more domestic than watchtowers. A great many more structures were crowded in behind them, rising up higher on the ascending slopes to each side, like building blocks stacked tightly together.

The pass itself was broader than it had appeared to Kahlan from a distance, meaning that the town partly built into the wall with more blocky buildings tightly stacked behind was larger than she had at first realized. The imposing wall stretched from the sharp rise of the mountain on the left to a similar soaring mountain on the right. Now that Kahlan was closer and could see that wall better, it was obvious to her that it was well built and looked quite formidable. Stained with water and age, it also looked ancient, as if it had been there for thousands of years.

As the trail led them closer to the base of the wall, they were finally able to spot a large, arched opening near the bottom. Two halves of a gate door stood open. The massive doors were made of wood held together with iron straps. Inside, beyond the doors, there was a portcullis made of crossed iron bars, but it was drawn up enough to easily allow admittance. The portcullis had spikes along the bottom to crush anyone if the heavy gateway were to be suddenly dropped on them. Through the tunnel that was the arched opening in the wall and beyond the portcullis, Kahlan could see broad steps bathed in moonlight.

Vika pointed with her staff. "What kind of tracks are these?"

Kahlan looked down and saw that in the trail they were following there were a lot of tracks from a big animal.

"Mountain lion," Richard said without even needing to look down.

"That's what I thought." Vika frowned over at him. "They go right into that opening in the wall up there. Why would a mountain lion be coming and going from this fortress?"

"I guess we're about to find out," he said, clearly not yet wanting to say what he seemed to already know.

Kahlan didn't especially like his answer that wasn't really an answer. He knew more about what was going on than he was saying. She had to admit, though, that she did as well. She guessed that she was no more eager to put words to her suspicions and fears than was he.

She glanced up from time to time but didn't see any guards patrolling along the top of the wall. As they went into the arched tunnel under the massive wall, it revealed at last how massively thick it was. The buildings up on top were obviously as broad as the wall itself. Everyone continually scanned the area, looking for trouble.

Kahlan thought it was just a little bit too easy for the gates into the wall to be wide open and the portcullis drawn up out of the way, like the maw of a beast inviting them in. As they started climbing the broad hill of stairs, Richard gave the Mord-Sith a hand signal. They spread out, some racing up the stairs, with others dashing off diagonally to the sides as they ascended.

When they finally reached the top of the long rise of stairs, Kahlan was stunned by what she saw. Spread out before them were row upon row of plants to each side of the wide path. Off in the distance beyond the fields of low plants were more of the blocky buildings, presumably homes. They were stacked along the base of the mountains to either side, all on top of one another, stepping their way up the steep slopes.

Richard paused and bent to lift a big leaf of one of the plants as he looked up at Shale. There was a long row of the plants with the same fist-shaped leaves.

The sorceress stared in disbelief. "Mother's breath."

Beyond the row of mother's breath, there were expansive rows of many other herbs, some tall and spindly, some short and lush, some with blue flowers and others with yellow. Bright blue butterflies flitted along over the plants in the moonlight, pausing at flowers, presumably to drink nectar. There were vast rows of different kinds of plants stretching off to each side of the cobblestone path. Kahlan recognized some of the herbs, but not most of them. Some of the plants were exotic, crooked shapes unlike any she had seen before.

Far out ahead, beyond the fields of herbs, up against buildings, there were pens with animals. Kahlan could see pigs and sheep. Given the size of some of the other pens, she was sure that there must be milking cows in some of the buildings that had to be barns.

The place beyond the fields of herbs and the animals was not a village; it was more like a small town. There were square buildings built of stone stacked up along the rising ground to each side of the pass. Out ahead in the flatter ground beyond all the fields and animal pens there were yet more of the blocky buildings crowded together.

While most of the buildings were small, some were larger, with two, three, and in some cases four stories, but it looked to Kahlan like it was possible that each of those square buildings was an individual home. Like the stone walls themselves, all of the windows were square and devoid of any exterior decoration. Nor were any of the buildings at all fancy or adorned in other ways. The roofs were uniformly tile, making all the buildings appear simple and much the same. A few of the windows had lamplight coming from inside, but most were dark.

"It's not cold here, inside the wall," Richard said as he looked around at the growing fields of herbs.

Kahlan looked around, then, too, realizing when he said it that he was right. Not only wasn't it cold, but there was no snow. It felt like a gentle spring night, with no sting of approaching winter. All the plants looked green and healthy. It was as if the wall also kept out the snow and cold.

Shale looked around in wonder. "The air is mild, mild enough to grow all these rare herbs."

"I think we all know that there has to be some kind of magic involved," Richard said.

The Mord-Sith all returned from scouting to form a protective ring around Richard and Kahlan. The ring tightened when they saw a man in the distance making his way toward them down the cobbled mountain-path road. He lifted an arm in a friendly greeting. He walked with an odd side-to-side sway to his gait, as if his knees didn't bend very well.

"Welcome," he called out when he was still some distance away, his arm repeatedly waving in greeting.

Despite his obvious difficulty walking very fast on his stiff legs, he did his best to hurry to meet the visitors. He finally came to a stop, wheezing a bit as he caught his breath.

"Welcome," he repeated. "We were expecting you tomorrow, not this late at night, but welcome anyway. I'm Iron Jack."

Kahlan could see where he got his name. He was quite stout-looking, with a thick neck, a full red beard, and a full head of wiry red hair. His thick features revealed that he was well beyond middle age, but he looked like a man made of iron, with his red hair giving him a rusty look, the kind of man who had been in many a battle in his years and had the scars to prove it.

Kahlan stepped forward, holding her hand back at her side in signal before Richard could say anything.

"I am the Mother Confessor."

Richard arched an eyebrow at her when the man showed no reaction, least of all reverence.

Cassia stepped forward as she spun her Agiel up into her fist. "Perhaps you are hard of hearing. This is the Mother Confessor. You should be on at least one knee, and two if you had any common sense."

He smiled as he gestured dismissively. "My knees don't work so well anymore. Sorry, but I'll not be able to kneel."

He didn't look at all concerned; Cassia did.

"Then maybe I can help you to—"

"It's all right," Kahlan said as she gently took Cassia by her upper arm and pulled her back. "It's clear that the man has bad knees."

Cassia looked in a mood to bite spikes in two. "His neck isn't bad. He can at least bow his head."

Iron Jack's cheerful face suddenly didn't look at all cheerful. "If it would speed matters along…" He performed a perfunctory bow of his head. "Mother Confessor. Welcome."

Out of the corner of her eye, Kahlan saw Richard use two fingers of his left hand to lift his sword from its scabbard enough to make sure it was clear. She had seen him do that same thing as a prelude to the possibility of violence countless times since he had become Seeker.

But this time, the sword didn't lift away from the scabbard.

Instead, the scabbard lifted with the sword as if the two were welded together. Richard tried not to betray his surprise, but Kahlan could read his reaction in the change of his posture. Kahlan didn't usually become overly concerned when someone didn't show the proper respect for the office of Mother Confessor, but with Richard's sword suddenly not available to him, her level of concern rose several notches.

She returned her gaze from Richard to Iron Jack so as not to draw attention to what was clearly a problem.

"What is this place?" she asked the man before her.

"Why, you didn't know?" Iron Jack lifted an arm and swept it around in grand fashion. "You have arrived in Bindamoon."

"Bindamoon? This is Bindamoon?" Shale asked with a frown of surprise as she took a step forward. "I know of Bindamoon."

Iron Jack's tense expression eased and he beamed again. "Then you know what a wonderful place it is."

Richard shot a suspicious look at the sorceress. "You're from the Northern Waste. How do you know of it?"

"Some of the people in the Northern Waste trade in Bindamoon for rare herbs. Healers consider this place sacred. They make pilgrimages here to collect the rare herbs they need."

Richard turned back to the blocky man. "You said that you were expecting us."

"That's right," the man said, as if no explanation were needed.

Richard clearly wanted to hear that explanation. "How is it that you were expecting us?"

"The queen told us that you were coming."

"The queen," Richard repeated in a flat tone.

Iron Jack twisted around to lift an arm toward an elegant, soaring structure built on a prominent rise of rock in the distance.

"Yes, the queen. That would be her winter palace, up there."

"We need to see this queen," Richard said. "Now."

Iron Jack, the mirth again vanishing from his gnarly features, lifted his eyebrows. "Oh, I'm afraid that isn't possible."

113

"And why isn't it possible?" Richard asked.

The man shrugged in reaction to the question. "It's the middle of the night, in case you hadn't noticed. No one would be wanting to wake the queen at this time of night, and I'm sure you wouldn't, either. You will wait until morning."

Richard clearly looked displeased. "The morning? You expect us to wait until morning to see this queen of yours?"

Iron Jack smiled without humor. "That's right. You may see her in the morning—if, that is, she wishes to see you, and when she wishes to see you. She is, after all, not at the beck and call of travelers. Until then, I will take you to our guest quarters, where you may await word on a possible audience."

"That sounds more than reasonable," Shale said as she tugged Richard's sleeve to get him to let her speak for them.

When he frowned back at her she gave him an odd smile as her eyes widened and she leaned toward him a little with meaning. Kahlan could see that the sorceress had her reasons for not wanting to push the issue and she wasn't going to say those reasons out loud in front of the stout man. She was simply hoping to get Richard to go along with her.

Richard finally turned back to Iron Jack. "Considering the late hour, I agree that it would be a rude imposition. Why don't you take us to these guest quarters?"

Shale looked relieved. Iron Jack appraised Richard with a sly smile. Kahlan thought for a moment that the two men might suddenly break into a battle right then and there among the fields of herbs and blue butterflies.

Iron Jack finally broke eye contact and turned to lead them off past the fields of herbs toward the mass of buildings. When they reached a series of paths that branched off, he took one leading to the right. It soon started ascending the steep slope into the town, wending its way among the tightly packed buildings that, while square and uniform, were placed askew, apparently wherever would work best on the rising mountainside.

Heavy wooden beams every few feet were set across the cobblestone path to make steps of sorts as well as help keep people from slipping in the wet as they climbed through the canyon of buildings.

Walls made of flat, tannish-colored stone set in dark mortar rose straight up to each side. The path wouldn't have been wide enough for a wagon. When they came to a small handcart sitting tight against the wall by a door painted dark green, they all had to turn sideways in order to squeeze past.

They finally reached a long, low, blocky building in a row of low, blocky buildings set in front of another. Since each of the buildings had a number of doors, the long buildings were apparently divided into a series of separate rooms. Iron Jack opened the first weathered, wooden door they came to.

"These are guest accommodations for visitors, merchants, traders, and those passing through Bindamoon and needing a place to stay for the night." He pointed to the row of doors in the low stone buildings. "There is a different room for each of you. I don't know what sort of food would be at hand at this hour, but I will have someone bring along something to eat to each of your rooms."

"Thank you, Iron Jack," Shale said, stepping in front of the others before anyone else could say a word. "We could all use a bite to eat and some rest."

He bowed his head with another sly smile as his gaze passed among all those watching him. "Have a good night's rest, then. I will come by in the morning to take you to the queen, if she is of a mind to greet visitors."

Once the man was gone, Richard ushered all of the Mord-Sith through the open door, rather than letting anyone go to one of the other rooms. He then urged Kahlan and Shale inside and, once inside, shut the door. The sorceress lit a lamp on a small table and another on a shelf in the stone wall. There was a bed, and other than a table with a bench on each side, not much else, not even a window.

"I don't want us splitting up and going to different rooms," Richard said.

"I have to agree with your sentiment," Shale said. "All is not right here, and not what it seems."

Berdine arched an eyebrow sarcastically. "You don't say?"

The sorceress turned from Berdine to Richard. "Iron Jack is gifted— maybe a sorcerer or possibly even a wizard. I don't know exactly what he is, but I do know he is gifted."

Richard shared a look with Kahlan.

"He's a wizard?" Kahlan asked. "You mean like Richard?"

"No one is a wizard like Lord Rahl," she said.

"But is he powerful?" Kahlan asked.

Shale shrugged unhappily. "I don't know a great deal about wizards and such. All I can say with any certainty is that he is powerful enough to cause us a world of trouble."

Richard slipped the baldric off over his head. He held the point of the scabbard out to Vika and Cassia.

"Take hold of the scabbard while I try to draw the sword."

Despite their looks of confusion, the two Mord-Sith gripped the scabbard and together spread their feet. Richard held on to the hilt and pulled the sword with all his might. The two women bent their knees and backs into it. As Richard pulled and they held on tight, their feet slid as he dragged them both across the wooden floor.

Kahlan was alarmed that the sword would not come free. She could see that the scabbard wasn't bent or dented. Richard finally conceded that it wasn't going to work.

Shale frowned with concern. "Here, let me see it."

When he handed her the sword with the baldric still attached, she held it in one hand and ran her other hand down the length of the elaborately engraved silver and gold scabbard.

She finally handed it back. "I can't tell the exact nature of it, but I can tell you that the blade has been locked in by a spell of some sort."

Richard tried jiggling the handle in an unsuccessful attempt to draw out the sword before looking up at her. "Can you break the spell?"

Shale arched an eyebrow. "You're a war wizard. Can't you break the spell?"

Richard's only answer was to smile. Kahlan couldn't understand the meaning behind the look. Before she had time to consider his expression, Shale shook her head in sympathy.

"It would take more power than mine to overcome the magic holding the sword in the scabbard. It was likely a relatively easy trick for someone gifted to merely weld it in, as it were, so that it can't be drawn. It would be a much simpler way to disable the magic of the sword itself than to actually defeat such immense power."

Richard simply nodded as he slipped the baldric back over his head anyway, apparently not willing to abandon the weapon even if he couldn't draw it for now. Kahlan had a hard time believing that he couldn't pull it from its scabbard.

"The Seeker is the weapon," she reminded him. "The sword is just a tool."

Richard smiled at her. "You're right."

"Iron Jack may be gifted in some way," Vika said, "but Lord Rahl is a war wizard. Lord Rahl is more powerful and can handle that red-haired fool. He has killed legions of Glee with his power. He can certainly pull the head off that obnoxious Iron Jack if he has to."

Shale sighed. "I hope you're right, and I don't mean to discount Lord Rahl's ability—I've certainly seen things that I can't begin to understand—but I think there is more to Iron Jack than meets the eye."

Kahlan stepped closer. "Like what?"

Shale shook her head, clearly distressed. "I don't know but think about why we are here."

"You mean the boundary?" Kahlan asked.

"Yes, and don't forget about the strange wood, among other things. The boundary was put up by someone or some group of people using Lord Rahl's gift. If they are that powerful, then…"

Vika planted her fists on her hips. "Then you think Lord Rahl isn't powerful enough to handle them?"

Shale looked anguished to be taken the wrong way. "I'm not saying that, I'm only bringing up the fact that people powerful enough to steal his ability and use it to create the boundary are at the center of this, so it seems obvious they manipulated us in order to get us to this place. I only mean to say that we are dealing with something profoundly dangerous, and we should not assume anything—not about Iron Jack or anyone else we might meet here. Bold people often end up dead."

Vika's glare eased. "Well, I would have to agree that Lord Rahl is often too bold for his own good. He would usually be better off if he let us handle things."

"Whatever is going on," Richard said, seemingly irritated by the way they were talking about him, "it is profoundly dangerous, and we need not to have tests of magic with anyone until we know what we're up against."

Shale nodded with relief. "That's all I meant."

Before they had time to discuss what they were going to do next, there was a knock at the door. When Richard opened it, a shy woman holding a tray looked inside and blinked in surprise. She then leaned back to look to the other doors. Richard leaned out for a look himself. Kahlan could just see through the open doorway that there were other women also carrying trays at the other doors, confused that their knocks weren't being answered. They all wore the same formal brown dresses with white aprons of servants.

"You aren't all in your rooms," the woman said with obvious surprise and uncertainty as to what she should do about it.

"They will all be going to their rooms in a bit," Richard told her in a friendly tone to ease the worry on her face. "We're all in here talking about our arrival at this amazing place of Bindamoon."

His words did the trick to put her at ease. The young woman finally smiled. "Bindamoon certainly is an amazing place."

"And how do you like the queen?" he asked, offhandedly.

The smile evaporated. She bowed her head, fearing to look up into his eyes. "I am but a nobody, sir. I have never met the queen, so I would have no reason to have any thoughts on her, much less an opinion."

"I see," Richard said as he took the tray with a bowl of soup.

Relieved of her tray, she took a step back to motion the others to bring theirs. As they filed in, several of the Mord-Sith took the bowls of steaming soup, pots of hot tea, and cups and placed them all on the table. Once they had emptied the trays, they glared at the women. The women, fearful of meeting the gazes of the Mord-Sith, bowed their heads as they tucked their trays under their arms and filed out.

The one who had come first bowed deeply several times. "Please enjoy your meal."

After she hurried away Richard shut the door. "I don't want us splitting up and going to separate rooms. I want all nine of us to stay together."

"I couldn't agree more," Vika said.

The rest of the Mord-Sith all nodded that they were of the same opinion.

Shale, over at the table, turned back to the rest of them after staring down into the soup. She stirred a finger over one of the bowls.

"I don't advise eating any of this."

"Is there a problem with it?" Kahlan asked.

"I believe that I can detect some kind of nasty magic floating around in it."

"You mean the food has been spelled?" Richard asked.

"Yes, I believe so, but I don't know what kind of spell it could be. It's possible that it could merely be an innocent spell to help us sleep, but I think it best if we don't eat it and find out too late that it is something more."

With the heel of his hand resting on the hilt of his sword locked into the scabbard by some sort of magic, Richard drummed his fingers on the wire-wound handle.

He frowned in thought as he looked around at the others. "Why are we here?"

"To see the queen?" Berdine asked.

Richard shook his head. "No. We came here because the boundary left us no other way around the mountains. But the path, while leading us into this trap, also revealed a pass that can get us over the mountains. That's what we need to do: get through this pass and cross over the mountains and into the Midlands.

"Why would we need to see the queen? What we need to do is leave this place before the Golden Goddess sees us through the eyes of people here and sends more of the Glee to kill us. We've been lucky up until now in fighting them. I'd rather not press our luck and have to fight them again."

Shale passed a worried look between Richard and Kahlan. "What about Iron Jack? He is gifted. And you can't use your sword because of some magic he has used on it."

"Hopefully he went to bed." Richard showed her a grim expression. "But if he tries to harm us and if I have to, I will put my sword, scabbard and all, through his heart."

"At last," Vika said, throwing up her hands, "you are finally making sense."

Her sisters of the Agiel all nodded their agreement.

114

Other than a skinny gray cat looking for a meal among the refuse in scattered piles and trash that had drifted into corners of buildings, the dark, narrow streets of the mountain-fortress town were deserted. Something about darkness gave the place a forbidding feel. Kahlan got the distinct feeling that Bindamoon was not a place where one would want to be outside at night.

Moonlight reflected off cobblestones worn smooth and shiny by countless feet. The variety of laundry hung on ropes strung between opposing windows overhead cast ghostly moon shadows across the passageways. Without any wind, woodsmoke from chimneys curled down the tile roofs to settle into the canyons and alleyways between the towering walls, looking like fog as it slowly crept along the ground.

Kahlan was relieved that there hadn't been guards posted at the guest quarters to keep watch over them. At least, there were none she saw. She supposed that they assumed the spells in the soup had rendered them helpless, or unconscious. Or even dead.

Shale had said that she didn't sense anyone near. Richard, worried about how the gifted might be able to use magic to conceal their presence, and not exactly sure of the extent of Shale's ability to determine such things, had gone out alone to scout the area anyway and make sure they weren't being watched. Once he was satisfied that there was no one about, he and Vika took the lead as they left the buildings Iron Jack had taken them to. They left the soup and pots of tea untouched and cold on the table.

Berdine shadowed Vika, with Kahlan and then the rest following behind. They stayed close together as they made their way through the cobblestone streets as quietly as possible. None of them spoke for fear of waking the sleeping residents or giving away their position if there were any watchmen in the city. She also knew of magic that could detect and even overhear distant voices, so they used hand signals when necessary.

The windows overlooking the tight, winding passageways were all dark. While there was a main road leading through the town, Richard didn't want to take it for fear of being spotted out in the open, so they took a route through the tight cluster of buildings stepping up the steep rises to the side of the pass. As far as Kahlan could tell, other than the main road through the pass, there were no large thoroughfares among the densely packed buildings, just a maze of narrow streets and alleys.

Those narrow streets and alleyways weren't laid out in any particular pattern she could discern. It seemed that the buildings were simply built where they could fit in atop the rocky terrain. That meant that to go in the desired direction, they needed to take a zigzag route among the stone buildings.

Every once in a while, they caught a view of the moon as they continued making their way generally west by way of twists and turns. As difficult as it was to navigate among the tightly packed buildings, Kahlan found it preferable to being out in the open on the main road through the pass. If they could be spotted by any of the people of Bindamoon, they could also be spotted by the goddess.

Richard pointed up at a window as he tiptoed under it. With his back close to the wall, he crossed his lips with a finger in warning. Kahlan glanced up and in the moonlight saw a heavyset man in a dark window scratching the back of his fat arm as he yawned. He stepped close to the window to look out at the mountains. He probably couldn't sleep. Kahlan wished she could; she was exhausted and, on top of that, being pregnant with the twins meant that everything required extra effort. Her fear of being caught by the menacing and gifted Iron Jack kept her moving without complaining as she, too, put her back up against the wall while passing under the window.

At the first opportunity, Richard hurriedly turned them all to the left around a corner and down a different street. He put a hand to their backs as they went by, urging each of them to hurry along so that the man wouldn't see them if he happened to look down. Kahlan breathed a sigh of relief to have made it past unseen.

The maze Richard took them through led them ever higher up the slippery cobblestones. The heart of the town was a warren of passageways, some of them with steps to climb the steeper alleyways. In some places there were courtyards to the side screened by solid wooden gates. Kahlan looked through the spaces between the wooden slats and was able to see small tables and chairs. There was nothing threatening in any of the enclosed spaces she looked into.

No matter how far they went, the buildings were all constructed the same way. The moonlight among the vertical stone walls was enough for them to see by, but barely, and not enough to banish the spooky shadows in angular, twisting corners. Kahlan worried about what might be lurking in those shadows.

In many places they had to step carefully lest they walk in the muck that people dumped out of the windows. Large populations of rats scurried along close to the walls. The alleyways stank of the waste thrown out from chamber pots. The streets didn't smell much better. The stench mixed with the woodsmoke creeping along the ground to make a pungent tang. In places the overwhelming smell made Kahlan feel sick to her stomach. She was eager to get away from Bindamoon and out into the fresh air of the surrounding forests.

As the sky began to brighten with the approaching dawn and they came to the top of a cobblestone passageway, they got their first glimpse between buildings at what lay out beyond the town. It wasn't a good enough view to satisfy Kahlan, but through the vertical slit between walls she was at least able to see open countryside. The expectation of getting away had them all hurrying to get beyond the buildings of the town and out into the concealment of the forests.

When they finally reached the outer edges of the town, where some of the buildings sat right atop the wall where it met the mountain, they all finally got their first good look over that wall and down the trail on the western side of Bindamoon. In the brightening daylight, Kahlan could see that the path went off into snow-crusted trees. She knew that anyone would be able to follow their tracks in the snow, but she also knew that the path would eventually descend below the snow line, where it would be much easier for them to disappear into the thick trees and brush among the rocky outcroppings.

She could see that lower down the pass there were dense green forests blanketing the slopes to either side that would help conceal them. In the center of the descending ground among the hills, far below, she could see a broad valley with a large stream snaking back and forth through flat grassland. She could also see the path in places as it wound its way down toward that expansive valley.

Beyond the grassland with that meandering stream, the countryside was open. There were no mountains to block their way.

What Kahlan was looking out at was the eastern ranges of the Midlands where it met D'Hara.

She felt a swell of excitement at seeing that open ground. Her heart beat faster. Each breath came quicker. She was almost home. She felt tears unexpectedly well up at the thought of finally being in the Midlands.

"It's our way out," she whispered to Richard with tear-choked words.

Richard circled an arm around her shoulders to give her a quick hug. "We will be to Aydindril before you know it."

Below them they could see that the road went through the opening in the western wall of Bindamoon. She knew, though, that once on that road they would be out in the open, where they could be easily spotted from either side of the town. To make matters worse, it was getting brighter, as the sun was close to rising behind them. It couldn't be avoided, so they hurried down out of the buildings to the road that would get them as far away from the town as swiftly as possible.

Once they were on the main road that led through the wall and out of town, everyone kept a watch all around. Fortunately, they didn't see anyone. Lights from lamps began coming on in a few windows behind them, but Kahlan didn't see anyone looking out.

The road led to an arched opening in the wall that was much like the one in the wall they had come through when they had entered Bindamoon from the east side, meaning that the town was a walled fortress with a wall guarding it from both sides of the pass.

Kahlan was relieved to see that the portcullis was drawn up. As they passed into the dark, arched tunnel through the wall, they all kept looking back to make sure no one was watching or following. Kahlan's gaze flicked from window to window, but she still didn't see anyone watching them. The huge wooden doors, like the ones on the eastern side of the town, also stood open.

She was alarmed to see, up on the wall, a small group of ravens looking down, watching them pass beneath.

Beyond the wall, the road dwindled back down to a well-worn trail. They hurried away as quickly as possible without running, putting distance between them and the town. As soon as they were out of the protection of the town, the cold air returned. With the mild conditions inside Bindamoon she had forgotten just how cold it had been outside.

Kahlan felt a sense of relief when they finally made their way in among sparse trees. Most were pine, and the ground was open. In places there were groupings of white birch. She could see that off ahead the woods became increasingly dense. She looked forward to getting into dense woods, where they couldn't so easily be spotted, although, she realized, the ravens would probably follow and keep track of them. Once they reached the Midlands and were away from Bindamoon, she thought, the ravens might finally abandon following them. She didn't care if they flew around outside the Keep once she got there.

Suddenly, without warning, the air around them turned green. Kahlan had been lost in her thoughts as they marched along; Richard thrust an arm in front of her to prevent her from inadvertently taking another step and walking into the world of the dead. As everyone lurched to a stop, the strange green glow was all around them. Going any farther would bring up the darkness of the underworld.

"Bags," he growled. "I was afraid of that."

It was unusual for Richard to curse. In this case, she couldn't say she blamed him. She shared the same frustrated rage.

"What do we do now?" Vika asked.

Richard backed them all away from the green wall of death. He glared back toward the fortress town.

"We no longer have a choice," he said. "The boundary completely blocks any way to get out. We're going to have to go back to Bindamoon."

Kahlan gestured off to the sides. "Maybe if we checked to the sides there might be an opening in the boundary wall—a way around it if not through it."

Richard shook his head in anger. "You know as well as I do that's a false hope. Someone wanted to get us here to Bindamoon and to keep us here. They were willing to kill any traveler or trader who might come along and walk into the boundary in order to make that happen. This place is a trap and they aren't going to let us escape it so easily."

When they turned back, off in the distance they could see Iron Jack, hands planted on his hips, standing on top of the wall, watching them.

115

With the boundary now blocking any hope for escape, they had no choice but to turn around and trudge back toward the tunneled opening in the wall. Satisfied to see that they were returning, Iron Jack turned and vanished from the top of the wall. Kahlan wondered where he was going.

Richard fumed in a quiet rage. His silence was telling. She knew that when he got like this it was best not to ask him anything unless it was important. The focus of his anger rightly belonged on whoever was doing this to them.

As was his way, he had first tried to avoid a conflict. Now that those who had created this trap had made avoiding conflict impossible, he was prepared to meet it head-on.

Kahlan struggled to put one foot in front of the other. She was exhausted, both physically and mentally. It seemed like everything was grinding her down. Her worry, though, was for the twins, not for herself.

It seemed like forever ago that they had started out from the People's Palace, and yet the distant Wizard's Keep seemed no closer. In her mind, the Keep had come to seem more an impossible dream than a place they would ever reach.

They had been traveling for so long her belly had grown quite large. She was relieved to feel the babies kick from time to time, because it meant they were still alive. Everyone sacrificed their own food to give to her, knowing she needed it for the growing babies.

Because they had lost an unknown stretch of time in the strange wood, she was no longer sure of when the babies would come, other than knowing that it was still a ways off. But with as big as she was getting, that time was clearly getting closer, while the Keep wasn't.

She reminded herself that she was still the Mother Confessor, and no matter her concerns and doubts, this was no time to show weakness.

She gestured to the sides. "There is still some forest here, outside the wall. I don't like that place inside the walls. We know they already tried to spell us—or poison us—with the food, and we know that the man up there bound your sword into its scabbard. Obviously, it's dangerous in there. Why don't we just go into the woods and set up a camp while we come up with a plan?"

Richard kept his gaze resolutely ahead as he continued to march toward the opening in the wall. "How is camping out here going to get us to the Keep?"

"I don't know," Kahlan said in a weary voice, "but how is going back in there without a plan going to get us to the Keep?"

"I have a plan."

Kahlan gave him a sidelong glance. "And what would that be?"

Richard didn't look over at her. "The people who are preventing us from getting to Aydindril by doing all these things to stop us, like the way they used my gift to bring up the boundary, are after those babies you are carrying. They are willing to let people who wander into that wall die. They are after the hope of our world and willing to kill innocent people to get what they want. I can't let this threat stand. I'm going in there and putting a stop to it."

Kahlan again stole a sidelong glance at him. "That's your plan?"

"That's all the plan I need."

Kahlan didn't think that was the case, but she didn't want to argue with him. He was not the one wanting to get her babies.

The witch woman looked distraught with concern. "But if they are powerful enough to do all the things they have done to draw us into this trap, and as you say they are willing to let innocent people die, do you think it wise to walk right back into their trap?"

Richard shot her a quick glare before looking ahead as he continued on. "They think they are smart and powerful because they have contrived to use my gift to put up the boundary to lure us to this place.

What they have actually done is to attract lightning, and that lightning is about to strike them down."

Out of the corner of her eye, Kahlan saw Vika and some of the others smile. They were eager to face the threat and put an end to it. Kahlan was as well, but it wasn't likely going to be as easy as it sounded.

Although it was a rather foggy memory, she knew that she had already started to miscarry once. She feared losing the twins. She had lost a baby before and didn't want it to happen again. In the past she never would have hesitated to back Richard, but now that she was about to be a mother, it added a complication to everything. She had always been willing to put her own life on the line, but now she had to consider putting the lives of the twins at risk, to say nothing of all the people of their world.

On the other hand, if they were to protect their children from the Glee, they needed to get to the Keep, where it would be safe to give birth. Of course, while they might be safe there, the rest of the world would not be. That meant that to protect her children, and everyone else, the situation actually demanded that she fight more ferociously than ever before.

How they would eliminate the overriding threat posed by the Glee she couldn't begin to imagine, but she knew that the worst thing they could do would be to hide forever in the Keep while everyone else faced the onslaught of the Glee. They had to stop the immediate danger, and once it was eliminated, they needed to find a way to stop the Golden Goddess.

That thought added resolve to her determination. It was time to show whoever was stopping them exactly why she was the Mother Confessor. Richard was right: whoever had trapped them in this place had to be stopped, one way or another. As for the threat of the Glee, she couldn't imagine how they could overcome predators who could simply come into their world at will, but in the back of her mind she knew that such a threat could be faced only by a war wizard.

The more she thought about it, the more she realized that Richard was right. They had to go back into the town and end the threat, or they would never make it to safety and then be able to find a way to stop the goddess. Their world would never be safe until they did. Unfortunately, she was pretty sure who was at the center of all their current problems, and that was the one thing she truly feared to face, but this time there could be no backing down.

They all marched resolutely through the dark tunnel and emerged again inside the town. None of the narrow streets and alleys were straight, so it was hard to know the best route. There was often a warren of sharp corners and wedge-shaped intersections confronting them. In some places they had to pass under arches with parts of the buildings crossing overhead and in other places go under lines with laundry. Richard didn't seem deterred by the maze. He took them on a route that headed ever closer to his destination: the tall, white palace.

As they came around a corner of a wider passageway, they were confronted by Iron Jack, fists on his hips, standing to block their way. To the sides behind him it looked like there was a converging intersection of several narrow alleyways. Kahlan had been wondering how long it would take him to make an appearance. He obviously had guessed where they were headed.

"I will escort you back to your guest quarters," Iron Jack said in a threatening tone.

"We're not going to any guest quarters," Richard said. "We are going to see the queen. Either you can take us there, or we will go on our own."

The burly man gripped his kinky red beard as he cocked his head to the side and peered at them with one eye. "That would require an audience."

"That's not a problem," Richard said. "I am the Lord Rahl, leader of the D'Haran Empire, and I intend to grant your queen an immediate audience."

"That's not what I mean," the man growled.

"No, but it's what I mean."

"I'm the gifted man who rendered your sword useless," he reminded Richard. "You would make a very big mistake if you think to defy me."

Richard didn't look to be moved by the threat. "You can take us to this queen, or you can stand aside and we will go see her ourselves."

Iron Jack's sly smile grew wider as his eyes narrowed. "I'm afraid that I can't allow that. If you try, I will put you down."

Richard marched ahead. As he did, he rammed the heel of a hand against the man's big chest, slamming him back up against the wall of a building with enough force to make his teeth bang together.

"Good luck with that," Richard said on his way past.

Kahlan hurried to catch up and then followed close on Richard's heels. Vika and the rest of the Mord-Sith, each with an Agiel in a fist, also rushed to keep up, adding their glares at Iron Jack on their way past.

Kahlan was glad to see that Iron Jack didn't follow them. She hoped he had gotten the point and wouldn't challenge them again.

Shale leaned closer to Kahlan and spoke in a low voice. "That man worries me."

"Why?"

"Because while I can't determine how gifted he is, I don't think I have the power to stop him if he comes for us."

Kahlan didn't look at the sorceress as she hurried along. "Richard does."

116

When Kahlan looked up between buildings, she finally got a good glimpse of the soaring palace. It wasn't dark and sinister-looking. Instead it looked light and elegant. While the base was obviously quite large, it didn't have a lot of grounds around it the way a typical palace would have had. It did, though, seem impossibly tall and graceful. Small, round spires, each with a conical tile roof and an arched window, stuck up here and there in various places along the towering height of the palace. Colorful pennants flew from each of those pointed roofs.

When they got closer, Kahlan spotted a flock of black-and-white wood storks, slowly flapping their broad wings and then soaring together in the clear morning air. She realized from how small the birds looked against the white walls of the palace that the place was both bigger and taller than she had thought at first. The scale of it didn't seem real.

She also realized, now that she was seeing the town for the first time in daylight, that most of the buildings were actually washed with faint color. There were a light mint green, pale pink, light blue, and soft yellows. All of the colors had faded over time so that the stone showed through.

Bindamoon was in many ways cramped and unappealing, even with the long-faded colorful paint, but the palace, glowing in the early morning sunlight as it overlooked the town, was actually rather magnificent. She realized that it was a mistake to ascribe a sinister aspect to a building inhabited by what could only be sinister people.

Considering all the twists and turns they had to make, there clearly wasn't a direct route through the town to the palace. That left them to try to find their way through the maze of structures as they worked their way ever closer to the palace rising up above them.

The buildings of the town seemed to have sprouted around the soaring palace like mushrooms around a tree trunk in damp weather.

As they got close, they didn't need the view between buildings; it loomed over them. Here and there Kahlan saw people in the windows of the surrounding buildings, looking out, greeting the early morning. In a few places, women leaned out to pull in laundry that had dried overnight. Occasionally, in the distance, she saw people hurrying among the buildings, but she didn't see anyone nearby.

As they were going up a cobblestone street that rose gently toward the palace, Iron Jack suddenly stepped out from a side alleyway to once again block their path.

"This is as close to the palace as you will be getting until the queen says otherwise," he announced.

Richard grew calm in a way that she knew all too well. Trouble was about to begin. She saw, then, several more men waiting in the shadows behind Iron Jack. Without being obvious about it, she pulled her knife from its sheath at her side. She saw Shale do the same.

She was surprised to see Richard reach over and grip the hilt of his sword. He couldn't possibly have forgotten that it was bound into the scabbard by magic, so she couldn't imagine what he was doing.

He stood for a moment, head bowed, eyes closed, the muscles in his jaw flexing, his right hand on the hilt of the sword at his left hip, the muscles in his arm relaxed. She realized he was letting the power of the sword flow into him, letting its rage join with his. She suspected he was also summoning his own gift.

And then he began to draw the sword.

The blade came out silky smooth. Its distinctive ring echoed through the canyons of buildings as the blade, stained black by the world of the dead, emerged from the scabbard. The gleaming black steel greeted the dawn, ready to do battle.

Iron Jack looked stunned. "You can't do that! I myself sealed the sword and scabbard into one with powerful magic!"

Richard glared at the man. "I am the Lord Rahl."

"Not my lord. I answer to no one but the queen."

"You, and the queen, answer to me and to the Mother Confessor," Richard said in a deadly voice.

Vika stepped up beside Richard. She made a show of spinning her Agiel up into her fist.

The rest of the Mord-Sith moved protectively around Kahlan. Each of them had her Agiel in her fist at the ready. They looked fed up with Iron Jack's nonsense and seemed more than pleased that Richard was as well. So was Kahlan.

Growing up, she had never had any interest in flaunting her authority. Her mother instilled a sense of responsibility as a Confessor, not self-importance. It was simply something she had been born with, not something she had that she would hold over others. As Mother Confessor, she knew how to wield that authority when it was necessary. And when it was necessary, she found that she didn't especially like that authority dismissed or disrespected, because respect for the Mother Confessor was not about her, it was about everything she represented.

Richard was much the same. He had never lusted after power. He never sought to be the Lord Rahl. But he had come to accept the responsibility and he, too, was fed up with his authority being ignored in something so important. He was, after all, the leader of the D'Haran Empire, and as such he ruled over these people. Including Iron Jack and the queen.

They were about to find out why.

As Iron Jack watched, Richard drew the sword across the inside of his forearm, giving the blade a taste of blood, something that made the sword's anger lust for more. Kahlan could see the sword's magic dancing in the Seeker's eyes.

Richard brought the blade up to touch his forehead. He closed his eyes.

"Blade, be true this day," he whispered.

"Is that supposed to scare me?" Iron Jack asked.

"This blade can't harm an innocent," Richard said. "It can only harm an enemy. I suggest you decide for yourself if you should be afraid."

Iron Jack ran a hand down his red beard as he took a step back.

Rather than accepting Richard's command to stand down, he suddenly lifted his hands with an attack of his own.

When he did, every one of the Mord-Sith around Kahlan toppled to the ground as if a rug had been pulled out from under them. Iron Jack had attacked, not with a blade, but with his gift. As they struggled unsuccessfully to get back to their feet, they were visibly in pain from the magic Iron Jack had used. He smiled in satisfaction at seeing them on the ground.

They all knew that Iron Jack had magic, but any of the Mord-Sith, when he used that magic against them, should have been able to capture his magic and use it against him. That none of them could clearly spoke to the unique power of his gift.

Shale moved closer to Kahlan, her knife at the ready, obviously not willing to put her faith in her gift against such a man.

Iron Jack defiantly spread his feet to show that he intended to block their passage. "As I said, no one sees the queen until she wishes it. You may have somehow overpowered the magic fusing your sword tight in its scabbard, but you will not overpower me."

The man again lifted his hands in anger.

Suddenly, in the distance, Glee flooded out from around the corners of buildings. In a heartbeat they took out the men in the background, before they knew what had hit them. Tall, dark creatures, all teeth and claws, raced down the cobblestone passageway.

The Glee weren't materializing out of thin air the way they usually did. Steam didn't rise from them as always before. They didn't come streaming into Richard and Kahlan's world all together for an attack.

This time, they were using a new tactic: they had been hiding in ambush and Richard and Kahlan had walked right into their surprise attack.

The Glee had just learned an important strategy. Ambush gives the attacker a tactical advantage. That kind of attacker gets to pick the place and the moment of attack, while the defender is caught unaware and forced to respond, which puts them at a disadvantage because action usually beats reaction.

117

Richard was pleased to see that Iron Jack's ire was so fixated on him that he didn't even notice what was happening back over his shoulder until one of the tall creatures raced in and crashed into him. As it did, it grabbed him from behind. The Glee's new tactic of ambush meant never letting the opponent see you coming. Iron Jack hadn't seen them coming. Before the stunned bearded man could grasp what was happening and react, dark, slimy arms had already circled around him from each side.

Jack twisted frantically in an attempt to get out of the bear hug, but the powerful arms held him in tight against the Glee that had him. Shards of light flashed from the man's hands as he tried to use some kind of power to get the better of his attacker. The Glee bent its head first one way and then the other to avoid each of the flashes of light, but another creature nearby was torn apart by the release of the man's gift and fell dead.

Before Iron Jack could do anything to get away, the Glee that had him sank its teeth into the back of the man's neck to hold him. The creature then pulled its claws in opposite directions as Iron Jack was being held by the teeth in his neck. One claw ripped open Iron Jack's chest. At the same time, the other claw pulled in the opposite direction to tear out his throat. He didn't even have time to cry out before the Glee dropped him in a bloody heap to come charging for Richard.

Fortunately, because they surprised Iron Jack first, Richard was ready, and the magic coursing through him from his sword was ready to respond with swift violence.

As the Glee charged in, Richard had already begun his counterattack. The tip of the blade came around with such speed that it whistled as it sliced through the air. When the creature saw the sword, it reflexively lifted its arms to defend itself. Richard gritted his teeth with the effort of the swing.

The blade took off both the creature's claws and its head in that one lightning-quick strike. Richard held the blade up straight and took a step back, at the same time turning sideways and out of the way. The momentum of the clawless, headless body carried it past him to stumble across the cobblestones and collapse.

With Iron Jack dead, the Mord-Sith were suddenly able to scramble to their feet, and none too soon. More Glee charged down the street. The Mord-Sith raced to cut them off before they could get to Kahlan. Needle-sharp teeth clacked in anger. Most of them held an arm and claws cocked back, ready to strike. They were met with either an Agiel in one hand or a knife in the other.

Claws flashed through the air. Mord-Sith ducked under those claws as they swept by overhead and then sprang up to drive in for the kill. The Glee were clearly as vulnerable to an Agiel as any person would be. Wounded Glee fell in agonizing pain, holding arms across their injuries, or turned to scribbles and vanished, bleeding, back into their own world. Dead Glee simply dropped to the ground. Their blood ran down the slope in between the cobblestones.

As Richard noted what the Mord-Sith were doing, he was already moving into the attack. He swung his sword with deadly effectiveness. The magic from his sword, the same magic he had summoned to help free the blade from the scabbard, raged through him, demanding the blood of the enemy. He gave it all the blood it could want of any Glee within range. As he drove his attack directly into the enemy, Glee fell all around him, many without a head, others cut nearly in two, and some run through with his blade.

He turned and saw that Kahlan already had her knife to hand. It quickly became clear that she was the one the Glee wanted. They had come to rip the twins from her womb. She spun around when she heard one of them that had snuck around behind her and drove her knife into one of the big, glossy black eyes. The creature covered its eye as it shrieked. At the same time, it stumbled back awkwardly and, as it did, vanished to its own world. Even as she was pulling her blade back, Richard was there to protect her from others charging in to get her.

Shale, too, turned her abilities, rather than her knife, to the attack. With her eyes rolled up in her head, she lifted her hands, her fingers slowly waggling. As she did, masses of white snakes appeared, slithering across the cobblestones, going for the Glee.

The morning air was filled with the screams of the dark creatures as the snakes sank their fangs into them. From their awkward, jerky, contorted movements as they were struck by the snakes, it was clear to Richard that not only were the snakes venomous, but the venom acted so swiftly as to be almost immediate in its action. Glee, with snakes firmly attached to their legs, arms, and bodies, stumbled back, gurgling in choking pain as the venom quickly began to paralyze their lungs.

Shocked people appeared in windows, looking down on the frantic battle. Some screamed and ran back into dark rooms. Some, their mouths hanging open and hands gripping the windowsills, leaned out to watch.

Knowing the snakes were Shale's and meant for the Glee, Richard ignored them. It was Kahlan most of the Glee were going for. She was the one they most wanted to kill. It was Kahlan he had to protect.

In that moment, as the fury of the sword's magic twisted together with his own and stormed through every fiber of his being, he lost himself to the madness of the battle. He became that madness. The Glee had come as hunters. Richard was now the hunter and they the prey.

As he responded to the attacks, he suddenly came to comprehend in a new and clear way how the Glee moved, the extent, the range, and the limitations of their movements. He began to see exactly how they used their claws to strike, with their teeth being their backup weapon. It was often a quick flick of a strike, but other times they used those claws to intimidate their prey for a fraction of a second to make the prey freeze just before they struck. That allowed them to be more accurate and deadly when they did strike.

The reason for the tactic, he saw, was that the Glee had most of their power when their arms were used in close combat. The farther they reached, the less power they had. The way they had killed Iron Jack had been their biggest strength—holding the prey in close as they tore it apart.

Once he grasped the technique in their strikes and how they set up for an attack, he was able to predict how they would move, which claw they would use first, and when they would strike with it, or instead, if their claws were not able to be used to their best advantage, use their teeth to try to kill.

He began to understand the fight with them in a whole new way. It all made sense in an entirely new light. He understood the battle from their perspective, rather than seeing it from his perspective, defensively.

Once he had the full scope of the realization, those attackers, rather than seeming like frightening creatures coming for him and Kahlan in a crazy, hysterical frenzy, became instead a part of the larger dance with death.

That meant he was no longer fighting them in the same ways he had previously. Now he was using their nature against them, turning it back on them, using their limitations and weaknesses as openings. For the first time, he was, in a sense, fighting them on their terms, and in that way, because he could anticipate what they would do next, he abruptly put them at a distinct disadvantage.

In that moment, he came back at them in a new way, in a way that completely overwhelmed their multiple tactical advantages of teeth and claws. Their limitations in range and movement became his advantages and openings.

In that moment, he stopped trying to kill them and switched instead to the quicker task of cutting off their powerful, deadly claws. It was a revelation. He didn't need to kill them. He simply needed to deny them their primary weapon. If the Glee didn't have those razor-sharp claws, they were nearly defenseless. They couldn't grasp or cut or rip or hold prey in order to use their teeth.

His sword spun through the air without pause, cutting at a dizzying pace. He moved around Kahlan, protecting her, disabling any enemy that came for her. She took out several with her knife as he momentarily moved around the other side of her. His sword lopped off claws as fast as they came within reach of his blade. He understood, now, where and how those claws would be coming, and which of the two were the actual threat. Severed claws tumbled through the air as he lopped them off at the wrist or forearm. The still-twitching claws littered the ground.

The creatures shrieked as they lost their precious claws. Some held out stubs in disbelief, and tried to reach out to grasp so they could attack with their teeth, but without their claws, it was easy for Richard to take off the heads of those determined enough to continue to come for him rather than escape back into the safety of their world. Seeing what happened when they came in at him, and seeing so many of their fellows with stubs of arms and no claws as they vanished back into their own world, they began to rightly fear to swing their own claws and lose them.

As they hesitated, the snakes struck and sank fangs into them. Once they had their fangs in the soft black skin, they would not let go. As that happened, Richard spun through their midst, taking the claws off the ends of their arms. Without their claws, they couldn't effectively try to tear at the snakes to get them off.

All around, panic spread among the shrieking and dying Glee. As their boldness and aggression turned to terror and timidity, those who still could started to turn to scribbles to flee back to the safety of their own world before Richard or the snakes could get to them.

Without a target, Richard finally paused, panting to get his breath as he let the tip of his sword lower to rest on the cobblestones. He looked all around, searching for any threat. The rage of his sword still thundered through him, demanding more blood. The ground was littered with hundreds of claws and dozens of heads, as well as the bodies of those that couldn't vanish before death.

118

With his sword, Richard gestured ahead for everyone to move on toward the palace and away from the scene of the brief but frenzied battle. While the Glee who went back to their own world would be testament to others of the trouble that awaited them here, tyrannical leaders, as the Golden Goddess apparently was, were often more than willing to throw the lives of countless followers into the fray.

With the battle over, Richard didn't want to be anywhere nearby in case the goddess, in a fit of anger, decided to send another wave of fighters. Attacking after a battle had seemingly ended was a good way to catch your opponent with their guard down. Richard didn't want to let his guard down, so he urged everyone away from the scene of the fight.

Though he might have won this skirmish, he knew that he had to solve the vastly bigger problem of stopping the goddess from sending any Glee at all. Winning a battle was of no use if he couldn't win the war. Every battle exposed them to the possibility that, this time, they might lose. If they lost, everyone in their world would ultimately lose.

Even if Richard and Kahlan could get to the safety of the Keep, that wouldn't provide any safety for everyone else. They would continue to be vulnerable. In the end, that was his weakness as a leader, and the goddess's strength. There was virtually no way for normal people to protect themselves, especially if the Glee came in massive hordes, and Richard couldn't protect everyone. People everywhere would be prey at the mercy of savage predators.

He took Kahlan's hand to help her balance as she stepped over the thick, tangled ring of severed claws and slimy bodies surrounding her. All those claws were now still, but it was a very visible reminder that they had been meant for her and her unborn babies. He knew that more would come. The Glee were relentless. He felt sick at not knowing if he was ever going to be able to stop them once and for all.

Richard let go of Kahlan's hand so she could help Shale, who looked weak and exhausted after unleashing masses of white snakes. The snakes she had conjured were gone now, either withdrawn by the witch woman after they were no longer needed or taken back to the home world of the Glee as they fled with the snakes still attached to them. Those snakes were in a way part of her, so when they were taken away with fleeing Glee, they were in a sense ripped away from her connection to them.

In the aftermath of the effort, the witch woman looked like she might collapse. Cassia rushed in on the other side and helped Shale stay upright as she stepped among the mounds of claws and the remains of the dead.

With the sword still in his hand, the magic of it still surged through him, filling him with rage. The sword hungered for an enemy; that was its way, its purpose. With the threat so fresh, the shrieks and howls still echoing through his head, Richard was not quite ready to relinquish the rage of the sword's magic spiraling through him. He wanted it at full force and at the ready just in case.

As the Mord-Sith started up the narrow cobblestone street, closely protecting Kahlan, he held back to reassure himself that there were no more threats lurking around any of the corners. Seeing none, he finally sheathed his sword and, in so doing, extinguished the rage. Once that fury of magic was finally cut off, it left him feeling weak and exhausted from the effort of the fight.

When the hair on the back of his neck tingled and stiffened, he looked up and saw a single Glee standing in the sun atop a two-story building, looking down, watching him. Somehow he had known that it would be there. The rest of those with him were helping each other and talking among themselves as they made their way up the narrow street. They didn't see the Glee. He didn't think that this lone creature wanted anyone but Richard to see it.

As he stood staring up at it, the Glee opened its arms a little and spread its claws to reveal webbing between its razor-sharp claws. Richard felt that it was a sign—that it was trying to convey the message that it meant no threat.

And then it bowed at the waist, as if out of respect.

He spotted, then, in those slow movements as it bowed, something he had never noticed before. There was a slight, iridescent, greenish sheen to this Glee's skin. It reminded him a little of the iridescent green sheen on the backs of some black beetles. He hadn't seen this quality to the flesh of any Glee he had fought.

Even though he hadn't noticed this slight greenish sheen on this particular Glee before, there was no doubt in his mind that this was the same individual he had seen several times before, when on previous occasions it had also signaled that it intended him no harm.

When the Glee stood back up, it shared a long look with Richard. From time to time as it stared, its third eyelid blinked across its big, glossy black eyes. It cocked its head a little, possibly as if appraising him. Richard felt a sense of peace with this creature.

He reminded himself of one of his most basic beliefs, that an individual was not guilty because of the crimes of others. It was something very personal for him, because he had once been hated as the Seeker because of how corrupt people before him had been when they had possessed the sword, its power, and the post. Because of their notorious behavior, it was assumed that all Seekers were evil. He had likewise been condemned as evil because of the sins of his father. He knew that although all the other Glee he had seen and fought had been trying to kill them, this one individual had not, so he had to remember not to judge it by their actions.

And then it turned to scribbles and in a fleeting moment was gone.

Richard wished there were a way to talk to that Glee, to find out its intentions and what it wanted.

Kahlan paused a ways up the narrow street and turned back. "Are you coming?"

"Sure," Richard said as he sprinted to catch up with the others.

"So," Shale finally said as they moved on up an even narrower alleyway to continue to make their way toward the palace, "tell me how you managed to get your sword out of the scabbard when it had been welded in there by Iron Jack's magic."

"Wizard's First Rule," he said.

Shale paused to turn back and give him a squinty-eyed look. "What?"

"I was always able to get the sword out," Richard said.

Shale flopped her arms against her side in frustration. "Well, if that were really true, then why couldn't you get it out before? You had Vika and Cassia hold the scabbard while you pulled on the handle. You couldn't get it out then."

"Actually, I could," Richard told her.

Shale clawed her fingers as she growled in exasperation. "No, you couldn't. I saw it. It was welded in by Iron Jack's magic and the three of you couldn't pull it apart. What's more, when I felt the scabbard, I could feel the magic bound into it holding it together."

Richard shrugged. "I could feel the magic, too."

Shale held her head with both hands as she growled again. "And you couldn't draw it! Why could you draw it now, but not back then?"

Richard finally showed her a smile. "Shale, I could have drawn it whenever I wanted. I asked for your help and you said you couldn't do it. As you said yourself, I'm a war wizard. But I wanted Iron Jack to think he had bested me."

The witch woman leaned toward him a little. "What?"

"I felt Iron Jack's magic tingling around the hilt. It was only Additive. There was no Subtractive element to it. So, I only pretended I couldn't get it out of the scabbard because I knew he would be able to sense if his spell was broken. For that reason, I was careful not to. I wanted him to think instead that I had tried and failed, so I was defenseless. I wanted him to believe that so he would feel emboldened. I wanted him to think he had everything under control so that he would lose his sense of caution and act true to his nature."

Shale straightened her back and stared at him for a moment. "You mean you were concerned that if he feared you, he might put on an innocent and friendly act?"

Richard smiled again. "Now you're getting the idea. I felt no need to show off and pull the sword when he thought his magic had locked it in the scabbard. I wanted to see what he would do when he thought he was in complete control."

Shale turned to Kahlan. "Your husband is a very devious man."

Kahlan nodded. "Annoying, isn't it?"

119

Richard didn't see anyone near the entrance to the palace. No guards, no supplicants, no staff. There was no insurmountable wall or any other method to keep people out as was typical around places of power.

Now that it was daytime there were lots of people hurrying about their business back in the narrow streets of the town. None of them came near the palace—not even close. It was obvious that no wall was needed.

If he was right, and he was almost positive that he was, they had good reason to give the place a wide berth, which would obviate the need for a wall, or guards.

While the palace was not massive in the sense that other castles or palaces he'd seen covered a lot of ground, it was nonetheless still sizable. Rather than being imposing by its girth, it was instead gracefully tall, taller than most palaces he'd seen. There was only one palace he could recall that soared to such heights with similar splendor. That palace didn't need high walls or guards, either.

He shared a look with Kahlan, and he could see in her green eyes that she was thinking the same thing he was.

As he looked up the soaring white stone wall, he could see in the places where it stepped back as the palace went ever higher that there were ravens perched on the edges of various levels, cocking their heads to look down at them.

Thirteen steps in gray marble with white swirls through it stretched out quite some distance to either side. At the head of those steps there was no grand entablature decorating the entrance; there were no intricate, ornamental moldings. Instead, atop the landing was an elaborate door set back into the white stone. The massive door looked to be made of bronze. The entire surface was covered in rows of orderly, embossed writing, designs, and symbols. Each row was unique.

When he led the others up the steps for a closer look, he saw that he recognized some of the lines of symbols on the massive door. They were in the language of Creation. He ran his fingers over the raised designs as he mentally deciphered their meaning. They were general warnings to stay away, but there were also some critically clear specifics.

With his fingers still on the symbols, he looked back over his shoulder at Kahlan. "This says that none may enter without first being commanded to appear."

Kahlan stepped up the final step to stand beside him to study the door. She gestured to one of the lines of the writing.

"It says the same thing there."

"Do you recognize any of the other writing?" he asked.

She scanned the door, then used her fingers to touch some of the lines of symbols to keep her place as she examined the strange designs. She finally gave Richard a grim look.

"At least a dozen of the languages here on this door are those used in the Midlands. That makes sense, given the location of Bindamoon right in the middle of the line of the mountains that divide the Midlands from D'Hara. And, as Shale said, even people from the Northern Waste came here. It would seem that many different people came here for the rare herbs they grow in those fields. It would make sense for there to be a lot of languages represented, so that anyone who came up here could read the warnings.

"I speak most of these languages. Each message is a warning that says the same thing as you read, that none may enter without first being commanded to appear."

Richard glanced back at the others. "I guess it's pretty clear by everything that's happened that we have been commanded to appear."

"With all those languages being clear warnings," Shale said, "do you think it wise to go in there?"

"Wise or not, this is the heart of the threat. We're going in and I'm putting a stop to it."

No one looked like they had any intention of arguing.

Richard turned a lever, then drew back a bolt. It made a dull clang when it reached the end of its travel. He put both hands against the tall brass door and pushed. He pushed, then pushed harder to get it to start to move. With a great deal of effort, and several Mord-Sith coming to help, the heavy door silently swung inward until the opening was wide enough for them to slip through and enter.

The hushed interior was not nearly as bright as it was outside, but there were a number of high windows that at least let some light stream down from above. Hundreds of candles in ornate metal stands all around the interior lent the place a mellow glow.

Their footsteps echoed softly back from the distance. If the outside of the palace was rather simple and plain, the inside was the complete opposite.

On each side there were a half-dozen steps up to raised vestibules. Above them were convex entablatures decorated with complex moldings. The massive stone structures were held up by rows of fluted stone columns that enclosed each of the areas. The capitals atop those columns were intricate, curling acanthus leaves carved from a pale greenish-gray stone Richard had never seen before.

Between the entablatures were enormous arches leading deeper into the side wings. Each end of those massive arches was held up with four fluted stone columns composing a single support structure. The bases of those arches were so sizable that they had small, internal arches on all four sides of their bases, each held by a stone column, all of them together holding up the more massive main arch. The whole thing was so complex it sent the eye dancing over the elaborate, involved, and interconnected shapes.

The windows beyond those arches were made up of what had to be hundreds of small pieces of beveled glass in a gridwork of stone mullions. That beveled glass sent prisms of colors scattering all across the walls and columns. Beneath and beyond those windows, Richard could see ornate side chambers, lit by countless candles.

In the center of the room, the arches before those antechambers formed a perimeter to support a central dome. Massive square support structures, with square, fluted pilasters, anchored each of the primary arched sections. Inside the top of the dome, small windows all around let in light from exterior rooms above and around the interior dome. All of the stone of the entire place was various shades of greenish-gray, giving the place a uniform, muted theme.

In the center of the massive room, beneath the dome, was a floor with cream and gray stone making up large squares that marched all the way around a central design of a wreath made out of gold-colored stone set against a background of white. In the center of the wreath were more concentric designs that stepped down in size. The floors to the sides, going off into the antechambers, were gridwork designs made of the same cream and gray stone.

In between the fluted columns and the fluted pilasters there were recesses with life-size statues in the same greenish-gray stone. Some were of people, but most were of strange, contorted figures that didn't look quite human—or possibly were people in great pain. All the figures were clothed in flowing robes carved out of the same stone. The carved robes were so realistic that it made it look like there was a brisk breeze blowing through the place.

Richard had seen a number of magnificent places since leaving his home of Hartland. This was up near the top in the sheer splendor of the complex yet graceful architecture. He had never seen cold stone looking so warm in its intricate stateliness. The whole place made him feel small and inadequate. He supposed that was really the purpose and the point of it all. Those who entered should be humbled before the master of this domain.

Richard and those with him, all standing in a close cluster, stared around at the ornate stonework of the arches and the dome. It was achingly beautiful, but at the same time it was a clear statement that they were in the place of powers not to be trifled with.

In the center of the circular design in the floor, under the dome, the mountain lion sat on its haunches, watching them, its tail slowly sweeping back and forth across the floor.

When the mountain lion was sure that they had all looked around enough, it stood. As they all watched, it turned and started walking away, deeper into the palace, clearly expecting them to follow.

120

Richard watched as the mountain lion casually walked off into the distance. "We're supposed to follow it."

"Why do you think that?" Berdine asked.

He gave her a look. "Because it was sent to fetch us."

Berdine's nose wrinkled up. "How do you know that?"

"Because I've seen it before at another important moment, and I don't believe it was a coincidence."

Vika turned a troubled look toward Richard. "So then you think it's the same mountain lion we saw up on the mountain when we found the mother's breath?"

"Of course it's the same one. When we found the mother's breath, it left to tell its master."

"And so you think its master lives here?" Berdine asked.

Richard gave her the same look again, as if to say it was a silly question. "Why else would a mountain lion be walking around inside this palace?"

"Oh," she said, "I guess I see your point."

"Odd choice for a house pet," Shale said.

"It wouldn't be the strangest one I've seen," Richard muttered under his breath as he started out after the mountain lion. "Come on. We don't want to lose sight of it."

Shale leaned in. "But—"

"Hurry," Kahlan said as she put a hand to the small of Shale's back to get her moving.

The mountain lion led them across the broad, circular design in the floor under the towering dome. The animal stopped before a vestibule of sorts in the distance. Curved staircases on either side surrounded it on the way to an upper level with rooms beyond and to either side.

The mountain lion looked back for a moment to be sure they were following, then ambled onward. That vestibule, with more of the greenish-gray columns to either side, stood before a broad passageway that wasn't as wide as the antechambers off to the sides of the domed area had been. This seemed to Richard more like it was an entrance into a central hall of some sort leading on into the interior. The significance of the central hall was evident from its elaborate architecture.

The same fluted columns of greenish-gray stone lined the long room. A great many ornate metal candlestands held what had to be hundreds of candles that not only lit the way ahead with soft light but lent a pleasant scent to the place.

To the sides, between pairs of fluted columns, inside stone frames, there were large square panels of incredibly beautiful red marble with swirls of green, gold, and black veins running through them. Each one of those massive red granite slabs seemed to glow in the soft candlelight.

It occurred to Richard that the swirly red marble panels reminded him of a floor covered with blood that had been cut out and then hung up for display. He paid closer attention to the red slabs as he passed by them, scrutinizing them to make sure they weren't actually patterns of blood. Even though he stared closely at each one, he still wasn't sure.

Farther down into the dark end of the magnificent but somber passageway, the pairs of columns were set closer together. Rather than the red marble that was displayed between the previous columns, between each of these there were faces, again carved in the greenish-gray stone. They were similar to the statues Richard had seen before, except these were only life-size busts. Each one leaned out, making it seem like they were trying desperately to come right out of the wall.

All of the grim faces stretching out from either side were distorted in agony, or longing, or terror. Some of them reminded Richard of the carvings of tortured souls he had seen in the Old World. Like those statues he had seen there, he had seen the real thing in the underworld.

Other faces looked like they might be human, but if they were meant to be human, they were ghastly examples of torment and torture. The others, the ones that weren't human, Richard couldn't even guess at, but they, too, had horrified expressions, with mouths opened wide as if they had been frozen in mid-scream. The farther they went into the ever-darkening passageway, the more grotesque and distorted the faces became, with flesh carved to look like it was torn open so that the bones and teeth beneath the ripped cheeks were visible.

The wide hallway was enough to sap the courage of anyone who got this far, but it didn't dim his determination. If anything, it reinforced his resolve to stop the person responsible for depictions of such horrors, but more importantly those responsible for what they were doing to Kahlan.

Shale looked from one side to the other, staring for a moment at each one of the faces looking like they were trying to push themselves out of the walls to escape.

"Why would anyone carve such awful things?"

Richard glanced back at her. "Well, I like to look at beauty, but there are people who choose instead to look at ugliness. That alone tells you a lot about them, don't you think?"

Shale looked from Richard back to the busts. She shook her head in disgust. "I fear to think what this tells us about the people who live here."

At the end of the long passageway, farther away from the light of the high windows and lit only by candles, Richard realized that the hallway didn't simply get dark, it actually ended in a dark opening, but not the kind of opening that went with the rest of the place. It was a hole crudely chiseled into the stone of the mountain the palace had been built into.

It looked like nothing so much as the rough opening into a mine. Or the underworld.

Unlike everything else he had seen in the palace that was ornate and highly detailed, this was merely a roughly round opening cut into the rock with crude tools used for excavation. The mountain lion vanished into that dark maw. He saw the tail flick up briefly, and then it was gone down into the darkness.

When they got close enough, they could see that there was a bit of flickering light inside from somewhere far down below. As Richard paused at the opening to try to see where the mountain lion had gone, he saw then that there were steps leading down.

"I don't think this is a good idea," Shale said. "We're walking right into the heart of this trap."

Richard turned back to her. "And how do you instead propose we free ourselves of that trap unless we face it and put an end to it?"

Shale's features twisted unhappily. "I don't know, but I don't like it. There are remnants of a spell of some sort lingering here."

Richard frowned at her. "What kind of spell? Can you tell?"

Shale shook her head. "It's just a trace of something, but I can't tell what." She sniffed the air. She frowned. "I can sense them, but I can't tell what sort of spells they might be. Whatever it is, it's interfering with my sense of smell."

"Well, we know that this trap was set with powerful magic," Kahlan said, "so there are bound to be spells lingering about this place. Sometimes magic does that—leaves traces."

Vika stepped ahead of him into the opening. "Rikka, Vale, come with me. The rest of you wait here. We will go down first and see if it's safe."

Richard gripped her arm and forcefully pulled her back before she could start down. "Are you out of your mind? Of course it's not safe. Now, stay behind me."

She looked so shocked by what he said that she did as he told her.

Richard started down with Kahlan at his side, expecting the rest of them to follow. Vika followed as close behind him as she could without stepping on his heels. Shale was right behind Kahlan. The others flowed down the steps behind them.

Only the first of the steps were carved well. On the way down, they soon became rough-hewn slabs in some places, and steps simply carved directly out of the stone of the mountain itself in others. Their uneven shape made footing treacherous. The treads and risers were different depths and heights, requiring care with every step they took. Sometimes it was a long stride and sometimes so short that they almost fell. Richard held on tightly to Kahlan's hand as he held his other out behind to urge the others to be careful. He didn't want them falling on top of him and Kahlan and causing them all to go tumbling down to somewhere far below.

As they cautiously descended the curving, irregular run of steps, he realized that the stairs followed the uneven excavation down along the rock walls. When they got farther down, he was finally able to see that they were descending to the edge of what was a vast, roughly circular chamber. He was astonished by how immense it was, both in width and height.

Like the opening above, the walls had been cut with excavation tools, leaving a rough, unfinished surface. It looked to Richard that in places on the walls great slabs of rock had collapsed down, actually aiding in the excavation. It resembled a mine more than a room, except that it was huge beyond any normal room, or any mine for that matter. He had seen chambers in natural caves that were this immense, but this was not a cave and not natural. He couldn't imagine its purpose.

Rather than it getting darker, they began to see flickering firelight from below that helped them see the steps better. Keen to find out what this place was and what was going on, he had to force himself to be careful and not to hurry. The fact that it was a trap, with the mountain lion leading them into it, also tempered his urge to hurry.

He started to realize that this strange underground chamber had to actually be the true purpose of the palace. The place above was merely a façade. Like a man irresistibly drawn to a beautiful woman with an evil heart, Richard felt that he had first been charmed by the beauty of the palace architecture, but he was now being drawn to the evil heart of this place.

The stairs turned as they approached the bottom. He saw, then, that they were coming down behind enormous statues of ravens that were at least three times his height. Their wings were extended in front to hold stone bowls of flaming oil that provided light. The smell was similar to that of burning pitch. It also left a haze to settle in the cool air of the pit.

When they reached the bottom of the rough stairs, and they came around one of the ravens, he saw that there were more of the stone ravens all around the room in a circle, thirteen in all. They all faced inward to the center of the chamber.

Between and beyond the stone ravens, he could see that there were caverns all around the base of the room, going back into the stone of the mountain itself. Torches lit the tunneled passageways, but he couldn't see what they led to.

Off in the middle of the room, he saw a line of intimidating people watching them approach. They were all women.

In the center of that line of silent women sat a tall, elegant throne. He could see the light from the burning pots dance and flare on the gold-leaf vines, snakes, cats, and other beasts carved into the arms and framing the tufted red velvet-covered back. A canopy draped with heavy red brocade and trimmed with gold tassels jutted out overhead, making an imposing statement.

The mountain lion sat beside the throne.

Richard had seen that throne before.

As he cautiously closed the distance, he recognized the woman sitting in the massive structure.

It was his mother.

121

Out of the corner of her eye, Kahlan saw Berdine's jaw drop. "Mama?"

Rikka lifted an arm to point. "No, that's my mother."

Vale went to her knees as her eyes welled up with tears. "Mother? Is that really you?"

"This is impossible," Shale whispered even as Kahlan knew that she, too, would be seeing her own mother.

When Nyda reached out in longing and started to rush ahead, Richard swept an arm around her waist and yanked her from her feet. He set her down behind him. Kahlan caught Rikka's arm to stop her from going any farther.

"Everyone stay where you are," Richard said in a commanding voice before any of the others could rush to the woman they all wrongly believed was their mother.

Most of the Mord-Sith looked in stunned confusion between the women and Richard. The woman sitting on the magnificent throne smiled benevolently. Kahlan knew that Richard, too, was seeing his mother. The only difference was, like Kahlan, Richard knew who this really was.

"Shota, stop it," Richard called out in a voice that cut through the hiss of the burning lamp oil and echoed around the chamber.

Kahlan had been pretty sure for quite some time who it was that had been drawing them into this trap. Richard had known as well, but like her, he had not wanted to put words to that belief lest that somehow make it true. They had both hoped they were wrong, and that it would turn out to be something else.

Kahlan's mother smiled, then, in a loving way, but Kahlan had already steeled herself against Shota's cynical deception. This was a witch woman playing her games; it was not any of their mothers. She didn't allow herself to let her emotions be twisted by what she knew to be an illusion.

Shale looked at Kahlan in wordless confusion.

"That spell you felt at the opening to this place?" Kahlan whispered to her.

"Yes? What of it?" Shale asked.

"It was to keep you from smelling witches."

Realization swept away the confusion in her features.

"Shota," Richard said again, "stop this cruel hoax."

Once Shota saw that Richard and Kahlan weren't about to play along, and that they weren't going to let any of the others be sucked into the deception, she stood and descended the three platforms the throne sat atop.

Her variegated gray dress gently billowed as if lifted by a gentle breeze. When she caught one of the points of the skirt, it was as if the breeze died out and it settled down. As the dress went still, her fabricated looks also died out, melding back into the face of the witch woman Kahlan knew all too well. She was glad, at least, that Shota was no longer taunting her with the image of her mother.

Kahlan glanced at the women lined up to either side of the throne. Their piercing glares were chilling. Even though they all looked very different, they all radiated the same aura of mystery and danger.

A self-satisfied smile spread across Shota's full, red lips. Her almond eyes sparkled with her smile. Kahlan had always thought of the stunning woman as a rose encrusted with ice crystals.

Shota glided across the room toward them, her eyes fixed on Richard the whole time. Kahlan found it irritating the way Shota had always acted a little too charming toward Richard. Richard, of course, didn't respond to her charms, but it nonetheless irritated her.

"Cruel hoax?" Shota asked in her silky-smooth voice.

Kahlan had never thought it fair that a woman as beautiful as Shota should also have a voice that could charm a good spirit out of the underworld.

"My intent was merely to bring a cherished memory to life so that each of you could once more look upon your beloved mothers." Shota arched an eyebrow. "How is that cruel? It was a gift created through great effort on my part."

"Your intent was to bring each of us pain and to crush our hearts," Richard said. "Nothing more, nothing less."

She smiled reproachfully. "Richard, a Seeker needs his anger. If you will recall, I've warned you before not to let it cloud your judgment. And yet, it is a mistake you have made too often in the past."

Richard didn't go for the bait and instead glanced around. "What is this gloomy pit? Why aren't you in Agaden Reach?"

Shota swept an arm around in a grand gesture as if to show him the massive room, all the while smiling at him. "This is my winter palace. Isn't it splendid? Do you like it?"

Richard never took his eyes off her, the same way he wouldn't take his eyes off any lethal threat. "Not really. I think I prefer the swamp you live in. It's more honest."

"Ah, well, the Reach is nice, I must admit," Shota cooed. "But I come here to Bindamoon, on rare occasions, when I have important business to conduct."

"We met the man you sent to welcome us," Richard told her.

Shota's brow twitched. "Man?"

"The bearded fellow with the gift. A gift he intended to use against us."

Realization came over her features. "Ah." Her expression soured. "Iron Jack."

"That's the one," Richard said.

She flipped a hand dismissively. "A sycophant, a stooge. He fancies himself useful to me, thinking it will earn him favors. He is always trying to impress me. He doesn't realize that he merely impresses me as a worthless freak. He is a bothersome little man."

"He won't be bothering you anymore," Richard told her. "He's dead."

Shota shrugged as she smiled. "Good."

Kahlan was a bit surprised by the reaction. She had thought that

Shota had sent him. Richard didn't mention that Iron Jack had been killed by the Glee.

Kahlan gestured, indicating the palace above them. "And so you have that place above, now, so that you can call yourself a queen? What are you queen of, exactly?"

Shota turned a cold look on Kahlan. "That is what the people in this place prefer to call me. Queen."

Kahlan frowned. "Why?"

Shota regarded Kahlan with the kind of penetrating gaze that only added to her menace. Shota had never liked Kahlan, and she took every opportunity to make that clear.

Shota glanced down at Kahlan's swollen pregnancy. It was not a look of approval. The witch woman's perfect shape made Kahlan feel fat and ugly in comparison. Against her will, she could feel her face start to go red.

"They choose to call me the queen because they fear to say my name aloud." The smile again spread on her lips, but failed to reach her eyes. She arched one eyebrow. "With good reason."

Frowning, Shale leaned closer to Richard. "Mind telling me what's going on?"

He held out an arm in introduction. "Shale, this is Shota, a witch woman Kahlan and I know all too well. Deluded by prophecy, she swore that if we ever dared to have children, she would kill them. That is the witch's oath that all along has been at the center of everything. That is the true witch's oath that has shadowed us, nearly gotten us killed, and in the end brought us here. The witch's oath had never been created by Michec. It had been Shota's all along."

Shota smiled at Richard and bowed her head in recognition of him grasping Michec's role. "He was a useful idiot."

Shale looked baffled. "But why?"

"Because," Richard said, "she fears our children. Isn't that right, Shota?"

Shota's eyes turned hot and dangerous. "I guess I can't fool you, Seeker."

Kahlan had noticed from the beginning that all the women to the sides of the throne were glaring right at her. She did her best not to look at them, but it was next to impossible not to. Each one was different, and each one, in her own way, looked intimidating.

Shota, annoyed that Shale had spoken before being spoken to, slowly stepped closer to her, her boot strikes echoing around the massive stone chamber. She came to a halt before Shale. She lifted her chin a little to look down her nose as she studied the sorceress's face for a moment.

"Well, well, what have we here?" she asked as she leaned forward then to peer intently into Shale's eyes. "A half-breed. How utterly revolting." She straightened back up. "Had you any shame, my dear, you would have long ago killed yourself." Shota's disapproval turned again to a mocking smile. "Not to worry." She cocked her head. "I will help with that when I'm finished with you."

"I can only assume that you are responsible for the boundary that appeared to force us to come here," Richard said to draw Shota's attention away from the sorceress. "That means that you are responsible for the loss of any innocent lives of the people who have been killed when they walked into it without realizing what it was. I want that terrible boundary brought down right now." Richard leaned toward Shota, fixing her in his raptor glare. "Right now."

Shota shrugged. "As you wish." She twirled a hand around overhead. "Done," she said in a voice that might have been used to announce dinner was ready.

Richard looked a little surprised to have her so easily agree, and a little dubious that she had actually undone something of such massive power. More than that, though, he was not at all happy about the boundary being put up in the first place. "How many innocent people do you suppose you murdered with that thing?"

Shota regained her imperious attitude. "I regret the loss of any innocent lives, but it was unavoidable in order to prevent what would be a much greater loss of lives. So, in that sense, you two are actually the cause of such deaths."

Richard continued to glare at her. "How do you figure that?"

Shota walked slowly to her ornate throne to stand for a moment as she gathered her thoughts.

She lifted a finger without looking back. "You saved me from the Keeper once."

"And this is how you show your gratitude?" Richard asked in a rising, angry voice.

After a moment, the witch woman turned and strolled back to stand before Richard and Kahlan. "I told you both that because of what you had done, I would be forever grateful. I meant it."

She touched her fingertips to the side of Richard's face. "I actually rather like you. You are a noble individual. You and the Mother Confessor both. You both have fought for the survival of your people, and in so doing fought for my survival as well. You have done good and brought peace to the world. For all that and more, I respect you both and wish you no harm."

122

"So you decided to trap us here because you *like* us?" Richard asked. "You put lives of innocent people in danger because you *like* us? You more than likely caused the deaths of unwitting travelers because you *like* us?"

Shota gently gripped Richard's throat as she glared with menace into his gray eyes. "I warned you that all the children a Confessor bears are Confessors. Over time it came to pass that most give birth only to girl children. I told you that if you give the Mother Confessor a child, it would be a boy, and that boy child would be a Confessor. Beyond that, even a girl child with Confessor power and the gift of a war wizard from two lines of wizards, one with Subtractive Magic, would be an abomination. I told you that for those reasons you must not have a child with this woman."

"So you're back to that, are you?" Richard folded his arms across his chest. "Back to the nonsense about prophecy?"

"It is hardly nonsense. Fathers wed to Confessors are supposed to have been taken by her power so that if by chance she happened to bear a boy, the husband would without question end its life. You changed all that by finding a way to be with her without being taken by her power. As a result, neither of you has the will or the strength to kill the tainted children the two of you conceive."

She paused a moment as her grip on Richard's throat tightened. "I have the will, I have the strength, and I am willing to use it. I gave you my word on that. I gave you a witch's oath on that. And you both defied me."

"It's our lives," Richard said in a surprisingly calm voice, as if trying to reason with her. "It's our children's lives. You have no dominion over any of our lives and no right to deny our children the right to live their lives. I will protect those children, as will Kahlan. We will teach them to be good people who care about others."

Kahlan could see that it was like trying to reason with a stone wall.

"You two have selfishly put your own wishes ahead of the greater good. Once they are old enough, the power those two children possess will be profound. Your teaching will not be able to control such corrupting power."

Richard's features hardened. "You need to stop this right now, Shota. I will not allow you to harm us or our children."

Shota slowly shook her head as she gazed into his eyes. "Better you battle the Keeper of the underworld himself, than me."

Richard gripped her wrist and pulled her hand away from his throat. "You think so much of yourself, do you? We already faced your witch and your oath in the form of Moravaska Michec. You should know that he died with my hands around his throat and Kahlan twisting her knife in his heart."

Shota flicked her hand dismissively. "A warlock. Such men are a poor excuse for a true witch."

"He was a witch man," Kahlan said. "You are a witch woman. A witch is a witch."

"Hardly," she huffed. "Witch women and witch men are from two entirely different lines. A witch man is not a witch by being born of a witch woman. Similar to Confessors, witch women don't give birth to boys. At least, none that live long. A witch man is the son of a witch man and a woman with no power. He does not carry the same heredity and power as a witch woman.

"While they like to think of themselves as more than they are, and while they certainly have great power and can cause a great deal of trouble, they are but a mere shadow of a *true* witch. His power was but a flea on the back of a wolf compared to mine. I let him have a try at enforcing my witch's oath, but in the end, he was an inferior witch and proved himself as much.

"He originally attached himself to Darken Rahl because he intuitively grasped the reality of his limitations as a witch and so he sought to add to his power through his association with a powerful wizard. Darken Rahl allowed him to indulge his sick desires because he was useful in the same way a vicious dog can be useful. Michec was a cruel man whom people feared—with good reason. But he made the mistake of thinking that because people feared him, that made him a more important witch than he actually was.

"With Darken Rahl gone, he sought an alliance with the Glee for the same reasons he had served Darken Rahl. He believed it made him a more powerful witch. His deluded beliefs ultimately proved to be his undoing."

"He was witch enough," Richard said, drawing Shota's glare away from Kahlan. "He was more powerful than you give him credit for. And we stopped him from carrying out your witch's oath, just as we will stop you if we have to."

Shota showed him an icy smile. "You think so, child? You can't begin to grasp how wrong you are about that. Michec groveled before me, the grand witch, as all witches do. He swore to carry out my oath, as all witches must. In his failure, he proved he was not a witch worthy of the task or my protection."

"I don't care what, in your vanity, you think of witch men," Richard said. "But I do care about your need to continue to pursue your nonsense about our children and what you saw while looking into the flow of time. Prophecy is dead. I ended it because prophecy is a corrupting influence and it was a danger to the world of life. Your blind obsession with it is proof of its corrupting nature."

Shota lifted her chin indignantly. "It was a true vision into the flow of time, into how events will unfold."

"The nature of prophecy is that it looks into possibilities that branch out endlessly from root events as the world moves forward and continually changes. You plucked one leaf from the tree of prophecy while ignoring the entire forest."

"The world may have changed, but the flow of time did not."

"You can't see into the flow of time anymore, can you?"

Shota squinted at him. "No, thanks to you. You destroyed one of our most valuable tools, a tool that belongs to witch women."

"It did not belong to witch women. It was an expression of possible futures belonging in the underworld. Once it was brought to the world of life, witches long ago latched on to it in order to deceitfully gain power for themselves. It was an underworld force that had never belonged in this world."

Shota took a threatening step closer to him. "I used the flow of time to know how certain events flow and unfold. I used it in the past to help you."

"And had we followed your advice born of prophecy, then on more than one occasion, we would all be dead by now."

"You were smart enough to use the prophecy I gave you to succeed in ways neither I nor you could foresee. But without that prophecy, you might not have saved anyone. That is part of the way the flow of time works. As you say, it branches into many possible futures.

"I know far more about that flow of time and prophecy than you ever will, and that flow foretold that if you have a child with this Confessor it will be a monster. Such a child would risk bringing back the terror of the dark times, and worse, considering the power these twins will be born with. They will be bonded as twins and by the power they would be born with.

"But you refuse to heed that warning of a dark future and instead would ignorantly visit upon the world a male Confessor. A male Confessor! You are selfish children, the both of you, without any care for how what you are doing would destroy lives of so many others if these monsters were to live."

She looked pointedly over at Kahlan, then turned back to Richard. "I won't."

Richard lifted his hands out in frustration. "You don't understand prophecy the way you so smugly think you do, Shota."

She arched an eyebrow. "You have used prophecy to survive."

"Yes, because prophecy was something that only a wizard with Subtractive Magic can rightly understand. That's because prophecy is an underworld element. I alone understood its changeable nature and thus its limitations. I acted within those limitations, not in defiance of them."

She dismissed his words with a flick of a hand. "This is a different form of prophecy, meant for a witch woman only."

"Prophecy is prophecy, no matter how you wish to dress it up."

Shota considered his words only briefly before ignoring them. "I used the flow of time to see that if you two conceived a child, it would be a monster. And now, you have conceived twins, the worst possible sign of the terrors to come."

Richard sighed in exasperation. "We're going around in circles. You said that we would conceive a monster, right?"

"You already know that I did."

He gestured expansively. "All right, for the sake of argument, let's say you were right." Richard held up a finger as he leaned toward her. "But what you may not realize is that your look into prophecy has already come to pass. That flow of time has run its course and is over. It already happened."

Shota folded her arms. "What are you talking about?"

"When the chimes caused magic to fail—caused the magic of the necklace you gave Kahlan to fail—we didn't know that your necklace wasn't working as you designed it, and as a result, we conceived a child. Unfortunately, Kahlan lost that child before it could be born. If your prophecy is true, that means the first child conceived, the one Kahlan lost, was in fact the monster you so fear, the very one you saw in the flow of time.

"That means that the prophecy you saw in the flow of time has already happened and has already been fulfilled. Since Kahlan became pregnant but lost that first child, that means the child you saw in the flow of time that would be a monster, is already long dead. The world has already been saved from the dark times you saw in the flow of time caused by that monster."

Richard gestured at Kahlan as he went on. "This pregnancy is now a different one. This time, these children Kahlan now carries are exactly what the world needs to survive. They are not the monsters that would destroy the world, but rather they are the other side of that prophecy, the balance to it that magic requires: the saviors of the world."

Shota scowled at him for a moment. "It is not possible for them to be saviors of our world."

"Yes, it is, because without them, our gift—mine and Kahlan's—will eventually pass out of existence when we die. The Grace each of us was born with will carry us and our gift beyond the veil. Right now, our gift, Kahlan's and mine, is what is holding magic together and preventing the Golden Goddess from completing her lust to take our world and kill everyone in it.

"Don't you see? Without our magic carrying on through these children of D'Hara, the Glee will be able to ravage our world. If you think the dark times were bad, you have not seen the terror visited upon people by the Glee. We have seen a small bit of it, and I can tell you that no one will survive. If these children don't live, then no one will.

"If you were to kill these children, you would, in essence, be killing everyone."

With her hands on her hips, Shota regarded Kahlan for a long moment before looking back at Richard and again folding her arms.

"That's a nice story, but I can't risk the world on a nice story. I won't risk it. I know of the Golden Goddess. What you don't see is that she is not my concern." She unfolded her arms to poke Richard's chest with a finger. "The Glee are your concern, your responsibility, as the Lord Rahl. It is up to you to protect our world, and as such it is your responsibility to deal with the threat posed by the Glee. It is as simple as that.

"My concern is the monsters you have conceived. It is my responsibility—since you abdicated it—to make sure the twins you two have conceived never come to be."

Richard's hands fisted at his sides. "I don't have any way to fight a threat from another world! Any hope for the future will slip away without these gifted children!"

Richard took a settling breath to compose himself before going on. "Shota, your fault, your flaw, is that you are so focused on your narrow belief, that you are not able to see the bigger picture. You are fighting the last battle from dark times long forgotten."

"It is you who are not seeing the big picture and the obvious solution," she said. "You simply need to stop the threat from the Golden Goddess and her kind, *wizard*. When you do that, then our world will be safe from the Glee. That is your duty as Seeker and as the Lord Rahl. Do your job. My concern is that these children are not allowed to live in this world. That is my job.

"Had you not ended prophecy, I would be able to look into the flow of time and see if anything has changed and if your theory could possibly be true. But because you took it upon yourself to end prophecy, that opportunity is lost to us. Because the consequences would be too grave to risk doing otherwise, the original prophecy must stand.

"My witch's oath stands. It will be carried out."

Richard's eyes took on the hawklike glare that Kahlan knew so well. "Shota," he said in a low, dangerous tone, "if you have forced us to come all this way so that you can kill us along with these innocent children yet unborn, you have made a very big mistake. You have no right to their lives or ours, and as the Lord Rahl of the D'Haran Empire, I am telling you once and for all to end your obsession.

"Believe me, you do not want to fight me." He gestured to Kahlan. "Nor do you want to fight the Mother Confessor. Have you ever seen a mother bear protect her cubs? I have. She is ferocious. You cross her at great peril."

123

Kahlan felt solace at Richard's words. Shota, however, looked like she was having none of it. Kahlan wondered how long the witch woman's patience would last before she decided to simply kill them.

Shota opened her hands as an empty smile spread on her lips. "Richard, just as you have so often misinterpreted my actions in the past, you misunderstand my resolve to be of assistance in this difficult time. You must believe me when I say that I have no malice toward you or the Mother Confessor. Nor do I have any desire to do battle with either of you. Most of all, I certainly have no intention of harming either one of you. I already told you: I am grateful to you both. Everything you falsely interpret as threatening is merely my desire to help you both."

Richard glared with incredulity. "You expect me to believe you are only interested in *helping* us? You want us to think that by murdering our children you are *helping* us?"

Shota stepped close so she could rest an arm over Richard's shoulder. She smiled warmly and batted her eyelashes, as if trying to charm him. Kahlan had absolutely no doubt that Richard was not charmed or attracted to the witch woman. Even so, it made her blood boil to see her trying to seduce Richard with her "charm."

"Think of me as doing a difficult chore for you, one that must be done, so that you don't have to do it," she said with a shrug. She idly ran a finger of her other hand down his chest, making Kahlan fume all the more. "I admit that my insistence on being of service to you could be taken the wrong way, but be assured, I certainly intend you no harm."

"If you intend us no harm, then why did you force us to come here?" Kahlan asked, drawing the witch woman's attention away from her husband.

Shota withdrew her arm from where it was resting on Richard's shoulder and turned to Kahlan, clearly annoyed to be interrupted in mid-seduction. "I brought you here so you could give birth to the children you carry. I will see to it that you will be safe and comfortable while you are here until then. Once you give birth, both you and Richard, and"—she gestured offhandedly beyond Richard without taking her eyes off Kahlan—"your gaggle of Mord-Sith, will be free to leave and go about your lives."

"My children will not be born here, in this vile place, so that you can slaughter them."

Shota's grin widened. "I'm afraid that you are once again getting the wrong idea. You see, you have no say in this. We will do our best to make you comfortable for the duration of your visit to my palace. After you give birth, as I said, you will be free to leave. But you will not be leaving with those children."

Kahlan's hands fisted with fury. "You can't have my babies so that you can murder them!"

Shota pressed the tips of her fingers together and bowed her head for a moment, as if patiently thinking of how to explain something to a stubborn child. Her head finally came back up.

"You claim to be protectors of your people. Well, so am I. Although we disagree about aspects of it, our goals are actually the same: the safety of our people. That is in fact what this is all about. You are blinded by maternal instinct, which is only natural, but it prevents you from having the vision and strength to do what is necessary for the greater good. I have both, so I am going to help with what must be done."

Kahlan fought back tears of rage. "The greater good?"

Shota's expression turned dark and dangerous as she leaned in. "I am finished with trying to reason with you two foolish children. It shall be as I say."

Kahlan knew how dangerous this witch woman was, but she was at the end of her patience. "Shota, if you do not withdraw your witch's oath and let us go, there will be no turning back—for either of us. Know that, as the Mother Confessor, I will grant you no mercy and allow none."

Shota looked amused. "You think your Law of Nines will help you? I'm afraid that it no longer applies."

Richard glanced around at the group with him. The Mord-Sith, all in their red leather, looked not only resolute but positively dangerous as they watched the conversation, waiting to be let off their chain.

"What are you talking about?" he asked.

Shota lifted her arm out behind, indicating the odd-looking group of women lined up to either side of her throne. "You see, I have come here, to Bindamoon, to my winter palace, to convene a coven."

Kahlan scanned the line of grim women to either side of Shota's throne. There were six on one side of it, and five on the other side. Although all of the women looked very different from one another, they had one thing in common: they did indeed all look like witches. They all fit the stories she had heard as a young girl from the wizards who taught her. And they certainly all looked dangerous.

She suddenly realized the flaw in Shota's grand scheme.

"I don't want to tell you your business," Kahlan said, "but a coven is thirteen witches. With you and the rest of these ladies, here, there are only twelve. You're missing your last witch."

"Do tell," Shota said with an amused smile.

Kahlan shrugged. "We killed Moravaska Michec, your thirteenth witch. Without the thirteenth witch, your call to coven can't authenticate the essential dictate so that you can initiate its power."

"Michec? A witch man? In a coven?" Shota said with distaste. She huffed dismissively. "Don't be ridiculous. He could not possibly be part of a coven. He's of more use to me dead than alive." She once more smiled as she leaned toward Kahlan. "But thank you for the suggestion of using him."

Kahlan couldn't imagine how Shota could use a dead Michec. Ignoring the distraction, she gestured to the women standing in the background.

"Well, I hate to tell you, but in that case you're a witch short of a coven. Like I said, including you, there are only twelve witches. Without thirteen witches you are not able to invoke the power of coven."

Shota smiled without humor. "Yes, I know. That's why I had you bring me the thirteenth witch."

Kahlan blinked, suddenly worried by Shota's calm confidence. "What are you talking about?"

Her eyes flashing with menace, Shota walked over to Shale. With her face mere inches away from Shale's, she pointed back behind. "Go and take your place with your sister witches."

Kahlan suddenly realized that Shale had been oddly quiet almost the entire time. Kahlan saw, then, that she seemed to be in a trance of some sort. She stared ahead without blinking.

Shota, still pointing back at the line of women, snapped her fingers. "Now."

Without a word of protest, or question, or even acknowledgment, Shale walked woodenly toward the women standing to the sides of the throne. When she reached them, she took up a place at the end of the line of five on one side of the throne, making six to match the six on the other side.

With Shale bringing the number in the line to twelve, and Shota making the total thirteen, Shota now had the witches she needed to invoke the power of coven.

"Shale," Richard called out, "what are you doing?"

When he started to charge toward her to get her back, Shota lifted a hand toward him, as if she were dismissing him. Kahlan didn't know what kind of power she had available to her with a coven, but she knew from stories wizards had told her that it was formidable.

Suddenly, Moravaska Michec materialized as if his corpse had been pulled directly up from the underworld. He looked as intimidating in spirit form as he had in life. Kahlan regretted now even having mentioned his name and giving Shota the idea. The dead man was semitransparent in his spirit form, but the part that was visible looked like half-rotted remains. Blood that had gushed from the wound in his chest where Kahlan had driven her knife into him covered his front, and his intestines hung out from a gaping belly wound, dragging across the floor as he advanced.

His mouth opened with a roar that shook the room and made Kahlan feel as if her eyeballs were rattling in her skull. Michec abruptly shot across the room, not on his feet, but through the air as if he had leaped, his intestines fluttering out behind him.

He struck Richard with enough force to catapult him back so powerfully that he stopped only when he slammed into one of the stone ravens. As he did, the spirit of Michec, his summons completed, dissolved back into the world of the dead.

Richard scrambled to his feet, refusing to be shaken by what Shota had conjured.

"Shale!" he called out. "Don't do this! Don't let Shota do this to you! Come away from them!"

Kahlan could hardly believe that the woman who had saved her life several times would suddenly join with Shota against them. She joined Richard in crying out Shale's name, pleading with her to come away from the others.

"If it pleases you both," Shota said in a surprisingly sympathetic tone, "know that this is not by the choice of your half-breed witch. It is by my choice alone, by my command alone, as the grand witch."

Her tone turned iron-hard. "But a witch woman with such a mix of powers is an abomination, as would be your children. I will use her as long as it pleases me. When I am finished with her, I will eliminate her, as I would any such crime of nature."

Kahlan could feel the blood draining from her face. "Shota, you can't do this. A coven invokes the underworld, and with it, Subtractive Magic. You said yourself that a witch with a mix of powers is a crime of nature."

Shota leaned toward her with a deadly look. "I warned you before. You did not listen. This is the consequence."

Kahlan knew that even in the best of circumstances, her gift and Richard's didn't work against witch women the way they did against others. Witch women had the ability to turn whatever powers you used back at you, often with fatal results.

But now that Shota had invoked coven, her power would make using their gift against her next to impossible.

She hoped that Richard remembered the warning Nicci had once given when explaining the complications of the magic involved when trying to use their gift against a witch woman.

Even so, they were being put in the position where trying might be their only option, since not trying would mean their death anyway.

124

Richard raced forward, going for Shota, but in response she again cast out an arm. A wall of shimmering light stopped him cold. He dropped to the floor, clutching his middle in agony.

As Richard hit the floor from what Shota had done to him, every one of the Mord-Sith spun her Agiel up into her fist. They had seen enough. All six of them, their single braids flying out behind them, leaped over Richard on their way to Shota. They screamed in lethal fury as they were still in midair.

They had only just started their attack when specters of horribly deformed dead appeared to catch each of the Mord-Sith in spirit arms. Like Michec, they appeared semitransparent, but they were solid enough to snatch up the Mord-Sith, the bones of the dead showing through their tattered flesh. Even as they were being lifted from the ground, each of the Mord-Sith attacked the specters with her Agiel in one hand and a knife in the other, but it had no effect on the phantoms from another world.

All of the Mord-Sith were swiftly carried backward, powerless to stop the underworld beings holding them, until each of the six were smashed into a stone raven, between its opened wings. A stone wing of each of the six raven statues swept around the Mord-Sith to trap them there. The spirits, their task completed, vanished back into the world of the dead.

The other wing of each of the six ravens held out its stone bowl of burning oil. The large stone wings were plenty big enough to hold the Mord-Sith fast. Dust and bits of stone drizzled down from where the stone wings had broken as they turned in order to grab and hold the Mord-Sith.

Out of the corner of her eye, as Richard struggled to get to his feet or possibly to conjure some kind of power to fight back, Kahlan saw two of the witches leave the line of their sister witches and start toward her.

Shota continued to hold the hand out toward Richard, as if pressing him to the ground, her power preventing him from getting up or doing anything else to stop her. She brought her other hand up when she saw Kahlan try to run to Richard. Whatever kind of magic Shota was using, she was effortlessly able to bring up a solid wall of air to prevent Kahlan from moving any closer despite how desperately she tried to push against it.

As Kahlan struggled to move through the thick air, her feet sliding against the floor as she shoved her shoulder against it, two women rushed up from behind and seized her arms. One was a short, squat, bulky woman in an outfit made of patches of different kinds of burlap sewn haphazardly together. It hung from her broad shoulders all the way to the floor, making her body look square. The wrinkles and lines of her face were pinched in toward her close-set eyes and wart-covered nose. Her downturned mouth made her look like she had a mouthful of bile she couldn't spit out. Her thin, frizzy hair stuck out all around her head like a dirty white thundercloud.

Kahlan tried to pull her arm back out of the witch's grasp, but the woman, while not tall, was at least three times as wide as Kahlan, and held her arm in the powerful grip of her fat fingers. Her mass made Kahlan feel like she was trying to pull against an oak tree that had her in its clutches.

The witch who grabbed her other arm was as thin as the other was burly. The tattered, hanging, dark dress she wore looked like she gutted fish in it daily and the filth had never once been washed off. The skin of her bare arms was wrinkled and withered, almost looking like tree bark. Her bony fingers had long, sickly yellowish fingernails that were ragged on the ends and scratched Kahlan's arms. The witch also had filthy rags wrapped around her head, one part around the top to hold in her shock of unruly, inky-black hair, and another part down and around her head going under her chin and tied back on top as if it was trying to keep her jaw from falling off.

A number of long strings of bones, teeth, and feathers hung around her neck, swinging back and forth and clattering as the witch yanked on Kahlan's arm. She had similar strings of collected animal parts around her wrists, some of them still in the process of rotting. The gagging stench of dead things was overpowering.

Her large, round black eyes did not look human. She had the dead stare of a corpse. Although she was much smaller than the woman who had Kahlan's other arm, she was, with that dead stare, more frightening than the blocky, angry-looking woman on the other side, and by the hand clutching Kahlan's arm, just as strong.

Together, the women began dragging Kahlan backward with an urgency she wouldn't have thought either could muster. She fought against them, but she was no match for their strength, and they were not even using their powers.

Looking back over her shoulder, Kahlan could see that they were dragging her toward one of the dark openings at the bottom of the towering wall. As they went past the throne, another witch left the line to join the other two and walk, leaning in, facing Kahlan as she was being pulled backward, her heels dragged across the stone floor.

This witch, unlike the two who had iron grips on her arms, was not monstrous. She was, in fact, shapely and, in a dark sort of way, pretty. She wore a black, formfitting bodice that was cut low and edged with black lace. Her skirt, which hung nearly to the floor, was made up of what had to be hundreds of knotted and beaded strips of leather. Some of the beads sparkled and reflected the light of the burning bowls of oil held by the stone ravens. They allowed her bare knees to part the strings and show through when she walked. Around her neck she wore a broad, black lace choker.

Her hair was red, long, and stringy. It mimicked the look of her strange, stringy skirt: the veil of small, ropy strands of hair hung down in front of her face the way the skirt veiled her legs. Beyond the screen made of the strands of hair, her pale blue eyes lined with black, despite their beauty, were far more menacing than any of the others' eyes.

As she walked close in front of Kahlan, leaning in, while she was being dragged backward by the two older witch women, the strands of her skirt swished around her legs, allowing the beads to clatter together, making a distracting, enchanting, almost musical sound. That beguiling sound for some reason made it difficult for Kahlan to think clearly. As they walked face-to-face, the young witch leaned in more, to within inches of Kahlan's face, with a look that made goose bumps race up Kahlan's arms to the nape of her neck.

"Stay green for me," she said in a low, smoky voice that matched both the beauty and the menace of her blue eyes, "until I can cut those squirming little brats out of your womb and twist off their heads and eat them while you watch."

Kahlan didn't know what "stay green" meant, but the intent was clear enough.

Kahlan was helpless as she was dragged backward toward one of cavelike openings at the bottom of the towering wall and into the labyrinth of tunnels beyond. With the third witch leaning in, her face inches away, the musical jangle of the beads wove a tune that made Kahlan feel limp.

Even so, with fear choking her breathing, Kahlan gathered all her strength as she drew a big breath and then screamed Richard's name.

Even as he was held fast by Shota's power, he managed to turn to the sound of her shriek, and the terror in it.

Richard's fury was evident at hearing the fright in her voice as she cried out his name. He threw his arms up as he screamed in rage. Whatever he did broke Shota's hold on him and staggered her back a step.

The witch woman's anger looked the match of Richard's. She again forced her hands out. At first, the air shimmered, but then spiderwebs of lightning ignited from her fingertips. As she did that, Richard did the same, but the crackling lightning coming from his hands was the black void of Subtractive Magic. The way it twisted and whipped around, it looked like it was tied to his hands and frantically trying to get away. Where it hissed and snapped against the walls, it cut through the stone. In places the stone above that had lost its support began to fall, making the walls look like they were beginning to come down.

And then they both halted what they were doing as they each seemed to gather their strength to redouble their efforts. They both cast their power out at the same time. Kahlan leaned her head a little to the side to look around the redheaded witch glaring at her. As they both projected their gift, Kahlan saw a wavering wall where that power collided suddenly come to life. The room shook with the thunder from the continual, flickering lightning they both were generating.

Neither of their magic could get past the other's wall of power, and the collision of their opposing powers created a blinding explosion of light in the center of the massive chamber. That sizzling light expanded outward in all directions, blasting into the stone to all sides—but far more critically, that sheer plane of power also shot vertically with a thunderous boom. Kahlan recognized that it was a hot brew of Additive and Subtractive Magic coming together. Both of their powers were clashing together in ways that weren't ever supposed to happen.

As the discharge of that explosive energy shot upward, it cut through the ceiling, the same as it sliced through the walls to the sides, going straight up through the entire palace, severing walls and floors above in the massive, ripping blast. Kahlan could hear the thunder of walls and ceilings on all the floors above collapsing inward.

And then, with so much above them destroyed, the ceiling of the massive chamber started caving in.

The other witches all ran for the safety of the caverns at the rear of the great chamber. Shota began retreating with them as she continued to use her power to hold Richard at bay and keep him where he was.

The redheaded witch in front of Kahlan slammed the heel of her hand into the center of Kahlan's chest to force her back. At the same time, the two holding her arms yanked her back with them into the darkness of the tunnels.

The ground shook and the air filled with rolling, choking dust as unimaginable tons of rock from the palace above as well as the mountain itself began cascading down into the vast chamber just as the witch women dragged her back into the safety of the labyrinth.

Kahlan tried to reach out as she screamed Richard's name, but even as she did, she knew he would never be able to hear her in the deafening thunder of everything from above collapsing in on him.

She lost sight of him in the cascade of stone and the swirling clouds of dust.

125

In the oppressive silence, Richard realized that he heard distant, muffled voices. He couldn't make out who was talking, or what they were saying. It didn't seem to be important to him just then, so he didn't dwell on it. His head hurt.

When he realized that he was beginning to wake up, he rather wished that he wasn't, because, besides his head throbbing, he was just beginning to realize that he hurt all over. In order to try to alleviate the discomfort, he attempted to reposition himself. But when he tried to move, he found that for some reason he couldn't.

In his mind, he did his best to determine if it was that he was being physically prevented from moving, or he was somehow paralyzed.

That sensation of not being able to move brought on a wave of alarm that woke him the rest of the way. He looked around but couldn't see anything at all. He felt with his hands, trying to figure out where he was.

In the pitch blackness, he felt something smooth, cold, and dusty mere inches above him. As he felt around, it seemed to be entirely over the top of him, but angled downward as it got closer toward his feet. There was more space under the thing above him up where his head was, so he was able to move his arms a little, but not his legs.

As he groped around, he felt ragged chunks of stone packed tight all around him. Everything was covered with what felt like a thick layer of dust. He regretted moving, because it lifted the dust into the air and he couldn't avoid breathing it in. He coughed, trying to get it out of his lungs. By the taste, he knew that it was stone dust.

As he was regaining consciousness, or waking up—he wasn't sure which—he began to remember seeing Shota unleash Subtractive Magic. He had known that if he didn't act quickly, he would be killed. But he remembered that it seemed at the time as if his legs wouldn't move the way he needed. Maybe it had simply been sheer terror that kept him in place and prevented him from running.

He wasn't entirely sure what he had done at that point, other than simply reacting out of instinct. His gift as a war wizard, from somewhere deep inside him, came forth and did what was necessary to save him.

But he did remember being alarmed at how the explosive collision of Subtractive Magic had cut through the walls and ceiling. He didn't know how far those voids went off into the side of the mountain, but he realized that they instantly cut all the way up through the entire palace. It had to have cut support structures and beams in addition to floors, ceilings, and arches all the way up through the towering structure.

He remembered the terrible shrieking blast of Subtractive and Additive Magic mixing and then the roar of the entire place coming apart as it started falling in, and not being able to make his legs work. Even as he started remembering it, though, the whole thing felt like something that happened long ago, or maybe in a dream, or even to someone else.

He was so thirsty he couldn't think clearly. He worked his tongue against the top of his mouth, trying to moisten it, but the dust in his mouth was turning to a chalky paste and only making matters worse.

Putting all the pieces together in his mind, he realized that the entire place and probably some of the mountain had come down on top of him and he was obviously trapped, probably under one of the slabs of a floor from above. A lot of the rubble was packed around his legs so tightly he couldn't move them.

He realized that while he was jammed into a small space, at least the thick slab above him had saved him from being crushed under what had to be the weight of the entire palace. As lucky as that was to have survived in the small pocket under the slab, he felt a rising sense of panic at realizing that he was buried alive. There was no hope of digging his way out from under a mountain of rubble.

He reached up and felt his throbbing head. It was wet. He put a finger to his mouth to taste the wetness. He could tell by the coppery taste that it was blood. That explained his head hurting. It felt like it hurt both on the outside and inside.

Again he heard the distant voices. He had thought in the beginning that it must have been something he heard in a dream, but now that he was fully awake, he knew it was a person calling out to him.

"I'm down here!" he yelled as loud as he could.

He didn't get a response, so he called out again, forcing himself to yell louder. He was feeling desperate as he fought back his growing panic. He called out again, louder yet.

"Lord Rahl?" came a distant voice.

"Berdine? Is that you?"

"Yes!" The voice came closer. "Yes! It's me! I'm here!"

He heard people frantically talking. The sound came closer until he could make out individuals. Apparently, whoever was up above with Berdine was excited that they had gotten a response. Now that he knew there were people out there somewhere, he started squirming, thinking he might be able to work his way out.

He soon realized, though, that it was simply impossible. The stone was packed in so tight that none of it would budge. He couldn't make any of it move so much as an inch. He was stuck solid in the rubble.

He began to remember his alarm as the entire palace above them had started to come down. Shota had somehow managed to touch off Subtractive Magic. The only way to prevent her from killing him had been to use a mix of Additive and Subtractive Magic to counter it. It had been his only chance. When those powers had come together, it had created a knifelike blast of Subtractive Magic that had cut all the way up through the palace and at the same time to the sides through the mountain under the palace.

He hadn't known that a witch woman could do such things. Apparently, from what Kahlan had been saying, a coven amplified her power and gave her additional abilities. For all of her assurances that she had no intention to harm them, she was quick to attack him with lethal power.

He remembered, too, that gifted people could join their abilities to amplify their power. The joining of the power of all those witch women had obviously managed to bring forth the boundary. That alone was a demonstration of the power that Shota now had at her disposal.

He could hardly believe that Shale had joined them. No, it wasn't her doing, he reminded himself. She was being used. He remembered that Shota had said as much. He could tell by the empty stare that Shale was not acting on her own.

"Lord Rahl!" Berdine's voice was closer, and more desperate. Even so, it still seemed like it was some distance away. "Lord Rahl, are you still there?"

"Mostly, I think. There is a big slab of floor, or ceiling, over the top of me. It created a pocket and kept me from being crushed. But my legs are encased in the rubble and I can't move them. How long have I been stuck down here?"

"This is the end of the second day," came the response.

Two days. Richard was stunned.

"Is Kahlan with you?"

This time the answer was slow in coming. "I'm afraid not. We haven't been able to find anyone other than you."

That answer sent a shiver of panic and pain through his heart. She had to have escaped. He told himself that she had gotten out in time.

"Who's with you?" he called out.

"All of us. When everything started collapsing, the falling ceiling toppled those big stone birds. They sheltered us from all the stone falling in long enough for all of us to run into the tunnels and escape. We only just made it in time. We had hoped you were right behind us. The entire palace fell into that underground room and with all the dust and falling debris we couldn't see if all the witch women escaped."

Escaped with Kahlan, she meant. Richard didn't know which would have been a worse fate—to have her die quickly, or have the witch women take her away to do what they intended. He knew that despite what Shota said, she was no longer willing to tolerate Richard and Kahlan being alive to disobey her wishes.

"Part of the mountain collapsed off to the side," Berdine called out. "We have a lot of town people up here with us. They are all helping."

He thought that was odd. "What do you mean, helping?"

"Helping dig you out. We've all been working for two days to dig through the rubble, hoping to find you alive. We were not going to stop, but we were beginning to give up hope."

"I'm stuck down here."

"I know. But a lot of the town people came right away to help us. We've been digging inward from the section of the mountain that fell away. Your power cutting through the walls caused a big section of the mountain to slide away, so we're digging in from the side. We've been searching, calling out, and digging for two days, day and night, hoping to find you. But a lot of the stone from the palace is in big, heavy chunks and some of it needs to be broken apart in order to move it out of the way. Now that we know you are alive, and where you are, we can concentrate on getting to you."

Richard let out a weary breath. He didn't want to tell her that his head was bleeding, and he was dizzy. It felt like the dark world he was trapped in was spinning and tilting.

"Don't worry, Lord Rahl. We're coming for you. Hold on. But I fear it will take some time."

Richard nodded, then realized they couldn't see him nod. "I'll wait right here."

"Lord Rahl, just try to relax. It will take us some time to get to you, but we won't give up. I can promise you that."

Richard felt tears welling up for Kahlan and their children. He feared to think what had happened to her.

For a moment, he felt overwhelmed by all of the insurmountable problems. In that instant, he thought that it would be better to just give up.

And then, he could feel his mind slipping into darkness deeper than the darkness of where he lay.

126

Richard heard people grunting with effort. And then, as a large chunk of stone was rolled aside, his dark hole was suddenly lit by a small shaft of light. It made him squint in the sudden brightness.

"Lord Rahl!" He recognized Vika's voice, and he could hear the desperation in it. "Lord Rahl!"

"I'm still here."

"Thank the good spirits," she murmured.

Richard briefly thought to ask her if the good spirits were up there helping them dig.

"Water," he called in a weak voice, instead. "Can you get me some water?"

"Water? Yes, we will get some," Vika said. "We've made a tunnel of sorts to get to you. It shouldn't be long before we have you out. Just hold on, Lord Rahl. We'll have you out soon."

"I need water," he mumbled.

"Rikka is running to get some. Hold on."

He could hear people grunting as they either lifted stone out of the way if it was small enough to handle, or rolled it back if it was too big and heavy to pick up. Hammers rang out against steel chisels as men tried to break up the larger pieces in their path. Others shouted instructions as they worked. Richard realized that he could hear a surprisingly large number of voices.

The light coming into his cavity in the rubble lit what he thought would be his grave with even more light as the people frantically worked to open the way in to reach him. The shaft of light revealed all the dust swirling around him. Richard wondered if they would be too late. He could feel himself losing the strength to remain conscious.

They had told him that he had been there for two days. Stuck in the dusty space under the slab without water, it seemed like forever.

From time to time he heard things above him collapse and large blocks tumble down the hill of debris. It sounded like more walls might occasionally be falling in, or maybe ceilings that had little support might finally have given way—or were starting to give way. He was well aware that if things shifted wrong, or something big enough were to fall, he would be crushed. The thought of that made his chest tighten with the embrace of panic. Every time he heard stone above groan, or fall, he held his breath, waiting for the end.

He constantly had to fight back dread at being trapped under a mountain of rubble, never to get out. To keep his mind from wandering into frightening thoughts, he remembered Kahlan's face, trying to recall every detail.

Suddenly, a hand touched his shoulder. He jumped right out of his memory.

"Lord Rahl, it's me," Vika said.

She was close. Grunting and panting, she had somehow squirmed her way through the little tunnel they had made to his grave.

Richard reached up and put a hand over hers. It was bloody from digging through the rough, jagged stone chunks and rubble.

"I'm here," she said, groaning with the effort of getting in close enough. He could hear her pulling something up along her body. "I brought you a waterskin."

He squeezed her hand. "Today, Vika, you are my favorite. Be sure to tell Berdine."

Vika laughed a little as she pulled her hand back. She pulled the waterskin the rest of the way up along her body and then pushed it through the final part of the opening, which was barely big enough for her arm. Once it was in, she pushed her arm back through and grabbed his hand. He didn't know if she was reassuring him, or herself, but he held on to the hand as he guzzled water while holding the waterskin with his other.

"Take it easy. Don't drink it all at once or it will make you sick."

Richard nodded and pulled it away to get his breath.

"I have to go," she said. "We need to make this hole big enough to pull you out."

Richard felt too weak to answer, so he didn't. Vika huffed as she worked her way back out of the tight hole. As soon as she was back out, the work resumed. He could hear people shouting and groaning with effort as they worked.

Richard took another drink, then had to rest again with the half-empty waterskin on his chest. It moved slowly up and down with his shallow breathing. The pull of the darkness was too great, and it gently took him again.

He was awakened by hands gripping his shirt and pulling on him. He cried out as they tugged, because his legs were trapped and it hurt when they tried to pull him. A wiry man wormed his way in under the slab beside Richard. His head was facing Richard's feet.

"Hold on, Lord Rahl. Let me see if I can free up your legs so we can pull you out."

He worked as quickly as he could, pulling the tightly packed rock and rubble out from around Richard's legs. He found a shallow place to the side where he could push some of it. For some he had to wiggle his way back out, pulling larger chunks along with him. He was soon back to continue the excavation.

After working at it for a time, Richard was finally able to move his legs.

"All right," the man said, "I think we have you clear. We'll go easy. Let us know if you are still stuck, but we need to get you out. There's no telling if the rest of what's above you might shift and come down all of a sudden."

"What's your name?" Richard asked.

The man seemed surprised by the question. "I'm just a nobody, Lord Rahl."

Richard smiled. "You are not a nobody. Right now, you are a very important somebody to me."

"I am Toby, Lord Rahl," he said in a gentle voice.

"Thank you for coming for me, Toby."

Toby patted Richard's shoulder as he backed out. "I'd do anything for the man what rid us of that cursed witch. Now you lie still, Lord Rahl, and let us do the work."

The man squirmed the rest of the way back out of the shaft they had made. Once again thick fingers gripped Richard's shirt. He felt himself beginning to move, and then they stopped pulling.

"Is everything free now, Lord Rahl?" Toby asked. "Nothing hurting when we pull?"

"I seem to be free. You can go ahead and give it another try. I'll let you know if I'm having a problem."

Once he was out a little farther, to the more open part of the little cave, other hands were able to reach in under his arms to help pull. Because they were on their stomachs, it was an awkward angle to pull from. They would pause and then someone would count down and say, "Pull."

They kept repeating the coordinated tugging. Inch by inch Richard was gradually worked out of his tomb and back through a jagged tunnel of what he judged to be a jumble of unstable debris. At one point, his boot dislodged a rock and the narrow tunnel back where he had been under the slab collapsed with a roar that pushed out a cloud of dust.

That made them pull all the harder and faster. The farther they drew him out, the more hands they could get on him to help. Richard finally emerged to see dirty, grimy faces in torchlight all around him.

Berdine rushed in to give him a quick hug. Legs in red leather were all around him. He saw that it was now night. Some people had torches, while others had lanterns. The sea of faces in the flickering torchlight was an eerie, but welcome sight.

An older woman pushed the Mord-Sith back out of the way and worked herself in through the tight crowd while holding out a lantern in one hand. With bony but strong fingers, she turned his head one way to have a look, then the other.

"He needs help," she announced back over her shoulder. "Lift him onto that litter and get him across the way and into the healing house so we can tend to him."

People rushed to do as the old woman said, lifting him by his arms and legs just enough to slide a litter under him. Four big men lifted the litter.

Trying to be as gentle as they could, they carried him down off the sloping rubble pile and into the narrow streets. Richard bounced up and down in the litter as they trotted along, all the while the old woman urging them to hurry. Looking up, Richard could see by the torchlight that they went around corners and down narrow alleyways until they crossed the pass road that divided the town, over to the side where Richard and his group of nine hadn't been.

They finally went through a doorway into one of the stone buildings and set him down on a raised platform.

The red leather reappeared around him; someone laid a hand on him as if to reassure themselves that he was alive. As they did, Richard's mind went back into darkness.

127

When Richard woke, there was daylight streaming in through a small window. He was about to sit up when he realized that he didn't have any clothes on. When he looked down, he saw that there was at least a towel covering his groin.

He sniffed the air, seeming to recognize an aroma, trying to place it. Finally, he remembered. It was the smell of an aum plant, something from back in his home of Hartland. It seemed like forever since he had smelled it. It was a difficult plant to find, but Zedd had taught him where to look for it. It usually grew in the deep shade of the forest under a nannyberry tree, which was easier to find first because of its thick crop of dark blue berries.

He reached up and pulled something wet off his head and held it out to look at it. It was a big leaf from an aum plant that had been crushed to make it pliable and conform to the contours of his head. That was what he had smelled. Aum both eased pain and, importantly, helped wounds to heal quickly.

Vika shot to her feet when she saw that he was awake.

"He's awake," she called out to the old woman.

The old woman turned away from what she was doing at a table against the wall and smiled down at him. "There you are. You are looking much better."

The room with stone walls wasn't large, but it was filled with tables, a long stone bench against one wall, and standing cabinets all across another wall.

The old woman picked up a stone bowl from one of the tables. She used the pestle in the bowl to crush and stir the contents, then tapped it on the side, removed it, and set it aside. She came close and lifted his head as she put the bowl to his mouth.

"Drink this. It will help you to clear your head."

Richard glanced at Vika. She gave him a reassuring nod, so he drank it. It had some pungent herbs in it, but it mostly tasted of honey diluted in tea.

When he was finished, she patted his shoulder. "I'll go get the others."

Shortly after the woman left, the rest of the Mord-Sith rushed into the room.

"Lord Rahl!" Berdine squealed. "You look so much better!"

Richard squinted up at the faces leaning in, looking at him. "Where are my clothes?"

"Your clothes?" Cassia asked.

"Yes, my clothes."

Nyda gestured. "They're over there. They were positively filthy with all that stone dust and dirt, so we had to wash them."

Richard frowned up at the faces leaning in over him. "Well, who took them off me?"

The faces all smiled.

Richard rolled his eyes.

"You were really dirty, too, from all that dirt and grime," Berdine said. She grinned. "So we had to wash you, too."

Richard could feel his face turning red.

The old woman rushed back in with half a dozen more old women, all of them in similar long, dark dresses with ample skirts. Richard was glad to have them interrupt the Mord-Sith.

The original woman who had given him the drink held her hand out to the others. "Lord Rahl, we are Bindamoon healers. We have all been seeing to your care. I'm Rita."

"So you have been healing me?"

"We all worked on you," Rita confirmed. "You were seriously hurt."

She lifted the stack of aum leaves off his forehead, to the side, to have a look. She turned briefly to allow the others to have a look at the wound on his head. They all seemed pleased. Rita laid the moist aum back down, patting it gently into place so it would be in contact with the wound.

He realized, then, that there were poultices in several places on his legs and a big patch of aum on the left side of his ribs. It was a pale yellow, similar to the poultice Zedd used to make, but it had a different smell.

"You're lucky to have been injured here, in Bindamoon," Rita said. "We grow some of the rarest herbs here, herbs very helpful for healing. Because of the herbs we have, people come to Bindamoon to be healed. Some we can help, some we cannot."

"Aum is hard to find back where I come from," he said. "You mean you actually grow it?"

Her brow lifted in surprise. "You know of aum?"

Richard nodded. "My grandfather taught me about it, and how to find it."

"Well, no trouble finding it here," she said with a smile. "It's a valuable medicinal plant, so we grow rows of it." She turned a little and pointed. "We use fresh when we can, and we tie the plants up by their stems and hang them up in drying sheds, over there, until they are cured for when it is out of season. We trade most of it to help support our town and use some of it for people who come here to be healed. You are in one of our healing houses where we tend to people."

Richard looked around and saw a variety of jars and canisters, along with a number of washbasins as well as a half-dozen lanterns on a well-worn, heavy wooden table supplementing the light from the small window. There were shelves under the cabinets with smaller bottles neatly lined up.

"How long have I been asleep?" he asked.

She let out a concerned sigh. "You were brought here two nights ago. Because of your injuries, we had to give you some things to keep you asleep. With so many wounds we feared infection. Some of the herbs we use work better when the person is sleeping. The medicated sleep helped you get over the worst of your injuries. They are now all nicely on the mend. Especially your nasty head wound. We couldn't be sure everything inside was all right until you woke, but we can now see that your eyes are clear and you don't appear dizzy."

"I truly appreciate your help," Richard told her. "But I really need to search for the Mother Confessor. She was—"

"I'm afraid she's gone," Vika told him. "The people told me that all the witches left with her."

Richard blinked. "Left with her?"

"On horses," Vika confirmed.

Richard looked up at Rita. "You have horses here?"

She gestured with gnarled fingers. "Over on this side of the road, opposite from where the palace once stood, there are stables— the queen's stables. The witch women all left and took the Mother Confessor with them."

Richard sat up in a rush, holding the towel over himself. "She's alive then?"

"Yes," Cassia said. "But we learned that they left with her that first night."

Richard put a hand to his head, trying to calculate how long it had been since he and Shota had their battle. "How long ago? How long have I been asleep, or unconscious... how long have they been gone?"

The Mord-Sith shared sidelong glances.

Vika's expression revealed her worry. "Quite a while, now, I'm afraid."

Richard stood, still holding the small towel in front of himself. "How long is 'quite a while'?"

"Altogether it's been over five days since they left," Vika said.

128

He turned to Rita. "Are there more horses in the 'queen's' stables?" She nodded. "Quite a few, but they belong to the queen. She never allows anyone in Bindamoon to use them. The people here must care for them for her. The man called Iron Jack saw to it that the queen's orders were carried out and no one from town was ever caught riding them. He was very cruel in that task, as well as others."

"Well, no one need fear Iron Jack any longer."

She leaned in. "Oh? I have heard rumors that say he was killed by demons. Are the stories true?"

"The man is dead, that much is true," Richard said as he held the towel over himself. "He can never hurt any of you again."

"This is wonderful news," one of the other women said. Several of the others nodded their agreement.

Richard gestured with an arm. "Out. Everyone out. I need to get dressed. I must get to the Mother Confessor."

The healers glanced at one another with renewed concern.

"I don't know if that is such a good idea just yet," Rita said as she held up a cautionary finger. "It would be best if you rested for a few more days in order—"

"There are vastly more critical things than me getting more rest. I've been sleeping for days. Believe me, I am plenty rested. Now, please, all of you, out, so I can get dressed."

The healers grudgingly gave in and filed out, looking back over their shoulders with concerned looks as they left. They closed the wooden door behind themselves. The Mord-Sith stood at ease and showed no indication that they thought the orders included them as well.

"You too," Richard told them with a swish of his hand. "All of you, please wait outside."

Berdine grinned. "Lord Rahl, that is rather pointless now. I mean, after all of us helped—"

"Out!" Richard could feel his face going red again. He briefly wondered if there was a way his gift could prevent that from happening. If there was, he wanted to learn the trick.

The Mord-Sith all let out deep sighs, as if he was just being silly, but to his relief they finally left him to get dressed alone, closing the door on their way out.

Richard found all of his clothes washed and neatly folded on a chair. His sword hung off one side of the back. His pack, bow, and quiver hung off the other side. His mind raced as he hastily got dressed. He needed to get to Kahlan, but Shota and her coven had quite a head start. He knew, though, that Kahlan would be doing what she could to slow them down, hoping that he would catch up—hoping, too, no doubt, that he was still alive.

Finally dressed in his freshly cleaned clothes, his sword at his hip, and his pack and bow each hanging over a shoulder, he pulled open the door.

He was not prepared for what greeted him outside.

The healing house stood at the edge of the town on the opposite side of the pass road from the palace. The hillside before him gently descended down toward the western wall below where he stood outside the stone building. The entire hillside was packed with people, all silently staring up at him. It looked to him like the whole town was assembled there.

The healers were off to his right, keeping watch, presumably in case he succumbed to his wounds and collapsed. The six Mord-Sith were there waiting for him just outside the door. Once he stepped out, they took up places beside him, with three to either side. Vika took her place immediately to his right, signifying that she was his lead protection.

The people looking up at him stared in silence. He had no idea what was going on, but he was pretty sure that they had never seen a Lord Rahl before, so he thought that maybe that was it.

Richard recognized Toby, but not the two big men in leather vests beside him. When Toby saw that Richard was looking at him, he glanced around, then took a few steps forward. He swiped the flat hat off his head and held the hat in both hands, nervously turning it around and around.

"Toby," Richard said, "I want to thank you and all the others who helped get me out from where I was trapped. You people saved my life. I am indebted to you all. I will never forget all you and the healers have done for me."

Toby shook his head. "No, Lord Rahl. It is we who are indebted to you."

"What do you mean?"

Toby gestured off across the pass road to where the towering palace had stood. Richard could see that the entire structure had collapsed. An enormous pile of rubble was all that remained of a once-elegant structure. It was a reminder of the tremendous destructive power of Subtractive Magic.

On the lower side of the mountain's prominence, where the palace had stood, the ground had sheared away and slid down to cover a number of the stone buildings. He could tell by the way the ground had dropped away on the downhill side that it had exposed the area closer to where the massive chamber beneath the palace had been. That was where Richard had been trapped. The Mord-Sith had been down in that chamber, so they would have known where Richard was. They had undoubtedly been the ones to direct rescue efforts.

It was fortunate that the rock of the mountain itself, having been sliced through and weakened by Subtractive Magic, had slumped down and off to one side the way it had, because it made it possible for his rescuers to dig in from the side, which would have been considerably closer to him, than to try to dig down from atop the enormous pile of rubble. Had they needed to do that, he knew, by the time they reached him it would have merely ended up being an effort to recover his body.

"I'm sorry that when the palace came down it buried so many of your homes," Richard said.

"You destroyed that terrible palace of the queen," Toby said.

"You mean Shota, the witch woman," Richard corrected.

People all through the crowd nodded at that. They had been afraid to say her name aloud, but now that he had, they readily acknowledged it.

"That's right," Toby said as he kept turning his hat in his hands. "The people in those buildings heard the powerful uproar of your magic, and the sounds of the palace coming apart, so they were able to escape before the whole place came down. Those homes can and will be rebuilt. I'm thankful that none of the people who lived there were hurt and they are all safe."

Richard nodded with relief. "That's good to hear."

Toby lifted his thumb to the side. "These are my two boys. They helped dig you out, as did many of the people of Bindamoon. We have lived our lives under the cloud of that witch and her sister witches, to say nothing of Iron Jack. Whenever she was here, in Bindamoon, we feared to even come out of our houses. Everyone feared that if she saw them, she might strike them down for any reason or no reason."

"Well, she's gone now, and Iron Jack is dead," Richard said. "She no longer has a palace to come back to. I intend to see to it that she never comes back here."

At that, everyone went to their knees. They all did it together, as if they were of one mind. The six Mord-Sith came around and in front of the people on the hillside, turned toward Richard, and went to their knees as well. Everyone bent forward, putting their foreheads to the ground.

Together, in one voice, they began.

"Master Rahl guide us. Master Rahl teach us. Master Rahl protect us."

Richard hadn't expected them all to give the devotion. He stood silent and tall as they continued.

"In your light we thrive. In your mercy we are sheltered. In your wisdom we are humbled. We live only to serve. Our lives are yours."

As all the voices died out, silence slowly fell over the expanse of the hillside. And then they repeated the devotion. When they were finished, they spoke it for a third time.

Richard felt a catch in his throat. This devotion was his link to people, a link forged through his gift. They were the steel against steel for him; he was the magic against magic for them.

He had used that magic to bring down the hated palace of the woman they feared to name.

More than that, the devotion was his protection for their world, linking all the magic of the world in a web of security that kept the Golden Goddess from coming unimpeded to slaughter everyone and feed on them as he had seen happen back in the lower reaches of the People's Palace.

His magic, and Kahlan's, was the protection for their world, and it linked them all together. The devotion was an acknowledgment of that shared bond.

The two children Kahlan carried were the continuation of that magic, that power, that bond that was the protection for their world.

Richard swallowed. "Thank you all. I can't begin to tell you what it means to me."

A cheer went up to let him know that it meant something to them as well.

"We've never been before the Lord Rahl to give the devotion," Toby said. "The queen—I mean Shota, the witch woman—wouldn't allow the devotion to be given."

"I appreciate everything you've done for me, both to dig me out of that rubble, and to heal me. I was in good hands. But now, I need to chase down those witches and put an end to what they are doing to destroy all our futures."

One of Toby's sons pointed. "The stables are over there." He grinned. "Since you are going after Shota, maybe you would like to take some of her horses to her?"

Richard returned a brief smile. "That's the idea."

129

With Vika and the rest of the Mord-Sith following right behind, the crowd followed them to the stables, eager to see to it that he had whatever he needed. Lord Rahl or not, Mord-Sith were fearsome, so they all preferred to follow at a respectful, and safe, distance. He hoped that these people had seen that Mord-Sith had been weapons used by evil men in the past, but that they were not the monsters they were once feared to be.

That deferential distance, though, pleased the Mord-Sith. Friends or not, this was the Lord Rahl, their charge. Their responsibility was to keep him safe. Nothing frustrated them more than when he, in their opinion, disregarded their protection and went out of his way to put himself in danger. In other words, live his life. He sometimes thought that they believed he should stay at the People's Palace where they could watch over him and he could simply rule from there.

The stable grounds were larger than Richard had expected. There were fenced corrals with lush green grass. The mild temperature of the mountain fortress provided the same perfect growing conditions for the grass as it did for the herbs they grew in large fields.

Richard and the Mord-Sith made their way among the complex of supply buildings and barns. He was eager to get going. His worry for Kahlan was a constant distraction.

As they were crossing the stable grounds, behind them Glee suddenly poured out from hiding places among the buildings. The dark creatures had let Richard and the Mord-Sith pass so that they could attack the massive crowd following them.

Richard instantly recognized that it had the makings of a massacre, which was exactly what the Glee had planned. He also recognized the method to their battle plan.

As the gangly creatures continued to pour out from behind the buildings, people shrank back in terror. The Glee quickly filled the gap between Richard and the crowd. Their tactics had evolved. This time the creatures wanted to attack directly into the tightly packed throng of people, both to kill as many as possible and to make it harder for him to fight back and stop them.

Richard knew he had only one chance.

He gestured to the Mord-Sith. "Wait until I tell you!"

He drew his sword as he raced through the band of Glee intent on attacking the townspeople. Running at full speed, he crashed right through the horde of dark, slimy creatures, knocking some of them out of his way when he had to, before they had time to react. They expected him to take up a defensive position back where he had been. They hadn't been expecting him to charge right through their midst. Though their legs were long, and they could run fast, Richard could run faster. Besides that, the sword whirling through the air, cutting them down from behind as he hurtled through their midst, surprised and distracted them, causing many to turn and slowing others down.

As soon as Richard broke through and gained the ground between all the people and the Glee, he spun around to attack them head-on.

"Now!" he called out to the Mord-Sith to be heard over the hisses and screeches of the Glee.

His sword whistled through the air as he sliced through the advancing invaders, swiftly lopping off claws as they used them to attack. Dark, glossy heads thudded down on the ground, bounced, and rolled among the advancing Glee. All of the severed claws and heads were a distraction that turned them away from their intended target of the stunned crowd. Infuriated, they instead all charged in at him. The people unwittingly helped him by continually falling back or running away, opening up fighting space and keeping the Glee from reaching them.

At the same time as Richard was hacking his way through the enemy coming at him, the Mord-Sith, now ordered into the battle, attacked from behind with Agiel in one hand and knives in the other. The Glee found themselves trapped between deadly attacks from the front and the rear at the same time. Many became confused, not knowing who to defend themselves from. Others began turning to scribbles to escape back into their own world to avoid certain death. Many more hesitated too long and it cost them their lives.

What Richard had learned about fighting them from the previous attack served him well. He had learned how the Glee moved their arms and claws, where those claws were dangerous, and where they were useless on their backswings or when their arms were extended. They also fought as individuals, not as a cohesive force, which made it easier for him to take out individuals.

Their main weakness was that each of them wanted to be the one to sink their claws and needle-sharp teeth into the helpless townspeople, not fight a battle. They each had their own agenda to be the first to get at the people and feed on them. As such, they had no regard for protecting one another, working together, or forming a united front. He scythed his way through their ranks, and claws, arms, and heads began to litter the ground as he perfected his technique of taking advantage of their weaknesses.

It became almost a game to him, a dance with death in which they had no chance to touch him as he spun and dodged through their midst.

At their rear, the Mord-Sith attacked them from behind and took down unsuspecting Glee, bringing surprised cries of pain as they were stabbed, or hit with the horrific power of an Agiel. Hearing the shrieks of pain, many turned to the new threat, which left them vulnerable to Richard's blade. Many realized that mistake too late to save themselves.

The creatures in the center of that hammer and anvil paused in confusion. They hadn't expected to be suddenly trapped between two dangerous threats interrupting their single-minded lust for the slaughter of the townspeople. They began to realize that what they had at first thought would be overwhelming numbers was not nearly enough and was dwindling by the second. As Glee fell dead, their assault began to fall apart. They had expected the panic of the townspeople to aid them in their attack, but now, instead, panic swept through their own ranks. They were quickly being overpowered by Richard's whirling blade on one side and the Mord-Sith dodging and weaving in to press their lethal attack from the other.

Even as the dark creatures were falling dead or seriously wounded all around them, the remaining Glee, gripped by terror, almost all at the same time turned to scribbles and vanished.

As soon as they were gone, the Mord-Sith moved quickly among the wounded on the ground and cut their throats. Panting from the effort, Richard scanned the area for any further threat, prepared for another surprise attack.

Exhausted not only from the physical effort but from the storm of rage pounding through him from the sword, he sheathed the weapon so that he could recover.

A group of healers in the dark dresses and full skirts rushed in and surrounded him.

"Hurry," Rita called out.

Richard could see a couple of others racing toward one of the buildings. The Glee were all dead or vanished, so he didn't understand what was going on or what they were so concerned about.

Rita and a gaggle of others rushed in around him and started pulling up his shirt. Not knowing what they were doing, he tried to push their hands away, but they were as persistent as a swarm of wasps. He kept trying to pull his shirt back down as a different woman on the other side pulled it back up.

He tried to lightly slap Rita's hands away. "What is wrong with you?"

She seized the tail of his shirt and shook it to show him. "It's not what is wrong with me, it's what is wrong with you."

Richard looked down and saw that the side of his shirt was soaked with blood.

130

The healers who had gone off to one of the buildings emerged and raced back with a variety of supplies.

Rita lifted his elbows. "Hold your arms up. Your wound has torn open from your effort at fighting and it's bigger now than before. We will need to stitch this up."

Richard was wishing he had Shale around to heal the wound with her gift. But then he remembered that Shale had become part of the coven, even if it was against her will.

Rita grumbled, reprimanding herself for not sewing the wound better before. She pushed the sides apart to open the wound so she could inspect it. It made Richard groan with pain. Another woman handed her a bit of poultice as another handed her a needle and thread. She immediately swiped some of the yellowish concoction into the wound and then set to work stitching it together.

Richard winced and held his breath each time she pushed the needle through his skin and drew the sides of the wound together. With each stitch she pulled the thread tight with a little tug. Each time she paused before the next stitch he caught his breath. When she was satisfied, she bent and bit the thread to break it and then tied off the ends.

"I hope that holds it," she muttered.

Another of the healers leaned in for a look. "It looks like it should. You did strong stitches. They should be more than enough to hold it tight."

"As long as he doesn't get into another battle right away," Rita said.

One of the others scooped another big glob of a different ointment of some kind out of a bowl. Richard could smell aum. Another woman dabbed the bloody wound over his ribs with a rag to clean it up. Richard winced and recoiled. It wasn't the stitching that hurt so much as the wound itself.

"Stay still," Rita groused. "Hold your arms up out of the way."

She obviously didn't appreciate that he had ruined her previous work. The woman with the ointment slapped a handful of it against the wound. As soon as she did, another pressed a folded cloth over it. As she held the cloth in place, Rita took a roll of binding material from one of the others and started wrapping it tightly around him. He grunted from the pain of how tight it was, but at least the aum was already beginning to numb the ache of the wound.

"I know that you aren't going to take our advice to rest for a few more days," Rita said, "so I had to put in extra stitches and it was necessary to make the binding tight. I don't want the wound opening up when you are riding horseback. I hope you don't need to get in another battle with those monsters for a little while at least."

Seeing that it was important, Vika grabbed the roll from Rita. "Here, let me help. I can make it tighter."

Vika was not nearly as gentle as Rita had been. She made the wrapping so tight that Richard feared to exhale lest she cinch it down when he did and then he wouldn't be able to breathe in again.

"Stop complaining," Vika murmured as she continued to wind the binding around his chest, concentrating on what she was doing.

"That's good," Rita said, taking the end from Vika once she had used the whole roll. She split the end, then pushed it through several of the layers of bindings and tied the tail so that it couldn't come undone.

"You are a natural at this," Rita told Vika. She shook a finger at the Mord-Sith. "I want you to keep an eye on the wound. If he starts to bleed again, unwrap it and put some more of this salve on it, then put a clean cloth over it. After that, wrap him back up. I'm afraid that is all we can do without him taking some time to rest and heal. But we all understand the urgency of going after the Mother Confessor."

Vika took the tin after Rita checked that there was enough in it before screwing on a lid. "I will. Thank you for helping Lord Rahl. I will watch over him in your place."

Rita smiled and patted Vika's cheek. "Good girl."

"We need those horses," Richard told Toby.

One of the men pointed a thumb back over his shoulder at the sinking sun. It was hovering over the western wall out to the pass. "It will be dark in a couple of hours, Lord Rahl. Don't you want to wait until dawn to leave?"

Richard glanced to the pass trail under the setting sun. "If I missed saving the Mother Confessor from that coven of witches by a couple of hours, or a couple of minutes, or even a couple of seconds, I could never forgive myself, and our world would never forgive me."

The man and those around him acknowledged what Richard said with solemn nods.

Richard intended to ride hard and cover ground as swiftly as possible. There were plenty of horses, more than he had expected, so he told the men that he wanted horses for him and the six Mord-Sith, and an extra for each of them so they could rotate their mounts when the horses got tired.

The crowd outside the stables watched as men led horses out of stalls in a couple of the stable buildings. A pair of men for each horse, to save precious time, helped get the horses saddled and bridles on. While they were doing that, other women and men rushed up with supplies for their journey and tied them to the spare horses. Richard could see men tying bags of oats to the spare horses as well.

"Let's get going," Richard told the Mord-Sith once he saw that the horses were ready.

As they all mounted up, Rita stepped forward and put a hand on Vika's leg. "Watch over him, will you?"

Vika smiled. "Like a mother hen."

Richard believed her. But he had to admit the support of the binding did seem to make the wound feel better. The aum helped as well.

"Lord Rahl, thank you," Toby said as he, too, stepped out of the crowd, hat in hand. "We are in your debt."

"And I in yours."

"If we can ever be of help, with herbs or anything else, everyone in Bindamoon stands ready to render any assistance we can."

Richard gave the man a nod of appreciation. "We need to get going. The children of D'Hara need me."

Without delay, Richard flicked the reins and gave his horse a gentle press with his heels. The horse responded immediately, charging ahead at a swift trot. The Mord-Sith stayed right with him. The extra horses ran behind on long tethers. He ran his horse down the trail road the rest of the way through the town and toward the western wall and its arched opening.

"Lord Rahl," Vika said as she rode up beside him as they went through the arched tunnel under the wall, "how in the world are we going to find that witch woman, Shota, and her coven?"

"That's the least of our worries. We simply need to head west."

"Why west?" Berdine asked.

"Because," he told them as he looked back over his shoulder, "Shota will be taking Kahlan to Agaden Reach."

Berdine wrinkled up her nose. "What's Agaden Reach?"

Richard passed a look among all the faces watching him as they rode. "A very bad place. It's surrounded by jagged peaks of the Rang'Shada Mountains, like a wreath of thorns, and then a dangerous swamp."

"Ah," Berdine said. "Of course it is."

131

A wintery gust of wind quickly reminded Richard how cold it was outside the town walls. It sent a shiver through his shoulders. He knew that he would soon enough become accustomed to the cold again, but in the meantime it was unpleasant.

He had to read the way ahead by how the snow followed the contour of a slight depression in the ground created by the trail as it wound its way into the snow-crusted trees. Once they were into the thick of the forest, the narrow but open area through the woods more easily revealed the trail. He knew, though, that once they got down out of the mountains, the snow would be gone, it would be warmer, and the path down from the pass behind them would be much more obvious.

The wound in his side hurt with each step the horse took under him. He did his best to ignore the pain. He checked a few times, relieved to find it wasn't bleeding. Vika watched him checking.

After the sun was down and it grew both darker and colder, Richard glanced over at Vika. "I'm not tired. The moon on the snow provides enough light. I'm going to keep going. I don't intend to stop unless we're forced to." He swept his gaze over the rest of them. "Is that a problem for any of you?"

Vika glanced over at him suspiciously. "You aren't planning on leaving us behind, are you?"

Richard frowned. "No, of course not."

Vika shrugged. "Then there is no problem. We are Mord-Sith. We will ride as long as you want to ride. If you get too tired to ride, you can ride on my horse behind me."

Even though Richard wasn't in a smiling mood, he smiled briefly at that. "Thanks. I'll let you know if I need you to carry me."

"Riding is a bit rough, though," she said. "You just be sure to let me know if that wound in your side starts bleeding again. If it does, I will need to fix it."

Richard turned his eyes ahead to the moonlit, snowy trail. "I need to be strong to stop Shota and get Kahlan back, so you just make sure I stay healthy."

Vika showed him an earnest smile. "By your command, Lord Rahl."

A few hours later, when Richard departed the trail and took a route leading down through a broad valley, Rikka rode up close to him. "Aydindril is to the north, Lord Rahl. Are you sure they aren't going to head there to take the Keep in order to be safe from the Glee? Surely even the witches don't want to tangle with the Glee."

"No, they're taking Kahlan west, to Agaden Reach." He gestured ahead to some of the depressions in the snow. "Those are their tracks joining us now, but they are days old."

Richard had assumed that they would follow the trail, so he hadn't taken the time to stop and look for tracks in the dark. He was a bit alarmed to see that their tracks were now intersecting their route. That meant that he hadn't realized the coven had somehow taken a shortcut up until that point. That would put them even farther ahead than he thought.

"I can't see any tracks," Berdine said. "It's too dark."

"I can see them well enough," he told her. "The wind and sun have worn them down over the days they had a head start, but fortunately there hasn't been more snow to cover them." He was angry at himself for not looking earlier for their tracks to cut away from the trail to take a shortcut. Even though it was dark, if he had spotted that deviation he would have seen where they had gone. "Even if it does snow, now, this confirms where they are headed. That is what matters."

For most of the rest of the night, they rode on through the dead quiet, snowy woods. They descended steadily through the mountainous forest and eventually down into the sparsely wooded hill country. As they got lower, tufts of long grass started to appear in open patches of the snow. Richard could see that in the distance, revealed by the pale moonlight, the valley out ahead was clear of snow.

Even so, they had to maintain a slower pace than he would have liked, because it would be dangerous to go too fast in the dark—snow or no snow. A horse could break a leg or easily come up lame if it stepped in a dangerous place it couldn't see. If they lost horses, they would lose a lot of time to the witch women they chased. If they had to take to traveling on foot, it would mean a disastrous loss of time to get to Shota.

The whole while they rode in silence, Richard's mind churned with questions about what he was going to do when they got to Agaden Reach. He ran through endless possibilities, trying to think through every likelihood, and even things less probable. None of the outcomes looked good to him.

When dawn broke behind them and gradually brought color and light to the landscape, and more open ground, Richard was finally able to pick up the pace. By midday, the horses were winded. He brought them all to a halt on a broad, flat plain so they could move the saddles over to the fresh horses.

The horses chomped on grass while they had the chance. A small stream meandering through the flat ground provided water for them to drink deeply. Berdine and Nyda broke out some of the fresh food from the supplies the townspeople had packed.

Nyda waited until he finished cinching up the saddle, then handed him some freshly cooked pork. Berdine gave him a chunk of cheese from a different pack. Seeing the cheese reminded him of the way Kahlan had hated cheese but craved it now that she was pregnant. That craving came from at least one of the unborn children.

He ate the cheese in three bites, washing it down with water, then held the chunk of pork in his teeth as he saddled up again. In mere moments they were on their way on fresh horses and with some much-needed food. None of the Mord-Sith had voiced a single word of complaint. Of course, they wouldn't even if they had any. Charging onward without resting was something they were used to.

By the second night a thick cloud cover had rolled in, completely blocking the moon and stars. It quickly grew so dark he couldn't see his hand in front of his face, much less the lay of the land. With a flint and steel he lit strips of birch bark from a stock of them he had in his pack and used that to light travel candles so that they could at least see each other.

Richard knew that he couldn't risk the horses in the dark over unknown terrain, so they were forced to stop for the night. Since they had not stopped to sleep the night before, they were all exhausted. There was no way to see if there was a good place for shelter, and Richard didn't think it was worth searching the surrounding countryside with a candle to look for wood to build a fire, so they all rolled themselves up in their bedrolls. Despite the chill, they all quickly fell asleep, all of them too tired even to eat.

The next day dawned overcast and gloomy, but it was warmer, and better yet they had made it down out of the mountains. Before them lay the rolling hills and broad valleys of the Midlands, which would be much easier and faster traveling. There were trees, but they were in scattered clusters along hillsides overlooking meandering streams through stretches of gravel beds.

They rode hard and switched horses at regular intervals to keep them fresh, using those opportunities to grab some food, which they ate while riding. Fortunately, the people in Bindamoon had packed oats for the horses. For the next few days there would also be grass for them to eat.

Richard knew that they would need to cross the Callisidrin River in order to get to Agaden Reach up in the vast spine of rock that ran northeast up through the Midlands. He wanted to cross the river north of Tamarang in order to avoid anyone seeing them, so that the Golden Goddess likewise wouldn't see them. They were fortunate that, so far, since leaving Bindamoon, they hadn't encountered any people. He was thankful they hadn't been forced into another battle with the Glee.

Richard pressed ahead as fast as they could throughout the day. As darkness began to gather, Vika rode up beside him. She reached over and put a hand on his forearm to bring him out of his brooding thoughts.

"Lord Rahl, we need to stop," she told him.

Richard gestured ahead. "We can still see well enough to keep going."

"You're bleeding," she said. "We need to stop so I can tend to your wound."

Richard put his hand on his ribs. His shirt was wet with blood. He sighed in annoyance. "We don't have time for this."

"We can stop, and I can take care of it while we get a quick bite to eat and let the horses graze for a bit, and then we can keep going if you want."

Richard knew she was right. "All right. We have a long way to go. I don't want this wound to get worse and slow us down."

"That's why I need to fix it now," Vika said.

"How much farther is it?" Nyda asked.

"It's still quite a ways," he told her. "But worse, not long after we cross the Callisidrin River, we will have to leave the horses and make it the rest of the way up into the rugged Rang'Shada Mountains on foot. Ordinarily it would take close to a week of climbing once we get to the mountains and have to leave the horses. If we're to catch up to them, we need to do it in less time than that. The last part of it up and into the Reach will not be easy."

Richard hoped that Shota and her coven would not be traveling as swiftly as he and the Mord-Sith had been and that he was closing the distance. They, too, had to make the same strenuous climb up into the mountains on foot, so he intended to press on as quickly as possible to catch them before they could do whatever it was Shota had planned.

She had said that they would wait until Kahlan delivered the twins, rather than simply kill her and thus the unborn babies. But since the battle at her winter palace, he knew that everything had changed.

The witches most likely intended to get Kahlan to Agaden Reach, where Shota would feel safe on her home ground, and then end Kahlan's pregnancy. He feared to contemplate how she intended to accomplish her ends.

132

The few rays of the late-day sun that made it through the thick balsam limbs reflected off a layer of long-fallen leaves, making a golden-colored path ahead of them leading the way between dark woods to each side. The beauty of the place was overlaid in Kahlan's mind by the sinister nature of where they were taking her. The smell of wet, decaying leaves piled up in corners of rocky outcroppings and under the dense brush only added to her sense of foreboding.

She was being taken to a place where she was told she would be held until she gave birth and then her babies would be killed. Shota said that she would then be released. While Shota was brutally honest about what she intended to do with Kahlan's babies, she didn't think Shota was being so honest about the second part of it. As if that mattered to her now.

When Kahlan looked up through the upper branches of trees, she finally saw the snowcapped peaks that were the formidable spires that surrounded Agaden Reach like a ring of thorns. The view was quickly lost again as they followed a trail that disappeared ahead of them into thick forest of fir and pine trees. She took out some of her frustration kicking pine cones out of her way as she hiked along the trail.

The canopy high above cut off most of the light, so the plants that grew in abundance on the forest floor, such as the ferns, were those that thrived in shade. Most of the brush, unlike the ferns that were turning brown, would keep their leaves all winter. They helped add to the shadowed gloom.

Kahlan could see that past all the women, out ahead, they would come to a branch in the trail, with the right fork leading lower and the left fork leading higher. Without delay or hesitation Shota took the left fork. The rest of them followed in a single-file line.

The witches following close behind Kahlan, and bringing up the rear, kept a close eye on her, making sure she didn't try to go another way or suddenly bolt and run. When they hadn't been looking, Kahlan had tried to vanish into the thick underbrush several times. The swift punishment taught her a painful lesson that escape was hopeless. At least for now. She was determined, though, that if she saw a chance to get away, she would take it.

Ravens followed them, as they had since they'd left the fortress town of Bindamoon, sailing effortlessly through open limbs of winter-bare branches of oaks, maples, and linden trees. In the thicker foliage of the weeping spruce, tamaracks, and red pines, where they couldn't easily sail, they swerved and darted through any opening they could find. Sometimes they flew above the forest canopy, only to swoop down unexpectedly, giving Kahlan a start as they suddenly appeared to surprise her.

The leaves, long since fallen, leaving the branches bare, blanketed rocks and in other places lay rotting in damp piles. The boots of the women ahead scuffed over rocks hidden under leaves. As weary as Kahlan was, when she wasn't paying enough attention, those hidden rocks sometimes tried to twist an ankle when she inadvertently stepped on them wrong. Thick lines of leaves suggested deep gaps in the rock that could break a leg, so she was careful to avoid stepping there.

The bull of a witch with the sour expression lumbered along just ahead of Kahlan, swaying from side to side to keep her low, squat bulk moving. Despite the obvious effort of walking, she didn't seem to tire and never complained. In fact, she had so far not spoken a word. The scary, bony one with the big, black eyes was directly in front of her. They were the two who had pulled her out of the way of the falling rock when the palace had begun to collapse. They had dragged her into the tunnels, saving her life and at the same time capturing her. As they were hauling her away, Kahlan hadn't been able to see in all the swirling dust if Richard had escaped the mass of falling stone. Since he'd been in the center of the enormous room, she didn't see how he could have made it out in time.

The scariest witch guarding her, while not at all ugly as most of the others certainly were, was the ill-tempered witch with the stringy red hair veiling her face. Kahlan had learned that her name was Nea. She followed behind Kahlan as they hiked through the woods, glaring at her the entire time, waiting for Kahlan to try to run, or to give her some other excuse to hurt her. For seemingly no reason, other than her bad temper, she occasionally murmured blood-curdling threats and promises. The worst were what she intended to do to her babies.

From the interactions Kahlan had observed during their journey, Nea was apparently Shota's lieutenant, her favorite, the one she trusted most, and the one she had put in charge of watching over Kahlan. Every once in a while, as they walked, Nea would lean forward and whisper in Kahlan's ear what she intended to do if Kahlan would just give her an excuse. Kahlan believed her.

Kahlan, though, wasn't so much worried about herself as she was for the two unborn children she was carrying, and she knew quite well what these witch women had planned for them. Kahlan couldn't stand the thought of the twins never having the chance at life.

When she saw soft ground with the leaves mostly clear from the center, all the witch women ahead of her walked off to the side to avoid the mud. Kahlan deliberately walked straight on through it in order to leave her tracks. She knew that if he had somehow been able to survive, Richard would come for her. He would recognize her tracks and know for sure where she was being taken. Sometimes, when a branch was close to her when she passed, she would break the tip and leave it hanging down as a sign for him.

She also did whatever she could along the way, from minor things like feigning having difficulty getting up a rise of rocks or having to often empty her bladder from the pressure of the twins, to bigger things like sitting and saying she needed to rest, all in order to delay them. She used all those little diversions to slow the coven down, hoping Richard would catch up with them. She didn't know what he could do to stop all of these witches, but, well, he was Richard, so she was sure he would come up with something if only he could get to them in time.

Kahlan did her best not to consider the possibility that Richard wasn't still alive, but her mind frequently didn't cooperate and fed her a steady stream of fears to haunt the dark corners of her thoughts. It would make her feel a sense of growing panic if she let herself think about him being crushed under a mountain of rubble, so she did her best not to.

After the trail went up a steep switchback and then doubled back on itself, she could look down and see through the branches of white cedar and spruce trees where they had just been a short time before. After they had doubled back, the path came to another fork. This time they took the one to the right. Knowing where it went, she dreaded the choice that was made for her.

The trail the witch women took immediately began an increasingly difficult climb up a series of switchbacks and up over ledges. In places it was so steep it required them to use their hands to hold on to the gnarled roots of the trees growing close in on each side of the trail. Those handholds helped them to continue to climb ever upward. The sour-faced witch woman ahead of Kahlan often had to wait for the assistance of the younger, stronger women ahead to help hoist her up.

The climb required that Kahlan frequently use her hands, so much so that the rough roots gave her cuts and increasingly painful blisters. The web of roots coming down the rocky ground surrounded chunks of granite, holding them in place like powerful, living claws so that it couldn't fall. Since they provided places for water to collect and moss to grow, the twisting roots frequently made for slippery footing, or slimy handholds.

More than once, Kahlan's boot slipped off a root and she had to catch herself with a tenuous grip on a rock or a root above as her feet momentarily swung free out in space. Each time it made her gasp. She worried about doing anything that could hurt the babies, so she did her best to quickly regain a foothold rather than let herself drop back down to a previous ledge. Once, Nea reached up, caught her ankle in a powerful grip, and placed her foot atop a shelf of rock so that she wouldn't fall.

Kahlan panted with the effort of the climb. She was drained and exhausted by the time she could again see the snowcapped spires around Agaden Reach off through the trees. But down in the dark woods where they were climbing the trail, it was growing increasingly difficult to see where she could put each foot to help support her when they had to climb. The farther they went, though, the more often she had increasingly open glimpses of that crown of thorns. She knew they would soon be up to the tree line and then they would have to make their way across open, windswept ledges.

When she reached a level place, Kahlan plopped down in exhaustion on a smooth piece of rock to get her breath.

Nea immediately was in her face. "What do you think you're doing?"

"Why don't you try climbing this steep trail when you're this far along in a pregnancy? See if you can do it."

Sorrel, one of the nastier of the witch women up ahead, gave the bull of a witch a hand up. Once she had helped the big woman up, she then knelt to lean back down over the top of where Kahlan sat. She had long, pointed nails, and both of her hands looked like she regularly dipped them in red wax. Her hair was done in neat rows of short spikes, all of them tipped with the same red wax, or paint, or whatever it was. At least, Kahlan didn't think that it was blood.

"No one told you that you could sit down," Sorrel growled down at Kahlan.

Kahlan looked up at Sorrel's black gums, revealed whenever she snarled, wishing she could drive her knife through the woman's heart. But they had taken her knife and her pack, lest she get the idea to use her blade on one of them. Shota didn't want to take a chance on losing one of the thirteen witches, because that would break the coven. That coven gave her powers over and above those she possessed on her own. The kind of magic she had used back in the chamber below the palace had made those frightening powers all too evident. As if Shota hadn't been frightening enough without them.

"I'm exhausted," Kahlan told Sorrel as she gestured to the side. "Look, there's a pretty level place, here, on this ledge. It's sheltered by that rock face you're kneeling on. I think we should stop for the night. Besides being spent, we can't climb this mountain in the dark. I could easily fall and split my skull."

Grinning, Nea put a hand on Kahlan's shoulder and pulled her around to face her. "That would solve everything, then, now wouldn't it? We are only keeping you alive because that's Shota's wish, not because it's ours."

Worry for her unborn babies immediately came to the forefront of Kahlan's thoughts. "Shota is the grand witch. You had better do as she tells you and keep me alive."

Kahlan didn't think that Shota really cared if she died, but it was a bluff that seemed to give Nea pause.

Nea reached up and parted the strands of hair hanging down over her face so that she could better peer out at Kahlan. "True, but if you took a nasty fall and broke some bones... who is to say it's the fault of anyone but your own clumsy feet?"

133

Shota pushed her way through the tight knot of witch women crowded around on the ledge just above Kahlan. She leaped down the last few feet, landing with surprising grace. She had fire in her eyes.

Kahlan stood. She didn't know exactly why. Somehow, she felt compelled to stand and face a coldly angry Shota, whether by her own volition or Shota's she wasn't entirely sure.

Kahlan remembered how terrified she had been the first time she had gone to Agaden Reach with Richard to face the witch woman. There had been times since then when her fear of the woman had ebbed and flowed, but at the moment, she was back to remembering how much she had feared that first encounter, when Shota had put snakes all over her. The witch woman knew how much Kahlan feared snakes. Had Richard not been able to stop her and make her remove her snakes, they very well might have bitten her, and she surely would have died. But Richard was not with her this time.

"Do you think I don't know what you are doing?" Shota asked in a smooth voice, suddenly looking and sounding like Kahlan's mother.

Such an image hurt Kahlan's heart, but she dared not show how much it got to her.

"I don't know what you are talking about, *Shota*."

Kahlan put emphasis on the witch woman's name to let her know that she wasn't going to break down in helpless emotion at seeing an image that appeared to be her mother. It was thievery of cherished memories from her own mind in order to use them in cruel trickery. As much as Kahlan had loved her mother, she didn't appreciate Shota using her mother's image in such a cold-blooded manner.

"Do you think I haven't noticed you deliberately leaving your tracks, or breaking a branch here and there so that Richard can follow you?"

"I don't know what you're talking about." Kahlan hooked some of her hair behind an ear. "I'm simply walking. I don't know how you expect me to walk and not leave tracks."

Shota, reverting to looking again like Shota—a very angry Shota—seized Kahlan's chin between her thumb and the knuckle of her first finger. She narrowed her eyes as she leaned in.

"Don't feed me that. I know what you're doing. I am also well aware that you have been trying to slow us down so that Richard can catch up with us and 'rescue' you."

Kahlan retreated to her Confessor face, showing no emotion.

"Why would you fear he would be alive?" Kahlan asked. "The entire palace fell in on him."

"Fear it? There is hardly anything to fear." Shota released Kahlan's chin, instead regarding her with an intense look that held her in no less of a powerful grip. "On the contrary. I made sure the palace fell in on him. But you foolishly hold out hope that he somehow got out in time. Am I right?"

Kahlan shrugged. "Well, you know Richard. He often manages to come out of impossible situations wondering why anyone would have been worried about him. So, were I you, I wouldn't be so smug that he isn't this minute coming up this mountain after you and your coven."

"You think so?" Shota nodded with a sly smile. "Well, I think you should know that down in that chamber beneath my palace, when I saw that everything was beginning to fall in, just before I escaped out the tunnel with you and my ladies, I turned back and cast a simple little spell to hinder his legs for just long enough to keep him from running to safety in time. He wouldn't have realized that my spell was there, and, because of it, he would have been unable to get away. As he stood there, momentarily helpless, the entire weight of the palace and a good part of the mountain all fell in on him."

Not wanting to give Shota the satisfaction of reacting with the horror and rage she was feeling inside, Kahlan maintained the Confessor face and didn't say anything.

"So you see, Mother Confessor, your husband, the man who fathered those two monsters you carry, is dead and buried in a grave so deep his body will never even be recovered for a state funeral. He is entombed under my palace, because of my spell. Quite fitting, don't you think, since he came to bury me."

"What's your point?"

"The point is, you no longer have a husband; we no longer have a Lord Rahl; those two children no longer have a father; and he isn't going to come to rescue you. So you might as well quit bothering with your little tricks."

Unable to maintain her Confessor face, Kahlan swallowed.

"You shouldn't be so smug about your safety, because if he doesn't come to kill you, I will do it myself—you have the promise of the Mother Confessor on that."

Shota straightened and folded her arms, looking down at her, amused by the threat. "Is that so? Well, I must admit, you are more vicious than I am. My intent is to let you live, not kill you. I simply want to eliminate the threat to the world posed by those two monsters you carry. Fortunately, with Richard dead, no more can ever be created."

Against her will, Kahlan felt a tear roll down her cheek.

"Now," Shota went on, "you can either get moving and get yourself and those unborn babies to Agaden Reach, where you will give birth to them, or I will see to it that you miscarry here and now."

Kahlan lifted her chin. "You mean like you tried and failed to do before?"

"With everything I have done, my aim was always to simply slow you down so that you wouldn't get too far away. Were you to get to the Keep I wouldn't have been able to get to you and do what is necessary for the greater good. I could have killed you any number of times, but I didn't. None of the things I did, such as that wood where you lost so much time, were an attempt to kill you, now were they?"

"You did something to make me start to miscarry after we were out of that wood, and after we were stopped from getting to the Keep by the boundary you put up, but Richard was able to help stop it. You were trying to kill me along with my babies."

"On the contrary." Shota couldn't seem to hold back a knowing smile, as if she were talking to an ignorant child. "I knew that if I cast a spell to have you start to miscarry, Richard would have to find you a plant called mother's breath, the only herb that could stop it. I made you start to miscarry and collapse in that particular place on purpose. I knew that when Richard went to look for mother's breath—mother's breath transplanted from the fields of Bindamoon and planted there for him to find—he would come across the pass trail, which would eventually lead you all to the pass and to me. My mountain lion returned to let me know that all went as I had planned.

"So, you see, it wasn't an attempt to kill you, but instead I went to a great deal of trouble to get you right to the spot where I wanted you. As I have told you, I don't want to harm you, but to simply eliminate the little monsters you carry.

"Unfortunately, Richard destroyed my winter palace. Now, I want you to finish the journey into my home of Agaden Reach, where you will be taken care of until you give birth. After that, you will be free to go. But like I say, if you are too difficult about it..."

Shota touched a finger to Kahlan's belly. She gasped with a sudden, powerful contraction. The pain was so intense that it doubled her over as Shota followed her down to continue holding the finger on her swollen belly.

"...then I will simply have you miscarry right here and now and be done with it. So what is it going to be, Mother Confessor? Do you want to finish the journey and give birth in comfort and with help? Or do you want to simply miscarry right here and bleed to death on this mountainside?"

Shota removed her finger. When she did, Kahlan sucked in a breath and a cry of agony. At last, the painful contraction eased.

"All right, you win," Kahlan said, swallowing between pants as she caught her breath. "I won't cause any more trouble. I will go willingly."

Shota stared long and hard into Kahlan's eyes as if to satisfy herself that Kahlan meant it before slowly nodding.

"Smart girl. Now, no more nonsense. We will not be stopping." The witch woman lifted an arm to point. "It grows dark, but the tree line is right there. Out of the woods and in the open, with the moonlight reflecting off the snowcaps, there will be plenty of light to allow us to continue.

"We will walk the rest of the night to cross that snowcap, and then in the morning we will reach the swamp that guards my home. Once through that foul place, we will head down into my beautiful home of Agaden Reach. It will be warm, and you will be able to rest until you deliver. But for now, we push on."

Kahlan was still experiencing stitches of pain, although they were easing. She felt helpless. She feared that what Shota did might harm the babies. She didn't want her to do anything like it again.

She nodded her agreement.

Shota looked around at all the witches seeming to hang on her every word, Shale among them. Shota gestured with a flick of her hand. "Let's get moving. Now."

Kahlan had been well aware that Shota had shown no fear of being within range of her Confessor's power. More worrisome, she could feel a subtle difference in the restraint that she always had to exert on that power within herself, lest it be unleashed accidentally. The coiled fury of the power felt... muted. It was as if that restraint had clamped down tight when Shota had finally established the coven with all thirteen witches.

When Shota glared at her, waiting, Kahlan grabbed a root for a handhold and started climbing, following after the rest of them, with Nea right behind.

Something fundamental in the back of Kahlan's mind was bothering her. She couldn't put her finger on it, but she knew that the pieces didn't fit. Something didn't ring true, didn't add up, didn't make sense, but she couldn't quite reach it. Despite her best efforts to pull that question out of the dark reaches of her mind to examine possible answers, it remained just out of her grasp.

She knew, though, that if she thought on it long enough, it would come to her.

134

Not long after dawn, after a long and difficult night of crossing the frigid, windswept lower slopes of the spires that formed the formidable wreath of thorns protecting Agaden Reach, Kahlan and the witches guarding her finally started a difficult descent. Initially, they trudged through deep snow to make their way down the slopes. They had to avoid what looked like easier travel over open rock because it was mostly covered with black ice. The snow at least kept them from slipping and falling out on the sloping granite ledges where they could easily crack their skulls if they fell wrong.

To avoid the danger of the slippery ice-covered rock, they instead had to plow down through the snow that collected between massive fingers of rock jutting up all around. It was not only a more difficult route, but a more dangerous one because of how steep it was in those white rivers of snow. There were times when Kahlan thought she might not survive the steep drops they sometimes had to slide down. A few of the witch women fell during those descents and tumbled a long way before recovering their footing.

Like the rest of them, Kahlan had to aim for the upright columns of rock and then slam her feet against the rock to break the slide and keep from accelerating and being carried over a cliff. Some of the others, like the sour-faced bull of a witch, were quite awkward at it, but they all made it. After using the tall stacks of open rock at the end of each of those runs down, they then had to traverse the slope to make it over to the next one that didn't end in a sheer drop where they would fall to their death.

Anyone attempting to get into Agaden Reach who didn't know the proper route through the maze of towering rock outcroppings would have a difficult if not impossible task to find the one true way down the dangerous slopes. Taking a wrong turn on the way down, one that might look good at first, if it didn't turn out to be a dead end could instead turn out to be a place where it would be impossible to stop, with nothing below for thousands of feet. It was just another of the many hazards protecting Agaden Reach.

Kahlan's teeth chattered the whole time they were out on the moon-lit, open ledges below the snowpack. But the worst of the cold had been crossing the snow. She had been so cold it made her hurt all over and gave her a crushing headache.

The muscles of her legs burned from the effort of the controlled falls down through the fingers of snow and then, once below them, hiking down off the steeply sloping shelves of open granite, then over and through debris fields of boulders and the jumble of fallen rock. Her ankles felt like they were about to give out, but she knew she had to keep going if she was to have any hope for the twins to survive.

She didn't know how she would save their lives once they got down into Agaden Reach, she only knew she would have to find a way. She knew she couldn't count on Richard showing up. It was going to have to be up to her.

When the sun was finally up, they at last entered the dark woods, where they were at least sheltered from the cold wind. As they moved down through the steep, forested mountainside, it gradually began to grow warmer. The farther they went, the warmer it got, until Kahlan's teeth finally stopped chattering and she didn't have to hunch her shoulders.

After a few more hours of making their way lower through tangled growths of tightly packed thickets of saplings and snarled vines, they at last reached the flat, swampy area that guarded the entrance to Agaden Reach.

Even though the sun had come up, it was dark and gloomy among the massive trees and vegetation, which grew thicker the farther in they went. Kahlan had always thought of this place as a moat, like those around some fortress castles, except this one protected Shota's home and was far more dangerous than any simple moat.

Kahlan remembered quite clearly going through these strange, hot, humid woods. After the frigid hike the night before, the oppressive heat was at first welcome. Before long, it became suffocating.

She remembered, too, how dangerous these woods were. The swamp had unseen things that would grab anyone unwary enough to wander into the water, and in some cases, if they simply got too close to it, they could be snatched right off the trail. It was not at all rare to see human bones in the bogs or sticking up from the slimy, green, swampy places that had trapped them.

Kahlan knew that a wizard had once come to take Shota's home. He was not killed by anything in the swamp. He had faced something far more dangerous: the witch who lived there and wanted her home back. She had used his hide to cover her throne. The same throne now buried under a mountain of rubble.

Kahlan prayed to the good spirits that Richard wasn't also buried under all of that same rubble.

As she plodded ahead, Kahlan was well beyond her second wind. She was spent and could only shuffle along, putting one weary foot in front of the other, her mind numb. But in these woods, she knew that she had to pay attention to every step, or it might be her last, so she focused again and tried to watch where she put her feet.

The hot, humid swamp smelled foul. They passed through a number of areas, though, where the stench was especially bad. She held her hand over her mouth and nose, trying not to breathe in the gagging smell of death and rotting flesh. She hurried until they were past the worst of it.

Birds screamed raucous calls that echoed through the wet woods. The ravens that had followed them for so long sat in a row on a long, dead branch, watching Kahlan approach. They cocked their heads and looked down at her with one black eye as she passed beneath them. Sometimes they flapped their wings and cawed so loudly it made her ears hurt. Then, they flew on to another branch where they could continue to watch her progress.

Here and there boggy patches of water spanned back in under the thick, overhanging growth. Vapor hung just above the murky black water. In places, it drifted out and across the path. It swirled around her legs as she walked through the thick, heavy mist. It came up only about as high as her knees and left the bottoms of her trousers damp. It also carried with it the smells of dead things.

In other spots, the tangle of thick vines coiled like snakes on the trees, killing them. In the boggy woods to the sides the roots of large trees were so thick, gnarled, and broad that in places they spread out over the path. She knew that if her ankle got caught in one of those gnarled roots, she might break it before she could catch herself, so it took time and extreme caution to cross those extensive webs of roots.

Off across the water, in the deep shadows, she could see glowing eyes watching them. Others followed from off in the trees and brush. A few dark shapes now and then leaped from tree to tree, following them from the shadows for a time.

In some of the wetter areas, large trees stood on skirts of tall roots, as if trying to stay above the dark water. Smaller creatures hid back in those standing roots. The gray trunks of those trees were smooth and bare of bark and their branches were bare of leaves. Instead, they were draped with long trailers of dead, brown moss hanging still in the stagnant, humid air. It made the trees look like silver specters haunting the trail, watching who dared pass.

The spongy path in many places was mere inches above the expanses of turbid water to either side. With each step, water oozed up out of the soft, mossy ground and over her boots. Sometimes the water to the sides rippled as something unseen under the surface followed them along for a time, then left a spiraling swirl as it submerged.

Off in the thick, dark, dense vegetation in the distance, unseen things whooped and howled. Every once in a while, Kahlan spotted a shadowed shape skitter through the lower branches or bound along the ground back in the brush. In the heavy air, other things off out of sight clicked and whistled warnings to others of their kind. Creatures she couldn't see and couldn't imagine noted the group's passing with apparent displeasure by growling low, guttural warnings.

In some places, the mist rising from the stinking, bubbling, thick black water carried with it the smell of sulfur. It was a smell strongly associated with the underworld, so Kahlan kept a wary watch whenever she smelled it, worried that something might appear from the world of the dead.

Sometimes the mist carried the gagging stench of rotting flesh. There was never any area where it smelled even remotely good. Kahlan was reluctant to draw a breath as her gaze continually swept the area to each side, watching for danger or the source of the stench. In places she saw the bloated, putrefied, half-submerged bodies of animals too rotted to identify. She didn't know if they had drowned in the foul water, or possibly succumbed to the toxic smells.

In a few places she saw rotting corpses that looked like they might be human floating only partly above the surface of scummy water.

Those ahead of her carefully picked their way over the tangled masses of roots of the gnarled trees. She remembered all too well that there were particularly dangerous roots in the swamp that no one would dare to walk across. The roots of those trees, the ones with squat, fat trunks, were tangled and looked very much like nests of balled snakes. Those roots had to be given a wide berth. She saw those every once in a while, but the path skirted them, and the witch women always walked on the farthest side of the path so as to stay as far away as possible.

And then, near one of those squat trees with the tangled roots that had to be avoided, Kahlan suddenly missed a step.

She stopped; her eyes went wide.

The thing she had been trying pull from the dark corner of her mind suddenly came rushing forward into her consciousness.

She realized what it was that didn't make sense.

135

One single question stood out in Kahlan's mind above all others.

Why would Shota want Kahlan to give birth just so she could kill the babies?

And why go to all the trouble to take her all the way to Agaden Reach to give birth? Not only that, but if she simply wanted to kill the babies, why not have her miscarry—which she had now twice proven she was entirely capable of doing—and then use a healer, like Shale, to help her recover if she really wanted Kahlan to live? If her intention was in fact to get rid of the babies and not kill Kahlan, that would be the easiest way. It would be over and done with.

So why would Shota insist that the babies must be born first, if she simply wanted them dead so that what she saw as the threat of their existence would be ended?

On the surface it made no sense.

But beneath the surface, it was starting to make sinister sense.

In the beginning, Shota had told Richard and Kahlan that she harbored no ill will toward them. She had even said that she appreciated the things they had done for their people, as well as what they had done that had saved her from the Keeper of the underworld. She had even said that she rather liked them, and that she didn't mean them any harm.

She had tried to paint herself as reasonable—kind, even.

She had said that after the birth they would be free to go.

And yet, she proudly admitted that she had spelled Richard's legs so that he couldn't get away in time and the palace would collapse on top of him. That certainly didn't sound like she didn't intend them harm. In fact, she had used her power in a surprise attack to try to kill him just before that. Richard hadn't struck first; she had. Despite her benevolent claims, it was clear that her intent had been to kill him, not let him go.

After all of that, why would she then go back to her original story that she meant Kahlan no harm and that she would let her go once she gave birth? She had said that she intended Richard no harm, either, yet she had clearly acted to kill him.

Why did Shota seem so intent on keeping Kahlan alive and having her give birth *before* she killed the children? What purpose would it serve to have the children born before she killed them?

It now seemed pretty clear from everything that had happened that Shota didn't really intend to let Kahlan go once she gave birth. She intended to kill her.

So, if she actually intended to kill her in the end, but wasn't admitting as much, which Kahlan now believed was the case, then the previous evening, on the mountain before they crossed the snowcaps, why hadn't she simply let Kahlan miscarry and bleed to death? It would have been a simple solution to the greater good she kept talking about.

For that matter, why hadn't she let Kahlan die way back when she started to miscarry after they finally got out of the strange wood? Killing the two unborn babies was her goal, after all, for that greater good as she saw it, so what difference would it have made had the babies died in a miscarriage and Kahlan died as well?

Shota's true intentions flashed like ice through Kahlan's veins.

Kahlan stood frozen with the sudden realization of what Shota actually wanted.

136

Kahlan was well aware that time was not on her side. If she was going to try something, it had to be now, when they least expected it. Later, down in Agaden Reach, with her time running out and the birth imminent, they would be expecting her to try to resist or flee.

The problem was, she knew that her Confessor power wouldn't work on Shota because the witch woman was now in command of the power of coven. That power protected her—protected all of them—as long as that power of coven was in effect.

The coven. Of course. With sudden realization, she grasped the only way that gave her any kind of chance against all of these women.

"Keep moving," Nea growled from behind, bringing Kahlan out of her headlong rush of thoughts.

She knew she needed some kind of excuse in order to create surprise. What had Richard always told her? If you had to act, if acting was your only hope, then act swiftly with maximum violence.

Thinking quickly, Kahlan saw her only opportunity. She went to a knee and bent forward so that Nea couldn't see what she was doing.

"I said to keep moving!" the witch woman screamed at her from behind.

Kahlan looked back over her shoulder. "My bootlace came untied. I have to retie it."

Nea folded her arms. "Well, hurry it up, then."

Sorrel, one of the more disagreeable of the whole disagreeable lot of witches, stormed back, shoving her way past the bull of a witch woman who had been just ahead of Kahlan. She angrily waved her arms. Her gums were dark, as were the rings around her eyes, adding to her already wicked looks.

"What's going on?" Sorrel demanded.

As the angry Sorrel had been charging back through the group of witch women, Kahlan knew she was quickly running out of time. She struggled with all her might, using her fingertips to try to pry the heavy rock out of the mud where it was half buried right beside her boot. She hunched over in such a way that the others couldn't see what she was doing and would think she was tying the lace on her boot.

She held her breath with the effort of pulling on the rock. The mud sucked it down tight and made it resist coming up. She wiggled the rock then pried it with all her strength, her breath held and muscles tight against the effort, knowing it was her only chance, but the portion of the rock under the muddy ground was larger than Kahlan had thought at first, making it far more difficult than she had expected. She knew that she dared not abandon the effort. It could very well be the last chance she would ever get.

Sorrel rushed up in a rage, screaming curses and waving her arms.

"Answer me!" Sorrel yelled, her face going red with fury, matching the red tips of her spiky hair.

The rock popped free of the mud.

Instead of answering the woman, Kahlan sprang up and whirled around in one fluid motion, bringing the rock with her. As she spun, she whipped the heavy rock around at the end of her extended arm.

Sorrel was just opening her mouth to yell something else when Kahlan slammed the heavy rock into the side of the woman's head. It made a loud crack as the thick skull bones shattered.

The witch's eyes went dead as her skull caved in under the speed of the heavy rock. Her right eye went glassy as it turned up and to the right. Her left eye, equally glassy, turned to point down and to her left. Kahlan imagined it looking to the underworld, where her soul was already sinking into eternity.

Sorrel dropped straight down into a limp, still heap.

As a pool of blood began to spread under Sorrel's body, the sour-faced bull of a witch—at first surprised, now looking livid at what she had just seen happen—suddenly rushed headlong for Kahlan. Her fat neck was sunken down into her broad shoulders, like a charging bull's, so much so that she couldn't easily look down at where she was going. Her angry scowl was fixed on Kahlan.

In a reckless rush, the big woman stumbled over Sorrel's body. In that instant, Kahlan seized one of her outstretched arms by a fat wrist and used the woman's falling motion and weight to swing her on around. With a grunt of effort, Kahlan propelled the witch woman's bulk out into the murky water.

She didn't fly far, but she flew far enough. Her angry cry was cut short when she hit the water with a massive splash that lifted not just the dark water but strings of water weeds and algae up into the air, some of it flopping out across the trail. The big woman popped back up to the surface, her hair matted to her head, coughing up water between gasps for air.

As she surfaced, splashing and paddling awkwardly to get to the bank, something apparently grabbed her leg, making her cry out. She screamed in pain, reaching for the bank at the same time. Whatever it was that had her abruptly pulled, and in a single big yank dragged her back and down under the water. She was gone in an instant. Bubbles came up from the deep as a blood slick grew at a rapid rate and spread across the rippling surface.

Almost at the same time, the bony witch with the big black eyes, who had seen what had just happened to her sister, charged toward Kahlan, careful to leap over Sorrel's body, intent on taking revenge. The witch's sticklike arms flailed as she let out an animalistic cry that was a shriek of anger and lethal intent mixed together in one. It was the first sound Kahlan had heard the woman make, and it was properly bloodcurdling.

Kahlan was just coming up from having dropped to a knee having lost her balance from the effort of tossing the bony witch's very large sister witch into the water. Without pause, as she stood, Kahlan seized a sticklike arm and spun the witch woman around, this time easily because she didn't weigh much at all. Kahlan wheeled completely around with her. As she did, the woman's feet, clear of the ground, sailed out as she flew around through the air like a bony rag doll.

As she came around from a full turn, Kahlan released her with a grunt of effort, letting her sail through the air and into the nest of roots of one of the squat, fat-trunked trees just off the trail.

When the bony woman crashed down in the midst of the roots, they instantly whipped out, knotting and coiling around her body the way a constricting snake would wrap its coils around a victim. Other roots captured her flailing arms and legs. Showers of sparks filled the air above the roots as the witch tried to cast some kind of spell, but it was too little too late.

Almost as soon as she had fallen in, the sparks died out as the witch woman was pulled under the mass of coils and writhing roots. Kahlan couldn't see it, but she could hear bones snapping and joints popping as the strange tree dragged her under its nest of roots and pulled her limb from limb. Almost as quickly as the roots had grabbed her, she was gone, and it was over.

At the same time, Kahlan heard Nea scream in rage and charge toward her from behind.

Nea was out for blood and revenge.

137

Kahlan turned halfway to the threat.

It was clear from the wild look in her eyes that Nea's rage had taken control of her senses. Surprisingly, she charged in with a knife—Kahlan's knife—rather than using magic. She apparently wanted to physically rip into Kahlan and take her down. She raced ahead knife-first, intending to slam the blade into Kahlan.

That was the last mistake the witch woman would ever make.

With the death of three witches mere moments before, the spell of coven was broken.

Kahlan's power was no longer suppressed.

Nea leaped toward Kahlan, throwing herself at her, intending to crash down on her knife-first.

Kahlan lifted her hand, palm out toward the blade, as if warding it off.

It all happened in an instant, but that instant was all the time it took.

The world went still.

Kahlan felt the tip of the knife, as it had just begun to touch her palm. Although it was a razor-sharp blade, to Kahlan it felt like no more than a breath of air on her hand. It was not necessary for her to summon her Confessor power; she merely had to withdraw her restraint of it, and she had already done that.

Time stopped.

The inner violence of Kahlan's cold, coiled power slipping its bounds was breathtaking. The astonishing magnitude of the force as it was unleashed was like touching the sun. It flared up from the very core of who she was and through every fiber of her being, lighting her soul with white-hot intensity.

Nea hung in the air, stopped dead before Kahlan, her hand with the knife outstretched, her feet clear of the ground, one of her knees parting the hundreds of knotted and beaded strips of her leather skirt. Kahlan could have counted the hundreds of stringy strands of red hair, lifted out in all directions, now frozen motionless in midair. It was like seeing a statue made of flesh and bone.

The rage in Nea's eyes had only just taken that first tick of transition to alarm. She had just begun to realize by Kahlan's posture, her resolute stance, her fearless bearing, that something was terribly wrong. Before she had been able to fully realize what was happening, it was already too late.

She was frozen in that instant of time just before the danger had fully registered.

Kahlan knew that behind her, the rest of the witch women were also still as stone, frozen in mid-movement. In the sky, a number of the ravens that had taken to wing at the initiation of the violence were impossibly stopped in midflight, their wings having just flapped, spread, or started to take another bite of the air, the fanned feathers at the back of their wings standing out individually, black, glossy, beautiful.

Something under the water to the side of the path had just disturbed the surface, and the ripples from it were now motionless. The mist drifting over the water had likewise stopped in place. The whole world waited, unmoving.

In the silent stillness of Kahlan's mind, she had all the time in the world, all the time she would need to do what she had done so many times before.

Nea's face was set in mid-snarl. Her teeth were bared. Beads of sweat dotted her glowering brow. Her pale blue eyes were wild, frozen in a picture of fury.

Of all the witch women, this one had been the one she had feared most because she always seemed dangerously deranged. Shota had put her in charge of Kahlan for a reason. She was not only Shota's next-in-command, but she was also ruthless and would not hesitate to take control of any situation, and she had the power to deal with anything.

Except this.

The control of what was about to happen now belonged entirely to Kahlan.

She knew that back behind her somewhere, Shota would be in mid-scream, trying to stop what Kahlan had already done to break the coven. That power was now lost to Shota.

The Confessor's power was now Kahlan's again.

She had yet to feel a single heartbeat. Even so, she had taken in the whole scene in excruciating detail. She knew where everything and everyone was, all stopped in space.

Kahlan wondered if this redheaded witch woman yet knew that her mind was about to be gone. It was possible that she didn't realize that a Confessor's power also took a person's mind, but everything she was, and everything she had been, was about to be wiped away in a lightning instant by the unstoppable force of Kahlan's power.

The woman's mind, once emptied, would be replaced with a frantic, burning desire to do what Kahlan, and only Kahlan, as the Confessor who was taking her mind, wanted.

Even with taking control of this one witch before her, Kahlan was well aware that her position was still one of great peril. There were a lot of other witches.

And then there was Shota. She would not take kindly to what Kahlan had done.

Even so, it couldn't be helped. The way things were going, if Kahlan didn't act, and soon, it would all end badly. This way, at least, she had broken the coven and changed the balance of power. It didn't ensure that she would survive, but had she not done it she would have had no chance. This at least gave her an entirely different field of battle, one in which she was not powerless.

As Kahlan gazed again into the eyes of this woman before her, she felt no hatred, no remorse, no anger, no sorrow, no pity. In fact, she felt no emotion at all.

This act was the embodiment of Confessor power, and the Confessor face reflected its cold nature, and in a way part of its purpose. This was reasoned action absent of emotion. It was a calculated act of aggression to change what would have otherwise happened. Emotion had no place in that, and was no longer necessary, so it was no longer a component of what had to be done. It was already decided the instant that knife point touched Kahlan's palm.

Nea had no chance. None.

In that singular moment, if Kahlan was the absence of emotion, then Nea was the manifestation of it.

In that infinitesimal tick of time, Nea's mind, who she was, who she had been, was already gone.

Kahlan did not hesitate.

She released the rest of her restraints on her gift to unleash the full, blinding force of her power.

Time slammed back.

Thunder without sound jolted the air—exquisite, violent, and for that pristine instant, sovereign.

The trees all around shook with the force of the concussion. The violent shock of it lifted the leaves, bits of plants, and sticks littering the ground and blew them outward in an ever-expanding ring around Kahlan. The dust and dirt and debris driven before the wall of power knocked the rest of the women from their feet as it stripped vegetation off the nearby shrubs and trees. As the force of that silent thunder ripped across the water to each side of the path, it drove a ring of water and water vapor before it. Trees shook. Small branches were torn off and blown back.

Nea gasped as the full force of Confessor power slammed into her.

Behind Kahlan, all of the women, who had been thrown from their feet and tumbled back away, were now grabbing their elbows, knees, or wrists in pain. She could hear them groaning in agony from having been too close to Kahlan when her Confessor power was unleashed.

Nea dropped to her knees before Kahlan. She looked up through strands of red hair, no longer in hate and rage, but in pleading.

"Mistress ... please ... command me."

Kahlan looked down, feeling no sorrow for the woman. Her life as she had known it was now ended. Her memories, her wishes, her hopes were gone. She had forfeited all of that and more when she tried to kill Kahlan.

"Please, Mistress," Nea begged. "Please, command me."

"Kill Shota."

Almost instantly, knife still in her fist, Nea scrambled to her feet and charged past Kahlan, going for Shota.

138

As Nea shot past, Kahlan turned to see all the rest of the witch women, including Shota, getting to their feet, most of them groaning in pain from being so close when Kahlan had unleashed her power.

Nea, screaming in single-minded, lethal fury, raced through some and leaped over others as she bolted toward Shota.

Unlike the others, who were slowly struggling up, Shota, who had also been knocked from her feet, swiftly swirled around as she rose with the grace of silk billowing in a breeze. The flaps and folds of her variegated gray dress whirled with her like trails of smoke behind the flames of a torch as she advanced in a blur with otherworldly speed.

Kahlan blinked and there was Shota abruptly standing before the advancing Nea. Nea was still screaming, intent only on carrying out Kahlan's command.

She lifted her fist with the knife to drive it into her former leader.

Before the knife made it to Shota, Shota calmly tapped Nea's forehead once with a finger.

Nea instantly stopped dead in her tracks. At the same time, all of her blackened and cracked the way a log in a fire turns black and checkers into pieces before it falls apart. All of those black chunks one moment made a very odd-looking Nea, and the next moment crumbled like coals collapsing in a blaze. In mere seconds, all that was left of a totally committed Nea was a heap of glowing embers.

Kahlan could hardly believe that just that quick, Nea was no more. She supposed she was actually no more the instant Kahlan's power had taken her mind, but still, this was a disturbing development. One second there was about to be a battle, and then the next second it was over. Of course, Kahlan hadn't thought that killing Shota would be as easy as simply ordering Nea to kill her, but she had hoped that it would result in a longer battle that would allow her to escape.

That was not to be.

Beyond Shota and the blackened, crumbled remains of Nea spilled all over the ground, Kahlan saw all the rest of the wide-eyed witch women, including Shale, standing close together, shrinking back in horror at having seen both Shota's power and Kahlan's used in such horrifying fashion, to say nothing of having also just seen four of their sister witches die violently in a matter of seconds.

The four dead witches had been vicious and seemed to enjoy their roles in Shota's scheme and as Kahlan's captors, glad to inflict whatever pain that control required or was commanded by Shota. It was apparent from the way the rest of them in the background stared that they were not nearly so eager for battle. Faced with such savage power unleashed so swiftly, and with such devastating results, they all had to fear that any of them might be next.

Kahlan knew that Shale, at least, was not there by her own wishes, but by Shota's command. She wondered if it was the same for any of the others.

Shota gracefully stepped around the smoldering remains of her former second-in-command and came to a halt in front of Kahlan.

"Well, well, Mother Confessor, it seems you have managed to break the coven." She tipped her head close and spoke in a low, deadly voice. "But in so doing, you have lost the ability to use your power again until you recover your strength, and we both know that will take a while. In the meantime, you have left yourself defenseless against my abilities." She gestured back at the smoldering ashes. "Abilities which, I believe you now realize, need no coven."

"Wars are rarely won in a single battle, or a single victory," Kahlan said. "It may take a while before my power recovers, but that power will soon enough return. On the other hand, you have lost the power of coven for good." Kahlan arched an eyebrow. "Unless you have four more witches hiding in your pocket?"

A slow smile came to Shota's full lips. "Nea was a very, very good witch, but she made the mistake of underestimating you. I don't make those kinds of foolish mistakes."

Kahlan didn't try to outsmile the witch woman. "Then you had best let me go, before I regain the ability to call on my Confessor power again."

Shota glared. "That isn't going to happen."

Kahlan shrugged. "Then you will have to kill me before my power recovers and I have you on your knees at my feet, begging for me to command you. So go ahead and turn me to a pile of smoldering coals as you did your trusted right-hand witch. I wouldn't delay long, were I you. I was named Mother Confessor in part because my ability recovers quickly."

Shota's smile returned and widened. Kahlan thought it looked almost like a smile of admiration.

"Kill you? I told you before, my dear, I don't intend to kill you. You are far too valuable to the world. No, you will come with me down into Agaden Reach, where you will rest in comfort and security until you deliver your two children. After that, you will be allowed to go off on your way."

"And how do you think you could possibly accomplish such a feat before I am able to use my power again and I kill you?"

Shota dismissed the notion with a gesture. "It took a great deal of time and trouble to assemble the witches needed to form a coven, and you may have broken that gathering, but you make a serious mistake thinking that weakens me to the point of being helpless against you and your power. I have not only my own power, but the power of the witch women behind me that I can link should I need to."

"Then you best do it soon," Kahlan warned.

The witch woman's smile changed from admonishment to amusement. "You are correct, Mother Confessor. Wars aren't usually won in a single victory, and although you don't seem yet to grasp it, you are destined to lose this war."

"I don't believe in destiny."

Shota sighed, weary of the game. She ran the tip of her finger along Kahlan's jaw.

"Maybe you are right, Mother Confessor, but I have made plans enough to predetermine that the outcome will be as I wish it."

Kahlan felt something abruptly tighten around her ankles. Without looking down, she tried, but couldn't move her feet. She was too angry to let herself panic.

"Clever trick, Shota. But I will soon end this war with you once and for all."

Shota arched an eyebrow. "I'm afraid you will never get that chance. You see, before you can recover your ability to use your power, you will be spelled into a deep and peaceful sleep and then taken the rest of the way down to my home, where you will not awaken before you give birth. Once you do, then I will kill those two children, as I have told you I would.

"I have given you enough chances to be reasonable for the greater good. For my own safety, since you have now vowed to kill me with your power once it recovers, after you give birth and your children have been killed, you will have to be put down for good. You will never recover from that peaceful sleep."

"You're a liar," Kahlan said.

"Do tell," Shota said, indulgently.

"You may indeed plan to kill me after I give birth—as you have actually planned all along—but you have no intention of killing my two children. None."

139

The smug smile vanished. "I don't know what you're talking about."

"Really?" Kahlan cocked her head. "If you really wanted these children dead, they would already be dead. You've just said you intend to kill me. So if your intent really is to kill these children, and you admit that you also intend to kill me, you would do to me right now what you just did to Nea. Then my unborn children and I would all be dead. Isn't that what you claim to want?"

Shota didn't answer.

"But you can't do that," Kahlan went on, "because you actually have no intention of killing my children, and if you killed me now you would be killing those two children—the children you so desperately want to be born alive."

Shota acted perplexed, as if such a notion was utterly outlandish. "Where in the world would you come up with such a fanciful idea? After I have for so long promised you that I would not allow the children you and Richard create to live, why in the world would you now come up with this crazy notion I would not carry out my promises and kill those two little monsters?"

"Because you intend to raise them."

Shota stood stock-still as she stared into Kahlan's eyes for a long, dragging moment.

"I can see that Lord Rahl does not wed stupid women."

"And certainly not one stupid enough to let you get away with it."

The menace returned to Shota's face. "Oh, but you are wrong, there.

I have already gotten away with it, we simply need to play out the final acts and it will be done. At least as far as your part in this is concerned."

"You seriously think I intend to let you raise these two children?"

"You no longer have any say in it." Shota gestured dismissively. "I will raise them in a way that you never could."

"You mean raise them as your two little underlings to follow in your footsteps, worship you as their mother, and do your bidding?"

Shota glared. "I have seen into the flow of time. I told you that I saw that you and Richard would conceive a monster. It is possible, although it is a remote possibility, that it is as you have said, that the child I saw in the flow of time was the one you previously lost. But having seen into that complex flow, I don't for a second believe that.

"One of the children you now carry is the monster I saw in that prophecy."

"Richard ended prophecy."

"That doesn't mean that prophecy wasn't real, or true, or that when it was here in our world I wasn't able to use it. You didn't see what I saw in that flow of time, and you can't begin to imagine it. Before Richard ended my ability to continue to use that flow, I saw this, saw what you two would create."

"Our children will be who we raise them to be. I told you, I don't believe in destiny. No matter what you saw, that doesn't mean one of these children will turn out the way you think."

Shota shook her head as she let out a weary breath. "You just can't grasp the entirety of this, can you? You see only your little slice of it, your naive wishes, hopes, and dreams. Monster or not, they are both gifted with power from each of you.

"You and Richard are not the ones to raise such a powerful pair—a girl with Confessor power combined with the power of her war-wizard father, and a boy war wizard with your Confessor power. Neither of you can begin to comprehend the enormity of what you have created.

"You say that these children are needed to protect our world from the Glee by maintaining the web of magic they provide, and you are right. The power these two hold will be a web of magic so intense that it will drive the Glee from our world for all time. It will protect our world and protect the magic of it.

"But you don't see the bigger picture beyond that which our world needs to free us from the immediate threat of the Glee. You and Richard are too weak, too softhearted, too indulgent of what people under your rule wish to do with their lives. Those ebbing and flowing wishes of the ignorant masses would eventually lead our world over the brink and into ruin that even the Glee could not accomplish.

"You two fought a long and terrible war against the Imperial Order. Do you think their destructive doctrine came from another world? No, it came from the people in our world, people who left to their own ignorant wishes will one day again fall under the seductive spell of such beliefs. It has always been that way, and it will always be that way, unless there is rule strong enough to exert control for the good of our world.

"These two children you carry, together, with the gifts they will be born with, will have the ability to rule the world with the kind of power and authority that will prevent that kind of thing from ever happening again.

"So you see, in a way, I, too, do not believe in destiny. I am the one who will prevent that terrible future from ever having the chance to fester and grow. What I do now saves countless lives in the future.

"With these two under my protection, care, guidance, instruction, and preparation, they will be the two powerful instruments to both expel the Glee and control our world so that it can never be allowed to fall into the foolishness of ignorant masses too stupid to know what is in their own best interest. I will control those masses. With those two children, I will protect the best interest of the world. It will all be done for the greater good.

"You and Richard do not have the strength to raise rulers like that. I do.

"I will be the mother children such as these really need. The boy will see me as a vision of Richard's mother, and the girl will see me as a vision of yours. They will both see me as their mother, think of me as their mother, and have total trust in me as their teacher.

"They will both depend on me for everything. They will learn from me everything. They will come to believe from me everything. I will forge them both into the powerful force the world needs, into the powerful rulers the world needs in order for it to continue without the mindless, destructive beliefs of fools being allowed to flourish. In the past when people were allowed to force unworkable ideas on nations, it cast the world into wars in which countless masses died. I will not allow that to happen again.

"These two will rule with iron fists and their power.

"I will rule them both with mine."

Kahlan blinked in stunned surprise. She had known that Shota wanted both children in order to raise them and use their gifts for her own ends, but she hadn't realized the full extent of her ideas.

Shota intended to turn the twins into weapons she would shape and wield. It was she who would be pulling the strings of her two puppets in order to rule the world. It was now crystal clear that Shota had put a great deal of thought, to say nothing of effort, into her mad scheme. She was convinced of the need of doing this. She believed in what she was saying and that she was doing it for the greater good. She thought that she was ultimately doing the right thing.

Richard had always said that the most dangerous person was the one who truly believed that their cause was right. Shota believed that what she was doing was inherently right. It was the greater good as she saw it.

Kahlan knew that she had to stop the woman now, before she used her witch woman's power to put her into a numb sleep until the babies were born. By then it would be too late.

Because it would still be a while before her power returned, she could see no other way to do it.

Since Kahlan couldn't move her feet, while Shota was still close enough and before she moved away Kahlan leaned out with lightning speed and just that quick had her hands around Shota's throat.

She gritted her teeth and growled with the effort of squeezing the life out of the witch woman.

But before she could crush her windpipe, Shota did something Kahlan hadn't considered.

140

Kahlan gasped in pain as she felt the shock of a flash of power hit her. The abrupt jolt of it sizzled through every nerve in her body, making her involuntarily release her grip, and then, as she pulled her hands back, she suddenly felt the terror of snakes slithering up in under her shirt.

Another snake, with multicolored scales, climbed up over her back and coiled its fat body around her neck, constricting enough that it made it difficult to breathe. She tightened her neck muscles as much as she could, hoping to protect the blood supply to her brain so that she wouldn't lose consciousness. She didn't know if that would actually work, but it was the only thing she could do.

Another, with a diamond pattern along its back, came around her waist, then moved up and over her shoulder. The whole time its tail rattled a threat. Several long, thin, black vipers with red and yellow bands slithered right up the side of her face and into her hair. Colorful snakes writhed everywhere on her, tightening around her legs as they pressed their heads against her back in under her shirt.

Shota didn't back away—she didn't need to. Kahlan was immobilized with fear. There were so many snakes everywhere on her that she feared to breathe.

The smile that Kahlan had come to hate spread once more on Shota's full lips. "I strongly suggest you don't move, Mother Confessor. Agitated vipers"—Shota leaned in a little—"bite."

Kahlan didn't have to be told not to move. She was too terrified to move. Her mind raced, trying to think what to do. When Shota had done this the first time they met the witch woman, Richard was

there and made her stop it. Richard wasn't there, now, to make Shota
withdraw her vipers.

Without looking away from Kahlan's eyes, Shota lifted a hand and
snapped her fingers back behind at the other witch women.

"Niska, come here."

One of the women in the group rushed forward, shuffling her feet
the whole way. Her shoulders were hunched in fear of the very angry
grand witch.

"Yes, Mistress?"

Niska wasn't at all malicious-looking, but she certainly was
strange, and Kahlan had no trouble whatsoever believing she could
be nothing other than a witch woman. She was youngish and slender,
wearing floaty, flimsy white robes pinned together above each
shoulder.

What there was of the robes left her arms and lot of her flesh
exposed, and every bit of that flesh was covered in writing.

It ran up her arms, line after line, on all sides. On her right arm,
from her biceps to her shoulder, the writing went in bands around
her arm. On her upper shoulders and chest the writing followed the
contours of her body. When she moved, and the material of her robes
parted, Kahlan could see that her thighs, too, were covered in line after
line of writing.

There were several lines of symbols down the bridge of her nose, and
horizontal lines of symbols following the contours of her face onto the
sides of her nose, where they met the lines coming down the bridge of
it. Line after line of the symbols ran all the way around her neck and
continued back under her fall of satiny black hair.

Kahlan could see in the light as she moved, by the way most of
the strokes had a welted look to them, that it all had been tattooed
in dark ink, not simply written or painted on her skin. Or else, she
thought, perhaps the lines of writing had been branded into her flesh
with magic.

Kahlan couldn't read the writing, but she did recognize the look of
some of the symbols. They looked very much like the ancient symbols
Richard had shown her several times. Those were the language of

Creation. These looked like they were as well. The significance of that alone was unnerving.

Niska stood meekly to the side and slightly behind Shota. Her shoulders were stooped, and her head was sunken down into those shoulders. She worried her fingers against one another as she stared at the ground.

"Yes, Mistress? Do you wish something from me?"

Kahlan could tell by the quality of her voice that although Niska was submissive in front of Shota, encountered by herself, this slight woman would be formidable.

"Yes, as a matter of fact, I do," Shota said.

Off behind Shota, the other witch women watched, not knowing what was coming but, after the things they had already seen, clearly fearing it.

"Niska," Shota said in her silky voice as she twirled a finger, "I'd like you to spin a sleep spell around the Mother Confessor. I want it to be irreversible."

"Irreversible?"

"Yes, irreversible." Shota shrugged. "We will not have cause to break it, since after she gives birth she will have to die, so yes, it may as well be irreversible. That kind is easier, and stronger, so we won't have to worry that she might come awake in childbirth."

Niska bowed. "As you wish, Mistress."

Niska took a few steps away from Shota to give herself room, then began chanting words under her breath. As she went on in the singsong rhythm of the unfamiliar words, she pointed down at the ground and slowly began spinning a finger around and around.

As she mumbled the strange words, and her finger revolved, her hand took up the turning, and then her whole arm began making circles as it hung like a pendulum from her shoulder.

As her hanging arm revolved round and round in circles, the beautiful but incomprehensible words gradually became louder. They seemed to echo back through the trees and thick vegetation, their power resonating with the wild things back in the shadows, with nature itself, calling power forth.

Kahlan began to see, off in that dense vegetation and out among the trees across the swampy bodies of water, a thickening mist all around begin to form and gradually start to revolve. As the strength of the words Niska chanted became stronger and deeper, the mist became thicker, and it gradually picked up speed as it circled around them all gathered there on the path through the swamp.

As the circle of that mist gradually began to shrink inward, Kahlan could tell that she was at the center of that low, thick ring of haze.

As she watched it closing in around her, she tried to move at least her feet, but she couldn't. Her feet were bound together with a spell, but worse, there were snakes, hundreds of them it seemed, slithering all over her feet and up her legs. They were so many that some of them had to slither over the tops of others. She had no doubt that if she moved, they would bite her, so she reconsidered her attempt to move her feet. The only slight doubt in the worry that she would be bitten was that if the vipers did bite her, her babies would die with her, and since Shota was determined to have those two gifted children, she wouldn't want to lose the opportunity. Still, as angry as Shota was, Kahlan didn't feel at all confident that she wouldn't let the snakes bite to kill her and the twins along with her.

As Niska chanted and the revolving ring of thick mist came ever closer, Kahlan felt increasingly desperate, but she was also beginning to feel so tired that she caught herself starting to nod off. Each time, she jerked herself back awake, knowing that once that circling mist completely closed in on her, it would overwhelm her ability to stay awake and that would herald the end of her, and the end of her children's chances to have a good life.

She knew that once she did fall asleep, Shota would simply have to bide her time a little while longer, until Kahlan delivered, and then she would have the twins all to herself.

As desperately as she tried, she could think of no solution to the spot she was in.

Kahlan blinked with sleepiness, desperately trying to stay alert even as the weight of drowsiness pressed in on her. When she forced herself awake again, she saw a big white snake rise up along the length of her, slithering its way onward among the writhing net of other snakes. All the rest were different colors and covered with patterns. Only this one was white.

Kahlan jerked her head again, trying to stay awake. She looked beyond Shota and Niska to the others standing together in a group.

Kahlan saw, then, that Shale's eyes were rolled up her in head and her fingers were moving.

Kahlan blinked in disbelief when she suddenly realized what that meant.

141

Kahlan instantly recognized that this was her last chance, and despite her paralyzing fear of the snakes slithering all over her and the sleepiness incrementally tightening its grip on her, she had to take it. She didn't know if Shota would let her snakes bite Kahlan, but she had no other choice but to act.

The white snake turned its big head to look at her, its red tongue flicking out. It was frightening seeing such a deadly creature up close.

Before it was too late, quick as a crack of lightning, Kahlan ignored her revulsion and snatched the white snake right behind its head. As she turned it and thrust it out, its mouth opened wide, exposing long fangs as sharp as needles.

Kahlan slammed the snake against Shota's neck before she had time to react. The fangs instantly sank in deep, hitting the main vein. Even though it already had its fangs in, Kahlan held it there, pressing the head against the witch's neck. She felt the snake's powerful muscles flex as it worked its mouth to pump venom into the jugular vein.

The witch woman stumbled back with a shriek of shock and fear. The white snake had its fangs fastened in her neck and was pulled away from Kahlan's grip as Shota staggered back. She grabbed at her throat, weakly trying to claw the snake away. As she did, it whipped coils of its white body around her arm and neck, preventing her from pulling it away from her.

There was no faster way for the venom to get to Shota's heart than the vein in her neck. Because that was where the venom entered her bloodstream, it acted all that much faster than it otherwise would have. Her heart would circulate it quickly to her brain and through the rest of her.

Niska gasped in shock at seeing what had just happened. She stopped chanting and quickly stepped out of the way as Shota stumbled back, both hands fighting the thrashing white snake that had her by the throat. Without the chanted words, the circle of mist began to evaporate, losing its grip of sleepiness on Kahlan.

Shota collapsed with the snake's fangs still sunk deep into her throat. She mumbled something in the delirium of the lethal venom pumping through her body. Her hands fell away from the snake even as it continued to flex and pump venom into her.

Shota gasped once, deep and desperate, and then the breath left her lungs with a sickening rattle. After that breath had gurgled out, she lay still and breathed no more.

Kahlan realized that the snakes that had been crawling all over her were gone. They had died out with the witch woman who had conjured them.

She stood stunned at how fast it had all happened. Grasping the relevance of the white snake, the near-instant crystallization of a plan, and the execution of that plan had all happened in a flash.

She blinked in surprise as Shale raced up and threw her arms around her.

"Mother Confessor! You understood! I was so hoping that you would realize that the white snake was mine."

In gratitude and relief, Kahlan embraced her tightly for a moment.

"I remembered the white snakes from when you used them before, on the Glee."

Shale pushed back and grinned at Kahlan. "That's right. I was hoping you would remember. Shota's power prevented me from using my gift against her—any magic used against her would only have reflected back to me. This was the only chance I could see to help you, so I had to take that chance while Shota was so focused on the snakes she had conjured. I knew she would have to watch what Niska was doing as well as make sure her snakes didn't recklessly bite you, or the babies would die as well. I knew she wouldn't want that to happen."

Niska came close and put a hand on Kahlan's shoulder. "I'm so sorry, Mother Confessor. I never wanted to be part of this. I would never have wanted to hurt you. Shota forced me to be part of her coven and do her bidding."

Kahlan nodded, tears in her eyes with happiness for her twins. "I know."

Kahlan circled an arm around Niska's thin shoulders and pulled her tight in a quick hug to let her know that she understood and didn't blame her.

142

The rest of the witch women all gathered around Kahlan, each of them briefly touching her in genuine sympathy as they explained how Shota had dragged them into her plans. They apologized for participating in the whole terrible ordeal. They all talked over each other, trying to explain that they had been living their own peaceful lives when Shota, as the grand witch, had summoned them with the magic of her oath and forced them to be part of her coven and thus her larger scheme.

One of the rather frightening-looking witch women, with one scarred, empty eye socket, a mangled nose, and no lips, approached. It took all of Kahlan's strength not to recoil at the horror of her face. She touched Kahlan reverently.

"I have been persecuted my whole life for being a witch." Her speech was halting and slurred because of her lack of lips, making it difficult to understand her.

The scar tissue where her lips had been cut off had thickened and tightened, pulling back from her gums and teeth, giving her a frightening look. The empty eye socket and the way her bared teeth grinned like those of a skull made it hard to look at her. She wet her teeth with her tongue before going on.

"I am named Yara. As you can plainly see," the woman said, gesturing self-consciously at her face, "I have had vile things done to me by people who think my gift alone makes me evil. I hate that every day I must wear the scars of that hatred for all to see on my face."

She choked up with emotion for a moment as a few tears ran down her cheek from her one eye. "But the one who was the most wicked of all was Shota, because she of all people should have known better. She knew what I had suffered, what I must live with for the rest of my life, and yet she used me anyway, used my face, to create fear in you. You have freed me, Mother Confessor. Thank you."

With a tear still in her own eyes, Kahlan put an arm around her shoulder and gave her the same kind of hug she had given Niska. Kahlan understood all too well people who in the past had thought her evil because of her Confessor power.

She tapped the witch woman's chest. "You keep your beauty in here, but I can see it."

Another woman stepped forward to touch Kahlan's arm. She was a lovely looking young woman, with unsettling birthmarks below each eye that made it look like blood was continually gushing from her eyes. While she was off-putting to look at, her gentle voice was the counter to the disturbing birthmarks.

"I am Thebe, Mother Confessor. All of us hope you can understand that none of this was our doing. We hold no ill will toward you and hope you can find it in your heart to hold none against us. We hope you can forgive us for taking part, even if it was against our will."

"We were being used," an older witch woman with long, wavy white hair said. She had a large wart on one side of her long nose. The tip of that nose drooped as if it were made of wax and she had let it get too close to a flame and it melted the end. "Shota used us much like the way she intended to use your two children, once they were born."

"She lied at first," another, very short witch woman said. She had wooden pegs for legs sticking out from beneath her tattered dress. "She had planned to kill you all along after you gave birth and keep your babies for herself. That is the most evil thing one woman could do to another, and to her children. She was using us as well, but what she was doing to you and the children you carry was much, much worse. I am so sorry for what almost happened."

"None of us would ever think to harm anyone," Yara said, as best she could without lips. "We have all been tormented by people for being born as witch women before anyone comes to know us for who we are. We simply want to be left alone to live our lives in peace."

"But there were a few among us who had evil in their hearts," Thebe said. "They were eager to participate in Shota's grand scheme, eager to cause you pain. Those are the four who are now dead, as is Shota herself. I don't think any of us ever dreamed that you would survive this plot, but we are truly thankful that you did."

"We realize you have no reason to believe our sincerity," another said, "but I swear to the good spirits, it is the truth."

"I can vouch for the honesty of what they are saying," Shale said. "I have spent time with these women. I know the heart of each. The hearts of the ones you killed were black, but these witch women are my sisters and their hearts are good."

"I understand." Kahlan spread her hands. "I am also sorry that all of you have suffered as well. Like my husband, I don't assign guilt because of the sins of others. We each should be judged for who we are and what we do. My hope is that all of you can now go back to your homes and live in peace. Know that I hold no grudge against you. My hope for you all is that others won't, either."

They whispered among themselves for a moment, until there were nods among them all.

"We have all discussed it," the one with the wavy white hair said, "and we all agreed that any of us will come to your aid should you ever ask us. We would be eager to try to make amends in any way possible."

"No amends are necessary, but I will remember your offer should I ever need your help." Kahlan let out a deep sigh. "Although she doesn't necessarily deserve it, Shota has in the past helped Lord Rahl and me, so in view of that alone, I think you should take her body down to her home, in Agaden Reach, and bury her there."

Heads tipped close together and whispering again broke out among them all.

"We will see to it, Mother Confessor," Niska said. "You are more thoughtful than she would have been for you."

Kahlan nodded. "I have known her for a long time, and while she intended to do something evil, the woman was more complex than this one act driven by the thought of such power going to her head. She has paid the price for that act."

"We hope your husband is safe," a woman in the back said, "but if he is not, we stand ready to help you in any way we can."

"There is one thing we could do," Shale said, looking around at the rest of the witch women. "When Shota made the Mother Confessor start to miscarry, Lord Rahl gave her the raw milk of mother's breath while I made up the preparation."

Worried whispers broke out among the women. They obviously thought that was troubling. They cast concerned looks at Kahlan. She fretted as to the reason.

Yara lifted a hand. "We could all join our gifts and cast a birthing spell to help ease your delivery, and also that the two babies might be born healthy."

Shale smiled. "That is what I was thinking."

Kahlan felt her worry ease a little. "I would be grateful for such a spell."

The women all gathered in a tight circle around Kahlan, their hands over each other's shoulders. They closed their eyes as they whispered a chant in unison. Kahlan didn't understand the words, but she understood the heartfelt intentions.

As soon as they had finished, they stepped back and, following Shale's lead, went to their knees and bowed forward.

Kahlan recognized the honor. She waited a moment in the silence and then said, "Rise, my children."

It was the Mother Confessor's formal recognition of those under her protection.

As they were coming up, Kahlan heard a sound and turned to see the red leather of the Mord-Sith emerging from the mist. In the gloomy swamp, such a flash of color was hard to miss.

She didn't see Richard.

143

Kahlan's eyes opened wide with dread as she saw all six Mord-Sith materialize out of the mist, but she didn't see Richard.

Panic started to rise up within her at seeing that he wasn't with them.

But then, off behind the Mord-Sith, she finally saw him emerge out of the swirling haze, like a good spirit come among them.

It felt as if her heart leaped up into her throat with relief at seeing him. She had been sick with worry that he was dead, but dealing with Shota was the problem at hand, so she'd had to set that worry aside to look after herself and the twins.

Kahlan cried out in excitement as she ran the dozen strides to meet him. She threw her arms around his neck and kissed the side of his face at least a half-dozen times. He squeezed her tight in return, momentarily lifting her from her feet. Finally, she separated from him and stood back to wipe tears of joy from beneath her eyes.

"What took you so long?" she asked him.

Richard shrugged. "Well, a building fell on me…"

She blinked in astonishment that he had survived such a thing and was actually alive. "Shota told us that she had spelled your legs so that you couldn't run to safety. She wanted the whole palace to come down on you. How did you get out?"

He didn't seem at all concerned about what had happened.

"The good spirits watched over me."

"Actually," Vika said as she gestured among the Mord-Sith, "we dug him out. I don't recall seeing any of the good spirits there, helping, but we did have a lot of help from the people of Bindamoon. Lord Rahl didn't make it easy, though. He managed to stand under the center of the palace as the entire thing collapsed, so it was a lot of trouble getting him out, I don't mind telling you."

"We knew you would be angry if we just left him there," Berdine said, offhandedly. "So we thought it best if we got him out and brought him along with us."

Richard rolled his eyes. "The people in Bindamoon turned out to be a huge help in saving my life. They were more than thankful to be rid of Iron Jack, the palace, and the 'queen.' But it was Rikka, Nyda, Cassia, Vale, Berdine, and Vika who organized and directed them in the rescue effort. I am indebted to them."

"As am I," Kahlan said as she put a hand on the forearms of two of the Mord-Sith. "I was so worried. Thank you for not giving up on him. I don't know what I would do had you…" Her voice choked up and she couldn't say the rest.

"Kahlan killed the five evil witches," Shale said into the awkward silence. "One of them was Shota." She grinned, then. "With her bare hands."

The Mord-Sith all looked a bit astonished, but proud.

Richard nodded with a serious look. "I would have expected no less. I'm just surprised it took her so long." He winked at Kahlan.

She gripped Shale's arm, then, and pulled her closer, as if presenting her to Richard. "I couldn't have done it without Shale. She gave me a snake to use."

"A snake?" Richard frowned. "You hate snakes."

Kahlan showed him a sly smile. "Not white ones."

"Ah, I see." He flashed a smile at Shale as he gripped her shoulder. "Glad you were able to help."

Kahlan turned and held her arm out toward the group of witch women all watching him with a mixture of awe and terror, fearing that, like so many others, he would think they were evil just because they were witches. Worse, they knew that he had the power to strike them down on the spot should he so wish.

"These ladies here were not willing participants in Shota's scheme. They were all forced to answer Shota's call to coven, the same as Shale. The ones who wanted to be part of it are now all dead."

"I know," Richard said. "I heard the last of it as we were coming in. I stayed out of sight and watched to make sure there wasn't going to be any more trouble. I wanted to be able to come in and surprise anyone who might still attack you. It turns out that, thankfully, it wasn't necessary."

"No," Kahlan said with a smile as she looked over at the women. "These women are all on our side. Shota was using them."

He bowed his head to the nervous women. "Thank you all for helping the mother of my children, my beloved wife, and the Mother Confessor. You have my most heartfelt gratitude."

There were giggles and nods as the witch women all finally stepped closer.

Richard turned to Niska, taking in the writing tattooed all over her flesh. He spoke words Kahlan didn't understand, but by Niska's wide eyes, it was clear she knew what he was saying. She bowed deeply.

"Thank you, Lord Rahl. Although I am their keeper, I have not heard these words spoken aloud since I was but a girl. It is a reminder to me of the importance of the messages I carry to preserve the ancient language of Creation."

"Keep yourself and the words safe," Richard told Niska. "Both are important for future generations."

With a slight smile, Niska bowed her head. "By your command, Lord Rahl."

He turned and gestured to the woman without any lips. "May I know your name?"

She bowed, too fearful to look up at him, or maybe too ashamed of her appearance. "I am Yara, Lord Rahl."

With two fingers, he beckoned her close.

Yara reluctantly stepped up to him, and then, upon his urging, up closer to him. Richard gently gripped her shoulders and turned her around. He leaned in and spoke softly in her ear.

"You know about Additive Magic, Yara, yes?"

She nodded. "Of course, Lord Rahl."

"Good. Now, I'd like you to close your eye for me."

She did, and Richard gently put his hand over her mouth from behind. As he held his hand there, he bowed his head until his forehead touched the back of her head. Kahlan didn't know what he could be doing, but as she watched, Yara brought her hands together in front of herself to twine her fingers together as if in anxiety, or maybe pain. She could see the witch woman's breathing grow short and sharp. They stood that way for quite a time, until Richard finally took his hand away from her mouth.

Kahlan was astonished to see that Yara now had normal-looking lips where there had been only lumpy scars before. Her disfigured nose, too, was restored to normal.

Her hand rushed up to touch them. She turned and knelt beside the water to look at her reflection. As she stood, she started crying.

"I'm sorry," Richard said as she turned to him, "but I don't know if it would be possible to create a new eye for you with Additive Magic. If it is, I'm afraid that I don't know how to do such a thing. But I could at least do this little bit to help fix some of the harm that was done to you by ignorant people."

Weeping, she fell to her knees before him and grabbed the bottom of his trouser leg, kissing it repeatedly.

"None of that, Yara," he said, reaching down to touch the back of her shoulder. "It's not necessary. It was my honor as the Lord Rahl to help you. More than that, it is my duty to try to set wrongs right where I was able."

She finally stood and returned to the others. Some of them touched her lips in wonder as they all expressed their astonishment.

Richard motioned then for the young woman with the birthmarks under her eyes to come to him. Holding her hands together, she approached him with her head bowed.

Richard lifted her chin with a finger to look into her eyes. "Those aren't birthmarks, are they?"

"You know?"

He nodded. "Yes. Someone marked you."

She nodded. "I am called Thebe. When I was young, I was cursed by a sorceress with these marks. She said it was to let anyone who looks upon me know that I am to be shunned as a filthy witch."

Richard shook his head in disgust, then turned her around and spoke softly in her ear. "You know of Subtractive Magic, yes?"

She nodded. "Underworld magic."

Richard smiled as he put a hand over her eyes. "Well, yes, but it is also part of my power. And, as far as sorceresses' curses go, this one is relatively simple."

After a moment, when he took his hand away, the frightening bloodlike marks under her eyes were gone.

"Thebe!" Niska exclaimed. "The curse marks under your eyes are gone!"

Thebe started to go to the ground before Richard, but he caught her arm first. "Not necessary, Thebe. It was a simple thing and I was glad to remove the marks for you."

She bowed. "Thank you, Lord Rahl, for removing this curse from my face. It has long made people shun me. Some even spit on me. It has caused me great loneliness. People fear and hate me without knowing me. They wouldn't allow me to help them with my gift."

Richard smiled. "I think they will shun you no more. In fact, I suspect you will find that a lot of young men are bewitched by your beauty."

She lowered her head with a shy smile.

Richard gestured at the woman with the two peg legs. She immediately held up both hands to ward him off.

"Thank you, Lord Rahl, but I do not wish to have my legs back. My knees used to hurt me so bad that I could hardly walk. With these, I can walk. They do me just fine if it pleases you."

Richard showed her a smile. "Then I would not think of changing them."

Kahlan wasn't sure if Shale looked amazed, or concerned. She leaned close to whisper to him.

"How did you do those things?" the sorceress asked. "I didn't know that magic had such powers. How does it work?"

Richard stared off into the swamp a moment before he answered. "I have no idea. Sometimes when I need it badly enough, my gift works. This was one of those times. I sincerely felt the need of it, the need of helping them, and it worked. That is the way with war wizards, I believe. Or at least with my power. It is brought to life by need."

He turned his attention to the group watching him. "I'm sorry that Shota pulled you all into this. Thank you for your concern for the Mother Confessor, and your help, but we must leave at once. We have a long way to travel and I want to get us where we are going before our children are born."

"Lord Rahl...?" Shale said, hesitantly.

Richard seemed to know what she was about to say. He dismissed her concern with a quick gesture.

"Of course you're coming with us, Shale. We need you with us. The children of D'Hara need you when it is time to be born, and after that, too. Besides, this is going to be a long and dangerous journey. We need to keep the Law of Nines intact. We can't do all that without you."

She sighed in relief and smiled as she gave him a single nod.

When Richard said that they needed to get going, Kahlan held the hand of each witch woman in turn, wishing them well on their own journeys home.

"Don't forget," the witch woman with the wavy white hair said. "If either you or Lord Rahl is ever in need of our help for any reason, we will always do what is within our ability."

Niska retrieved Kahlan's knife from near Nea's remains. Her pack was not far away. She brought both back and handed Kahlan her knife, handle-first. "We will do as you have asked and bury Shota down in Agaden Reach."

Richard rested the palm of his left hand on the hilt of his sword as he looked at all the women watching him. "Do you all know about the Glee?" There were worried looks all around. They obviously all knew what the Glee were. "The Golden Goddess, their leader, continually tries to get into the minds of people in our world in order to find out where the Mother Confessor and I are so that she can send the Glee to kill us and prevent these babies from being born."

"What can we do to help?" Niska asked.

"You can all guard your minds. If you sense a power probing your thoughts, use your gift to shut it out."

All of them nodded and spoke up to say that they would be careful.

144

Richard put an arm around Kahlan's and Shale's shoulders and moved them away from the witch women over to the group of Mord-Sith standing a short distance apart under a dead tree draped with sheets of moss. He wanted to have a confidential conversation. He didn't necessarily distrust the witch women, but he didn't want to let anyone know his plans for where they were going, or the route he intended to take.

"Besides nearly killing us all," he told them once they were all back together with the six Mord-Sith, "Shota greatly delayed us in getting to the Keep. The diversion exposed us to attacks by the Glee. With Kahlan so far along, she is even more vulnerable. We need to avoid any more of those risky battles. Not only that, but Shota has caused us to go a long way off course in the wrong direction in order to come up here to Agaden Reach. It put us a long way from Aydindril."

"How far do you think we are from the Keep?" Shale asked.

Richard stared off to the northeast, as if he could almost see the Keep from where he stood. "We are farther from the Keep, now, than we were when we were at the People's Palace."

Shale clearly looked disheartened. Richard couldn't say he blamed her. They had already had a long and difficult journey, not even counting the time in Bindamoon and now up near Agaden Reach. They were all exhausted from that journey, and it turned out that for all practical purposes, the journey was only now beginning. They now had farther to go than when they started.

"We are going to need to hurry, then, if we are to get to the Keep before the babies come." Shale passed a look of caution among them all. "We certainly don't want to be traveling when the Mother Confessor gives birth. The Glee are danger enough, but if they ever caught us when the Mother Confessor was in labor, well, I think we all know how bad that would be."

Richard nodded. "I think we all agree on that. Fortunately, we brought plenty of horses with us from Bindamoon. They couldn't make it up here, of course, so we had to leave them down the mountains a ways. They are eating grass and hopefully resting up for the long and difficult ride ahead."

"Are you sure they will still be there?" Kahlan asked.

Richard had no trouble reading the concern in her voice or on her face. He reassured her with a nod. "We made sure they will stay where they are until we get back to them. We left them in a good-size box canyon. There's a stream through it, so they have water, and there is plenty of grass for them to eat. We made a quick fence of sorts with some deadfall to close off the narrow entrance to the canyon. They aren't going anywhere." He smiled at Kahlan. "I brought along a mare that is especially gentle riding for you."

She didn't look to care about that. She was obviously worried about bigger issues than an easy ride. "How far?" She ran her hand over her swollen belly. "We need to be on our way to Aydindril. How long will it take us to reach the horses so we can set off in earnest?"

Richard was probably more impatient than she was, but he was trying not to show his concern over the distance they still had to travel before the babies came so as not to discourage her. He didn't want Kahlan to worry they wouldn't make it in time, but it was a legitimate fear.

He could see that she looked spent from the battle with Shota and the other witches she had fought and killed. He knew she wouldn't give up easily, but he also knew she would be concerned about the twins. Carrying them, added to the difficulty of traveling, would have to wear her out all that much quicker.

He didn't really have an alternate plan if they didn't want to try to make it to Aydindril in time. There was no substitute that could begin to provide the same level of safety. That meant that they had to get there, and they couldn't afford to waste any time.

"You just went through quite the ordeal," he said. "Are you feeling strong enough for a difficult walk down these mountains?"

"I'm fine," she said without hesitation, almost sounding annoyed that he would think of her as fragile. "But I will be a lot finer when we get to Aydindril. Stop worrying about me—I can rest all I want once we get there. Now, though, is not the time for resting. Now is the time for riding. Get us to the horses, would you please?"

"All right," Richard said with a sigh at her determination. "If we push hard, I think we can reach where we left them by dark. It's a good place to camp. I saw wild boars on our way up here. I know where they will be bedding down late in the day. If we're lucky, I can get one with an arrow and we can have a good meal tonight and meat for our journey. We're going to need our strength, and our supplies of travel food are running low."

"Which way?" she asked, eyeing the path back through the gloomy and dangerous swamp, not seeming concerned about the details that worried him.

"I found a way that will keep us from having to go back up the peaks and over the snowpack that you used to get into this place. I saw your tracks," he explained when she looked over at him with a quick frown.

"That would be good. Then what?" she asked.

Richard flicked his hand toward the east. "Once we get back out of this swamp, we need to head east down out of these mountains as quickly as we can to get back to the horses. After that, we ride east."

Kahlan gave him a puzzled look. "Why not northeast? Aydindril is northeast of here. Northeast would be the straightest route."

"This spine of mountains runs northeast all the way up through the Midlands. You're right that it's the straight route, but it would take forever to pick our way through these mountains. Not only that, but we couldn't take horses if we went that way.

"Once we are down and out of these mountains we will head east, cross north of Tamarang to reach the Callisidrin, then we can follow the river up to its headwaters. That will be the flattest traveling, where the horses can make better time. After that, we jump east again between the worst of the mountain ranges over to the Kern River basin. Following that north will take us right to Aydindril and the Keep."

"Sounds simple enough," Shale said.

Kahlan looked over and arched an eyebrow at the sorceress. "Not so simple. Most towns and villages are along rivers. We don't want people to spot us. I really don't want to encounter any more Glee. If one of them hooks my belly with a claw, it's all over."

"Kahlan is right," Richard said. "That means we're going to have to stay close enough to the rivers to make riding easier and faster along relatively flat river valleys but stay far enough away from any of the towns or villages where people could see us ride past. We simply can't afford to let any people spot us before we get to the Keep. That won't be easy, but it's not so impossible."

"We're wasting time," Kahlan said. "By your lady's command, take me away from this dreadful place and get me to your keep, wizard. Our children are asking to be born."

Richard answered with a smile that made her smile in return, and that, more than anything, lit his world. He wanted to hug her and kiss her, but they needed to be on their way, and besides, he didn't want an audience when he finally had the chance.

They quickly wished the witch women safe journeys home after they buried Shota; then they traced their route back out of the swamp. Once into the vast forests of the rugged mountain country, they ascended steep climbs through clefts in the mountains to get through a confined, narrow pass that Richard had found before. It was a difficult climb but, in the end, it turned out to be a lot easier than the frigid way into the Reach by going across the snowpack and then over the windswept, open ledges. The thickly forested cleft in the mountains had steep rises to each side and jumbled rock up the middle, so it sheltered them from the worst of the winds but was hard work that tired their muscles and at least made them warm with the effort.

Once through the pass, they were finally able to start down out of the mountains. The trees were thick, but that meant that the forest floor, so sheltered from the sun, was relatively barren, making travel quick and relatively easy.

Ahead of them lay a long and dangerous journey.

Richard intended to outrun any trouble.

145

As the nine of them rode through a woodland of massive oak trees with low spreading limbs, now bare of leaves, Kahlan worried about the people in Aydindril who had seen them arrive. They had taken out-of-the-way routes and bypassed main thoroughfares. Doing so enabled them to avoid being seen by most people, but they still had unavoidably been spotted by some. There was no telling how many more had looked down a rise, or out a window, or up a street and seen them race through the city. Still, it was only one of her worries, and not nearly the biggest one.

They all knew that being spotted created the danger of the Golden Goddess being able to look through the eyes of those people in her search for Richard and Kahlan, and then she would be able to find them. As soon as she did, there was no doubt in any of their minds that she would send hordes of her kind to finish them before they could reach the safety of the Wizard's Keep. But they were close and would soon be under the protection of the defensive magic of the Keep.

All the way from Agaden Reach, they had traveled as fast as possible and the whole time managed not to be spotted by anyone. It had been a swift and exhausting journey up through the Midlands. She only wished that the original journey from the People's Palace to the Keep had been as swift. Without the interference of the witch's oath, it would have been.

Aydindril, however, was another thing altogether. It was no longer possible to avoid detection.

There were also people out on the road, both on foot and on horseback, as well as in wagons as they went about their business. They were all surprised to see their group ride past. Many of those people waved. Some cheered. Word of the sightings of the Lord Rahl and the Mother Confessor, pregnant no less, would quickly spread throughout the city. By morning it was likely that everyone in Aydindril would know that the Lord Rahl and the pregnant Mother Confessor had finally returned. There would be rejoicing.

But with the Glee sure to attack at any moment, any rejoicing would soon turn to terror. While they would be safe up in the Keep, the people of Aydindril would have no such safety. Had it been possible to take a way in to the Keep without being seen, they would have done it, but there was no such way in. It had been inevitable that they were going to be seen, and even if it had been by only one person, that was enough to bring the Glee.

Kahlan's spirits lifted a little as she at last saw the magnificent Confessors' Palace. Set on an expanse of vibrant green grounds, the white stone of the palace atop a hill seemed to glow in the light of the setting sun. She slowed her horse to momentarily take in the sight. It had been so long since she had seen it that she had come to fear she never would again.

This was the ancestral home of the Confessors. It was where she had been born and where she had grown up. She ached to go straight there. More than anything, she wished the twins could be born there, where she had been born. Some of the same staff she knew growing up likely still lived and worked there. She knew they would be overjoyed to have the children of the Mother Confessor be born there, and to have little feet once more running through the halls. Kahlan wanted to bring life back to that home of the Confessors.

The palace, in addition to being the ancestral home of the Confessors, was also a seat of power for the Midlands. The larger lands of the Midlands had palaces down in the city for their ambassadors and members of the Central Council, which had ruled the collective lands of the Midlands. As the Mother Confessor, the last of a long line, Kahlan had reigned not only over the other Confessors when they were still alive, but, when need be, over the Central Council itself.

It was an authority that the Mother Confessor exerted only when the council could not reach agreement, or when they reached an agreement that she couldn't accept as the best course for the Midlands. Some of the larger lands occasionally manipulated the council to the disadvantage of other, smaller lands. When that happened, the Mother Confessor would intervene, but otherwise she let the council manage the Midlands.

Even so, her authority was such that kings and queens sought the Mother Confessor's advice and counsel. They were well aware that they ultimately answered to her, as did every ruler of every land of the Midlands. The council was the intermediary step to her final authority, and handled most of the mundane, day-to-day affairs. Kahlan used her role to sometimes speak for those in the Midlands who had no voice on the council.

That didn't earn her any friends, but Confessors, and the Mother Confessor in particular, didn't have friends anyway, because everyone greatly feared a Confessor's power. Richard had been the first real friend she'd ever had, the first one not to shy away from her because of that power, the first to stand with her and protect her willingly for the person she was, not because of her ability or status.

The irony was that wizards had always protected Confessors, and Richard was a wizard, although he hadn't known it at the time.

Up on the towering mountain beyond the palace they got their first glimpse of the dark, imposing walls of the Wizard's Keep. While the Central Council ruled the Midlands, and the Mother Confessor had authority over that council, it was the dark, brooding Keep embedded high up in the rocky face of the mountain that was the dark threat backing the word of the Mother Confessor. The Wizard's Keep had provided the wizards who always accompanied Confessors, including the Mother Confessor herself. The Keep, in a sense, was the muscle behind the Mother Confessor's authority. While it hadn't always been that way, during Kahlan's lifetime the wizards at the Keep chose not to use their power in order to rule, preferring instead to let the Central Council rule the lands.

As they rode higher up on the road to the Keep, it offered spectacular views of the city of Aydindril spread out far below. Smoke came from many a chimney, as most places had fires going not just for preparation of food but to ward off the cold. Lamplight glowed in most of the homes and buildings, making the city seem to sparkle in the gathering dusk. People, carts, and wagons filled the streets of the city. The view of the city from the road up to the Keep had always been one of Kahlan's favorite sights.

As they rode silently up the mountain along a series of switchbacks, the road finally emerged from a thick stand of spruce and pine trees before the bridge spanning a chasm that had always seemed to her like the mountain had split open, leaving a yawning abyss.

Beyond the bridge, the Wizard's Keep above them was embedded in the rock of the massive, imposing mountain. The complex of the Keep was vast, and it seemed to be perched menacingly on the side of the mountain, as if ready to pounce on any threat. The Keep was enormous, and its walls of dark granite looked almost like cliff faces rising up before them, as if it were a part of the dark rock of the mountain itself. Above those imposing walls, the Keep was an intricate maze of ramparts, bastions, towers, connecting walkways, spires, and high bridges between sections of the structure.

Wispy clouds drifted past some of the higher spires and towers, making the place seem as though it lived in the clouds.

Out ahead, off across the stone bridge, Kahlan could see the gaping entrance of the arched stone passageway where the road tunneled under the base of the outer Keep wall. The portcullis was up.

Kahlan brought her horse to a stop to take it all in. The site of the Keep seemed to bring her mood to a low point of despair. They had spoken little the last few days, mostly because Kahlan had not been in a mood to talk and everyone seemed to realize it. When they saw her stop, everyone else slowed to a stop as well.

Kahlan turned in her saddle and looked back at Shale. "How long until I give birth?"

The sorceress was ready with an answer. "From my experience, the babies will come any day now. It is difficult to say precisely when, but I don't think it will be longer than three or four days, at most."

"You've been awfully quiet for the last few days," Richard said. "What's wrong?"

Kahlan felt tears well up. Fears she had been keeping to herself wouldn't let her have a moment of peace. Even when she slept, those fears haunted her. And now those fears were about to be realized.

Richard, right beside her, pulled in the reins and rested his wrists on the horn of his saddle. When he glanced back at the others, they waited back where they were.

"Kahlan, what's wrong? I know you and I know that something is bothering you. This should be a joyous time. Our children are about to be born. We have reached the Keep, where they will be safe."

She nodded, too ashamed of her fears to speak. Richard's words only seemed to bring it to the surface, making the tears start to flow all the harder.

Richard leaned over in his saddle to get closer so he could speak privately, assuming it was something she didn't want the others to hear. "Kahlan, what's wrong? You can tell me."

Kahlan couldn't bear to tell him. How could she? These were his children, too, the children of D'Hara, the children the world needed.

Or were they?

"Kahlan, please tell me what's bothering you," he pressed in a whisper.

She couldn't hold it back from him any longer.

"You know what's wrong. Shota said that one of our children will be a monster. She saw into the flow of time. While she got her prophecies wrong in the sense of how they would come about, you know as well as I that in the end they always proved true. She was positive about this one because it was so clear-cut. I want these children so badly, but I'm terrified that one of them is going to be the monster she predicted."

Richard relaxed a bit. "Is that all?"

She wiped a tear from her cheek. "Is that all? It's everything. It's everything we have wanted, it's everything our world needs, and yet one of them is destined to be a monster who will destroy lives."

He smiled a little. "I don't believe in destiny any more than I believed in blindly following prophecy, and neither do you."

"This is not destiny. This is a vision from a witch woman who had seen it in the flow of time. Now that their birth approaches, I can't bear the thought of one of them being that monster that we bring into the world."

Richard took a deep breath and let it out as he considered a bit. "Do you think me a monster?" he finally asked her.

"You?" She frowned at him. "No. What does that have to do with it?"

Richard shrugged. "Darken Rahl was a monster."

"So what?"

"His father, Panis Rahl, was a monster, as was his father, and his father before that. The House of Rahl was a whole line of tyrants. Every Rahl who became a Lord Rahl was a monster and each bred a monster for a son."

"What does that have to do with it?" she said.

"I am the son of a monster. By that logic, I should be a monster as well."

"But you were raised by a good man and so you didn't turn out to be like Darken Rahl."

Richard winked at her. "Exactly."

Unsure, Kahlan squinted at him. "What's your point?"

Richard smiled. "Had Shota looked into her flow of time when I was conceived, what do you suppose she would have seen? Yet another monster in the making. Prophecy, after all, is in many ways merely the essence of potential. Though it would have been possible, I'm not the monster she would have seen. Monsters aren't necessarily bred and born to be monsters. Evil people are mostly created by how they grow up—either by the terrible way they were raised, or by the terrible things they experienced that shaped them into who they turn out to be.

"Our children will grow up to be good people because we will raise them to be good people."

Kahlan stared at him a moment. "Are you so sure of that?"

His smile widened. "Kahlan, if it wasn't true, then I would be a monster the way all of the men in the Rahl line of rule were monsters. But I'm not like them because I was raised differently, by a good man."

She gave him a look from under her brow. "Your brother was a monster."

Richard drew a deep breath. "True enough. But I don't think it was because of birth or that he was predestined to be a monster. I think he was weak and didn't use his head. He made a lot of bad choices. His friends and the people he associated with encouraged those bad choices. In a way, they urged him on to be the evil person he became. But I don't think he was born a monster the way Shota meant."

Kahlan finally smiled over at him as she wiped away the last of her tears. "You always make me feel better when I think things are hopeless. Please don't ever stop making me feel better."

Richard bowed his head to her. "By your command, my lady, it shall be so. Now, can we get you into the Keep so that you can bring our two children into the world?"

Kahlan leaned over and touched his arm. "You are going to be a good father."

At that, they started out again. The rest followed behind.

146

Kahlan rode close beside Richard as they crossed the stone bridge. She felt as if a weight of dread had been lifted from her. She had been secretly terrified that Shota's prediction that one of their children would be a monster would turn out to be true, but she hadn't wanted to burden Richard with her fears. The world had seemed a dark and threatening place. She had felt doomed, without a way out.

Richard had just made the sun come out again. Her spirits had been cheered to the point that dread suddenly turned to expectant joy at the thought of the fast-approaching birth. In the past, Shota's prophecies had always turned out to be true, but in ways that never brought about the kind of doom she had predicted. With this one, like the others, they could work to make sure that things turned out well.

He offered her a smile, reassuring her, but she could see in his gray eyes that he was worried about things other than one of their children being a monster. She knew that, like her, he was worried about the lives of all the people down in the city once the Golden Goddess found out where they were. They both knew that she would use the lives of those people to try to force them to give themselves up.

On the one hand, she felt dreadful that their coming to Aydindril could result in the death of so many people in the city she loved. But on the other hand, if they didn't retreat to the safety of the Keep, then they and their children would end up being hunted and eventually slaughtered. If that happened, then in the long run, everyone in the world would be naked before the onslaught of the Glee and everyone in their world would be hunted to extinction.

That was always the dilemma with hostages, but the end result of giving in was why Kahlan never submitted to hostage negotiations. As cruel as it seemed on the surface, sacrificing hostages was for the greater good.

She hated that such a phrase was what Shota had used, but in this case, it was the cold reality. Giving in to such evil only resulted in more death in the end.

At least at the People's Palace there had been a lot of soldiers of the First File to help protect people. Even so a great many of those people had died. Here, there was no large force like that. There was only Richard, and he couldn't be everywhere at once.

The only solution she could see was that the threat from the Glee had to be ended by force, but she had absolutely no idea how they could accomplish such a thing. The Golden Goddess, after all, was off in another world. Even if they wanted to try to kill her, they had no way to get at her.

Kahlan smiled when Richard looked her way again, feeling better at least about how he had said they would raise their children. What he said made sense.

As they rode over the bridge, she looked down over the edge of the bridge's stone wall at the side. The rock walls below the bridge dropped away seemingly forever. In one place on the far wall of the chasm, a thin stream of water, as usually happened for several days after rain, emerged from a crack in the rock. The water tumbling down turned to mist before it ever reached the bottom far below. There were often clouds floating by below the bridge, but there were none this day.

"It's good to be home," she said to Richard.

He nodded. "It's been a long time, and a long journey."

It seemed too simple a statement for all the effort of finally arriving after deciding to leave the People's Palace and all they had gone through, from Michec to Shota to all the battles with the Glee.

Once across the bridge, they quickened their pace up the road. When they were almost to the opening in the outer Keep wall, and before they went in, Kahlan turned to have a look at the city she had so missed.

When she did, her breath suddenly caught.

Everyone else heard her gasp. They all wheeled their horses around to see what she was seeing.

To their astonishment, there on the bridge where they had been only moments before stood a lone Glee.

"Dear spirits," Kahlan said under her breath.

Everyone else drew their horses close together, both to protect Kahlan and as they prepared for a fight. All their heads swiveled as they frantically scanned the countryside for others, looked for the rest of the Glee about to ambush them before they could get into the safety of the Keep. The Mord-Sith all had their Agiel in their fists. Rikka and Cassia threw a leg over their horses' necks and leaped to the ground, drawing their knives in addition to the Agiel they had in their other hand.

Unlike Shale and the Mord-Sith, who looked ready for the expected battle, Richard merely stared at the single dark figure on the bridge. Kahlan was surprised that he didn't look alarmed. She could see that his posture was relaxed in his saddle as he watched the Glee. Much to Kahlan's surprise, he merely studied the creature, which was just standing there looking back at them.

"Something looks a little different than I remember about the Glee I've seen before," Kahlan finally said when no one else spoke, "or maybe I just never before saw them standing still like that for so long."

Shale frowned back over her shoulder. "What do you mean? Different how?"

"I'm not sure, but I don't really remember them having that slight greenish iridescence across the tops of their heads."

"That's because the others you've seen before don't have that sheen of color." Richard sounded calm and not the least bit worried.

The way he said it made Kahlan think he had seen a Glee like this before.

She frowned over at him. "What are you talking about?"

Just then the Glee did the strangest thing.

It opened its arms out a little to the sides, and turned its claws palm-out, toward them. When it did it spread its arms a little. She saw webbing she had never noticed before between the individual claws of the Glee.

And then it bowed its head.

Kahlan, Shale, and the Mord-Sith stared in astonishment.

Richard let out a sigh. "Bags," he said to himself, but loud enough that Kahlan heard it.

"What in the world could this mean?" she asked him.

Richard finally looked away from the creature and regarded her with an expression that bordered on regret.

"It means I want you all to get into the Keep."

Kahlan's frown tightened. "You know this creature, don't you? I can't imagine how, but you know it."

Staring off at the Glee again, Richard nodded as the Glee stared back at him.

"Get inside," he said. "All of you."

Kahlan grabbed his shirtsleeve in her fist. "Richard, what are you going to do? The twins are due any moment. I need you here. Our children need a father. I don't know what you're thinking, but I can see in your eyes that you are getting one of your crazy ideas."

He finally looked back to her with an iron determination in his raptor gaze. "I need to end this."

She shook her head, as if trying to clear what didn't make sense. "End it? What in the world are you talking about?"

"I'm not sure." He stared off again at the dark creature. "I want you all to get inside. I will be back with you as soon as I can. It may only be a few minutes… but I have a funny feeling it may be longer."

"Longer? What are you talking about? How much longer?" Kahlan quickly glanced around at the others all staring at him before she leaned closer. "What are you going to do?"

Shale was looking apoplectic. The Mord-Sith all looked back and forth between Richard and the creature, unsure if they should go attack it, or stand their ground. A firm look from Richard told them to stay where they were.

Kahlan again grabbed his shirt. "Richard, answer me. What are you going to do?"

He had that look she knew so well. The ferocity of it softened when he turned to her, but it didn't leave entirely.

"I don't know yet, but I suspect that this is a sign that the city is about to be attacked. I have to stop it."

He kissed the ends of his first two fingers, pressed them to her lips, and then pressed them to the twins.

"Richard—"

He gathered up his horse's reins. "I have to see what I can do, or this ordeal will never end, and countless people will die. I am the Lord Rahl, the leader of the D'Haran Empire. It is up to me to protect our people. I intend to do just that. Now get inside. All of you. Shale, I am counting on you to take care of Kahlan when the babies come."

"You mean you will be gone that long?" she asked.

"I don't know, but if I am, I want you to take care of Kahlan when she gives birth."

"Of course, Lord Rahl."

His gaze slid from Shale to the Mord-Sith. "Do as I say. I want you all to get Kahlan into the Keep where she will be safe. Don't delay for anything. Do it right now. The people in there will help you protect her."

"Only if you take Vika with you," Kahlan said.

"It's not his decision to make," Vika told her. "That decision has already been made. You had better do as he asks and get inside the Keep where you will be safe. I promise you, I won't leave Lord Rahl's side."

147

Richard dismounted and handed the reins to Berdine. Nyda took the reins to Vika's horse as she slipped to the ground. He gave the rest of them a commanding gesture to get into the Keep. They all recognized the seriousness of the command. Reluctantly, they all followed his orders and rode off toward the arched opening in the Keep wall. He watched Kahlan, with Mord-Sith surrounding her, ride in under the arch and then inside until he knew she was no longer in danger.

Just before she disappeared inside, she turned back to give him a last, brief look. Finally, she disappeared through the opening in the wall, to be greeted by people he could see waiting inside. He wasn't able to see who they were, but he hoped there were Sisters of Light among them who would be able to protect her. He hoped Chase was still at the Keep. He would certainly protect her.

"Lord Rahl, what are you planning?" Vika asked. "The Mother Confessor said that you have a crazy idea."

Richard nodded as he continued to share a look with the lone Glee. "She isn't wrong."

"So, what is your crazy idea this time?" she asked with a long-suffering sigh.

He flashed her a smile. "I think that Glee wants to talk to us. Let's go find out what it has to say."

"The Glee don't talk. They only come to kill."

"My crazy idea is that I don't think that this one intends us any harm."

She nodded as she started after him. "That is indeed a crazy idea. If you are wrong, and it's a trap?"

"Then we will deal with it."

Together, Richard and Vika walked back down the road toward the bridge, scanning the area for trouble as they went. He looked back over his shoulder, up at those ramparts and crenellations in the walls he could see from such a low perspective, but he didn't see anyone. Kahlan was now safe inside the fortress.

The Glee on the bridge had not moved from where it stood, waiting. Richard continually swept his gaze in every direction, looking for a mass attack, but not actually expecting one. Vika also kept up a sweep of the area, especially the woods, but unlike him, she did expect an attack.

Each time he looked back at the Glee, it hadn't moved. It watched him coming with big, glossy black eyes. Occasionally its third eyelid would blink across the surface to keep it wet.

The creature, with its soft, moist, mottled black skin, hairless head, big glossy eyes, two small holes for a nose, and wicked claws, looked completely alien standing there on the bridge built by men. Glee weren't typically anxious. But given how uneasy this one appeared, he thought it must be here for a reason it felt was important enough to overcome its apprehension.

As Richard slowed to a halt in front of the dark creature, he held his hand back and out to the side a little to let Vika know that he wanted her to stay back out of his way and give him room in case he needed to draw his sword. He really didn't think that was going to be necessary, but as he had learned so often before, it was better to be prepared to act and not need to, than to not be prepared and find out all too suddenly that you should have been ready.

The Glee tipped its head to the side and blinked with its third eyelids, as if studying Richard's face up close for the first time. It was a disconcerting appraisal by such a dangerous creature. At least its lips weren't drawn back to expose its needle-sharp teeth.

"I am called Sang."

Richard blinked in surprise. While it hadn't said the words out loud, and its mouth hadn't moved, Richard could clearly hear the words in his head. It was an unnerving sensation to have a voice talk to him from inside his own head.

Vika gasped. "I heard him talk in my head!"

"We can both hear him," Richard told her under his breath. He looked back at the Glee.

"How is it that I can hear you speak in my head"—he tapped a finger to his temple to show what he meant—"but you make no words that I can hear with my ears?"

Sang cocked his head the other way. *"It is how we communicate. The goddess comes into the minds of your kind in much the same way so that she may look through their eyes to see where you are. She has talked to some of you in the way that I talk to you now, in your mind. In that same way, I can speak into your mind in a way that you understand."*

"Can all of your kind do this?"

"Yes. This is how we communicate with each other. I have tried to speak to others in different worlds in this way, but they could not hear me in their minds. Only you and your kind can hear us speak in this way, as some have heard the goddess."

"Why did you try to speak to those others, in other worlds?" Richard asked.

"For the same reason I speak now to you. But they could not hear me and unlike you, they could be of no help."

Richard didn't like riddles but decided to let it slide for the moment.

"I have seen you before, Sang," he said aloud.

"Yes. I have watched you fight a number of times now."

"Why have you watched me fight but not participated in those battles with the rest of your kind?"

"I am also Glee, but I am not like those who attacked you. I watched because I wanted to learn about you."

Richard found that rather worrisome, but at the same time, it was what he had been beginning to believe.

"What have you learned?"

"I have watched and seen you finally discover how to fight the Glee. It is not easy, and no other has ever been able to learn what you have learned. The Glee are very, very dangerous. But you have grasped the way of fighting them effectively. You understand what I am meaning?"

Richard nodded. "Yes. I have learned that their claws, while deadly when used for ripping and tearing at people, are not really made for fighting. I think they are meant for something else. Even so, those claws are obviously very deadly. I have learned how those who fight us use them, and how to defeat them by using their weaknesses."

Sang cocked his head. *"And what are their weaknesses?"*

"Most of their arm strength is in close range, not when they extend their arms out to slash. Their shoulders and upper arms are not as strong when extended. I have learned the limitations of their movements, and where in those movements they are slowest and more awkward, and thus most vulnerable. The farther they reach, the weaker their ability to use their arms and the more cumbersome their strikes."

Sang nodded. *"Your kind thinks we are deadly, and that is obviously true in most cases, but in reality, you, Lord Rahl, are more deadly by far."*

Richard was somewhat troubled that Sang knew his name and title, but on the other hand, it told him that this individual shared information with others of his kind, which from what he had observed was rather unusual among Glee. This was obviously a thinking, reasoning creature, even if very different from him.

"Is there a point to all of this?" he asked. "A reason you have been watching me?"

Sang tapped his claws together several times, as if to demonstrate something. They made a clacking sound.

"My kind uses our claws to feed. We eat water plants called flutter weed and float weed. We harvest it with our claws. The webs between our claws help us to maneuver in water.

"We also use our claws to eat muscle snails that stick themselves down to rocks and can hold tight. They are at least as big as your hand and have a broad, powerful foot to hold themselves against rocks. They provide us nourishment.

"We must get our sharp claws in under their broad, shallow shells and then pry and pull them off the rocks. We use our teeth—" He drew his lips back to expose his tightly packed, needle-sharp white teeth. *"—to rake the muscle snail's meat from inside the recess of its shell.*

"We also eat other kinds of water plants, delicious varieties of thick, ruffled plants that grow low and tight on rock. We use our teeth to scrape

them from the surface of rocks. It is the only way we are able to collect and eat them. We also eat a variety of other snails and use our claws to extract the meat. Mostly, though, the flutter and float weed and the muscle snail are our staple foods which grow in abundance and what our kind has lived on for as long as any of us knows."

"But something happened, and as a result of that event some of you developed a taste for the flesh of creatures from other worlds?"

Sang let his claws drop back to his sides as he let out a kind of hiss that Richard took for a sigh. He looked somehow remorseful.

"Yes. Some time back, before any of us now living were alive, we were visited by a race from another world. We thought of them as gods. These gods left us a gift. With this gift, we were able to visit other worlds much like they did. In these worlds the Glee visited, they eventually found other things we could eat.

"At first, it was a wondrous device to explore worlds with different kinds of edible plants. In some of these places the Glee found the kind of water weeds and snails that were similar to our favorites and they brought them back for our young."

Richard and Vika shared a look.

"You mean to say you care for your young?" he asked.

"Of course. We love our young. A male and female Glee will together care for and protect her eggs until they hatch. From the time they hatch, the mother and father bring them food until they grow enough to be able to learn to gather food for themselves." Sang cocked his head again. *"Did the goddess tell your kind something different?"*

Richard let out a troubled sigh. "As a matter of fact, we were led to believe that the Glee simply reproduce, somehow, but that you don't experience love and bonding the way we do. From what we were told, it sounded like your kind didn't pair together, and producing young was not a meaningful act."

Sang looked distressed. *"That is not true. When we find a mate, we bond for life."*

Richard hooked his thumbs behind his belt as he stole another quick glance at Vika. "This is not what the goddess led us to believe. She gave us a picture of a cold-blooded race that cared only about collecting other worlds and hunting creatures in those worlds for sport as well as to eat. She made it seem that they were born for this purpose and it was all they cared about. We were told that even if the goddess grew old and died, it was not important because they are all the same and of a like mind and basically interchangeable. She said her death would not matter because there would always be another to take her place."

Sang let out the same kind of hissing sigh as he had before. *"The one who calls herself the Golden Goddess lies as easily as she breathes. She lies in order to strike fear into the hearts of those she intends her followers to hunt. They have developed a taste for the flesh of other creatures, including, most of all, your kind."*

"A taste for people?"

Sang nodded. *"You are the only thinking creatures we know of that are in some ways similar to us. We have so far discovered no others. The other worlds we have discovered have at most lower creatures such as insects and other small creatures without the ability to understand our voice, much like float weed and muscle snails cannot hear our voices.*

"The goddess and her followers find great satisfaction in hunting down, killing, and eating your kind more than any that has been found before in the worlds she collects. She will tell anyone from your world anything that makes it easier for the Glee to succeed in hunting and killing, hoping your kind never learns any of our weaknesses, as you have. Creatures that are terrified don't fight back effectively. That makes them easier to kill.

"The goddess and her followers have come to highly desire the flesh of other creatures more advanced than the muscle snails of our world, and especially after the game of hunting your kind. The hunting has become the purpose of many, and they do not even devour all they catch. The fighters the goddess sends out to other worlds are all males, like me. They bring some of their kills back to feed their females, the young, and the goddess.

"Those of us like me find the idea of eating thinking, reasoning creatures like you to be not only wrong, but abhorrent. Those with the goddess don't care about our objections, and as you have seen, they have embraced violence and they now eat your kind exclusively. They are even willing to use violence against their own kind in order to hold power so that they may continue doing as they wish."

Richard was disturbed to learn how much of what they had been told wasn't true. It changed everything.

"I have noticed that unlike all the rest of the Glee, you have a greenish iridescence to your flesh, especially over the top of your head."

Sang nodded. *"It is because of the flutter and float weed as well as some other plants of our world that we eat. Those plants we prefer to eat have this same shimmering green color. Those who have turned to eating the flesh of creatures in other worlds, especially your kind, no longer eat the food from our world and so they quickly lose this coloring."*

That certainly explained the color Richard noticed on Sang that he hadn't seen on the other Glee. "I'm glad that there are some of you who don't want to eat us. I would much rather cooperate with you and those like you."

"It is the same with the others who side with me. You are the first creatures that I found who will fight back, which, of course, excites those who follow the goddess. And among your kind, you are the most effective at fighting and killing the Glee to stop them. I have been looking for one like you for a very, very long time, hoping all the time that I would find one."

"For what purpose?"

"To help us kill the goddess, of course."

"Of course," Richard said.

148

"*The Golden Goddess is smart, cunning, and knows how to win followers. She prizes the power she has. She craves the loyalty of her followers and is pleased that they would do anything for her. They would die for her. As you know so well, many have already died for her. As we speak, many more are preparing to come here and slaughter all the people living in this place.*

"*Those like me, who believe in consuming what our beautiful, wonderful world has to offer in abundance, have tried many things to make the others see that what they are doing is wrong. But they see us as simply weak and too timid for the dangerous hunts of your kind.*

"*More than for the food, they enjoy their power over your kind, much as the goddess herself enjoys her power over her followers. After trying everything to reason with the goddess and her followers, we now realize that there is no way to turn them back from their new ways.*

"*If they are not stopped, she will see to it that the Glee come to roam this world and hunt your kind until there are none of you left. They think of eliminating your species as a goal and as an accomplishment. Finding new worlds for her followers to hunt, especially this one, gives the goddess power over them.*"

Richard stared into the large, glossy black eyes. "So why, exactly, are you are telling me all of this?"

"*Because for your kind to survive, they must be stopped. For my kind to survive, they must be stopped.*

"*To stop them, the Golden Goddess must be killed. There is no other way.*"

Richard leaned back a little as he tried to judge the truthfulness of Sang's words. It was possible, after all, that there was a power struggle in Sang's world and he was just as bloodthirsty as the goddess, and simply wanted to win Richard's sympathy in order to help eliminate his opposition for power.

Richard supposed that it was even possible that Sang was trying to win Richard's trust in order to eliminate him for the goddess.

On the other hand, what Sang was saying did seem to ring true, and if it was true, this could be the key to ending the threat that Richard hadn't previously thought was possible. More than that, not ending the threat could very well result in the end of everyone.

"We were told that this goddess is merely one of your kind that takes the position of goddess, as others before her, and that if she is killed, another will simply take her place, and then another, and so on, so that killing her is not a solution to stop this madness."

Sang didn't hesitate to answer. *"It is true that if she is killed, her followers may not stop simply because she is killed. Hunting and killing has given them a taste for power, so another leader will likely emerge to take her place. If killing her would stop this war with other worlds and what she is doing to her own kind, we would have tried to kill her ourselves if we could.*

"But she is very powerful, with many who believe in her and do what she tells them. She teaches them that through eating the flesh of intelligent beings, like your kind, they will gain the strength and wisdom of those they eat, making them superior beings. Unlike eating our traditional food of float weed and muscle snails, they find a thrill in the danger involved. It gives some of them the chance to rise to be champions of the kills. Champions gain the favor of the goddess. That means that if she is killed, another would very likely want to take her place.

"Those with me could never succeed in stopping them because they have learned to fight, and they are vicious at it. Those who believe like me that what they do is wrong are not fighters and we don't have their fighting skills.

"But on the other hand, if she is killed and if her followers are dealt a severe enough blow with many in their ranks killed on their home ground, they may then for the first time fear for their lives, fear for their world, fear for their offspring, and they may go back to the way we have traditionally lived for as long as any of us knows."

Richard studied Sang's emotionless face for a moment. "It's also possible that even if she and a number of her followers are killed, they could still hold to their belief in collecting and hunting other worlds, gather followers and revert to this savage life."

Sang nodded. *"Yes, this is true, and this is why, besides killing the goddess and enough of her followers as only you would be able to do, there is another important aspect to what must be done."*

Richard had thought there had to be more to it. "And what would that additional thing be that would need to be done?"

"The device that allows them to go to other worlds must be destroyed once and for all. If they are denied any possibility of ever hunting other worlds, they could not win over followers, and without followers—believers—they could not continue."

Richard felt goose bumps ripple up his arms to the nape of his neck. He didn't like the idea of being an assassin. He remembered telling Zedd once that if he took the sword, he would not be an assassin. Zedd had told him that he could be whatever he wanted to be. Not only the world, but he himself had changed since he'd taken the sword. He now understood that there were times when it was necessary to stop a deadly threat and that killing was often the only way to do that. The difference between him and those he had to stop, like the goddess and the Glee, was that they killed because they wanted to; he killed because it was the only way to survive and prevent killing from continuing.

"I presume you are here, then, to ask me to somehow return to your world and kill the goddess for you along with enough of her followers to discourage them."

Sang bowed his head. *"Yes. You have it exactly right."*

"Let's just say for the sake of argument that I agreed. So then, if I went to your world and could accomplish such a thing for you, you would then send us back here and you would then destroy the device so it could never be used again?"

"No," Sang said with a sorrowful shake of his head. *"You must also destroy the device with that weapon you carry."*

"How could I possibly destroy a device that I don't even understand?"

"*We cannot destroy the device because there is nothing in my home world that would be powerful enough to harm it.*" With a claw, Sang gestured to Richard's left hip. "*I have seen you use that weapon. I have seen it do things that I find hard to believe. I have seen it do things that nothing else could do. We do not have anything like it. I believe it is the only weapon that could destroy the device.*"

Richard was feeling a rising sense of dread. "If I were to agree to come to your world and I succeeded in defeating the Golden Goddess and her followers, and then destroyed this device that allows them to go to other worlds, how could I come home, to my world?"

Sang reluctantly shook his head again. "*There would be no way. With the device destroyed, you would not be able to return to your world.*"

149

Richard swallowed, trying to moisten his suddenly dry mouth, not entirely sure he had heard Sang correctly.

"You're saying that I could never return to my world? Never? There would be no way for me to return?"

Sang nodded sorrowfully. *"Yes. I am sorry. Once you destroy the device, you would not be able to return here. I am sorry, but it is the only way."*

Richard shook his head, not wanting to believe that he would have to stay there, in Sang's world.

"I don't know if I could leave my world for yours to fight for those on your side who can't—or won't—do it themselves, and then, even if I succeed, never be able to return home to my mate, my offspring, my people, and my world. That is too much to ask."

"I am sorry, but there is no other way," Sang said. *"But it would not simply be that you fight for those like me, it would be for the survival of those in your world as well."*

Richard blinked in disbelief. "I don't see how I could live in your world."

"I can tell you that of all the worlds the goddess has collected, none can begin to match the beauty of my own home world, so you would at least have that. Your world, here, is a harsh, dry place. My world is lush and warm and beautiful beyond anything you have ever seen before."

Richard had to remind himself to hold back his rising anger. This wasn't personal. Sang was trying to find a way to end the bloodshed, even if the solution he had come up with was unacceptable.

"I don't care how beautiful it is, it's not my home. Everyone I love is here, in this world."

Sang cocked his head to the side. *"But this is such a dry place. I don't know how you are even able to survive here. We have much trouble coming here because of how dry it is. We must put the jelly of the scrum plant on ourselves to help keep our skin moist while we are here, or it would dry out and crack. Then we would bleed, and we would die."*

That explained the gelatinous masses that Richard had seen slide off of them when the Glee first arrived, as well as the wet appearance of their skin.

"Sang, I'm not sure I could ever agree to such a thing—to leave everything I have here and everyone I love, never to return. As you may know, my own offspring are about to come into the world."

"I do know about the imminent arrival of your offspring. Please believe me when I say that I sympathize with your reluctance," Sang said, sounding sincere. *"If the situation were reversed, I don't know that I could stand to live in your world, never to return to mine."* He gestured at Vika. *"But you would have this female with you, at least."*

"That is not enough, nor is it a solution." Richard gestured up to the Keep. "My mate is there."

"I am sorry, but while I do admit to wanting my kind to return to their ways and no longer be able to raid other worlds, the more important thing I am telling you is that this is the only way if you wish your kind here in this world to survive.

"As we speak, the Golden Goddess is right now preparing to send the largest number of Glee yet to come here to kill all the people of that place down the mountain. She wants none left alive to punish you for going into that place of magic to hide, rather than surrender. When that is finished, they will then be sent to other places in your world to hunt the people there until there are no more of your kind. This will not be attacks such as you have seen and fought against before. This will be mass attacks in many different places at the same time.

"The goddess knows of and fears your magic, and she also knows that when you retreat into this place of magic, here above us, she will not be able to reach out and take you, your mate, or your unborn children. But she also knows that with you hiding in there and not able to fight, or at least not able to fight in all the places of your world at once, there will be virtually

no effective opposition to her and her forces. There will be the sport of some opposition of course, but the Glee enjoy some resistance. People in places all over your world will not be able to withstand the attacks. The resistance they put up will not be enough for your kind to survive.

"The goddess knows that your magic protects the magic of this world. If your offspring live, their magic will do the same.

"Yet, as you hide and protect them in this place, she will see that vulnerability and exploit it. With you stuck in there protecting your mate and offspring, it gives her and her followers an opening to come here to this world in mass to hunt and devour your kind until there are none left other than you and those few with you in this fortress of magic.

"Although you may in that way be able to preserve magic in your world, and the few people inside there with you, there will be no people left out in the rest of the world. They will all be dead. Your world will be a dead place."

Richard looked over at Vika. When she realized the full extent of what was in store for their world, some of the color had left her face. What was coming was no less than the cataclysmic end of everyone and everything.

Sang was right; even if they stayed and fought, they couldn't fight in every city, town, and village all over the world at the same time. He might be wildly successful against the Glee he faced, but he was only one man in one place and could not face nearly all of them.

"I am afraid that I am not offering you the ability to return to this place and the people you love," Sang said. *"Once you destroy the device, it will not be possible for you to return to your home. But what I am offering you is the possibility of destroying the threat that otherwise will hunt down and slaughter everyone in your world. You have seen what they have already done, how many they have slaughtered, and what they are capable of. They know no mercy and will grant none.*

"They will not stop unless you come with me and stop them, and then destroy the device to prevent them from ever again coming to this world. You can only do those things in my world.

"What I am offering you is the possibility of saving the lives of those you

love and everyone else in your world. I will not deceive you; that is all I am able to offer.

"I understand the sacrifice you will be making, but you must decide now because they will be coming soon and if you don't come with me and stop them there, it will be too late."

150

Richard stood unmoving, terrified at the thought of never being able to see Kahlan again. She was his world. He would never see their children, never be able to teach them and watch them grow. Never see them have the life he and Kahlan had fought so hard for them to have.

He would never see Kahlan's special smile and her beautiful green eyes again.

Richard had never been so frozen in fear and uncertainty before.

Through that fear, though, he realized that if he didn't do this, it would be the end of his world and the end of Kahlan and their children's world. If he didn't take this chance, how could he ever look Kahlan in the eye again once she knew he might have been able to stop the slaughter of everyone in their world, and he hadn't tried?

Richard looked over at Vika. "What do you think?"

She arched an eyebrow. "You are the Lord Rahl. You care about everyone in this world or you would not have sacrificed everything you did to win freedom for everyone. You fought those long wars for those who depend on you, and because you care that they have a life.

"I know you are going, and I know that nothing I could say would stop you. So why are you even asking me?

"But I am going with you and that is final. I will fight beside you in the struggle you face there, in that world, no less than I have in this world."

Richard swallowed as he nodded. She was right, of course. She would also be sacrificing everything she knew and the possibility of what the future might bring for her.

He had only entertained the idea of not going as he desperately tried to think of another solution, but deep down inside, just as Vika said, he knew that he had no choice. This was the only way of ending the threat. He had to go, no matter what it cost him, personally.

The lives of everyone in the D'Haran Empire were his responsibility. Not only that, but he cared that the people of his world could live their lives as they wished and in peace. The Grace told the story of each of their lives and it needed to live on. It was not simply a matter of being the Lord Rahl and it being his responsibility. He sincerely wanted people to be able to live their lives as they wanted, to achieve their hopes and dreams. If he didn't do this, they would know only terror and death.

He was still filled with questions, though. Some, he knew, had no answer, but at least some did.

"How did you get here from your world? You had to have used this device you spoke of, but isn't it guarded by the goddess or her followers? That device is their way to raid other worlds."

"The device is in a high place that is very dry," Sang said. *"No one guards it because no one uses it except the goddess and her followers. Only they wish to go to other worlds, so there is no reason to endure such a dry place except when they use the device. They know that it cannot be destroyed, so there is no reason that they would need to guard it.*

"Other than her followers, I am the only one who has used it. I went to other worlds they raided to try to find help but I could find none until I saw you fight. I needed to use the device to come here to observe you and see if I thought you could possibly be the one to help stop this. I finally came to know that you are the one."

"So then you simply went up to where it is and used the device to come here?"

"Yes."

As Richard considered it, he thought that it made sense. "But the device is not here, in this world, or any of the worlds the goddess collects for hunting grounds. So how do you return to your world without the device to send you back?"

"It is hard to explain."

"Do your best."

"You have seen my kind when they fear being killed and they simply vanish?" Sang asked.

"Yes. They sort of turn all scribbly and then they disappear. We all assume they are returning to their own world."

Sang nodded. *"They were. When the device sends us somewhere, it creates a link to our minds. So, when I desire, because I am connected to it through my mind, the device knows my thought that I want to return, and it pulls me back. It does the same with all the Glee you have seen vanish."*

Richard grasped the general idea but couldn't imagine how it could work. It sounded like magic of some kind, a very powerful, advanced, and incomprehensible magic.

As if he could see that Richard was having trouble understanding it, Sang idly clacked his claws as he tried to think of a better way to explain it. *"The way to think of it is that we become attached to the device by a lifeline that it creates when it sends us to another world. Imagine if you went in dangerous water, and you suddenly wanted to go back to shore. When you called out, others pulled you back to shore by that lifeline. In much that way, when we want to go home, the device pulls us back by that lifeline."*

Richard nodded as he considered, still not entirely satisfied. "What you expect of me will not be so easy. If I agreed to come to your world with you, would those who believe as you do fight with me to defeat the goddess and her kind?"

Sang stared at him a long moment. *"I cannot say for sure. They are not fighters."*

"This is about their world and their way of life," Richard pointed out with a rising sense of angry frustration.

Sang nodded. *"You are a great leader in your world. Leaders become leaders because they are able to convince others to follow them. The goddess is like this. Although those with me are not fighters, I believe that they might be willing to follow you. At the very least, they can help you in many ways, such as getting you to the goddess and her followers."*

"I need a lot more than having them point me in the right direction." Richard drummed his fingers on the handle of his sword as he considered. "I think I can understand what you say about how you are able to go back. But how could Vika and I go there, too? We don't have that link, that lifeline as you called it, for the device to use to pull us there."

"That is the easy part. When a number of injured Glee returned, they confirmed a theory many of us have. One time when they attacked your people, one of the women with you used magic to create snakes. Many of those snakes bit the Glee, and while we do not fear the snakes in our world, these snakes from your world were killing those Glee with venom. The snakes, once they bit into a Glee, would not let go. The Glee being bitten panicked, called on their lifeline, and the device pulled them back. All they needed to do was to merely think to return, and the device that had sent them was able to know that wish, and it snatched them back to our world."

"What about this theory you had?"

"The important part is that when they returned, the snakes were still holding on tight to them. That confirmed our theory that if I hold on to something from this world, it will return with me. I myself tested this by holding a rock when I returned, and it came to my world with me. This was also confirmed when some of the Glee returned with parts of your people for the Golden Goddess and their offspring to eat. Those body parts were also used to convince others to join with her."

Richard remembered quite vividly how the Glee down in the bowels of the People's Palace had dismembered many of the bodies.

"You are saying, then, that we would hold on to you and we would go there with you to your world when you return? You think it is really that simple?"

Sang gave him a single nod. *"Yes."*

Richard considered for a moment. He couldn't imagine a device with such power, but then, on the other hand, he had sent those who didn't want to live with magic, including his half sister, to another world without magic. He also had used a device that created a star shift and sent their entire world to another place in the sky. He had seen devices, such as the boxes of Orden and the omen machine, that had unimaginable power, power over the world of life and the world of the dead, so he supposed that even if he hadn't seen the device the

Glee had, he knew that such powerful devices existed. He didn't really know where most of those devices came from, or who could have made them. For all he knew, it might as well be these same gods.

He looked over at Vika. She simply shrugged.

"If I were to agree to this crazy idea, what would we have to do? Simply hold on to you and we would be pulled back with you?"

"More than that," Sang said as he stared at Richard for a long moment with a haunted look in his big black eyes. *"It is more than simply being pulled back by a lifeline. There is more to it."*

"What do you mean?"

"We must go into darkness."

151

Richard's brow tightened. "Into darkness?"

Sang nodded again. *"I am afraid that it is the only way."*

"I don't understand. What do you mean we have to go into darkness?"

Sang stared off again with a haunted look. He seemed to be looking again into that place that obviously frightened him.

"That is the only way I can say it for you," he finally told them as he looked first at Vika and then at Richard. *"There is no way I can explain such a thing in a way that would make you truly understand. The only way I can say it is that we must go into darkness. It is what happens when we use the device. Once you have done it, you will understand. You will know what those words mean. If you have not done it, then there is no way for me to make you understand."*

"Into darkness," Richard said as he stared at Sang.

Sang nodded. *"Into darkness. That is really the only way I can begin to describe it, yet the words are so hollow. Into darkness is something such as you have never experienced before. It seems to consume you. It is falling into darkness, and it is... terrifying. You think that it will never end, that it never could end. Each time I go into darkness, I fear that this is the time it will not end, and I will forever be in that place of darkness."*

Richard wondered if it was anything like the underworld.

"So," Richard finally asked, "is there a risk that we would be lost there, in that darkness? Especially since we aren't attached to the device by this lifeline?"

The Glee bowed. *"To find what you seek, you must sometimes go into the darkness, even though there is always the risk that you will become lost."*

Richard thought that was a pretty vague philosophical answer. It didn't really tell him anything. He shared a look with Vika. He had of course been to the world of the dead. For that matter, he had actually *been* dead and then managed to return. In a way, he had been pulled back by his connection to those still living. That was a place of eternal darkness. A lifeline of sorts had pulled him back.

He couldn't imagine any place or experience that could be darker than that, but he got the impression from what Sang said that this place might be darker even than the world of the dead. Although he didn't think that Sang had ever been to the underworld to judge the difference.

Vika had been to the cusp of that world. She had looked into the dark world of the dead. He could see by the haunted look in her eyes that she was remembering that experience.

"The longer you think about it," Sang said, *"the greater the risk grows that the others will go to the device in order to come here before they can be stopped. If we delay too long, we risk arriving as they come up to the device, and then you would have to battle them when you are disoriented from having just come out of darkness and into my world. That would not be good. All three of us could be killed before we are able even to run."*

Richard knew Sang was right. To have the element of surprise, they needed to get there and meet with those who were on his side first to come up with a plan. The longer he considered, the greater the risk grew that the goddess and her horde would arrive in Aydindril first.

Plus, he had no idea how confused he would be upon arriving in that world. He knew that when he came back to the world of life after being in the underworld, it was difficult to again get his bearings. Light and colors and sounds were all overwhelming at first.

But this sounded somehow worse. He found himself immobilized with fear. Not with fear of going into darkness, although if he knew exactly what that meant maybe he would fear it more, but with fear of leaving everyone he loved forever.

It was fear of never again being with Kahlan.

He just didn't know if he could do such a thing.

It would be a living suicide.

"If you say no," Sang said, *"I would not blame you. I don't know that I could come here to your world and never be able to go home. But if you are*

willing to do this to have a chance to save the people of your world, then the time is now upon us when we must act."

Richard steeled himself. He hooked his bow over one shoulder and his pack over the other. Vika hoisted her pack up over one shoulder.

Finally, Richard reached out with his left hand and put it firmly on Sang's right shoulder. His skin was cool, soft, and moist, more like the skin of a salamander than that of a person. He looked over at Vika. When their eyes met, each of them placed a hand on the other's shoulder; then she put her right hand on Sang's left shoulder.

Sang reached up and laid a claw over each of their shoulders. Once he had, they were all locked together into a circle of three—an important component of the Law of Nines, Richard reminded himself. He hoped that added bit of magic would help him and Vika survive going into darkness.

"Do it," Richard said. "Call your lifeline."

152

Almost as soon as he said it, he thought of Kahlan and wished he could call his words back. But at the same time he knew he had to be strong if Kahlan and everyone else in his world were to have a chance to live free of the Glee. Besides, even as he had the thought, it was already too late.

Everything all around him—the stone bridge, the forest, the Wizard's Keep above them and the city of Aydindril below—all started to look scribbly.

Only Vika and Sang seemed solid. The air itself had streaks of empty darkness slashing through it, as if the fabric of the world of life were shredded apart. The whole world around them was rapidly dissolving into scribbles as holes tore open into voids in the very reality of existence.

Those voids suddenly expanded explosively.

All light, all sound, and everything else that made up the world around him seemed to be sucked out of existence, ripped away, leaving a universe of nothingness. Not even Sang and Vika were there with him.

He was totally alone as he was sucked into that darkness.

It felt in a way like tripping in the darkest night and tumbling off a cliff.

Richard felt himself falling without end.

He kept expecting to hit the bottom, or to hit something. He knew he couldn't fall this long without soon slamming into something. His muscles tensed and his nerves burned with the agonizing expectation of that sudden, bone-shattering impact.

It was terrifying. An eternity of fear was compressed into every second that he felt himself helplessly falling into darkness.

That fear of hitting the bottom—or of falling forever—became everything.

Richard worked at talking himself out of the panic that was clawing at his emotions. He tried to see his hand but couldn't. He tried to touch it to his face, but he felt nothing, either from his hand or his face. He felt nothing at all.

He put all his effort into focusing on reasoning out what was happening. As he did, he realized that he wasn't really falling. Once he concentrated and tried to make sense of what he was feeling, or rather not feeling, he became aware that there was no down, no up, no hot, no cold, no light, and actually no sensation of any kind. It was complete and total suspension of all sensation. There was nothing other than his own, free-floating thoughts.

He couldn't feel anything that made him feel alive. He couldn't feel his heartbeat or his breathing or anything that made him feel that he existed at all anymore. In fact, it felt as if he didn't exist, as if he were merely thinking that he had once existed. It was even becoming hard to remember his world.

Rather than let himself be pulled under by the overwhelming emotion of feeling that he no longer existed, and since he had absolutely no control over what was happening, he let himself relax as he tried not to think.

He lost track of how long it had been, and as he did, it began to feel like something he was all too familiar with: the eternity of the underworld. That place, too, was darker than dark, and it, too, went on forever.

But this was a different kind of darkness. Not only was it a physical darkness, it was also a kind of inner darkness. The totality of it was different from the underworld. This was not a sense of being in the world of the dead, but a void of existence itself. The only thing that seemed to exist was his thoughts.

In the underworld there had at least been constellations of souls and he had been able to will his soul to travel through them. Here, there was nothing to travel through and he was not able to will himself to go anywhere. There was no "there" within this darkness.

Suddenly, it ended.

Existence imploded in on him from all sides.

He felt his own weight, and with that, solid ground under his feet.

He opened his eyes and as scribbles all around him were just vanishing, he saw a strange world of desolation beneath a heavily clouded sky. All the clouds were different shades of dark red, darker and thicker the lower they were. Ruddy rock rose up in towering, otherworldly formations, seemingly shaped by the hot, moist wind that swirled around them. The muddy-reddish clouds that rolled by low overhead looked almost like smoke.

Everything in this world was some shade of sullen red. Richard felt like he was looking out through a piece of red glass that tinted everything.

It made him wonder if his eyes or even his brain had somehow been damaged by the journey from his world and maybe they weren't working properly, and as a result he could now see things only in shades of red.

He breathed in deeply. The air was damp and warm. So damp that in comparison to his own world it was heavy, humid, and uncomfortable. It felt almost thick. He could see why Sang said that his world was a dry world. This was an oppressively clammy, sticky, and moist world. He already longed for dryness.

They were standing in an area of sand that reminded him very much of the area of white sand in the Garden of Life in the People's Palace. Although, the sand here looked white only in that it was less red than everything else.

With all the smooth, towering rock formations, it felt almost like an eerie cathedral of stone sculpted by wind and weather. That muggy wind moaned as it moved through the strange, smoothly curved surfaces of the rock.

Vika was still holding his shoulder on one side and Sang on the other. Their arms were all still locked together. It had seemed he was totally alone once he went into darkness, but that wasn't true. The other two had always been there with him, he just hadn't been aware of them.

He finally released Vika's shoulder, and she his as they straightened. He could tell by the look on her face that she had experienced the same thing he had coming to this brooding, reddish, windswept world. He let his hand drop away from Sang.

He leaned toward Vika and whispered, "What colors do you see?"

She looked around. "Everything looks red. At least my outfit fits right in."

Richard nodded. "That it does."

As he looked around, he could see from the clouds between the reddish rock formations that they were someplace high. Over the edge, down below them, the ground was obscured by the rolling, roiling clouds drifting swiftly by the high place where they were.

"Come," Sang said to them. *"We must get away from this dry place before the others come."*

He turned and made his way between some of the surrounding rock formations. They were striated in layers of different colors of dark brownish reds and looked like the wind had eroded the soft rock, making smooth, round depressions and curving edges. It was disorienting to look at.

Richard could see by the clouds down lower that they were high up in some kind of desolate, mountainous terrain. There was absolutely no vegetation. He remembered Sang saying that it was a dry place. The wind carried a lot of moisture and made a ghostly moaning sound through the strangely shaped rock formations. Apparently, the air, as damp as it was, was not damp enough for the Glee.

Trying to focus his eyes in this reddish world was giving him a headache. The sand he and Vika were on was the least red thing he could see.

"This is my home world," Sang said as he waved an arm, urging them on, *"the home world of the Glee. We have arrived safely. Now we need to get down out of this place."*

153

"Where is the device?" Richard asked, grabbing Sang by his arm before he could leave. "Is that it?"

Sang stopped and looked across the sand to what Richard was pointing at: something that definitely did not belong in this strange, windblown landscape of organic shapes.

There, across the way on the edge of the sand, stood a square piece of stone, each side about the length of his arm from his shoulder to his fingertips. It wasn't tall. It wouldn't quite come up to his rib cage. The top was slanted, so that if you stood before the stone at the edge of the sand on the other side, you would have been able to have a good look at that slanted top, but Richard couldn't see it from where he was.

The stone looked smooth, but not smooth in the same way the sculpted rock all around them was smooth. This thing was absolutely square and straight on all sides. And while it was smooth, it was not polished like so much of the stone in palaces.

With everything some shade of red it was hard to tell what color it might actually be, but Richard thought it would be dull gray in his own world. There were markings all over the stone. He was too far away to know what kinds of markings they were, but he could see that they covered the entire stone.

Richard wondered if he should draw his sword and destroy the device before the goddess could send more Glee to his world.

As if reading his thoughts, Sang was gesturing urgently. *"Hurry. We must get away from this place for now and get to those who side with me, against the goddess. I told them about you and said that I was going to see if I could get you to come back with me. They will be waiting."*

Richard and Vika followed Sang as he rushed off between the labyrinth of smooth, flowing shapes of the towering rocks surrounding the white sand. Once they were through the meandering gaps in the rock walls, the descent rapidly became steep. There was a path of sorts between the standing forest of rocks, at times with crude steps cut into the soft rock.

Below them, Richard could see a thick blanket of clouds covering the ground far into the distance.

As they moved down from the place with the device that sat at the edge of the area of sand, they gradually descended into that dark reddish cloud. As the visibility grew less and less, it was similar to moving down into clouds below high places in the mountains in Richard's world, and having those clouds turn to a dense fog once you were inside them. It was the same here, except the fog was a dirty reddish color.

The farther down they went, the wetter the air became with mist. At some point, the mist turned to drizzle. Even before the drizzle, the heat and humidity had Richard's shirt soaking wet.

Vika unbuckled some leather straps so that she could open her outfit at the neck. This was definitely not a place to be wearing leather, although the red fit right in. In fact, the red leather stood out brightly in the murky red world.

Sang looked relieved when they finally got into the heavier drizzle. He used his wrists to rub the water collecting on his arms around on his body, seeming to luxuriate in the wetness that he had missed for so long. He looked back at them and drew his lips back to show his teeth.

Vika glanced at Richard, wondering what it could mean.

"I think he is showing us a smile," he whispered to her.

She gave him a look of silent incredulity.

If it really was a smile, it was about as grotesque a smile as he had ever seen.

After about a couple hours of moving quickly down slopes of loose scree that slid out from underfoot, over ledges and down through canyons of towering rock walls, and then over yet more rock, but this time harder and more jagged, they emerged from the bottom of the cloud cover into a strange, wet-looking world. The ground for as far as Richard could see was relatively flat. The only mountainous area was behind them, as was the one they had just climbed down from out of the clouds. Haze and drizzle made the visibility toward the horizon poor, but he didn't see any hills or mountains off that way.

There was scattered, low vegetation among open swampy areas, and there were a lot of rather tall plants that resembled lush ferns. Mostly roundish rocks, most small, covered much of the ground where there wasn't the water or areas of the low vegetation. Among those small rocks were a few smooth, round rocks no bigger than about the right size to sit on. The rocks covered most of the dry areas above the water. In fact, they littered the ground endlessly. Some of the expanses of water in the distance looked larger, but most of the water nearby was in patchy areas much like the swamps he had seen before, but without the trees.

In the distance were peculiar trees with long, crooked, bare trunks. High up each tree had a single, dense clump of leaves. Widely spaced here and there, the trees seemed to march across the landscape beneath the cloudy red sky. They were the strangest-looking trees Richard had ever seen. None, though, were very close.

Flocks of birds moved through the air like current in a raging river. As some swept down closer, he could see that they weren't actually birds. They were large bats flying in colonies.

As they reached the bottom of the climb, Sang walked right into the first body of water he could get to until it was up to his neck. Richard could see several snakes writhing just below the surface of the water. Sang stretched out and swam for a bit, as if to refresh himself.

"Sang! There are snakes in the water!" Vika called out in alarm.

Sang kept swimming for a moment before turning back to them. *Don't worry. The snakes are friendly.*

"Friendly? What if they bite you?" she asked.

They eat small insects. They don't bite us and they do not have venom, like the snakes in your world. The only animals that sometimes cause harm to us are the boars. They are big and mean, and sometimes even kill Glee.

"Boars?" Richard asked. "You mean you have wild boars?"

"They live in the muddy places." Sang gestured off beyond the immediate swampy water. *"But sometimes they attack us. They are dangerous. They are big with tough hides our claws can't cut through and have sharp tusks, bigger than our claws. We must always watch for wild boars when we are not in the water. They like the mud, but they don't go near the water."*

He then busied himself at the edge of the water, dredging up water plants with round nodules dotting their entire length. They were a sickly green color, with a slight iridescence to them. When he had an armful, he flopped them over on the rocks.

"Float weed," he told them.

As soon as he was free of his load of float weed, he started using his claws to pry at a large, flat snail stuck tight to a rock at the waterline.

"This is a muscle snail," he announced as he worked at prying it away from the rock. *"I want you to be able to try our delicious food."*

Richard thought the place smelled rather rank, like most any swamp he had been in; not as bad as some, worse than others. Vika looked around at the strange and forbidding reddish desolation, then looked over at him and spoke in a low voice that Sang wouldn't hear.

"He's right. This place is an absolute paradise."

Richard half huffed a laugh in answer.

"Sang," he said, "we're not hungry right now. More importantly, we don't have time for this. We need to stop the goddess before she sends her hordes to my world to kill people. You said that there were those of your kind who wanted to see me if I returned with you."

Sang blinked up at him, then walked up onto the rocks. The water sluiced off him as he emerged from the swampy water, some of the string algae draped over a shoulder.

"Yes, you are right. My apologies. I was just so happy to be home that I wasn't thinking. I was eager to show you some of the wonderful things about my world, so that you would not be so afraid that you must remain here."

"Where are the others?" Richard asked, getting right down to business as he scanned the other swampy areas. They were dark, and it would be hard to see any Glee if they were in the water. "We need to talk to those who believe as you."

Sang stretched up on his webbed toes and peered into the distance. He pointed with a claw.

"There are some of them over there, on those rocks, harvesting muscle snails. I will go talk to them and ask them to gather the others right away."

"Good," Richard said, as he took Vika's arm and guided her up onto some of the rocks that were a bit flatter and easier to stand on without their ankles twisting.

In the distance, he could just make out the dark shapes of other Glee near the edge of some of the swampy areas. They were hauling up float weed. In other places he saw a few Glee swimming through larger bodies of water. They were so graceful in the water that they hardly disturbed the surface.

Richard was beginning to feel frustrated and annoyed. He had come to stop the Golden Goddess from sending the Glee to slaughter the people in his world. He and Vika had given up their futures—their lives—in order to accomplish that vital mission.

He hadn't known that he was going to end up playing mother hen trying to gather up groups of distracted Glee.

154

Sang met with Glee that were close by. They kept staring over at Richard and Vika. He then went off to talk to others. A crowd of Glee began to come over, gathering around Richard and Vika. The way they blinked as they leaned toward him and stared, they were making him feel like some kind of curious specimen.

By the time Sang returned with yet more of the Glee, a crowd of large black heads had spread out before him. They watched him, looking like maybe they expected he might fly, or breathe out flames or something. As they all crowded in around him, they made a kind of low hiss as they looked around at each other, as if mumbling, but he didn't hear any words in his head. Richard thought they must be talking to each other and they chose not to let the words come into his mind.

Richard and Vika shared a look, not knowing what to expect.

Sang finally stepped through the gathering of tall, black creatures. He held his claws in tight to his stomach so as not to accidentally catch on them, and they did the same as they allowed him to pass. Sang turned to the Glee assembled before them and held out a claw toward Richard and Vika as he waited for all those gathered to fall silent and pay attention.

Richard watched all the Glee, still wary. He was trusting Sang's word that they wanted his help, and that this wasn't some trick to get him away from his own people so they could eliminate him. He didn't really think that was the case, but he studied all the Glee before him, one at a time, looking at each face for any hint of trouble.

"*These are the ones I spoke of,*" Sang finally announced. "*This is Lord Rahl with the weapon he carries on his hip, and the female is Vika, one of*

*his warriors. Unlike us, their females fight alongside the males, and I can tell
you, from having watched them fight, that this female is deadly.*

*"They both have given up their lives and those they care for, given up any
hope of ever returning to their world, in order to come here to finally stop the
Golden Goddess and her followers. Lord Rahl has even given up caring for
his new offspring not yet come into the world in order to come here to protect
his world and ours."*

This news seemed to create a lot of conversation that he and Vika
couldn't hear, but he could imagine it well enough as Glee faced one
another, nodding among themselves and occasionally glancing up at
him and Vika.

Their animated gestures finally subsided until no one seemed to be
saying anything, unless they were talking to Sang and only he could
hear them in his mind. Richard didn't especially like the way the Glee
could choose for others to hear them or not. He worried that if they
were saying anything threatening, he wouldn't have any idea that he
was suddenly on the verge of being attacked. If that were the case,
there was nothing he could do about it before it happened.

"If we are to stop the goddess," Richard said aloud to get their
attention, "we are going to need your help."

That seemed to send a fright through the group. A number of them
started slowly moving back. A few at the edges of the crowd slipped
into the water and glided away.

"They are afraid," Sang explained. *"These are not fighters, like the others.
They are against what the others do, but they are not fighters. They don't like
cruelty."*

Richard looked out at the sea of inky faces watching him. At least
they weren't showing their teeth. As he scanned the group, he paid
particular attention to one individual near the front. He was standing
just behind a few others.

Richard pointed to that one. "You. Come here."

All the Glee looked confused. The Glee Richard had pointed to
glanced around self-consciously but didn't move.

Richard stepped down off the rock he was standing on and gently
urged several Glee in the front out of his way. Before anyone knew

what was happening, he snatched the Glee he had been watching by the wrist, above the claw, before he could slip away.

The Glee twisted and turned first one way and then another as he tried to back away from Richard's grip. Richard turned the wrist over and increased the pressure on it. He was glad to find that it had the same effect on the Glee as it did on people: it forced the Glee to his knees.

"What are you doing?" Sang's voice in his head sounded frantic and frightened.

155

Richard twisted the Glee's wrist harder. Doing so worked just as well as it did on a man, causing the Glee to squeal in pain as he cringed before him on his knees. Richard continued to apply pressure to keep him immobilized.

"This one here is a spy sent by the Golden Goddess," he announced to the shocked crowd.

At his words, the mass of Glee all moved back away from the one Richard had by the wrist as they hissed in fear, confusion, or Richard didn't really know what.

"She sent this one to watch the Glee she considers traitors to her kind. She considers all of you a threat. This one was watching and then intended to report back to her on what he heard you saying. Once he did, it would only be a matter of time before she moved against you."

Sang looked confused as he glanced around at the others watching them. *"What are you doing? What makes you think this?"*

Richard showed Sang a small smile. "He doesn't have the green sheen to his skin that all the rest of those gathered here have. This one does not eat flutter weed, float weed, and muscle snails. He eats the flesh of those from other worlds."

Along with everyone else, Sang stared at the Glee Richard had on his knees. *"Is this true?"*

"No!" the Glee screamed in Richard's mind and, he was sure, in the minds of all the Glee gathered around, watching.

"You are lying," Richard said as he gave Vika a meaningful look.

Without hesitation she spun her Agiel up into her fist. She went to one knee to get down closer to the Glee, and without a moment's hesitation she gritted her teeth and rammed her Agiel into his midsection.

The Glee shrieked out loud, twisting, trying to get away, but Richard held him tight with pressure on his wrist as Vika kept the pressure on her Agiel. She finally pulled back away.

She leaned in, then, putting her face close to the Glee. "Tell everyone what you are doing here."

"I don't know what you are talking about," the Glee cried out in their heads. *"I am no spy! I am not with the goddess!"*

"We don't do this kind of thing to one another," Sang said as he held his arms out, trying to urge Vika and Richard to stop. *"This is not the way we behave to each other."*

Vika looked back over her shoulder, giving Sang the kind of look that only a Mord-Sith in a rage could give. He went silent as he backed up a step.

"We gave up our lives to come here," she said. "Lord Rahl gave up his wife and children who are about to be born to come here. He can never return home. All for you, all for the Glee. All to help you stop your own kind from killing and destroying your way of life. We are doing this as much for you as for the lives in our world. And I have to tell you, after sacrificing my life and my world, I am definitely not in the mood to be lied to."

"I would tell her what she wants to know," Richard told the Glee he was keeping on his knees.

The Glee defiantly shook his head.

Vika reacted by ramming her Agiel into his midsection again. The Glee twisted and shrieked. The first time had been a warning to talk. She held it there longer the second time and pressed it in harder. When she finally pulled it away, the Glee sagged, one arm raised up only because Richard had a firm grip on his wrist. Tears of agony ran from his big black eyes.

Vika held the Agiel up before the panting Glee's face. "The next time, unless you start answering our questions truthfully, I am going to shove this in your eye, blinding it, and when you don't answer, I will blind your other eye. If you still don't—"

The Glee held up his other claw. *"No! Please! I will tell you what you want to know."*

Richard lifted up on the arm, still putting pressure on the wrist, until the Glee was standing on trembling legs. "I want you to tell everyone the truth of what you are doing here."

The Glee looked around. He glanced timidly at Vika before beginning.

"The Golden Goddess sent me, just as this one said. She is gathering a large force to begin a mass attack." With a claw he gestured out at the crowd. *"She considers all of you traitors because you do not support her. You are traitors! She has promised those with her that she is going to let them hunt you for the sport of it and then eat you all. She will no longer tolerate any of you who talk to her followers, trying to get them to change their ways. She believes it would be better if you and your offspring were all dead."*

Loud hissing that Richard took for a kind of collective gasp of shock spread through all the Glee watching. They clacked their teeth and claws, apparently in a display of anger.

"Why are you here, now?" Richard asked.

"A spy up near the mountain saw that Sang was bringing two of the creatures from the other world down to here. The goddess sent me to find out your plans so that she might stop you. She is very angry. She wants your blood."

"I would be glad to tell her my plans," Richard said to the Glee. "In fact, I want you to go back and tell her my plans."

The Glee nodded eagerly. *"Yes, I will tell her what you say."*

"Do you know who I am?"

The Glee shrugged a little. *"The one they call Lord Rahl?"*

"Yes, that and more," Richard said for all to hear. "I am also the one called *fuer grissa ost drauka*."

"Fuer grissa ost drauka? *I don't know what that means."*

"It means 'the bringer of death.' I want you to tell your Golden Goddess that besides being *fuer grissa ost drauka*, I was born a war wizard. War is my calling. I live for fighting wars."

The Glee nodded furiously. *"Yes, I will tell her."*

"I want you to also tell the Golden Goddess that she has sent her kind to my world to kill us. Because of her, I have gone into darkness.

"Now I am here, and I mean to make war."

"Yes," the Glee said, still nodding. *"I will tell her your words."*

"I want you to also tell her that I demand she surrender her world to me."

The Glee winced a little as he shrank back as much as he could with Richard still holding pressure on his wrist. *"Surrender her world? What should I tell her are your conditions?"*

"No conditions. Her surrender must be unconditional. There will be no negotiations. If she does not surrender her world unconditionally, I will come and kill her and all of her followers."

The Glee seemed to wince a little as he nodded again. *"I will tell her. Fuer grissa ost drauka. The bringer of death. She must surrender our world unconditionally. I will tell her."*

"One more thing."

"Yes?"

"Tell her that I am going to enjoy hunting and killing her."

Richard suddenly released the Glee's wrist. As he did, and before the Glee could leave, he drew his sword. The rage of the sword's magic instantly surged through him. The unique sound of steel rang out across the swampy water. Before anyone could say anything or had a chance to move, the blade flashed through the air and lopped off the Glee's claw.

The Glee stumbled back in shock, clutching the arm without a claw to his chest with the other as he shook.

"You tell the Golden Goddess that her kind has shown my kind no mercy, and I will show her none. Now go before I take your head in addition to your claw."

156

Richard watched the Glee stagger away and then gradually break into an awkward, stumbling run. As he watched the Glee leaving, he felt the magic of the sword pounding through him, matched by his own anger at how many people the followers of the Golden Goddess had killed in his world. He raged at what they had done to Kahlan's life, to his, and the lives of countless others left without a loved one. He finally slid the sword back into its scabbard to extinguish its fury.

He was glad, though, to learn that the sword's magic had joined with his and had worked in this world. His bond had also worked to power Vika's Agiel. It had confirmed that his own gift would function in this alien place. If he knew how to call upon it at will, that would be even better, but he had rarely been able to do that. He was relieved, however, that even though there were only the two of them, at least his magic would be there for him if he was in desperate need. He hoped that would be enough to see them through what lay ahead.

He turned back and looked out over the stunned crowd of Glee watching him.

"That Glee, had he not been discovered, would have betrayed you all. You could all have lost your lives before you even realized that the goddess was planning to send her followers to kill you. Now that you know they don't have the same greenish iridescence as all of you have, you need to be on the lookout for others. There is no telling if the goddess might have sent more than that one among you."

The Glee all looked around at those nearby.

"We will do as you say and watch for them," Sang said.

"I need to know the lay of the land and where the goddess and her followers are," Richard told them.

"It is some distance that way," Sang said as he pointed in the direction the lone Glee had run off into the thick brownish-red haze that continually drifted past. *"She and her followers are off that way. It is an isolated area. There is only one way into the place where they are. There is not a lot to eat in that location, like there is here, but it is well protected. She does not care about what there is to eat there because her followers prefer to eat creatures from other worlds rather than the food our world has always provided for us.*

"But now that you have sent her spy back without a claw, she will be angry, and she will be expecting you to come for her. Her followers will be on alert and massed to protect her. I don't see how it would be possible to attack her now that you have told her that you will be coming for her."

Richard briefly glanced into the distance where Sang had pointed. "There is only one way in?"

Sang nodded. *"Yes. She chose that place because there is but the one way in, so it is easy to defend, should any others think to take her power."*

"Or think to end her ideas of taking other worlds," Richard said.

Sang nodded along with a few others. *"She will be preparing for you and prepared to protect the place."*

Richard rested a fist on his hip again, thinking, as he looked off in the direction Sang had indicated. It was a gloomy, reddish landscape of swamps and low vegetation. In the distance there were more of the strange tall trees with the leaves in tight clumps at the tops of their long, crooked trunks. Colonies of the large bats flew among the trees.

In the far distance he could also see some higher ground, along with some imposing cliffs. He presumed that higher ground must be what protected access to where she and her followers were gathered. He looked back at Sang.

"What do you mean, there is only one way in? Why? Why can't we go around to come in another way, on another side?"

Sang and all the other Glee seemed to shrink back a little. *"It is impossible to go around and come in from another way."*

"You already said that. Why is it impossible?"

"Because," Sang said with a kind of whine that Richard could hear

in his head along with the words, *"that way is far too barren and dry. Nothing grows there, and there is no water. None of us could survive there. We would die."*

"What do you mean, you would die? You came to my world, and you said that was dry. You didn't die there."

Sang shook his head with conviction. *"This is a different kind of dry place. Do you remember the sand we were standing on when we came back from darkness?"*

"Yes. What of it?"

"All around the place where the Golden Goddess and her followers live is that kind of ground. Sand, as you call it. Nothing but sand and many towers of rock. In between those high rock walls there are hills of sand. Expanses of wind-driven sand make up all the ground there. When the wind comes up stronger, it creates a storm of sand and wind on the ground. Nothing can survive there."

Richard nodded. "Good. Then that's the way we will go."

There were gasps from the Glee and they turned to one another, seeming to murmur their fears. Richard ignored their obvious concern and instead squatted down and pushed some of the smaller rocks aside to clear an area of muddy ground.

"Here, draw a map for me. Show me where everything is located in relation to us."

Sang leaned in and looked at the bare ground. *"I don't know what you mean."*

Richard pointed out at the areas of swampy water, then drew a quick map of the ponds in the sandy dirt. "Like this. A picture on the ground of where places are. See this?" He pointed again out at the nearby landscape. "I have drawn a map, a picture on the ground, of where the water is"—he gestured—"out that way. See each of the areas of water I drew?"

Sang and the others looked back at the water, then leaned in to peer down at the map Richard had drawn on the ground.

"I see what you mean, now," Sang said.

Richard smoothed out the ground, covering the map he had just sketched. "Now, you draw a map of where we are, where the goddess is, and the kind of land around her place—what is the area of dry sand. Try your best to show their relative sizes."

Sang squatted down and lifted one single claw out and away from the other two, like pointing with a finger. Richard hadn't known they had that much dexterity with their claws. Sang then used the single claw to sketch out a lay of the land. All the while he was drawing, he pulled his lips back over his sharp teeth, the way some people stick out a tongue when drawing.

"This," Sang finally said, tapping the ground with the single claw, *"is the area of sand and tall rock. Here are mountains that are too high to climb. Here, on this side, is the way that the goddess and her followers go in and out of her place to then go to the mountain with the device they use to travel to other worlds. All of this, around here, is the impassable area of sand. We would die if we tried to go that way to get to the place where they are gathered."*

Richard studied the map and then tapped a finger on the area that Sang said was impassable. "Good. We will go in this way. They won't be expecting us."

All the Glee gathered around looked at each other, again hissing their fright. Sang held up his claws to ward off the very notion of Richard's idea.

"You can go that way to kill the goddess if it is your choice, but we cannot guide you into her place if you wish to go that way around. Besides, even if we could go that way with you, we are not fighters. This is why I asked you to come to our world to kill the goddess. I have seen you fight. We, here, cannot fight the way you do, or the way those with the goddess have learned to fight and kill. We are peaceful."

Richard raked his fingers back through his hair as he let out a sigh of angry frustration. "Look, I intend to do my best, as I said I would. I have proven my willingness to help end this threat to both of our worlds by coming here, to your world, with you. But this is not my fight alone. It is your fight as well."

"But we cannot—"

"This is about your future more than mine." Richard gestured off in the direction of the goddess and her followers. "You heard what that spy said. The goddess intends to slaughter and eat all of you for disrespecting her. What if I die in the attempt to kill her? Then what? What will you do then? Just let them kill you all?

"Brutal leaders like the Golden Goddess cannot long tolerate those who don't believe, follow, and do as they are told. She views all of you as a disease that could spread to her followers if she does not cut you out before she loses any of her followers and then her power. She cannot allow you to live. She will send her followers for you and they will kill every one of you, along with your females and your offspring. You don't need to believe me. You all heard what that spy said.

"I have fought wars before, and this one is really not all that different. Such brutal leaders always seek to eliminate any who don't believe in their cause.

"You all are a bigger threat to her than I am. If I am killed, she continues to rule. But if you are not eliminated, you all pose a continual threat that could make her followers turn on her. Leaders need the support of those they lead. All of you threaten to cause her to lose her support. For that reason, she must kill all of you.

"It is not up to me to do it for you. You all must be a part of your own futures if you want to protect not only your own lives, but the lives of your offspring. If you do not help me, your offspring will have no future."

One of the Glee in front gestured to be heard. *You told that spy that you are a war wizard, the bringer of death. You said that war fighting is what you were born to do. We are not war fighters. We were not born to do this. This is something you alone must do. We cannot fight.*

Richard fought back his urge to yell some sense into them.

"I realize that," he told them, trying to maintain his patient, reasoning tone, "but you all need to listen to me. You are a gentle race. You are peaceful. You love your young. You do not wish to harm others.

"I understand all of that because I was once very much like you. I did not want to fight. I learned hard lessons that if I stand aside, then those I love lose everything. They lose their lives. I have seen many good friends die.

"I learned that to save those I love, and even others who believe in peace as I do, as you do, I had to fight even though I did not wish to fight. I am telling you this from my harsh experience. If you wish to survive, you must fight for your own lives. I can help a great deal, but I can't do everything for you. This is about your lives, and the lives of your kind. If you don't take your world back from the goddess, she will take everything from you.

"She already has plans to come and kill you all, so, in a way, you all are already dead. Your only choice now is to decide to live."

157

S ang looked around at the silent Glee watching them. They seemed to be shaken by Richard's words as they looked at one another, but Richard didn't hear their voices. At least they weren't running away. He wondered if they were talking among themselves or voicing their objections to Sang alone, or maybe even arguing among themselves and they didn't want him to hear.

It was even possible that they were all about to decide that they couldn't, or wouldn't, fight and in the end they would all walk away, leaving it to him. He couldn't do this alone with only Vika to help him. He feared that they were so shaken by all they had heard that they would end up saying no. He knew that once the Glee had made that switch to hunting and killing, they lost all reluctance, but these Glee had not made that transition to being killers.

He knew that he might be able to kill the goddess, but that would not by itself stop the beliefs that she and her followers held. If these Glee would not fight for their own lives, then in the end, the most realistic thing he could do would be to save the people in his own world by destroying the device that allowed them to go to different worlds to hunt people. That might be enough to save his world, but it would not save this one, and he and Vika were going to have to live out their lives in this world.

Finally Sang turned back to Richard, as if having heard what the others had all had to say. *"Lord Rahl, we understand and appreciate the very meaningful sacrifice you have made to save your kind, and your world, as well as to help save our world and preserve our way of life. We have helped you in coming here so that you might stop the goddess and save your world. We also understand the threat the goddess poses to our lives.*

"But even if we agreed to do this, you must understand that we would die out there in those barren, dry, empty lands. It is too far for us to travel away from here, away from the water where we gather our food and live. We could not survive out there. We would die."

"And what you need to understand is that I know about fighting wars. I'm telling you, if the goddess believes there is only one way in, then that is the only place she will guard and the only place they will stand ready to fight. If we could instead go in behind where they least expect us, and surprise them—"

"I am telling you, we could not do it," Sang said, lifting his arms in frustration. *"We would die out there."*

"Not necessarily," Richard said.

Sang shook his head in apparent exasperation. *"We cannot go that way and hope to live to fight them."*

Richard smiled. "That's what the goddess believes. That is why it would give us the element of surprise on our side, and surprise is one of the best weapons you could have in a fight. Surprise will help all of you prevail even though you are not experienced at fighting. It would be even better if we could come in at night. When does it get dark here?"

Sang hissed his frustration that Richard just didn't seem to get the point. He gestured to the sky. *"There is always at least some light in the sky. When the sun goes down, there are moons that provide light."*

"Moons?" Richard asked. "How many moons are there?"

"Two. It does get darker when the sun goes down, but with the light of the twin moons it never gets to be such a dark night like it sometimes does in your world."

"Is that when they sleep? When the sun goes down and it's darker?"

"Yes. When the sun goes down and day grows still, we all sleep then. When night comes, we sleep partly in the water to stay wet, and also to be safe. The wild boars like the mud, but they are afraid of water, so they won't come right up to the banks to attack us."

"How much longer until then?" he asked. "Until they sleep?"

Sang looked to the sky, shielding his eyes with one claw. With such thick, continually heaving and rolling clouds, it was hard to tell where the sun was, but apparently the Glee had learned how to judge it. Sang thought a moment, trying to think of a way to explain it. Finally he did.

"You know how long it took us to come here from the device on the mountain? It will be the quiet time when the Glee sleep in probably three of those journeys. That long. We have never crossed the drylands, but it would be at least two days and nights. We could not survive that long there."

Richard pinched his bottom lip as he considered. It was a problem that it wasn't darker at night. Still, if the goddess and her followers were asleep, that helped. He consulted the map Sang had drawn on the ground, and again looked at the sky.

"Then we must go now, around the way they would not expect us, in order to arrive at their place when it is dark," he announced to the crowd watching him.

Sang shook his head along with many of those in the crowd watching. *"You are not listening to my words. We would die, so we can be of no help to you in fighting them if we go that way. If you wish to go that way, then you and Vika will have to go alone."*

"If there was a way that you could cross the drylands, without getting too dry or suffering, would you all agree to come with me, show me the way, and fight with me against them? If there was a way, would you help me for your survival and your world?"

Sang looked around. A number of the Glee finally nodded. Richard knew that they were probably all nodding because they felt it was impossible, so they could easily commit to something they thought they would never have to do.

Sang shrugged. *"If there was a way, then yes. But there is no way for us to do this, so we cannot go with you."*

Now Richard knew for sure that he had just gotten them to commit to something they all thought was impossible. It was easy to agree when you never thought it was possible and so you wouldn't have to do it. He was about to use that commitment to his advantage.

He looked over at the pile of float weed Sang had pulled up before and thrown on the rocks. He turned back to Sang.

"I would like you to show me the water plants you use to get the jelly that protects you when you travel to my world."

"*The scrum?*" Sang asked.

"Yes," Richard said. "Collect a big pile of the scrum plants for me."

158

Richard watched as a few dozen or so of the Glee waded through the swampy water, bending down and pulling up water weeds here and there. As they collected it, they threw their loads on the bank beside the pile of float weed.

While they were doing that, he directed others to collect more of the float weed and an even bigger pile of flutter weed. They had no idea why he wanted them to do it, and he knew that they possibly thought he was crazy, but as he and Vika watched, they all went along with his odd request and collected the water plants. As they worked, the piles grew quite large. Every time they asked if they had gathered enough, he had them continue adding more to the piles.

As the Glee brought ever more of the water weed up onto the bank, Richard finally squatted down and pulled some of the scrum plants from the pile. The plant was tough and fibrous, and almost transparent. The broad, flat blades were almost as wide as his fingers would be if he spread them all the way out. Each piece was longer than he was tall, and a relatively uniform width.

The most remarkable thing about it, though, was how slimy the long blades were. If he pulled one through his fingers, he could collect globs of the sticky, gelatinous coating. The broad leaves themselves remained quite slimy despite some of the coating being removed.

The other plant, the float weed, had groups of nodules that apparently caused the ends of the plant to float, probably so that they could reach up to get more sun. Below the nodules, the broad blades of the plant were almost as wide as the scrum, but it was only slightly slimy, as was any plant growing in water, and the leaf texture was thick and strong. It was hard to tear.

The flutter weed was similar to the float weed, but without the nodules and even more flexible. Both sides of the broad blades were wavy, but they were pliable enough that they could easily be flattened out.

Richard looked up at the puzzled Glee watching him. "I need the help of one of you so I can demonstrate what we are going to do."

Looking around at the others and not seeing any more volunteers, one of the Glee finally stepped forward. *"I am Iben, Lord Rahl. I will help you. What would you like me to do?"*

Richard stood, bringing up a bundle of scrum plants in one hand. "I would like you to simply stand there so I can demonstrate to everyone that it is possible to protect yourselves so that you can survive a good long time in any dry land."

Iben shared a look with Sang before finally coming up to stand in front of Richard. Richard immediately began layering the slimy scrum plants over and around Iben's body. Next he wrapped his arms and legs with lengths of the wet, slippery plant. He draped some over Iben's large, black head and around his chin and then around his neck. He directed the others watching to pay attention as he explained how to lay down the strands to weave the long plants together in order to give them more strength together and hold them in place.

All the Glee watching were fascinated. Richard thought that since they so enjoyed being wet, this must be something that felt luxurious to them. A few of the Glee stepped up to help by smoothing down the scrum in a few places or filling in missing spots. As they did, Iben made a low, guttural, cooing sound.

"Now," Richard told his eager audience, "over the top of the scrum, we are going to do the same thing with the float and flutter weed. On the flutter weed, pull off the round nodules, like this. We don't want that part of the plant. We only want the long, broad parts."

When he did, several of the Glee scooped up the discarded nodules and tossed them in their mouths. He could hear them softly pop as the Glee chewed them.

As they watched, Richard began covering Iben in the same way he had done with the scrum plants, but this time covering it over with the thicker types of water weeds. He wove the layers together so that they had strength in all directions.

"How does this feel, Iben?" he asked.

"Actually, quite wonderfully wet."

"Good. Now, walk around to make sure it stays put."

Another Glee called out for them to wait. Soon, it brought long, thin, flexible vines out of the water. They were about as thick as string, but stronger.

"Use this," the Glee said. *"Put it around and around to help hold the scrum, flutter weed, and float weed in place."*

Together Richard and the one who had brought the vine used it to quickly weave a net of sorts to help hold the water weeds down on Iben. Richard remembered quite well how the gelatinous material always slid off the Glee when they arrived in his world. Now the flutter and float weed, layered over scrum, kept the slime against Iben's skin so it couldn't slide off.

Richard gestured. "Move around. Run and bend." Iben hopped about, following the instructions. "See how well it stays in place?"

Iben demonstrated his new suit of water weed to the others, walking among them so they could inspect it. It worked better than Richard had dared hope.

"Now, I want all of you to do the same thing with each other. Put the scrum on first, as I showed you, and then the other weeds over the top both to hold it in place and to keep it from drying out. This way, even if the top layers of flutter weed dry out, it won't matter because underneath it will still be wet and comfortable."

The Glee were all eager to try both being the one wrapped and the one doing the wrapping. It almost seemed a game to them, something new and unheard of. They cooed excitedly.

With an eye to the sky, keeping track of the day and how much time they had before dark, Richard saw that the afternoon was wearing on. He urged them to hurry. If Sang's map was at all accurate, it was a long journey across the drylands, and Richard wanted to arrive at the enemy camp while they were still asleep.

It never ceased to surprise him just how much dexterity the Glee actually had with their big claws. They could pinch the first two on one hand together to hold things, much like fingers. Of course, without thumbs, it was still somewhat difficult, but they managed and were obviously good at it. In fact, maybe because they were used to handling the water weeds, they were faster at it than Richard had been. Along the way, they perfected the weaving technique, making the suits of water weed fit snugly yet still allow them freedom to move.

As they worked at wrapping each other, more of the Glee collected the water plants needed. Before long they had an entire trade in full swing. The Glee found the wrapping exciting and interesting. None voiced any complaints. He knew that when they came to his world, if they became too dry, they could always activate their lifeline and return to their own wet world. Out in the drylands, they would not have that ability.

He was sure that somewhere along the line, they had to have figured out what he had in mind, and why he was doing this, but if they had, none of them balked or refused to join in.

As they worked, he realized it was building a sense of camaraderie, like soldiers working on their armor to get each other ready for combat.

He hoped they would maintain that sense of spirit when they headed out into the drylands, and even more so, when they met the enemy.

As they were wrapped, the Glee drew their lips back to show him a kind of frightening smile. He returned a similar smile, hoping it satisfied them despite his not being able to quite match the display of teeth.

Sang came up to him, completely wrapped from head to toe. *"I am amazed by this, Lord Rahl. I thought crossing the drylands would be impossible for us, but I really think this will work. Not only now, but in the future, after we are rid of the goddess, this will give us a way to expand our world and discover new places and more food."*

Richard put a hand on Sang's slimy shoulder. "I'm glad to hear it. But the day is wearing on. We must hurry. We need to get to the goddess's followers while they are still there and before they leave to come here. We still have a long way to go."

Sang nodded. *"As you say, we must get started, then. You are right that it is a long way around through the drylands in order to get to the place the goddess holds. Unfortunately, none of us has ever traveled there, so we are not exactly sure of what that place is like or what we might encounter there.*

"We will not be able to get there in one day. We will have to stop along the way tonight for some sleep for at least a little while, because it will be a longer day tomorrow and then tomorrow night we will arrive there."

Richard looked around at all the Glee, wrapped in water weed, watching him. "You all look wonderful. Let's get moving."

159

S ang had been right. As the sun set and night descended on them, the two small but bright moons certainly did provide enough light to see by, especially out in the windswept drylands. Everything, though, was a different shade of gloomy, dark red that seemed to weigh down Richard's spirits. He wanted to rub his eyes to clear away the bleak shades of reddish color to everything. He had never really appreciated color so much as he did after being in this place. He longed to see the simple colors of his world again.

Thick, heavy clouds frequently scudded past to sometimes obscure the moons, but when that happened they were backlit by the moons and in that way provided enough light to see where they were going. When the moons came out from behind the clouds, it was about as bright as a night with a full moon in his world. It was easily bright enough for their journey, especially in such an open, sandy landscape.

Although the ominous clouds scudding past looked thick and heavy, they didn't bring rain to this desolate place, and didn't look like they ever had, making Richard wonder if they could actually be more dust than rain clouds. If they did carry rain, he guessed that for some reason they didn't release the rain they carried until they reached the swampy parts of this strange world.

Richard had thought at first that the sand would be hard to walk across, but he found instead that in many places it had been packed hard by the howling winds that left ripples in their wake across the face of the dunes. In other places, especially on the lee side of the dunes, the sand was deep and loose, making progress difficult and time-consuming. They hadn't been traveling long and Richard's legs already ached from the effort of walking through the places of deep sand.

Enormous, soaring rock peaks thrust up through the sand to impossible heights in random spots all around them, like islands in the sea of sand. The massive stone monarchs watched them pass at their feet. In places when they passed close to the stone towers it hid the two moons, casting them into gloomy shadows.

The rock of those strange peaks was so rough and rugged, composed of faceted, stacked, sheer cliff faces, that Richard couldn't imagine they could be climbed. He was happy to instead make their way past in the shadows of those rocky peaks.

It looked to Richard that those craggy, monumental prominences of rock stood so tall that they often pierced up into the dark, ruddy clouds continually sweeping past, and that had over the ages caused them to crumble under the forces of wind and weather. All the decaying rock created both the sloping skirts of crumbled rock, and the sandy surface between each of those monstrous stone outcroppings. As the decomposing rock gradually and continually added pieces of debris to the low places between them, the wind tumbled it around and around, breaking it down, until it all turned to sand. Once it was small and light enough, the wind lifted it and carried it across the face of the landscape, shaping it into dunes.

Some of the dunes couldn't be avoided without a long detour and had to be climbed. The windward sides were sloped gradually enough to be an easy climb, but the lee sides were often quite steep and the sand soft. They had to run down the steepest sections to keep from falling face-first. A few of the dunes were quite high. At the top it gave them a good view of the bleak landscape out ahead of them. From those views, Richard thought it looked endless.

That landscape greatly concerned the Glee, but in their wet wrappings of water weeds, they at least weren't complaining about being dry. The weeds were tough and were proving surprisingly durable. Richard thought that they were surely mostly worried about fighting the followers of the Golden Goddess. These were not warriors, but they seemed to grasp the necessity of what they were doing and were so far willing.

Some of the followers of the goddess had already visited Richard's world and fought the people there. Those that hadn't yet had that experience were probably eager for it. The Glee with Richard were not at all eager to fight.

None of them carried weapons, but of course they didn't need to. They had wicked weapons at the end of each arm. He had discovered just how skillfully those claws could handle the most delicate of tasks. He hoped that when the time came, they would also be able to fight with them. Their lives would depend on it.

As if reading his thoughts, Vika leaned close. "Do you think they will fight, or run?"

Richard leaned over slightly to speak to her in a low voice. "To tell you the truth, I've been wondering that very thing myself. I think, though, that their usefulness may actually be in the shock value they will provide.

"It's a sure bet that the other Glee with the goddess will never have seen anything like these Glee all wrapped in water weeds come walking out of the drylands. I'm hoping that surprise will make them stop and stare. That hesitancy will give you and me the opportunity to get to the goddess."

"You're thinking, then, that if you can take her out quickly, that may take the fight out of her followers?"

Richard nodded. "I'm hoping so. If nothing else, it should cause a lot of confusion. Confused people—and Glee—are easier to take down."

"What if another one of them is eager, once they see her killed, to become the leader?"

Richard tucked his head down and turned to the side as he leaned a shoulder into a hot gust of wind-driven, reddish sand. He had to wait for it to die down a little before he could answer.

"Then we will simply have to take out any of them who think they would like to become the leader. I have my doubts that the Glee with us will have the nerve to do that. It's going to be up to you and me. If a different Glee steps up to be in charge only to swiftly meet our blades, I'm hoping that will take the fight out of any of the others who would think to be a leader, and the ones who would be followers willing to fight. If they don't have a leader, then their whole defense may very well collapse like an army without officers."

Vika lifted an eyebrow. "Well, that's not the craziest idea you've ever had, but it's certainly one of the more optimistic ones."

Richard didn't want to tell her his doubts and fears. "I'm glad you are with me, Vika."

She smiled. "I wouldn't have it any other way."

The thought of living in this strange world for the rest of his life had hopeless depression continually clawing at him to take over his emotions. He tried his best to tell himself to worry about one thing at a time. For now, they had a big enough problem to overcome with a fighting force of Glee that had never fought before and seemed more kind and cooperative than vicious. He worried about what they would do when they saw their kind dying.

"When this is done, I need to get back to the device and destroy it," he told her. "If there are Glee that escape during our attempts to get to the goddess, they could eventually get the same notion as the goddess had to travel to other worlds. We can't allow the Glee to ever again get to our world."

"You will get no argument from me."

Richard glanced over at her. "When that time comes, before I destroy the device, I am going to first have Sang activate it so we can send you back."

Vika stopped in her tracks and glared at him. "You are going to do no such thing."

"Vika, there is no reason for both of us—"

"Yes, there is every reason. I am Mord-Sith. I have sworn to protect you with my life."

"I don't want you to sacrifice a future you could have in our world."

Vika stepped closer as she flipped her single braid forward over her shoulder and gripped it in a fist, as if deciding on using that instead of pointing her Agiel at him.

"You gave me a choice in the beginning of how I wished to live my life. This is how I wish to live my life—at your side, protecting you. I never wanted anything else. If I returned without you, my life would have no meaning. This, here, is the choice I made for my life."

Richard would want her to return and then devote herself to protecting Kahlan and the twins but decided that this wasn't the time and place to task her with that duty. She would say that there were other Mord-Sith to do that. He didn't want to argue with her. She still existed partly in that place of madness.

The Glee behind them had slowed to a stop, waiting.

"But you would have a life, Vika," he said, simply.

"It is my choice, not yours, and besides, maybe I like this world much better than a world full of people. I often find people intolerable.

"You once told me to choose what I wanted to do with my life. I am here by that choice. Do you now intend to revoke your word and deny me the right to choose for myself what I will do with my life?"

Richard slowly let out a deep breath as he scanned the horizon. "No, Vika. I will not deny you the right to choose what you want to do. If it is really your wish to stay here with me, then I will be happy not to be so alone."

"Good."

Sang came a little closer and pointed to an outcropping of rock. *"That place there will protect us from the wind so we can get a little sleep. There is still a long way to go."*

It was deep in the night. Richard knew they were all tired. He nodded. Sang started back to the others, motioning for them to gather in the protection of the rock for a bit of sleep.

Vika gestured to a spot in the shelter of an overhang of rock where the Glee were headed. "Now that that subject is closed, let's get some sleep. We have a war waiting on us tomorrow."

160

The next day, after hours of walking, rocky areas began to break through the sandy ground. Here and there off to the sides, enormous rock towers also appeared to erupt up through the sand and thrust toward the sky. Their size made Richard feel very small. The debris that had gradually fallen as the rock decayed had accumulated over eons around their bases, creating massive slopes of scree that gradually became almost vertical near their tops. The way it rose up ever more steeply, it gave the rock monoliths a flared appearance at the bottoms, but it was really their rock faces gradually shedding material.

Between two of the towers off to their right, one of the moons between the massive rock mountains lit the billowing clouds that seemed to boil up from the distant landscape, the reddish color making them look almost like smoke from distant, raging fires. With those silent monoliths, that sand, the rolling clouds, and the moons, it was a frighteningly beautiful, if ominous, sight. The isolated islands of massive rock towers reminded Richard of the plateau that held the People's Palace rising up from the Azrith Plain, except these in this world rose up considerably higher.

It had been a long journey from that palace, a journey unlike any other that had taken him to a different world. It was turning out to be a journey that could never see him reach home again. It was depressing to think that this world of sand, desolate rock, and in places stagnant swamps, would be where he had to live out the rest of his life.

Richard had to put those thoughts from his mind. Being distracted by turbulent emotions was a good way to die in battle. He had to stay alive at least long enough to be sure his home world would be safe from the Glee ever coming there again. He had to make sure that Kahlan and their children would be safe.

As they went farther into the drylands, he understood the fear the Glee had of this desolate place. While the areas where they lived were swampy, there was abundant life there, providing food and safety. For good reason they were most at home there. This was an empty place where it would be all too easy to die a very lonely death. If they died out here, it was unlikely that anyone would ever come along to bury their bones. Eventually those bones would be ground to dust by the wind-driven sand.

The one good aspect of what they were doing was that he could see why the Golden Goddess and her followers would never expect that anyone would come around this way into the place where they lived. They wouldn't be expecting Richard, Vika, and the Glee with them.

"How are you doing?" Richard asked Sang.

Sang held his arms out, wrapped in water weeds with just the claws sticking out the ends. Water weeds were also draped over and around his head, so that his eyes could barely see out of his suit.

"I thought that you were foolish to think we could cross this land, but this way you thought to wrap us with the water weed is working. It is amazing for us to explore this strange dry land we have never seen before. My skin is warm and wet. I no longer fear that I am about to die."

Richard thought that maybe Sang should reserve judgment until they met the enemy.

Areas of rocky ground breaking through the sand became ever more frequent, with large stretches of the rock joining with others until before long they were walking over jagged, uneven rock rather than sand. The rock was pitted and sharp. The terrain was even more harsh, and that worried the Glee with him. As they continued onward the rock seemed to tilt upward so that they had to continually climb the ever-rising, massive shelf of rock.

Having never been through the drylands, the Glee didn't really know much about the terrain and could offer no advice other than general guidance about the direction they needed to go to reach the area held by the goddess and her followers. Richard worried about what other surprises they might encounter in the vast trackless drylands.

As they went farther, many of the enormous peaks began to line up, with numbers of them joining in chains of towering rock making it appear that they were one long mass of rock wall rather than individual peaks. In some places the rock did completely cease to be individual towers, becoming long, sheer rock walls hemming them in. By their size and orientation across the landscape, those rocky outcroppings seemed to bend the wind, deflecting it off to their right, rather than channeling it through the drylands the way they had up until then. Those winds, while still hot, became heavy with moisture and felt stuffy. Richard could see the thick overcast being funneled past the walls of rock to head off away from them.

The uneven ground, littered with sharp, pitted, crumbled rock, was difficult to walk on. They all had to be careful lest they twist an ankle. He was worried that the Glee might fall and tear their suits of weeds, as well as their soft flesh.

As they came to the crest of the rising ground, they all slowed to a halt.

"*There,*" Sang called out, pointing off into the distance. "*That place down there is where the Golden Goddess and her followers live. They like this place because it is near the mountain with the device, it is wet, and there is a lot of room for their great numbers to assemble.*"

Richard nodded as he studied the landscape out ahead. It looked to be a low, swampy area, with abundant vegetation. It was indeed a vast area that would hold great numbers of Glee. In the far distance, he saw more of the tall, crooked tree trunks with the single, high clumps of foliage.

"When we get down there," Richard told the Glee in a low voice as he scanned the area in the distance, "I want you all to stay behind me."

"*Why?*" Several Glee asked in his mind at the same time.

"Because if things get rough, anything in front of me is going to die."

That seemed to bring the seriousness of what they were doing into sharp relief for them. Richard urged them back a ways, out of sight of any of the Glee down below that might happen to look up. If they did look up, they would easily be able to see them silhouetted against the sky. Once back a ways, they all watched as he quickly strung his bow.

"What are you doing now?" Iben asked.

Instead of answering, Richard gave him a meaningful look and then nocked an arrow. Without a word, he drew back the string, let out a deep breath, settled his aim. He drew the target to him as he had long ago learned to do and then let the arrow fly. Even as the arrow left his bow, in his mind, it had already hit its target. Several seconds later reality caught up with what he was seeing in his mind.

The arrow went right through the head of a Glee sitting on a rock outcropping down closer to the swampy area. He had been looking away from Richard and his group, keeping watch from higher ground toward the only way they believed others could enter their home ground.

Watching the Glee crumple in the distance seemed to sober those with him even more. None spoke, but they glanced around at their fellow Glee, having never seen anything like it.

"That one was standing watch," Richard whispered to them. "Had he turned, he would have seen us. We don't want any of them to sound an alarm. We need to catch them by surprise."

"We will let you know if we spot any others standing guard," Iben said. A few others nodded their agreement.

161

"Where do they sleep?" Richard asked back over his shoulder after he had moved forward in a crouch and taken a peek.

"We like to sleep in beds of water weeds where it grows thick on the banks of the water," Sang told him, *"often with our legs in the water."*

"So then most of them will be sleeping right beside the areas of water?" Richard asked.

"Yes," Sang said. *"That is where Glee like to spend the night. It is comforting."*

Richard found the concept disturbing but didn't say so. "But these Glee don't eat the water weeds or the muscle snails like you eat," Richard told them. "These Glee eat those like me. So do you think they would still sleep on water weeds the same as they used to do?"

Sang thought about it a moment. *"Now that you mention it, I'm not sure. But I believe they would still want to sleep the same way as Glee have always slept. They still want to keep their skin wet, and stay where the boars won't come."*

Richard nodded, thinking. He turned back and peered into the distance, trying to spot any of them sleeping at the edge of the water. Richard finally looked back at the others as they waited.

"The Glee who have been eating people from my world don't eat the float weed anymore, so they lose the green sheen to their skin that all of you have."

"Like that spy you found," Iben noted.

"That's right. All of you have that green coloring. The ones down there won't have it."

Iben nodded. *"Now that you showed us that with the one you caught watching us for the goddess, we can easily know any who are followers of the goddess.*"

"That's exactly right," Richard said, "so remember that if things get confusing in a battle. I don't want any of you to accidentally slash those with us if some of you lose the water weeds wrapped around you." After another quick look, he turned back to the Glee with him. "Is there a way to tell the goddess apart from the rest of the Glee down there?"

Almost all the Glee were nodding even as he was finishing the question. Iben stretched up, looking over the rise to be sure of the lay of the land, and then gestured off toward the swampy areas.

"I don't see her," he said.

"But how would you recognize her?"

"The one who calls herself the Golden Goddess hatched in a nest of eggs that had unknowingly been built almost on top of a rare plant," one of the other Glee with them said. *"It was the first thing she ate when she emerged from her shell. She then broke open the other eggs and ate her sibling offspring so that she could grow fast and strong."*

"None of you eat the other eggs in the nest with you, do you?" Richard asked.

They all looked horrified at the very notion. Just about all of them were shaking their heads, not wanting to be associated with eating their siblings.

"That is not something our kind does when they hatch," Sang told him. *"The parents would prevent it. I don't know why her parents did not, but maybe she did it while they were asleep."*

"What does all of that have to do with recognizing the goddess?" Richard asked.

Iben spoke up first. *"That rare plant growing by her nest, the one she ate when she first hatched, is somewhat poisonous. As a result, it scarred her skin and gave it a golden color unlike any of the other Glee. Also, she is big for a Glee, at least a head taller than any of us. Her whole life she has always used her size to torment and intimidate others."*

Richard realized then that all the Glee were very similar in stature. They were all lean, and their skin all looked the same. From the description it certainly seemed like he would have no difficulty at all recognizing the goddess.

Although, he couldn't imagine how she would look golden in this world. Everything was tinted some shade of red. Only Vika's red leather outfit looked normal to him. But the rest of her was tinted red. Her blond hair was a rather lovely rose color.

He guessed that maybe the golden color was simply relative to everything else. But finally, with an easy way to recognize the goddess, Richard felt like they at least had one advantage on their side.

"Do you think she will be down there with the others?" Vika asked.

"*Oh yes,*" Sang said, nodding confidently. "*She likes the others to see her among them so they can admire her. Her golden skin color is the envy of all for its exotic appearance. She likes others groveling and seeking her approval, so she is always among them.*"

"*Besides, she never likes the others to be out of her sight,*" Iben said. "*She doesn't easily trust that they will stay loyal.*"

Not wanting to waste what darkness there was, preferring to have that on their side along with the element of surprise, Richard finally gestured for them to move out. With Vika beside him, he started out in a crouch, heading down the long slope into the place of the goddess and her followers. He worried about their numbers. When they had attacked back in Richard's world, there were sometimes large numbers of them, so they were likely to encounter even more of the enemy Glee here.

All the Glee wrapped in water weed followed Richard down the rocky slope. None of them seemed to grasp the concept of sneaking up on an enemy. He urgently signaled for them to crouch down the way he and Vika were doing. They did their best considering the wrap of water weeds but found it awkward.

The Glee they were after were quite familiar with being vicious. Most of the Glee with Richard and Vika apparently had not yet met any of their fellow Glee with such a capacity for brutality. The spy had said that they were coming to kill Sang and all those who weren't followers of the goddess. This was going to be a savage encounter.

To say that he greatly feared for those with him was an understatement, but this was their world, and this was about their lives and future. Richard couldn't simply fight this war alone and then hand them their freedom from the Golden Goddess, or others who would eventually spring up from her legions of followers to take her place. Sang and his group had to take part in stopping the threat to their world and way of life.

He hoped that when it came right down to a battle, they would show the same capacity for ferocity as those they were about to face.

162

Richard moved in a low crouch from one thick growth of vegetation to another, relieved that, since they were coming in from an unexpected direction, they had managed to get down close without being spotted. He knew that the closer they could get before they struck, the greater the surprise, the more confusion it would create, and the more effective the attack would be.

Vika was close behind him as he silently slipped through the moon shadows, going from cover to cover. He had told the Glee to stay back a little because he wanted room to draw his sword and fight. If he had the chance, he would rather use his bow to take the goddess down from a distance than engage in close combat with her. He already had an arrow nocked and ready.

He had learned to fight Glee, but he had no idea what her capabilities might be. She was taller than the others, so she very well might be stronger as well. But Richard was also tall, a little taller than the rest of the Glee.

The biggest problem would be their numbers. It would be hard to take out one individual, the goddess, if masses of her followers were charging in all around him. It would be much better if he could simply drop her with an arrow and then they could deal with her followers.

It tended to take the fight out of followers when they saw their leader be the first to fall. If he could, he wanted to dispirit them by killing the goddess first, before he had to fight the rest of them, or before the Glee with him had to engage in battle. He wanted the important part over first. He knew, though, that in battle things rarely went as planned. In such unfamiliar territory, that made the situation even more difficult.

So far, they hadn't seen any sleeping Glee, but they were still some distance from the areas of water. The ground back where they were was muddy, but Sang and Iben had said that the Glee favored sleeping in the wet water weeds on the banks and often partly in the water.

All of a sudden, there was a loud squeal, and it wasn't from a Glee.

Richard turned just in time to see something low crash through the thick brush close to him. He heard grunts and high-pitched squeals. When he spun to the sound, he saw several Glee upended, their legs knocked from under them as they were flipped through the air.

He just caught sight of a bunch of piglets scattering through the underbrush in every direction. Almost immediately he saw the sow charging through the brush to protect her young. The sow was bigger than any wild boars he had ever seen. The tusks were enormous, and no doubt lethal. The sow charged at the Glee with Richard. Fortunately, they were all able to dive out of the way just in time.

The piglets' piercing squeals seemed to be all the louder in the stillness of the night. The sow let out angry snorts as she wheeled and charged the Glee before racing through the dense brush toward the squeals from her young.

The boar was not the problem, though. The squeals and screeches of all the piglets were the problem because the sound pierced the quiet night air.

Richard heard the warning cries of the Glee rising from their sleep, furious at discovering other Glee sneaking up on them in a surprise attack. He saw frightening numbers of the dark shapes rising up everywhere out of the swampy areas and then the shadowy shapes of all the Glee were suddenly racing toward them.

Searching frantically, he finally caught fleeting glimpses of the Golden Goddess as she raced through the dark masses of Glee. Iben had been right. There was no mistaking her. Her long legs carried her faster than any Glee Richard had seen before.

Richard tracked her as he let the first arrow fly. Although the aim was true, it hit another Glee that got in the way of the shot at the last second. She charged ahead without pause, pushing some of them out of her way as she wove through the throng of her followers, clearly infuriated. The same thing happened with the second and then the third arrow as others passed in front of the arrow before it could get to her.

Richard realized that his plan to take her down at a distance with an arrow was not going to work. There were simply too many Glee in the way to have any hope of getting a clear shot and she was closing the distance fast.

As he momentarily lost sight of her, Richard threw his bow to the ground and drew his sword in a rush. The unique sound of the blade that had been touched by the world of the dead rang out across the swamp. That clear, pure sound could easily be heard above the mass of angry howls as it announced the arrival of a lethal rage of its own.

Some of the advancing Glee in the front stopped in their tracks at the sound as those behind kept coming, packing them together even tighter. Maybe some of them had heard that sound before, or heard descriptions of it from returning Glee, or maybe the danger it represented was simply obvious.

Off to Richard's right, Iben raced out ahead, calling out, bent on urging the Golden Goddess to stop and listen, hoping to stop the battle before it could begin.

The goddess suddenly burst through the throng of dark Glee and with one powerful swipe, tore out Iben's throat.

Shrieking her anger, she turned and raced toward Richard even as he was charging toward her.

As they came together, she swung at him with a claw. He dodged to the side and it just missed his face. Without pause, he brought his blade around and severed the claw before she could withdraw it. The sword flashed in the moonlight and just as quick the other claw was off.

She stopped dead in her tracks as her big black eyes blinked in stunned surprise.

While her followers had gone to Richard's world to fight, she never had. Because of that, she was all angry bluster and intimidation without the fighting skills or experience to back her threats. She had never come face-to-face with anyone like Richard who was not intimidated by her.

Before she could react, Richard was already using all his strength to power the blade around in an arc. It severed her head in one clean strike.

The goddess's head, as it flew up and back, made one slow turn through the air as strings of blood were pulled around after it. Glee stood frozen as they watched what they could never have imagined.

The clawless, headless Golden Goddess dropped straight down as if she didn't have a bone in her body.

The crowd pushed back to be out of the way as her head completed several revolutions in midair before it thudded down heavily on the rocks in their midst and took a few odd bounces before rolling to a stop. Her stunned followers backed out of its way as if it might bite them, or yell at them.

All the howling rage and fury came to an abrupt halt.

A number of the Glee with Richard cried out then and fell to their knees around Iben's body. Their distress at his tragic death was sad to see.

Richard immediately turned to the threat from the goddess's followers, expecting a furious onslaught of claws and teeth. Instead of charging in to fight them, he stopped as he saw them slow to a stop. They all briefly gazed down at the body of the goddess before moving on to come forward and stare at the dead Iben.

Glee wrapped in water weeds protectively surrounded their dead friend, many on their knees beside him, weeping. They all crowded around, reaching out to touch their friend, clearly devastated that he had been so violently slain by one of their own kind.

After Sang, grieving, had gently touched Iben's body, he stood in a rush to face the enemy. Tears of rage ran from his large black eyes, his third eyelids trying to blink them away, but more continued to flow.

He gestured angrily with a claw down at Iben's body.

"Look at what you have done! This is what you all wanted? Look at what you all have done to one of your own kind! Look! Glee should never

harm Glee! Never! Your Golden Goddess did this! You all did this! You are all responsible!"

If Glee could look shamefaced, those Glee watching him standing over the body of his friend certainly did. Many hung their heads. Others looked away in disgrace.

"This is what you wish for our world?" Sang cried out as he swept an arm out in anger. *"This is what you wanted? This is your way, now? To kill other Glee?"*

Other grieving Glee behind Sang stood after touching the body to gesture down with a claw, demanding that the enemy look at what they had all been a part of.

"Is this how you want to live now?" one of the others asked as he got up from kneeling by Iben. *"This is what fills your hearts? This is what you wanted? Your own kind to be murdered? This is what you all would do to other Glee? To us? None of you are as good as this one was. He rushed forward because he wanted to tell you all to please stop your ways and return to the way we have always lived. But you instead killed him! What kind of beasts have you become?"*

The guilty Glee stood around, watching but not interfering, some holding their claws behind their backs, while others hung their heads, all of them clearly not knowing what to do.

The fight had been taken out of them.

Finally, in the unbearable predawn silence, one of the enemy slowly approached and pointed with a claw. *"You are covered with water weeds. Is that so that you were able to cross the drylands to come in and surprise the goddess?"*

Many of the Glee who had come with Richard nodded.

Then, the masses of Glee that had been hanging their heads began to step forward and do the strangest thing.

163

At first, a few of the enemy Glee slowly, timidly, began approaching the Glee still kneeling around their fallen friend. When the first reached Iben's body, the Glee who had been kneeling stood and moved back so that the others could see what their beliefs had wrought. Many of Sang's Glee bared their teeth as they hissed. Richard thought that their meaning was clear enough.

The first Glee to slowly shuffle up to Iben went to a knee beside the body. Richard and Vika shared a look, wondering what it could mean, and what was going to come next, but with that look they wordlessly decided to let it play out and see what happened. Richard still had his bloody sword in his hand, so if things suddenly turned violent, he intended to show them what violence really was.

The twin storms of rage were still roaring through him. His blade had come out in anger and tasted blood. It wanted more. This time, if a battle broke out, they were already in their home world and would not be able to vanish to escape certain death.

The Glee that approached first and went to a knee gently pulled off a strip of the float weed from Iben's body. As Richard and Vika watched along with all the silent Glee, he ate the piece of water weed.

To Richard, it looked almost like some kind of sacred ceremony or statement that this one Glee, at least, wished to give up the path he had been on and return to their traditional ways.

As that Glee stood and moved aside, another came forward and took his place. He, too, pulled off a short piece of water weed and ate it while the Glee with Richard stood back beyond Iben's body, out of the way, and watched.

Soon, all of the Glee were lining up to come and kneel before the dead body of one of their kind. Each in turn took a piece of float weed and ate it in a kind of reverent expression of their sorrow. Richard took it as a wish to return to their ways.

Before long, the flutter and float weed, and the scrum under it, had all been eaten, except for the layers around Iben's neck that were covered with blood. There were still a vast number of followers of the goddess who hadn't had a chance to eat some of the water weeds that had protected Iben, so instead, they began mingling in among the Glee who had been with Richard, looking like they wanted to take pieces of the water weeds off of them as a suitable substitute. The Glee covered in water weeds all held their arms out so that their former enemies could all partake of the water weed in a symbolic gesture.

If any of them were speaking, they were not doing so in a way that allowed Richard and Vika to hear anything they were saying. He supposed they didn't want outsiders to hear their apologies and pleas for forgiveness.

It took quite a while for all the Glee to come up and take a piece of the water weed. As they gathered around, waiting their turn, some of the Glee wrapped in the weeds began pulling off strips and handing them to the ones waiting their turn in order to speed up the process.

Richard didn't see a single Glee leave, or express defiance. They all looked genuinely remorseful at the death of one of their own kind.

He finally sheathed his sword. He was thankful that it had done enough.

He also didn't see a single Glee pay any attention to the body of the Golden Goddess lying in a heap by itself. None of the Glee mourned her death. There were so many of the Glee, it took over an hour before all of them were able to collect and consume a symbolic piece of the water plants that had long been part of their staple diet and way of life.

"I have never seen anything like this," Vika whispered as she watched the silent ritual. "I'm sorry that Iben had to die, but I am thankful to be able to see others make the kind of decision I once made."

Richard put an appreciative hand on Vika's shoulder. Having been prepared for a bloody fight to the death, and now seeing that fate turning aside, he feared to test his voice.

The piglets had all run off and the sow had gone after them, so the scene was hushed as each of the Glee ate some of the water plants after they paid their respects to the dead Iben and finally greeted their long-separated brethren.

Richard, too, was sad at the death of Iben. He had been open, friendly, and eager to help, and along with Sang had completely turned Richard's view of the Glee upside down. They were not all what he expected. They were far more than that.

Iben had wanted to talk his fellow Glee out of violence against their own kind. He had wanted to try to get them to stop and think about what they had been about to do. He thought he could persuade them.

In the end, he had.

164

Late in the afternoon, the Glee took turns using their claws to dig a grave. When it was finally deep enough, they gently placed Iben's body in it and covered him over.

After they had put Iben to rest, they then slashed the body of the Golden Goddess until it was covered with ribbons of deep cuts. Richard and Vika couldn't imagine what they were doing. Once satisfied, they threw the body and the head into one of the swampy lakes. The body floated for a short time among standing reeds before small creatures Richard couldn't see began tearing at the flesh. After a few hours most of it had been eaten, leaving only bones. It was apparently a disrespectful burial to show their displeasure with what she had brought to their kind.

The strange celebration and socializing went on into the evening. As it grew dark, the Glee began finding places to sleep. Some curled up in thick beds they made from fronds. Others laid their heads down on the banks of ponds and let their legs float out into the water. Whatever had eaten the body of the goddess apparently didn't bother with living Glee. They slept peacefully with half their bodies in the water.

Richard and Vika found a place nearby beside a beautiful bush that was more like a small tree. They gathered fronds to make sleeping mats. Neither one of them liked the idea of both of them sleeping at the same time, so they took turns taking naps while the other stood watch. Richard wondered how long they were going to have to do that in their strange new world.

By late morning of the next day the odd reunion was still going strong, with the Glee mingling together and talking with one another. Richard and Vika weren't aware of much of what was being said, because while they occasionally heard some of the talk, most of the Glee chose not to have their voices, or possibly their confessions, heard by these strangers from another world. Richard wasn't overly concerned, though, because everything appeared to be friendly enough, but he did wish he possessed that talent to deny others the ability to hear his words. It could come in handy at times.

As he casually watched, he remained vigilant and ready to draw his sword at the slightest sign of trouble. He didn't think it looked like there would be trouble, but he felt it best to be ready just in case. He saw Vika idly spinning her Agiel on the end of the gold chain around her wrist as she, too, watched.

He and Vika stood out of the way, not wanting to intrude. From time to time many of the Glee slipped into the water, where they seemed most at home. Groups congregated in the water as they floated together. Others would periodically bring bundles of water weeds to the banks, where yet others could take some to munch on. Others, apparently tired from the reunion and celebration, rested their chins on a pillow of their folded arms while the bottom half of their bodies floated in the water. Yet others sat cross-legged on the banks to talk. Richard supposed they had a lot to talk about.

Richard had been to a number of fancy banquets and gatherings of officials. This seemed very much the same, other than the trappings of power and social standing, and of course the claws and needle-sharp teeth. Other than those trappings, he recognized the body language and the interplay of different personalities. The whole thing was, in a word, weird.

Richard was getting hungry himself. He wondered what he and Vika were going to be able to eat in this strange world. He certainly didn't have any cravings for the smelly water weeds. He supposed he might be able to catch some fish, or he could hunt wild boar. There might even be fruits and berries that they could eat. Fortunately they still had some travel rations in his pack, but not a lot. As they watched the Glee, he and Vika idly chewed on strips of dried meat.

It occurred to him that as time went on maybe the Glee could provide the meat of some muscle snails for him and Vika to roast over a fire or smoke. He glanced around and realized that he didn't see much that they could use for firewood.

All the Glee Richard had brought through the drylands were easy enough to spot, because their skin had the green iridescence. They seemed somewhat somber that Iben had died, but also recognized that his death had resulted in the end of the reign of the Golden Goddess. Iben had been the catalyst that had brought all the Glee together again. Richard didn't know if, or how long, that would last. He hoped it did, but he worried that it wouldn't.

He was also all too aware that at some point after those former raiders of other worlds ate enough water plants, it would give their skin the same green iridescence. He worried that once that happened, he wouldn't be able to tell the formerly hostile Glee from the peaceful ones. If they ever turned hostile again and decided they wanted to eat Richard and Vika, he would have no way of telling them apart. That would put surprise on their side.

Richard supposed that, while he didn't want to die, he didn't really have much to live for anymore, except the one thing that he was growing impatient to finish.

As he and Vika watched, some of the former followers of the goddess came up to them and made a point of telling them that besides ending the tyranny of the Golden Goddess and her oppressive rule over their lives, what Richard had done had lifted them from a terrible future in which they abandoned their traditional ways and instead went to other worlds to hunt for food where many of their kind had been killed.

Some told him of beloved offspring that had been eager for the adventure of going off to other worlds and had only ended up dying there. Richard wondered if he had killed some of those Glee, or offspring. They had been vicious killers and had died as such. He hoped their minds didn't turn to revenge.

Those engaging him in conversation explained that they had done what they had done because the Golden Goddess made them do it. Richard didn't necessarily believe a word of it, but he let them have their excuses in order for things to remain friendly. If that was what they wanted to claim in order to soothe their consciences, he didn't really care as long as it meant an end to the fighting.

At this point, stuck in their world with Vika, never to be able to return home to Kahlan, he didn't really care how they justified to themselves what they had done. He only cared that it stop. Now that it had, he was relieved that he didn't have to face yet another protracted war in which he and Vika would be vastly outnumbered.

But this new peace still had to prove to him that it could last. It was possible, or even likely, that there were Glee among them who harbored very different sentiments and they simply hadn't come forward to express them. He realized that he might never again be able to sleep with both eyes closed.

He had always been skeptical that when the time came, those Glee who came across the drylands with him would actually fight. Now, he didn't need to fear that bloody conflict, or all of them being slaughtered. If, that was, a new leader didn't rise from the ranks of the former followers of the goddess.

Richard's patience finally came to an end. He pulled Sang aside to talk to him privately.

"Before any of these former followers of the goddess start to think that maybe they might like to have the power she had and be in charge of a vast army that could raid other worlds, we need to destroy the device so that can never happen again."

Sang nodded, looking apologetic that he had forgotten all about it, and handed the long piece of the float weed he was munching on to one of the others passing by.

"Everything is back to the way it was, thanks to you and Vika. I don't think we could ever adequately express our gratitude. With peace restored, we have nothing to fear, now. We can take care of the device any time. There is no longer any worry or any rush."

"There is to me," Richard said in a firm voice. "I want it taken care of now. I don't want to have to worry that I might have my throat torn out in my sleep by followers of the goddess who decided to resume their ways and will then go to my world and kill the people there."

"I don't think you need to worry about—"

Richard held up a warning finger. "I came here to do what was necessary to protect my world. I sacrificed my life with my kind, my wife, and my offspring to do this—both for my people and for your kind. I have nothing left for me, now, other than a lonely future here in this world where Vika and I don't really belong.

"I made that sacrifice to be able to destroy that device that made all of the terror and bloodshed possible. That job is not yet done. I want it finished."

Sang could see the determination in Richard's face and hear it in his voice. He nodded.

"Of course, Lord Rahl. I understand. Of course you are right. We will go there now. I will show you the way."

Richard would simply have left the days-long celebration and gone there on his own, and he actually would have preferred to do that, but with the clouds obscuring much of the landscape, he wasn't sure exactly how to find the place up in the mountains. They had come into the territory of the Golden Goddess via a long, roundabout way through the confusing maze of rocky spires in the drylands in order to surprise the goddess and her followers. With the clouds, the wind-driven sand, the maze of rock towers, and not being able to see exactly where the sun was in the sky, he wasn't confident that he had been able to keep track of direction or distances.

He had a general idea where he could find the mountain where the device was located, but with visibility so poor, and the low clouds always obscuring mountain peaks, he feared that if he looked for the site on his own it could end up taking him days to find the small trail. He knew that Sang could show him the way and then he could destroy the device much sooner.

He worried about the possibility that in the meantime, if it wasn't quickly destroyed, it might be used again without him being aware that some of the Glee had snuck away to travel to his world. He didn't want to risk it existing any longer. Better to destroy the device once and for all. That was the only way to make sure Kahlan and everyone else would be safe.

Sang spoke with some of his followers, apparently letting them know that they were leaving to go to the mountain where the device was located. But as they started out, Richard saw that a large number the Glee were following behind—both Sang's followers and many of the followers of the goddess. He didn't know why, but as long as Sang got him there so he could use his sword to destroy that strange square block of stone, that was all that mattered.

His sword had cut through steel before. Not all that long ago his blade had cut through massive stone pillars and blocks to get at Moravaska Michec down in the complication.

Neither steel nor stone ever proved to be any obstacle to the Sword of Truth, so he had no doubt that it would cut through the stone device.

Although, in the back of his mind, he realized that it was possibly neither steel nor stone. It was, after all, a device that allowed travel to other worlds, so it was possible that it only looked like stone and would in reality prove much more difficult to destroy than he had at first thought.

When he looked back over his shoulder at the line of Glee following him, it reminded him of a funeral procession.

In a way, that's exactly what it was.

165

A warm rain accompanied them along the climb up the mountain. It made the air wet and heavy, and difficult to breathe. At times it came down in sheets, harder than any rain he had ever known before, almost like standing under a waterfall. It was so heavy that they could barely even see.

When the rain increased to an intensity that Richard and Vika found unendurable, they had to crouch behind some of the forest of rock towers that had overhangs enough to shelter them somewhat. Sang warned him to stay out of any low places because this kind of rain often created flash floods that could sweep him away before he realized what was happening. It could easily be disastrous to be rolled down the mountain in such floodwaters. From time to time they came to those kinds of sudden, rushing, muddy rivers and had to find a way around them.

The Glee didn't at all mind the rain, at times standing in it with their arms held out and their faces turned up to the sky, but Richard and Vika found it miserable. Traveling into the heaviest of the curtains of rain was arduous. It was also hard not only to see where they were heading, but also where they were stepping. He worried that either Vika or he might fall and break a leg. Richard had grown up outdoors, and so he was familiar with walking in challenging terrain, but Vika hadn't, so it was harder for her to walk among the jumbles of rock during the downpours.

There were no healers that he knew of among the Glee, and he didn't think that they had any. They seemed to be too simple a species to have healers. If he or Vika was injured, there could be no help. They had only each other, and while he knew about healing, both with magic and with herbs, he could certainly heal Vika, but she couldn't heal him. He also didn't know if this world had any healing herbs they could use.

The landscape they had to travel through was completely devoid of any kind of life; there was just rock and, in the rain, mud, much of it rushing down at them. There were no plants, not even a blade of grass. Just continual rain. Since starting up into the mountains, he hadn't seen a single bird, or even one of the bats that he had seen in large groups down in the swampland. He remembered that Sang had said that where the device was located was a dry place, but getting there beneath the leaden overcast certainly wasn't dry. He was looking forward to getting up into the mountains above the clouds that were dumping so much rain on them.

A lot of the rock was sharp and crumbly, making walking difficult. This world was a strange mixture of lush swamplands, sandy drylands, and desolate, lifeless mountains. The skies seemed to be an odd mix, too, of dark clouds that carried no water and heavy, wet overcast. From what he had seen so far, it seemed that nothing lived anywhere other than the swampy lands down lower, where all this water running down the mountainsides eventually collected in the swamps.

Richard came across holes in the upslopes of grainy rock. They appeared almost big enough that he might be able to crawl inside. He wondered if they might be able to be enlarged and in the future provide some kind of cavelike shelter for him and Vika. He stuck his head inside one of the holes, trying to see how deep it was. All he could see was blackness.

Suddenly, Sang put both claws around his arm and urged him back out. Richard pulled his head out of the hole and turned to look back at Sang. Sang shook his head in warning. It seemed clear to Richard that Sang didn't want to talk about whatever lived in those caves. Richard could tell from the looks of the others that whatever was in the holes scared the other Glee speechless.

Right then, the device was Richard's priority, so he didn't want to waste the time to be concerned about the holes and what might be in them. He would have to ask later.

After he nodded his thanks for the warning to Sang, he turned back to the trail and kept going. But now he was concerned about what lived in those holes that he and Vika might one day have to deal with. Unlike the Glee, the two of them weren't equipped with claws for protection.

Lightning flashed nearby, and the ground shook with a sudden thunderclap. While the rain didn't bother the Glee, the lightning clearly made them nervous. It made Richard nervous as well. The Glee looked around, as if they thought they would have time to run if they saw lightning. Some of them sought shelter behind rocks whenever there was a particularly bright flash and crack of thunder. Richard knew that hiding like that was pointless, because by the time you saw a close bolt strike, it was already too late to run from it. Richard disregarded what some of them did and kept climbing.

"Being up high like this is dangerous when there is lightning," Sang said, almost apologetically.

Richard looked back over his shoulder as he pulled himself up over a projecting shelf of rock. "I understand. I know the way from here, so you don't need to go the rest of the way up to the device. You can all go back, now, and when I'm finished destroying it, I will come back and join you."

As he and Vika waited, Sang consulted with a number of others. Richard couldn't hear that debate in his mind, so he didn't know what was being said, but he was hoping they would turn back. He didn't particularly want an audience. Flashes of lightning lit clouds from the inside in a frightening display of the power of the storm that was rolling in on them. The heads of some of the Glee sank into their shoulders as they cast worried looks to the sky.

Finally, Sang returned. *"We will go with you. I want to see the device destroyed, and so do many of the others. It has ruined many Glee lives. We want it ended once and for all. The ones who used to follow the goddess wish to go as well."*

Richard worried about those Glee, but didn't want to get into any kind of disagreement that could prevent him from destroying the device. So, he simply nodded and then turned back to the trail up through the rocks.

They had to scramble up steep areas of scree, almost running in order to make progress against the ground sliding away underfoot. The rock was loose and difficult enough to climb in the dry, but when it was wet it was even harder to get up because the water coming down helped it to slide out from underfoot. After an exhausting climb up through the loose, wet rock, they finally made it up into rock that was still slippery in the wet, but at least solid and much easier to climb. Richard's legs ached, but he didn't want to stop to rest. He could rest once the task was completed.

As they climbed higher into the low clouds, the fog became so thick that it was difficult to see very far. Richard could see Vika's dark shadow behind him, along with a couple of the Glee, with what looked like ghosts following them, but the rest were lost in the poor visibility.

Thunder rumbled almost continually through the desolate landscape. Lightning flickered somewhere off in the distance, illuminating the cloud they were in. Because they couldn't see where it was coming from, the light and sound instead seemed to be everywhere. It was unsettling.

Richard didn't like the idea of being on a mountain in a storm with such violent lightning, but his need to destroy the device made him ignore the danger and drove him onward. After he destroyed it, they would be forever trapped in this awful, wet world.

After hours of climbing, they finally began to emerge above the cloud cover and into the strange, dry forest of small rock towers. The sun was still obscured by an even higher layer of clouds, but at least it wasn't raining, and it was brighter. The lightning moved some distance away along with the huge, dark, billowing clouds, but Richard could still see the near-constant flickers of lightning inside those clouds down below them, lighting them with an eerie reddish, firelike glow.

He didn't know that he would ever be able to get used to this strange world, but he knew that he didn't really have a choice. It made him wonder if life would be worth living here after he destroyed the device.

As Richard and Vika wove their way through the maze of rock spires that had been carved, shaped, and softened by the weather, they finally reached the cathedral of those stone shapes surrounding and

overlooking the device. It sat across the way at the edge of an expanse
of white sand.

He could tell that Vika, not usually given to emotion, was feeling as
despondent as he was at the prospect of destroying their way back to
their own world. But it had to be done.

Richard drew his sword.

166

The sound of the blade being drawn from its scabbard rang out, echoing back from the complex shapes of the stone walls all around them. It was the forlorn sound of finality, of all his hopes and dreams ending. That distinctive ringing sound caused the massive crowd of Glee following them, who had seen the sword kill the goddess, pause with concern before backing away. Many moved back among the safety of the standing stones.

In his mind's eye, Richard could see Kahlan's smile. He had to force the image from his thoughts lest it be too unbearable or even prevent him from doing what he knew he had to do to protect her and all the people in her world. He hoped that one day his home world would again have a Lord Rahl, one who cared about his people: his son. One day it would also have a new Confessor to help protect them: his daughter.

For now, though, Richard was the only protection for that world, and to protect it, he had to destroy the device that allowed the Glee to go there. None of his people would ever know what he had done to save their world, and one day the Glee would only be a terrible memory. New generations would likely not even know anything about them or the horrors they had brought to the world.

He looked up overhead when he noticed that it was getting brighter. He saw that the clouds had parted enough to give them a rare glimpse of the sky. The sun itself wasn't in view, but the sky was a bright reddish orange. Because it was still late in the day, he thought it likely that it was near sunset. He couldn't yet see the stars, but if he could, he knew that he wouldn't be able to recognize them from a strange world he didn't want to be in.

So far, since he had arrived, the sky was rarely visible. The continual, heavy, rolling, boiling clouds seemed to make this world all that much gloomier. He didn't know if it was simply a seasonal weather pattern, or a habitual one.

Kahlan was out there, somewhere, among stars he couldn't yet see. He wondered if in her world, when she looked up, she might one day look toward the forsaken place in the sky where he would be forever stranded.

His joy at having a glimpse of the reddish sky instead of the continual overcast vista was short-lived when his gaze reluctantly settled on the device waiting for him across the sand.

"Are you sure you want to do this?" Vika whispered from close behind him. "Once you do, there is no going back."

He looked over his shoulder into her blue eyes. She questioned his choices and decisions quite often, sometimes in the form of a cutting remark, but he knew that it was her way of testing his confidence in a course of action, a way to get him to reaffirm his decisions within his own mind. When it came down to it, he knew that she had complete confidence in him.

This time, it was a critical, consequential question.

"What choice do I have?"

Vika's face said it all as she nodded slightly.

"None, I guess."

Richard could feel the power of the sword storming through every fiber of his being. That power pulled and tugged at him, wanting his anger to join with that power. But this time, he knew that venting his anger on the device that would forever separate him from Kahlan seemed out of place. This was an instance more of solemn duty than rage.

Besides, Richard couldn't seem to bring forth any anger of his own to join with that of the sword, or at least none he dared unleash.

Finally, he decided that it was best to simply get it over with and not dwell on it, so that he could at last rest easy in the knowledge that it was done and that Kahlan and their children would not have to live in fear of Glee coming to slaughter them. So many had already died a horrific and senseless death. He couldn't realistically do anything for them, but he could at least see to it that the ones still alive would be spared the terror the Glee could bring.

As he crossed the expanse, with the tip of the sword dragging through the sand behind him, he was reminded again of the round area of white sand in the Garden of Life at the People's Palace. That was a place of great significance. So much had started there, and ended there, and now it was all ending in a similar circular area of white sand in a world far away.

As Richard got closer, something about the symbols on the stone device made him pause for a moment, staring. He moved closer then to have a better look, to see if his initial thought could actually be possible.

When he realized that he was right, he sheathed his sword.

Vika looked suddenly concerned. "What's wrong?"

Richard hardly heard her as he dropped to his knees in front of the stone and reached out to run his fingertips lightly over the symbols on the smooth surface.

"Lord Rahl, what is it?"

He could hardly believe what he was seeing.

"These symbols are in the language of Creation. It's not precisely the same as the symbols I've seen before, but they're awfully close. I can tell right off that most of them are substantially the same. There are some differences, but they're close enough that I think I might be able to translate them."

Vika rushed up and fell to her knees beside him. "Really? What does it say?"

"It's not that simple."

"Well, if you can recognize it as the language of Creation, and you understand that language, then it only makes sense that it must be something you can read, right?"

"Yes, I think I can. Some of it, anyway. From the parts I am able to read, what it says is incredibly complicated."

"What do you mean by complicated?"

"Well, in many ways, it reminds me of a complex constructed spell."

"A constructed spell?" She leaned closer to him with an astonished look. "You mean magic?"

Richard nodded as he tried to decipher one of the symbols having to do with intersecting lines of power.

"Yes. Like magic."

Vika let out a sigh as she sat back on her heels. "I'm afraid that I can't help you there. But are you sure? How could magic possibly be involved with this device?"

"Magic is involved with all the devices I've seen before."

"You would know a lot more about that than I would," she said. "I try to avoid anything having to do with magic. You seem to always be involved with it in one way or another."

He nodded, not really hearing her as he leaned in and frowned. "It's saying something about a ring."

Vika stared at him. "A ring? What kind of ring?"

Richard ran his fingers over the symbols, trying to understand what he was reading out of order and out of context. Doing so always made translations much more difficult. The language of Creation was not easy to read as it was, but a lot of it had to be read in context to be understood.

He searched for the beginning to try to read it from where the description started. The problem was, he wasn't entirely sure, yet, exactly where that starting point was.

He read several of the symbols looking for the beginning when he recognized something. He looked to the sand at the sides of the stone.

"It's talking about a ring beginning and ending here."

"What could that mean?"

"I'm not sure." He pointed beside the stone. "Dig in the sand, right there, and see if there is a ring of some kind."

As Vika did as he asked, Richard went to the other side and started digging with his hands.

"I found something," Vika called over to him.

As he dug, his fingers touched something hard and smooth. "Me too."

He started clearing away the sand, exposing what was buried there. He brushed sand away to expose more of it. Vika was doing the same. In a few moments they each had uncovered gleaming metal. It was the color of gold and perfectly round, about as thick as his forearm. It was not cold to the touch like some metals. It felt more like real gold.

As he and Vika both followed it along, uncovered more and more, they began to see that it went out in both directions from the stone, and by the way it curved as it moved away from that square stone, it soon became obvious that it was a gold ring that, from what they had so far uncovered, looked like it encompassed most of the round area of sand.

"What should we do?" Vika asked.

Richard was using his hands to sweep away sand from the top of the ring. "It's not buried very deep. Let's uncover it all and confirm if it really does go all the way around in a ring."

They worked with urgency to solve the mystery. They both felt driven by the discovery, wanting to excavate it to see if it told them anything important. Richard couldn't imagine, though, what use it could be to them. After all, the whole thing would soon be destroyed.

The hundreds of Glee watching them from around the whole area and back in among the stone formations didn't say anything or try to interfere, but it was clear that they were as astonished as Richard and Vika. They had lived with and used this device all their lives, and yet they had never known that the ring was right there, connected to it, just under the surface of the sand.

In a short time Richard and Vika had uncovered the entire ring. Both of them stood and stepped back to look at it.

Richard thought that it was either made of or covered with gold. The golden ring went in a full circle, interrupted only by the stone sitting at one side of the sand. The ring was polished and so perfectly smooth that Richard could see his distorted reflection in it. It was simply a smooth, polished golden surface. It had no writing or symbols on it.

Richard looked over at the stone. It had a massive amount of writing on it.

He rushed across the white sand to see if he could tell if the writing on the stone might reveal something about the purpose of the golden ring.

167

"Anything?" Vika sounded impatient. "You've been looking at it long enough that you must be able to read at least some of it. You should be able to tell something from the symbols, right? So, what does what you've translated so far say?"

Richard sat back on his heels and looked over at her. "The Glee are wrong in calling it a device."

"Really? Why? What is it called?"

"It's called a gateway."

Vika stared at him a long moment. "A gateway?"

"That's what it says."

Vika gestured at the stone. "You mean... like a gateway to other worlds?"

Richard nodded. "It would seem so."

She frowned as she considered. "I guess that makes sense. But it seems like an awful lot of writing just to say that it's called the gateway. Does it really take all of that to say it's called the gateway?"

Richard let out a deep sigh as he looked back at the stone. He gently ran his fingers over the symbols as he considered them.

"No, that's only a small amount of what this says. There's a lot more to it. The symbols are similar to those in our world, and many are the same, but not all are and there are key differences from any I've seen before. Some of the more complex symbols are meant to convey concepts by using underlying elements, but not all of those use the same elements as the ones I'm familiar with. Even though it's in many ways different, it's still hauntingly similar to what was once a common form of writing in our world."

"You mean it's the same as the writing all over that witch woman,

Niska, back in our world? The one in the swamp by Agaden Reach where we caught up with the Mother Confessor."

"The very same. And it's close to the same as in a lot of other places in our world. It predates everything else. All other writing, which involves words rather than pictorial elements and concepts, came after the language of Creation."

Vika gave him a blank look. "So... what, exactly, are you trying to say?"

Richard shook his head with a sigh as he looked back at the stone. "I don't know. I'm just saying that this has to be very old. But more than that, don't you think that it's more than strange for the language of Creation to be on this stone in another world besides ours?"

"It has been here for a very long time," Sang said from back beyond the sand, trying to sound helpful. He had stepped a little closer, away from the others watching. Richard had forgotten that the Glee packed in among the stone spires were listening. *"Maybe that is what you mean? That it has been here for a very long time?"*

Richard knew that Sang didn't grasp the significance of what he had discovered. There was no way he could. He wasn't in the mood to give lessons, though, so he kept it simple.

"Longer than that."

All of the Glee looked to be confused as they whispered among themselves. They clearly had a hard time grasping anything Richard was saying. The language of Creation, after all, had no meaning for them.

Vika slapped a hand onto the stone. "But it could be that this thing, this gateway, may have once come to our world and given us the language of Creation, don't you suppose? Much like it came to this world?"

Richard shook his head. "I have absolutely no idea, Vika. That seems like it could be true, but I don't think that's the case. I simply have no way of saying for sure. What I do know is that these symbols are instructions."

Vika withdrew her hand from the stone as she leaned close to him. "Instructions?" she whispered. "Instructions for what?"

Richard leaned in toward the stone again to put his fingers on the symbols. "I'm not ready to say, yet. I need to read some more so I can try to piece it all together."

Vika stood to leave him to it. She walked the perimeter just beyond the gold ring. Richard thought she looked like she might be making sure the Glee stayed back out of the way. The more he read, the more he thought that might be a very good idea.

On one of her rounds, as she went past him, she bent close. "Anything useful, yet?"

Richard looked up at her. "Tell Sang I'd like him to come over here. I want to ask him something. Be casual about it. I don't want the others to hear me."

When she strolled back with the tall, nearly black Glee, Richard stood.

"What is it?" Sang asked. *"Why are you not destroying the device? I thought that was why you were—"*

"How did you use this device to come to my world? You came a number of times. How did you do it? How did you make the device work for you?"

Sang was taken off-guard by the question. He thought about it briefly, and then looked over at the device.

"There is a place on the top, on the other side, that I used to make the device work so that I could go into darkness. That is how I reached your world."

"Show me," Richard said.

Sang nodded and then led them around the square block of stone to stand just outside of the ring, facing the slanted top. Richard came around with him and watched.

Sang spread his right claws to extend just the first one, much as a person would extend their first finger to point.

"When I wished to go to your world, I would put one claw into this place, here."

Sang used the claw to tap the sloped top of the stone. There was a slot right next to where he tapped. It looked like he would be able to fit the single claw all the way down into the slot. That was what Richard had thought from what he had read so far. But he knew that there had to be a lot more to it.

"How did you know where to go? When you went into darkness, it didn't just spit you out somewhere at random. How did it allow you to come to our world?"

"In the beginning, long before we all came alive, it is said that Glee would sometimes try putting their claw into that place. They were never seen again. No one knew what happened to them. So maybe, as you say, the device sent them someplace where they died. Or maybe it sent them nowhere at all and they long ago simply vanished into darkness.

"The Golden Goddess, besides being bigger than other Glee, was also smarter. She was the first to learn that she could ask the device to send her to other worlds where she could survive. I believe that was the key. The device then picked places like that.

"She learned right at first that she could return by what we now call the lifeline. She would travel to other worlds and then come back and tell others what she had discovered. As she found worlds for them to raid, they came to call her the collector of worlds.

"After she found a world she liked, she would then insert one claw, and think of the place she wished to go back to, and the device would send her into darkness until she arrived at that world. They began to call her a goddess, much like they thought of the ones who had left the device as gods. Because she alone knew how it worked, she began to gain followers who called her goddess, and then the Golden Goddess. She liked having followers who worshipped her.

"After a time, she would stand here, where we stand now, and in that way send her followers to the places she had found where they would hunt for food. That eventually evolved into sport for them."

Richard knew that when the gods, or whoever it was, had brought the gateway to Sang's world and left it where it now stood, it had to be adjusted so that the Glee could use it. It had protocols, shown in the symbols, that had to have been set so the Glee could use a single claw to activate it. From what Richard had read, once it had been set for the new use, such as had been done when it had been left here in this world, nothing else would work.

Until the gateway was reset.

From what Sang had just told him, the Golden Goddess was the first to finally figure out how to make the gateway work successfully. Now, all the Glee knew.

The implications were racing around in Richard's mind as he tried to piece together all the things he had so far been able to read on the stone.

"Thank you, Sang. That explains a lot." Richard lifted his sword halfway from its scabbard to show it to Sang. "You better go stand back there with the others where it will be safe."

Piecing together what he had read so far, and what Sang said, Richard knew just how dangerous this gateway was in the hands of the Glee. It had to be destroyed.

Sang nodded, having seen the destructive power of the sword before, and rushed out of the circle of sand to stand back with the others among the rock formations.

Richard stood staring at the symbols on the stone gateway for a long moment. He let the sword slide back down into its scabbard.

Vika frowned at Richard and lowered her voice. "Lord Rahl, what's going on? Are you going to destroy this terrible thing or not?"

Richard rubbed his chin as he looked from her to the stone and back again. "I'm getting an idea."

Her brow tightened. "What kind of idea?"

"The crazy kind."

"Is it going to get us killed?"

"Probably."

168

"What kind of crazy idea is it this time?" she asked, sounding weary of such ideas and the likelihood that it would get them killed.

Richard waved off the question. "Do me a favor and keep making sure the Glee stay back. I need to be left alone for a while to study these symbols. They're complicated."

Vika waggled a hand at the stone. "What do you think all those are for? What is their purpose? You said before that they're instructions, but instructions for what?"

Richard looked into her blue eyes. "Instructions to reset the gateway."

"What do you mean, reset it?"

Richard wiped a hand across his face. He was already weary of this damp world. He dreaded the thought of living out his life among the Glee in this hot, red, often wet world. He supposed he wouldn't have to live too long until one of them eventually got the idea to eat him.

"Well, when whoever brought this gateway here left it for the Glee to use, they had to reset it so that it would work for the Glee."

"Maybe they didn't really intend to leave it here," she suggested. "Maybe the Glee captured them and forced them to reset it so they could use it. After all, we know all too well how vicious they can be."

Richard pulled his lower lip through his teeth. "I suppose that's possible, too. There is no real way to tell for sure."

"So, what are you considering?"

He waggled a finger at the stone. "I'm thinking that if I can figure out enough of the symbols to activate it, I may be able to reset it."

Vika cocked her head as she suspiciously scrutinized him with her left eye alone. "Why would you want to reset it? For what purpose?"

"Well, think about it. If I'm able to reset it so that it works differently, then they could never again use it to go to our world—or any world for that matter. They wouldn't have the means to reset it to work for them, so that would render the gateway inert."

Vika's mouth twisted as she tried to follow his train of thought. "Why bother with all that? Wouldn't it be a lot simpler to just break it apart with your sword? If you did that, they certainly wouldn't be able to ever use it again, right? I mean, you wouldn't need to understand the symbols to do that. If you simply break the stone apart with your sword, that would be the end of it. Forever."

Richard glanced over at the stone before looking back at her. "We don't know what this thing really is."

Vika was giving him a wary look, like she was trying to figure out what he could really be thinking. "You said it's called a gateway. Obviously, it's a gateway to other worlds. That's what it is."

"Yes, but what I mean is we don't know what powers it, what makes it work. How does it send people"—he gestured with a hand in the direction of the throng of Glee watching them—"or Glee, or whatever, to another world? What if it uses some kind of magic, or what if inside it has mechanical components powered by magic like the omen machine used to have?

"I've found things in our world that are incredibly powerful and in many cases I have no idea exactly how they work or who could have made them or, for that matter, even where they came from. But I learned that they were profoundly dangerous, and had I tried to simply destroy them with my sword so that no one could ever use them, it could have caused unimaginable consequences. Some of those devices could have destroyed the world of life. In some things involving unknown magic that has the potential to be profoundly dangerous, such as this, here, you have to think it through before you do anything that can't be undone."

Vika glanced over at the stone in a new light. "So, you're saying that it could be so dangerous to try to destroy it that you think it might kill us all?"

Richard shrugged. "I don't know. From what I know about magic that's a possibility. If I hit it with my sword it could kill me, or, for all I know, it might even unleash enough power to destroy everyone for miles around, or even render this entire world a dead rock." He leaned closer to her. "Or, for all I know, it might even act as a weapon and send that destructive power to the last place the Glee used it to visit—to our world."

Vika flipped her braid forward over her shoulder and held it in her right fist as she considered.

"You mean, you think it could possibly be dangerous to try to destroy it, even dangerous to our own world, so instead you are thinking it might be safer for us, and our world, if you try to reset it so that the Glee can't possibly use it, and that would accomplish the same thing. It would render it useless and prevent them from ever harming our world again."

Richard gave her a firm nod. "That's right. For all I know, it could kill me if I try to destroy it, and then it would still be here and still work and remain a threat to our world."

"Well," she said with a deep sigh, "that's not crazy, so it's obviously not what you are actually thinking of doing. What is the crazy thing you are really considering doing?"

Richard showed her a small smile and gestured off to the other side of the ring. "Would you please go keep an eye on them. Once I start, I think I may need to keep going and I don't want to have any nosy Glee interrupting me."

Vika studied his face for a moment. "What are you not telling me?"

"I'm not telling you what you don't yet need to know."

Vika folded her arms as she looked at him from under her brow. "I'm here alone in this world with you. Forever. I'm going to grow old and die in the world along with you—if we live that long. We are in this together. Tell me."

Richard pursued his lips. "We are starting to sound like an old married couple."

She kept the look leveled on him. "Tell me."

He sighed. "All right. Well, first of all, if I simply reset the gateway, it's always possible that someone else could come along, figure it out, and reset it back again. If that happened, then they could use it for who knows what purpose. There's more to it, though."

"Like what?"

Richard gestured toward the gateway without looking over at it. "These symbols are starting to look to me like they could actually be a constructed spell."

169

With her arms still folded, she shrugged. "That's the big deal you couldn't tell me? That it might be a constructed spell?"

"If you mess with them and accidentally do the wrong thing, some constructed spells can kill everyone within dozens of miles."

Her arms came unfolded. "Oh."

"They can also be incredibly dangerous in other ways as well. Unexpected ways. If it really is a constructed spell, or even if it isn't but it functions something like one, it's not any kind of constructed spell I'm familiar with, and yet it has many of the routines and protocols I recognize. On top of that, not all the symbols are close to the same as those in the version of the language of Creation that I'm familiar with. That makes it hard to know precisely what each of those protocols means, how they function, and if there is a specific order to using them.

"Some constructed spells have fail-safes built into them that can kill you if you do the wrong thing at the wrong time. I will need to study it some more, first, before I can say for certain exactly what we are dealing with, here."

Vika looked at the stone and then back to him. "But if it really is the language of Creation, you should be able to understand it, shouldn't you?"

"I believe that the language of Creation may have different dialects. The markings here might simply be one of those different dialects, and that's why I'm having trouble understanding it. That makes it a little more difficult to translate all these symbols. It won't prevent me from translating what they say, but I first need to be sure of what some of the more familiar ones mean. Once I'm sure of the meaning of the symbols in those, that will help me translate others. That's going to take me some time. I don't know how much time, but I need to be left to it."

She shrugged. "All right, so study it."

He gave her a meaningful look. "I would appreciate it if you went over there and watched the Glee to keep them from getting too curious so I can concentrate in this."

"Oh. All right. Well, why didn't you just say so? But if you really think it is a constructed spell, wouldn't that mean this thing is powered by magic?"

Richard shook his head, feeling frustration that he had a hard time explaining all the technicalities. "I don't know. Maybe. I understand constructed spells, and I know how they function. I've even made a number of them myself. This looks in many ways like it could very well be a constructed spell, but in other ways it's different, so I'm not yet entirely sure.

"It may simply share some aspects with a constructed spell. It may be a coincidence that it looks like one to me in part because I'm not able to read all the symbols. I might also be reading too much into it. I just don't know yet. But these symbols are the key to learning how this thing functions, and if it actually is a constructed spell, so that's why I need to study it. Got it now?"

"What difference could that make?" She frowned at him. "If you simply reset it so they can't use it, that's all you really need to do, right?"

"Sure, unless someone comes along who can recognize the symbols or figure them out and then reset it for themselves so they could use the gateway. I'm trying to figure out if there is a way to lock in the reset, or better yet, use a fail-safe. So, unless you know how to work a constructed spell or you understand the language of Creation, would you please go over there and watch those Glee? And be prepared in case something happens."

Vika glanced to the Glee and then back at him. "Something like what?"

"Are you going to ask questions all the time for the rest of our lives in this awful world?"

Vika only smiled.

Richard looked over at the Glee out of the corner of one eye. "I don't know for sure what might happen, but if this thing really is a constructed spell powered by magic and something happens, they may become alarmed."

"What should I be prepared for?"

Richard let out a weary sigh. "Vika, Sang is going to soon grow impatient that I am not destroying this thing. I don't know what the other Glee will do if this stone starts making noises or something. After all, they seem to regard this thing as some sort of sacred object given to them by gods."

Vika finally relented. "All right. That makes sense. But if I have to start using my Agiel on them, things could get messy."

"Well, I don't want you to do that. Just keep your eye on them. Strike up a conversation or something. Divert their attention. Ask them about their offspring. Parents love to talk about that."

As soon as he said that, he wished he hadn't.

"I'm not all that experienced at small talk, but I'll give it a try."

"Is life with you in this world always going to be this difficult?"

Vika smiled again. "You wouldn't want life here to be boring, would you?"

Richard shook his head before turning back to the stone as Vika walked over to Sang.

170

Richard glanced over to check and saw Vika talking to the Glee. Things seemed peaceful enough. They looked interested in whatever she was telling them. He turned his attention back to what he was doing, bending close to continue studying the series of symbols and emblems on the stone, trying to figure out what the parts he didn't recognize meant.

He rubbed a temple with a finger as he worked to understand the connecting links. They were in fact different in a number of ways from the language of Creation he had learned, but he hadn't told Vika everything he already knew about them. He wasn't sure she could understand it—or would care to. Mord-Sith were famous for their dislike of anything to do with magic. Richard wasn't yet positive that this gateway stone really did possess magic, but the symbols certainly did have a lot of the characteristic elements of magic as expressed through constructed spells. He almost had a hard time believing it could be something other than magic.

In large part, they did comply with the precepts of a constructed spell. And yet, in some ways, they didn't.

He had created constructed spells before, and in his studies, he had learned a great deal about their complexities and how they functioned through principles of magic, both Additive and Subtractive. He knew a number of their key provisions. But that hardly meant he knew everything about them.

While this was in many ways the same element he knew, and understood, there were differences he couldn't yet fathom. He traced components of things he knew, struggling to identify exactly how this was different so he could fill in the blanks.

In his studies of books of magic and in working with constructed spells he had access to, he had also learned a lot about his own gift. For reasons that eluded him, he had an easier time using his gift with constructed spells, perhaps because they were so technical, and the steps made sense. When he followed the steps in constructed spells in the proper way, the spell came to life. In other situations when he needed his gift, it didn't always respond, so he naturally gravitated toward the type of magic with structure he could analyze.

He also suspected that those technical aspects that required him to concentrate distracted him enough to call upon his gift without really thinking about it when his magic was needed in procedures along the way. When he was relieved of the conscious pressure to call forth his gift, it simply naturally worked as required to assist him. Importantly, one of the things he had learned in his studies was that it took his gift not only to work with constructed spells, but to understand them.

It had always been difficult for him to call up his gift consciously, except in a certain kind of crisis, but here, with these emblems, he could sense them with his gift. It seemed like here, in this world, with this complicated spell he was able to touch his gift in order to understand elements in ways that were difficult or impossible to do back in his home world.

He realized that it felt to him like he was having much the same kind of ease with using his gift as he had experienced before, only in the underworld.

Because constructed spells were so rare, he hadn't been able to study a lot of them. Having seen only a relative few, that left a lot of questions in his mind with the gateway.

He came to realize that, rather than trying to decipher every element of every symbol along the way to understand all of the language of Creation the way it was written on the stone, if he simply assumed it was a constructed spell and treated it as such, that very well might be the best way for him to come to grasp the entirety of what all the writing meant.

As he became more familiar with the symbols he hadn't seen before, he began to learn by their context that it wasn't really all that different from the language of Creation he already knew. This simply said things in a slightly different way. It might use the symbol for a bat to express flight, rather than the bird symbol he was familiar with. But it suddenly clicked in his mind that the larger concept was really the same. They were both referring to the concept of the air, or the sky. That realization helped him start to make faster progress in deciphering the overarching meaning of what he was reading.

When he glanced up, he noticed that the Glee across the sand were starting to look restless. Vika was walking back and forth, talking to them, distracting them. He certainly couldn't afford to have the Glee suddenly decide that they didn't want Richard messing around with their device, as they called the gateway.

But what was worse, he now realized that he was going to need to ignite a verification web if he was to learn more of how the gateway functioned, and he didn't know how the Glee might react to that. He finally decided that there was no other way around it. He was simply going to have to do it.

Richard finally located the sequence of symbols that would initiate the verification web. He touched those symbols with a finger in the proper order, letting his gift flow into each of them to begin to unlock the constructed spell. It should work if the symbols were what he believed they were.

He held his breath and briefly tapped the last one to let a bit of Subtractive Magic feed the emblem.

Suddenly, all the symbols on the entire stone lit up as if they were made of glass and there was a light inside the stone. Every one of the symbols glowed a pale bluish color that stood out all the more because of everything else being some shade of red. More alarming, the thing started giving off a low humming sound.

Richard didn't know if he had merely activated the stone in some way, or it was doing what he intended. He quickly went back to the symbols and tapped the next series in the proper sequence to add Subtractive Magic to them in order to find out if this really was a constructed spell. Subtractive Magic would break the necessary seals if it actually was a constructed spell. If it was, then something should happen to give him some kind of indication.

At first, nothing happened.

He held his breath as he waited.

All of a sudden, one of the emblems on the top of the stone, on the side opposite the sloped top, lit with red light. He touched it with a finger, letting it have a bit of Additive Magic. As soon as he did, it abruptly threw a series of lines through the air similar to the way a fisherman would toss out a net. But instead of sinking to the ground, this net of lines hung in midair over the sand. The lines all glowed the same pale bluish color as the other symbols on the gateway stone. That was a sign, but not yet the right sign.

He heard the Glee across the sand, crowded in among the rocks, start to hiss. It sounded to him like a hiss of impatience.

He glanced up at the intricate pattern of the lines hanging in midair only to see Vika rushing back to him.

The alarm on her face was clear.

171

Richard motioned frantically to get Vika to go around the glowing lines rather than run straight toward him and through them. She had no idea how dangerous they were, but fortunately she instinctively avoided anything having to do with magic, so as soon as she spotted the glowing lines she dodged to the side and changed course to avoid going into the gold ring altogether. He breathed out a sigh of relief.

She skidded to a stop beside the stone. She put a hand on it for support as she panted.

"Lord Rahl—"

Richard pushed her hand off the stone. "Don't touch it. It's active. I don't know what it could do if you touch the wrong thing."

She drew her hand back as if she had touched fire. "Lord Rahl, the Glee are not at all happy about what they're seeing."

Before she could elaborate, Sang raced up behind her. *"Lord Rahl! You must not do this,"* he shouted in Richard's mind. *"You said that you intended to destroy the device. That is what you must do. The others, the others who were followers of the goddess, are growing angry. They consider this device a sacred gift from the gods."*

Richard frowned up at Sang. "Then why didn't they object when I came up here to destroy the thing?"

Sang looked back at the massive throng of Glee among the rocks on the other side of the white sand. They were all waving their arms, apparently arguing among themselves. He looked back at Richard and bent down as if to speak confidentially, although the Glee had already proven their ability to have others hear them selectively. Or maybe it was only an ability to make Richard and Vika selectively not hear them.

"They did not know that you intended to destroy the device."

"What?" Richard rose to his feet. "You mean you didn't tell them what I intended to do?"

Sang shook his head. *"No. I dared not. You must understand that we have only just been reunited with them after you struck down the Golden Goddess. I thought you would come up here and do the same thing with the device and it would be over before they realized what you were going to do, and in that way have it ended once and for all before they could object."*

"What did you expect them to do once had I destroyed it with my sword?"

Sang hesitated. *"I thought that since it would then be over and too late for them to do anything about it, we could more easily convince them that it was for the best. With the Golden Goddess dead and the device destroyed so we could no longer go to other worlds, I thought they would then realize they had no choice but to go back to our traditional ways and then they would come to be at peace with it. I thought they would even realize that the fighting and violent death of so many was finally ended and be pleased."*

Richard realized that even though they had the ceremonial eating of the water weed from Iben's body, they hadn't fully committed to giving up all their beliefs or using the device to go to other worlds. They had enjoyed the sport of hunting, and they had developed a taste for the flesh of people. There were probably Glee among those watching who craved power and were waiting to later use the device to win followers to themselves.

"This is more complicated than I realized," Richard told Sang. "I can't simply use my sword to break this stone apart. It's not just a piece of rock. If it were, I could shatter it. But it's a powerful device that uses magic to send you to other worlds. If I use my sword to try to destroy it, it could end up killing us all, or even killing everyone in this world. I need to disable it in another way."

"Do what you must, but hurry," Sang urged. *"If you do not destroy it quickly, you may never get another chance."*

"I will go as fast as I can, but it will take some time. I need you to go back and convince them that they need to stay away because these lines you see above the sand are dangerous."

Sang looked across the sand toward the Glee for a moment and then back to Richard. His third eyelids blinked across his large, glossy black eyes.

"What lines?"

172

Richard was shocked. "You mean to say you can't see the glowing lines above the sand?"

Sang briefly looked again and then back at Richard. He shook his head.

"I see only sand and beyond it, the Glee who are growing angry."

Richard hadn't expected that the Glee couldn't see the lines of light. He knew that everyone in his world had at least a spark of the gift within the Grace they were born with. That spark, even though it usually wasn't powerful enough in most people to use it to do magic, still allowed them to see and interact with magic.

The only explanation was that the Glee had no such spark of the gift. They were completely devoid of even that infinitesimal spark. That was why the goddess had been so fearful of the magic of Richard's world. She had never experienced it before and didn't understand it. It was a fearsome unknown to her.

Sang drew back his lips, exposing his needle-sharp white teeth, as if in apology.

Richard gestured. "Can you see the symbols on the stone light up?"

Sang leaned past Richard to look at the stone. *"Light? I see no light. Only the markings as they were always there."*

The sun had set, and it was rapidly getting darker. Sang should have had absolutely no difficulty seeing either the glowing lines of light above the sand or the glowing symbols on the stone gateway.

Richard looked over at Vika. "You see them both, right?"

She shrugged her confusion that Sang couldn't see them. "Of course. I don't know what the lines over the sand are, or what they mean, but I can see them."

Richard was at least relieved by that much of it. "It's the initial stages of a verification web. The lines mean that I was able to get the gateway to ignite its constructed spell. There's no explanation I can see other than whatever this gateway is, it uses a constructed spell. It's built right into it."

"What is a constructed spell?" Sang asked.

"Magic," Richard told him. "Dangerous magic."

"Dangerous to you, or to us?"

"Extremely dangerous to the Glee," Richard told him. "You already know that this device has the ability to send you into darkness. That should tell you something about how powerful it is. That power is dangerous."

"But we have used it since long before any of us were alive," Sang said. *"It never harmed us."*

"It was never activated before, but now it is. Because it uses a very powerful form of magic, I need to use that power built into the device to destroy it. It's the only way."

Sang gestured back across the sand. *"But the others are angry at not knowing what you are doing with their device, and they may soon decide they must stop you."*

"You need to go talk to them. Tell them how you have seen the power of magic in my world. This device uses that same magic. If you want to, tell them that the device is malfunctioning, and it is about to kill anyone up here. You need to get all of the Glee away from here or they might be killed. Get them all to go back down the mountain to safety."

"I don't think they will want to leave you alone with the device. It is too important to them."

Richard growled his frustration. He gestured up at the darkening sky. "It's getting dark. You need to go now while it is still light enough to see your way down the mountain or you will all be stuck up here in this dry place all night." Richard leaned toward him. "All night. Without water."

Sang touched a claw to his lip. That concerned him, but he was still hesitating. Because he couldn't see the glowing bluish lines, Richard didn't know if he understood and feared the magic of the gateway, but like a boulder falling off a cliff from above, you didn't need to see it to be killed. He knew, though, that fear of being stuck in this dry place overnight was probably more alarming to him than anything else. He looked across the sand to the others. Some of them were clacking their claws in a threatening manner.

"Sang," Richard said, drawing his attention back to him, "something is about to happen that will likely kill all of you up here. You need to convince them they must leave, right now. You need to tell them that darkness will soon trap them here in this dry place and they must leave now, while they can still see the path down. Tell them they can come back tomorrow if you have to."

Sang nodded. *"I will try. I will tell them what you say about being trapped up here in this dry place where it will soon be dark. That may convince them to go back down from here right away."*

"I'm serious," Richard said. "Dangerous magic is about to begin and if anyone is up here when it does, they will die.

"If they refuse to leave, then you and your friends must leave as quickly as you can or you will be killed, too. You must believe me, Sang. You must leave now. I don't want you or your friends to be harmed. But if they stay up here, you all will die."

Sang again touched the tip of his claw to his black lower lip as he studied Richard's face. Finally, he nodded. *"You have done what we needed to stop the Golden Goddess. You have helped us. I will tell those with me that we must run. I will tell the others, too, that it will soon be too dark to see, and they will be trapped here so they must leave until tomorrow. They will be warned. If they don't leave…"*

Richard put a hand on Sang's shoulder. "You have been a friend, Sang. I wish you a good life."

Sang's dark skin bunched above his big black eyes in a kind of grotesque frown. *"Are you saying that you will be here when the magic starts, and you will die?"*

Richard continued to gaze into those black eyes. "I'm afraid so. This is what I need to do to protect my world. Thank you for your part in this, and for coming to help me protect my people as well as yours. Now go. Hurry. Get to safety."

"You have been a friend to me and to my friends."

Sang laid a claw on Richard's shoulder, as if to thank him, and then he quickly turned and rushed away. He paused once to look back, and then he ran to the others off among the forest of tall rocks to warn them that they must leave at once.

173

Vika leaned close to Richard once she saw Sang join the others. "This is it, then? We are really going to die?"

Richard glanced over at her. "If my crazy idea doesn't work, most likely."

She frowned in a way that only Mord-Sith could frown. "And if your crazy idea does work, then the gateway will be destroyed, and we will have to face who knows how many thousands of angry Glee that will want to rip us apart for destroying their precious device?"

"Maybe they will cool off once they get back to their ponds."

Richard didn't want to tell her what his crazy idea actually was.

"So, if your crazy idea doesn't work, we will likely die in the attempt, and if it does work and doesn't kill us, the Glee likely will."

"I tried to get you to stay back there in our world," he told her. "You are the one who insisted on coming with me."

Vika made a sour face as she folded her arms. "I guess coming with you was my crazy idea."

He showed her a small smile that was more forced than real.

She looked across the sand at the Glee. They were all engaged in an animated discussion. There was even some pushing and shoving. Sang threw both arms up in the air as he jumped around, frantically trying to make his point. They didn't look to be convinced. He gestured at the sky and then toward the way down the mountain, urging them that they had to leave before it was too dark.

The former followers of the goddess who had followed them up the mountain didn't look like they had any intention of leaving before it was too dark, apparently more upset about Richard messing with their precious device than anything else. The way they were pointing across the sand, they looked like they were more set on stopping Richard.

The Glee Richard had brought across the drylands finally heeded Sang's urgent warnings and started for the path down the mountain. Richard looked up and he could already see the first stars. They soon wouldn't have much light to help them make it down the mountain. The moons would help, but only until they were in the dense fog of the heavy cloud layer lower down the mountain.

"I don't know what you have planned," Vika said, "but you had better hurry up before they decide to come over here and kill us to keep you from harming their sacred device."

"I know, but I need time."

"Time for what? How much time?"

"I already activated the verification web." He gestured toward the sand. "That's the bluish lines in the air above the sand. It doesn't tell me enough about what I need to know to reset the gateway. In order to understand the gateway and the process to reset it, I need to do an aspect analysis of the verification web from an interior perspective."

"Oh, of course." Vika rolled her eyes. "I don't know why I didn't suggest that in the first place."

"Vika, this is serious. This is our only chance. I'm going to have to use both Additive Magic and Subtractive Magic. It's the only way to activate an interior perspective."

That sobered her. "What do you need me to do?"

"Once I ignite that kind of power, anyone up here is going to die."

"I hope you don't really expect me to leave with Sang."

"No." He gestured to the bluish lines above the sand. "I want you inside that web with me. It's the only way to protect you."

"Inside magic?" She looked at him like she thought he had lost his mind. "You want me inside some kind of powerful magic with you? That's your crazy idea?"

"You need to trust me. You have already let me take you to the world of the dead. Compared to that, this should be a breeze."

"Sure, a breeze." She glanced briefly at the glowing lines above the sand. "I don't know a lot about magic, but what I do know is that mixing Subtractive Magic and Additive Magic is beyond dangerous. If you need reminding, that's what brought Shota's palace in Bindamoon down on top of you."

"I know, but this time there is not a witch unleashing the same thing at me."

"Will we be safe in your web thing?"

Richard nodded to reassure her. "Yes. I've done it before, and I know how to do it. But there is a problem."

"Of course there is." She let out a deep sigh. "What's the problem?"

"While I know what I'm doing with the constructed-spell portion, I don't know for sure how the gateway is going to react to a mix of that kind of power."

She gestured across to the sand. "Well, whatever you're going to do, you had better hurry. I don't think Sang is convincing those angry Glee of anything."

Richard saw that she was right. The last thing he needed was to get into a battle with Glee in the middle of complex protocols. He grabbed hold of Vika's upper arm and urgently pulled her with him toward the center of the maze of glowing, bluish lines, working his way carefully but quickly through the maze without touching it to get to the center. Fortunately, there weren't yet a lot of the bluish lines; that was why he needed to do the more extensive interior perspective from inside the verification web.

Once there in the center of the sand, Vika looked all around at the glowing lines, like they might bite. She wasn't necessarily wrong. But they were far from as dangerous as they were going to get.

"I don't have magic," she reminded him.

"You have the bond to me," he told her in a distracted voice. "I have magic. That gives you all the magic you will need. You will be protected by that bond."

She looked around at the lines. "If you say so."

"I do."

"Well, do I need to do anything?"

"No. Just try not to move around too much or touch the glowing lines. Stay close to me. Once everything starts, don't move away or try to run."

She gestured. "Sang is still here, trying to convince them to leave."

Richard turned. "Sang!" he called out. "You have three heartbeats before anything living up here is killed. Go now! If they won't go with you, leave them!"

174

At Richard's urgent warning, Sang and the rest of his followers still up on the mountain raced away and disappeared through the contorted rock spires toward the path that would take them down the mountain. A few of the other Glee looked about and then changed their minds when they saw the others running for their lives. A number of them decided to go with them. Many more watched them go but didn't follow.

Richard had given them a chance to get to safety. They refused to take it.

He saw the masses of Glee that were left behind, apparently wary because of Sang's warnings about dangerous magic, cautiously begin to move out from between and behind the smooth, flowing shapes of the rock. Cautious or not, he recognized Glee with murderous intent.

"Lord Rahl—hurry!" Vika yelled.

"Don't stare at the lightning," he told her.

"What lightning?"

Instead of taking precious time to answer her, Richard simply reached out and touched two separate primary intersections of converging, glowing, bluish lines and then closed his eyes. To cast the proper interior perspective of a verification web, he needed to use his gift. He could feel the power of the gateway's constructed spell as it pulled his gift up from the depths of his soul.

He knew by the way it functioned that the gateway had to be powered by a constructed spell. It was clear that it was simply a type of constructed spell he had never encountered before. That being the case, he hoped that everything at least worked in the same way with the same procedures he knew.

As he felt the power from those bluish lines radiating up his arms, he didn't try to resist. They were seeking within him what they needed. He knew that without Subtractive Magic the verification web would be sterile. He quickly opened his mind to what they were trying to pull from him and released his restraints.

His gift responded with such a rush of power it took his breath.

Time and movement outside the golden circle seemed to stop.

Inside that circle, almost instantly, both Additive and Subtractive Magic ignited from his outstretched arms with a deafening thunder-clap. From his right hand, Additive Magic flashed in a twisting arc that would blind a person were they to stare right at it for more than a brief glance. Beyond the gold ring, Glee tried to shield their eyes with an arm. They might not be able to see magic, but this kind of power was something that even they could see. With his eyes closed, Richard could still see the bright, searing lines of the lightning right through his eyelids.

Almost at the same time, from his left hand, Subtractive Magic thundered into existence, shaking the ground. Unlike its opposite, it wasn't at all bright. His eyes were closed, but he had seen it enough times that he could sense the cold void in the world of life that was blacker than death itself.

Now that his gift had responded and the full verification web had been ignited, Richard held both arms out as he squinted just enough to see the blindingly bright threads of crackling Additive lightning and shrieking threads of totally black Subtractive threads flickering and twisting all around him and Vika. Those threads of power arced upward from his hands and then cascaded down to the golden ring. The way they each turned and tumbled, they reminded him of wild beasts on a chain.

In his peripheral vision Richard could see the dark shapes of the Glee that had started racing toward the gold circle suddenly stop where they were as they saw power they couldn't comprehend exploding into existence before them. They didn't run, maybe because they were waiting for an opening to attack to save their precious device, or maybe because they couldn't understand what it was they were seeing, or maybe because they were simply paralyzed by fear.

The whole perimeter of the golden circle that he and Vika had uncovered in the sand drew a network of thin Subtractive threads of inky black lightning as well as blindingly bright threads of Additive Magic, all of them flickering as they jumped and raced around the entire perimeter of the gold ring as if it were alive and trying to find a way to escape. But the golden circle prevented any escape. At least for the moment.

Richard closed his eyes again and swiftly raised both arms. Using all the power of his gift he abruptly brought the main trunks of those crackling, flickering discharges of Additive and Subtractive Magic up with his hands feeding them everything he had. Both of those arcing streams of thunderous power slammed together, rocking the mountain.

Instantly, all around the perimeter of the gold circle about waist high, a burst of dark energy powered by Subtractive Magic exploded outward in an ever-expanding ring. As it shot off in all directions, it instantly cut cleanly through the Glee where they stood and the rock towers behind them as well as those all around the mountaintop.

Richard saw what had just happened as if watching from outside his own body. With the threat stopped, he immediately used his gift to pull the Subtractive Magic he had allowed to escape back within the boundary of the gold ring.

The Glee had all been sliced cleanly in two and were dead before they tumbled to the ground. Some of the tops of the rock towers, suddenly separated by a void cut cleanly through them by Subtractive Magic, dropped straight down with a thud and stayed there, as if joining into one again. Others that were out of balance slowly began to tip over until they crashed down. Any of the Glee that had been behind the rock had also been cut in two and killed. No Glee that had come up on the mountain, other than those with Sang who had fled, escaped alive.

Everything had happened in a blinding flash of pure elemental power. What only a second before had been a dangerous threat, was no more. With the threat eliminated, Richard turned his attention back to the procedures for the ignition of the interior perspective of the verification web.

He allowed both kinds of lightning to twist and dance together. Countless threads of the combined power crackled all around them, forming a dome shape over Richard and Vika. The ends of all those thrashing threads grounded on the golden ring, like lightning drawn irresistibly to a tree. It didn't seem to do any harm to the ring.

That part was unlike any verification-web procedure Richard had ever seen before, or heard of, but he realized that just because he hadn't seen it before didn't mean it was wrong, and was no reason to stop.

Within that dome of crackling power, all around Richard and Vika, the constructed spell rapidly built a network of yet more lines, confirming that everything about the spell was unfolding properly and as he had expected. As Richard concentrated on giving those lines the power they needed from his gift, they traced their way through the air, building a three-dimensional series of glowing lines.

Unlike the previous lines, these glowed orange, which was a rather discordant contrast in the red world. The bluish lines from before turned green when the orange lines intersected with them, changing them and adding to their structure. Lines of light raced through the air to support and reinforce geometric shapes. Triangles merged and formed complex angles and shapes of pure white light that lit the remaining towers of rock all around them in their soft glow.

The lines swiftly grew in purpose, creating an intricate web around Richard and Vika. Richard understood those lines and the elements of magic they represented. As they multiplied, the glowing lines continued to build, crisscrossing around the two of them at a dizzying rate. As they did, Vika pressed her back to his as yet more lines shot like arrows through space close in around them.

The lines, Richard knew, were routines of the spell-form, protocols that created the web to confirm what elements made up that spell-form. They were, in essence, a three-dimensional diagram of the constructed spell.

The lines continued to trace their routes with purpose and precision as the dome of crackling lightning overhead protected them. The symbols on the stone flashed in sequence. In the fabric of the web around them made of orange, white, and green lines, in the angles and junctions, Richard could read purpose and procedure, revealing how the spell and the strange power used by the gateway functioned.

Even though it was unlike any constructed spell he had seen before, in the complexity of glowing lines all around them, there was profound beauty of purpose.

Richard now understood how it all fit together and the underlying mechanism for how the gateway worked.

And, he now understood exactly what he had to do to alter the gateway.

175

R ichard looked back over his shoulder at Vika. "Are you all right?"
"Peachy," she said above the crackling noise of the lightning
flickering all around them.

Richard smiled. "Good."

She cast a worried look around the dancing and glimmering dome
of power, then gazed back at him. "As far as your crazy ideas go, this
one might be the craziest."

"Well, I have to tell you, I haven't yet gotten to the crazy part."

She carefully avoided touching any of the glowing lines as she used
her hands on him to twist herself around until she was facing his back.
She circled one arm around his waist to make sure she stayed close
enough in case he moved. He was glad, at least, that she was taking the
danger of the glowing lines seriously.

"What?" she yelled out. "This isn't the crazy part?"

"No. I just wanted to make sure you are all right because I'm about
the do the crazy part. I'm going to need your help to do some of it
with me."

She shook her head. "Sure, why not. I have nothing better to do."

He gestured around at the complex network of luminous blue,
green, orange, and white lines of the verification web. "I'm going to
have to extinguish some of these glowing orange lines in order to open
up a corridor of sorts that you and I can move through to get to the
gateway device."

"Should I go with you?"

"Yes. Once I clear away enough of the lines, then when I start to
move toward the stone, I want you to move with me, like you are my
shadow. Can you do that?"

"Of course. But that doesn't sound like it's the crazy part."

"It's not. When I'm ready and we start to move, keep your arms in close. Be careful not to let any part of you touch the lines, because they will cut a slab of flesh right off you."

"I understand."

"I'm going to extinguish some of the lines, but I can't get rid of them all quite yet or the web will collapse, and I still need it, so it will be a narrow space and we will have to be careful."

"I understand. But there is something that I think you should know, first."

"What's that?" he asked.

She pointed down. "We're not touching the ground. We're floating about a foot above it."

"I know. It's part of the process. When I extinguish some of the lines, we will settle down to the ground and be able to walk to the stone."

Once he was sure that she wasn't going to panic and do something that might get her killed—he realized as soon as he had the thought that Mord-Sith didn't panic and they didn't necessarily fear getting killed, as long as it was in service to protect him—he began reaching out and touching his first finger and thumb together at key intersections in the web. Since the lines were in part a creation of his own gift, he knew that as long as he was careful, they wouldn't harm him the way they would harm Vika.

As he touched the first intersection of lines above and a little to the right, two of the lines crossing in front of him vanished. He continued to pinch off primary junctions of lines, in a way cauterizing the flow of power so that it wouldn't bleed away, and the web would remain viable.

As he pinched off intersections at the proper nodes, it extinguished lines in midair between him and the stone at the edge of the ring. With each that vanished, he could reach farther in to touch other prime points where complex networks of glowing orange lines came together. As he worked, he and Vika gradually sank toward the ground.

Once their feet touched the ground, he spoke to Vika back over his shoulder. "I'm going to move closer to the stone. Stay close."

"Don't worry. Just think of me as your shadow."

Richard worked as he moved deeper until he had an adequate corridor opened to the stone. It wasn't roomy, but it provided enough space for them to get through. Once there, he started clearing the glowing lines from all around the stone to give himself the access he would need to all the symbols.

"All right, I'm ready for the next part. Don't be alarmed."

"Nothing you do alarms me anymore."

He smiled as he pulled his silver-handled knife from the sheath at his belt. It had an ornate letter "R" on it for the House of Rahl. It was a reminder of home, Kahlan, and all he had left behind, as well as his responsibility to his own world.

As Vika watched over his shoulder, Richard gritted his teeth and drew the razor-sharp blade across his forearm, cutting deep enough to bleed sufficiently to provide the blood he would need. He ignored the stinging pain of the cut and wiped the knife in the blood, turning it over, collecting all of it he could on the blade.

He held the knife level so that the blood wouldn't all run down and drip off. Leaning over, he touched a series of three emblems in the language of Creation with just enough Additive Magic to initiate a reset of the gateway. Each one he touched confirmed that touch of magic with a slight vibration and a tone.

Once done with that, he held the knife over the stone to let the blood drip from the tip of the blade into the slot on the top where Sang had shown him they put their claw.

"What are you doing?" Vika sounded apprehensive.

"I thought you said that nothing I do alarms you anymore."

"I'm not alarmed. I'm Mord-Sith. I'm curious."

Richard held the knife steady to make sure all the blood continued to drip into the slot. "I'm altering the protocols with my blood so that the gateway will only recognize a Rahl from now on."

"That's actually not crazy."

"Just wait," he whispered.

"What?"

"Nothing."

Richard swiftly stroked the edge of the blade up his arm again to collect more blood. Once he had, he quickly held it over the slot, letting more of his blood drip from the tip into the slot. He didn't know how much would be needed to accomplish what he wanted to do, but he decided it would be best to be sure it was plenty rather than risk having too little.

As he dripped the blood in the second time, the ground began to rumble like distant thunder. A soft glow appeared in the air over the sand within the gold ring.

Richard looked back at Vika. "Now comes the crazy part."

Her mouth dropped open. "You mean none of this was the crazy part?"

"No, not really."

"What are you going to do?"

"I don't have time to explain. The reset is active. I need to complete the series."

"What can I do to help?"

"I need to hold an arm around this stone. I will reach back with my other arm. I want you inside the gold ring as close as you can get to the center of that glowing light and still be able to stretch out an arm and hold my hand."

Seeing his grim expression, she nodded. "All right. Anything else?"

"Just don't let go of my hand no matter what happens."

"I won't," she said earnestly before she started carefully working her way back through the corridor in glowing orange lines. She turned and stretched her arm out, waiting for his hand.

Richard put his right arm around the stone, with his wrist hooked up over the top on the other side so that he could hold the knife, still dripping his blood, over the slot in the slanted top of the stone.

With his left hand, he reached down and touched the reset sequence with his palm. He used enough of a flow of Subtractive Magic to close the verification web. As soon as he felt the final emblem vibrate under his palm, confirming that it accepted the instruction, all the glowing lines instantly turned to smoke. Those lines of smoke swirled a little in the air before they quickly began to vanish. In a moment they were gone.

But in their place the softly glowing air within the golden ring began to vibrate with an ever-increasing roar that hurt his ears.

Richard looked back at Vika. She was wincing against the pain of the thundering roar.

"You will need to bend over a little more to be able to reach me!" He had to yell to make sure she could hear him over the strange vibrating, rumbling noise.

She nodded as she did as he asked, bending at the waist and stretching her arm out toward him while keeping her feet in the center of the sand. She held the position, waiting for him to grab her hand.

With his left hand, Richard quickly pressed his palm to the final reset authentication emblem. It pulsed a bright red to confirm that it recognized him. As soon as it did, he immediately stretched his left arm back to Vika. She grimaced against the pain of the sound as she grabbed and then gripped his hand like her life depended on it.

It did.

He again read the critical emblem in the language of Creation that was facing him. Because it was so important, the same emblem was on all four sides of the stone so that it couldn't be missed. Each emblem was the same. It translated roughly to "Keep your target in mind."

He didn't need to know what that meant to tell him. He understood it from using a bow and arrow. When he shot, he called the target. That was what the gateway meant him to know. As strange as it seemed, it felt to him as if the gateway, now that it had his blood, was reading what was in his mind and using what he already knew in order to guide him.

It was like they were now of one mind and one purpose.

Richard looked back at Vika. "Once more into darkness!" he cried out over the roar.

Hugging his right arm around the stone, target firmly in mind, he reached over the top with his right hand and slammed the silver knife down into the slot in the stone.

176

The air within the gold ring that had been glowing with a roar abruptly began to flare with points of light packed together so tightly that it almost looked like the air itself was burning white hot. All of those sparkling points of light gave off a crackling sound that replaced the roar but was just as loud.

Richard hugged the stone with all his might as he gripped Vika's hand as hard as he could. He dared not lose his grip on her hand. He thought he might be hurting her, but she was squeezing back just as hard.

He closed his eyes, trying to empty his mind of all the thousand worries questioning everything he had just done. No one had taught him these procedures. He had learned them from the gateway itself through its verification web. In essence, the gateway had shown him what it needed at each step.

His grandfather Zedd had taught him that many dangerous things of magic had fail-safes that prevented anyone who wasn't supposed to from using them. He worried that maybe the things the gateway had revealed it needed to function and reset might be one of those fail-safe traps to not only prevent him from successfully using something that he was not meant to use but kill him in the process.

Many fail-safes were, after all, lethal.

He mentally ran through everything he had done, trying to make sure he hadn't overlooked anything. He knew he had done a thorough analysis and as a result he had disarmed all the fail-safe sequences he had found from the interior perspective of the verification web. He tried to think if it was possible there had been any that he could have missed. But if there were, it was too late now.

He knew he needed to focus, so he finally put those concerns from his mind.

He called the target.

He tried as hard as he could not to let any other thoughts but that target enter his mind. Around the fringes of his awareness, though, a continual stream of little things nagged and nibbled, calling to him, trying to pull him away to think about each of them. He redoubled his effort to put them from his mind.

As he did when he shot his bow, he saw the target in his mind, centered on it, and pulled it toward him.

He didn't feel anything trying to force him from the stone, or Vika from his grip, but he dared not loosen his hold on either. He had to remind himself what mattered and put both of those thoughts from his mind as he concentrated on calling the target.

He stole a quick peek. It was hard to see anything through the sparkling points of light, but he could detect the windswept stone all around them rapidly getting increasingly wavy. He thought it might be that his eyes were watering, so he blinked and returned to concentrating on calling the target.

He had done everything to the best of his ability. He knew he could no longer dare to spare the mental effort to worry about any of it. Now, he simply focused on calling the target. That was all that mattered. It was everything that mattered.

Suddenly there was a thunderous rumbling sound, low, intense, powerful. Even with his eyes closed, he could see the flash of light that had caused it.

The next thing he was aware of, before he could begin to understand what had just happened, was darkness beyond dark.

Abruptly, there was no longer any sound at all. The profound silence rang in his ears until it hurt, and then even that sensation was gone.

Richard felt nothing. It was a complete lack of any sights or sounds or sensations. He couldn't tell up from down.

He couldn't feel if he still had hold of Vika's hand or if he was still holding the stone. He desperately hoped that he was. If he wasn't, then it had all been for nothing and he would go forever into darkness until even his thoughts gradually disintegrated into nothing and became part of the void.

He had absolutely no sense of time. He didn't know if it had been minutes, hours, or even days since the silent darkness had abruptly collapsed in on him. Even that sensation of falling and the awful expectation of hitting the bottom left him. Having done this before made it easier to do again. He told himself that this was no different than it had been last time.

But somehow, in some indescribable way, this was different.

Very different. Profoundly different.

Despite having done this before, it was a sensation of no sensation that left him feeling hollow and lost.

Since he had done this before, it was relatively easy to talk himself out of any panic. He knew that eventually it had to end—in one way or the other—so he tried his best to disregard the sensation, or rather, the lack of sensation, and focus only on calling the target. That was his only job, now.

To keep his mind from wandering into disturbing places even as he concentrated on calling the target, he thought of Kahlan in the background behind the target.

He pictured her face in his mind.

He smiled when she smiled.

177

Suddenly, light and sound and sensation slammed in all around him. It was such a powerful awareness that it made him gasp. It was so totally different from the void of all sensation that the abrupt weight and light and sound hurt.

He could feel himself still holding Vika's hand and he still had his other arm around the gateway stone.

Richard opened his eyes, afraid he would see the same terrible place in the Glee's world.

Instead he saw his target brought to life all around him.

Despite having expected it, he blinked in surprise.

Vika turned all the way around, her eyes wide with wonder.

"You did it! You did it! Lord Rahl, you did it! You got us home!"

The gateway stone was right there beside him the way it had been, except that now wisps of vapor rose off of it. The gold ring sat in the white sand, like it had been before. But this sand was white. Really white.

All around him, in all its glory, was the Garden of Life.

He could see the stand of trees off to one side, with the path meandering back through them. It made him feel so good to see trees again that he thought his chest might burst. When he looked up, he saw the glassed skylight overhead that let in the sunlight... sunlight of his world. The sky was a clear, bright blue, not red. All around him there was color—greens of every shade and browns and whites. Color had never looked so luscious, so vibrant before.

He and Vika stared around at the place. It didn't seem possible that it could be real.

This was the target he had called, and it was all around them, and it was real.

They were in the People's Palace. They were home again in their own world.

Vika finally gripped him by his shoulders as she looked into his eyes. She had to swallow to be able to use her voice.

"Lord Rahl, I will never ever again, for as long as I live, doubt any of your crazy ideas."

Richard smiled as he used a thumb to wipe tears from under her eyes. "Don't be so quick to make that pledge. You have not yet heard what other crazy ideas I have."

By the look in her eyes, she didn't care. He turned more serious.

"I expect all those I love to occasionally doubt my crazy ideas, because questions from ones I care about and trust make me have to be sure, for their sake, before I act. So don't ever stop questioning my crazy ideas."

She smiled. "All right. But now what? I'm afraid that we're back where we started. The Mother Confessor and the rest of them are a long way off at the Wizard's Keep."

He looked over at the gateway stone sitting beside him. The vapor was finally beginning to abate. It was still making a soft humming sound, as it had back in the Glee's world when he had activated it.

Vika gestured at the slanted top. "Don't forget your knife."

Richard could see that several of the emblems were still glowing red and a couple were blue.

"I'm not done yet. While the reset process is still active, I have to put in a fail-safe."

"A fail-safe?"

"Yes, a procedure that prevents just anyone with the gift from being able to reset it or use it. Believe it or not, if you activate the gateway in the way I've done, you can actually create a duplicate."

Vika frowned. "What for?"

Richard shrugged. "I don't know. Maybe so that you can play that you are gods by gifting a gateway to other worlds. Maybe this one is a duplicate and that is how the Glee came to have it. Maybe the ones who gave it to them wanted to play at being gods."

"But you know for sure that there was no duplication this time, right? Are you sure this device is the one from the Glee's world, and that they don't have one anymore, maybe a duplicate of this one?"

"I'm positive. The procedure for creating a duplicate is completely different. This is the original from the Glee's world and there is no duplicate left behind. The Glee are going to be trapped in their world. They can never again travel to other worlds. I think Sang and his friends will be happy about that."

"And only you can ever do that with this one?"

Richard nodded. "Only a Rahl, yes, with fail-safes to prevent just anyone from figuring it out and using it. The knife I used is only used by special people. The gateway will recognize only it, the same way it was set to recognize the claw of a Glee, before. That's one safeguard. My blood created another protocol so that the gateway will only recognize Rahl blood."

"That should be specific enough, shouldn't it?"

Richard shook his head. "With something this dangerous, you can't be too careful. It needs something more, another fail-safe that no one would likely know to use. Something that only the right person would know."

"Like what?"

Richard flashed her a smile before squatting down before the stone. Most of the symbols in the language of Creation glowed a soft blue. One of them in the series of final emblems still glowed red, indicating that the reset was still open. He knew that once he touched it, the protocols would lock in and set.

Before he put his hand on the pulsing red symbol, he reached down to another series of emblems designed to accept additional properties. He recognized that this was a way he could set a fail-safe protocol.

He tapped that lower emblem once each time he counted out loud.

"One, two, three, four, five, six, seven, eight." Each tap elicited a soft chime along with a pulse of brighter light. He tapped the emblem one last time. "Nine."

He spread his fingers to touch two green emblems at the same time. The gateway stone made a soft dull sound as it recognized and accepted the new fail-safe.

Finally, he pressed his palm against the glowing red, pulsing symbol. He felt it make a soft vibration to confirm that the fail-safe was set and all the new protocols he had initiated were locked in.

Vika leaned close, looking at the symbols as the light within them gradually faded away and finally went out. The gateway stone once more looked like the inert stone it had seemed to be the first time they had seen it. It now appeared to be nothing more than a smooth but not polished stone, with symbols inscribed on it.

Vika looked puzzled. She gestured at the gateway stone.

"What were you counting?"

"This thing is obviously dangerous. As dangerous as the most dangerous magic. I'm not sure how to destroy it, or what harm it could cause if I tried, so instead I decided to make sure that it will be incredibly difficult for anyone to ever use.

"To make the gateway work, I locked in protocols that one now has to use a special knife like the one I'm carrying, and Rahl blood. But it's always possible that those requirements could be met, even against the will of a Rahl, by using a knife like this to kill him. This kind of knife, with Rahl blood on it, would meet the initial procedures. But it's too dangerous to leave it at that.

"So I set into the gateway a protocol that, in addition to this kind of knife and Rahl blood, the Law of Nines is also required for the gateway to work. Without the Law of Nines, no gateway. It will remain an inert piece of stone."

Vika rose up. "You are a devious man, Lord Rahl."

Richard let out a deep breath now that it was finalized. "You've said that before."

"It bears repeating."

He looked to the path out of the Garden of Life. "We need to get to the Wizard's Keep. Kahlan was about to give birth back when we left her there."

178

"It was a long and difficult journey getting to the Keep the last time," she reminded him. "We had better get some fast horses."

"I have a better way," Richard told her.

"Another crazy idea? Please tell me you don't intend to use the gateway to get us there."

Richard shook his head at the very notion. "Dear spirits no. I'm not sure that would even be possible. But I know a better way, and it's not crazy at all. Let's go."

As they went through the double doors and out of the Garden of Life, there was a very surprised knot of men of the First File standing right there. They all stepped back, stunned at seeing the Lord Rahl and Vika.

It looked as if they had heard sounds and were all gathered by the doors. At seeing him, all of them snapped to attention after stepping back and clapped fists to their hearts.

One of the Lord Rahl's personal guard stepped forward. The man was even bigger than the rest of the men of the First File. He was armored with fitted leather and had metal bands around his massive arms, just above his elbows. Those bands had razor-sharp projections on them that were used in close-quarters combat. They could tear an opponent apart with ease in short order.

The big man blinked in astonishment. "Lord Rahl, we weren't... expecting you."

"I suppose not," Richard said. "To tell you the truth, I wasn't expecting me to be here ever again."

When the man only frowned in confusion, Vika showed him a smile. "We went into darkness to get here."

He clearly didn't have a clue as to what she could mean.

"We've been keeping extra guards on this place since you told us to before you left," the captain of the guard said. "Not a soul has gone in there, but we heard noises and thought that maybe it was more of the Glee." He leaned over to look around Richard and through the open doors into the Garden of Life. The man looked painfully puzzled. "How did you get in there?"

"I just returned from the world of the Glee," he told them. The eyes of all the men widened. "They were killing people in our world, and they killed a lot of people here, at the palace. I had to make sure they can never come here to harm anyone again."

The captain looked grim. "There was an attack not long after you and the Mother Confessor disappeared, some time back, but none since then, thank the Creator."

"That wasn't the Creator's doing," Vika told them. "It was Lord Rahl's."

Richard ignored her and addressed the captain. "I'm sorry to hear about that, but at least there is no longer any need to ever again have to worry about attacks from those monsters. They will never be able to come here to our world again."

The captain frowned his concern. "Lord Rahl, how can you be so sure of that? Those demons could just show up out of thin air—we never knew when or where. How can you be sure they will not come again?"

Richard gestured back through the open double doors. "Because I stole the device they used to travel to our world and brought it back with me."

Jaws dropped. "Weren't they angry you did that?" the commander asked.

"Well, yes, actually they were, but the ones who objected are now dead."

They all looked at Vika, like maybe she could explain the incomprehensible to them. "I know, it sounds crazy," she told them, "but Lord Rahl sometimes does crazy things. If he didn't, we would be the ones who were dead by now."

The captain cleared his throat. "We are certainly happy to hear that you are safely back in our world with us, Lord Rahl. But what of the Mother Confessor? You were going to the Keep for her safety."

"Yes, well, and therein lies the problem. I wanted to bring the device I stole from the Glee here, where I know it will be safe under the protection of the First File. Now that I've done that, I need to get to the Keep as soon as possible."

"What can we do to help?"

"Get me to the sliph."

At that command, he sensed Vika tense up, and he saw her glance down at the Sword of Truth.

He showed her a small smile. "Since the sword had been touched by the world of the dead, and this time there isn't any risk to Kahlan's pregnancy, I can take my sword with me in the sliph."

Her expression eased. "That's a relief."

Richard nodded his agreement and then turned to the captain. "The fastest way to the sliph, if you please."

The man clapped a fist to his heart. "Come with us."

Richard could see in Vika's face that she had lost weight. They had eaten hardly anything in the days they were in the world of the Glee. He was feeling weak himself. He knew that the sliph would take at least a day to get them to the Keep.

Before they started out, he took one of the other soldiers by the arm. "It's going to be a long journey. Please bring me and Vika something to eat. Nothing fancy or anything that would take time to prepare. Some kind of meat. Whatever is already cooked. Bring it to the sliph and be quick about it."

179

*B*reathe…

Richard had traveled with the sliph a number of times, and as was usually the case it was both breathtaking, in more ways than one, and utterly terrifying.

The only difference this time was that he didn't need to be told twice to breathe when they arrived and the sliph pushed him to the surface. While the sliph could be an experience of profound wonder, his sense of urgency meant that he didn't care about any of that. He simply wanted out.

He threw one arm over the side of the sliph's well to hold himself up as he forced her fluid from his lungs, returning it to her, and then pulled in a deep breath. The shock of air made his body want to reject it. Despite the burning discomfort, he quickly pulled another deep breath as he grabbed a fistful of red leather as a limp Vika bobbed to the surface nearby.

He pulled her up from the churning silver liquid to the edge where he was holding on with one arm over the side of the stone well. Slipping his other arm around her, under her arms, he helped keep her head up above the sliph's quicksilver surface. She was limp and unresponsive. The silver fluid sluiced off her hair and red leather.

"Breathe!" he yelled in her ear.

He knew from experience that the sliph would be telling her the same thing, but in her mind, much the same way the Glee had talked to them. She didn't respond.

He put his mouth closer to her ear. "Vika! Breathe! I need you! Do it for me!"

She abruptly opened her eyes wide and exhaled the silver fluid as if she had just been surprised awake. She gasped a deep lungful of air and immediately winced in pain. The first few breaths after breathing the sliph were painful, not just physically but also mentally, because all your mind wanted was to stay in the velvety silver dreamworld.

She coughed, spitting up a little blood. In her mind, he knew, she didn't want to breathe air again and at first had to force herself to do it. The quicksilver-like fluid of the sliph was an otherworldly, spectacular experience unlike any other. It was a release from the bounds of the world of life, a sensation of free-floating, flying, and drifting all at once. It was in a way like being with a good spirit in a different kind of existence, where the concerns of the world no longer mattered. Once in the sliph, breathing her silver fluid, you never wanted it to end.

Except this time Richard had been eager for it to end.

Richard threw a leg up and over the side of the stone well. He pulled Vika up, helping her to get her arms up and over the wall. She was still limp.

"Breathe, Vika."

"I'm breathing," she complained.

The silver fluid in the well swelled up in the center, pulling upward until it formed into a beautiful, shiny, reflective face.

"Were you pleased, Master?"

"Yes," Richard said. "Very pleased."

"I know how painful death was for you, but I am glad that your sword now knows death as well so you can take it with you when we travel again."

"It is always a pleasure to be with you."

"Then come. I can take you many places. Where would you like to go? You will be pleased."

"I would like that very much. But I have some business right now. Maybe later."

"When?"

"I'm not sure yet. But really, it was wonderful. I was pleased."

The silver face smiled. "I am glad, Master." A bit of a silver frown formed. "You are sure you were pleased?"

"Yes," Richard said, nodding, as he hauled Vika's upper body over the edge. As she finally got a leg over, he helped her down to the ground. "Very pleased. You may go back now and be with your soul. I will call on you again just as soon as I wish to travel."

"Thank you, Master, for traveling with me. I enjoyed it. When you wish to travel again, I will be waiting for your call."

With that, the silver face melted down into her churning silver waters. The reflective fluid began sinking down inside the well. Richard looked over the edge to see the choppy surface receding at an ever-increasing speed until in a blink it was gone down into the darkness.

When he looked back, Vika had her fists on her hips. "That was just plain weird."

"I know, traveling in the sliph is a strange experience."

"No, I mean that conversation was weird. Why were you talking to that thing like that?"

Richard waved off the question. "It's a long story. Come on. Let's go."

They raced out of the sliph's room and along the railing around the pit with the dark rock sitting in the center of dark water. Their sudden appearance caused small creatures on the rock to leap into the surrounding water.

The lower reaches of the Keep were dark and gloomy. Occasionally there was a long shaft that reached to the outside to let in light and fresh air.

Richard took them the shortest way he knew to get to the massive lower chamber that was kind of like a central hub. From there, one could go to any number of different places and levels in the Keep. The chamber was so long that he couldn't recognize a person's face from one end to the other. It wasn't nearly so wide, but it was immensely tall. Up near the top there were long openings that let the Keep breathe, changing the air down deep in the place and letting it flow through the halls. It also let birds and bats come and go. Both came for the bugs.

It was a long climb from the lower Keep. They went up both narrow, dark stone stairs and more elaborate staircases. Together they raced down passageways and through elaborately decorated rooms.

Higher up in the Keep, when they finally rushed around a corner, Richard heard voices. He looked down a broad hall to see two women standing at a window, looking out and talking.

Richard trotted down the hall with Vika at his side. He slowed to a breathless stop near the women. Both stared with wide eyes as he and Vika caught their breath.

"Sister Phaedra, right?" he finally asked.

She curtsied. "Lord Rahl, it has been a very long time. I am surprised you remember me."

Both women stared at the red leather. "This is Vika," he told them as he held a hand toward her in introduction.

The Sister likewise lifted a hand out to the side. "This is Jana, one of the women from down in the city who come up here to help out at the Keep."

Richard offered her a quick tip of his head in greeting.

She blushed, and then performed a shaky curtsy, too intimidated by the Lord Rahl to speak. It was something that he'd gotten somewhat used to. He didn't have the time to talk her out of her mute fright.

"Where's Kahlan?" he asked the Sister. "She is—was—pregnant. Did she have the babies yet? Is she all right? Where is she?"

The woman blinked at the burst of questions. She turned to the window and pointed out.

"She went down there. She said she wanted to have her children where she was born."

"She went down to the Confessors' Palace?"

Richard was astonished that she would take that risk before knowing that she would be safe from the Glee.

"That's right," Sister Phaedra said. "She has been down there for quite some time now."

180

As he and Vika raced into the majesty of the Confessors' Palace, two of the women who lived and worked there were already rushing toward them, skirts held in a hand as they ran.

"Lord Rahl! Lord Rahl!" one of them called out, waving an arm overhead to make sure they saw her.

They both ran up to meet Richard and Vika as they came into the bright, airy, grand central entryway. "Lord Rahl—"

"Yes?"

"I'm Ginny. This is Nina."

"A runner just arrived to tell us that you were on your way," Nina put in as if it were exciting gossip, or maybe she was just excited to see him.

Richard had been in a hurry to get there, so he was surprised to hear it. "A runner? A runner beat us here?"

"Rachel," Ginny said with a grin. "She knows the shortcuts."

Richard frowned. "Rachel? You mean Chase's daughter? That Rachel?"

Ginny nodded. "Yes, she is such a big help to everyone. She has long legs, that girl. She was so excited to tell us that she had spotted you and a Mord-Sith that she had to race all the way down here as fast as she could to tell the Mother Confessor." She pointed toward the ceiling. "She is up there with her now."

"Where is Kahlan? Has she had the babies yet? Has—"

Ginny held her arm out, directing him. "Come. Everyone will be so excited that you have returned. To be honest, we all, well, we all thought you were dead. Everyone except the Mother Confessor. She said…"

Richard wanted to strangle the words out of her. "She said what?" He looked over at the other woman instead. "What did she say?"

"Well," Nina stammered, "she said that you weren't dead, that you would…"

"Would what?"

Nina blushed furiously. "She said that you would get some crazy idea and be able to come back to us. I guess she was right. Oh! I don't mean she was right that you would have a crazy idea—I'm sure your ideas aren't crazy—but that you would return."

When Richard swished his hand to urge them to get moving and show the way, Ginny immediately turned and led him and Vika up a grand stairway of white marble to a spacious balcony that ran most of the way around three sides of the palatial entryway. Around one side of that balcony they went up a second stairway to the third floor, and then turned down the central hall.

As they hurried down a wide, elaborate hallway with comfortable-looking chairs in groupings, Shale came racing around a corner out ahead. "Lord Rahl!" She rushed up and seized him by his shoulders. "Dear spirits! We thought for sure that you were lost to us!"

Vika cocked an eyebrow. "He got a crazy idea how to come back."

Shale stared at her a moment, but had no answer. She turned back to Richard. He was surprised to see her in such a fine dress.

"The Mother Confessor will be relieved to see you. She was so worried, but she would never admit it. Whenever one of us would look at her, concerned for her and what she must be fearing, she would just smile and tell us not to worry. That you would be back."

Richard threw up his arms. "Where is she! Bags, would one of you take me to her?"

Ginny and Nina blushed at the language.

"Come on," Shale said, rolling a hand to urge him to follow. She started him down the hallway toward another grand stairway.

Richard was beside himself. "Has she had the babies yet? Are they all right? Is Kahlan all right?"

"Just come on and you can see for yourself."

Shale led Richard and Vika up the stairs two at a time. Ginny and Nina hastened along behind. The palace was white and quiet and beautiful, but it was all a blur to Richard. He hardly saw any of it. He just wanted to get to Kahlan.

And then as they came to another hallway, he saw a group of people all milling around down the hall. He recognized the Mord-Sith, but they were all in white leather, which was a shock after having seen them in their red leather for so long.

Berdine spotted him coming and broke into a dead run. When she got to him, she leaped up into his arms, nearly knocking him down. She threw her legs around his waist.

"Lord Rahl! Lord Rahl! You're back!"

Richard grabbed her by the waist and set her down. He flashed a quick smile as he turned her around and pushed her ahead as he rushed onward to the group outside a doorway.

He saw Chase there, with his wife Emma. He paused long enough to squeeze the big man's arm in a silent greeting.

"Richard!" Rachel cried out as she suddenly hugged him. He ran a hand down the back of her head of long hair. He was surprised to see that she was now nearly as tall as him.

Richard looked around at the small group. "I need to see Kahlan."

Shale smiled as she opened a white door with ornate carving on it. She held the door open for him and motioned him in.

Richard stared at her.

Shale grinned. "Go on, then."

181

Richard walked into a beautiful room decorated with cream-colored curtains with a textured pattern and white frame and panel walls. The reflector lamps mounted on the walls were all silver, but none were lit. The carpets were leaf patterns in various shades of off-white. It wasn't a large room, considering the size of the palace, but it looked special. The bed had four posts draped over the top with a white, filmy material that hung down on each side near the headboard. Through the open window Richard could hear birds chirping outside. In the distance the looming Keep looked down over them, a dark protector of the Confessors.

From that bed, Kahlan's green eyes were locked on him from the moment he walked through the doorway.

His heart hammered as he stared at her.

She was so beautiful he felt tears well up in his eyes.

In each arm, she held a bundle. He could just see the tops of the babies' heads.

"Are you all right?" he asked in a hushed tone, feeling stupid because he couldn't think of anything better to say.

"Now that I see you, everything is good," she said in a soft voice. "Everyone was so worried. But I knew that you would find a way to come back to me."

"I'm sorry it took me so long. I wanted to be here when the babies came. But I—"

She was still smiling. "You are back with me now. That's all that matters to me."

"You don't have to worry about the Glee coming after us ever again. No one in our world ever has to fear them again."

"The Golden Goddess is not the new golden age, then?" she asked.

Richard shook his head. "No. A golden ring helped me get back to you and make our children safe. That golden ring is with us, now, here in our world. I think that is what it really meant when I promised you the beginning of a new golden age. That's where that promise really comes from. I wanted you to know. It's nothing else, nothing bad."

She nodded against the pillow she was propped up on. "One day you can tell me about your crazy adventure, but right now, come and meet our children."

At long last, Richard carefully stepped to the edge of the bed, close to her. He didn't think he had ever felt more nervous and expectant all at once.

Kahlan smiled with bliss, with tranquility, and in weariness. It somehow calmed him. Her green eyes calmed him.

"Lord Rahl, I would like you to meet your children." She lifted the one in her left arm, on the other side of her from Richard, out a little. "This is your daughter, Cara Amnell."

He stared in wonder a moment at his sleeping daughter.

Kahlan looked down as she lifted the other one, asleep in the crook of her right arm, out a little. "And this is your son, Zeddicus Rahl."

Richard stared at his son a moment, then bent and gently kissed the top of his head, then leaned farther and kissed the forehead of his daughter.

At last, he finally kissed Kahlan, making everything he had been through melt into nothing.

He straightened as he smiled down at her. "Their names are perfect. They are perfect. You are perfect."

Both babies reached a tiny hand out, then. They looked almost like they were searching for each other's hands. Using her fingers on the bundles she held, Kahlan gently smoothed their hands back inside the blankets.

She smiled her special smile at Richard as her eyes closed.

Shale came up behind him and took his arm to urge him back.

"She needs to rest, now," the sorceress whispered. "You can talk to her again after she gets some much-needed sleep."

Richard didn't want to leave, but he wanted all three to rest.

182

Once they were outside the room, Shale gently closed the door. "She wanted so much for you to see the babies that she has been trying to stay awake until you came back to her. She knew you would be back. And she wanted to see that you were safe. She can rest easy, now."

The Mord-Sith were all beaming at him. Vika put a hand on his back for a moment, a touch of congratulations that meant more than words. In that simple human act, Richard saw far more. He saw a journey back from madness.

"She looked so tired," he said. He gave Shale a meaningful look. "Is everything all right? Did it go well? The birth, I mean."

Out of the corner of his eye he saw the Mord-Sith all share a look. Shale glanced over at Rachel as an excuse to divert her gaze for a moment. She finally looked back up at Richard.

"Yes. The babies finally arrived. They are all well."

"Why is she here, at the Confessors' Palace?" Richard asked suspiciously. "We went through a lot of trouble to get to the Keep so she could give birth where she would be safe. What is she doing here?"

Rachel touched his arm to answer. "She said that she was born here, and she wanted her children to be born in the Confessors' Palace as well."

"But the danger of the Glee—why would you all let her come down here to give birth?"

"Have you ever tried to tell the Mother Confessor no?" Shale asked. "It is not so easy, let me tell you."

Richard realized that he knew the truth of that.

"We tried to tell her to stay in the Keep where she would be safe," Berdine said, "but she said it wasn't a problem because you would see to it that she and your children would be safe."

"But—"

"He did," Vika said. "He saw to it that they were safe. He didn't let her down. He didn't let any of us down."

Richard looked back at the sorceress. "You helped her, then, when the babies came?"

"I did," she said as she was overcome with a peaceful smile. "As I promised you. I wouldn't let you, or her, down."

Richard could sense an odd tension in the mood of all those in the hallway.

"Was the birth difficult?"

Cassia, standing next to Shale, turned her back on Richard and whispered to Shale. Richard could just barely hear her say, "Tell him."

Richard looked back at Shale. Her smile faltered.

"What is it? Was there a problem with the birth? I should have been here. I'm sorry. I came as fast as I could. What is it? What happened?"

Shale folded her fingers together, holding her hands together in front. "Well, to be honest, it was a difficult birth. Partly because of all the mother's breath we gave her. But there was… more to it. Kahlan was in labor for days. She finally gave birth not long ago."

"But… she looks all right. She looks just fine. The twins look beautiful and are sleeping peacefully."

"No, no, she is fine. That's not it. The babies are fine as well."

Richard gestured as he grew impatient. "Well then, what is it that all of you know about and none of you are saying?"

Shale cleared her throat. "The thing is, Lord Rahl, she had a very difficult birth. The babies…"

"You already said that. The babies what?"

Shale glanced away from the intensity in his eyes. "The babies had a difficult time being born."

Richard had been with Zedd when he had helped with a few difficult births. He knew how tense that kind of situation could be. "Why? What was the problem?"

"Well, actually," Shale said, "I've never seen anything like it before, so it's rather hard to explain."

Richard was at his wits' end. He threw his hands up in the air. "What was the problem? What happened?"

Shale cleared her throat again. "The thing is we were having a difficult time helping her in delivering the babies."

Richard looked from face to face. "Were they breech?"

"No, that wasn't it, exactly," Shale said.

Richard planted his fists on his hips. "What was it, then? Why was it difficult? Tell me."

Shale finally looked back up into his eyes.

"When the twins were being born, they were holding hands as the Mother Confessor was trying to give birth."

Richard stared at her a long moment. "Holding hands."

Shale nodded. "We had a very hard time getting them to let go of each other so they could finish being born. After we finally pried their hands apart, Cara was born first. Zeddicus came immediately after. For a time we didn't know if we would be able to get their hands apart so they could both be born. It was a tense situation."

Richard frowned. It didn't make any sense.

"They are newborn infants. How difficult can it be to pry their little fingers away from each other?"

Shale looked up at him from under her brow. "You do realize they are both gifted, right? They were holding on to each other not just with their hands, but with the power of their gifts."

ABOUT THE AUTHOR

Terry Goodkind was a #1 *New York Times* bestselling author and creator of the critically acclaimed masterwork The Sword of Truth. He wrote over thirty bestselling novels, was published in more than twenty languages worldwide, and sold more than 26 million books.

The Sword of Truth is a revered literary tour de force, comprising seventeen volumes born from over twenty-five years of dedicated writing. Terry Goodkind's books are character-driven, with a focus on the complexity of the human psyche. He had an uncanny grasp for crafting compelling stories about people like you and me, trapped in terrifying situations. Goodkind brings us into the lives of his characters; characters that must rise to face not only challenges, but their deepest fears. For that reason, his characters speak to the best and worst in all of us.

While The Sword of Truth and its siblings The Nicci Chronicles and The Children of D'Hara are confirmation enough of Goodkind's storytelling abilities, every bit of his masterful voice is also clearly evident in his contemporary thrillers set within our own world. The bond built between the reader and one of the world's great authors rises above worlds and settings, mere backdrops for uniquely intricate stories of life, love, challenge and triumph.

'To exist in this vast universe for a speck of time is the great gift of life. It is our only life. The universe will go on, indifferent to our brief existence, but while we are here, we touch not just part of that vastness, but also the lives around us. Life is the gift each of us has been given. Each life is our own and no one else's. It is precious beyond all counting. It is the greatest value we can have. Cherish it for what it truly is… Your life is yours alone. Rise up and live it.'

TERRY GOODKIND (1948–2020)
from *Confessor*, volume 12 in
The Sword of Truth

THE SWORD OF TRUTH

TERRY GOODKIND
THE NUMBER ONE BESTSELLING AUTHOR

WIZARD'S FIRST RULE
SWORD OF TRUTH 1

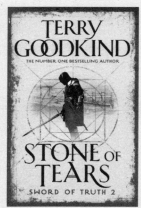

TERRY GOODKIND
THE NUMBER ONE BESTSELLING AUTHOR

STONE OF TEARS
SWORD OF TRUTH 2

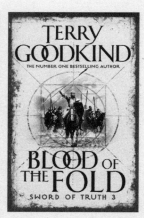

TERRY GOODKIND
THE NUMBER ONE BESTSELLING AUTHOR

BLOOD OF THE FOLD
SWORD OF TRUTH 3

TERRY GOODKIND
THE NUMBER ONE BESTSELLING AUTHOR

TEMPLE OF THE WINDS
SWORD OF TRUTH 4

TERRY GOODKIND
THE NUMBER ONE BESTSELLING AUTHOR

SOUL OF THE FIRE
SWORD OF TRUTH 5

TERRY GOODKIND
THE NUMBER ONE BESTSELLING AUTHOR

FAITH OF THE FALLEN
SWORD OF TRUTH 6

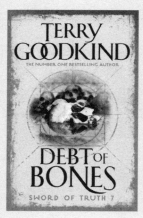

TERRY GOODKIND
THE NUMBER ONE BESTSELLING AUTHOR

DEBT OF BONES
SWORD OF TRUTH 7

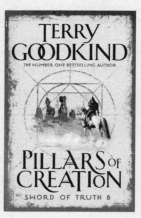

TERRY GOODKIND
THE NUMBER ONE BESTSELLING AUTHOR

PILLARS OF CREATION
SWORD OF TRUTH 8

TERRY GOODKIND
THE NUMBER ONE BESTSELLING AUTHOR

NAKED EMPIRE
SWORD OF TRUTH 9

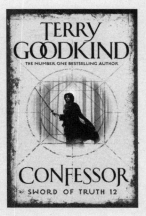

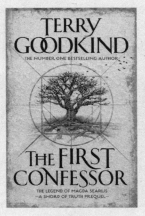

Twenty-five years in the making, seventeen books
published, numerous #1 *New York Times* bestsellers,
printed in over twenty languages, and with more than
26 million books sold worldwide, The Sword of Truth
is an extraordinary adventure, unlike any other.

THE NICCI CHRONICLES

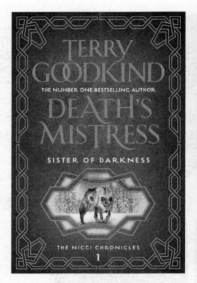

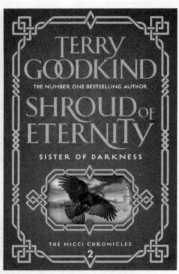

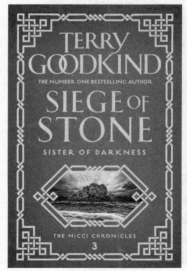

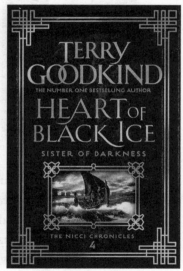

Centred on one of Terry Goodkind's best-loved characters,
the fiery sorceress Nicci, The Nicci Chronicles takes place
in the world of The Sword of Truth.

OTHER WORLDS

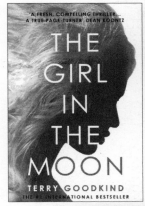

Beyond The Sword of Truth, The Children of D'Hara, and The Nicci Chronicles, there are entirely new worlds to discover. Author Terry Goodkind defies expectations with stunning stories that will leave you gasping, mind racing, heart pounding, palms sweating, and eager for more.